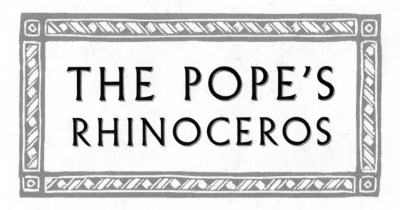

THE POPE'S
RHINOCEROS

Also by Lawrence Norfolk

LEMPRIÈRE'S DICTIONARY

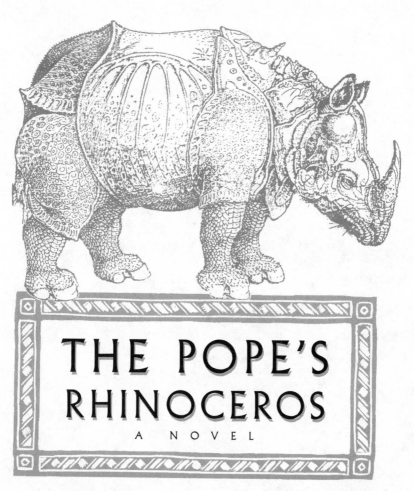

THE POPE'S
RHINOCEROS

A NOVEL

LAWRENCE NORFOLK

Harmony Books / New York

Copyright © 1996 by Lawrence Norfolk

All rights reserved. No part of this book may be reproduced or
transmitted in any form or by any means, electronic or mechanical,
including photocopying, recording, or by any information storage and
retrieval system, without permission in writing from the publisher.

Published by Harmony Books,
a division of Crown Publishers, Inc.,
201 East 50th Street, New York, New York 10022

Random House, Inc. New York, Toronto, London, Sydney, Auckland

http://www.randomhouse.com/

Originally published in Great Britain by Sinclair-Stevenson in 1996.

HARMONY and colophon are trademarks of Crown Publishers, Inc.

Design by Lynne Amft

Printed in the United States of America

Library of Congress Cataloging-in-Publication Data is available upon request.

ISBN 0-517-59532-X

10   9   8   7   6   5   4   3   2   1

First American Edition

For Vineeta

ACKNOWLEDGMENTS

Thanks are due to Thomas Harder for his translation from the Italian of Iacopo Modesti's eyewitness account of the sack of Prato and to Professor Hermann Walter of the University of Mannheim for a copy of Sigismondo Tizio's *Historia Senensium* found in the Vatican library by his colleague, Ingrid D. Rowland of the University of Chicago.

CONTENTS

I   Vineta   1

II   *Ro*-ma   113

III   The Voyage of the *Nostra Senora de Ajuda* from the Port of Goa to the Bight of Benin in the Winter and Spring of 1515 and 1516   351

IV   And the Ship Sails On....   405

V   Nri   439

VI   Naumachia   509

VII   *Gesta Monachorum Usedomi*   569

All fishes eat. All fishes spawn. Few fishes spawn where they eat.

—Arne Lindroth

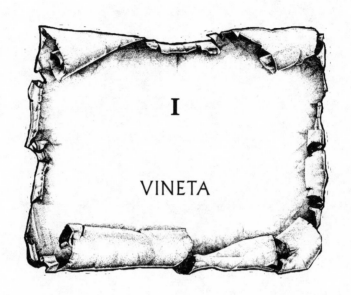

I

VINETA

*T*his sea was once a lake of ice. High mountains overlooked a glacial plain frosted with snow and scoured by the freezing wind. Granite basins curved up from under the ice-tonnage to rim it with irregular coasts. In ages still to come, boulder waste and till will speak of the ice pack's tortuous inching over buried rock and sandstone; moraines and drumlins of advances and recessions that gouge out trenches and shunt forward ridges. The sea-floor here was prepared long before there was a sea to cover it. In the interim came the governance of ice.

Fault lines and fractures healed and welded, grew invisible, until the Gulfs of Bothnia and Finland, of Riga and Gdansk, were indistinguishable from the central basin that joined them. Northerly blizzards left their drifts of snow, which compacted down and thickened until the earth's very crust tilted under the weight. Veins of frozen oil ran like the hawsers of a ruined fleet, looping and meeting in the dark far below the surface. Grit speckled the ice pack as though blasted out of the earth and suspended in midair, boulders shattered and hung immobile in the dark of this catastrophic freeze. Nothing breathed here. This must once have been the deadest place on earth.

This surface interruption: a pale disk of light germinating in the snow-flecked sky suggests a radical tilt to the axis below, gales cede to gusts and vicious whirlwinds, ice giants shout in the night. An inch of silt marks a thousand years, an aeon means a single degree of arc, and by this scale a thaw is under way. There will be a century of centuries of snarling ice, an age of glacial strain until the first crystal's glistening melt to liquid spreads and seeps and creeps north across the frozen surface to make of it a mirror wherein the sun might see its face. Light slaps and dazzles the ice, sends thick fronts of heated air against the polar cold. Meltwaters dribble between ice and rock, refreeze and melt again. The nights are cold enough to strip the lungs of any beast foolish enough to venture on this wasted acreage, the wind that blasts across the vista turns hide and flesh to stone. An ice-blink sky glares down at the nights' reverses, which are boulder waste, scree and brine cells locked in rime. There are shelves where the sun never reaches, and salts forced by the pressure lie as powder on the surface.

But the days grow longer, water-sheets spread, mean temperatures rise and vent mists that boil off the blazing ice. Secret cables of water are trickling down and prising the frigid bole from its case of rock, meeting and joining on the stony floors that the sun cannot find. A thousand miles of ice floats in an inch of water.

Different orders are coming down the line. Crevasses and canyons rive the surface and snake forward, cutting loose immense crystals that shatter and collapse. Water runs at the bottom of ravines a thousand meters deep, eating out the lowest levels of the ice pack and rising until the whole is cut with rivers fed by their own corrosive increase. The landscape resounds with the crash of ice-columns and ice-arches, the unheard thunder of a million wrecks. Glassy ridges sink and settle in pools that lengthen and rise, become fissures, until this territory of waste is neither solid nor liquid, but an archipelago of drifting icebergs dwindling in a sea of their own dissolved bodies and a fog so thick with damp, it is neither air nor water. Unhinged mountains collide in the green subsurface light and send up rafts to the surface, where the sun can melt them. Small floes bob and rock in the water's cradle while sunbeams draw them into the sky as clouds, which spread in filaments, snap, and shrink to nothing. Where there was ice, is water.

Still, this is an empty expanse. More temperate, more fluid, but the gulfs sprawl north and east, the central body curls south, then west, much as they did before. The change is local, confined to the westernmost strait, or most perceptible there. Are the northern mountains less towering, the Aland islands less numerous? Is the Landsort Deep sunk lower than before? The rise in water level is a matter of feet in a landscape of leagues, the product of differing coefficients—water expands, ice contracts—and yet this alone is not enough to drown islands and creep up cliffs. The movement runs deeper, reaches back farther. A compacted weight has lifted, an oppressed floor is rising, tilting back, and tipping water south and west toward the Belts and Sound of Zealand. Low rocky sills seem to shrink before the slow surge of the lakewaters, are overrun as the thaw reaches the northernmost coves. The breach is made and water races west to join the seething gray of an ocean that has waited some million years for the arrival of this, the last of its tributaries. Rocky lowlands offer little resistance to the forward flood; these shelving plains were always meant to be seabeds. Faster now, welling up and spilling over the scarps, forced on by the tilting basin at its back, the flood follows the lowest contours to meet the greater ocean. The battered coast is outflanked and overrun in one extraordinary moment as the first tongue of water trickles out of the dunes and runs down the shore, laps at the lapping waves, and tastes the ocean's unfamiliar salt for the first time. An hour old and raw from the breach, it is the youngest sea on earth.

The thousand-mile ridge of rock that bars the northern gulfs from the ocean collects snow all through the dark of winter. Spring brings meltwaters tumbling down the mountainsides to boil in the ravines. A water table of distant plateaus and barren fells feeds great rivers to the north and east. Showers are frequent, though rarely sustained for long. Short hot summers give way to drizzly autumns. The first men to gaze on these waters would have found a placid, temperate sea, thick with reed-beds. About its southernmost coast—for they came from the south—the waters meandered haphazardly, prising intricate spits and bodden out of the coast, baring reddish sandstone to the blast of the odd winter gale. Healing drifts of clay covered the ice-scarred granite of the seabed, purple heather shaded the long humps of eskers and drumlins back into a boggy foreshore. They were easy waters, and the thick forests of oak and beech through which they must have traveled might have supplied the timbers for a vessel. But something deterred them and sent them east along the shore rather than north across the sea. Some journeys are irresistible, some no more than the thudding of feet. They set their sunburned faces toward the interior mysteries and left behind them vague currents, placid convections and stirrings. Drift.

This strange and gentle sea, reed-fringed and resting in a granite cradle still rocking in the aftermath of ice, dotted with islands and bounded with stony northern coasts, fed by melted snow and rainwater, almost enclosed behind the jut of the peninsula, yet appears somehow lacustrine, an outbreak of water arrested at the edge of the ocean, frozen in the moment of joining. The bulk and heave of brine calls from beyond the strait, but its newest dominion still clings to an earlier being, of a freezing and preservative stillness. Weak inflows through Skagerrak and Kattegat signal distant oceanic storms, but mostly the sluggish currents roll under the impetus of debouching rainfall and snow. These yeasty yellow waters are almost saltless, almost tideless, almost stagnant in the deeps of Arkona or Landsort. The northern gulfs still freeze over five winters in ten. This sea will always keep something of the character of ice.

The first men never returned. Peat-bogs, beech scrub, and moorland lay undisturbed for centuries while fish entered by the Belts, spawned in the brackish waters, grew fat on sea snails, brown shrimps, bristle worms, and soft-shelled crabs. Atlantic salmon sped east with the sea trout and grayling to spawn in the great rivers whose mouths in summer would choke with the bodies of spent lampreys until shrieking gulls and goosanders plucked them from the water. Flounder, dab, sand eels, and lumpsuckers grazed the saline bottom waters while gudgeon, pike, and dace hovered about the freshwater outflows. Cod spawned in Arkona Deep, grew huge, ate each other. The spring and autumn herring founded their colonies in the nearby shallows off the islands of Rügen and Usedom. A million undisturbed existences floated, swam, spawned, and died before the first keel cut the waves above and the nets descended to haul the sea's fat harvest ashore. Invasions, battles, and slaughter were a vague clangor, dim thuds in the deathly air; the pale bodies sank quietly, watched by lidless, curious eyes. Spars and planks drifted off the exploded coast. Dim shapes sank amidst the skerries.

Herring-lives circled such interruptions; supple cycles of eating and breeding stretched to allow their passage. Storms had brought no more than the puny challenge of barrel staves and broken oars in the past. As the rising wind churned the surface they would sink, whole shoals diving for shelter in the lee of the cliff, until the swell died down and they could rise to feed. This storm was different, its course bending away from them, its first shudders familiar enough, but then exceeding all they had known before. They dived and waited, but the storm only roiled and thudded overhead, a bludgeoning throb reaching deeper than ever before. In the deep off Usedom, they shook as the tempest tore loose sea-grass and kelp, sent fogs of clay billowing out of the trenches, buried its violence in the depths. They never suspected the transaction taking place above, so stubbornly held by the spit running off the line of the coast, so violent a wresting as the waves clawed this gift for them from the land. The thrashing surface-creatures above were yielding up a surpassing tribute to the waiting shoals, greater and more intricate, different in kind as well as scale, and more enduring.

The herring knew the coastal cities as compacted secrets, the ends of tunnels emerging at night under a moonless sky. Looping wakes converged there, linking each to each, one confirming the next as the vessels passed overhead with their dim shouts and the pressure of the hulls fumbling dully in the depths like minor showers on their way to somewhere else. The herring tracked them home to port, suffered gray death in the nets that were hauled aboard with the full-grown fish strung about the middle, trying to jackknife free and drowning as the threads tightened over their gills. A foaming cloak of scum protected these places from prying herring eyes, thickening about the piers, breaking up in the wash beyond the headlands. Such a traffic, such a thickening of these solitary creatures. Hungry places, these cities. But beyond the vague maw, the strange tightening and deadening of currents, where were the teeth, the gullet, the stomach?

This: felt first as a distant disturbance in the storm's fury, a vast crumbling or drawn-out collapse. Out of the battered cliff, great shards of clay were coming loose. Slabs of sandstone tumbled free, crashing down the sheer edge and dropping into the deep. The sea took great swings at the spit, cutting away until the weight above drove down its own foundation and followed it into the waters. A massive submergence, a vast pulse of pressure, clay misting and clogging their eyes and gills, clearing and revealing to them the scale of the displacement. Greater than the greatest vessel, this awaited mystery still locked in the aftermath of its deliverance, too strange and exceeding them all as it lowered itself to the seabed. There it was, laid out below the shoal, with all its people, buildings, carts, and livestock stretching farther than they could see with the reek they had tasted before only from a distance. Here it was thick and strong, all the tantalizing stenches blended together and curling thickly through the water. They waited and felt the surface grow calm. They saw each other's fat silver bodies turn this way and that before the yielded gift. And then the first few flipped their tails and descended. The thrashing creatures above had delivered as tribute a city.

The older herring swam with its citizens, circled their temples, and overlooked their marts. Paddling in and out the doors and windows, they sought out the clumsy giants in flowing robes who promenaded through the drowned streets. Lurching in the waters' flow, they were more like plants than men. The herring rose, and sank, and rose again. Other shoals gathered about them. The upper waters glittered with fry. They would never forget the pact forged in the storm. The city would grow familiar to them as the sea-floor itself, and in time indistinguishable.

Gifts and years: bladderwrack creeps closer to the shore, loamy soils flocculate and wash away. Near tidelessness means the survival of low landscapes and improbable islands. Sharks' teeth and whalejaws are the oldest bones in the sea. Weed rafts drift and are blown by northerly gusts into estuaries and lagoons. Sinking canvas wheels down into the darkness, goblets and bracelets glitter and are eclipsed. Spear shafts, scabbards, rope-ends, and corn sacks take their own trajectories through the fathoms. Smashed hulls lurch while mastheads dive, but all are voided and deposited on the seabed. Surface-creatures drown. If the ice was a barrier no object could breach, then the sea that took its place will accept all; a subtler poison, for everything sinks in the end. The herring understand. Not since the city—and that was a hundred generations before—have they clustered so thickly and so curiously as now. The tribute from above is always puzzling and clumsy, always awkward and misshapen; this is no exception. And yet it neither floats nor sinks, seeming to hover in the water like themselves. They move closer, and it begins to shake. They feel the waters agitate around it. A booming sound resonates with their otoliths, and their fins begin to twitch. It is almost invisible in the murk of these depths; something hangs beneath it. What? Is this finally the key to the mystery of the city? Something snakes away above, tautens as they circle slowly, comes loose, and disappears. The larger fish butt against the intruder. These are herring waters and this is the coldest water-layer. But perhaps they were mistaken, for it seems to be sinking now, tumbling down out of sight. Some turn away as deepwater currents take the intruder, weird tribute from above, drifting in the saltless tideless waters fed by meltwater springs, racked by memories of ice, scourged by serrated coasts, darker and deeper and farther down toward the city. Lost? No, not quite. Blunt herring noses butt against its sides. Their curiosity sustains it; its own weirdness buoys it up. But what? In this sea a barrel is sinking, and in this barrel is a man.

They had practiced in Ewald's pond, amongst the greasy weeds and fishbones. Islands of leafmold drifted in from the beech copse and stank along with the part-dried fish and stagnant black water rising off its scum-flecked surface. It lay behind the herring shed set back fifty yards from the shore. The summer before last Ewald had tried to drain it. To the left, the ground fell away; a trench cut through the turf and sodden earth beneath would draw the pond water off, but the sides of the cutting had collapsed a day later and the pond filled up accordingly. Returning from the market at Wollin, Ewald had contemplated his pond's reappearance. He had fetched beer and sat at the back of the herring-shed. When he had drunk himself into a morose rage, he had primed his fox-traps, then thrown them one by one into the stagnant water so he would never be tempted to try so foolish an enterprise again. They were still there, unsprung. He had warned the two of them, tried to discourage them, but they had gone ahead anyway.

"Higher, Bernardo! Higher!"

They had built a derrick, but it had not worked well, so now three poles lashed together in a tripod with a longer one balanced in the fork served the same purpose. From one end of the pole a barrel was suspended over the pond. From the other hung Bernardo, who clambered up and down its length as muffled commands issued from within the tun. They had caulked its staves and cut a tiny window in the side into which fitted the glass filched in Nürnberg, then cased the whole in leather with lacings for the window and the top.

"Now down, Bernardo! Down!"

He heard a *whump* as the barrel hit the water, felt it sink, then settle with six inches of barrel showing above the surface of the pond, the waterline cutting his viewing hole in two. The barrel had been borrowed from Ewald's store—inevitably, it stank of fish. It gave him splinters, too. He saw the pole from which he was suspended running back overhead and Bernardo clinging to it like an overgrown sloth. He tried a wave, and the barrel rocked alarmingly. The ballast-rock would cure that. Bernardo waved back, a great extravagant wave, which was actually Bernardo losing his grip, falling, and releasing the pole, which reared up at one end and fell heavily at the other. He braced himself—*dunt*—a direct hit on the barrel, which tipped slowly onto its side, then overturned, and he found himself upside-down in utter darkness and panicked.

Afterward, prising the fox-trap off Bernardo's foot while they dripped and shivered before the fire, contemplating the necessary repairs to their vessel, lying leaking by the pond, he was forced to concede that punching out the glass had been the course of action most likely to turn mishap into disaster.

"That was coming here in the first place," muttered Bernardo. He yelped as the trap came free.

It had been so sudden, so swift a descent in the lightless water, and the dark so close; choking him in an instant, the water and his own terror somehow dissolved in one another and the world turned upside-down. He could not stand it for a second, had to get out. He had punched out the glass and the water had rushed in. He was nailed inside the tub. He had begun to fight and scream, but only barked his knuckles, and the water had a dreadful thickness to it, like molasses. He had punched out the glass in a panic, and Bernardo had strode in there to rescue him.

"Shut up, Bernardo," he told him now. He had been lucky. Not so much the rescue—Bernardo did not know fear, and fox-traps would not teach him—no, in a crisis Bernardo's presence could be counted on. Nor in the manner of the rescue, which was straightforward, a simple lifting of the barrel and its contents from pond to shore. But in the man himself, there fortune had favored him. By himself he could barely shift their contraption when empty and on dry land. His partner stood almost seven feet tall and was built like an oak; he had lifted the vessel over his head, filled with water and himself, then waded back to shore with a fox-trap on his foot. Bernardo was not clever, but he was big.

Later, hungry and cold as they lay in damp clothes, breathing smoke from the temperamental fire, the two men tried to rest. For a while the hut was silent but for their tossings and turnings. Neither slept. Tomorrow they would restore the glass and experiment with the ballast-stone. They would work with a strained enthusiasm to ready themselves and cheer their spirits, and in his own case to banish the fear that had got a grip on him with their late mishap. He was thinking that the pond was nothing to the sea, whose waves had advanced on the near inlet throughout the past weeks' effort, seeming sometimes to beckon him on and sometimes to warn him off. The day after tomorrow Ewald had agreed to lend them the boat. He shifted irritably on the damp earth and heard Bernardo do the same. At length, the other man rose. They were both awake, and there was no use pretending otherwise. He knew what would follow.

"Tell me again," Bernardo said. "Tell me about the city."

They had practiced in Ewald's pond, but it had not gone well. It was deep and still and black as night, and he had almost drowned. He drew a deep breath and stared into the fire. The city . . . They were too close now not to believe in it. The day after tomorrow he would be in the barrel, sinking down the fathoms to Vineta. There would be no one then to carry his lumpish craft to safety. There it was, leaning against the wall, the severed head of a monster, its black mouth open to swallow him. The glass glinted on the ground beside it. Oak chips crackled in the fire and sent a harsh white smoke into the rafters, where Ewald's herring hung on strings. It was the same smell, the same sight. Salvestro thought back to his mother twisting her knife in the fishes' white underbellies, spitting out the guts like a mouthful of worms.

"Well?" demanded Bernardo.

He sighed inwardly.

"There was a city," he began, "and to the men and women who lived there it was the greatest city on earth. There was a war that lasted a hundred years and a storm that lasted a night—"

"Stop!" Bernardo interrupted him. "You've missed out the part about what the city was like."

"How many times have I told you this story, Bernardo?" he retorted. "If you know it that well, why don't you tell it yourself?"

"Just tell the story properly," said Bernardo. "Without leaving bits out. What about the people who lived there?"

"They were a water people," Salvestro resumed. "The people who lived here then were fishermen, boatmen, pirates, and they made their homes in the marshlands. They built great cities to guard the river mouths, and the greatest of them all had walls built of huge tree-trunks and broken by four great gates. The slave market covered an acre and traders came to barter there; by ship from the lands of ice to the north, by horse and foot from the dry valleys of the south and the plains of the east. It grew to become the wealthiest city on earth. . . ."

He had found his stride now. This happened. That happened. The story rolled forward. He said, "The people of this city loaded their temples with silver, and in every house in every one of its stone-paved streets a table groaned under the weight of the food. Merchants flocked from every port to share the spoils, and in time, its very name came to mean abundance. This city was called Vineta, the most prosperous and peaceable you could imagine."

"That's better," Bernardo muttered approvingly. "That's one of the best bits. About the food, and the temples with all the silver."

"Yes," said Salvestro, nodding. He remembered his earlier self leaning forward across the fire to catch his mother's words as she told him of their ancestors' city and its riches. Fabulous visions of it had formed in the firesmoke, bursting the walls of the mean hut that was their home. Now it was Bernardo who strained to catch the same words.

"Then the newcomers came," he resumed.

"Henry the Lion," said Bernardo. "And his army."

"No, you're muddling it up, Bernardo. Henry the Lion was later. Either listen or tell the story yourself. The first of them were . . ." He paused, unsure whether his mother had told him what they were or not. Perhaps he had forgotten.

"Planters," he declared with authority. "They called the lands here the New Plantation. There weren't very many to begin with. They built churches and drained the marshes. Anyway"—he was picking up the thread again—"they felled the forests and sowed grass for their cows. More and more of them came, and they hated the people who were here before them. They muttered curses against their temples, and against their god Svantovit until Svantovit cursed them back. Then there was a war."

"The war that lasted a hundred years," said Bernardo.

"Yes," said Salvestro. "A hundred years, a thousand battles, and it ended here, on the island. When Henry the Lion reached Vineta."

Sometimes his mother had paused there. Sometimes she had gone on directly to what had followed.

"They camped on the mainland—near the place where we crossed, Bernardo."

Bernardo nodded quickly, eager for him to get on with it. But he was reluctant now. This part of the story was stranger than that which preceded it.

"They could see the smoke from Vineta's fires, and the water was frozen to ice. They could have crossed that night, but they stopped. I don't know why. They pitched camp on the mainland, and that night there was a storm."

He thought of the women, the children, the priests, the last of their beaten armies all cowering behind the walls of the city amongst their jewels and their silver, great chests of treasure consecrated to the gods who could not save them.

"There was a storm," he repeated.

"The storm which lasted a single night," prompted Bernardo.

"It came from the north," Salvestro continued, gathering his thoughts. "A terrible storm, the worst they had ever seen. Waves broke through the ice and the winds flung boats into the air. The ice itself was broken into huge slabs. . . . It was the most fearsome storm that any man had lived through, and Henry and his army could do nothing except pray for it to end—"

"And God answered their prayers," Bernardo interrupted then.

Salvestro glared at him. "Yes, Bernardo, he did. The storm died away as suddenly as it came. When dawn rose, the sky was clear. They crossed the broken ice. They marched across the island. Vineta was built on an arm of land that stuck out into the sea. They climbed up to the point—"

"And what did they find then?" Bernardo burst out.

Salvestro regarded the big man across the fire. He was agog, his thumbs twiddling with excitement, though he knew the answer as well as himself.

"Nothing," said Salvestro. "Vineta had disappeared. Where it had stood there was only water. The storm had torn it loose with the land on which it rested and cast them both to the bottom of the sea."

His mother had usually stopped then. He would be left suspended, rooted to the top of the point and staring down into the water as though he were actually amongst the conquerors and prey to the same bafflement. He looked across at Bernardo, who was rocking back and forth on his haunches.

"And Vineta is still there," he murmured, "with all its temples and their treasure. . . ."

And its people, too, his mother had said. Our people. When the water was clear, she told him, you might see them walking in the watery streets. Svantovit was down there with them. He could not save them, but neither could he desert them. Salvestro's thoughts drifted.

"So what was that ruin?" Bernardo broke in, and for once Salvestro was grateful for the interruption. He did not want to think about Svantovit. He did not want to think about his mother.

"Ruin?"

"On that cliff, where you said they were all looking down at the water. There's a ruin there."

For a moment he did not understand. The previous day they had stood on the beach and Salvestro had pointed down the coast to where the land rose and extended out for a little way into the sea. The point ended abruptly, as though the storm had cut it off with a sword. "There—" He had indicated the patch of water in front of it. "Vineta lies there." Bernardo had stared and nodded, then looked inland again, to the top of the point.

Salvestro's puzzlement disappeared. "It's not a ruin," he told Bernardo. "That's the church. They built it after Vineta sank. To stand guard, so the islanders say. Monks live there."

A suspicious look that Salvestro knew only too well spread slowly over Bernardo's face.

"If it's a church," the giant replied, "how come half of it is in the sea?"

The church *had* looked different, Salvestro reflected. It had been so many years since he had last seen it and even more since he had paid it any attention. There was a monastery built about it, but no one ever went there. And no one, so far as he could remember, had ever seen any of the monks, except as distant figures clothed in gray, patrolling the precincts of their domain.

"Perhaps it collapsed." He shrugged. "It doesn't matter, anyway. The monks won't bother us. Let's get some sleep. Tomorrow we'll fix the barrel and have another go in the pond, then I'll talk to Ewald about the boat."

There was silence. The fire hissed softly.

"And the beds," said Bernardo.

"What?"

"You'll talk to Ewald about the beds."

"Bernardo, I never—"

"The beds you promised when you said, 'Bernardo, we'll have plenty to eat, a roof over our heads, and proper beds to sleep on.' Those beds. The beds your old friend Ewald was going to give us, along with the roof, which leaks as it happens, and the food, which so far as I can see is fish, and more fish, and more fish after that. In fact, Salvestro, I'm sick of fish, and I'm sick of sleeping on the ground, and I'm sick of this stinking shed. A dog wouldn't live here."

"It's not a 'shed.' It's a hut, and anyway it's not so bad—"

"Not so bad!" the giant erupted. "It's cold. It's damp. I'd rather be back at Prato lying facedown in that bog. I'd rather be in the snow on top of a mountain. You promised beds, and what we get is this. I'd rather be in a ditch than here. How can you tell me it's not so bad?"

"Just shut up, Bernardo."

He was tired. He did not want to hear this.

"No, really, I want to know." Bernardo sat up now and gestured around him angrily. "How can you think that this is 'not so bad'? Eh, Salvestro?" The big man thumped the ground for emphasis and spat into the fire.

There was a short silence before Salvestro replied.

"I suppose, Bernardo, I think it's not so bad because I'm used to it. This is where I was born."

The short silence was succeeded by a rather longer one.

"Here?" Bernardo said eventually, trying to keep the incredulity out of his voice and failing. He sounded hesitant. The fight had gone out of him, Salvestro reflected. Bernardo's fits of outrage never lasted long.

"We lived here, once," he said. "My mother gutted fish for Ewald's father."

Bernardo grunted, digesting this fact.

"And that's how you and Ewald are friends."

"Yes," said Salvestro.

He looked up at the fish strung high above their heads, row after row of them. How many had he strung by the gills and hoisted up there? Hundreds? Thousands? Whole shoals. . . .

"He didn't look very pleased to see you," Bernardo ventured then, "seeing as how you're such old friends. He didn't look happy at all to me. In fact, he looked shocked."

Salvestro shrugged, thinking back two weeks to the moment when he had knocked on the door of Ewald's hut. What had he expected from the man who had opened it and stood there, not recognizing him at first, then his face falling when he did, his jaw dropping? Joy? Ewald had looked from himself to the giant standing silently behind him. The expression on his face had been worse than shock. Dismay?

When Ewald had finally recovered himself he'd offered a belated and half-hearted welcome. Bernardo and he could stay in the drying-shed, Salvestro's old home. He loaned them the barrel, some old blankets, even the use of his boat when the fishing season ended. The day after tomorrow. . . . Another thing he did not wish to think about.

"He thought I was dead," said Salvestro. "But we were close once. It was a long time ago."

More than just close, he thought. Ewald had been his only friend on the island. And the island might as well have been the world. Now, across the fire, he saw Bernardo yawn. The giant was losing interest. Whatever substance it was that his complaining was rooted in was sinking, or dissolving, or seeping away. The hut *was* damp, and cold. It did stink of the fish and always had. He remembered his mother sitting where he sat now, one hand cradling a silver body, the other holding the knife.

She gutted fish for Ewald's father and another man. When they brought the catch he and Ewald had to wait outside, so they used to play in the woods. Sometimes they fought, but Ewald always lost. He showed his friend three ways through the peat-bog and how to get into the Haases' loft to steal cabbage. He tried to teach him to swim. They told each other their secrets.

He ran to meet the boat when it came, but Ewald would not speak to him with his father there, and the other man crossed himself and looked away. He spent his other days wandering the island, looking for things to tell his friend. Greengages grew wild on the eastern side in an orchard overgrown with nettles and whippy ash trees. Little sticklebacks swam in the peat-bog, and eels came ashore at night to cross the narrow band of land, winding through the stringy grass near Koserow. He could swim underwater with his eyes open and hold his breath until he fainted. He told all these things to Ewald, but his best secrets were not his at all. They were the things he heard from his mother.

She told him wolves ran in packs. They had yellow eyes and could see in the dark. In shape they were much like dogs, but bigger and with longer legs. They were frightened by fire. Bears were frightened of nothing. They stood twice as tall as a man, could run like the wind, climb trees, and loved to eat children. They could not swim, though, and for that reason there were no bears or wolves on the island. If attacked by a bear, she told him, run for the sea. These things were on the mainland, where he had never been. Sometimes, from the south side of the island, he saw men riding up and down the coast road. He watched the fishing boats sail east in the morning and west at night. They berthed in a great port farther down the coast, his mother said.

She told him these things while she gutted the fish. She worked by firelight. By touch. He watched the knife slide down the belly until it found the vent, then, one two, up and down very quick, with a twist to cut them loose, and the guts would shoot out. He strung them by the gills and hung them in the roof. He sat in front of her when she worked, and if he talked too much, she made a quick movement with her hand and the guts would hit him in the face. She never missed. Once they landed in his mouth. He watched her hands moving in the gloom of the hut, the white of the fish-belly, the quick glint of the knife, the silver of her bracelet as it bumped about on her wrist. He told her she should take it off, but she said someone else had done that once and lost it forever. She had found it washed up on the beach after a storm. He could not remember how old he was then. Did he want to know where it came from?

He had nodded.

That was the beginning, he thought now. That was what had brought him back, or perhaps had driven him away in the first place. His eyes wandered around the hut where she had told him these things. She had been shunned by most of the islanders. They were different, she and her son. Vineta made them different. Vineta and her gods.

She told him about Svantovit, who had a hundred eyes and lived in the sky. He used to sleep on the smoke from their fires, she said, but when the fires were put out he fell into the sea and drowned. Now all you could see were his claws. The people who lived there now thought they were islands, but she knew they were his claws. He had tried to drag himself from the sea, but the water pressed down on his back and held him there until he drowned; but there were still places on the island where he was strong. He nodded, pretending not to understand. She meant the holm oak grove. One night he had followed her there, creeping noiselessly through the undergrowth. He crouched down under the brambles and watched her pick up sticks around the clearing. The oak in the center rose high over the beeches, the weight of its branches pulling them almost to the forest floor. He saw her stoop and straighten, moving closer and closer to the tree. His mother had the blackest hair on the island. He heard her cry out words he did not understand. He had crawled backward, watching her until all he could see was the great oak's trunk and a blur of white wrapped about its base. He had fled.

Then she said that Svantovit had once been strong all over the island, and the mainland, too. The people who had worshiped him built a great city here. But there had been a war and a storm. The city, she said, had been called Vineta.

After that she told him everything, and as many times as he wished until he knew the whole story by heart. He began to comb the northern beaches, quartering the sands under the eye of the monastery that stood at the limit of the point, a grim keep overlooking the sea. The fishing boats rarely cast their nets in the waters there. When Ewald's father said they came up empty and often torn, he thought of Svantovit ripping them open and feeding on the catch. He never found anything on the beach except driftwood and crabs. He tried to imagine Svantovit himself, but if his mere claw was the size of the island, then the rest of him exceeded anything he had seen, except the sea and sky. He threw stones at the goats until the neatherd drove him away, watched boats sculling over the Achter-Wasser, pissed in the pond behind Riesenkampf's manse until it stank. Svantovit and Vineta were the best secrets he had ever heard.

He had been waiting under the beech trees as usual. He watched the men pulling the fish-barrels into his mother's hut, Ewald dawdling behind them. When the men were inside he waved and Ewald ran across to him. He was out of breath, but instead of talking he simply grabbed him by the wrist and they both ran off into the woods. Ewald had a secret to tell him, something better to show him than eels and sticklebacks.

They ran and ran, past the herring-shed, past the Ronsdorffs' hives, until Ewald pulled him up short and told him what he was about to see was his best secret, he must never tell anyone, and swore him to silence. He nodded eagerly. He had no one to tell, in any case.

They ran again. They slipped by the monastery. They wove a path through the strange mounds about Krumminer. Behind the next rise was the Stenschke farm. They crept along the side of the chicken run and through the yard. The Stenschke dog knew Ewald and hardly raised its head, but he was scared. Stenschke had let the animal loose on him once when he had walked along the top of his field, and his daughters had screamed that the Savage was coming to get them. That was what the other children called him. All except Ewald. The dog had bounded after him, but he'd lost it in the peat-bog. Ewald squatted down and pressed his face to the wall. He could hear the low bubble of talk inside. Ewald rose and beckoned. There was a crack for him to look through. He crouched and took the other's place. Inside were Stenschke's daughters. They were pouring water over each other and the steam was all around them like clouds while they scrubbed and rinsed and unwound white sheets from their bodies, which were naked. He watched and felt Ewald watching him. He thought of his own confidings: plums, peat-bogs, eels, swimming. Ewald's was a different kind of secret.

They walked back by the path through the woods. Scrubby little ash trees started tripping them up and Ewald wanted to go around the longer way, but he kept on walking. Ewald said he was definitely going to marry Eva; his father knew Stenschke pretty well, and he used the boat sometimes. Erica was all right, too. Why didn't he say something?

He thought of the three girls pouring water out of the jug, their arms plump and red from the steam, the dog chasing him into the swamp, his running away. Ewald was right beside him, but his chatter was distant and tinny. It was almost dark and the trees were black skeletons jumbled together in the sky. They were almost at the clearing. He stopped and Ewald stopped, too. He knew the secret he was going to tell. He exacted the same oath from Ewald he had sworn himself, and they crept forward in silence until they stood before the oak. He took off his clothes and told his companion to do the same, then they joined hands about the tree and he began to tell Ewald about Svantovit. When he told him about the islands and Svantovit's claws, Ewald started to cry. Then he tried to get free. The oak seemed to grow colder. It was dark, and the moon was hidden by clouds. Ewald was struggling. His chest scraped against the rough bark and his hands were clamps about the wrists of the other, who was jerking to get away. Words were coming from his mouth, harsh and guttural, the same chant over and over again. He heard them fade and be replaced by forest silence, the clash and scrape of wind-stirred branches, the secret creak of roots. His hands released their captive. He saw Ewald run howling into the wood. He dressed slowly. Walking back to the hut, he began to wonder what he had done.

But he knew what he had done, he thought now. Bernardo was motionless, perhaps already asleep. I knew even then, he thought to himself. He had told Ewald his best secret because Ewald's secrets were better than his own.

The following week the catch did not arrive. It had never happened before. He waited under shelter of the beech trees for his friend to arrive until darkness fell, but no one came. His mother had to call him in. She waited through the week that followed, but when Ewald's father failed to appear for the second time she told him to build her a drying-rack. The stench in the hut was overpowering. The herring were beginning to rot. He set to work where the trees ended and the cleared land in which their hut stood began, carrying bundles of staves back and forth from the woodland. Dropping the final bundle, he looked down and saw that there were footprints in the earth, a confusing jumble of them, and, a little farther on, behind an alder bush, a pair deeper than the others, as though a man had stood there for hours without moving.

He should not have told Ewald his mother's secret. Dead leaves crunched underfoot and brambles snagged his shirt as he stalked the woods about their home. He left the paths and crept through undergrowth, his gaze sweeping left and right. Each night he quartered the wood, and once he thought he saw the figure of a man, far off and barely visible through the moonlit trees. But as he watched, the man turned and melted into the night. Perhaps it was the man who left his footprints by their hut, perhaps another. He knew why these men were here and whence they came. Svantovit was angry, so he had sent these demons to frighten him. He dreamed of heads rising out of the sea, bodies marching up the beach, men coming to get him and drag him down to Vineta. He was fearful of what he had done. They were waiting for something, and he wondered what it was. If it was not himself, then it was his mother. He wanted to tell her everything, but he did not. He said nothing.

When the third week came, she rose unexpectedly one night and left the hut. He almost told her then, but instead he waited until her footsteps had faded into silence and followed.

It was late summer and the moonlight fell in white shafts where the canopy opened. He crept forward into the wood, imagining that at any moment his mother would leap out and collar him and march him back to the hut. He was some way short of the grove when he saw them, two men standing stock-still amongst the tree-trunks, barely distinguishable at this distance, facing toward the clearing. He stopped dead in his tracks, then ducked behind a bush. The two men turned to each other, and he saw that one of them was Ewald's father. They moved forward. He thought of skirting around them. A thicket of little elder trees would hide him, he could run and not be seen. He could reach the clearing before them. He rose and was about to run when a hard hand grasped him about the neck, another clamped his mouth, and he was hoisted into the air. It was the man from the boat, the one who shunned him, and with him was another. He twisted like an eel, but there was no escape. The two of them waved across at the other pair, and then he was lifted and held under the man's arm. He tried to cry out, but the hand stayed over his mouth. As they started back for the hut he saw the other two move forward toward the clearing.

He struggled against his captor with all his strength, but the man carried him and contained his rebellion with ease, striding forward in grim and purposeful silence. At one point he was set down and hit three times on the side of the head. The blows dazed him and made him feel sick. The moon kept swinging about the sky, a strong white glare reaching deeply into the darkness, disappearing, reappearing. Out of the wood's blackness a thin shriek was rising, climbing high into the bareness of the sky. His own? They were going to put him in the water butt. He felt himself lifted by the ankles, his arms pinioned for the moment it took to lower him, then the water closed about his head and he was upside-down in darkness, trapped, his arms thrashing and his head thudding madly against the barrel. He was drowning.

It was Ewald's father who saved him. He was lifted out and thrown on the ground to choke and puke up water. When he looked up all four men were staring down at him. On the far side of the clearing, other men were twisting a white shape with flailing limbs, tying her up with something. A hand muzzled him, as it muzzled her, staring at him until he was dragged off, down to the shore where a small boat waited. He was too frightened to run.

The boat pulled away from the shore. One man rowed, the other sat facing him. For a time there was silence broken only by the dip of the oars and the hoarse breathing of the oarsman. He saw the island shrink to a dark strip off the stern. Then the other man began to mutter that he was the luckiest vermin alive and they should have dealt with him properly in the water butt. His kind were nothing but heathen vermin, the spawn of the Devil. His kind loved nothing more than to foul the souls of Christian children with their filth.

They had rounded the point of the island. The line of the coast fell away and they were moving into open water. The other man shouted at him not to look him in the eye, he knew all the tricks his kind liked to get up to.

He was numb, and the words were no more than a noise, like the breathing behind him. The oarsman said nothing. He watched as the man drew two lengths of cord from his pocket, and he was rigid, as if they had already bound him hand and foot. The oarsman stopped rowing. He felt the boat shift. Then, as the man's hands reached to grasp him, his limbs unfroze. He sprang forward and hurled himself into the water.

For the second time that night he felt the shock of the cold. He dove deep and swam forward until the blood thudded in his head and his chest would burst unless he rose. He broke the surface thirty feet from the boat. They were standing one on either side, looking down at the surface, waiting for him to appear. The mainland was less than half a mile by his estimate. They would never catch him. He struck out for the shore. Cutting through the gentle swell with the sea's black liquids buoying him up, the general drift sweeping him across the face of the coast, he felt invincible. He swam like a fish, then like a seal. He could swim like this forever. He floated on his back and gazed up at the sky while the wash of currents slid under him. The sea held him softly, burbling and murmuring, until he fancied he heard the hum of jumbled voices rolling up from the depths. He might dive beneath the surface and swim the fathoms to the city, or he might float here, bobbing between sea and sky, in the shift of their agreement. They were a water people; water would always favor them. And this was a strange sea, almost saltless, almost tideless, carrying him in safety toward the shore.

"And they are still there, Bernardo. All still there with everything they owned, their houses, their streets, their temples filled with silver. Vineta sank entire. Do you hear me? . . . Bernardo?"

Bernardo slumbered beneath his blanket, a giant with his mouth agape. His companion listened to the rhythm of his snores, their thunderous advances and recessions, until he heard beneath them a different wash of sounds, latent in the quiet of the night: the dying echo of storms returning to calm or the muted shudder of water turning to ice. He thought of the first men to cast their unbelieving eyes over the waters' expanse, then the army of newcomers, who stood at the limit of the point while the city's disappearance rose in a backwash, scending the cliff to reach it. He shifted, mind drifting and sinking, allowing the fraying thought to unravel under the sea's bland interrogation, to come apart as liquids dissolve in other liquids or purposes fail in wider needs. Vineta answered, climbed out of a still sea to gather in the soldiers' lack: unrealized city, waiting to engulf them and drown them in themselves. He was hung there with them, held in the moment's fierce suspension, in the soundless geal of their frustration.

Henry the Lion and his captains, their sergeants, and the platoons of March-men crossed the smashed, refrozen ice of the Achter-Wasser expecting Wendish blood on their weapons, a sky stained with purple-black smoke, a final cathartic cleansing. They had fought their way through marshes, rivers, forests; survived hunger, cold, and disease. Ice, they believed, was no different. But they stumbled on the island's frosted glacis, the few remaining horses skidding and laming them-selves on the jagged ledges and unexpected scarps, freakish reminders of the pre-vious night's violence. Behind their broken progress lay the families left behind the Elbe, the pressing host of colonists come from Holstein, Frisia, as far away as Zealand, the rhetoric of bishops urging them forward against the verminous enemy "until with the help of God either their faith or their nation be extermi-nated," memories of the fleet burning at Lübeck and Niklot's squadrons firing the banks of the Trave, their weariness and the winter damp settling in their bones, crusted blood on the faces of the monks with crosses carved in their skulls driven through the villages, their crossings and recrossings of the Elbe, advances and their repulse with the name of Kruto a battlecry their grandfathers' grandfathers would flee still ringing down the years from when Mistivijoi's slaughter and Bishop John's bloodless blue-tongued head, mounted on the altar of the Veletians and eaten with the maggot-years would cry them on to setbacks and laments, sad stumblings over broken ground, dead counts, and the nameless margraves gath-ered about Otto's spiritless corpse in the silence of the chapel to recount the Saxon's deeds, his mournful *comitatus*. . . .

For these all but exhausted soldiers, the buckling on of swords and the for-ward march are crumbs to the ravenous appetites that have driven them onward and farther until here, the shoreline of the island, where ice became land and they halted to await the stragglers at the rear, light fires, to pitch and strike the last of a thousand camps.

The storm rolled over them. The skies lightened. They marched north across the island in good order, their feet bound in rags against the cold. The peat-bog crunched under their footsteps. Frost shaken off the branches of the beech copse fell as snow and dusted them in white. Somewhere beyond the treeline lay the city. The coasts swung in from east and west. The land narrowed to a point. They broke cover and stood there storm-scoured, rimed only with the memory of their dead, to find a crumbling cliff, placid water, a resigned silence broken by flaking shards of clay as they crashed and sank in the sea. Where the isthmus should have projected and broadened to form the platform of the city, they found a wound, the mark of a single and final severance. They stood back from the edge with the island behind them, the whole Nordmark behind that, with its marshes, swamps, and forests marked out with the crosses of their graves, the silent groves

covered in leaves of red and yellow, and beneath the corrosive earth the bodies of
their ancestors serried and layered with the years. The Lion and his men looked
forward and down and saw nothing but water. The city had disappeared.

Previsions return, now hoisted out of forgetting on the point of a contemptuous lance. Their voiceless rage has its almost muted precedent: Szczecin, which
they will rename Stettin, not sixty miles from here and its siege not twenty years
before, which gave them a taste of this almost saltless sea, a mere drop on the
tongue expecting brine. Veterans of that campaign are dotted amongst these
silent, resentful ranks and recall to themselves siege engines mired in the black
mud of the Oder, the clerics hammering crosses into the swampy earth, Bishop
Zdík's shrill encouragements while they drew up the ranks of hauberks and the
horsemen cantered behind the line. The palisades were low and unspiked, the
faces that peered from within seemingly puzzled rather than grim. This would be
an easy conquest, a rarity, for God and Saxony against the heathens. The momentum was unstoppable. They were ready, on the brink and toppling, eager again to
dip their hands in godless blood. Freedmen heft the shafts of their weapons,
horsemen tighten the reins, all coiled together, waiting, when a whisper runs
through the ranks. A shudder of puzzlement. Matters are not as they first appeared, and their own expectations seem to turn on them. . . .

They looked up and saw crosses rising on the palisade; the gates were opening, and striding toward them over the glacis was a figure in full pontificals, Adal-
bert, Bishop of Pomerania, his every footfall dragging the conflict away from
them into some haven of confusion and twisted purpose—an enemy they never
understood—untwisted as Stettin's conversion to the cross some hundred years
before. They have converged on the point where opposites meet and cancel one
another. A foretaste, the unhelpful rehearsal of this situation on the cliff where
they found their purpose tangled once again, darker this time and inextricable as
ever. They were masters of the island, and their goal as remote as ever. Where
could they go from here?

The truncated limb of the point ended in a sheer drop, a clay-red rawness
prickling with blood, and beneath lay only the water's endless and opaque balm.
Somewhere below its surface was the city they had come to sack, the temples to
raze, men and women to cut down, children's heads to dash against vanished
walls, all disappeared, sunk out of reach, still to be done. The wound never bled.
They were alone, and every man foraging in his soul found an appetite only
sharpened by the stark disappearance set before them. A promise had been made,
but the victory was ill defined and beyond them, in some inconclusive region of
convections and sluggish movement. The last ditch should have been the city and
every life within it, never this yellow-gray monotone, this limitless vista of nothing. A promise was made, and broken. Never the sapping extent of the sea.

They would build a church. They would carry stones from quarries as far
away as Brandenburg to build this monument to their bafflement. They spurned
the local sandstones and sent south and east for granite. Full-laden barges plied

the Elbe and Saale for five summers until the foreshore of the island was paved with gray-black stone. Wagons loaded with toises cut to the length of a man a hundred miles hence crept laboriously about the Achter-Wasser, across the island to the limit of the shortened point. Foundations were laid which sank in the soft earth until piles were driven underneath and the creeping collapse arrested. Wooden outbuildings, hasty sheds, and shacks straggled inland from the site. The lodges of the stonecutters and masons spread until they cut the road to the works, were demolished and rebuilt nearer the beech copse. A stables was thrown up, and dormitories for the laborers. The smithy sent the tannin-reek of oak chips billowing into the sky while nails, pegs, tie-bars, horseshoes, ironwork for the carts, and tools for the workmen piled up at the back of the forge. Caskwood, roof-beams, rough planking, and scaffold poles lay stacked in depots next to the tiles. Workshops were built, and wheel-hoists. Ropes were measured and cranes constructed. The laborers dug their trenches with ease in the island's soft substance. In spring, the carpenters arrived.

Not stone but wood will form the first of this structure's guises: the skinless skeleton of a church. Groin-vaults, arches, towers, and walls rise from the foundations through the inference of scaffolding and lathes, a trellis for the church to grow into. The site is crowded with workmen: a hundred, then two, more when the work is at its height. Mortar makers grind lime in pestles, hands scarred white from the burns, sand, gravel, water, stiffening to the paste the mason's trowel can spread and layer; the stonesetters wear gloves and their scars are different, crushed fingers, jagged and crudely healed cuts, bruises welling under the thumbnail, calluses hard as bone. Treadwheels turn and the stones are raised. Hardcutters saw at the facing blocks, sanders sand, plumb-lines swing and fall. Soon, elevations rise off the plan and the walls begin to climb skyward.

Two winters pass. Two towers face the sea. Roofers scramble across the beams and hammer pegs to hold the tiles. Ribs are being carved to replace the caskwood supports within the nave. The last year has been a year of haste. Now the laborers are slipping away, the masons tamping down whichever stone comes easiest to hand. Work will begin at Strassburg within the year, five hundred miles south from this eerie, deserted place: no easy journey. Plasterers work from before dawn till after dusk. A window is cemented inside out and left. Statues are misplaced. The priest to consecrate this church arrives by boat from Lübeck and speaks before the altar of victories over the pagan, of abundant seas and fertile lands. Winds blow off the water, find the unplugged eaves, and whistle in the echoing roofspace. Plaster dust rises off the floor. Twenty workmen listen in silence while the prelate battles with the wind. They watch him leave, then leave themselves. The church stands silent and deserted, empty on an empty island.

It was the decision of distant bishops; they could not have foreseen the indifference of Flemish and Saxon settlers to herring. Boats and nets are alien tools in hands used to the ax and plow. There is the border to be reckoned with, too: the very shoreline is under dispute. From the east, Boleslav will move his squadrons across the Oder to challenge the Lion's crusaders, and God will be claimed by both. There will be meetings between Bohemian and Saxon bishops at Stargard and Hamburg, but the ragged coast about the mouth of the Oder resists the compromises drawn up in their ill-tempered conferences. About the Trave, islands seemed to loose themselves from the foreshore and drift ambiguously into the sea—discrete landmasses, sandbars, shoals, tiny peninsulas cut and rejoined and cut once more—the confusion baffles their efforts to apportion it until the whole morass is dispatched south, to Rome for elucidation, and sent back with the Pope's blessing and acceptance of their gift. Further ill-tempered conferences: they had not foreseen this particular solution; more, they resist it utterly. The decision stands. The Holy See will create the missionary diocese of Kammin to minister to the heathens' needs and collect their tithes. There is a Bishop, it is rumored, but he is not seen at Kammin, Wollin, Stettin, across the Oder, and east as far as Stargard, nor even on the island that lies like an ill-fitting stopper in the mouth of the estuary: Usedom. Yet he must have existed, his permission would have been needed. The monks who were to take up residence in this place must have sought him out and found him somewhere. In name at least if nothing more, this was, after all, his church.

They crossed the Achter-Wasser in boats hired farther down the Peene. They came from Prémontré in the forest of Coucy and spoke neither the glottal dialect of the Flemish nor the guttural accents of the Saxons, let alone the gibberish of the Slavs. They retraced the steps of the Lion's army, the toings and froings of the workmen who followed, north across the island until they reached the site of their new home, the church built to mark the Saxon triumph. They brought chalices, missals, psalters, breviaries, copes, crucifixes, and censers. Their Abbot bore a chest filled with books wherein he carried hopes of a library, together with the implements and parchment to add to it. Their thoughts were of a famed and feted foundation, the beginnings of a northern Rome. It was Saint Martin's Day, and brilliant winter sunshine pierced the canopy of beeches. A psalm echoed among the tree-trunks, and their hearts were filled with happiness as the monks broke through the scrub. They saw the ground rise and narrow, and at the limit of the point they found their church.

It was a shell, a tomblike accumulation of stone sticking up like a single rotted tooth with its substance eroded, its lines awry, and the whole structure frozen in a seeming stagger as though it were lurching toward the sea.

The masons had worked through the winters without troubling to cover the stones in straw. Now the frost had cracked and flaked them. Some had been laid across the grain, and those nearest the foundations had crumbled under the weight of those above. The walls bulged out and the roofline sagged. Winds blowing in off the sea had lifted tiles so within this echoey shell rainwater stood in stagnant pools. The plaster had drawn damp out of the air and fallen off the walls in slabs. Fragments of mortar lay scattered on the flagstones of the floor. On the seaward side, one of the towers leaned alarmingly toward the overhang. Its piles had sunk at the corner and the foundations disappeared into the clay. Thirty white-robed monks and their Abbot slung back their cowls to view the church that was their home. They climbed the stairs of the one sound tower and cast their eyes south and east across the deserted island, saw peat-bog and beech copse, mixed forest and scrubland cut haphazardly with tiny streams, minuscule islands standing off the landward coast. To the north, the sea. Their own presence was the result of distant, protracted debate to which they had never been party. They had not been told the island was deserted, their church a new-built ruin. Their Abbot felt his heart being fingered by despair.

They set themselves to the work of rebuilding their crumbling domain: mixing new mortar and plaster, repointing the walls, resurrecting the smithy to forge claw hammers and roof-pegs, replacing the tiles, cutting timber to buttress the leaning tower and the western wall of the church, which leaned, too, as did the south, though less, and the east, though less still, and the north, which they only suspected. They ordered stone from the quarries of the Uckermark, built a dorter and the beds to fill it, a refectory, a kitchen, infirmary, and chapter-house to enclose a cloister behind the church. They drained water from the nave, watched it seep back, drained it again, and again, finally lifting the flagstones to discover them laid on bare ground more resembling mud than earth. So they dug drains, and more drains, culverts and a channel for the reredorter. Still the floor of the church sagged, as though it were fashioned from planks floating in a lake of liquid, and the arches of the bays sank under the load of ill-conceived masonry.

Their Abbot began a history of their works on the island, *Gesta Monachorum Usedomi,* a rough account scratched out in a cursive hand, which he would write by candlelight in the hours between Lauds and Terce.

Sent by Abbot Hugh de Fosses in the year of Our Lord twelve hundred and seventy-three to found a monastery on the isle of Usedom, we arrived on these shores on Saint Martin's Day of that year. Much toil awaited us. . . .

The monks planted vegetable gardens, barley fields, and plum orchards. The first settlers arrived and they collected rents, but the tower still leaned, the whole place sagged, and the Abbot watched his income dwindle and disappear into sodden foundations, collapsing roofs, and all manner of improvements that somehow failed to improve. His *Gesta Monachorum Usedomi* grew to become a never-ending list of building works, and when the Abbot noticed that he had written *This week was spent by the brothers relaying the stones of the cloister* three times in as many months and *Straightening one corner of the chapter-house has pulled the others out of true* five times, then he gave up his history and consigned it to the chest containing the books intended for the library, which somehow he never found the time to unpack. He felt the same fingers of despair tighten about his heart and began to believe that even the task of maintaining their church was beyond them. The Lion's endowment was long spent, his monks exhausted from their labors—surely Norbert himself had not intended his order to dissipate itself in such labors? He sent to Magdeburg for help but received from the Archbishop only a message describing Usedom and its monastery as "peculiar": meaning subject not to his jurisdiction, but to that of the diocese of Kammin and its Bishop, if there was one, and if not, then to the Curia and thence the Pope; meaning no. His absences at the annual seminars of abbots at Prémontré were noticed but not discouraged.

The Abbot wrapped his isolation about him like a cloak. At dawn he would absent himself from the chapter-house and climb the easternmost tower to watch the sea fogs roll over the foreshore, engulf the island, and be burned away by the midday sun. He sought God in a desert of water, this puzzled stylite, but saw only the Hansa cogs sailing to Gdansk and the mouth of the Vistula. The sea itself remained unchanged, a contemptible sea, weak tides, brackish, yellow near the coast. Fishing boats toiled from nearby Rügen and sometimes landed in the cove on the far side of the island. He should levy something. The settlers minded their pigs, goats, and barley fields, tended beehives and chickens. Every Quinquagesima Sunday past they had laid the refectory for a dinner of salted pork, but no one ever came. The settlers spoke a tongue his monks could barely understand, and vice versa. Their fields and farmhouses dotted and parceled out the island, but most of it remained forest, swamp, and scrub. Some of the original inhabitants were rumored to live still in the woods, survivors of the Lion's zeal, and the storm, and the city's disappearance, which was why the church was built, or why it was built so badly. Yesterday the roof of the chapter-house fell in; tomorrow the kitchen chimney pot would follow it. It was the pieces of a church.

He descended, resigned to imperfection and its toil, as others would resign and descend. Oblated infants would pass from the gatehouse to the choir, from the choir to the order, from the order to the infirmary, and thence to the cemetery, which lay to the east of the gatehouse. The lines of graves would lengthen until the bodies of twenty-three abbots lay side by side, each worn out by the struggles of the soul and the battle against their church, which tilted farther toward the sea with every successor to the office until a cup placed on the floor of the nave would roll its length unaided and continue into the presbytery. Winter squalls would eat away the foot of the cliff, prising free the shoring timbers and carrying them out to sea. The monks would descend in their wake to rebuild the buttresses, and it was then that they would find the true foundations of their church: rings, goblets, silver chains, and bracelets, the glittering detritus hauled by the storm from the city beneath the sea. The cliff was shored anew and the benison carried to the Abbot; almost a casket of it now. But the church continued to lean, an inch, two inches a year, until the bells found their own notion of perpendicular jammed fast against that of the towers and fell silent.

The island was no Rome, or Jerusalem, or Santiago de Compostela. No pilgrim routes had swept the alluvia of cathedral lore to accumulate on Usedom. No Abbot Suger was willing to clad his soul in stone on this remote outpost. Perhaps some imperfect prevision of Strassburg's facade found its echo in the lurching towers, of Ebrach's groin-vaults in the malformed bays of the nave, but for all its faltering three hundred and threescore years it remained a hasty gesture of permanence, a conclusion stamped on molten ground, on the Lion's thwarting, his bafflement at the disappearance set before him.

And now, as before, the Prior of this monastery dwells overlong on bafflement. He is alone in this meditation, and the thought is unconfessed, welling unstoppably in the hours of darkness. It has been with him a year or more. He sees the rotations of the monks through their services, the ceaseless rolling maintenance, their severance from the incomprehensible islanders. He hears the unvoiced rage of the Lion and his ragged, long-dead army. He traces the dwindling circle of minor acts and observances, repetitions and services, nearings, evasions, and returns. Their routine appears the cement of a permanent church, a mortar laid down long ago, too quickly mixed and crumbling invisibly between the stones. He lights a second candle and pushes the cowl from his head. He hears his brother monks shuffle to the church. Only he can see it, waiting for them all while they spiral toward its center, while their devotions run their course.

Nocturns and Lauds are the offices of night; lanterns and candles move up and down the nave in their pools of light. The cantors chant and the Lauds of the Dead ring out through the church. He hears the Lion's rage in a plainsong rising to the resonant vaults, an echo redoubled in the darkness above their heads. Monks and novices shuffle from the church to the chapter-house, to the refectory, to the church, to their beds in the dorter. Terce follows Lauds as day follows night, then Sext and None. The bell should have tolled for Vespers next, but the bell is stilled, the towers lean, bell-pulls snag on the crumbling stones: clay is no foundation on which to build a church. Compline is sung before dusk. Masses are sung after Terce and Sext, then work in the gardens or the fields, on the fabric of their crumbling church. Ropes have been strung from the porch to the altar, for the tilt is visible, palpable, and walking up the nave is a struggle. The rhythm of the day is a changeless round. Cantors chant, he hears the choir sing out, but clay is colloidal, a yielder to load, and the church is a load, hence the tilt, hence the ropes. The Lion's gall drips from the ribs, works channels under flagstones, suffuses the structure. The choir sings out and Nocturns is the first of the offices of night and it is dark in the church, only pools of light, yet the change is waiting, only difficult to see. Clay is a sediment and not yet stone. Henry the Lion rages at nothing but the city's failure to remain. The prior hears a different music dripping through the stones, a corrosive music of rage and thwarted purpose. Voiceless in face of the city's disappearance, stopped up by the church's crumbling plug, he listens for its leakage, hears the drip of its return.

Lauds: the Prior fails to attend. A plainsong reaches him at work in the chapter-house. He hears the choir sing out and bends his thoughts to the lesson. *Thou art Peter and upon this rock I will build my church.* . . . He hears the voices fall quiet and the murmur of the sea slide from under the monkish song. Father Jörg knows the sea is weak, rising inches through the year from neap to spring. Yet their timbers shift out and come loose from the cliff. He feels shudders that others do not feel, suffers nameless fears. There is a devil in the sea with an unseen face. *And upon this rock* . . . The church is a fort, he will tell them that. But a faltering fort, an ill-manned garrison at the edge of the world. He will preach vigilance, and wariness, and labor—he always does. But the moment is near, the collapse is waiting. Nameless fears shared by no one else. They will not understand, and so he waits through the nights, listening, holding his breath. He stands in the center of the chapter-house, rapt in his thoughts, drifting between the lesson and his private fears, and then, quite suddenly, he lurches.

And falls. He comes to himself as the sounds flood through his ears.

He hears the voices start up, the cantors cry out, he is right, it is true, and the church is shifting, shuddering below. He hears the clay slide out, like the ebb of a tide of a sea filled with clay. He knows the weight of the stones, the invisible loads. His ears seem to pop with the force of the din. He hears the rumble of a massive collapse, the clangor of the sack which the commander should have heard: the crack of a spine, screaming priests, and the struggle to escape. He runs to the door as the monks spill out, runs in and falls on the heaving floor. The church is moving. A terrible grating growls up from below. The church is breaking at the end of the nave. He rises to usher panicking monks to the safety of the chapter-house. The floors are shaking, tilting, breaking halfway up the church, the altar dipping out of sight. He rises and climbs forward up the nave to the line of the break. The roof gapes open and tiles rain down. Before him, the floor slopes steeply away. He watches as the far wall of the apse topples backward out of sight. Stones fall away and tumble out. The back of the church is peeled away. Down the vault of the church he sees the surface of the sea and hears the crash of the stones as they break it. He crouches there until the roof-beams begin to creak above his head. Stars prick the sky through the broken roof. Moonlight foils the pitch of the sea: different kinds of darkness with their different kinds of light. Himself, balanced between them. Even through the crash of timber and stone, tiny slaps of wavelets prickle in his ears from the water below. Stiff fluids throb and roar in his skull. There are slower convections, deeper currents. Beneath even these lies the loss that the church could not recoup.

Looking down through the barrel of the backless nave to the waters a hundred feet below, Jörg sees no more than the Lion saw. He feels his heart fill up with the dead man's rage, brim, and spill its waste in the splintering of beams, toppling masonry, the clatter of tiles as they shatter on the broken floor. The Lion stands again on the jut of the point, sees the yellow-gray waters crawl slackly about the coast, his single coordinate invisible, unreachable, as he searches for missing walls and ramparts, lost temples and their idols, a disappeared people and all their vanished works, buildings and wide paved streets, the hum of voices, clatter of footsteps: the uncity's clangor, of Vineta. His church is broken and the crisis is here. The moment has come again. This time Jörg knows what must be done.

A dim rumble rolled across the Achter-Wasser, through the narrow strait of Twelen, was squeezed by Gormitz and the Gnitz and funneled in a muddy roar to reach Wilfried Ploetz sleeping in his hovel. No light reached down the chimney hole, and with no birdsong or screeching of gulls to break the ensuing silence, he rubbed his eyes, yawned, realizing that dawn was hours off yet and he was fully awake. Now he would be denied his rightful rest and instead of snoring would toss and turn until dawn squeezed some light out of the stubborn autumn skies and he rose hollow-eyed to reluctantly embrace the day. Such injustices never arrived by chance: a big noise of some kind, perhaps a distant storm. He yawned and stretched. Yes, his mind was turning over, whatever it was still rumbling around in his head; unbidden, unwelcome, unexplained. Ploetz cursed.

The question still vexed him as he tramped across the island some sleepless hours later, still irritated him as he reached the Brüggeman farmhouse, knocked, waited for Mathilde to rouse her husband, Ewald, his employer, faded to an irksome itch while they dragged the boat down the foreshore, was forgotten in the tedium of disentangling nets, and might never have been remembered if Ewald had not turned the boat to starboard, heading northeast along the coast, instead of to port, where the fishing was easier. Who was he to argue? His father had never argued, and if he had, Ewald's father would have thrown him off the boat. But the morning mists were thicker here and the waters more difficult; the nets would snag and sometimes tear.

Ewald signaled for him to cast. He threw, but clumsily, felt the water pull as the net cords grew sodden. Ewald shifted to the starboard side; he felt the boat lean over, then right herself as he hauled up the catch, the two men balancing to hold the boat true. He bent, heaved, and then the load was aboard, the bottom of the boat alive in a moment with a glittering spillage of herring and sprat. But a quarter of a barrel, no more than that. Ewald frowned, and Ploetz thought back to the moment before. To drop the nets then would tilt the whole boat; Ewald would fall and be over the side. The balance of a boat was a delicate matter.

They moved farther up the coast, and the mist grew thicker. The nets were cast and drawn in once again, both men sweating in the clammy morning air. Three more weeks and the boat would be beached for winter. Ploetz felt firm, slippy herring-bodies sliding about his ankles as he took the oars to row the next hundred yards. They would be passing Koserow by now, but the coast was invisible, still clouded out. In came the nets, out went the nets; Ploetz worked to a rhythm. An hour passed, another, and the fog began to thin. A plank floated past. Brüggeman was busy sorting herring from sprat, and the tide was inaudible, negligible, little more than drift. Neither man noticed their nearing the coast. Ploetz threw a dace back over the side, pulled some weed from the net, then stood to piss off the back of the boat. The splash of his urine was the only sound. Another plank drifted into view. Then another, and another. Soon the boat was surrounded by them. Not planks, though. Beams. A floating lumberyard all bobbing in the water. Ploetz stared, then frowned. Brüggeman was intent in the bottom of the boat. The first beam bumped, Brüggeman started, and both men looked up. A vast dark shape loomed vaguely above them.

Their boat had drifted beneath the jut of a cliff, and on Usedom there was only one. They had reached Vineta Point.

Ploetz knew this cliff, a sheer face of clay shored with crude, massive beams and the back of the church just visible atop. But the overhang was changed, its shoring swept away, and the base of the cliff had disappeared, gouged out so the rest seemed to stand on nothing. The two men looked higher and saw through the mist, a hundred feet above, a ragged black hole pointing down toward them. It seemed to teeter on the brink, arrested and frozen in the moment of falling, a great vault tilted downward, gaping down at the boatmen like a massive stone throat. The two men were staring up into the nave of the church.

The news spread quickly, and by late afternoon most of the island was stationed at the beach to witness the aftermath of the disaster. Like an anvil, thought Ronsdorff. Like the prow of a ship, thought Haase. The islanders gathered on the shore by Koserow to look along the coast and view the newly shaped cliff. Perched on top, the church appeared hinged at the middle, half on, half off. Like the boathouse at Stettin, thought Matthias Riesenkampf. Like a half-broken loaf, thought Otto Ott. Werner Dunkel brought his pickax and Peter Gottfreund three shovels. From time to time, from their vantage point a few hundred paces along the shore, they saw odd stones topple from the broken bell tower or shoot forth from somewhere within the nave, as though the church were spitting pebbles into the sea. Of the monks themselves there was no sign at all.

Winter advanced and began to send the two boatmen its warnings. Waves coiled loosely in the placid autumn swell, rolled up the beach, and began unfurling frigid whites and starker blacks. Winds chilled in the northern gulfs swept south, gathered pace over open water, and whipped waves from the normally placid surface, pushing them farther out from the coast for fear of being driven aground. The days rattled and collided in the loose vaults of the season, and each morning found Brüggeman and Ploetz rowing out from the shore in the teeth of the wind and hoisting the sail to return in the evening. The catches were growing thinner, and most years, Ploetz knew, Brüggeman would have beached the boat weeks before. Yet they persisted, against their better judgment and Mathilde's protests, while the waters grew darker and more turbulent by the day. They worked off Vineta Point. They cast and drew in the nets, soaked and chilled to the bone. They looked inland to the cliff and the scurrying specks of gray that labored in its shadow. They watched the monks try to save their church.

The first week had seen them recover the beams. As the winds blew them in, the monks had thrown lines and grappled them ashore with hooks. A depot was built and ropes thrown down from above. A tripod was raised, anchored underneath the cliff, then another, then a third. Other beams were hoisted, lashed together, and braced. A scaffold was rising underneath the jut, an enormous prop to underpin the church. Ploetz watched as it rose upward to the overhang. It grew day by day but seemed never quite to reach. A puzzle, a conundrum, which kept him wondering at night while he drifted into sleep. He dreamed of towers being sucked beneath the sea, hungry mouths gulping invisibly beneath the waters, and he realized that it was the yielding ooze of the seabed that would defeat them; the gap between their effort and its success was widening, not closing, and their scaffold was sinking even as they built it. Still the monks persisted. They built a raft, a strangely fashioned craft with a hole in the middle, to drive in piles. Monks leaped about its deck to manhandle logs, making it lurch wildly, while small waves rocked it up and down. The fishermen watched as piles were fed down through the hole, knocked about by the raft, lost, then retrieved and inserted once again, until one was held in place for long enough to drive. Ploetz wondered what plan they had formed to free their raft from the firmly anchored beam that now stuck up through the deck. He saw their craft knocked about by the rising swell, bumping against the pile, which bent this way and that, loosening under the battery, finally coming free of the seabed's soft mud. And above this minor disaster, he noticed now, the greater scaffold was not only sinking, but leaning, too, outward, away from the flaking clay of the cliff toward the ever more vigorous sea. This would be their final day before the boat was covered, before the year wheeled about and spring returned with calmer waters, a warmer sun, and boatloads of newly grown herring. It was growing rougher and colder. The gray-clad bodies were still at their labor. As the sun began to sink, the fishermen hoisted their sail, let the boat swing about, and left the monks to their hopeless engineering, their church to the coming bad weather.

There was little to do through the drab winter freeze, no fishing, no work, little reason to do more than cut wood, build fires, eat sparingly and carefully, wait for the coming of spring. Gray skies rolled north over Usedom, broke up over water, and let the sparse winter sunlight waste its warmth in the sea. It rained. It froze. In the offshore waters herring hung motionless in the clay-stained waters, lidless eyes set in slick fat bodies, mouths opening and closing, feeding on the fruits of the sea. Salmon raced east like an army of knights in glistening mail. On the island, nothing set these days apart but the arc of a struggling sun.

Then, with the drip of melting frost spattering the floor of the forests, birdsong, the squawk of goosanders and gulls breaking the stillness of the air, the frigid days would seem to unfreeze, to swell and grow warmer with the strengthening sun. And it would seem to the islanders, rising, yawning, cracking their joints, setting out once more for their manses—repairs are waiting, there is ground must be broken—that along with its usual shoots and crescent growths the spring had brought a hybrid to flower, the result of unnatural conjunction. Something unheard of and troubling; an unaccountable nearing of a dependably distant landmark. The monks.

Before long, every man, woman, and child on the island had a tale to tell of monkish visitation. They would appear from nowhere at any hour of the day, always in a group, mumble a sentence or two, then move on to the next reluctant islander. The greetings were uttered in odd, stilted accents and seemed to serve no purpose at all. "How fare your wife, your sister, and her friends?" "Your father and mother are well?" "Well plowed, plowman!" Some strange animation seemed to grip them as they uttered these phrases, a weird fervor that drove them to rove about the island in this unprecedented fashion, engaging people in halting intercourse and interfering with their tasks. It was suspicious and unwelcome. What did these wakened sleepwalkers want?

Tithes, in the opinions of some, lay behind this outflux of monks. Tithes were left at the gatehouse on feast days: a chicken, a ham, half a bushel of wheat. But since the monks never left the confines of their monastery, save to work at their garden or harvest their fields, since the topsoil was thin and the summer months short, the livestock scraggy, the hens often broody, the oxen hungry, and the barley grew short, and since the islanders preferred to eat rather than not, tithes had tended to shrink. Tithes, then, or rents, or some other form of debt, or their sinfulness in general drove the monks to this lackluster crusade. Yet tithes, rent, and sin figured little in their bizarre interferences, which grew less bizarre as the months wore on and the brothers became positively fluent. "How's the family, Haase?" or, "Your furrows look like eels, Riesenkampf!" Which they did, his ox being blind in one eye. Some islanders chose to hide beneath a touch to the hat or a wave and swift retreat. Others engaged in plodding conversation, offered them beer and sometimes ham. By late summer the children were steeling themselves to throw rotten pears, their mothers to apologize, their fathers to hail these singular fellows as a matter of course while they wandered about the island.

Apprehension gave way to novelty, novelty to grudging acceptance, but the question returned and returned. The monks had been there before any of them, the island was theirs by the Lion's grant, and if they had chosen to shun it for the past three hundred years, why should they not reclaim it? Why should they not take long pointless walks, engage in this purposeless talk, pursue some inscrutable end? Why not? Or rather, and maddeningly, why?

Jealousy of the church at Wolgast, thought Mathilde Brüggeman. Of the better one at Stettin, thought her husband. Still the tithes, worried Riesenkampf. The rents, opined Ott, while the rest of the island thought of sinfulness, charity, preparations for the Second Coming, one, some, or all of these, or something else like them, some explanation to drag them each morning through the monastery gatehouse and send them the length and breadth of the island. It was not divulged in the ceaseless greetings, nor in the pattern of their movements: some undivined need lay beneath their cowls, behind those tight white faces and unblinking eyes.

When spring came around, the Quinquagesima feast was announced. For the first time in centuries, islanders were ushered through the gatehouse and served by the monks with slices of pork dripping with grease, steaming rutabagas and parsnips. The Prior rose before grace to commend them for their welcome, to welcome them in turn and wish them good appetite. He watched them lean forward eagerly for the merest hint. But the reason was not given and their earlier guesses foundered as though they were snared in a parable whose meaning would reveal them, too late, as Doubting Thomases, unenlightened Sauls, Jonahs, to each other. What had brought the monks from out their monastery? And what had ushered the islanders in? It was a test of some sort, but too obscure, so they speculated, changed their minds, disputed, and discounted their neighbors' theories to erect more fanciful ones of their own. Confusion swamped the truth just as the sea concealed and ate into the cliff. Stationed off the coast, as the nets sank down, Ploetz would pause in his work and look along Usedom's shoreline, past Koserow to Vineta Point. He saw the wreckage of their scaffold, the gouged-out cliff, the ruin balanced on its brink. He thought of the monks' hopeless labor in the freezing gray waters. What else could drive them to break their isolation? What else if not the ruin of their church?

True, he could do nothing in the darkness of the chapter-house, nothing to succor them while they cowered together in the center of the floor and his fear enclosed them. That night he could only stand and wait, listening with them to the shatter of tiles, the crash of stones in the sea, crumbling and toppling certainties. The brothers held each other in their arms while Father Jörg strode about the gradines, tapping walls, stamping on floors, assuring them the structure was sound. The novices whimpered, the brothers muttered prayers, and Jörg's mind raced forward alone.

Daylight. Ropes. Brother Gerhardt's high wail drifting back through the nave as they haul him back from under the cliff. The damage is worse than any suspected, the red clay crumbling, their foundations sinking. Brother Wilhelm is found shuffling, lighting candles in the church. Their Abbot will not leave his cell. Jörg sees the brothers slump listlessly, stunned in the chapter-house, faces gray from the shock with no service to rouse them. Torpor pinches their souls with fingers of ice, milking them of hope. Jörg feels his impatience rising, turns and leaves, walks by the sagging cloister to the garden, and finds himself scrambling down the slope that fronts the coast. Morning fog rolls across the sea and thuds soundlessly against the cliff, a muffled hammer as he looks across at the face. At its base the clay curves steeply inward; the sea has advanced twenty feet or more. Their shoring timbers bob up and down in the tiny waves. Brother Gerhardt will want to retrieve them, to start again and raise a buttress to the overhang. Impossible. Madness—which will goad Brother Gerhardt, make him more determined than ever. Very well, very well. His notion will keep. The brothers must be won over, and the Abbot too must be persuaded. Sunlight is bleaching the cloudy air, disturbing and turning in on itself. Silent giants hover in the vapor and ring Father Jörg as he sits in the midst of his thoughts.

A mast? Yes, he squints through the fog, and there a boat, moving in toward the coast. A small one-master floats in amongst the beams, almost beneath the cliff itself. Two fishermen are standing, staring up at the church, mouths open, faces agog. He notes their amazement. Feast your eyes, thinks Jörg. Tell your chattering wives and your curious children, your gossiping neighbors and your friends. Tell everyone, for I will need you all. Tell every soul on the island.

They held services in the chapter-house, but all through that first winter their true worship was performed in the sea. Jörg watched them labor in the freezing waters, building hoists and cranes, raising beams and joists. A raft was constructed, though it failed, and the piles they drove in the mud beneath the waves seemed never to find a foundation. Brother Gerhardt's cell was a mass of scrawls: braces and crossbeams, buttresses and counterforts. But as his confident tripods lurched sideways and sank, his scantlings came loose and the struts fell away, as the psalms they sang grew more quiet, then stopped, the weather got worse and his fantastical scaffoldings fell into the sea, it would seem to the builder monk that he was building a staircase that sank with every step taken upon it. Looming above them as the wind chapped their faces and the water turned their fingers blue was the flaking overhang and their toppling church. Unreachable. Impossible.

Brother Gerhardt scrawled by day and night: arches, vaults, towers, columns. He needed angels to power the cranes he designed, ropes pulled by the arms of Christ, prayed for them, cursed them, and the north wall of the cloister became a mass of white, a sheer blank to which he pointed: "See! See!" There was the solution, a plan plain as day, yet all the monks saw was whiteness; an illegible palimpsest. Gerhardt's consuming fury. He scrubbed the walls bare to the gray of the stone and pointed again. He traced fabulous arcs and soaring verticals, tremendous arches in rising tiers. "No horizontals. No horizontals, understand? Horizontals are the work of the Devil. . . ." But their beams and buttresses were so much wreckage in the water, and his workers saw nothing but stone the color of the sea.

Jörg watched and waited. At length he gathered the brothers and novices in the chapter-house and had the Abbot carried from his cell. It was spring, and they were exhausted. Despairing faces turned to him from their seats. Brother Gerhardt would look away furiously as he spoke, all his efforts come to nothing. He would never be Abbot; that, at least, had been settled. Jörg spoke and heard his words roll and spring like acrobats in the interior of the chapter-house, beguiling and purposeless. Old and young alike listened in silence to their mission. They did not understand. The islanders? How were the islanders able to help? Bright words dancing and tripping on their brows, a diversion for them, a novelty. The first of their several new worlds. He strode up and down, haranguing and cajoling, spreading his arms, pointing, addressing each in turn, drawing them in. He described the perilous state of the church, the collapse of the church's foundation, their labor and its failure. But as the walls of their circumstances rose like a prison around them, he drew upon their stones a different vision: of great plains and rivers, pasture dotted with fields of barley, high snowcapped mountains, and bustling, crowded cities. The world without the monastery. He looked about them, but their faces were blank and uncomprehending.

They would not understand, not when he sent them out through the gate-house, nor when they returned, still baffled, with stories they muttered amongst themselves of the islanders' reluctance, their malformed speech and strange customs. They were adrift, unanchored in this wider world, undermined in their own. Brother Gerhardt resisted utterly and would spend that year rebuilding his raft at the foot of the cliff. He toiled alone but was watched by his fellows, who saw in his futile efforts a last door closing on their former existence. Every day of their excursions was taking them further from their familiar paths, of worship, contemplation, and building. Always building. Through it all, their Abbot never uttered a word. They sat him in his cell, overlooking the sea, where he remained, gazing out over his old enemy like an aged, defeated commander.

Jörg would question them on their return and they would tell him of the beech forests and marshes, little ponds and lakes that dotted the island, the slopes of tussocky grass that led to reed-beds and weed-fringed shelves of gluey black mud. Beyond them, always, the sea. The islanders, he insisted. Tell me of the islanders. They spoke of rebuffs, evasions, children running shouting across the barley fields, figures disappearing below ridges at their approach. Women hiding under tables. He needed more, and better, pushing them out through the gate-house until they brought back snippets of conversation, vague tidings, the flotsam of life amongst the islanders. Ronsdorff's honey was better than Ulrich Meister's. Otto Ott had a liar's face but was honest. He demanded more. Stenschke's daughters had all married well. They bossed their husbands. Old man Stenschke was mostly lucid but going mad. Sometimes he walked about naked. Better, thought Jörg.

He began to ask for news and learned that the fishermen he had seen in the aftermath of the disaster were Ewald Brüggeman and his underling, Wilfried Ploetz. The other boats were beached on the Stettiner Haff, across from Wolgast or else from Wollin. A daughter of Werner Dunkel's was pregnant, but no one knew by whom. Wittmann, perhaps, or Peter Gottfreund, but the brothers were more inclined to Haase. When half a dozen of them returned drunk on Riesenkampf's beer, Jörg shouted and raged but knew his work was proceeding. And when he closed his eyes on the night of the Quinquagesima feast, heard the brothers chatting amiably, the islanders chatting back as they stuffed their stomachs and slapped one another on the shoulder, listened there to the easy commerce of monk and laity, he thought the first part of his task might almost be complete.

Jörg rose and slipped quietly past the monks carrying empty tureens, out into the cool of the cloister. The night was almost clear, only thin shreds of cloud silvering the harsher white of the moon. He walked carefully over uneven stones past the dorter to the cells. The Abbot sat as he always did, in silence, eyes fixed on the dim play of moonlight bouncing off the waves. Jörg knelt by the side of the chair, allowing the room's silence to gather for a minute or more. The Abbot's breath rattled. He had urinated where he sat. "Am I right?" he whispered. "Do you believe me right?" But the Abbot made no sound or sign. Jörg sighed and rose. He had not come for sanction. The chests he sought lay on the far side of the cell.

   Sent by Abbot Hugh de Fosses in the year of Our Lord twelve hundred and seventy-three to found a monastery on the isle of Usedom, we arrived on these shores on Saint Martin's Day of that year. Much toil awaited us. . . .

   The hasty characters had almost sunk into the parchment. Jörg had to squint to make them out as the first Abbot's chronicle told him of collapses and repairs, subsidence and restorations. He shuffled through the leaves, but they were unvarying, the events relentless, and though after a few more pages the chronicle simply stopped in midsentence Jörg knew that its story continued, sunk invisibly within the parchment, the chest whence it came, the stones of the cell that surrounded him, and the fabric of the monastery that had soaked up their efforts as the parchment had the ink until they were only gray-robed ciphers, illegible in the church's mere continuance. Its collapse had saved them.

   Jörg reached across the Abbot to his desk and quickly cut a quill. The Abbot had not touched his accounts since the night of their catastrophe. Jörg moistened the ink-cake with his spittle, scraped the quill in the well, and scrawled quickly, *When their church collapsed, the monks of Usedom were sent by their Prior to mingle with the people of the island. Much bafflement awaited them. . . .* And there the ink ran out, so he stopped. He had not come here to write his own *Gesta Monachorum Usedomi.* His thoughts swept wider than Usedom, further and higher. Father Jörg reached within the chest for the books that had lain undisturbed beneath the chronicle since the days of the very first Abbot. The library they were to have founded had never been built. One after another he lifted them out, wiped the mold from their covers, and placed them carefully on the floor. The Abbot ignored him as he staggered under the weight, never turned as the door swung shut, only watched the sea where black waves and white moonrays seemed to play together, waiting for daylight to blend them to gray.

   In the weeks that followed, the brothers were to find their island excursions inexplicably curtailed. Ulrich Meister's pigs had been fattened on acorns, and Brother Walter had hoped to help with the slaughter. Brüggeman had told Brother Florian of wild greengage trees somewhere on the far side of the island, ideal for grafting, but the far side of the island was hours away and by order of Father Jörg every monk was to return to the monastery by midday. Brother Gundolf had taken up fishing, and Brother Volker was breeding bees with Stenschke. Brother Heinz-Joachim was charting the ponds of the island, Brother Joachim-Heinz the woods. All these activities would now have to wait. Brother Georg felt the lack of his circuitous morning walk around the peat-bog to Haase's manse, while Brothers Wilf, Wolf, and Wulf came to miss their tricornered chin-wags

with Riesenkampf's wife. Already, from within their hesitant footsteps and bewildered trampings new measures had emerged. Brother Bernd worried over
Riesenkampf's ox rather than the crumbling casements of the dorter. The cycles
of service and labor had expanded to encompass the island and its denizens, and
now their ambit was narrowing, drawing them back, returning them to their
church. The brothers found themselves surprised at their own disappointment,
resentful once more of their Prior, who spent his days closeted in his cell and
his nights the same. Brother HansJürgen brought him his meals and was told to
leave them at the door. Mucky yellow light seeped out as he burned tallow
candles until dawn; alone in there, unguessable, under siege from their unframed
questions.

He read, breathing in damp and the chalky smell of mold as he slid his nails
under the pages and bent his head to the fading script. The candles' thin convections sent the musty years spiraling about his cell. He coughed, scratched, rubbed
his eyes, reached the end of one book, and picked up the next. The days began to
lengthen, and outside, on Usedom, the harvest began.

Tar barrels burned for Saint John on the mainland, sending up thick black
smoke columns in a lazy slant, high into the dispersing air. The islanders cut their
corn with long-handled scythes, their women gathering and sheaving behind
them. Old gods marched ahead of the harvesters, Roggenmühme scaring the
children, who ran shouting into the cool of the beech woods. They picked
berries and stripped bark from the oaks for tanning. Ronsdorff scraped the honey
from its combs, and Haase gathered resin from the fruit trees. Dunkel's daughter
gave birth to a girl who howled in the thick summer heat.

All through the harvest, Jörg squinted, sneezed, and read on. He sweated, and
sometimes the characters would swim on the page as he bent his head to the
book. His orbits swung out beyond the island and mainland to the countries at
the ends of the earth. He frowned and worried. His days were filled with heat
and distance; his nights with dreams of strange animals. On Saint Lambert's Day
he called Brother Herbert and told him to plaster the wall of the chapter-house;
on Saint Sequanus' Day, to paint it. He thought of spiny-backed dolphins leaping
over ship masts in the waters of the Euxine, of enormous sea tortoises, of elephants tramping the plains of Africa guided by the light of the stars, and the sin-
gle-horned asses of the Indies. Their stupidity, their fierceness. Sometimes he
wondered idly what these creatures might look like, but his dreams gave him only
shape-shifting and fakery. And the brothers were impatient, Gerhardt stirring
them up. They did not understand—how could they yet? All in time, he thought,
and heard the sea's clepsydra washing away the clay. Seconds ticked in the cliff's
subsidence, days in the lazy swipes of the tide.

When the paint and plaster had dried, he gathered the brothers in the chapter-house. Twenty-nine pairs of eyes fixed him from the tiers of the gradines. He
stood before them, holding a baton. Behind him, marked upon the wall, was a
circle and within it a T, which divided it in three. He thought of their widening

circuits about the island, their commerce with the islanders. Perhaps this was their limit, and here was where their impetus would stall. Here was the challenge that Usedom had thrown down, the same but writ in letters the size of continents, bellowed babel-tongued and louder than the ears of man might stand. Would their curiosity help him now, draw them further, take them with him? Twenty-nine baffled faces watched him carefully while he traced the circumference of the circle, then tapped the three areas within it. They awaited his explanation.

"The world," said Father Jörg.

To the north, Rügen's chaotic shorelines straggled in and out, intersecting and breaking, forming tenuous capes and headlands within a jumble of spits and bays. Balkers stationed on the distant cliffs were dancing insects, directing the fishermen west. Tiny rowboats were rounding the thick nub of Stubnitz on their way to Cape Arkona. South, offered the flat sweep of Usedom's seaward coast, its sheer extent broken in half by Vineta Point—what remained of it—the ruin of the church atop. He tugged on the nets, and Brüggeman lifted himself to free them. His employer was distracted, preoccupied. Ploetz cast. They were off the coast at Greifswald, half a league out from the Oie. The net arced out over the side of the boat, the impact slapping on the surface, spattering seawater like the briefest, most local of rainshowers.

Submergence then, disappearance and unseen distortions. Nets trace the motions of an invisible sea: twisting, curling, pulling pocks from the lattice. Sea-heat and sea-cold, rolling convections and subsurface currents collide and recoil, mingle and subside. The buffered thud of water masses percuss the sea-depths and merely add to the turmoil. Moving water needs ciphers and signals; scraps of reed, shells of whelks, flotsam, sea-grass, a waterlogged spar. Or a net. Water has its own kind of darkness, its endless equivalence. Brine too needs its badges of state. It sinks, this net, silently and stressfully, the banner for an army of armies. Every competing stipple and thrust, swell and outflow, diving seiche and deepwater stillness means a ripple, a jerk, a new twist to its fabric. Mere descent means the weights tied at its edges; but everything else, every twitch and shudder, ripple and yaw, means the sea. It is the servant of too many masters, this diving sea-flag, waving downward into the fish-filled depths. Its meshes open like a battery of mouths, wide to swallow herring.

Which scatter, mostly. Flight from nets is an instinct strong in herring. The shoal hangs decked in the fathoms, layer upon layer, row upon row. The very last of the autumn fry vibrate the surface waters; below them are the fattening sprat. Herring flesh muscles itself with the years, moving down through the layers little by little: all herring tend to descend. In the midst of the shoal are the full-grown fish, millions of them, billions of them, spawning, feeding, slowly sinking. Many never see the open waters, surrounded by the colony from birth to death: they are their own landscape, a herring-sea. Plankton and spawn are the currencies here, but below, farther down in the lightless depths, a different commerce is carried on. From far beneath the shoal come the sounds of crustacea being cracked, of fish spines being crunched. Of the eating of copepods and sticklebacks. Of herring feeding on herring. Dark-backed bodies twist in the darkness and swirl about near the bottom. They rarely rise. As sprat, these demersal predators passed from a diet of plankton to a diet of fish, ate themselves huge, and sank. Now they swim the deepest waters. They look like herring and would taste like herring, though they are seldom caught. Contact with each other is avoided—not much unites them; even together they are alone—and their swimming is a graceless business of lurches and lunges. They are giants to the sprat, monsters to the shoal. Shunned and feared by those above, these nightmare fish are cannibal herring. As the net descends they feel the waters twitch. The shoal breaks up, shooting sideways, upward, downward . . . Downward is good. The cannibals stir, then circle up slowly. The waters pop with aimless herring-panic, lone slivers of silver darting back and forth, lost in these depths. The cannibals cruise, picking off the stragglers and gulping them down. The net hangs above them, hovering and waving, but they are gorged and torpid, barely noticing as it balloons and starts to rise out of sight.

Uppp . . . through the layers of fish, catching full grown, near grown, leaving sprat and fry. Ploetz strained on the ropes. Ploetz heaved in the net. Ewald stared at the bottom of the boat. He bit the flesh around his nails and scratched at his cheeks. Ploetz lugged. Ploetz tugged. The boat lurched and bobbed. Brüggeman stared at the cloudy sky. A dark mass of herring grew brighter and nearer, rising through the water. Ploetz hauled, intent, working hand over hand. The catch was good, the net almost full. He braced himself, grunted. The gunwales dipped, the whole boat lurched, unbalanced. Ewald started, looked across, saw, knew.

Too late.

The boat tipped them both into the freezing sea, rolled, and almost capsized. Ploetz gasped from the cold, shouted, spat mouthfuls of water, striking down with his feet as the water filled his boots. Brüggeman surfaced like a madman, lunging at the hull. Underneath their bodies the net was opening, wriggling, unsnagging. The herring were escaping and diving back to the shoal.

They would right the boat and clamber back in. They would gather dead fish from the waters around them and row to shore. Ewald would curse him, but the balance of the boat was a matter for them both. Ewald would know this, know too he was worried, lax on the job.

Later, when they had dragged the boat up the beach and the two men had sunk soaked and exhausted beside it, Ploetz turned to the vessel's master.

"You tipped us in," he said bluntly.

Ewald nodded absentmindedly. He was gazing out over the water. Another week now and the boat would be out for winter. Perhaps they should haul it up now? His heart was not in it, and he told the other man as much.

"Don't tell me you don't like the work," Ploetz burst out. "We both hate the work. If you've got two vagabonds in your drying-shed, that's your concern. Turn them out if they trouble you, but don't turn me out of the boat. We might have drowned out there, and for what? Because Ewald Brüggeman doesn't like his new lodgers!"

Ploetz snorted.

"It's worse than that," Ewald replied after a few moments' silence. "If they were just vagabonds . . . It's worse, that's all."

"Worse? What do you mean, 'worse'?" Ploetz made no attempt now to hide his contempt.

For the first time in the exchange, Ewald met the other's eyes. "It's Niklot," he said. "One of them's Niklot. He calls himself Salvestro now. He asked for the use of the drying-shed, and to borrow the boat. . . ."

"Niklot? You mean the Savage?" Ploetz's voice was incredulous. "But they drowned him! How can he . . . What does he want with the boat?"

Ewald was shaking his head now, saying, "The other one is a giant. I don't know what they want with the boat. I don't know why they came here. I don't know what they want with me. . . ." His voice died away.

Terrified, thought Ploetz.

Aloud, he said, "You should have told this before, Ewald. Our fathers knew what to do with his kind, didn't they? . . . Eh, Ewald?"

He would tell them of the world beyond Usedom, of Europe, Asia, and Africa, which lay joined together in the midst of an illimitable ocean. The center of the world was Jerusalem. To the south, in the desert wastes of Africa, lay the torrid zone, so hot that no man might cross it. To the east, in the Indies, were manticores and elephants, single- and double-humped camels, serpents that swallowed donkeys. Summer and winter came twice a year, and on the easternmost edge of the world were the Serians, who made silk and bartered it in silence.

"How?" asked Brother Joachim-Heinz.

"I do not know," replied Jörg. He considered briefly. "Hand signals."

His diagram had grown cluttered as he marked in the islands of the Middle Sea: Sardinia, Sicily, Corsica, Candia, Nigropont, and Pharos. East, and the world breathed harder, tides grew stronger, rushing past Icaros, Melos, Carpathos, and Rhodes to dolphin-filled Hellespont, where Christendom faced the Indies. Thrace was where the fearsome cranes drove the Pygmies from the third coast of Europe. Every winter they flew east carrying stones for balance, led by one bird, then another, as their exhausted chieftains fell from the sky. On the island of Ortygia the quails would arrive in autumn, cluster in a flock, and fly low across the sea. Nothing would deflect them, neither sails nor boats, which would be shredded or capsized, such was their fury. Even the goshawk would be turned aside, the leader flying wide to offer himself in sacrifice that his fellows might alight in safety. . . .

"I see it!" Now Brother Volker had leapt to his feet. Jörg inclined his head. "The mystery of the quails is very simple to penetrate: the quails are souls who fly alone in their confusion. Only together can they find the true path. Their leader is Christ, who sacrifices himself that the rest might be saved and the boats and sails are their travails on earth, which they must pass through to reach the heaven of the island. . . ."

"Heretical nonsense!" Brother Georg rose from his seat. "Heaven cannot be on earth. The quails are sinners led astray by their prophet, a false prophet justly slain by the sword of the church. That is the true meaning of the goshawk."

"Surely not," riposted Brother Bernd. "Surely the goshawk is a test, and the quail which flies too wide has strayed too far from the path. . . ." Brother Walter nodded sagely. Brother Hanno disagreed. Brother Christoph thought it ridiculous and Brother Harald clearly true. Soon everyone was debating, disputing interpretations, constructing hypotheses, and quoting the *Psychomachia* at one another. The island was a paradise, an Eden, a second Promised Land. Or a fleshpot, a Sodom, a hell on earth. The quails meant angels to some, agents of the Devil to others. Saints, thought Wulf. Sinners, thought Wolf. Wilf did not know.

"No! No! No!" shouted Jörg. "Can you not understand? The quails do not mean anything. They are, quite simply, quails!"

But they did not understand. They sat blankly, baffled in the chapter-house while he told them of Scythia, where the blue-faced Tartars wore the skins of their enemies as clothing, where the white-haired Albans of the coast trained dogs to bring down bulls and lions, even elephants. The brothers' response was to talk of popes converting Ostrogoths to the service of the Church. The bulls were tyrants, the lions Moors, the elephants were other tribes of the East. When he told them of the elephants of Mauritania guiding hapless travelers out of the wilderness, the elephants became Moses, horned on Mount Sinai, and when he spoke of the same beasts marching in the armies of the Indies, then they were the Pharaoh's armies that pursued Moses and were drowned. Jörg grew vexed.

"The elephant is a beast of surpassing size," he told them. "He is as large as a house and has the tail of a rat. He has a hide of armor, but his belly is soft and his enemies will always attack him there. He eats trees, stones, but loves oats above all else. Crossing seas, he will not go aboard without firm pledges to return and can only be tamed with malt beer. His enemy is chiefly the dragon, which sucks the coolness from his blood till the scaly beast be bloated, and many times the elephant will fall upon it and thus it bursts. This is the nature of elephants."

But he had lost them. He traced the lands of Ethiop, Numidia, and Egypt, described the rivers of Oxus, Indus, and Ister. The brothers took them for ciphers, symbols, abstractions. The terrible camelopardalis was a figure of rapacity, the chameleon an emblem of apostasy. He talked of parrots, popinjays, tigers, and tapirs. Then he would wait for Brother Bernd to rise, or HansJürgen, or any of them.

"Father, the tapir then would be a beast connoting lust?"

"The tapir is simply a tapir," he would intone. "It is a pig with hooves and lives beyond the isle of Taprobane."

There would be a short silence then, and following it, a brother would venture, "Taprobane, I believe we determined, would represent a false and beguiling paradise, not the earthly Paradise of the legends of the East, but a jewellike imitation to tempt men from . . ."

"No," said Jörg

". . . the path of righteousness."

"You are on the wrong path entirely. It is not a point of doctrine, but an island. This is the world wherein we live."

Privately he knew it was not so. For all their trampings about the island, their accustomed contact with the islanders, his monks remained locked within their church. Bent within its round they saw no farther than its walls, and now the church was failing, its foundations giving way beneath them all. He imagined it pitching slowly down the cliff and sliding into the sea with his monks perched atop like so many bickering commentators:

"Fear not, brothers! Our church is meant for a second Ark, which we will sail to the Ararat our Lord has raised for—"

"No, no. We are all Jonahs and our church is the whale sent to pluck us from our fellows."

"Nonsense! The Lord has cast us from his garden as sinners. Feel. This water is very cold, is it not? Brothers? Brothers! . . ."

In his own darker moments Jörg would envision the day of the church's conception, when Henry the Lion, his margraves, and their armies stood together at the limit of the point, baffled, frustrated, suddenly arrested when they needed above all to continue, forward over the cliff into the steely gray waters below. Their church was a dam, the final halt for an army of dead men. Still they pressed forward, driven by the need to finish what they had begun, which had led them too far and would not stop, farther into Vineta's oblivion. Yes, Jörg too would be there as they careered down the cliff, adding his voice to the pointless debate, "We are crusaders, Christ's soldiers, sent to finish what was begun, to break the stalemate of Henry's thwarting"—bleating his own doubtful gloss while the nef pitched forward, its splintered prow breaking the surface, and the cowled mariners squabbled aboard their sinking ship of fools. He saw such battles play their havoc across the faces of the brothers as they filed past him out of the chapter-house, fought his own in the secrecy of his call, endured them, won them, watched them return. Brother Gerhardt watched him from his place on the gradines, contributing nothing, waiting for his failure.

He persevered, leading them in a flattened loop about the shores of the Middle Sea from Pontus to the pillars of Hercules, thrusting inland, chasing vistas of burning sand and blistering heat, lands of perpetual ice where the sun would rise but once a year and a single night outlast the winter. He drew paradises of lush green grass and restorative fountains, infernos of blazing black rivers and fire-spitting mountains. His voice grew louder, his gestures wilder, as he traced the world's extremities. Their puzzlement only deepened. Each day they gathered dutifully after Sext to hear him rant of monsters and marvels, listening in near silence, their occasional comments as wrong-headed as ever. Each day he would notice a few more avert their eyes from his own as they left for their chores or some errand about the island, he would see the grin beneath Brother Gerhardt's impassive features broaden, and alone in his cell his own doubts gathered force. He needed their curiosity, at least. His plan was going awry, foundering before any one of them had set a foot beyond Usedom's shores. They were blind, or would not open their eyes. They would stumble and fall. He returned to his books, poring over them until the candlelight ringed his eyes with strange aches and the characters clouded and merged. He could not find what he needed, and the brothers were whispering, conferring amongst themselves. He had pressed their faces against the island until they could not help but accept it. Beyond it, they understood nothing.

Autumn came, and the festivals of thanksgiving. Coppery beech leaves drifted on the forest floor, and approaching winter began to suck the sunlight out of the sky. His lectures continued through the shortening days while the islanders turned to the mending of fences, digging of ditches, their women to preserves for the months ahead. The island's pulse beat slower, and Jörg too found his turning thoughts slow, as though he were not yet resigned to the failure that was their conclusion. He could see no way forward but could not bring himself to stop. The brothers were a weight he could pull no farther. He was emptied and all but stalled. Then, on Saint Bruno's Day, with the sea and sky meeting in gray equivalence on the winter's drab horizon, Brother HansJürgen climbed slowly up the steps to his cell to inform him that two strangers had arrived on the island, soldiers, in flight from a war far away to the south.

Jörg nodded slowly at the distraction. Soldiers and a distant war. What of it? But then his thoughts quickened. His mind jumped and began to spin. Of course, he thought, yes. A thousand times yes. His heart began to pound as the thought gathered force. Behind him, in the semilight of the doorway, the monk waited patiently for his response. These vagabonds might prove his deliverance, prayed for even unknowing, the makeweight for all their shortcomings. When he finally spoke his voice was neutral, casual seeming, and bled of all intent. "Concerning these new-come ruffians," he said, "I would have you find out more, Brother." HansJürgen nodded acceptance of the commission, turned, and left the Prior to his studies.

In the days that followed, the monks would note in Father Jörg a moderation of his choleric humor, a most welcome calming of those passions that had led

him to bellow the names of distant islands and peoples, to beat upon the wall
with his stick, and even to galumph up and down the chapter-house in imitation
of the manticore—a figure denoting promiscuous gluttony, as they recalled.
When he told them of the tree-living Hyperboreans—who signaled, they decided, the state of the eremitic soul in its passage from earth to heaven—it was in
quiet, casual tones. And when Jörg described for them the thirstworm and sleep-
worm of the deserts beyond the Nigris, their conclusions as to the meaning of
these serpents—obviously, drunkenness and sloth—went unchallenged but for a
murmur that those actually bitten might differ from this view. They took his calm
for resignation, a sign that he would soon give up his lectures altogether. From his
post in front of the chapter-house wall, he noted a softening in the serried faces
of his monks. He fancied he saw the first hint of condescension in Brother Gerhardt's increasingly elaborate salutes. They were marking time, merely waiting for
his madness to run its course, and believing he was doing the same. Wrong.

He sat before his opened books while the candle on his table filled the cell
with tallow smoke, seeing nothing, engaged in nothing more than listening for
Brother HansJürgen's footsteps. If his lectures had diminished in passion, it was
from distraction rather than neglect. His thoughts were elsewhere, not yet fixed,
gathering and forming anew. Charters and grants that had swapped the
monastery between simonical and pluralist and absentee prelates centuries before
lay scattered and unread before him. His church lay somewhere in the transactions they hinted at, unanchored, lost, wrecked. When the monk arrived, Jörg
would ask simple questions, feign near indifference at the answers, then charge his
envoy with discovering more. If Brother HansJürgen suspected more than idle
curiosity, he betrayed no sign of it. The ruffians had arrived by boat from the
mainland and were camping out in a herring-shed of Brüggeman's. They had
fought with the Spaniards, it was said. The darker-skinned of the two was a giant,
standing more than a head above his companion. They were engaged in some
practice involving a barrel, in the pond behind the herring-shed. One of the
Ronsdorff boys had seen them.

"A barrel?" His casual query drifted with the tallow smoke. "I would know
more of this, Brother."

So HansJürgen had persisted with his quest, tramping the length and breadth
of the island, rain and shine alike, echoing his master's questions. The barrel, it
seemed, was intended as a vessel. The smaller of the two would climb into it,
whereupon the giant would lower it into the pond. They had constructed a kind
of crane for this. But inquiring beyond these bare facts, he came up against an
odd resistance, a calculated vagueness. His normally garrulous acquaintances
feigned ignorance or disinterest. If there was a purpose behind the vagabonds' exercise, he could not discover it. And as to the islanders' reticence, he garnered only
impressions of a baffling anxiety.

"I believe," he said after Jörg had approached him on the latter question from
several different angles, "that the islanders are in some way afraid of these men."

"Afraid? A whole island of able-bodied men afraid of a pair of vagabonds?"

"It is an obscure kind of fear. I cannot fathom it."

And then, inevitably, "Plumb deeper, Brother. Reach the bottom of this mystery." Jörg paused and considered the turn of events. "Talk to Ewald Brüggeman."

HansJürgen's sandals clacked on the stone floor, strummed on the flagstones of the cloister, fading until Father Jörg was left alone with his speculations. The barrel bothered him. So wrenched from its normal usage (wine or tar—no, herring—whose else could it be but Bruggeman's), it betokened purposes outside the island's limited ken, his own, too, truth to tell, which was part of his fascination with this pair of ne'er-do-wells, these outsiders. What on earth were they doing with such a contraption? Lowering each other into ponds. And a crane! He wondered if Brother Gerhardt had learned of these rival engineers. His fingers tapped on the page as he turned these thoughts over. They led him nowhere. The candle was guttering, spilling yellow wax across the table in a spreading, congealing pool. It was almost time for Nocturns.

End of autumn drizzle turned paths hard-packed through the months of summer by the tramping feet of the harvesters to straggling mires and glutinous shallow ditches. Puddles gathered and sank into the island's softening substance. Mud spread. Weather-afflicted, vaguely caught up in the penumbra of the island's anxious silence, Jörg's proxy marched purposefully through pools of standing water, leaf-mulch, decrepit oak and beech scrub. Brother HansJürgen skirted the edge of the Achter-Wasser—drab, boatless, wind-jarred—before veering back toward the seaward shore and the copse of brine-stunted alders that marked the limit of Ewald Brüggeman's manse. A fire was burning, its smoke rising out the chimney in a column that would break and disappear as gusts blew in off the sea. He shivered, approached, and knocked.

"Out there."

Mathilde Brüggeman's surly countenance was not about to invite him in. She stood there, blocking the doorway, with her thumb pointing back over her shoulder. Out there. She meant the sea. She meant "Not here." And go away. His unwelcome questions withered in his throat. Brüggeman's children had been playing by the fire. They stared up at him from within the room, frozen and openmouthed. The door was closing before he turned his back. He walked around to the back of the house, thence down to the shoreline, and sat himself down to wait.

Spiky wavelets bristled landward and boiled away in the shingle of the beach. A mizzle swirled in as the gusting wind scooped at the water's surface, and soon his face was sheened with moisture. An hour must have passed. A mile down the coast he saw the cantilevered church, perched improbably on the brink of the cliff, pitching forward. Wintry gray skies seemed to grudge the earth below its measure of daylight, and soon the church was fading, merging into a murky half-light that draped the whole island in its fog. Sea, land, and sky bled into one another to reach a dull equivalence, and the monk squatting on his haunches on the

beach shivered in his habit as he scanned the horizon for Brüggeman's boat. The
intruders must have sought his permission, or extracted it somehow. Why
Brüggeman? There was no shortage of greasy, evil-smelling ponds on Usedom.
Something bound Ewald Brüggeman to these men, something untold, lying
somewhere in the island's silence.

Something white out there. A sail? Yes, and barely fifty yards out. More audible than visible as the wind sucked and slapped at the canvas. Brüggeman and his
man were both hunched toward the stern. HansJürgen rose to his feet and waded
out to help the fishermen drag their craft ashore. Both were soaked to the skin
and shivering violently. Brüggeman was scolding his helpmate for some obscure
mishap—Ploetz, a sickly-seeming individual, who offered no defense against his
employer's halfhearted remonstrance. A thin catch was offloaded, and HansJürgen
waited for the opportune moment to begin his interrogation, ladling herring
from the bottom of the boat with the two men. Brüggeman betrayed no surprise
at his presence. Ploetz kept looking across at him but said nothing. With the nets
unraveled, pleated, and laid across the boat to dry, Ploetz gave his master the
merest salute and disappeared over the brow of the slope. The two of them were
alone.

HansJürgen seized his chance, immediately launching into a string of questions as Brüggeman lifted his single sack of fish, hoisted it onto his shoulder, and
strode briskly up the beach. The monk followed, his queries growing more urgent. Brüggeman had yet to acknowledge his presence, but now he was waving
him away, it was far too late, almost dark, and the monk would lose his way unless
he set out for the monastery now. He was cold, too—listen, could HansJürgen
not hear the chattering of his teeth? He was frozen, famished, finished for the day,
and had no use for questions. Not now. Tomorrow? No, not tomorrow, either. Tomorrow he was off to Stettin, and the day after that he was back on the boat, and
anyway there was nothing to tell. He was soaked through, see? He was shivering,
too, and now he was at his own door, where, HansJürgen knew, they would certainly part company with nothing learned at all except Brüggeman's brittle irritation, a nervy brusqueness he knew too well would produce no more than the
same clumsy half-truths and ill-rehearsed evasions he had been hearing the island
over the frustrating fortnight past. Mathilde Brüggeman's stony glare, the same
openmouthed children, as though all three had waited motionless for his unwanted reappearance to unfreeze them. Ewald Brüggeman ducking beneath the
brawny arm of his spouse and the door banging shut in his face. Nothing.

He stood there for a few moments more, listening to the urgent muttering
within, which faded as they moved away from the door. He had discovered nothing at all. The drizzle turned abruptly to rain, and the monk turned to retrace his
steps back across the island. It was almost dark, and several times he slipped on the
treacherous path. Brüggeman's concern had been no more than a diversion, but,
caked front and back with mud, now soaked himself, and alone in the dark,
HansJürgen began fervently to wish himself back at the gatehouse of the

monastery. His teeth began to chatter, and all this to learn only what he knew already—that the fisherman was frightened, perhaps of the soldiers themselves, perhaps of something else entirely. He lost his footing again, fell heavily, and groaned aloud. The rain fell steadily. He had almost crossed the island at its thinnest point, and once he reached the Achter-Wasser the way, he knew, would be easier. He heard a movement somewhere away to his left and looked about but saw nothing and no one. He continued, stumbling, then heard it again. This time he shouted. There was no reply. As he reached the edge of the wood, the monk halted and looked back into the darkness. When he turned again to continue, he started and cried out in shock. A man was standing not ten feet from him, sheltering calmly in the lee of a beech trunk.

"Told you he was off to Stettin tomorrow, did he?" the figure said. Shaken, squinting against the dark, the monk could only nod his confirmation.

"Lost his head then, didn't he? Nothing new there," the figure continued in a sarcastic tone as he moved nearer the monk. "Since when was there a fish market on a Sunday, eh? Bloody stupid! You want to know the truth of it? That what you're here for, monk? He's scared. That's all you need to know about Ewald Brüggeman. He's scared out of his wits!"

It was Ploetz.

The rain would stop an hour before dawn. Brother HansJürgen staggered from Ploetz's hovel as first light pushed its cold gray fingers into the mass of night. Gormitz hauled itself clear of the bay's sluggish surface, and the first birds chirped shrilly against the receding gloom. He was fuzzy-headed, glassy-eyed. He had listened through the night to Ploetz's caustic drawl, snatching the facts he needed from a looping litany of injustices and scorn for his weak-headed employer. Oddly, he felt an increasing sympathy for Ewald Brüggeman while, without Ploetz's dismal little hut, the rain fell in sheets and dripped through the holes in its roof. The fire had smoked, spluttered, and fizzed. Come his departure, he was no drier than before.

"Ploetz?"

Father Jörg was still asleep when he reached the monastery. The monk shook him gently by the shoulder.

"Wilfried Ploetz. Brüggeman's man, on the boat." The Prior rubbed his eyes and rose from his pallet. The boat, of course. He had seen this Ploetz, though at distance, the morning after the collapse. Jörg listened intently as the monk told him the substance of the last five hours in as many minutes.

"So they drowned her for a witch, and now the son returns. No wonder they are frightened. How did he escape?"

"They set him ashore that night. The giant they do not know, but he frightens them. Brüggeman especially. He believes they are here for him. It was his father, Ploetz's, Stenschke, and another man, Ploetz thinks he came from Rügen."

"Old Stenschke?"

"The same."

Jörg pursed his lips. "The sins of the father. If Brüggeman is fearful, why is Ploetz not?"

"Brüggeman and the witch's boy grew up together. The bond was stronger, the cut deeper, perhaps. When they arrived, it was to Brüggeman they went first."

"But for shelter, which was given them." Jörg paused and thought again. "I do not believe these men have come for revenge, Brother. Do you?" HansJürgen shrugged, undecided. "The barrel. The pond. The crane. That is why they are here," he stated with sudden conviction. "Nothing you have told me explains these things."

"Ploetz knows only that the barrel is intended for a vessel, that they climb within it and sink it in the pond. And that they have the loan of Brüggeman's boat."

"His boat? Brüggeman's charity knows no bounds." The Prior paced slowly across the cell to the embrasure. A listless wind was gusting in. Sea fog thickened and thinned in accordance with the fitful breeze, opening to show him short-lived vistas of near dead water. The clouds looked waterlogged, too heavy to do more than lurch and come apart over the sea surface. A barrel would be a clumsy vessel, even in a pond. The mildest sea would sink it in a moment. And with a boat, what need for it at all? They fitted together somehow. Some greater contraption awaited the conjunction of these lesser ones; a larger beast, shy and elusive, lurking somewhere in the recombinant clouds. Beyond him.

"And when is this loan to be made, Brother?" he inquired, still gazing out the window. "When is Brüggeman's charity to be put to the . . ."

But his voice fell away, and he did not need to hear the monk's answer. Dimly, then more definite, covered and uncovered by the slowly swirling clouds, lolling with its badly loaded cargo and the antics of its handlers, Brüggeman's boat emerged out of the fog before his question could be framed. A hundred yards out, no more, and aboard were the giant, his companion, a barrel, and what appeared to his straining eyes as an enormous coil of rope. Jörg stared in silence as submerged thoughts rose and broke the surface. Drifting fog thickened and thinned about the lurching vessel to throw weird shapes and images into his wondering mind's eye: a crumbling fortress, dissolving islands, the emergent features of a massively figured animal eyeing him out of the gloom, towering, graying, and then gone. Contraptions and misdirections, ill-conceived and failing vessels floating off Vineta Point.

"Fetch Brother Gerhardt," he snapped to the waiting monk, who hesitated, startled by the turn of events. "Quickly, Brother!"

Crunch, crunch, splash, crunch . . .

Terra firma on the littoral means water-sheets, shingle ridges, water damped with sand or sand suspended in water, semblances of solidity, and shifting extents of gray and brown crazed with wriggling gullies and brine-filled channels—a various and troublesome terrain for the would-be mariners Bernardo and Salvestro as they trudge along the beach—ambiguity and mud.

... *squelch, splosh, crunch, crunch, gloop* ...

This pocked and stippled no-man's-land, teetering before the tilts of the sea, is strewn about with slimy sea-grass, reeking kelp, wormy and piddock-bored flotsam, chitinous debris, wave-stripped gull feathers, wind-scoured razorshells, the crunching bubbled mucus-rafts of pelagic snails, and—

*cru*UNCH!

"Ow!"

Mole crabs.

Tracking the weak flood tide up the shallow gradient of Usedom's shore, a colony of tendril-waving spume-straining mole crabs have suddenly decided to drill out of the sand and chase landward after the protein-rich surf, intent on food-capture farther up the beach. Consider, the thousand versions of crab-surprise at Bernardo's horny-soled foot descending into their midst. Enormous, white—a brine-scrubbed cow skull washed up some months back is a distant point of comparison, but crab memories are short, crab tempers shorter still. They attack.

"Salvestro! Crabs!" His fox-trapped foot, too, still tooth-marked, too swollen to get a boot on.

"Are you whining already, Bernardo? Pick up the barrel and come on!"

They continued, sullenly, along the tide-squeezed beach, crunching over the pebbles and sploshing through the pools, bound in silence and mutual irritation for Ewald Brüggeman's boat.

Off the coast, the previous night's rainclouds had descended to settle on a turgid sea. Great clods of fog stirred and lumbered before a breeze too weak to clear them. It would be sunrise now, could they but see it. Salvestro tried to shrug the rope higher up his shoulder. It kept slipping down. He only hoped it was long enough. He scanned the beach ahead as vapor swirled in from the sea. His stomach growled. They had breakfasted on herring.

Soon, a vague lozenge appeared some fifty yards ahead. They drew nearer, and the lozenge grew more boatlike, the dark bar of her mast rising out of the fog.

"Here she is, Bernardo." Salvestro slapped the boat approvingly. "Stow our own craft here by the mast. The *mast,* Bernardo. That's it. Now drag the boat into the sea and let's be off."

Bernardo bent, took hold of the stem-piece, and heaved. A few pebbles crunched underneath, but the boat barely budged. He tried again, straining harder, with as little success as before. "It will not move."

"Put your back into it, come on!" Another heave followed, and another, the boat remaining fast. Bernardo straightened, caught sight of his companion, and glared.

"Get out, Salvestro."

"What?"

"Get out of the boat and push."

Some minutes later Bernardo was rowing powerfully into open water. Salvestro sat facing him, shouting directions. Both men were soaked to the thigh. Fog blew over the boat in waves, thickening one moment, thinning the next, to allow him glimpses of the shore. They rowed east, keeping the face of the island to starboard, Salvestro growing gradually quieter and more somber until the only sounds were Bernardo's grunts as he pulled on the oars, the slap of water against the boat's sides, the faint thuds and dunts of the barrel as it knocked gently against the mast. From time to time he glanced down at it anxiously. The thongs, the glass plate, the signal line, its leather sheath and black insides. Darker than he remembered.

"Faster, Bernardo!" he barked abruptly. "We'll be here all day at this rate."

But Bernardo was intent on his rowing, a novel and interesting activity in his view, and would not be roused to argument. Salvestro contented himself with rehearsing their signals and giving his final instructions.

"Remember, one pull for down, two for up, three and four for forward and back. . . ." Forward and back, thought Bernardo. Like rowing.

"And mind your balance," Salvestro recalled Ewald's warning. "Keep the weight of the barrel opposite your own. Use the rope, Bernardo. You on one side, barrel over the other. Don't forget." Something troubled him about this arrangement, but he could not put his finger on it. "And pull smoothly." Perhaps that was it. Bernardo grunted his assent without breaking stroke, and Salvestro lapsed once more into silence.

Gazing through the gaps in the fog, he watched the coast unwind in a hazy gray strip. At first it seemed hardly to hold sea and sky apart, but as they continued east it thickened and firmed. Ashore, the ground was rising. He screwed up his eyes, trying to pierce the vapor's shroud. The spectral foreshore grew more definite, became a ridge, then a steep-sided bank, rising higher still, until there, he saw it: a sheer face of dark red clay, the cliff's ruddy wound, with the church on its summit just visible through the mist.

"Stop rowing, Bernardo," he instructed. They had reached Vineta Point.

Both men rose, Salvestro to uncoil the rope, his partner to manhandle the barrel. The boat rocked alarmingly. Salvestro checked his pockets for candles and tinderbox, then moved to inspect his craft: the seal about the spy-hole, the firmness of the glass. Bernardo had the lid off and was tapping his knuckles against the staves. He stood back as Salvestro tied the rope to the eye-bolt and the boat lurched more wildly. Both men sat down quickly. When the boat had steadied herself, Salvestro stood up gingerly and looked down into the barrel. It smelled dank and fishy. He felt his breakfast climbing out of his stomach.

"Well, then," said Bernardo.

"Right, then," said Salvestro. A moment's contemplation before he climbed inside. His earlier unease returned, stronger this time. Something about the boat. About balance. He crouched down, drawing his knees up to his chest. Bernardo took hold of the lid.

"Should we say a prayer?" he ventured. Salvestro was motionless, staring fixedly at the wooden wall an inch away from his nose.

"The lid," he said.

Dirty gray light bulged in at the windows set high in the wall, pressing on the interior gloom. Humped on pallets lining the length of the dorter, monks in various stages of wakefulness stirred at the sound of footsteps. HansJürgen tiptoed between the two rows. There was a time they would all have risen as one at the tolling of the bell, but now the bell was silenced they began the day when it pleased them. Some rolled over to eye him resentfully. Some ignored him altogether. It was barely daybreak. Some snored. Some lay silent as the dead. Laxity of discipline, in HansJürgen's judgment, a slackening in the monastery's round. It seemed so long ago.

His intrusion rippled slowly over the slumped bodies. A belch sounded. Sphincters began to loosen and release farts into the cold air. Unwashed mouths breathed stertorously and added evil-smelling clouds to the fug. Urgent rustlings ceased abruptly at his approach, were furtively resumed as he passed farther down the dorter. Fingery sins were being committed under rank-smelling coverlets. It was on the increase; fumblings and yieldings in the dawn's gray silence, Onan's sin at the dousing of the lights. HansJürgen blamed the Prior. His lectures stirred up the younger ones and threw their humors out of balance. A loud, ill-concealed grunt resounded from somewhere behind him. Spillage. Young dogs.

The senior monks slept at the far end of the chamber. He passed his own pallet, undisturbed that night. Beyond it, Brother Gerhardt was already dressing. He betrayed no surprise at the summons, and the two men strode out quickly together, watched by two dozen pairs of eyes. They crossed the cloister in silence. Behind them in the dorter, rumors would already be taking flight. Gerhardt would see him as the Prior's creature, not party to his own circle of supporters; an enemy. Their sandals clacked on the cobbles and clattered up the stairway. Gerhardt, Hanno, and Bernd: they kept themselves close, those three. A shifting handful of younger monks made up the outer circle of the clique, all pledging nominal allegiance to the old Abbot. They entered the Prior's cell.

Father Jörg was standing by the window as before.

"My eyes cannot pierce this gloom, Brother," he said, indicating for HansJürgen to take his place. "Welcome, Brother Gerhardt," he added. Gerhardt nodded without speaking. "Tell me now, what do you see?"

HansJürgen waited for a thick patch of fog to pass. The boat was stationed where he had seen it last, a quarter mile or more out from the foot of the cliff. He spied a figure aboard, but no trace of his companion.

"I can see only the giant, Father," he said. "One of them has disappeared."

"He is in the barrel. That much I saw before this cursed fog thickened."

An inquisitive face had appeared at the door. Brother Joachim-Heinz's.

"Yes?"

"I came to offer my assistance, Father."

"Brother Heinz-Joachim, too, no doubt." The monk nodded and was joined by the other. "Very well. Now, Brother Gerhardt . . ." Brother Gerhardt nodded.

"The giant is attempting to lift the barrel, Father," said HansJürgen. Brothers Hanno, Georg, and Bernd appeared, shunting the first two farther into the room. "He has fallen over, Father. The boat's motions are too wild for him, I fear," reported the monk.

"Right. Now, Brother Gerhardt, I recall during your endeavors of three summers ago . . ." Brothers Florian and Reinhard were sidling past Hanno and Georg, trying to peer over HansJürgen's shoulder on the far side of the cell. "Now what?" asked Jörg.

"We came as soon as we could," said Florian.

"To help," said Reinhardt. He stumbled forward as Gundolf, Matthias, and Harald pushed their way in.

"Help? With what?"

"The giant has righted himself," relayed HansJürgen. "He is waving his arms, I think—no, he is shouting at the barrel."

"With the giant," answered a small group at the back of the room (Brothers Egon, Ludwig, and Volker).

"With the boat," answered those behind them, moving forward (Brothers Henning and Horst). Brother Christoph lost his balance as they entered and bumped against Brother Gundolf, who elbowed him in the ribs. Someone shoved Matthias.

"We're here," said Brother Wulf.

"Here we are," said Wolf.

"All three of us," said Wilf. "Over here."

"Stay there," ordered Jörg. "Now, Brother Gerhardt." Gerhardt nodded.

"He has it!" cried HansJürgen. "He is going to drop it over the side. No, he cannot. The boat will capsize if he does. . . . Ah. He has fallen over again." Volker and Ludwig crowded nearer, pushing their way between Christoph and Harald, who pushed back, and someone kicked Matthias.

"Concerning your endeavors, Brother Gerhardt, of three winters ago, I recall you built—"

"The giant is going to try the stern. The nose will rise, though, I know it. There it goes. Yes, I was right. Pardon me, Father."

"—a raft." Brother Gerhardt nodded. Brothers Walter and Willy had arrived and, finding the doorway blocked and the room beyond it solid with monks, now decided to climb over Henning and Volker, who threw them off as they grew sensible of this plan, landing them abruptly on top of Gundolf, Florian, and Reinhard, who all fell over, bringing down Hanno, Georg, Berndt, Wulf, Wolf, and Wilf. Someone punched Matthias. Finding the cell momentarily cleared above waist level, Jörg pressed on with his request.

"Now, Brother Gerhardt, we have need of a vessel to fetch these unfortunates to safety. Any vessel." He paused and scratched the side of his mouth. "Your raft, in short."

Florian jumped to his feet at this. "I will man the tiller," he said.

The other monks were picking themselves up off the floor. At Florian's offer, several more volunteered their services: "No, I will. . . ." "Me!" "No, me. . . ."

"The raft has no tiller," retorted Gerhardt, "nor decks, nor mast, nor fabric of any kind. The raft is rotted and utterly unseawor—" But the other monks were already offering themselves as midshipmen, captains, boatswains, third mates, helmsmen, and ship's carpenters, jostling forward to catch Jörg's eye.

"The rope!" HansJürgen cried out suddenly. "Of course, he will swing the barrel out with the rope. Here he goes. Heave it now, that's it. . . ."

"Ship's beekeeper!" petitioned Brother Volker.

"Ah no. He has hit the mast. He will shout at it now, I know it. Yes, there he goes."

"Oarsmen," appealed Jörg, and the monks clamored to be taken on. He chose the ten largest: Egon, Reinhard, Gundolf, Walter, Willy, Georg, Hanno, Henning, Volker, and one more—he cast his eye over the excited monks—Harald. "Good. Now obey the orders of your captain, Brother Gerhardt, and all will be well. Come now. . . ."

"The giant is very vexed now," said HansJürgen as a scramble began for the door, Christoph and Johannes barging each other aside, Florian slipping between them, while Wulf, Wolf, and Wilf hovered about, blocking Walter's and Reinhard's paths and diverting them into that of Georg.

"He is picking up the barrel now, yes, up it goes. What strength!"

Bernd fell against Horst, who fell against Henning as Joachim-Heinz and Heinz-Joachim stumbled, rose, and rushed forward, only to collide with Harald and Hanno. Gerhardt nodded. Egon and Christoph shunted Gundolf and Hanno, while Ludwig, Hubert, Volker, and Horst kept bouncing off the rear of the pack. Matthias burrowed directly into its midst, drove forward for the door, was tripped, and fell flat on his face. Someone trod on him.

"He has it over his head now. He is swaying. . . . Keep your balance, giant! Good, good. He is going to hurl it into the sea, Father." Matthias picked himself up and scurried out last, leaving HansJürgen alone, still relaying his comentary from the window.

"Here he goes, one, two, three . . ."

"NnnGAARHH!"

Bernardo heaved the barrel and its contents head-high—teetered in the pitching boat, tottered as it yawed—then threw, the barrel catching the very edge of the wales and crashing into the water, *bang, ker-sploossh!* The splash caught him full in the face as he fell and landed with a thump in the bottom of the boat. The rope and signal line were already running quickly over the side, pulled by the sinking barrel. He grasped hold of the rope and put a turn about the oarlock. The boat rolled sideways. Balance, remembered Bernardo. To do with sides.

He leaned back, the craft settled, and he began to pay out the line more steadily. When thirty feet or more had disappeared into the water, he stopped and gave a tug on the signal line. The morning fog seemed to be clearing. He waited for his companion's response, but the line remained slack. There had been a bang. There had been a splash. Had there been a third noise in the course of the launch? A dull report sandwiched between the bang and the splash? The seconds lengthened, and Bernardo began to grow agitated. His launch had not gone as smoothly as anticipated. Swinging the barrel by its rope had been Salvestro's notion. When both had crashed against the mast he had peered anxiously through the spy-hole. A furious face had risen out of the blackness to press against the glass and shout at him. Flustered, he had shouted back. Simply throwing the stupid contraption had been his own idea. Catching the side of the boat was just bad luck. He tugged again, more violently this time. That second thud. The sound, perhaps, of bone on wood, of a skull dashing itself against barrel staves. . . . Bernardo waited. It would be better, he thought, if Salvestro were up here on the boat, directing his efforts and telling him what to do as usual, rather than down there, where he was silent and invisible, quite possibly dead and no help to him at all. Salvestro had dragged him to this muddy little island, hatched this stupid expedition, then left him to cope when it all went wrong. Yes, this was Salvestro's fault—not his—and he was about to start hauling up the body in its coffin, when it came: a tug, a faint answering pull damped by the intervening fathoms. He tugged back with vigor. A single pull, was it? One, he recalled, meant down.

Gnaarshter-rummpssh . . . shudders down the fathoms and mushrooms over the stony sea-floor. The signal rolls and spreads, dissolves and dies. Something is coming down. Surface crashings grow cloudy down here, blunt themselves, and disperse through the almost empty waters. The shoal has moved west along the coast, leaving the spawning ground to winter amongst the more temperate shelves of the Belts. Now only the stragglers remain: undernourished sprat, the oldest and sickest fish, which dart and scatter as the intruder plunges past. As the freeze moves south, a vanguard of gales sweep down from the northern gulfs to suck up autumn heat. The sea grows barer, thinner, less sustaining. Young fish freeze. Old fish die. Sick fish weaken and sink toward the bottom. Odd swirls of current rise up to meet them. Big-bodied movements down there, in the dark.

Indifferent to season and oblivious of spawning, the cannibal herring are sluggish for now. Eels will arrive again with the turn of the year, and the herring shoal a little time after. In the meantime they resort to crunching fishlice and chasing the faint blue puffs of night-feeding ostracods, nosing the odd whiff from the bottom-sand and nipping each other's tails. They hover about the lip of the ledge. Below them lies a lightless chasm. Above, the prospect of choicer fare. It is all a matter of lurking.

Dull twitchings and vibrations alert them first. Somewhere above, something descending; herring-thoughts turn to eating. Patrolling begins. And waiting, until there, overhead in the light-shot water, a wobbling blot appears. The cannibals gather as it grows larger and darker. More waiting. Further descent. It is fish, perhaps. Or meat. They have known meat, but rarely. Usually floats. Meat, then? Fish?

This: an awkward, hesitant, defenseless intruder plunging down the fathoms to hang on the very lip of the ledge. Below is the darkness where they dare not venture. Cannibal herring circle slowly about, nosing, tasting. Its attributes spell food, and yet . . . It is too big. Too hard, and strangely shaped—utterly unfishlike. Utterly unmeatlike. Juices curdle disappointingly in their stomachs. They cluster more thickly. It has tendrils—one thick, one thin—which grow up toward the death-light and twitch, *plick,* in the shielding water. *Plick, plick.* It has an eye, or a vent, set in the middle of its stomach, which spews a murky yellow glow. Wintering is the time of waiting, of weathering, of thinning the shoal. But this . . . This has always been out of season, always out of kilter. Its freakish reappearance is almost to be expected. Their own frustration stirs them up, reawakens appetites, provokes a dormant curiosity in the creatures overhead: the sea-crawlers and wave-thrashers, the gougers and sinkers who batter their way from nowhere to nowhere. Blunt-nosed herring butt against the dangling trespasser. Ever since the first leaky skin-boats and hacked-out klovaskepps nosed gingerly out of the river mouths and scuttled across the face of the coasts, they have been sending down such tokens. At other times, in other guises, this has been here before.

Old memories rise like bile. Cannibal herring and their ancestors have watched cold-eyed as pine dinghies, umiaks, and plank-built jekter hop between the bays. Farther out, harpoonists stand on the prows of gut-sewn karves, white sails hoisted high to attract the dull-witted basking shark, while oarsmen beat the surface and send their thuddings into the depths. Viking freighters, byrdingers, and knarrs dart across the open water to the islands of Bornholm and Gotland; flat-bottomed scaphas prefer to hug the coasts. Coracles swell into coasters, galleys into snake-headed longships. In Usedom's lee, the *Long Serpent* is surrounded by Harald's dragon-ships, boarded, and cleared, her crew put to the sword, and blood drips off her clinker-built sides to stain the Achter-Wasser a tasty red. Olaf Tryggvasson leaps overboard, sinks in his chain mail, rots on the bottom with his slaughtered bondsmen. Nothing is learned. The sea is air-loss; the air sea-loss.

Floating and sinking are the functions here. Surfaces are murderous. Simple enough: some herring must die for the good of the shoal. Is it then their *own* compelling cull that leads these creatures to lumber forth in their cumbersome tubs, to pitch and yaw and overturn, to thrash and drown so consummately? And why are their sacrifices so often made during storms?

It is a puzzle, or rather the pieces of a puzzle. Hulks and caravels lurch and split and spill their cargoes into the sea. Prams spring leaks. Barges overturn. Menapian traders pull snarling bears out of the Finnmark for service in the circus of Rome; short swords and Gaulish wine travel north in return. Imperial courtiers send up from the Moselle for feathers, fur, and slaves. Colleges of *nautae* carry glassware from Cologne, Samian ware, and terra sigillata. Old amber routes are rediscovered and grow crowded as the counts of commerce in distant Moesia and Illyria usher Frisians, Franks, and Saxons through the tariff gates. Border patrols and river flotillas on the Rhine and Danube cannot stem the flood of bronze, iron, wine, olive oil, a hundred forbidden trade goods; the Pax Romana is not so balmy these days. The northern sea grows thick with sinking freight as the Abodrites and Rani move north and west to cut the Geatish trade routes and force the merchants afloat: Pontic beaver skins, Birka jars of wheat and wine, rolls of *pallia fresonica,* wax. And threading passage through the Åland islands from the distant marts of Persia, overland, and up the Elbe from the cities of the south come all the coins to pay for them—sesterces, dirhems, dinars, soldi. The turning faces of emperors and caliphs mix, glitter, and sink together in the water's terminal democracy; Hadrian and Caliph Walid, Augustus and Hisham, King Ivar Widefathom and Louis the Pious. Cracked-open casks from cracked-open hulls spill beer and stain the surface muddy brown (investigating herring grow wobbly and sink). Below, the darkening liquids urge strange meetings and conjunctions, of Frankish swords and Saxon plowshares, wolf pelts and lambskins, Charlemagne and Harun al-Raschid. Pearls and cowries deck the waters in tropical jewels, salt-cargoes turn it saline. This sea wears the clothes of its disciples, eats their food, drinks their wine; chokes on their generosity. Its swimming minions pay a wary attention, listening as finless beasts roar, bellow, neigh, and bleat from within the punctured holds. They watch, puzzled, as woolly creatures leap the rails to follow their leaders down the fathoms. They scatter, sensibly, as furious bears and panicking horses kick, and claw, and drown. They track a barge under escort the length of the coast, east from the mouth of the Vistula River, by the Gulf of Danzig and Cape Arkona on Rügen, through the Mecklenburger Bucht to Lübeck. Aboard her decks is a camel.

It is more than odd. Marten and sable skins unfold and flap down through the shoal's tight ranks. They taste the bittersweet of pine-honey and smell the deathly stench of *liquamen.* Downwardness and dispersal apart, it is difficult to relate these things, and when the great storm came and the city sundered and offered itself entire—its surpassing shudder still palpable, echoing dimly even now in herring-memories—they could only stare blankly at the purposes laid bare before them in the streets and crowded marts of Vineta. The very volume presses upon them purpose, but what can these thrashers and sinkers hope for from so various a tribute, a profusion so incoherent? So massive a plumb, the very question so mazed in detail, the need behind it clogged and baffled as it thuds down into the depths. Such persistence signals enormous cause, its expressions only lumpishness: millstones, ring money, walrus hides, and soapstone. Where is the question these foreign bodies frame? Bone, horn, flesh, skin; the surfacers themselves. Off Usedom's coast some twenty winters back, two men and a boatload of their netted fellows. What can they want? What are they fishing for down here? Wondering herring note the rupture of delicate cycles: spawning, feeding, the sea's exchanges and slow circulations. Water-layers balloon out of true with the crash of cargo, which shakes and unsettles them and unhouses them from themselves. Two years before, billowing red clay from the foot of the shoreward cliff fogged the night waters, massive stones crashed down from nowhere and bedded themselves in the soft offshore ooze. An altar followed. A cross. And now this.

The intruder tilts. The cannibals are drawn to the creature's dim yellow eye. Tilting and toppling are perhaps those mechanisms of the air that have brought them their useless harvest. This is, perhaps, the awaited key to the drip of tribute. They peer in at the glow, and yes, this might be it, for there is a surface-creature within. A live one, too. Feeding is briefly forgotten while they observe its measured, intent maneuvers. Fascinating. Surely its queer activity will now begin to link and pattern its predecessors, to extend tendrils as far-reaching as those that stretch up toward the surface, which twitch, arc, flex, and now seem to drag its body in lurching hops across the bottom, toward the mouth of the chasm?

The cannibals follow. A herring with peeling scales and yellowish gills drifts down. They eat it. The creature teeters on the lip—there is no doubt now where its destination lies. There is no specific prohibition on the black mouth below, no known danger down there. And yet, since that first meandering investigation many winters ago, no herring has turned tail, flipped, and swum down. Quite why eludes them. This particular blackness has nothing to with the soft squirts of spawn, or the straining of creature-rich waters, or even the chomping of other herring. If another sick fish should choose this moment to offer itself, that would probably suffice to divert their curiosity. The creature seems almost to be waiting for them, hovering there while its tendrils thrash more urgently. They cannot resist as it wavers and leans, then rights itself with a jerk. Its tendrils straighten as it swings out over the edge to begin the plunge. They follow.

A more active sea would have healed this gash. Turbid currents should have shunted flocculated clays and argillites over the lip of the ledge to drift down gently as the barrel and its herring-escort do now and build up in oozy layers. A light dusting every few days or so over forty millennia would have filled this canyon to the brim. Dumping down a city smacks of impatience and desperation. Steady accumulation is the key. But, vague and island-obstructed outpourings from the debouching Oder and Peene apart, the bottom waters hereabouts are almost motionless, almost airless, too, hence the mad flappings of the cannibals' gills as they dive with this challenge to their dim comprehension down the ice-scoured, plantless sides of the chasm, peering in at the creature within and seeing their own agitation mirrored in its fluttering contortions—holding its head, waving its arms, voiding its food—cannibals, big creature, creature within the creature, all of them sinking down the fathoms to Vineta.

Salvestro comes to in darkness, head throbbing from a swelling the size of an egg. Water is pooled about his feet. He feels for the candle and tinderbox. Illuminated, the inside of the barrel seems smaller even than before. Peering through the window gives him his own reflection superimposed on a vista of utter blackness. The air is already foul. He reaches down for the guide-rope and gives a single sharp tug. There is a long pause, then a lurch, and succeeding it a strange swaying motion as his craft begins its descent.

His head quickly begins to throb more painfully. He tries to fix the candle in its holder, but, perhaps due to his shivering, perhaps the odd motions of the craft, he seems unable to marry the stub to its hole. He begins to feel nauseated, but also strangely unconcerned. The candle simply will not go in its hole, and the water in the barrel simply will not stop rising. Up to his chest now. His eyes are playing little tricks on him—swiveling the wooden walls of his chamber about, turning the air yellow. Amusing? Something is wrong.

Trailing his arms in the rising water, Salvestro begins to laugh to himself. It seems very funny that he cannot find the guide-rope and, when found, hilarious that it is slack. He laughs and laughs—until he cries, until he gasps and then pukes in a sudden yellow spray of fish-bits and bile. His breath is coming very hard, his laughing head seeming to wrest itself free from his convulsed shivering body, to rear up weightlessly and peer down into a landscape of twitching tubes, trembling membranes, the lungs' flooding and draining sponge. Air-starved blood gluts the lacework of his lights, bulging and swelling, offering taut surfaces and eager membranes, but there is no air, or not enough. Salvestro's blood chokes on the barrel's dead gases, his eyes roll in their sockets, and his body begins to turn in on itself. His gullet is a glistening chute leading into ventral darkness. The prickling surfaces of his lungs are interfaces of air and liquid, the press of a night sky on a night sea, and suspended between them a body with skin white as bone—the moonlight, perhaps—a child's body floating on the Achter-Wasser. Vineta calls, and this time he descends, becomes the creature he did not become then. The child floats on, unconcerned, unknowing, to be washed ashore at Greifswald, to crawl exhausted into the forest and find the first of a thousand roofless sleeping-places. The sun will wake him next morning, buried deep in the undergrowth. He will walk deeper into the forest. He will lurk at the edge of villages, keep to the woods. He will be the face glimpsed at dusk, or in the penumbra of the fire-light, by which parents frighten their children into bed. The winters will drive him south, this scavenger, a denizen of outskirts and the forest.

Through the Achter-Wasser's strange refractions and distortions, the other path he might have taken winds beneath the water's surface; the creature he might have become watches him shrink and disappear. Not properly of air or water, the shape of a Water-man waits in the shadows of shallows, in the breezes scooping troughs from the sea's surface. He is one of the secrets the waves whisper amongst themselves, here now, spectral, still half-realized but growing more definite with the fathoms, of a piece with drowned Vineta. Thickening with the press of the depths, the Water-man molds himself new limbs, strikes attitudes, grows congruent once again with the flesh and blood that abandoned him in the Achter-Wasser all those years ago. . . .

Is it the deadness of this unconvected watermass, an oxygen-starved twitch of apprehensive herring-brains? Are they deceived as their dorsal lines shudder at the pressure pulse that presses from the chasm's ill-defined sides? The watermass seems suddenly to shunt itself upward. Surely they have already passed that particular band of sediment? A weirdly deferred rumble succeeds the water-shudder, growing, building, shaking the eyeballs in their sockets. Stunned cannibals gather their wits and reorientate; the creature is still sinking, its tendrils speeding past them. Oddly, they can see it more clearly now, etched against a thinning of the sea-floor's darkness, a glow punctuated by flashes of light, as of objects puncturing the surface and sunlight catching the splashes. Small chunks of cliffside are coming loose and impacting on something down there—they are traveling with a few lumps themselves—but what exactly? The water is growing absolute, airless, utterly liquid, and they should turn back, ascend, get out. They continue, blood thickening, organs pumping, the light seeming to pulse as the pressure inside them swells. The creature is plunging on and the flashes now appear to them as eyes, hundreds upon hundreds, all opening and closing. The water has a fist around them, and up is no longer possible. There is a burst of brightness as the creature crashes through, and they are following hopelessly, knowing now that this was an error as they dive on after. Absolute water is a mouth closing over their gills in the lightless fathoms; absolute air signals choking in the sky's high brightness above—or below; the two are confused. They have arrived at both and found them hinged together like jaws. The creature sits motionless, still mysterious, booming dully as they flop and drown about it and the city creeps over the curve of their lidless eyes. The Water-man gathers himself above, hangs there. The rope that spears him through the midriff jerks and straightens, seeming to slice him in two. He dangles and shivers as the creature tips, then begins to rise.

The rope quickened its slither over the side, then stopped as suddenly. Bernardo hitched the remainder securely about the oarlock and settled back to wait for the next signal. Salvestro had reached the bottom.

More times than he cared to remember he had fallen asleep to the sound of his companion's voice telling him of this city beneath the sea. It had soothed the blacknesses of mood that would overtake him and goad him and that he could not marshal. Even unseen this sea had dissolved his frustrations a hundred times before now. Sitting about the low campfires with the black rocks tumbling in his brain, he listened, and Salvestro's voice would reorder his thoughts and lead them toward dulling sleep. The urge was a hunger he could soothe but never satisfy. Never remember satisfying, at any rate. Even after Prato. "This will be good," his companion had told him as they stood on the boggy foreshore and looked across the Achter-Wasser to Usedom. He had nodded, for as someone had once told him, a starving man will eat coal.

Lazy troughs spread themselves in shallow basins about the gently rocking boat. Waves curled and relapsed. He was alone. Bernardo busied himself with re-coiling the little that remained of the rope. Only minutes before, Salvestro had plunged overboard and sunk beneath the waters' crawling surface. It seemed like hours. Years. Another age, already the day he would remember as the "the day when . . ." Too distant. He began uncoiling the rope, then sat in the center of the boat, the boat itself surrounded by sea: a pointless speck in the expanse of gray. The signal line tautened and slackened with the boat's motions. Pull, he silently urged his sunken partner. He felt very faintly sick, from the boat or hunger he could not tell. Possibly Salvestro had drifted directly to the richest of the promised temples. He would be counting the treasure they would raise. Estimat-ing weights and loads, like their rehearsals in the pond. Organizing matters prop-erly. That was still possible. But it was growing less and less possible with the passing minutes. Salvestro had discussed the matter of air with him; he had for-gotten the exact nature of the problem. Not enough, perhaps. And balance, an-other problem. He had liked the rowing and that was good, and the launch, too, apart from the bump; but the line remained still and he wished Salvestro were here to make this particular decision that the minutes were pressing upon him, for he did not like it and gave the water about the boat a great roar of frustration.

Bernardo reached across and gave the line several fretful tugs. It came free with the last. Or snapped, perhaps. Most probably it snapped. He was too big and too stupid. His caresses too often became assaults. Necks could snap like candles. He began to sniff and sob a little. Salvestro was a certain bastard, but without him he was hesitant and unsure what to do. There should have been a signal. He had been promised signals. Perhaps it was not too late. He moved to brace himself crosswise between the oarlocks. He untied the rope, took hold of the free end, and heaved. Somewhere below, down the black fathoms and through the waters' dragging bulk, he felt the weight of the barrel and its occupant rise off the bot-tom as they began their passage to the surface. The fog was almost lifted now. Hand over hand, Bernardo hauled in the stiff wet rope and sweated in the wintry sunlight.

His labor found a rhythm, a capable *one two, one two,* counted out in a mutter as the barrel's weight grew more definite somewhere in the water below him. He heard first of all some irregular shouts, some splashes, on the shoreward side, but intent on his task, he accepted these sounds with the quiet sloppings and wave-slaps and went on with his efforts. The sounds grew sharper, impinging more urgently. *One two, one two,* thought Bernardo. Then a barked command, louder, breaking the set of his concentration. *"Wait!"*

He brought up his head, his hands frozen about the rope, and he saw them streaming down to the waterline in a long scurrying line. Gray-robed figures were scrambling down by the side of the cliff. Monks. They were shouting to one another, and several had already reached something he had earlier registered as driftwood; it looked like a bird nest built from logs. They were climbing aboard, one, the one who had shouted for them to wait, now struggling past his fellows to order some of them off and marshal the remainder with, what, they looked like paddles. Yes, paddles, most definitely, as a curtain of spray was raised and the raft lurched out from the shore. The monks aboard—ten, perhaps twelve—were vigorous but inexpert. Their raft wallowed and veered about wildly. The shouting monk yelled and waved his arms. His paddlers moderated their strokes. Bernardo watched openmouthed as the strange craft lunged one way, then the other, up the coast, down the coast, back toward the cliff, but more and more toward himself. The rope began to slip through his fingers; the barrel was sinking back. Bernardo looked down into the water, then up at the monks, and recalled himself to his task. *One two, one two . . .* The shouting distracted him, his long arms jerked at the rope, and the barrel seemed to shift position as the boat swung about. He grew frustrated and apprehensive. The monks were gaining some semblance of control over their vessel, and its course seemed set on collision. Bernardo yanked and heaved, the weight growing more definite by the second. More focused. His companion would be directly below him now. He breathed deeply, trying to shut out the commotion heading toward him. *One two, one two . . . Thunk!*

Bernardo leapt to his feet and the boat tilted violently. The top of the barrel had surfaced under the boat's curving side, knocking against the strakes. He fell back, then cinched the rope and advanced more gingerly, peering over the side and seeing their craft turning freely in the water. He manhandled the barrel about until the spy-hole was uppermost. Water topped with a yellow froth slopped against the glass, then a white shape rose out of the barrel's interior darkness: eyes, an open mouth. Bernardo pressed his nose to the glass and watched as the face sank back beneath the liquid. He shouted again, then hammered with his fists.

"Ho there!" reached him across the water. He shut it out. Think, he told himself, then lunged for the barrel, and the boat tipped, hovered for a second between capsizement and relapse, fell back. Balance, he told himself, and braced himself once again to heave on the rope. But the barrel was wedged firmly under the angle of the side.

"Ho! Ahoy there!" Again. He ignored it, straining at his impossible task, thinking of the bloodless and slack-jawed face, the watery confines, Salvestro drowned or drowning. But the barrel would not rise, he knew it already, and the boat would not hold him as he plucked it from the sea, and so he bellowed at the

water, at the sky, at the monks, and kicked at the bottom. At the filthy island. The
raft was almost on him. Rage and frustration hurled stones in his head. He stood
upright as the monks paddled up. Ten. He flexed his fingers. His own familiar
anger, closer now, closer, all ten of them as their captain started waving and pointing at the barrel, just a few more feet before he might jump the gap between
them; he tensed, steadied himself.

"... grasp the end! Do it, you lumpish dolt!" The command stalled him. The
raft collided with a clatter of waving paddles, and the shouting monk was shouting at him and pointing to the barrel that knocked and rolled between their vessels. He bent down, still uncomprehending, quite overtaken by the turn of events.
Other monks were reaching down, and then he understood. Hands, thin and
white from the raft, huge and red from the boat, grasped either side of the barrel,
heaved it up, Bernardo thrust forward and the monks fell back, the tun rolling
over the deck of the raft, where other hands fell to cutting away the leather and
smashing in the lid. Greenish, evil-smelling water topped with a yellow scum
spilled over the deck. An arm fell out, the back of a head.

"Salvestro!" Bernardo jumped the gap between the vessels. The whole raft
tipped beneath his weight, he almost fell.

"Silence!" the monk's leader barked, then turned to his companions. "Walter!
Willy! Hold the drowned rat by his ankles. Higher, good. Now, Brother Gundolf,
punch him in the stomach."

A monk stepped forward and began to pummel the lifeless body. The others
clustered around. Ignored, Bernardo felt his rage replaced by apprehension. This
had happened before; now it had happened again. He was alone amongst
strangers with no one and nothing for company but the aftermath of a disaster. It
was not his fault. Salvestro had gone and left him here and died. The bastard.
What was he supposed to do now? They were going to be rich and live like
princes. Like kings. He was exceedingly hungry, tired in his head, and he would
like to simply curl up and sleep and awake to find himself far away from here.
Home, wherever that was. He had been promised. Bernardo felt the raft yaw
under his feet, watched the gray habits move about its deck, heard the monk's fists
thud against unfeeling flesh, and sniveled into his sleeve.

The corpse shuddered. Bernardo's head came up. The corpse vented seawater,
bile, fragments of half-digested herring, coughed, then puked, spattering the
monks, who lowered him quickly to the deck. Bernardo shoved aside the nearest
and knelt on the deck by his heaving, choking companion.

"Alive!" Bernardo shouted at the expressionless faces looking down on them
both. "Did you find it?" he hissed. "Tell me, whisper it in my ear. . . ." The shouting monk was standing over them.

"Are you Niklot, son of the witch who once practiced abominations on this
island and gutted fish for Brüggeman, was tried by water, and perished?" he demanded of the figure groaning on the deck.

"He is called Salvestro," Bernardo said, but the monk ignored him.

"Are you?" he asked more sharply.

"I am," managed the body on the deck. "Or was." He looked up at his inter-rogator and saw a thin, ageless face topped with a mat of blond hair. The man might be thirty or fifty.

Bernardo looked blankly from one to the other. The monk turned away to shout orders at his brothers, and Bernardo bent his head closer.

"Whisper it now," he whispered, and pressed his ear to his companion's lips. "Tell me what you found." His companion gasped for breath and let loose an acrid belch, then a great convulsion seized him. He puked, heavily, finally, the last of his stomach emptying itself down the side of Bernardo's face.

"Nothing," he spluttered. "I found nothing."

They expected more. He saw it in their faces, in the ebbing flush of excite-ment, the strain of mere exertion, as Gundolf, Reinhard, Harald, and the others dug their paddles into slack water and propelled the raft to shore. He ordered the giant and heathen into their own vessel and towed it off the stern, where it dragged and rolled. The heathen seemed to have recovered well enough, lying back with one elbow propped insolently on the wales. The giant appeared incon-solable, staring down at his feet and muttering to himself. A boat, two vagabonds, and a barrel of seawater: not much of a catch to the innocent eye. He felt his own heart jerk and shudder at their prize.

Paddles plashed to either side of him, and the rotting ropes below the deck's planking chafed against the logs. Jörg's eye wandered over the ruin of the church, down the cliff to its foot. There was Gerhardt, flanked by the remainder of the brothers. They were drawn up along the waterline, still sentinels in gray, the is-land's defenders. Only a little farther now. He glanced back at the boat lolling in their wake and the men within it. The giant seemed quieted.

Ashore, Jörg directed Florian and Matthias to clean and clothe their guests. Gerhardt was speaking with his back to him. A group of brothers was listening. The raft and boat were made fast, and then he moved quickly to scale the slope. Gerhardt blocked his path.

"I would have words with you, Father. . . ."

But Gerhardt's words were chains, weights, sapping loads. He was too close for distractions, for Gerhardt's sour face and his pique at losing the captaincy of the raft, and he muttered, "Not now, not now," pushing past the man and hearing an answering mutter start up behind him as he strode up the side of the point. The prize needed to be better, and would be if he could only impel them to grasp it, to leap over their fears and reach it. They were close, but still too far. Brother HansJürgen was waiting for him in the cloister.

"Take our guests to the beet loft," he told the monk. "Give them straw and a slop bucket. They may take their meals there. Bring the one calling himself Salvestro to me before Vespers."

More monks appeared, then the paddlers, breathing heavily from their exertions and the steepness of the ascent, and last of all Brothers Florian and Matthias with the giant and his companion. HansJürgen followed as they were led to the well and watched as they stripped to have buckets of water poured over their heads. Naked, the giant looked if anything even bigger than before. His companion was rather puny. HansJürgen found it difficult to connect him with the islanders' ill-defined fears. What had these vagabonds hoped for? What had they sought out there, beneath the sea's opaque surface? He waited as they dried themselves and dressed, then led them through the cloister, past the dorter to a stone lean-to tacked onto the back of the kitchens.

The beet loft was wider than it was deep and higher than it was wide, perhaps twice the height of a man. Lines of lathes on which the beets had once rested were set into the back wall, pointing out horizontally and rising in cobwebby shelves up the back wall. Three kinds of confusion—momentary, resigned, fundamental—peered through the door, for between it and the lathe-ends there was barely room to stand.

"You will stay here," HansJürgen told the two men. "You will be brought straw and food later. You may remove these sticks as you see fit."

Sounds of hesitant, then determined destruction followed him as he walked back through the cloister.

Once Bernardo had removed the last of the lathes the two men entered and sat down. The beet loft smelled of dry rot and long-abandoned chicken coops. Gloom descended.

"Nothing!" Bernardo burst out after a minute's silence. "How could there be nothing?"

Salvestro looked up absently. "Not nothing," he murmured to himself.

"What, then?" demanded the other.

Salvestro did not reply. They could sell the rope, he calculated. The market at Stettin was held on a Saturday, or had been when last he heard. Today was Sunday. Ewald's boat would have to be returned and Bernardo's other boot fetched from the drying-shed. Barns, woodsheds, caves, stables, scrapes, and bivouacs; in the forest beneath the boughs of the trees, the open sky. Now a beet loft. All the miles since Prato had fetched them up on a packed-earth floor with a view through the open door of a pile of sticks and a flat muddy field. Little enough. But down there, in the blackness and the disorder of his wits . . . Something. He had pulled back. He fingered the bump on the back of his head, which began once more to throb. Seated opposite him, Bernardo shifted on one buttock to release a long-withheld fart. Salvestro looked over at his companion, who prodded the ground aimlessly with his finger and would not look back.

"There is a market quite near here. We'll be able to sell the rope, and there's a good few suppers right there, that's just for starters."

Silence.

"Listen, Bernardo. These monks didn't fish us out just to throw us back in. They probably need a couple of fellows like us about the place. We can winter here as well as anywhere, and in the spring—"

"I don't like it here," Bernardo said abruptly. "I didn't like it when we arrived and I don't like it now." He paused and thought. "It's a shit hole."

"It may be a shit hole, Bernardo, but it's a shit hole with a roof, with walls. . . ."

"That fish shed was a shit hole, too. I don't care if you were born there or not. This island's a shit hole, and that dump we stopped in on the mainland before we got here, now that was a real shit hole. . . ."

And Salvestro listened with diminishing interest as Bernardo began listing the watering holes, villages, and the scattering of wayside inns and camps that had served as the stations of their flight north, separating them into "shit holes" and "real shit holes," beginning with "that bog you led us into outside Prato," where they had spent the first night of their journey spread-eagled on the quaking frangible surface, listening to the shouts of the Colonel's men as they searched for them around the marsh's periphery, not daring to move until dawn showed them safe passage, and following it with the remembrance of an ill-chosen hiding place to which they had resorted with a whole village chasing after them (was it Ala? Serravalle? Somewhere before Trento, certainly before the mountains . . .) following Bernardo's theft of a swan, and which, inasmuch as it was a silo built eight feet high, might be termed "a hole," and which, inasmuch as it was a manure silo . . . Well, Salvestro admitted privately, it fell fairly and squarely into the second of his companion's categories. The swan had proved delicious, though the "shit" in that particular "shit hole"—being actually shit—had added its now faint but still unscrubbable stink to the others in his weeds: old sweat, cooking grease, tiny bits of food more easily rubbed in than wiped off, beer splashes, milk . . . Milk seemed so innocuous at first, he reflected, but then give it a couple of warm days and it smelled worse than puke. Funny stuff, milk. Most lately herring. Under them all the smell of the woman at Prato, soaking into him, her fish-cold flesh sucking the heat out of him. That smell. Prato. No sense in dwelling on that.

He cocked an ear once more to his companion, whose rambling lament had gathered speed and now leaped a German mile north for every Italian one south, or vice versa, jumbling Cisalpine shepherds' huts with Franconian hamlets, nameless clusters of hovels with the great marts of the Nordmark, redrawing the jagged line of their northward progress according to his own touchstones: Had they eaten? Had they been warm? Had they been chased? Hunger, cold, and dogs figured large in Bernardo's imagination. For him, their journey had been little more than endless trudging through varying obstacles and discomforts. His companion had never really grasped that it had a purpose, a destination, and when they had finally stepped off the small boat that had ferried them across the Achter-Wasser and he had said that they would stop here, they had arrived, Bernardo had become a child overwhelmed with gratitude and surprise, as though to merely stop were a gift too great to be longed for and its receipt an all-surpassing miracle. "Well, here we are. Here we are at last!" he had exclaimed over and over as they'd tramped across the island to the north shore. "Now, tell me"—he was beaming, standing there on the beach and drawing great breaths of the sea air—"where is the city?"

". . . and Nürnberg. Nürnberg! Another shit-hole. . . ."

Salvestro picked at his nose. It had been for his own good, for the both of them and to save their skins—there was no knowing how far a man like the Colonel might pursue them and thus no knowing where exactly their progress had ceased to be a flight and become a journey—and Bernardo, the lummox, had wanted to stay. . . . But, had he—Salvestro—omitted a certain fact that, had it been known, might have severed the rope by which he had dragged Bernardo north? Emerging from the ravine that the Freiburg road took on its way to Dresden, he had pointed down the gentle slope of the valley and across the broad swath of the river to the great walled city on the far bank, saying, "Once we reach the island, Vineta is as near as that." They were outside a little village called Plauen, which, an old man who gave them water there assured them, had long ago lent its name to the much larger city they had passed through some days before and never got it back. He was furious on the subject. An hour later they had crossed the Elbe and were walking through crowded, narrow streets. "As near as that. . . ." It was true, but was it the truth?

Bernardo had scanned the gray expanse before them, southeast to northwest, where his eye alighted hopefully first on Greifswalder Oie, then behind it the heights of Göhren on Rügen, the headland of the neighboring island just peaking out from behind that of Usedom's own. Neither looked like the promised city of Salvestro's tale, and the latter was pointing in the other direction, to where the sea lay unbroken before a truncated point of land on which some stone buildings huddled together all higgledy-piggledy. Not a city, though, and beyond it only the sea. . . .

"Where is it?"

"There."

"But I can't see anything. Just water. . . ."

There was a short silence. *As near as that. . . .* Had he, on one crucial point, as it were, deceived his reluctant companion?

"Underneath," said Salvestro.

Bernardo had begun complaining that night, clinging to his grievances like so much driftwood from the wreck. This latest lament was nothing new and would run its course now as it had before.

". . . then that raft, making me get on that thing. That G'litcz fellow, eh? A right pig in a poke till we sorted him out. Down that river . . ."

Two rivers, thought Salvestro. The Neisse and then the broad flood he had been waiting for since . . . Since he had fled this place all those years before and emerged from the forest and followed its banks upstream, south, away from the island and into other arms and all the years between. Island-obstructed and riven with false channels yet broad enough for all, they had found G'litcz in its tributary, run aground in midstream aboard a great raft of Bohemian oak trunks destined for the mart at Stettin, abandoned by his hirelings and squawking for help before the current should smash his vessel to ungovernable splinters. . . . They had shouted terms from the near bank, then Salvestro had swum out to take a line to shore, Bernardo had pulled him off, and they had continued on, the three of them poling downstream to the great confluence past Guben, where their course joined the thick muddy flood of the Oder.

There G'litcz had claimed to have lost his satchel in the river, and with it his purse. He had been a short wiry man. How could he pay them? They had watched impassively as this story spilled out a league or so short of Stettin. Salvestro had pointed to the rope.

G'litcz's rope. A piece of glass filched from a workshop backing onto the Schmiedegasse in Nürnberg. A barrel. A boat.

"And then I thought you were dead!" Bernardo burst out suddenly, a leap in the catalog of his misfortunes that caught Salvestro by surprise and seemed to add new energy to the other's accusations. "That was just typical, to leave me high and dry in a boat, on my own, after you promised this and swore by that and . . ."

While the promises he had made scattered like sinking cargoes into regions of dark and doubt, never to be recouped. Never to be lost, either. The jolts of the surface, tidal surges, and heat-sapped convections add their slack echoes and seiches to the purposeless flux below: whorls, tilting waterfronts, skittish eddies peeling off the mass that drift and disperse their entrusted vessels . . . Where? It's unpredictable, to do with remote sea-motions, invisible storms, gales striking over the horizon. These are distant resolutions. A boy, bone white, diving and washed away one night. A man diving in his fool's coat of wood and rope, finding a boy's promises down there, the water still thick with them. An inner skin had been waiting for him, but its smooth invasion had been too cold, too final, for him to gulp down. He gulped air instead. He spilled his stomach on the deck, telling his eager friend, "Nothing. . . ." Nothing? Something. His clothes steamed gently as his blood's heat dried them. There was the rope to sell. There was the boat to be returned. . . . What else?

"Straw," said a voice that was suddenly not Bernardo's.

"For bedding," said another.

"Brother HansJürgen told us to bring straw for your bedding," said the third.

Peering in at the door were three monks, younger than the one who had conducted them here earlier, all three struggling somewhat under identical loads of straw. Salvestro jumped to his feet. "And very welcome, too," he said quickly. "Right here—" He indicated the floor.

Settled on their beds of straw, the two men watched the gray afternoon light drain west and disappear. Cooking smells reached them through the walls, and though Bernardo quickly resumed his complaints, his heart was no longer in it. "I never asked to come here in any case; we should have done like I said. You wouldn't listen to me though, oh no. I told you what we should've done. We should have stayed with *Groot,*" he finished up.

"Groot is dead," Salvestro said then, and after that his companion was silent.

The same three monks reappeared a little later, two of them bearing large bowls filled with a kind of broth, the third a small oil-lamp. They watched by the flickering light as the two men ate hungrily and collected the bowls when they were finished. Salvestro looked up at the trio, who hovered there as though they had been charged with some task and were unsure how to go about it. A fourth, older face appeared behind them. It was the monk from that morning. Brother HansJürgen beckoned to Salvestro.

"Father Jörg will see you now," he said.

Small ponds will freeze, but not the sea, the winter being too mild. Such snow that fell by Michaelmas fell in heavy sopping flakes that melted at the first touch of sun. The northeasterly winds blew weakly. It was a sodden winter.

They could be seen rounding the marshy precincts of the Schmollen-See or paddling the sheltered waters of Krumminer Wiek, splashing ashore at Eigholz to tramp north as the sun dipped below the dark mass of the mainland. They came in twos and threes, muddying themselves in the marsh behind Stenschke's place, threading their way through the bare and unfamiliar woods, which thinned to beech scrub a little before the slope of the foreshore. They called on Ploetz once or twice, but he only shook his head as though to say he had worries enough already. Brüggeman's were no business of his.

Ott, Ronsdorff, Riesenkampf, the Krumminer Wittmanns and the Buchen-wald Wittmanns, Haase, Peter Gottfreund, others, too, they all turned up on one evening or another, grunted a greeting to Mathilde, and took their places around the hearth. She watched them clear their throats and spit in the flames, shifting their buttocks on the narrow benches. Their weather-scoured faces were bristly and red in the firelight. Heavy silences descended and enveloped them in an inhibiting pall. They were dour gatherings. Brüggemann could count himself lucky to have neighbors like them. He should have dealt with the matter himself.

She remembered the first sight of them. Two men had stood there, the giant behind, both silent until Ewald had appeared behind her and recognized the foremost. He had come back.

Her husband had offered them the herring-shed. Later they had asked for food. And then a barrel. When the boat had disappeared she hoped without truly believing that this might be the final price of their forbearance and they were gone or drowned. When the monk's knock came at their door, she had cowered, fearing it might be they. Then a voice she knew was not theirs sounded, asking who was within.

A monk stood there, a little older than her husband, tall, quite alone. "You are Brüggeman?" She saw her husband nod. She hung back, catching only fragments of what passed between them: they are with us, at the monastery . . . our Prior too trusting, foolish even. . . . The monk moved his hands quickly and surely. They were working hands, callused, with thick stubby fingers. She heard him say, "You are a good man, Brüggeman. You islanders are all good men. . . ." The children lay very still, but they were awake, only feigning sleep. Other children lay awake in other beds about the island. "You have just cause. Remember the Lion, Brüggeman. . . ."

The first of them came at dusk the next night. Their neighbors, though their relations were strained to something else now. Mathilde would pour them mugs of broth. She listened and nodded. When the fire burned low she sent her husband out to the woodpile, and his exit uncorked the bottle they had waited these hours to taste: *Just a boy at the time. God alone knew what that bitch and her whelp had done to him. They had shunned him for it, as boys, that is: Ewald did it with the Savage. . . . But that was just teasing.* Whatever it was that had gone on, it was no laughing matter now. If it was down to Brüggeman, it was down to them all; their own fathers should have finished the business.

Toeing the door open and peering over the faggots piled high in his arms, Ewald saw their faces turned to him, half-shadowed in the glow, and heard the familiar silence descend. He took his place on the low stool he reserved to himself and waited once more for the punctuation of grave assertions and grunts to shape the unspoken act before them: *Isn't that right? There's no avoiding it, eh? Eh, Ewald?* They would come to it easier with him out of the way, but he was at its heart, somehow essential. The thing they were coming to could be come to only here, sitting around his, Ewald Brüggeman's, hearth. The closer they came to it the more he nodded. He had nodded to the monk. It was Ewald whom the witch's boy had led into the woods that night. Now the witch's boy was back. The monk had warned them. Now his warning had come true.

The bones of the Michaelmas goose were soup, foaming in the kettle over the fire. She had opened the door and there he was, and though her heart was in her mouth as she stammered that, no, Ewald was not at home, she had known too that there would be no further doubts that it must be done. Not here, she repeated. She slammed the door shut and waited, leaning with her back to it, listening as he left. She waited for her husband to return. She stirred and skimmed, hardly looking up as he entered, waiting for him to settle himself, holding herself in. He dipped a finger in the bowl before him.

"He was here," she said.

"Who?"

"The witch's boy. The Savage."

"What of it?" Face like a liar.

"He is to return the boat. He means you to help beach her."

He nodded, and she saw that he was as frightened as herself. They had looked at each other in silence.

"Get the others," Mathilde told her husband.

"Right, I'm going," said Bernardo.

He watched the big man stomp off across the field, still limping. It had become a habit in the week it had taken Salvestro to muster his energies and walk the short miles across the island to retrieve his companion's boot. Nothing had changed in the herring-shed. The pond was much as it was before, though someone had pushed over their derrick. He swung back toward the shore. There was the smoke from Ewald's chimney, there the chimney itself, then the hut as he cleared the trees and waded through the scrub, coming to the door at a run down the slope. He hesitated there. He had put it off for a week. He knocked.

Sixty yards away, Bernardo had reached a stand of beeches and was looking about him, seemingly confused.

Mathilde had faced him across the threshold. He was thrown suddenly. At a loss to what to say, he mumbled something about the boat. It was not why he'd called; he had expected Ewald himself. He wanted to talk with the husband, not his wife. Now he would have to return the boat, which the monks had dragged up the slope and beached against the east wall of the church. Kind enough, except that they had left it uncovered, it had filled with snow, the snow had melted to water, the water had frozen solid, and now it was filled with ice. He should have seen to it himself. He should have seen to Bernardo's boot sooner, too. He blamed the Prior for these misfortunes.

Sixty-seven yards away, Bernardo was manhandling beech trees, which were obstructive and larger than himself. The sky was a collection of dull grays, rain possible but unlikely. Bernardo swiped at low-hanging branches, ducked, and disappeared within them.

That first night, HansJürgen had climbed two short flights of steps broken by a corner that brought them to a passage running above the cloister's north ambulatory. The monk's sandals clacked ahead of his own near soundless footfalls, the oil-lamp held before the monk's chest throwing a great swath of shadow that gathered him in and drew him along behind. They passed three doors set at regular intervals in the wall to their right; a fourth faced them at the end of the passage. A rod of light tapered itself between the lower edge and the threshold's worn sill, flickering and fanning out over the flags' tiny pits and slopes, dying in the passage's outer dark. He could hear the sea very faintly; any of the rooms they had passed would overlook it. The monk had stopped. Salvestro thought to himself with sudden conviction, I have been here before.

At Prato, Groot had led him through the gates of the palazzo, across courtyards and through reception rooms echoing with their own emptiness, trumpeting abandonment. There are rooms behind such rooms, chambers dedicated to shier purposes. Deniable rooms. The summons' aura is perfumed with a fine blend of obligation and threat that will dissipate and adapt new shapes here: a private word, a dubious proposition, the privilege of a shared secret. Privy wares are set out amongst simple, hastily arranged furniture. A sergeant had asked them if they were the Colonel's men. He was like no sergeant Salvestro had ever seen before, fine-boned and well-spoken, a silk-and-feathers sergeant. He sensed the half-veiled distaste at this pollution of the sanctum; authority's resentment of its instruments. What was the task they had been designed to perform for this strange sergeant's colonel? The ritual continues with grave nods, half-truths. He and Groot are being escorted out, anointed, spat out. Days later he is fleeing a slaughterhouse, he is lying in a marsh. Remembering . . . Authority's resentment raised suddenly to fury and pursuing them over mountains and rivers. Stringing up Groot by the neck. Himself running north with an imbecile in tow. . . .

Bernardo. Where has he got to now? Having emerged on the far side of the stand, crossed a shallow bog, and entered the woods proper, he was surrounded by beech trees, moving in a direction whose gist was south, but which also contained strong elements of southeast, east, and southwest. There were even hints of west, when the terrain became particularly vindictive. Distance? One hundred and seven yards.

"Come," had sounded from within. HansJürgen pushed open the door. His summoner was bent over a table covered with papers, the monk from that morning, their leader. Simple furniture. His hand was raised and frozen in a beckoning gesture that seemed to both invite and stay his entry. He looked up at the two of them standing in the doorway. A room behind other rooms. What did he require?

One hundred and twenty-four yards south-southeast from where he sat (remembering, imagining), undirected bellows were erupting through the tangled branchwork, disturbing winter birdlife and small arboreal mammals, such as squirrels. Bernardo has encountered a thornbush.

The giant had been unsettled and difficult in the days following their arrival. Discontent had centered about his boot, its absence, Salvestro's reluctance to fetch it, but its roots were in their idleness. The monastery was a currentless place. They heard singing come from the chapter-house. They smelled cooking as it seeped through the wall. The monks themselves would congregate at odd hours in the cloister, walk about in twos and threes, talk together in tight, unwelcoming huddles. Their own meals arrived twice a day: an unvarying diet of black bread and broth (the morning) and black bread and broth and salted meat (the evening), delivered by the same youthful trio that had brought them food on the first night. Dried fish on the Friday. Bernardo had struck up a number of halting conversations with them, which invariably ended with his describing the food as "real rotgut stuff, thanks all the same." The three novices seemed to find this funny.

Others shunned them completely, seeming to look through them as though they did not exist. There were alliances and private hatreds at work. He had walked down the slope to the shore one afternoon, then looked up at the gaping hole that had once been the nave of the church. He saw the clay beneath it was sodden. When summer came it would dry and crumble. A few blocks of stone showed above the water's surface and bore witness to the earlier collapse. More would follow. He wondered if the monks were aware of, or even cared about, this fact. They never seemed to venture down here. He looked around him: the coast running northwest, gray sea, the coast running southeast. Farther: the slope of the shore steepening as it neared him, the path down which he had walked, and then, at the top of the path, a monk. The monk was watching him, and he felt suddenly that he should not be here, that he had been caught at something. He waved. The monk's face appeared strange in some way, but at that instant he could not make it out. There was no answering wave. The figure turned abruptly and stalked off. The crumbling cliff. The collapsing church. The face, Salvestro realized belatedly, had been contorted with something close to rage. Even without the why or how, he knew then that here was the fault running through his new lodging. The sea lapped placidly at the foot of the cliff; it was this that splintered the monks into little cliques and factions. He scrambled his way up the slope, passed by Ewald's ice-filled boat, and walked quickly across the cloister. He did not go back.

"Thank you, Brother HansJürgen." The monk had withdrawn, closing the door behind him. There was a stool. "Sit." Salvestro sat. The Prior bent his head to the sheets of parchment. Salvestro saw squiggly black marks, curled corners, two wooden blocks placed to prevent the sheets from rolling closed. The man before him gathered his thoughts for a second, then said, "You came back here to make mischief for Brüggeman, did you not? You used to be his friend."

Bernardo's boot was the Prior's fault. The delay in fetching it. He had been preoccupied, mulling over such questions, anticipating others. There had been a second summons since that first one, and others would follow. He stood on the brittle crust of the present while the Prior's interrogation pressed down on his head and the thin plate beneath his feet warped and shuddered. Beneath that was Then, and Then was dark and bottomless. He would sink in Then.

"No," he had said.

"Then why did you come back?"

The Prior's table was strewn with quills, little earthenware pots, stoppered bottles, amulets whose meaning he could not divine. Above all, papers. He had prepared a speech for this occasion, for this inevitable question, a proud speech with flourishes and intrepid expressions. He had returned to uncover Vineta, a thing no other man had done. He was an adventurer, restless and impulsive. He needed an anchor to ground his spirit, a task. The undersea city was it. The Prior would then ask if he had found the peace he sought, if his spirit was quieted and

harnessed. No! would be his answer (perhaps tearfully), and they would pray together side by side. He knew a prayer or two. He would revile his life, if necessary.

But he had barely embarked on this course when the Prior, eyeing him
across the table, held up his hand as though his words were the screechings of two
battling cats. "You are a liar. Out."

He sat there rooted for a moment. "Out!" He rose.

HansJürgen was standing in the passageway, as expressionless as before. As he
turned from the door to face him, Salvestro saw two other monks carrying tapers
and a bowl appear at the far end of the passage. They disappeared within the first
of the doors they had passed earlier. The monk turned, and Salvestro understood
that he was to follow. Wan candlelight shone through the doorway ahead. The
monk stopped and stared.

"What are you doing there? That is Brother Florian's task! Who gave you
permission . . . ?"

Salvestro looked over the outraged monk's shoulder. He saw a cell furnished
much as the Prior's was, a little larger, perhaps. The two monks were sitting on a
low bed that rested against the far wall. Between them they supported a wizened,
skeletal creature, a man, dressed in a stained nightshirt and thick wool stockings,
whose head lolled back and whose mouth hung open. The skin was blotched and
stretched tight over his bones. Even wedged between those of the monks, his
arms and legs were limp. They were trying to spoon food into his mouth, but he
would not or could not swallow, and most of it was spilling onto the already filthy
shirt. The only parts of him that moved of his own accord were his eyes. These
rolled from side to side as though trying to catch sight of his tormentors.

"Brother Florian is unfit to care for him," one of the monks replied shortly.

"By whose authority!" demanded HansJürgen again. "Gerhardt's?"

But the monks ignored him, simply spooning food into their patient's
mouth. When he repeated, "Gerhardt? Is that it?" the same monk looked up and
said, "Since you take more pains with your ape than your Abbot, Brother
HansJürgen, why do you not lead him back to his cage now? Or does our Prior
plan to return him to one of his distant lands?"

HansJürgen had led him to his lodging in thunderous silence. He had lain
down on the hard earth; Bernardo had filched most of his straw during his absence and now snored loudly on the other side of the beet loft. That day had
begun with the two of them walking down the beach to Ewald's boat, which
seemed long, long ago. He had much to think about that night, and the following
days had given him more. He had had no time for boots, but Bernardo's complaints had eventually reached an unignorable pitch, culminating in the usual
threat that "he had had enough and was off." Without his boot this was impossible. With it, the compulsion was removed. A mind more vindictive than his own,
Salvestro reflected, might have taken more pleasure in the conundrum.

He took none. He thought of the Prior. The second summons had come two
days before the Quest for the Boot. Again he climbed the same steps and fol-

lowed HansJürgen past the Abbot's door—closed this time, the cell within unlit—and along the passage.

The second meeting went much as the first. He sat on the stool. The Prior fixed him with a stare and asked, by way of variation, "Tell me how you came to assume a false name?"

He had anticipated this. "Niklot" was a common name; that was his curse. There were other Niklots. One even resembled him somewhat. Unfortunately, he was a thief. From his lair deep in the forest, this outcast would snake out in the night to lift a chicken, a few eggs—once even a young pig—from the farms and manses thereabouts, leaving himself, the true Niklot, to take the blame. This impostor would trample corn, break fences, appear out of the greenery to frighten farmers' daughters at their bathing, throw stones at their cattle . . . There was no end to his devilment. No one could catch him, either. He melted away like water into sand, leaving a damp stain that the sun would dry in minutes. What was he, the true Niklot, to do? After much thought, and many unjust accusations (none proved), he had decided to change his name. Henceforth, he would be "Salvestro."

He began this recitation with high hopes. He was establishing the fact of there being other Niklots when the interruption came.

"Enough!" The Prior was glaring at him in exasperation. "More lies. Out!"

Walking back once more to the beet loft, following the dim pool of light cast by HansJürgen's lamp across the cloister, he was struck by a thought. He considered it briefly. It was absurd. Once again, Bernardo had stolen his straw. Tomorrow he would again not fetch Bernardo's boot. He lay down but could not get comfortable. The Prior vexed him. If he, Salvestro, did not know what the man wanted, how could he be expected to give it to him? An account of some sort, certainly. Something believable, consistent. It was hard to credit, but it was almost as if—and here the Thought jabbed him again—he wanted to hear the truth. And, harder still to believe, turning it over in his mind now, he, Salvestro, was almost tempted to accede, to in effect be frank, even candid, as it were, with reservations, of course, but on the whole not, perhaps, or perhaps not . . . an extraordinary Thought then, this, which was, at least as a possibility, to, well, actually to tell the truth. The truth, yes. Could he? Might he . . . ? No.

The next day he considered the matter further. He wandered absentmindedly into the cloister. A group of monks were standing by the door of the chapterhouse. As he approached, one scooped a handful of water from the stoup there, ran up to him with a strange, tight face, and threw it over him. The monk stared at him as though the water had been molten lead and he should fall to the ground and shrivel to a cinder. When he did not, the monk backed away fearfully. He turned about and resumed his deliberations. So long as he did this, the Thought, by and large, left him alone.

It was back soon enough. Indeed, more insistently on the following day, and Salvestro caught himself muttering angrily to himself, "No! Stupid!" He found himself at the edge of the field. The Thought prodded him. The Prior seemed somehow to know when he was lying. In the Prior's eyes, he was already a liar. He kept walking. Soon he was at the herring-shed. The Thought, obviously, had been lying in wait for him. It swung out of the roof and knocked him to the ground. He struggled, but the Thought pinned him down. He wrestled, but it had him firm. He fought back, but at that it only pounded and pounded. . . .

Bernardo's boot lay on the floor of the herring-shed. He picked it up. The boot, then the boat. Thoughts of Ewald, the scene rolling round again. He called on the man, got his wife. The boat, then the boot. He walked back. Bernardo stalked off in a meaningless sulk, but Bernardo would always come back. He was happy enough, for the moment, to be alone.

The Thought circled him mistrustfully. He was resolved, yet the notion that he might actually follow this course of action shook him to the core. It went against the grain. He wavered. He had faith. He doubted. He believed. It was brilliant, irresistible, inspired. . . .

He envisaged a voice asking questions in tones that tell him they will not be repeated, a near future voice having the Prior's ring. Shivers underfoot; cracks snake forward and outpace him, split and peel the floor from its foundations, themselves already fallen away and sunk. Long-settled conflicts skinned this boggy earth in wood and stone, called it "Land." Misplaced faith at best, and importunate. Soils and shy clays shrink away to leave hollows, cavities, brittle vaults that unmindful feet pound from above; the skin itself dries, grows paper thin, stretched over nothing. The catastrophe waits while, as prelude, stones tumble away one night into a void that only daylight calls the sea. Vanity scrapes at the defining rind, and that which conceals itself in the very blandness of the cell, in the coming banality of such questions—Jörg's questions—this is a version of "Then." They will begin, he imagines, like this:

"How did you come to be 'Salvestro'?"

And he will answer, he imagines.

Like this.

Sunlight woke him on the shore of the Achter-Wasser. He rose and walked forward into the woods. Standing and fallen trunks, dry and dying underbrush, leaf-drifts, scrub . . . The forest's victors and defeated parted ranks to admit a damp and scrawny refugee. Hungry, too: his teeth ground tuberous stems, tongue twitched and wettened, throat gulped, sap-heavy crowns burst against his palate. He pulped stringy roots, swallowed soapy juices, bolted acorns, wild garlic, a dead crow once, in experiment, and his excrement crawled with worms. He stole eggs from the farms thereabouts, a chicken, followed the banks of a great river, upstream, until the forest sucked him deeper and farther in. Scabs and rashes bloomed on his arms and legs. He shod himself in calluses. Distance was a thickening of shadows, an opacity. By the island's measure he was ten years old walking into this place; by the forest's, a newborn baby.

For it scoured him, and he forgot himself within it, and his memories when they came at all would come at him like appetites. He ran, jumped, clung, hung . . . Two holm oaks stood in a clearing opened by the deadening shade of the greater one's canopy. The younger stood beside it, gangling as a new foal. It shot up in a dash for the sunlight, crescive and skinny-limbed. How many seasons before its elder would starve it down? The needy suck of its roots, the pump of the supple trunk . . . He swung, felt the bough he clung to half-bend, half-break, felt it yield, snap, and drop him to the ground, where he twisted and pulled, jumped again, and gnawed at the fibrous splinters until it broke clean away at last. He thought of the years' growth rippling up the trunk, along the boughs, fattening like a wave. . . . He saw a bear once. A shambling sack of fur crashed about in the undergrowth quite near him, searching for something. Deer clattered away, smelling him. Unseen creatures twitched and bolted. Sunlight prickled the dark canopy above, and the wind when it blew was a terrible thrashing and scourging, a frightening violence from which he was immune. He cowered anyway and fled the winters, too, feeling the endless ache, the bone-freezing chill, of each season a little less than the last—moving south, as he would later understand it. By chance the forest might give out, a sky yawn open, and he would be standing at the edge of grasslands, a moor, open ground. Huts appeared as little bricks with thin plumes of smoke disappearing into the abrupt blue. He would turn back, blend with the forest's interior stillness, disappear again. He was incurious and uncatchable and invisible and unknown. . . . But he liked to watch fires.

"What?" (The Prior's expression will be quizzical, one eyebrow raised, a little tilt of the head.)

Heart thumping against his ribs, mouth filled with spit, he liked to creep close, out of earshot but close, smell the carcass roasting over the glow, see the red flames flicker, watch the hunched figures shuffle about and nod to one another. They excited him, these wounds in the forest's play of soft lights and shades and subtleties of dark. He liked to blind himself with the glow. The forest was briefly nothing then and would unclasp him, cut him loose to drift and blink the hot light out of his eyes. He liked to crawl about the camp, circle it inch by inch, slowly drawing spirals in the forest's rustling growth. . . . He wanted always to get close, and closer, and closer still. That was how they caught him.

"Who?" (Put bluntly, a retraction of the earlier hint of curiosity. The Prior will not be curious. He will be businesslike and matter-of-fact.)

"Pull him out by the ears!"

"Bark his shins!"

"Box his ears!"

Perhaps these were the words they shouted, which he heard as sudden noise and chaos and terror while they beat him. It was a whirl of light and huge faces looming in and out of view, of noise, above all noise. . . . They brandished themselves like clubs, knocking him about, colliding amongst themselves with great thuds. If he flattened himself against the earth, he could disappear in the shadows and they would forget him, walk away like the bear or clatter like the deer. Flatten himself. Disappear. *Run, run to the sea. . . .* They were huge booming men, strange smelling and deafening. He clasped his head in his hands to shut them out, but they were stubborn and forceful. They refused to vanish. One punched him on the ear. Another kicked him on the leg. He was rolled up in a resistant ball. They unrolled him. He was almost naked, he realized, and as tall as they. How had that happened? He wondered about this, amazed and somewhat hopeless.

There was a night of this, and then a dawn. There were great explosions of din and racket. Days fell out of the sky.

He remembered a sloping ridge of ground choked with grasses into which his feet sank spongily as they traversed and rose to the crest. It was sunny and he was being led along on a length of twine. Just that.

Another time, he was sleeping, near the fire for once, and dreamed that heavy sheets of material were being draped over his body, like animal skins, growing heavier and heavier. Mice burrowed beneath him and produced fantastic litters of young. Dozens upon dozens of squealing bodies.

Here was a different place, where the turf had been worn through to the damp black earth beneath and thus a path was etched between little hummocks and anthills. He lengthened his stride over the long thin puddles and added his own footprints to those already printed in the impressionable earth, for he was marching along near the back that day. A meadow ran up to the very edge of the forest, and the tree-trunks with the darkness beyond them appeared as a palisade forbidding entry or the bars of a monstrous cage roofed with green.

Another time they entered a village with fierce whoops and shouts. There was a long low interior in which the air had been breathed over and over until it smelled of the insides of men. One of them was scrabbling about on the floor, where meat bones, corn husks, crusts, and bottles were scattered. Three others spoke together in low tones at the far end, falling silent as he came near. These men were different and strange, smelled different. They were not his men. There was a table running almost the length of the room. The scrabbler rose from beneath it and placed before him a large pile of scraps. He was suspicious. The other mimed eating and then, when this produced no response, plucked a bone from the pile and commenced to strip the remainder of its meat with his teeth. He understood then and fell on the pile like a wolf. The three men murmured to one another, and from outside there was shrieking and a few shouts. Opposite him, his companion pointed to himself and made a sound like *Aar-aar-Oood.* They left there in the night, quietly, disturbing nothing. He liked that. He was the quietest of them all. The next morning, though, the din began again.

For there was always noise. The air looped him in quick eruptions and outbreaks of clatter such as *Nnunng* and *Tz-ztts* and *Lull-ooll.* Differing sounds startled him and made him nervous: louder and softer grunts, grunts ending in sharp claps and hissings. . . . He began to nod when these little thunderclaps passed near him, to duck almost, as though their chatter were a physical force, the rustling, or crashing, or slithery approach of a hundred different animals ten or twenty times a day. There were regular sounds that went back and forth between the wagging tongues, others that seemed to keen or stutter. Sharp yaps and little strings of yips. He twisted about, jumped and started at their barking, and after a time they even stopped laughing at these nervy antics, so familiar and predictable had they become. And then, weeks after his "capture," months even, perhaps—he was rolling a water bottle between his knees and one of the men was throwing little pebbles at him that were bouncing off his head—a sound came at him all suddenly, like *SSoss-O!,* which he had heard aimed at him before, and then two little gobbets of noise, like a half grunt, *Oer-tt,* and then a groan, *ooOower . . .* Like that. And he felt the muscles in his cheeks and tongue ache, the muscles he used to maneuver mashed food into position before swallowing, and he felt his tongue do something like peel itself dryly from the roof of his mouth, like skinning a very dry animal, and he opened his mouth and said, quite clearly, "Geddit y'self." Then a gulp.

"Shit."

Everyone stopped. An amazed hush swelled suddenly, an abrupt luxuriant silence that engulfed the odd creature he had spat at them, swallowed it whole, and his utterance wallowed and floundered about for footing. He blinked with the strain and said the same thing again. Their blank surprise trembled like a wall of deadening liquid behind which his tiny noise was unweighted and soundless. Then someone broke it with, "So Salvestro ain't a deaf-mute," and everyone else started laughing. He looked about blankly. "Well, what else was we to call you?" It was the same man, the one who had called to be passed the bottle, which now lay forgotten on the ground in front of him. "Groot," he said, thumping himself on the chest. He was Groot. "Eh, Salvestro? Mister Geddit-Yourself-Shit, eh?"

SSoss-O! Oer-tt-ooOwer!

Salvestro. Water. He rolled the words in his mouth. Geddit 'self. Groot. Groo-oo-oot. Behind him, the forest was a jumble of little rustlings and sussurations; unguessable, without meaning.

And these renaming vagabonds, who were they?

They were: Fante the Dagger and Umberto the Pike, Shiner, Horvart, Hurst (or 'Urst), who was imperturbable, Heinrich Von Bool, dubbed Drool, for he had no tongue, and the Bandinelli twins, who, though they were near doubles of one another, had grown up in the same village and bore the names Aldo and Tebaldo, were unrelated. A certain Corprochet titled himself "the Admiral of the Adda"; Pandulfo was "Il Dottore" and alone of the company could read and write. He was composing an epical history in song of their exploits in the wars to the south. There was Criparacos the Greek, Low Simon, Sigismundo of the Fiery Eyes, and the Chevalier Gianbattista-Marcantonio di Castello-Molina di Fiemme. The one with the unnaturally smooth and garishly colored face was Powder Jack. But most fearsome of them all was the Teeth.

Groot pointed them out and described them to him, advising him of their foibles and failings and explaining that these were not ordinary men but soldiers, tuned for combat and unpredictable in their humors. "Always approach from the front," he warned, "and avoid shouting." For in the days and weeks since he had rediscovered his speech, Salvestro had taken to yelling nonsensical phrases at the top of his voice every few minutes or so to keep his new faculty in trim.

Their leader, known only as Il Capo, was a black-bearded, blue-eyed, jolly-faced gentleman of fifty years or more who was carried about in a wicker basket construction resembling in equal parts a very small boat and a large but legless chair. Il Capo had no feet.

"The Christian Free Company, m'boy. That's us. A nasty bunch of bastards we are, nasty as any you'll meet this side of hell, the Alps, and Kingdom Come. Don't forget that, young Salvestro. And don't forget this, neither." Il Capo leaned forward in his throne, wheezed, gathered himself. "By Christ, we hate the French!"

It was dusk. It had rained earlier. On the far side of the clearing, Powder Jack and Sigismundo of the Fiery Eyes were building a fire that stubbornly refused to ignite. Il Capo stared at him as though expecting an answer.

"The French," said Salvestro.

Il Capo nodded approval. "Hate 'em!" he hissed. He rocked back into the basket's inner gloom. There was a rustling then, the sound of him rooting around, several dull clanks. "You'll be wanting to see 'em, then," came from within.

"The French?" said Salvestro, surprised. He had conceived "the French" as some kind of animal—noxious, probably large, unlikely to be found in Il Capo's basket. In any case singular. What was "them"?

"Those bastards? Good Christ on the Cross, no!" exclaimed Il Capo, emerging from the interior clutching a silvery metal box in each hand. "No, I meant you'll be wanting to see the Feet."

"Vitelli cut 'em off him after Buti fell," Groot explained later. "He was lucky, mind you. The arquebus men lost their hands *and* eyes. Did he show you the toes?"

The Feet had been yellow and shiny, odorless, in a perfect state of preservation. Slightly shrunken, perhaps. The toes had followed, each in its individual box. A little stump of bone protruded where the flesh about it had dried and the toenails had detached themselves from their cuticles. The toes were a slightly darker color than the Feet, as though they had been stubbed shortly before excision.

"The toes I don't find so impressive," Groot confided when Salvestro nodded, "but the Feet . . . the Feet, I think, are a miracle."

Salvestro looked across the gloomy camp to the barely visible hummock that was Il Capo. His wicker lodging would sit inertly wherever they had decided to pitch camp that night, and from it would issue bellowed proclamations and commands: "Thirty lashes for anyone fouling within the perimeter!" or "Post guards! 'Urst! Drool! Jump to it!" Fires would be lit, lookouts chosen and dispatched. Camps were pitched and struck. They moved on, stopped, moved on again. Ordered to "jump to it!" by Il Capo, the men of the Christian Free Company by and large jumped. But try as he might, Salvestro was quite unable to see why. The source of Il Capo's authority was deeply mysterious. It had something to do with the Feet, he felt.

Come morning, and all day long if they were on the march, it was Groot's task to carry Il Capo in his basket. Two poles extended stretcher fashion front and back. Groot was short and powerfully built. He took the front. Bringing up the rear was one more powerful even than Groot and standing two heads taller. Salvestro had become aware of him in a wary fashion, seeing that the other men treated him with an odd mixture of disdain and mocking affection and wondering if the company did not after all include one even more lowly than himself. Il Capo's rear porter was part scapegoat and part mascot. Amongst the confusion and clangor of his early days, Salvestro remembered the youth—for he was little older than himself—setting a pile of scraps before him. More recently, venturing into the underbrush to empty his bowels, he had come upon the giant standing patiently by the path leading to their camp. He had been there two or three hours already, sent by Simon to meet the Chevalier, who would be coming that way, having scavenged "a vital longweight." The Chevalier was intermittently visible in the camp behind him, but the giant had drawn no conclusions from this. Salvestro had tried to explain that the men were playing a joke on him.

"Not Longweight. Long *wait*," he explained.

"That's it," said the giant.

He had left him standing there and gone to shit. That night, sleeping, deep in the loose clasp of a pleasant and watery swimming dream, he had been awakened by something akin to a shovel striking him violently in the back.

"Longweight," an enormous face, inches from his own, had exclaimed with delight. "Long"—the face paused for effect, dimly recognized now through the dark and blear of his sleep—"wait!" The face had begun to laugh.

Now, in the cool afternoon light that offered itself between the lintel of the beet loft's doorway and the mire of the field beyond, he observed his companion plod back in desultory fashion, limping theatrically in protest at his prodigal boot. It had shrunk, or his foot had swelled. The face retreated into memory with its idiot cheerfulness, returned again, blankly this time. Bernardo toting his end of the basket. Bernardo bringing up the rear. They had arrived a league or two short of a little village somewhere west of Innsbruck, and strange preparations were afoot. The village was called Muud.

"The village is called Muud," explained Il Capo, flurries of action already welling up about him. Sigismundo and Horvart were stripping hazel saplings out of the hedgerow and the Chevalier was trimming them with a hand ax. Low Simon disentangled numerous short lengths of rope from one another, and other members of the company were unrolling and applying filthy bandages to their limbs. Powder Jack moved amongst them, daubing rust-colored paint over these rags or else administering dollops of bright red paste to proffered arms, legs, and foreheads, which would then be bound up and and the paste seep through as though open wounds were bleeding beneath. Hovering about the fringes of all this, the Teeth lurked, inactive and menacing as usual. There were rehearsals of limping, and several crutches appeared.

"Look lively!" shouted Il Capo. "Full bellies tonight!" Low Simon was tying the saplings into large square grates, then tying the grates together—a boxlike structure was taking shape, with an improvised door on top and poles slung beneath to lift it—a cage. Powder Jack had taken out a *mouchoir* and was scraping at the caked powder on his face, which came away in lumps and slabs to reveal, on his left side, a landscape of deep pockmarks and craters, and, on his right, a deforming jagged valley running from ear to neck so deep that it seemed it must cut through the cheek altogether. Then Salvestro saw the Chevalier call to the Teeth and open the door of the cage. The Teeth approached, and then, without a murmur of protest, he climbed up and lowered himself inside.

The Christian Free Company then set off at a smart hobble, which slowed and grew more pitiful as they approached nearer to the village of Muud, 'Urst and Drool leaning more heavily on their crutches, the Bandinelli twins swapping rhythmic *oohs* and *aahs* of discomfort, bandages being given a final smearing of paint, poultices moistened and refreshed, stringing out along the track until, when they reached the common, the four rangy cows grazing there looked up from their deep stupidity to stare at a column of stumbling casualties and the tethered goat ignoring the thistles it had been staked there to devour and instead busily destroying a stand of myrtle saplings left off its gleeful vandalism to eye a band of beaten warriors, bravery leaking from their wounds, carrying the glamour of the unfairly defeated, coverers of ignoble retreats, the outnumbered driven reluctantly from the last redoubt of honor. . . . There was also a measure of threat, it has to be said, for there was the cage, and within the cage was the Teeth. And tied behind the cage was Salvestro. The imagery was various and multiple.

There was too—and crucially—an element of urgency in the company's limpings and hoppings, a strong signal of transience and wanting to be off. Of pursuit and even, did their obvious staunch and steadfast courage and reckless heroism not mitigate absolutely against it, something of their being in flight. Something horrible was out there, over the bluff behind them, beyond the village's limited purview and ken, and yet in full view, bleeding through the bandages that the villagers assembling dully in their doorways eyed fearfully as the men dragged their spent bodies forward. Villagers conferred amongst themselves in low whispers as the company came to a halt before the well. The Wars, which they had heard as titillating whispers and scraps of rumor, other people's horrors in the wilderness beyond the Alps, had come to Muud.

"Water!" cried Il Capo. "Water for my men! We cannot tarry. Will no one give us water?" There was silence for a moment, before a black-bearded villager nodded to one of the others, who trotted to the well and began drawing a

bucket. "God bless you," Il Capo thanked the man, who stepped forward hesitantly, glancing to left and right at the desperadoes, to the cage and the youth tied
up behind it.

"Water's free to him who asks," said the man.

"God preserve you," responded Il Capo, motioning for Groot and Bernardo
to set him down.

"What brings you to Muud?" asked the Beard.

"Ah, my friend," began Il Capo, "there's no need to mock us, even beaten as
we are. We must be off, and if you. . . . Well, we must be gone. We thank you for
the water. . . ."

"Mock you? I asked civilly enough," protested the man. "Tell me now, what
brings you here?"

"Can you truly not know?" A little knot of men and women was forming
about the man, watching anxiously as these words flew back and forth. "Can
Innsbruck blaze so fierce and its river run red and still you do not know?" One or
two of the villagers shook their heads. "It is the Wars that have brought us here!"

"There's no wars here," the Beard said stolidly, but his voice carried no
weight.

"And then at, at—" Il Capo gestured down the road as though the name
were too painful to utter.

"At Slime?"

"Slime!" It was a howl of anguish.

"Slime is but a day from here!"

"Slime *was* but a day from here, my friend. Today it is no more. They were
too many, and too well armed, and the acts committed . . . We are hardened soldiers, not good men like yourselves, we too have killed when necessary, but the
acts committed on the good people of Slime . . ." Other villagers had been lured
from their homes by the prospect of juicy tit-bits of gossip. They surrounded the
black-bearded man and swathed him in an appalled silence. Il Capo seemed to
gather himself within the horrors of Slime. "The main body will not find you; set
your mind at rest on that, my friend—"

"Main body? Main body of what?"

"—but the forage parties will be here tonight, perhaps tomorrow, or perhaps
they will miss you, too. We tried to beat them off, but . . . But . . ." It seemed that
Il Capo might almost be sobbing. "Yesterday I captained a hundred men. A full
hundred!" He choked back his tears, and suddenly his voice came like a clarion
out of grief and disorder and dark violence: "Pray with me!"

"What!" the man exclaimed, but behind him his own kinsmen and women,
children, friends, neighbors, enemies, were bending to kneel in the mud of
Muud, and in front of him the gallant wounded of the Christian Free Company
were groaning in pain as they did the same, and so he too knelt.

"God!" Il Capo's voice rang out over the impromptu congregation. "God!

Receive into your arms the souls of my brave hundred, good men who died in protecting the poor villagers of Slime.

"God!" Il Capo sounded a desolate tocsin of waste and horror. "God! Guard and watch over the poor villagers of Muud, gentle lambs to the lion's claws, for they are innocents and do not deserve their fate, it being so terrible.

"And God!" Now he was wrathful, a fire-hardened sword of vengeance hanging over bestial skulls. "God! Flay their flesh and grind their bones, let their souls be racked and tortured with hot irons, as they did to the poor villagers of Slime, without mercy and eternally, for they are abominations, *abominations!* Vile creatures, scum, filth, they are the . . . they are the . . ." Il Capo stuttered, spluttered, choked on the hateful syllable.

"What?" asked a villager.

"They are the, the . . . I cannot say it, I cannot. We must go. We have stopped too long."

"You cannot leave now!" a woman's voice cried.

"For the love of God, protect us!" came another, and soon the whole crowd began to clamor, many already weeping and begging for protection, in the midst of which Il Capo resumed his prayer.

"They are," he declaimed in a voice of dread, hauling himself forward out of his basket and upright, wobbling, turning to gesture at the only one not to have knelt, the prisoner in his cage, the Teeth, whose jaw muscles Salvestro saw from behind as they swelled into great muscled knots, whose bared rictus he saw reflected in the villagers' stupid, terrified faces, in their horror of what was to befall them, "the French!"

Pandemonium.

It usually went like that. After the hapless villagers had implored their reluctant saviors to stay, sentries would be posted and travelers on the routes leading to the village would be encouraged to take some other path by men supposedly shivering from a terrible plague raging unchecked farther up the road. They would stay a few days, a week at most, but it was that first moment, that crisis of terror in which the villagers' placid world seemed on the brink of shattering and crashing about their ears, that gave, as Il Capo termed it, the best yield. Rings would be slipped off fingers or from around necks. Little boxes would be unearthed from the packed dirt of hovel floors and their contents magically presented. There was sometimes a stone or two, fake often enough, but touching and accepted.

Thereafter, a slow decline. Feasted like kings to begin with, by the second or third day the company was usually supping on vegetable stews, and the beer or wine that had at first flowed so freely now suffered puzzling accidents, souring, spilling, simply disappearing. Then, when another day had gone by without the promised apocalypse, the villagers would begin to mutter amongst themselves, to avoid the men who camped idly about their miserable huts and barns, to wonder if they had perhaps panicked too soon. The women would skirt about them, the men eye them uneasily, and sometimes the sentries would pick up a boy slipping through the line with a basket of eggs and an implausible tale, and Salvestro, the "captive," with the Teeth the visible evidence of an invisible peril, would feel the aura of the villagers' fear peel off him and crumble like Powder Jack's facepaint. Il Capo was tuned to that. The villagers looked at Salvestro and the Teeth. Il Capo looked at the villagers. The company looked to their leader. He knew. When the moment came they melted away like darkness chased by light, and then always, one morning, they would be gone.

Salvestro gathered wood, built fires, watched their embers flare and pulse with the whims of the wind, ebbing to dull glows and sinking into the surrounding darkness. Sometimes around dusk the Chevalier would rise, seek out the Teeth, who sat alone and apart, and the two of them would stalk off together. He followed them one night and saw the Chevalier's blade flashing and mazing the thickening dark, the Teeth a little way off, and then the blade swung flat about, hissing at the other's head, which neither flinched nor jerked but made a tiny quick movement as a hand moving to crush a fly in midflight, and there was a dull, jarring sound. The Teeth had caught the blade in his mouth. He released it and both men nodded satisfaction before resuming their strange mock duel.

Sometimes Pandulfo read to him from his poem, bloody battles and strange, contextless heroisms: Il Gran Capitan smashing multitudes at Cerignola, Paulo Orsini drowning in his armor after Gaeta, the inexplicable calm of the Count of Pitigliano watching Trivulzio's men cross the Adda . . . Each episode ended with the beating of a desperate retreat covered by mysterious forces that, although Il Dottore did not say so, might well have been identified with themselves, the Christian Free Company. Either that, or the cutting out of the French from the body of Italy "like a wart," one of his favorite expressions. Bernardo would often listen, too, though he seemed more mesmerized by the sight of Pandulfo's eye and index finger moving over the black squiggles than by the story itself. Only during the harangues against the French, which were lengthy and numerous, did he pay any attention to the words, thumping the ground softly with his fist and saying, "That's right, that's right," until Salvestro would tell him to shut up.

Most of all, though, he would sit with Groot and Bernardo. In a previous incarnation, Groot had been, or had always wanted to be, a baker. "Up in the morning before everyone else, stoking those ovens, rest of the world asleep," he would ramble fondly. He knew a great deal about different flours and meals and would draw fine distinctions between them. His share of their loot would be spent on bricks and mortar, a little shop with high chimneys, earthenware mixing bowls too heavy to lift, long-handled spatulas . . . He described how one could tell if a loaf was baked through by tapping a knuckle on the bottom and listening for a sound like a drumstick striking stiff leather. So they passed their evenings gabbing, with Bernardo throwing in confused recollections of a woman, a stone hut on a hot rocky hillside, a man he had seen from the rail of a boat that took him away over the sea. But when it came to Salvestro's turn he found himself at a loss, unable to rake the coals from a fire dowsed in distant, placid waters and buried in a pathless forest, unwilling to offer the hard grit of memory or invent substitutes, and so, in place of his past, he spoke about Vineta.

From Muud to Krems, from Krems to Schlien, from Schlien to Wys, and on to Orbach, and Cruuen, and Grunewald, and on: clusters of hovels with their gaunt livestock, and conniving inhabitants, their woodpiles, mud, and treachery. Winters made the villagers meaner, less credulous, and the company overbold. Four times they had fled with torches fanning out over the fields behind them and the thud of hooves and shouting in their ears. Two of those times children had been found, a boy and a girl, their necks snapped and the bodies otherwise untouched, left carelessly, in full view. The villages were Proztorf and Marne: the Proztorf girl, the Marne boy. No one talked about them. There had been alarms and hasty retreats.

Salvestro had soon rebelled against his role in the pantomime. Being tied to the cage was dull and uncomfortable. He preferred to swagger about with the rest of the company, wearing a broad-brimmed hat with a feather in it and a large, blunt machete. Once he had a woman in a barn. It was late summer, a blazing heat, the air was choked with the smell of straw. She was older than him, with red hair and very ugly. She rolled him onto his back and galloped him until the sweat poured off them.

The Christian Free Company passed peddlers with their mules loaded high with boxes and bales, little bands of pilgrims, shepherds moving their flocks up and down the pastures. They took drovers' trails and forest paths, weaving east and west through the forested plains and lake-spattered aprons of rock and grass behind which the mountains lay like chipped, ice-scoured teeth, the bones of long-dead giants. One summer they crossed those mountains.

The foothills rose in successive ridges and peaks, their calm grassed slopes rising and breaking about outcrops of granite, growing harsher and more fissile with the altitude. Mountain pines with stunted branches forced their roots into the thin soils. Springs gouged deep channels and ravines, splashing the gray boulder waste with jet black. Salvestro thought he had never felt water so cold. They had spent the first winter this side of the mountains on the high slopes in the thin air, and it had killed Low Simon. The second had driven them south into the Duchy for the hardest months. They crept east and then south, left the road after Ferrara, and struck out across country for the Valle di Comacchio. They came to a tiny hamlet called Viemme.

"The village is called Viemme," Il Capo announced beforehand. It was wrong from the first. The villagers were sullen and too dull-witted. Il Capo had blustered, haranguing them for a full hour before the good people of Viemme had turned to each other in doubt and worry, another hour before the bargain had been struck, and thereafter they had been ignored as though this transaction were no different from buying a yearling or a hogshead of young wine. Viemme sat in swampy ground some hundreds of yards from the shore of a vast lake. The land about was as flat as the water, and they had posted no sentries. Salvestro overheard Sigismundo talking in a low voice with Il Capo, who said in reply, "Nor me. We leave tomorrow night."

They awoke surrounded by soldiers.

How much did this Prior desire to know? How much must he dredge up to satisfy him? The Thought was still present, but quiet now, attending him in this deliberation. He remembered the Spanish captain's words as Groot and Bernardo bent to pick up Il Capo: "Not him. Leave him." They had been marched in column with the crossbowmen to either side. He had looked back at the first cry. The villagers had wasted no time. Il Capo was on all fours, trying to crawl away. A few villagers, five or six, measured and deliberate in their motions, were taking turns kicking him. He heard high wails cut off abruptly by the softer reports of the kicks, a moment of silence, the noise start up again, stop, start up again, kicks and screams and kicks and screams. Eventually there was silence.

"And then?" (Merely helping him along by now; this mild interrogation will be delivered in the blandest of tones.)

And then the camp, which was the shouts of brutish men called Sergeants, idleness and disease. Horvart died there, and the Bandinelli twins simply disappeared, slipped miraculously past the sentries and vanished into thin air. After the camp, the battle, which was Ravenna, when they stood across the rough moorland from the French lines, too distant to be frightening, and 'Urst said, "I see nothing here to perturb me," seconds before the bombardment began and Salvestro saw him literally explode and disappear in a spray of blood and bone. There was smoke and noise and terror. Groot dragged him into a rillet with Bernardo. His sense of direction had disappeared; he had no idea whence the cannon were firing—he had not even seen cannon—nor whether the stumbling figures in the smoke were friend or foe. A covered cart rumbled out of nowhere and disappeared again with its team bridling and rearing, no sign of a driver. Toward the end there had been a thunderous flash and his face had prickled with heat. He had fouled himself but could not remember when. Bernardo and Groot wore black faces, powder-burned like his own. It was a glorious victory.

They had spent that night stumbling about the battleground, making for a little line of fires that might have been twenty miles away for all they knew, coughing gunsmoke out of their lungs and avoiding the gangs that roamed the field looting the dead and dying. They came upon a man-at-arms, helmetless, kneeling as though about to pray. He breathed and regained his balance when Groot nudged him slightly, but that was all. A crossbow bolt fired from below and behind had found the soft channel where the skull meets the back of the neck and driven itself up into the brainpan. The knight's head had ballooned to near twice its natural size. He wore a cloth cross, but they could not make out its color. Groot was for taking his sword, but Bernardo and he were already walking away. He could taste the smoke, his head full of it and pounding, his snot bright yellow. The din of the bombardment still echoed in his skull, along with occasional sharp cries as icy hands went about their work under cover of the darkness. Dawn revealed a fluttering clump of colors, with men stumbling toward it from all directions, a few marquees. No one seemed to be in charge.

They were marched to Bologna. He thought that he spied the Chevalier and the Teeth as they entered the town, amongst a group of Spaniards lounging near the statue in the Piazza del Nettuno, but he never saw them again. The rest of the Christian Free Company seemed to have vanished from the face of the earth. He, Bernardo, and Groot listened to a fine speech by the Viceroy of Naples and joined a company of pikemen composed mostly of Sicilians who spent their days insensible from drink and, when they woke, loved nothing more than to stab each other. The company articles were read to them, an oath administered, and fifty soldi completed the process. Later they were issued with pikes, and three days a week they marched out of the town to practice on the fields of the *campagna*. By late summer, with the muster still growing, the swelling soldiery lodged in Bologna were ejected and took up residency in those fields. Bales of canvas were unrolled and slung over timber frames to form tents, a gibbet erected, hay stacked, fires lit, water fetched. Strings of horses were led about and heavy carts drawn up in endless rows. The camp-wives followed, contemptuous, furious women who swatted at each other and screamed at their men, seeming to fear nothing. One who rode about on a horse was dubbed by the Spaniards Nostra Senora d'Espuela for the spurs on her boots, by the Sicilians as La Cavallerizza Sanguinosa for the uses to which those spurs were rumored to be put, or perhaps the red of her hair, which was bright copper. Salvestro eyed her from a distance but had no money for women and was cowed by her in any case. Dismounted, she swaggered about like a man, would disappear for a few days, then return to shout insults at her lovers around the camp, who were numerous and tight-lipped on the subject of her charms. One of the Sicilians told Salvestro that she carried no weapon but a small hook-knife that was used for only one purpose. He dreamed about her hair dragging across his face and blood welling up where their crotches were joined, her amazement.

By the end of summer, gun carriages were arriving, and their arrogant bombardiers, and the camp had spread until it took an hour to walk from one end to the other. Tongues wagged of a return to Ravenna, of digging in at Bologna, or sacking Florence, *La Crasa Puta,* as the Spaniards dubbed her. The rumor-mill ground idleness and boredom into a cloud of whens and wheres: tomorrow, or a week hence, the feasts of Apollinaris, or Domenico, or Cosmas and Damian. There was wild talk of Paris by Martinmas, or ringing in the New Year in Jerusalem, but when they were finally formed up in lines and saw the Viceroy Cardona and Cardinal Medici canter past holding cross and sword, when those lines began to inch forward and Salvestro marching near the back of the long column could see its distant head only as ants through a thin haze of dust, when the baggage train rumbled out and the field was bare of everything save the black scars of the campfires, rumor had yet to be replaced by fact, and Salvestro had the sensation that he had enlisted in a grim, unstoppable pilgrimage to a shrine that could never be reached. And when, eight days into the march, outside a town called Barberino, their destination was cried through the camp, the fact itself proved slippery, escaped them, leaped ahead, and lost them, for it would turn out that they were marching on not Florence—as they were told—but Prato.

Enough.

Bernardo would return soon, for the familiar cooking smells were creeping once again through the wall. The light would fail soon, too. Sometimes the winter sunset would catch the surface of the sea and swoop up in a great wash to flood the eastern sky in reseda and pale turquoise. Garish pinks and reds would play out a gaudy pantomime on the western horizon, but the greater dome of the sky would be imperturbable and luminous, undisturbed by stars in these brief minutes. Then the perfectly even light would fail, or the teetering ember of the sun would drop, or the sea suck the sky's rival ocean dry to its bed, or darkness would fall and this twilight end, and so it was that night.

There he was, having reemerged from the left side of the copse (a distance of eighty-two yards), hugging the straggling line of the fence, walking back in hang-dog fashion, fit of temper forgotten or fading into forgotten. . . . Salvestro felt the Thought swell tightly in his skin, congruent now. He thought about the two islands that were called Usedom and the years that held them irreparably apart. He thought that soon the three young monks would come with their supper and that after them the monk called HansJürgen. He thought he would sit in front of the Prior once again—tonight, perhaps—and perhaps many times after that in this strange ruin of a monastery, answer the questions put to him simply and directly.

"Pretty thick back there." Bernardo tramped past Salvestro, reentered their makeshift quarters, and sat down. "Trees and whatnot," he added as though the other had sent him to reconnoiter.

Salvestro nodded. He thought too that, branded twice as a liar, the Prior would listen to those answers and either explode with indignation or not believe a word. But the Prior's reaction, when it came that night, or the next, or in any one of the subsequent interrogations that stretched ahead of him, draining and inevitable as the winter whose nights they would fill, proved quite other, for far from throwing up his hands in horror at the rapacious beast squatting in his cell or recoiling in disgust at a tale whose incidents were chiefly of murder, theft, and rape, the monk would fix him with long unblinking stares punctuated with near imperceptible nods and occasional unsurprised *hmms* that suggested, if not acceptance, then a bland indifference, and if not indifference, disinterest, and if not that . . . As the winter wore on, Salvestro would realize with a mounting sense of resentment that not only were many of the elements of his life already known to this Prior, but most of the remainder elicited only nose-scratching, inspection of

fingernails, the picking of imaginary specks of nothing in particular from the surface of the paper-strewn table over which his words seemed to lose their impetus
and fall lifelessly into his interrogator's all-accepting boredom.

He would leave puzzled and troubled by the pointlessness of it all, picking
over the midden he had happened to pile up that night, scratching up the occasional prize: Jörg's leaning forward in his chair as he related the Christian Free
Company's passage over the Alps; his impatient, "Go on," as he detailed the correct method of traversing a bog; the sharper nods that prodded him through the
navigational problems encountered in rafting down the Oder, and then, again,
boredom, as he described its course northward until it debouched into the very
sea whose soft suckings and slaps, audible outside, hushed him eventually and on
each of these occasions to silence. Tedium again, and bafflement: unintended the
one, the other unwanted, both of them his own.

Jörg read:
*On Saint Leonard's Day, or the day after that, the monks of Usedom espied from their
house a strange craft at work in the sea before them. Two adventurers were rescued from their
folly, which was to disturb and loot a city sunk here many years before, by name Vineta, and
brought ashore to rest here through the winter for the sake of charity. . . .*
That last was not quite true, Jörg thought to himself as he read over the man-
uscripts of his *Historia*. He had taken up his account again a week or more after
fishing this catch from the sea. That evening, the one called Salvestro had grown
frank, even effusive, and had been ushered out, not expelled as twice before. He
had cut a quill and scratched the lines before him now in a strange excitement
whose origin he could not then fathom. Leonard watched over captives of war
according to a passage copied from the *Vita* and bound into one of the battered
volumes locked in the case behind him.

*They go by the names Salvestro, which I know to be a lie, and Bernardo. This "Sal-
vestro" is of middling height, his features flattish but not unpleasing, white in color but with
black hair. I believe him sly and full of deceits, though they are small for the most part. His
companion is swarthy and broad in the chest and legs, stands two full heads taller than any
of my brothers, Volker and Henning excepted, and is weak in his wits, like a child.*
My brothers. That may have been true then. How true was it now? Gerhardt's face swept past his mind's eye attended by viperous acolytes. He himself
moved less freely about the monastery's precincts than before. Conversations
buzzed and stuttered to a halt at his approach, started up again behind him. Backs
were turned on him. Hands turned against him? He had long given up his lessons
in the chapter-house. Athos-shadowed Lemnos, vineless Carmania with its fish-
skinned natives, Ægypt, where the year was calculated by, what was it, the passage
had moved him, by "driving beasts into a holy grove where, when the motion of

heaven is come to its determinate point, they express their understandings by such signs and talents as they are able. Some howl, some low, some roar, some bray, diverse run together into the mire and wallow. . . ."

He wrote:

Today is the first day of February fifteen hundred and fourteen years after the death of Our Lord. Tomorrow will be Candlemas, but no Candlemas will be sung on Usedom. The monks of Usedom have grown neglectful of their offices. Few enough heed their Prior, and their Abbot has lain sick all this past winter.

He had thought the winter would be harder, and he had thought that the Abbot would die. HansJürgen had taken his silence for indifference, he thought, but the few times he had ventured into the cell at the end of the corridor and looked at the creature that huddled on the bed, heard the resentful rasp of its breath, he had wondered how something so nearly dead might yet live. He could not, or would not, stand, or speak, or even chew. But he continued—a bundle of sticks wrapped in papery, liver-spotted skin—and while he did, Jörg might rest secure, for even Gerhardt would not dare to contend the abbacy with its incumbent still alive. After that, he did not know, and did not care to know. After that, he thought, it would not matter. If he was ready, that was, or if the brothers were ready. He thought again of Saint Leonard and of the swordless war whose captive he was—they all were, even Gerhardt—of Paul amongst the Corinthians, worrying "lest there be debates, envyings, wraths, strifes, backbitings, whisperings, swellings, tumults. . . ." There had been all but the last of these things, and were swellings now. HansJürgen advised him of them daily. Only the tumults remained.

He wrote:

Yet the monks are not blameworthy. They have been unanchored as a ship might be in a storm and misled by false lights, having no others in the darkness of their unknowing. They await a pilot before they might leave their useless tossings and find their bearing.

And their pilot awaits a chart, he thought, blotting the page before him with the sleeve of his habit, turning to the case at his back and reaching behind it, using his forearms to spread apart the rolls of a parchment and reveal upon it the labor of the long candlelit hours that would have followed Compline if Compline had still been sung, but now followed only the departing back of his unwitting informant, Salvestro. At the top, farthest from him, was a wavering outline above which he had laboriously rendered an approximation of waves. In those waves, set side by side like a pair of claws reaching out of the sea for the coastline, were two islands, one of which was Usedom. Lower down there were forests marked upon it—better drawn, these—and cathedrals with little pointy steeples, and mountains, and rivers, and towns. His draftsmanship had improved through the winter. A thick irregular line ran from top to bottom, skirting the forests, swerving east jaggedly through the great range of mountains, blotted black with intention as his pen had paused at the confluence of rivers and the parchment leached ink—this way? that way?—razor thin where the choice was clear, continuing on, south, marking a road.

The weeks now are inclement and interim. Winter strips its sopping tarpaulins off the frost-bruised sods and tender soils, scrapes gray muck out of the sky in the form of rain. Brief warmths blow in off the mainland, lose much of their heat in the waters of the Achter-Wasser, reaching Usedom as tokens of an advancing, still distant spring. The sky is undecided on its blueness, retracting it with bewildering haste to be replaced with rain and unhappy birds: chaffinches, robins, swifts, noisy crows, which scatter up and drop to find shelter amongst the bare branches and battered-looking evergreens. The raindrops make a noise like *Sploo-ot,* perhaps a little softer. Afterward there is fitful sunshine, dazzling and worrisome.

"Why do you take his part in this business? His mind has failed, which you know better than any of us, Brother." Gerhardt spoke mildly but bluntly.

"His soul is battered from without, taking the brunt for all of us. . . ." Hanno indicated vaguely toward the far end of the chapter-house, to the church, which had begun once again to drop fragments of its substance into the sea now that the preservative winter freeze had ceded to a destructive thaw, ice-riddled cements cracking and plunging downward, meltwaters sheaved among the blocks pushing lines out of true. Cherubic effigies break ranks, peer out over parapets, pry themselves loose, fall . . . The weather is always relevant.

"Saint Christopher himself would have buckled, taking on such a burden," added Georg.

Their faces were close to his, stubbly like roughly cut corn, red with cold. They had cornered him here in the chapter-house, where he had come to gather his thoughts alone and to pray, perhaps.

"He is unsound, our Prior," said Gerhardt. "There it is, HansJürgen."

They had sought him out, as he had known they would. Catching sight of them across the cloister, advancing out of the dorter, rounding unexpected corners, this or that face—the number of Gerhardt's supporters who might be termed close had grown through the winter's whispers and huddles—had sent him on suddenly remembered urgent business in the opposite direction. He did not want this.

"No," he said.

"The brigands, though," Gerhardt murmurs, shaking his head. "Here in our midst, served by novices. . . ."

"We love you for your loyalty, HansJürgen," said Georg. "You have no enemies here."

"Our Prior has not been honest with you about them," Gerhardt went on.

"The islanders know more than they would readily tell, about the smaller one. . . ."

"Salvestro," said HansJürgen. "He is contrite."

"I have spoken with the islanders, as I say. It is not a pretty tale, though the victim lives. They know what must be done even if we ourselves cannot. When our Prior falls beneath the heathen's spell and our Abbot sickens at his presence . . ." His voice wandered into some region of sadness, already mourning, inaudible. "None here are innocent," he murmured.

"Will you stand with us, Brother?" asked Hanno.

Or against us?

"If there were some design in his plotting, if there were a purpose discoverable in his giving sanctuary to these outsiders . . ."

If? It seemed to HansJürgen that the winter had driven his Prior deep within some cave of private purpose, that every time he escorted Salvestro from the beet loft to the cell at the far end of the passageway, its denizen would look up in blank abstraction, an engineer at work on some fabulous contraption whose arm reaches blindly for the one tool needed and has eyes for nothing but the monster that consumes him. To HansJürgen's suggestions that he take up services once more in the chapter-house, or that he speak with his restive monks, he returned bland, acquiescing nods and did nothing. To his reports of his fellows' various derelictions and slacknesses, he offered sad shakes of the head. The Abbot interested him more, if only because his death would raise the question of who was to assume the mantle and, HansJürgen suspected, were that question to be asked, its answer would not favor Father Jörg. On several nights HansJürgen had come upon him squatting on his haunches by the invalid's bed, gazing impassively into the imbecilic face that seemed not to register his presence—or anyone's—the two of them awaiting some sign or event. Jörg scribbled on a kind of chart, which he would snatch up quickly if HansJürgen approached, shamefaced at its contents or their implication, or the impression of secrecy itself. He kept it hidden behind his bookcase. HansJürgen had seen it. A map. It told him nothing.

Not "if," then, but "what." For Gerhardt had been right to aim his sharp face at the vagabonds lodged at the Prior's behest (and no one else's). There was little else to do in winter but become accustomed to unpleasant realities, yet they unsettled the younger ones and aroused deep suspicions and resentments in the rest even now. Gerhardt's hand had rested on his arm as he rose to leave, their cajoling turning to thinly veiled threats. He looked down at the tracery of little scars on his fingers as the monk asked him finally, wonderingly, whether he was truly with *them,* "them" being the beet loft's creatures and their Prior, too. He wanted to shout that no, no, he was not. Never had been. It was too late somehow, striding out like a mad old saint into a pointless martyrdom to be alone with God. Was Gerhardt right? Jörg? *Do not presume. . . . Do not despair. . . .* A thief would steal him, bind him, and carry him off. But which thief?

And when? There would be no angels or trumpets. *And the sea will give up its dead. . . .* Not that, either. There was the soft tocsin of the church's crumbling, the gravelly breaths of its Abbot, the noiseless sundering of the monks, like two islands whose coasts had fitted, bluff socketed to inlet, headland to bay, now floating apart to create a marvelous channel, a gulf, an expanse of new sea that widened until only the eye of God might compass them both.

As the quick rainshowers of Usedom's spring ceded to the more familiar drizzles and fogs, HansJürgen found himself seized by an obscure wanderlust. The winter caged him. Vegetable plots and fruit cages should be turned over and repaired, the roof of the dorter needed patching, too, but . . . But he too was seized with the sloth, the sense of indirection, that had come over all his brothers and found himself unable to muster the vigor to galvanize and organize a work-party. And even if he did, who would join it? In the cloister, Henning and Volker would still seek him out and greet him; Florian, too, and Joachim-Heinz. Heinz-Joachim? Perhaps. But who after these? Only novices.

So he walked the island alone, striking out toward the north and west, following the shore for a mile or two before turning inland, through beechwoods that brought him to the near shore of the Achter-Wasser—a little above Ploetz's hovel—where his pace slowed and he skirted the island's margin at a dawdle, looking over at the mainland's wooded foreshore and seeing the smoke plumes of unseen fires rise into the sky. Then he turned once more into the woods. The path here served as a watercourse after heavy rains, rising gently with the land, then curving east about the slope's contour. When the woods gave out he found himself traversing little plots and fields worked by the islanders—the path threaded a diplomatic passage between them—then the huts and outbuildings of the workers themselves: Ott's, one of the Wittmanns', others belonging to he knew not whom. The route grew familiar as the weeks went by, seeming to welcome him with little bouquets of early snowdrops, then bluebells, the frost-hollows slowly giving up their morning dusting of powdery ice. Splashes of shocking green spread among the trees' black branches. After the winter confinement, his solitude was strange, strangely calming and then strangely broken.

It happened three times. First with Ott, then with two others whom he did not recognize. He would be taking the path through the fields when a distant figure would disentangle himself from some task—fence-repairs, brush-clearing—rise and walk briskly toward him, taking the long arching strides that the sticky mud demanded, an arm raised in greeting until not only the figure but the face too came in clear view. And at that point the figure would come to a halt. He thought each time he could see puzzlement on the thick features or vague alarm, confusion. Something, but whatever it was, the man would then turn and walk back to his task without looking back, and he, HansJürgen, was left with a sense of incompletion, a strange unease, as though his would-be accoster had told him something in a language he could not understand. Something vital that he had missed.

He would stand there for a minute or two, then continue, tramping the last two miles to the seashore and follow it back up the coast to the monastery. Odd stunted trees were dotted along the shore here. A carpet of neatly cropped grass draped the low humps and gentle troughs up and down which he paced, the smooth green surface forming a raised strand. The resentful sea foamed weakly below and out of sight. He kept clear of the edge.

It was on this final stretch of his circuit, a cold early March day, that he saw himself, or so he thought for a split second—the light gray habit, the man's build similar to his own. He was ahead, quite tiny in the distance, at the margin of the island's grassy apron, about to make the last short climb up the point and disappear within the muddle of buildings that was the monastery. But, as he watched, the figure turned to the right and finally vanished not into the monastery, but behind the point. HansJürgen gained the same place a few breathless minutes later, already certain that this was the man the islanders had expected and thought themselves greeting before his own features told them of their error.

A cluster of outbuildings—most now abandoned—were set back a few yards from the edge. One could continue between them and the edge to the transept whose cracked wall blocked the path finally. HansJürgen rounded the corner of what had once been a wood store. The wood itself had long been sunk in efforts to buttress the church. Stringy grass, patches of mud, blocks and fragments of stone, and the vagabonds' boat. It had lain here through the winter. Someone was hunched over it, scooping at the standing water inside. He moved nearer, puzzled, the clothes wrong, something wrong. The man heard him and turned. It was Salvestro.

One night he heard airy voices singing, and their sound was like golden threads, coppery red in the dark of the beet loft.

"Christ is born," Bernardo muttered grumpily. He had been sleeping.

"What?"

"Christ," his companion repeated, then added, "You heathen."

He looked up in surprise, though the loft was dark. Heathen—that was the epithet bestowed on him by Gerhardt's men, the little conclave he gathered about him each morning in the cloister. HansJürgen too was a kind of focus in the muted resentments of the monks. Gerhardt stared at him glassily while his lieutenants scowled and brushed past him in heavy silence, but the current of these hatreds ran over him to other destinations. Heathen. That particular fragment of alluvial grit had formed its pearl in Bernardo, who cherished it, while the stream itself ran on, bitter, its surface dark and glossy, debouching over the Prior, who was hardly seen in daylight, over the church, or its disrepair. Or the place itself, the whole island? It was undivinable. He thought to ask the Prior. Their meetings had grown almost fraternal—he would sit without being bidden and sometimes bring the evening to a close by yawning and, asked if it was not perhaps time to sleep, would nod, rise, and make his way back to the beet loft unescorted. He thought to ask but somehow never framed the question. *Tell me, Father, why is it that your monks hate you? . . .* No. Impossible. The Prior was a low humped boulder, half-concealed and worn smooth by the turbid waters about him, well bedded in and offering no purchase to their lather. *Because, my son, I took in two murderers. . . .*

The place, then. The place itself. Nothing worth stealing in it, nothing not nailed down, anyway. Crumbling, a lot of it. They all hated it, though in different ways, and their feuding was a muffled business, all straw padding and blunted swords. He didn't understand it and awaited the coming spring, thinking vaguely that east might be a good direction, thinking too of the barrel, which rested in an outhouse with the rope, of Ewald's boat, leaned carelessly against the outer wall of the church and still icebound (albeit from within), of Ewald himself.

The singing ended.

Winter loosed its grip slowly that year. He remembered these days—his mother had called them something. Tricky gods used them to lure out the dull-witted to inspect their winter wheat or even turn a little topsoil. Get them out there in the open, get them grinning up at the blue of the sky, mopping at a dribble of sweat somewhere out in the fields, the dark red earth turning pink as it dried. . . . Then a deluge falls out of the sky. Ha, ha. Rainwater spattered in the mud outside the door. They would leave soon, one way or another. They might have left already, Bernardo's sharp appetite for inaction notwithstanding. His friend had spent the cold months sitting on his arse, eating, and complaining of what he ate. He had moved a large pile of stones from the north side of the monastery to the south at Brother HansJürgen's curt request. That was it. In fact, their continued residency puzzled Salvestro, his own acquiescence in it. These thoughts were like planks and beams sent up from a stricken ship, knocking dully together in the water just below the surface. Unfinished business. Like Ewald, and Ewald's bloody boat.

"She tends to loll," Ewald had warned him the week before his ill-fated plunge in the barrel. "Keep the weight amidships." He had been nervous, fingers drumming on the wood of the stern, though whether this was at his own presence or for the safety of the vessel, Salvestro could not tell. "She is old, but she is sturdy," he had said. "My grandfather built her when our fields were poisoned with salt." Salvestro had waited to hear the remainder, but Ewald had been quiet for a minute or more, only tapping his fingers against the strakes, gingerly, as though frightened of awakening a large, irascible animal. "This boat was his revenge on the sea," he had said at length, and then he had begun to ramble, as though once his mouth was open every memory he held of the vessel before them had chosen this moment to make its escape in a great scramble of complaints and long-nurtured resentments.

His grandfather had built a boat. Alder was light and pliable, easy to work, and plentiful on the mainland. Skiff-steering, punt-poling inland watermen threading their craft through the bodden and stagnant marshes about Stettin and Wollin, skimming over the swampy shallows of Greifswald, humping their lightly timbered scows over the Frisians' dikes and dams, all swore by alder. But, from the rainswept safety of his cabbage field, Anselm had seen black-hearted squalls blow up out of nowhere, whip a five-foot swell from the usually placid water, and thrash the cogs west across a heaving sea. The smaller boats always seemed to have disappeared some little time before, but Ewald's grandfather's landlocked soul had quailed. He needed adamantine walls to save him from the hurling waves, a bulwark made of mountains to brook the sea's capricious fury, a palisade to cower behind while the water did its worst. He made his boat from oak.

Clinker-built and stoutly braced, with a sail to run before the wind and oars to row back in, Anselm captained the sturdiest smack on the water. It would take a whirlpool to spin it, a broadside of cannon to break it. It would take two men straining their shoulders from the socket to shift it an inch. Oak, he discovered, was heavy. Ewald, when he eventually inherited the vessel, discovered this, too. Hence his employment of a good-for-nothing ne'er-do-well who would tramp the width of the island each morning to help him launch and handle his seaborne pride and joy, his helpmate and general scapegoat: Ploetz.

With Ploetz aboard, Ewald ventured out for his first season afloat, hallooing and waving to join the fleet and exact his due from the brine. Fishing would be his sweet revenge on these sour waters, this soil-poisoning sea. But, breasting the swell, casting his net, steering his vessel in pursuit of the herring, Ewald soon noted that his boat was bigger than the others, rode lower in the water, rolled more, and despite a sail twice as wide as a man, seemed to have trouble keeping up. When the shoal moved farther out from the shelf, or darted along the coast, the Rügen boats would quickly spin about and scuttle after. If a gale got up, they merely scudded in to a sheltering lee, darting out once more when the wind died down. Ewald's boat lumbered. It wallowed, and Ewald cursed Ploetz for his scrawny arms and lack of speed. And when a squall did blow up—half dreaded, half hoped for in Brüggeman's violent secret dreams, a chance at last to pit his vessel against the damnableness of the sea—the Rügen boats simply ran before the wind and were gone, while his own more bravely built craft lurched about in a sea of glue, invariably catching the worst of the rain as they slogged the final league home. They would reach shore drained of strength and up to their knees in water, often too tired to drag their vessel beyond the negligible reach of the tide, which pulled at it, and tugged at it, and sometimes dragged it out to sea. It never seemed to drift far. He named his boat the *Stormhammer.* The Rügen men dubbed it the *Anvil,* but after the first season they did not see it often. Ewald and Ploetz fished alone.

Some ugly aura hovered about the the *Anvil's* wales, something eerie about this particular death-tub. Oak is too heavy a wood for these fluxey waters, too obdurate for a sea mindful of its icy history. Pitting the strength of its grain against the rare flexings of these waters' muscle, it is a craft more suited to shore than sea, a bearer of landlocked dreams. Afloat, and despite Ewald's tinkerings with ballast and the height of the mast, it wallowed and lurched, getting itself into all kinds of watery trouble.

Contemplating it now, Salvestro reflected that it might be just as troublesome ashore: over the course of the winter the overgenerous heavens had spilled a small and somewhat mad sea into the uncovered vessel, its stillnesses and agitations, freezings, meltings, and refreezings telescoped into a single season. He looked down gloomily at a brimful boatful of rain.

The Boat Sea was muddy brown, with bits of straw floating on its surface. The bowl he had reserved for bailing it out was put to work, and soon the ground about him was swampy with water. He had worked close to an hour, and the Boat Sea's level had fallen no more than three inches. Several times already he had tried to tip the boat onto its side. He tried again now. No luck. The vessel seemed to be made of lead. His bowl was small and awkward to hold. It was an unhappy afternoon. At least it was not raining.

"Good day, Salvestro." The voice startled him. He had heard no approach. Standing by the edge where the ground gave out was Brother Gerhardt.

"Brüggeman's boat," the monk continued when Salvestro said nothing. He caught sight of the bowl. "You would be better served by a siphon."

Salvestro nodded, not knowing what a siphon was, shifting uneasily in the mud as Gerhardt moved nearer.

"You are to return it?"

He nodded again, and the monk turned to look out over the sea, which swirled about and slapped at the red earth twenty feet below. He turned back.

"How?"

Over the past few evenings this question had been meditated in the dark of the beet loft: a rope would be needed, a winch mechanism of some sort or a brake, perhaps as simple as a stoutly anchored post with a couple of turns of the rope around it, Bernardo on one end, himself on the other armed with a pole to push himself clear of the drop, for the boat would swing and spin if dangled over the edge like that, would collide with the face, possibly. He thought of himself clinging within, Bernardo letting down slack artfully so that the prow would rear up at the moment of hitting the water. There was the mast to consider, too. It would get in the way. Masts did. And Bernardo would have to be instructed, drilled. . . . He thought of the launch of the barrel all those months ago.

"I don't know," he managed at last, still somewhat tongue-tied at being addressed by this person, the very person about whom his vaguest and most pervasive fears and misgivings had coalesced in the previous months.

They contemplated the boat, then the Boat Sea slopping in its hull, united for a moment in the conundrum.

"Bail her dry. I will have Hanno, Georg, and some others carry her down to the water tomorrow after Nones. Do you know when that is?"

"After midday," Salvestro hazarded. The monk nodded, then abruptly continued past Salvestro, past the side of the church, disappearing from view around the corner as Salvestro thought to shout, "Thank you," which was ignored. He had expected to be accused of something. Perhaps Brother Gerhardt was not so bad after all. Bail her dry. Right. He set to work.

Scoop, *splosh*, scoop, *splosh*, scoop, *splosh*, scoop, *splosh* . . .

Hanno and Georg. That was good. Gerhardt's offer meant Bernardo's services were no longer needed. That was good, too. He would want to come. He would have to be put off. Ewald would not want a great lump like Bernardo splintering his chairs and frightening his children. There had been children, hadn't there? Now that was a strange thought. Ewald, and Ewald's children.

Scoop, *splosh*, scoop, *splosh*, scoop, *splosh*, scoop, *splosh* . . .

For he wanted to see Ewald alone. Why? (Scoop.) Had wanted to since first planting his foot on the island, in fact; just the two of them *(splosh)* like old times, just as he had imagined. Then, the door opening, himself standing there, Ewald clapping him on the back (scoop), come in, come in. . . . But, as it had actually turned out that first day of his return, it was not Ewald at all but Mathilde who had looked the two of them over—with something like horror. *(Splosh.)* And Ewald, too, come to think of it, appearing in the doorway behind his wife. Horror. And no wonder! No wonder at all, considering the appearance of Bernardo. And so far as Ewald knew, he himself had been dead, drowned years ago. Obviously Ewald would be shocked. Yes, not horror, but surprise. And if he had been a little tight-lipped after that *(scoo*—a fumble, recovered—*ooop)* and puzzlingly absent sometimes, then that was undoubtedly for some similar reason. Shock, yes. He should have thought of that before. That was it. That was it for sure. He did not blame Ewald. He did not blame Ewald for any of it.

"You!" *(Splosh.)* The forgotten bowlful spilled down his front as he was jerked from this reverie, and for a moment it was as if time had twitched and fallen in overlapping folds, for there was the same gray-habited figure, standing in the same spot, shouting at him, "What are you doing here?" But it was not Gerhardt.

"Well?" HansJürgen insisted.

"Emptying the . . . Tomorrow I am to return Brüggeman's boat. Brother Gerhardt will help me get her down to the water. . . ."

"Gerhardt? It was Gerhardt here?"

Salvestro nodded, which seemed to throw HansJürgen into a sudden ill humor, and waving Salvestro aside, he stamped off in the same direction as his enemy.

Scoop, *splosh*, scoop, *splosh*, scoop, *splosh*, scoop, *splosh* . . .

When there was no more than three thumbs of evil-smelling water standing in the bottom of the hull, Salvestro was able to tip the boat. He watched the last of the Boat Sea dribble out and add its moisture to the quagmire about him. It was almost dark. Later, it began to rain.

There was a commotion that night, a few shouts being enough in the hush of the monastery to wake the two of them. Then calmer voices muttering together, two or three of them somewhere outside the beet loft. Salvestro thought he caught the question "How long?" and its answer "Not long. Tomorrow." A sudden silence followed, as though their own invisible presence had been wordlessly indicated. Footsteps moved away. One of the voices had been Gerhardt's.

Tomorrow came. Monks were huddled together in little groups in the cloister, darting glances at one another, one occasionally marching to a neighboring group. A few looked up as he stood there, but he was paid no more attention than that. Some of the monks were talking in intent whispers, hands being placed briefly on shoulders. An unfamiliar urgency was in the air. One of the youngsters, Wulf, brushed past him, followed by Wolf, whose sleeve he caught hold of.

"What is happening?" he quizzed the novice.

"The Abbot," replied Wolf, white-faced.

"He is dying," added Wilf, red-eyed, bringing up the rear.

The trio hurried off again. At that moment shouts were heard, heads turned upward, and Gerhardt hurried in from the other side of the cloister, accompanied by Hanno, whose face was dark red with rage. In an instant they were engulfed, but no, no, no, the moment was not come, he was waving them off, making little placatory gestures with his hands. Salvestro turned away and walked back to the beet loft.

Midday came and went. Wanting to know what was so obviously in the air, Bernardo had hauled himself upright and gone to find out. "How would they know?" had been his question when Salvestro had told him that the Abbot was about to die, and his companion had struggled to answer. Pulling the dimwit out of Prato, he had offered the wisdom that he would rather die on the island where he was born than at a wool market turned slaughterhouse. Then Bernardo had asked what difference *did* it make? He had a genius for such questions. What difference did it make? Dead was dead was dead. An hour passed, and he had given up the notion that today the boat would be returned, when one of the younger monks whose name he did not know poked his head in the door and told him that Brothers Gerhardt, Hanno, and Georg were all waiting for him and he had better hurry himself up.

"Ready?"
"No."
"Wait . . ."
"One, two . . ."
"Ngggh . . . No."
"Right?"
"Down."
"Uhhh."
"Oooof."
"Three!"

From the boat, Salvestro watched the three monks' retreating backs. He watched the mast wave about above him as the boat slowly settled, then reached for the oars and began to pull into open water. Soon he was fifty yards out, the boat more lumpish even than he remembered. The monastery was a scrape of gray cement and stones, the church a black wound in its center. He turned northwest, dabbing ineffectually with a single oar, the prow obstinate in its inertia.

A thin cry reached him across the water. "Where are you *going?*" It came again, the same shout of distress. Bernardo's voice. He pulled hard on the oars, one, two, one, two . . . Gerhardt had clapped him on the back when the four of them had made it down the slope. Hanno and Georg had not looked at him; had avoided his gaze, in fact.

Where! One, two, one, two . . .

Steadily, gradually, the shouts, the land, both fell away until he was alone in the boat in the sea and, beyond the plash of brine, the dull knocks of the oars in the row-locks, the suck and gasp of his breath, there was silence. The sky was birdless and the air hung in cold columns that parted before him. The smudged coast inched past to his left. Above, a great flat plate of cloud extended almost to the horizon, where a knife edge of light reddened, and pinkened, and then the sun fell through, a deep orange, and the clouds darkened to heavy blues. Soon it would be night. He pulled harder.

Pewter and bread. Excrement pooling in his bed. This is how we die, thought HansJürgen.

Two times Florian had taken the sacrament from the pyx. Twice he had coaxed it down the Abbot's throat, and twice the Abbot had vomited it out. Two times Florian had eaten the vomited sacrament.

Before dawn, Gerhardt and his men had hammered on the door. They had repelled them by shouting dire warnings and by prayer. Hanno had shouted that they would be back.

Hours later, when the sun rose finally and threw a short-lived ray of light into the cell, the Abbot writhed like a blindworm uncovered in the damp earth beneath its stone. The light seemed to stir the dead air about them. Florian had been in prayer. He himself had been waiting, perhaps for the old man to die, perhaps for this very eruption. Jörg had said nothing for hours when Gerhardt's men returned.

"State your business here, Brother," Jörg said mildly, his body blocking the doorway from Gerhardt's men, Georg, Hanno, others filling the passage outside. For a moment HansJürgen thought they would barge past their Prior, simply knock him aside, and he saw Jörg's body stiffen as though he had read this thought in Gerhardt's face. That point was not far away now. Again, it was Hanno who shouted, furiously, madly, barking that they were killing their Abbot before

Gerhardt turned on his heel and strode off. The noise and the brothers' animosity, naked now, sapped him of something. His head fell into his hands. When had he last slept?

The Abbot grew more peaceful with the hours, seeming to sleep for a few minutes at a time, then retching and coming awake, falling back exhausted. Florian tried again to administer the host by crumbling it into the chalice of wine. The Abbot would not take it.

"It is correct enough that he should look upon the sacrament if he cannot swallow," said Jörg. He seemed unperturbed by Gerhardt's intrusion. "Count Albert received it through a wound in his side which healed before he died. I read of it once."

Florian nodded.

"The host is the most precious of our miracles," Father Jörg continued. "The company of angels, immunity from death. . . . I believe in these, though the process is more complex."

HansJürgen looked up wearily, feeling his patience stretch and at last snap. "You must face them," he said. "You must show yourself, at least. Next time, they will break in. . . ."

"Saint Giles did not absolve Charlemagne of his incest, it was the host. The host did that. When I was a novice, I believed I saw the infant once. He was new-born and crying, though I could not hear him. He was in the wafer, just before it was broken. Then he disappeared."

"Do you even hear me, Father? There is no more *time.*" HansJürgen took Jörg by the shoulder. "You must act now."

"Where are our guests?" asked Jörg, looking at him as if the thought had just struck him. The question took him by surprise, Florian, too, turning from the bedside to look up, puzzled, bewildered.

"Guests? The heathens? I do not know. In their quarters, I imagine. But why should—"

"You must find them, Brother, and when you have found them, take them to my cell. Hide them there. Quickly, HansJürgen. I need them safe if . . ."

"If what?"

"I need them, that is all."

The cold air outside shocked him after the cloying fug of the cell. Even filtered through a covering of cloud, the light was dazzling. He felt weightless, light-headed. He had barely entered the cloister before the monks' faces were in his own, huge red faces, yellow teeth, questions, and more questions. In the end he barged through them blindly, stumbling out past the dorter and into a paddock one side of which ran along the cliff edge. There he found Bernardo seated on a large stone.

"Where is your companion?" he demanded. The giant seemed gloomy and perturbed in some way. Without looking up, he pointed out to sea.

"Brüggeman's boat?" asked HansJürgen.

"He left me on my own," Bernardo said bitterly. "Again."

"Come with me," HansJürgen said, and the giant rose obediently, towering over him. He had not counted on this, on Salvestro choosing this day amongst all others. But he had known, of course. Salvestro himself had told him.

"Come with me," he said again. They stood there together. Salvestro was important somehow in the game that Gerhardt and Jörg were playing, had some significance that he was unable to see.

"Where are we going?" asked Bernardo after a minute's silence had passed. Where? echoed HansJürgen to himself, remembering the islanders seen on his walks. Here they come, arms up in greeting, stumbling over the clods. Ott, others. It was Gerhardt, of course, Gerhardt toward whom these swaggering approaches were directed. He was so tired. It was almost sunset. And then the words remembered from the chapter-house: "Our Prior has not been honest with you about them" and "The islanders know more than they would readily tell, about the smaller one. . . ."

The smaller one was Salvestro; and then, "I have spoken with the islanders. . . ." Of course he had. HansJürgen imagined him tramping the island through the winter, homestead to homestead, hovel to hovel. For what purpose? "They know what must be done even if we ourselves cannot . . ." What must be done. He needed food in his stomach, sustenance of some kind, a splash of water. But the islanders did not know "what must be done," did they? So they had been told. By Gerhardt. It was afoot, happening now, the key to it in Jörg's "I *need* them," which somehow Gerhardt had guessed or deduced. How exactly did they fit together, these fragments? What was the act they formed, the precise nature of the dance so carefully choreographed?

"Wait here," he told Bernardo, and strode back toward the monastery, a conviction growing, trying to remember Gerhardt's amongst the whirl of faces pressed against his own. Where was Gerhardt? He gained the cloister. Hanno, yes. Georg, yes. But Gerhardt was nowhere to be seen. He turned away, ignored now by the herd of them. Bernardo again: gloomy, perturbed, anxious, on a stone both broad and flat. Gerhardt and the islanders together, adding them up to produce. . . . Then he knew: the conviction freezing in his stomach. What must be done. What must be done. . . .

"What?" Bernardo's voice broke in on his thoughts. "What must be done?"

Had he been thinking aloud? He was tired, emptied. The giant's face was tilted up at his, mildly curious.

"They mean to kill him," he said.

It was odd, the way his old friend drank. Ewald had served them both mugs of small beer, flat and warm, delicious after his exertions. Nearing the beach after two hours or more afloat, he had seen Ewald standing there, waving him ashore. He had strung his boots about his neck, and then the two of them had lugged the monster up the beach, shouting directions to one another as the water foamed about their thighs, finally flopping down in a sweat, thirsty. They had guzzled water from the butt, splashed a bit on their necks, then gone inside for beer. No sign of Mathilde or the children. Their hoses steamed in front of the fire now.

Salvestro lifted his mug, slurped, sat it down, then waited to see if Ewald would do it again. After a few seconds, Ewald started. He glanced quickly across at Salvestro's mug, then down at his own. Grasping it in both hands, he raised it to his lips and gulped at the contents. As before, a little spilled down his chin. He had drunk three mugs so far to Salvestro's one. He twitched and looked about as if someone were moving behind him. He had done this throughout Salvestro's chatter.

"Bit of a shock, me and Bernardo turning up like that, eh, Ewald?"

Ewald stared at him for a second. "Well, it has been so many years. . . ."

"I meant, thinking I was dead."

"Well, I was told afterward. That's what I was told." He paused. "I was only a child. There's no need to bring up all that, is there?"

"No, no, no. No need at all. I was just thinking back, that's all."

He drank again, and again Ewald gulped. The beer was weak, but having touched nothing stronger than cold water through the winter, he found that it was going to his head. He asked if there were more. Ewald drained his own and refilled them both from the keg, his bare white legs a little unsteady. The room ballooned about him.

The two men drank on. Salvestro began to tell Ewald about his time with the Christian Free Company. Ewald said nothing, merely nodding when that seemed to be required, his eyes drifting again and again toward the door. Three times already he had got up to open it and peer briefly outside. It was quite dark now.

"Is something the matter, Ewald?" he asked finally. The other shook his head. Salvestro went on with his story. Soon, he and Bernardo were rowing across the Achter-Wasser.

"So what did you think, when you opened the door and there we were?" Salvestro persisted.

"I was . . . surprised," said Ewald.

"I'll bet!" roared Salvestro. The beer was excellent stuff. More, gulp. "Now, tell me . . ." He leaned forward. "Why do you think I came back, eh?"

It was fun, making Ewald squirm. He was like a younger brother, really. Tickle him till he wet himself. Put an eel in his bed. . . . But there was something in the question that snagged him, something in that white face behind the woman's, in the doorway. He wanted Ewald to tell him what he had been thinking. It was simple.

"Come now, Nico—" Ewald began.

"I'm not called that anymore," Salvestro broke in, a little belligerent now. "I haven't been called that for a long, long time." He leaned back in his chair. "So tell me, why? Why did I come back?"

"You know why you came back," replied Ewald. His eyes would not meet Salvestro's.

"Of course *I* know." He was badgering, moving his head about to intercept Ewald's gaze, which drifted evasively over the walls and up to the lathes of the roof. "But what did *you* think?"

"Nothing." Ewald gulped quickly at his beer, draining the mug again. The fire spluttered. Salvestro picked a log from the pile by the hearth and placed it on the embers. A small yellow flame popped up. His hose was dry, or dry enough. He struggled in, more drunk than he thought. He remembered pulling his clothes out of the underbrush after the first attempt at teaching his friend to swim. One of his secrets. Years ago. Now Ewald reached for his own hose, and soon his toes were tangled in one leg. He fell over. Salvestro straddled him, then sat down quickly, twisted an arm behind his back. Ewald twisted violently, but to no effect. They were boys again, swimming, mucking about, wrestling on the floor of the woods. He pulled Ewald's head up by the hair, then bent forward to whisper in his ear, "I came back for you, Ewald."

Instead of exclaiming "Get *off*," in the bored-irritated tone he had adopted for such events as a boy, Ewald remained silent.

"And now I'm going to slit your throat. . . ."

Salvestro peered down at his adversary's face. It was the color of ashes. He looked at Ewald's eyes. Ewald's eyes bulged. Salvestro jumped up quickly.

"Ewald! It was only in play!"

Ewald was stumbling to his feet, marching to the back of the room, talking to himself in a mumble, rooting about back there. He turned and there was an iron hook in his hand, its shank as long as his arm. "Calm down, Ewald," he said, but Ewald seemed not to hear.

"So you're going to slit my throat, are you, you filthy savage?" spat the other. "I'll deal with you myself."

He swung the hook in front of him, his eyes seeming to fix on Salvestro, then to lose him, to find him again. His face was bloodless, and Salvestro realized that he was terrified, panicking, and these words were for himself.

"Come now, Ewald. It was a stupid joke. Why would I kill you? Don't be so stupid. . . ." As he spoke, Ewald stepped forward and swung. He ducked, the bow of the hook glancing painlessly off his head.

"They should have drowned you like they said. Like they did your mother. That's what we're going to do. Drown you, or hang you on this hook and burn you."

He was edging around the table.

"You had to come back, didn't you. Well, I was waiting for you. And now I've got you." He swung again. Salvestro rocked back, not thinking anymore, only watching the other's movements, weight shifting from foot to foot. "Why do you think I came back?" Ewald's voice was a whining imitation of Salvestro's. "I know why you came back. We all know why you—"

Salvestro moved forward suddenly and caught Ewald by the throat. His other hand drove forward into the stomach and up under the ribs. Ewald bent forward, choking. The hook fell with a clang to the floor. Ewald followed. Salvestro looked down at him, then dropped, sitting astride his chest, knees pinning the winded man's arms to the dirt floor. He picked up the hook. Nice heft, sharp.

"Please . . . ," Ewald gasped, but Salvestro seemed not to hear him. He waved the hook to get the feel of it. He was tired, his stomach full of beer. If he were to drive the hook through Ewald's eye, he would be able to drag the corpse around like a log. This hook was for dragging logs. That was its purpose.

"I came back," Salvestro said, looking about him, "because . . . I didn't come back to kill you, Ewald."

"Liar," hissed Ewald.

"If I'm lying," said Salvestro, "why haven't I stuck you through the eye with this hook?" He got up, throwing the hook on the table. "You always were a coward."

There was a long silence. Then a few snuffles started up. Ewald's. Ewald gathered himself.

"You have to get out of here," he said. "Leave the island. Now. Tonight."

"Tonight?"

The sounds of the sea were very faint, soft rolls of noise somewhere outside. Nearer, a breeze slid through the scrub, scratching dryly at bare twigs and branches. There were little rustlings and silences. The embers hissed and popped in the hearth. The next instant, these sounds were overtaken by a shout from outside the hut. Several voices together, but shouting a single word.

"*Heathen!*"

"*Heathen!*" The second shout came louder than the first. HansJürgen stopped, cocked an ear, then moved forward again.

"What are we doing?" asked Bernardo for what seemed like the twentieth time.

"Lead the way," HansJürgen directed.

The giant moved more stealthily than he would have believed possible, picking a way through the undergrowth, seeming to sense the low overhanging branches and, when they had quit the path, swerving about impenetrable sprawling bramble patches to find narrow channels and gaps, paths of least resistance. The moon was low and miserly, disappearing for long minutes behind banks of invisible cloud. It came into view now, blank and luminous, gauzed in vapor. The ground rose before them, then steepened. A tracery of branches tessellated the dimly lit sky. Bernardo's broad back swung and dipped before him as they climbed the bank. He was a large, patient animal nudging aside the whippy trunks and branches. From the brow they looked down onto the beach. Brine and wood-smoke in the air. Brüggeman's place was a block of darkness and showed no lights. His excitement was feverish and papery over the deep well of his exhaustion. Bernardo ran down the bank, bringing himself up short at the bottom. He followed, the turf having the dead feel of the coarse sand beneath. The sea lapped and washed at the shore fifty paces away. The door was half-open. Little scraping sounds came from within.

The fire was almost dead. Ewald sat on the floor at the far end of the room. He was trying to pull himself upright as the two of them approached. One of his eyes had closed; the other watched expressionlessly until Bernardo towered over him. Dried and drying blood were mixed on his face. His head jerked to the right, once, twice. Something had been poured into his hair. The two men stood in the near dark, looking down at him, hearing the wheeze of his lungs. Ewald shifted again, winced. His mouth was puffy and shapeless. This time he used his arm, indicating again to the right. HansJürgen saw that they had broken his fingers.

Outside again, along the beach, which was striated with bands of shingle and fine sands running in strips along the shoreline so that the two men would pad noiselessly for a minute or two until a spit of pebbles thickened and spread to cross their path along the strand and the shingle crunched beneath their footfalls. Then they moved up the beach. Bernardo had said nothing after Brüggeman's place. HansJürgen panted after him, the sand sucking the strength from his legs. He was falling behind when he saw them, a red glow of torchlight in the darkness ahead of them. And in that moment he saw a silhouette pass between that light and themselves, a figure habited and cowled like himself. Bernardo's footsteps quickened and he could no longer keep pace with the giant. The darkness swallowed him and he was alone.

He stopped and rested his hands on his knees. He wanted to lie down in the cold sand and sleep. He wanted to sleep more than anything else in the world. Farther up the beach, the cluster of torches appeared to him as an eye of fire, shifting and melting in the black of the night. It was moving toward the sea, down the beach. He began again to walk. From time to time, men's bodies would pass before the shapeless glow. The figure bent double in the middle would be Salvestro. They were marching him down to the water. It was not too late. Nearer: he would fall as they clubbed him about the legs and head. They would club him as he rose. Their shouts were audible now, though echoless and flat on the beach. Then came the much larger shape he had been waiting for, the torchlight seeming to crowd and throb about it. He gathered himself and ran forward as fast as he was able, toes stabbing into loose shingle, throat burning. Now the torches were scattering and whirling no more than a hundred paces away, the shouting at once louder and abbreviated to yelps and sharp cries. Faster and faster he ran; faster and faster and faster, hardly able to keep his head raised, to look ahead, even, blind to the dark pillar whirling out of the night, rising out of the sand, falling like a sky of granite to meet and fell him with a single blow, which seemed to brush him softly, for he felt nothing, and which seemed a phantasm of his own suspicion made hard flesh and bone, for it was Gerhardt he met in the soundless clangor of their collision. Then his falling began, which seemed to go on and never to end.

"Is he dead?"

"No."

Large crabs painted fiery red like torches shifted and slid about in the black sand, grouping and scattering, melting into one another, then shooting apart. Two moons hung in the sky, wearing faces like the men leaning over him. His sense-lessness was imperfect, lying there.

"He's dead."

"Shut up, Bernardo."

"What shall we do with him, then?"

"Get him off this damned beach. Us too."

He had come to in the different darkness of the woods, slung over Bernardo's shoulder like a sack of fish. His temple throbbed where he had been struck. Several times, the two men had stopped and crouched low, saying nothing until the source of their alarm, whatever it was, had passed them by. At the eastern lip of the sky a tongue of light slavered and drooled blue. HansJürgen asked to be set down. Salvestro's face was swelling badly and his left leg dragged. Otherwise he appeared unharmed. Dawn was breaking as they reached the monastery. Florian awaited them at the gate.

"Where were you?" he asked as soon as they approached.

HansJürgen ignored the question. "The Abbot?" he demanded.

Florian looked away. "An hour ago. It was very violent at the end." Florian had been his confessor. HansJürgen touched him on the arm. Florian shook himself. "Gerhardt has declared himself already. They are all in the cloister now."

"Father Jörg?"

"Not him. He is in the Abbot's cell, in prayer."

The cloister fell silent as they walked in. Gerhardt was expressionless, watching the four of them. HansJürgen motioned for the others to stay and walked across alone, the monks parting before him, closing behind him. He felt their eyes on his back, their coldness. What had Gerhardt sucked out of them? He climbed the steps.

Jörg was kneeling at the Abbot's side. He crossed himself as HansJürgen entered, then rose.

"Are they safe, our guests?"

"They are."

"Good. Your face is bruised." The Prior had changed, had reached the moment where his purposes might be understood. HansJürgen imagined smooth pebbles heated to unimaginable temperatures burning in the other's chest. "Gerhardt means to oust me, you know that?"

HansJürgen nodded. There was a short silence.

"He will not," Father Jörg said abruptly. "Assemble them in the chapter-house. I will address them there."

HansJürgen turned to leave. Sunlight was stabbing at the clouds as he regained the cloister. Again the monks' eyes fixed him, colder than fishes', and his words seemed to sink in wet sand, so silent was their reception. But Gerhardt was smiling, his moment come, too. He was ushering his followers through the doors, the disdain as they passed him unmistakable on their faces. The Prior's creature. He wanted to shout that he was not, that he was as unsettled as they.

HansJürgen slipped in behind them and took his place on the gradines. Gerhardt's men shunned him, Gerhardt himself moving to and fro among the monks, whispering urgently, persuasively. The younger brothers twisted about on their seats, the elders watched hawk-eyed. They understood the transaction taking place here. He saw Florian amongst them. Lines were being redrawn, and the chapter-house buzzed and hummed as Gerhardt's faction swelled. The ruffians slumped outside the door were inexplicable as the islanders, as the Prior's scrawlings in this very hall. As the collapse of the church. The brothers craved explanation. Hurry, HansJürgen urged his Prior. Georg glanced over at him with ill-concealed contempt. Yes, there was no doubt now: he was tainted, infected, wedded to the madness of their Prior's impenetrable schemes. Gerhardt's sanity would have no place for him. The Prior's creature: how had he become that? What had he been thinking, chasing rumors around the island? He looked down at his lap, and the whispers grew louder, doubting tongues flapped harder. Then, quite suddenly, there was silence. Father Jörg stood in the doorway.

"I say with Cyrus of the House of God, Let the house be builded, the place where they offered sacrifices, and let the foundations thereof be strongly laid. Will any man here speak against me?"

There was silence. Their eyes followed him as he walked the gauntlet between the tiers, then turned to face them again.

"I say with the Lord, to Jacob as Isiah saw, To the cities of Judah, Ye shall be built, and I will raise up the decayed places thereof. That saith of Cyrus, He is my shepherd and shall perform all my pleasure: even saying to Jerusalem, Thou shalt be built; and to the temple, Thy foundation shall be laid."

Again he paused, and this time the question was written on his face as he scanned the faces before him. No one spoke.

"Henry the Lion stood here once. Stood here, I say, and saw a church. And built the church he saw to stand guard over a heathen city. This church, my brothers. Our church, where we have prayed and labored together. The lives of the Israelites were made bitter with hard bondage, in mortar, in brick, and in all manner of service in the field: I feel your weariness, my brothers. We have surveyed the forests and marshes, tramped the shores and fields, walked among the people, and the scales have fallen from our eyes. We have unrolled the world's fabric and spread it over these walls and wondered at the sights we saw therein and been sometime dazzled: I stand in your blindness, my brothers. Now will you stand with me in mine?"

Again his eye roved over the faces turned toward him. HansJürgen felt himself flush as the Prior's gaze swept past. Gerhardt's head was inclined to Georg, who sat behind him and murmured in his ear. He was nodding imperceptibly. The other monks kept glancing at him and looking away.

"In my blindness I see a city of towers, and bells within them and fair churches below them," said Father Jörg. "I see us in the streets which wind between these churches. We are returning home, for this is a distant city and difficult to reach. A hard journey lies ahead of us, and yet our hearts are light. For our church will be restored. Our church will be built up by masons and laid on a new foundation. The ruler of this city has sent them to do our bidding, which is more than we might do alone. They are his gift to us; they are our petition to him. He is whom we must seek. In my blindness we have found him. We are looking back on this day and laughing at ourselves for ever doubting that we would. We are forgiving those who doubted most and praising those who doubted least. I share your doubts, my brothers, but the church is broken and will not mend. We cannot stay. Walk with me in my blindness, my brothers."

The Prior stopped. His demeanor had changed, his words seeming to gain weight in the silence that followed. Gerhardt broke it. He stood, and the monks swiveled on their seats to see what he would say.

"Such a city, and such a King. Where are we to find them, Father? How are we to reach them? Why should they avail themselves? We have our salvation. Here"—he held up his hands—"and here"—he gestured to the monks—"and here"—his arms flew out to indicate the island. "You would send us in search of a fool's paradise when it is our own garden requires tending, our own walls rebuilding, our own foundations relaying." A murmur had got up amongst the monks. Some were nodding at these words, others simply staring. Heads turned now to Father Jörg, who spoke more sharply.

"It may be, Brother Gerhardt, you have gazed too long on wood and clay. Head of one, feet of the other, when our church falls into the sea you will prove most ambiguous, both floating and sinking as you will. I have watched you, and waited for you. I have seen you labor and mix your sweat with the sea. I have seen your scaffolds fail, your ropes snap, and so I have sent you and your fellows across the length and breadth of the island to learn the customs of the people here. I have told you of the stranger peoples and more distant lands that we may find beyond these shores. And I have found guides to lead us through them. . . ." At this, the monks began to stir. They looked to one another, then around the chapterhouse as though the men they sought might be perched aloft in the rafters.

HansJürgen saw Gerhardt's face soften for an instant, the merest hint of a smile pass across it to be replaced with a glare.

"The heathens!" he exclaimed. "He means the heathens. You would have us guided by soldiers and murderers!" Father Jörg was trying to ask whom Gerhardt might otherwise suggest, but the monks had caught their brother's tone. HansJürgen heard "No" muttered up and down the gradines as the brothers saw shock fill the faces of their fellows. The Prior was talking of foundations, of collapse, of their ruin if they stayed.

"Alone, we have no means, no hope," he pleaded. "There is only one who may help us found our church on rock. . . ." But his words lacked their earlier weight and chased weakly after his audience. Gerhardt pointed to him and spoke in acid tones that rang though the hall.

"I say with Jeremiah, O the hope of Israel, the savior thereof in time of trouble, why shouldst thou be as a stranger in the land, and as a wayfaring man that turneth aside to tarry for a night? Are you savior or wayfarer, Father? Would you have us save our church or leave it?" Gerhardt's voice had become a shout. Some of the monks were thumping on the floor with their feet. Father Jörg's eyes blazed and his cheeks were flushed.

"Your rebellion is as Korah's revolt against the Prophet, whom he would leave to journey alone. Your hot words too are as his, and I say with Moses, It came to pass, as he made an end of speaking all these words, that the ground clave asunder that was under them. And the earth opened her mouth and swallowed them up." The two men stood staring at one another. HansJürgen looked from one to the other, then, rising gradually all around him, the questions began. Why must they go? Where would their travels take them? What would await them at the journey's end?

"An authority higher than mine," Father Jörg replied. "An army as great as the Lion's, but armed with trowels and spades, with plumb-lines and angles. . . ."

"With coxcombs and motley, with bladders nailed to sticks," Brother Gerhardt broke in. "More fools to lead the fools you will become in following this one." His scorn was naked, paraded before the brothers, who shifted awkwardly in their seats and rumbled their doubts and fears, and more questions. Hours spent in the freezing winter sea hauling on Gerhardt's ropes and beams, or plumbing the bottomless mud that would crust them to the waist as they tramped up the slope to the church, fed their whispers of disbelief. Had their own efforts now sunk to nothing in the clay? How might these masons find the solid ground they themselves had failed to discover?

"The church itself must be moved entire. Stone by stone, beam by beam . . . ," Father Jörg said flatly, and the monks gasped.

"Why not the island?" Gerhardt scoffed. "Tree by tree, sod by sod, or the sea in which it sits, or the world you drew so prettily on the wall behind you?" The brothers murmured their assent, "Why not, why not . . ." and still the questions came, rippling through the ranks and breaking as sudden crests of sound above the general murmur. Scornful questions and doubting questions. Curious questions.

Of course, HansJürgen thought. Their trampings about the island had nothing to do with custom, everything with curiosity. Beyond the monastery was the island, but beyond the island, what? He sat hunched in the gradines and listened as the whys of the doubters contended with the hows of the curious, why and how, why and how, running and tumbling through the lines of the monks, Jörg and Gerhardt battling through their proxies, but the Prior was losing. He could feel it, hear it. The balance was tilting, tipping, pouring weight behind Gerhardt's contention that they should stay, and the questions were growing, widening, and deepening, becoming the pit they would all fall into unless he acted now against the gathering whine of doubt, which grew louder and louder, until he stood and heard a single clear voice cut through the babble and reduce the monks to an abrupt expectant silence, and the voice, he realized suddenly, was his own.

"How?" said Brother HansJürgen. "By faith. And why? Because our Prior asks it of us. I say with Paul to the Hebrews, By faith Abraham, when he was called to go out into a place which he would after receive for an inheritance, obeyed; and he went out, not knowing whither he went. By faith he sojourned in the land of promise, as in a strange country, dwelling in tabernacles with Isaac and Jacob, the heirs with him of the same promise." The monks had all turned to look at him. He saw his words register on their faces, then drew breath and said, "For he looked for a city which hath foundations, whose builder and maker is God."

The monks looked down at their laps, all except Brother Gerhardt, who stared across the chapter-house at Brother HansJürgen and wore on his face a look of unconcealed disgust.

Father Jörg cast his eye over the heads bent before him. The hall was utterly silent. He thought of this place on the night of the collapse, himself padding about the gradines, thinking on the sermon he would deliver to the monks at prayer in the church. There was a darkness in the semilight, a latent clatter in the soft footfalls of his round. Soon the monks would finish their devotions and file out to take their places before him. But the splintering beams, the stones splitting on the floor of the nave, the clay sagging under them all . . . He would take two winters to find them in the moment under this moment, but here they were, gathered together as they should have been before. A city which hath foundations. Had HansJürgen somehow divined his purpose? The monk was still on his feet, glaring his defiance at Gerhardt.

"Who will journey with me?" Father Jörg asked simply of the heads bent down before him. And with that he clasped his hands before him and, looking neither to left nor to right, walked slowly between the tiers of benches to the doors and out into the cloister.

For a long moment no one stirred. Then HansJürgen looked away from his adversary across the hall and began to edge his way out. Wilf stood to let him pass, and Wulf, who sat on the end of the row, moved out, then found Wolf doing the same. He continued down the steps to the floor, hesitated as though not at all sure how he had arrived, then walked toward the door, followed by Wolf, then Wilf, and last of all, silently urging them forward, HansJürgen himself. There was a second pause, and then the tier below followed suit, then the tier above, led by Joachim-Heinz. Gerhardt looked about wildly.

"What! You would follow these fools, these . . ."

HansJürgen barked from beyond the doorway, "You have said enough, Brother!"

The noise jolted them. Heads came up and eyes blinking as though awakened from sleep saw gray habits walking toward the doorway. On both sides of the hall, monks began to rise and shuffle along the rows to join the band gathering outside in the cloister. At the last, Gerhardt was left standing alone.

"So, Brother Gerhardt," HansJürgen spoke when the last man had passed beneath his arm, "will you stay or will you come?" But that question had already been answered. He waited while the monk shuffled slowly along the empty row, past the empty seats, his slight movements amplified now by the deserted hall's echo, until he too bowed his head beneath HansJürgen's arm and HansJürgen pulled the door shut behind him.

Father Jörg moved among them, laying his hand on a shoulder here, clasping a hand there, murmuring greetings and meeting gazes. He was a ransomed commander reunited with his troops. They formed themselves about him in a rough crescent, and a hard, cold sunlight beat down on the stones of the cloister. Come nightfall, the puddles that gathered in the hollows of the cobbles would freeze once again, but for now they were sheets of glaring light and the mirrored blue of the sky. A weight seemed to have lifted from the monks, who stood at ease, stretching and blinking, settling into their decision. Then a voice came from the back.

"Father, pardon me." A young voice, and Jörg craned his neck to find the speaker. "Here, Father." It was Heinz-Joachim. He nodded for the monk to go on.

"Father, I wondered, when you spoke of the city of towers and churches, the city we shall journey to, I wondered which city this would be—"

"And I, Father, I too wondered this," a second voice broke in. It was Joachim-Heinz. "I wondered too as to the King, the King we will petition. Forgive me, Father, but how is this king called?"

He recalled their terror, their huddling together on the floor of the chapterhouse while the stricken church bellowed and shuddered from its wounds. They had climbed from the wreckage, but slowly, becoming trepidant pilgrims about the precincts of the island, restive schoolboys on the gradines they had left behind now to follow him. He was invested in their raiment, crowned with their new horizon, a racing halo whose penumbral rim of gold sped west over the ragged marshes and brackish lagoons, out into the freezing black Atlantic, east to the thin soils of the plains and mountains tufted with scrubby grass and blasted pines, north where the winter will be bitter this year and the next, where men will stand dumbstruck at the sight of wolves crossing the frozen northern gulfs while ice creeps farther down the shoreline to rime even the coast of Usedom; no matter, they will be long gone by then, and this moment, when Jörg turns to answer his questioner and, sitting unnoticed behind all the monks, Salvestro whispers to Bernardo, "This will be good," this will be part of the clutter of a past to which none will return before the sea-ice has become water twice more, groaning and cracking in the frail warmth of spring as though some beast were trapped alive beneath it. They are men without shadows. Their thoughts have already left this place and are chasing forward, leaping rivers, scaling mountains, traversing the plains that divide them from their arrival. The monks gasp as the city's ruler is named, and then the city itself gives them the bearing. The journey is tugging at their feet. They are a tiny army, no more than a vanguard, standing in silence at the limit of the point. The city they came for is so close, a matter of fathoms away, but ahead lies the grayness of a saltless, tideless sea, which brings them up short, and the church to be built here will never make of this rejection a journey's end: they must go on. They are heirs to the Lion's error, but now that error will be redeemed. They will turn and tramp back across the island, these swordless soldiers of Christ. They will cross the Achter-Wasser and head south because the ice long ago unlocked a sea and a city sank beneath it, because the Lion's march could not be halted and their church would prove a fragile bulwark. Because they are unhoused and Vineta will not have them.

"Rome," said Father Jörg.

II

RO-MA

A slow flood is moving up to the barricades. In the east, an invasion is under way. The ground is prepared, shuddering and waiting below. The vault of heaven is tented and empty, its commanders fled. A central pivot soaks pressure out of the enemy camp: finitude and light take a toll, but there is no sudden breach, no obvious horde to overrun the gates of these high spaces. Seepage and calm marshal the invader's open declaration, and the sky is a broad, undefended front. Clouds hanging in the field of operations might be giants, huge animals, ships, engines of God. The night is blind and cannot see the erosion of its edges. The sky is cut and angels cannot close the wound. This is a battle without surprises: another dawn is rising over the city.

God's face is made of light. Light rears in a tangent above the curving earth, a gathering wave of gray becoming blues and yellows and pinks. All about the eastern horizon the night is breaking down. The advance is cautious, but all resistance has disappeared. The encircled camp is deserted, its black defender already dead of fever and the body consumed. Or concealed somewhere where the light is unable to find it. The sky is quartered, but the body is nowhere here. Uneasy light drenches the high, featureless vault. Clouds burn away. Empty sky. The night is in hiding, waiting for the slow moment when it will return its defeat in kind. For now it is sunk and drowned. The light wheels and turns. The earth is a dark haven from the sky's unending wars, a place for the defeated. Then the wave breaks and the light descends.

There is a city here, a stony purple bruise that wells out of the ground to meet its invader. Scarred targets, outcrops, and promontories mount the air as the vessels burst and pump upward out of the earth. This city fell from heaven into a sea of darkness; air flayed the light from its bones. Scarred and healed a thousand times, floundering and reaching up to empty heaven, darkness pours off the city's surfaces and crevices, down its walls, through its streets, alleys, lanes, and out its gates. A dark sea drains and flies away. The seabed is land suddenly, and now light touches the first of its outposts, its highest points, which are old hills spattered with ruinous arches and towers: the Palatine, the Aventine, the Capitoline, the Coelian, the Esquiline, the Viminale and Quirinale. Across the river whose bend this city abuts, the long hump of the Janiculum emerges out of the earth's shadow. Sunrise.

Sunlight creeps down the Torre delle Milizie atop the Palatine, down the Torre de' Conti, down the towers of the Lateran, of San Pietro in Vincolo, the palace of the Senate on the Capitol, and San Pietro in Montorio. The night is in recession, pouring through the channels that divide them and that they punctuate as fingers of rock whittled to sharp angles by the flood. Cupolas poke the sky as though some second, protecting skin might tent the city in safety. But the bastions are lost and fend off nothing. The skin is stripped away. Sunlight reaches deeper into the city's secret folds, inching down the east-facing walls into the narrow alleys and runs, finding out basilicas and palaces, running over the rough pasture of the piazzas, and drawing mist off the marshy valleys that run between the hills. Long shadows emerge, run west, shrink as the sun climbs higher and the city is overtaken, turned to stone, overrun by its invaders. From the east, light. And now, from the south, a baking and penetrative heat.

The ground is clogged with bodies: cadavers and their sepultures. The earth is heavy with oils that bubble as the heat finds them. The circuses are wrecked, and arches raised to older triumphs are fallen in defeat. Now out of the old city's burial come the survivors. In the Pincio, San Rocco melts in the dawn half-light. A bronze torso flops in the Campo de' Fiori, Pan clambers from the ruins of the Satrium, which curls itself about him, and Venus scatters fish-heads in Pescheria. Marforio chatters with Pasquino, and the sick are already gathering around the fount of Juturnus, newly risen and steaming in the magical morning heat. Groups of figures haul themselves out of the molten ground, their long interment suddenly no more than a blink of the sun's eye and forgotten as quickly. The wall of the Scrofa splits open, and a sow clambers from the wreckage of her crypt, her litter squealing, slack belly dragging in the mire of the road as she hunts stupidly for the hopeful augurs to welcome this second foundation. Across the Campo Marzio, brushwood, creeping weeds, and hybrids find their abandoned roots and rise again in the Garden of Sallust.

The old city is staggering to rise, but the sun is a strong disperser of its half-lights. The night leaves its silt in the cracks and eaves. Columns of smoke from the lime kilns stand high in the still air above the Calcaranum. Heat moves in a crescent across the districts of Ripa, Sant'Angelo, Parione, and Ponte, over the Tiber, and through the drab precincts of the Borgo to the gardens of the Belvedere, where panthers will stretch, rise, piss in their cages. A great gray body lies seemingly lifeless in the shade of the plane trees. Overlooking them all, in the Stanza di Eliodoro in the palace of the Vatican, heat and light batter the sleeper's uneasy dreams and a thick body stirs beneath its coverlet. The face of God is pressed against the city, and the morning is a clarion of light calling excavators to the depleted ruins of the Capitol, butchers and horse-traders to the market in Navona, swineherds and fishmongers to Campo de' Fiori. Haulers trundle salvaged columns and marble slabs through the narrow streets to the lime kilns, Tiber boatmen ferry wine to the *sensali* of Ripetta, millers feed their island mills, and the cardinals slumber in their palaces. Innkeepers are throwing back grease-stained curtains, and pilgrims are rising from beds and straw palliasses the city over. Buildings faced with travertine glare over marshy courts. Stations of faith beckon differently to drive the honest devotees up the Holy Steps, blood soaking through their knees, and the next, and the next. A chamberlain knocks softly; a fishwife shrieks at a Jew. In the Via delle Botteghe Oscure, thick slabs of tufa soak in the morning heat while curio-sellers erect their stalls and booths before the workshops of the jewelers. Now the sun is high, but for all the purpose and bustle of the awakening city, an inhibition hangs over the workaday efforts of its inhabitants. Something latent, not visible yet. They are marking time, hurrying through the motions. Waiting.

Rain in June? Random downpours have drenched the city these two days past, turning the plazas into lakes, the alleys to minor tributaries flowing into the swollen river proper. Puddles still stand under the open drum of Saint Peter's and the square outside. To the north of the city, bright sunshine lifts a murky steam off the mire of the Piazza del Popolo, where a small herd of cattle mooches over the sodden humance, hooves squelching and sinking in the mud. Neatherds stood in hunched gangs under the awning of the German print shop to watch their wading charges suffer the downpour in silence while the pelting rain turned pasture to swampy mud, mud to shit-stained pools that glare in the succeeding sunshine and stink in the heat. Delays were inevitable.

Now, while the arriving warmth shrinks puddles to salty residues on the flagstones and heats the mud to steam, two of this city's thoroughfares turn from quagmires covered with water to quagmires covered with people. The Via Lata and Via del Popolo cut a wedge out of the city to meet at the plaza, intervening *macchia* forces them farther apart as they reach back into the city and rough pasture cedes to hovels and sprawling tenements, stables, and barns. Pilgrims, minor clerks, and the whole flood of skiving tradesmen follow in the hoofmarks of curious riders who braved the rain and cantered up and back to report what they could of the embassy beyond the gates. At first the spectators pick careful paths to avoid the deepest basins, but the roads are quickly ruined and the following, cursing crowds sink in the muck and wade through pools of stinking water. Flies whirl in figures of eight about their struggling legs, and the freshening stench wrinkles noses from the Porta del Popolo to the heart of the city: cowshit and goatpiss and their own breaking sweat. The marshy square grows crowded, and more crowded, and still the influx continues. Trampers through the mud slow and slow their pace until the roads themselves are jammed, the surrounding slopes stiff with people, and the few mean houses that mark the sections of this churned surface fill and spill onto balconies and porticoes, with everyone elbowing for a view. The impatient city is emptying northward and westward, harried by heat and light. Huge water-wheels thrash the yellow waters about the Tiber island, while buffalo watch their masters decamp across the river and empty barges knock against the piers. Straw-sellers and innkeepers have left their precincts in the Borgo, excavators and lime-burners upped and followed the general drift northward through the crowded alleys and shambles of Ponte and Parione. The banks are closed. The churches are empty. At Campo Marzio, the tenements and shambles give out and odd buildings stand in strange isolation amongst the scrub, wild grasses, and ruins. Or stood. Crowds in the distant plaza have already swelled and fed back along the Via del Popolo, so now the flood of the curious is stemmed farther and farther from the spectacle they await. They stand shoulder to shoulder on the rising ground to left and right, all their sweating faces turned north, from where the procession will emerge, although now they see only more of themselves, curious, expectant, blurring in the distance.

Peter's city jabbers in a hundred dialects, a thousand irritated conversations. Outriders shout down at pilgrims who still mill and jam the narrow lanes about Sant'Angelo. Various vanguards drive wedges through monks, apprentices, insolent boys, and dogs. But the way is blocked, the alleys, courtyards, and dismal runs all stoppered up and stuffed with shuffling bodies. How many of them even know where they are going? Their irritation is solidarity enough, mere number an irresistible compulsion. The distant plaza is a heaving mass of Roman flesh, women are fainting and children being trampled, but all of them are craning for a view toward the ruin of the gate. The roads are solid and still the city feeds them forward, thousand upon thousand growing blacker and denser until the northern districts are silted solid and the crowd must layer itself about the girth of the gathered citizenry, a swelling bole of bodies bulging into Parione. Ponte is already solid, and the latecomers must swing west, farther back into the cradle of the Tiber bend, then up toward the Borgo and the grim frontage of the Castel Sant'Angelo. Even here the going is heavy and the slow coagulation of pilgrims and clerics hardening. Horsemen trying to force their way through the crush swerve back and forth with the crowd's surges as they make for the span of Ponte Elio that links the castle to its city. Disgruntled bodies move sluggishly before the onslaught, then more smartly as other horsemen join the first, diving for their lives at the last—a phalanx of horses is driving forward, insensible of the bewildered pilgrims and beggars, galloping headlong for the bridge, while in their midst a gang of foulmouthed angry old men dressed in scarlet shout at the crowd and each other. Watching from the balcony of Castel Sant'Angelo, the papal datary turns to tell his master the cardinals are coming.

Trumpets and drums to the north. The spectators have waited, sweated, grown ill-tempered, then quiescent, suffered the blazing day and their neighbors, but now their patience seems set to be rewarded. Snippets of gossip have flown around the crowd. The rumored beast stands as high as a house, eats only oysters, and drinks the blood of virgins. Hootings and bangings beyond the gate draw their heads about until the whole of the plaza is focused on the break in the city wall. They are silent now, and the trumpets louder. Soon the first of the drummers appear, and following them on horseback, a bearded man, very erect in the saddle and oblivious of the gaping onlookers. More drummers, and trumpeters, and more men on horseback riding four abreast and fifty deep. A miraculous passage opens before them and seems to draw them on, but it is not for these marchers and riders that the crowd has waited. Hooting, marching, banging: the city's palate is jaded with these. Crumbling plaster arches and tattered pennants still mark the Medici Pope's late *possesso*. Smashed, abandoned floats litter the courtyards, and dead echoes of *Palle! Palle!* are spattered over walls. Rome is inured to carnivals and triumphs, yet today its citizens jostle and strain for a view. A new hunger is being fed, a wide gullet opening in the plaza and Via del Popolo, and down this pressed, impossible corridor the splendid embassy advances in regular wide-spaced files. The crowds forget their discomfort and impatience. From farther up the route waiting spectators hear perfunctory cheering, which gradually dies away to be replaced with a weird silence. The trumpeters, drummers, and liveried horsemen are a necessary prelude, no more. Fractious neighbors grow calmer and quieter, anticipation clears the packed road, and now only dogs trespass on this luxurious space. Everyone is waiting.

Even the Pope. Seated in the center of the loggia of Castel Sant'Angelo with his cardinals to left and right, the ambassadors behind, the Servant of the Servants of God overlooks the crowd below. They, in return, look up. The Pope seems calm, composed, on his little dais. Flanking cardinals are more restless, perturbed perhaps by the promised spectacle. Then, too, waiting is unfamiliar to them; unsettling, even. Their clerks wait, their households wait. Cardinals do not, save on the Pope. And the Pope is calm, or seems so. The cardinals are reassured. They press nosegays to their faces, swat at insects, shift about in their chairs. On the stairs their officers eye each other up and vie for precedence. Cardinal Armellini's men have the topmost steps and are operating an unsanctioned customs post. Unhappy servants carrying trays of sweetmeats and silver pitchers of wine have protested their devotion to Cardinals Riario, Grimani, Soderini, Vigerio, Della Rovere, Del Monte, Accolte, De Grassis, Sauli, d'Aragona, Cornaro, Farnese, Gonzaga, Petrucci, Remolino, Serra, Challand, Schinner, Bakòcz, and Bainbridge. They are cowed and disgruntled porters who reach Armellini's ruffians and struggle through, much depleted, to serve the thirsty prelates. A conclave is assembled here to elect the lumbering symbol that approaches from the north. The Pope is self-possessed, a model of patience. The crowd below is abandoned. Between them both, the cardinals urge God's speed on the invisible embassy. They hear weak cheers and, succeeding them, an indecipherable silence.

Stiff Tiber mud caked on the piers of Ripa tells of succeeding and overlapping washes, rising levels and late recessions leaving their alluvium on the city fringes. A central spring is sprung and moves along the Scrofa, but noise leaves no silt and silence no mark. Overleaping cheers are an airy vanguard, easily broken under the sun's boot. Tomorrow there will be nothing of this but tavern gossip and lies. The smart ranks of infantry will be a thousand Scipios, or ragged mountaineers; turbaned keepers will be captured kings or monsters with heads the size of houses. The procession will balloon in the heat, or shrivel to wizened fruit, or change into something quite different, something rarer. The strange, failing cheers send these specters forward into the city, where spaces wait to be filled: shifting, swelling, and shrinking volumes, new colors. The embassy advances in overlapping waves, succeeding one another and draining into the parched sands, disappearing, melding, sinking below the surface. The crowd's appetite is dry as dust, drawing on the spectacle to taint and dissolve and fuse. A new amalgam hardens under the baking sun. Their bodies are rigid figures grouped about the beast's abandoned path, held in place by all the spaces of its bulk. There is nothing to see, yet they look on still. They are different people and changed, or ready for change.

Here, on the balcony of Castel Sant'Angelo with the rabblement of cardinals and in their midst the Pope; now, after the first flurry of expectation has become merely waiting, before the embassy of the Portingales is arrived, scarlet robes flap and wave like banners over the crowd, goblets glint in the sun, while the Bishop of Rome sits still in his composure. The minutes tick by and the prelates' gabble and banter quietens and finally dies away. The Pope sits patiently. His cardinals strive to emulate him. But their silence is disconcerted, their noise suppressed. Their Pope, they know, should be clamorous and impatient by now. His silence is a signal they ape without understanding. He seems hardly aware of them, blandly overlooking the throng below, the cluttered roofs, the infinite tent of the sky, while distant trumpets hoot thinly as the procession nears the Borgo.

Drums beat in the Via Recta, past Navona and the Tower of the Sanguigni. Cheering and the same succeeding silence float past the embassy as it passes the low hill of Monte Giordano. The musicians and outriders, the Ambassador and his guard, seem to disappear as their charge comes slowly into view. On they march, marooned in silence and the crowd's blindness, to the Canale di Ponte, where floodmarks chart strange coasts along the walls. They can smell the river and see the piazza, and behind them they sense the animal that has reduced the city to silence driving them forward toward the Pope, a dot of white amongst the red of his cardinals; immaculate on the balcony.

Porticoes and staircases crowd together over the street, casting inky shadows so that the Pope sees vague movements: an advance of heralds, perhaps; he cannot make it out. A second piazza swells and opens in the first as people spill back. Trumpets glint in the murk as odd rays of sunlight strike the street; the drums are louder. A man on horseback appears, outriders and men marching in long files behind them. The cardinals are watching him, watching for his reaction. They glance across the piazza, then quickly back. Drummers, trumpeters, riders, marchers: the embassy stretches the length of the square, and still it is not finished. He blinks in the strong light, his patience ebbing faster. He wants to urge the procession on. A shape is swaying in the overhung street. Slinking creatures led on chains by turbaned men precede it, emphasizing its bulk, its mass. The shadows clear, and he can feel the eyes of his cardinals upon him. He fidgets in his seat, cannot keep still, wants to, cannot. The beast advances out of the dark corridor, and the Pope's eyes widen. It halts in the sudden sunlight and raises its head to the sky. The Pope rises, raising his arms as though to clap in acclaim. But the moment lengthens and his hands are frozen, his mouth half-open as though to speak, eyes rolled back into his head. He is caught in neutral space, his expression half-formed. The cardinals glare from either side. The animal waits. But the Pope is stalled between happy recognition and unease. He can see himself standing there before them all, offering himself up to their ridicule. He is an imbecile in a white gown. He cannot decide. The crowd is silent, waiting. Still he remains with time ticking away, sand running through his fingers, ebbing, falling back. He is impotent. Far below, flanked by its escort and the silenced spectators, the animal stirs and the Portuguese divide before its shambling, swaying gait. The Pope looks down into the silent afternoon. Red, sweating faces blur and merge. Livery of green and gray. He is frozen, watching the animal moving toward him.

And he saith unto them, Whom do men say that I am?

And he saith unto them, But whom say ye that I am?

The night before his birth, a beast leaps into the dream of Clarissa Orsini. She will remember a huge and docile lion. Such animals are fitted into the design of the bed's canopy. She has lain and stared up at them for days on end. But the lion of her dream is heavier, more powerful, and its head more massive than those decorative figures that flee the chasing huntsmen above. He paces before her, tail swatting the air. The yellow eyes are fixed upon her, and the tongue is lolling. The sleeping duchess wraps her arms about her belly. The lion patrols back and forth, his heavy paws thudding on the ground, rearing slightly to turn, and all the time his eyes watch her in expectation. She is unafraid. He might be her jailer or guardian, or the portent they have sought these last months. She does not know, and cannot ask, for her dream is silent. The lion stops. The duchess moves forward. The lion turns and she wants to follow, but her belly is huge and tight as a drum. The lion begins to run, and she tries to rise. A hand holds her back. Other hands press cloths soaked in cool water to her brow and cheeks. The maids are chattering, and the midwife's face is huge above her own. Lions lead huntsmen into the dark wood, where blue birds fill the trees. Quick seizures grip and release her midriff. The bedclothes are already soaked. She gasps suddenly, fully awake. Her waters have broken. The midwife takes her hand.

"I dreamed of a lion," the duchess says.

"Then the child will be strong," the woman tells her.

He will be told this story many times.

And thou art he whom thy brethren shall praise. Lion's whelp, and old lion. Who shall rouse him up?

Abed, still supine yet awake, the Pope considers the blue birds in the trees that border the canopy of his bed. Points of sunlight prick the paneling in the bedchamber. Boars and stags and hounds are pictured alongside animals with towering necks, long curling tongues, and teeth. Bizarre beasts fringe the scene: gross unicorns, gryphons, basilisks. Mournful lions cluster around an orange tree, and other lions lead to the far corner. The hippopotamus cheers him.

Every morning he awakes to the animals' muster. Perfunctory artisans labored over this tapestry; the needlework is undistinguished. As a child he recalls garish scarlets and blues. Now, rust and pallid watchet struggle out of the gray dawn light. The animals are fading. The birds keep the cobalt of their first plumage, but the splendid hippopotamus is barely visible, growing drabber with every succeeding day. His eye roves about the scene. To each of the Medici his animal. He has been dutiful, mindful of his mother's dream. He has kept faith with the lion, as his father with the giraffe, but the kinship remains unfelt. The great gray ruminants afford his affection an easier purchase. The Pope is drawn to bulk.

Nero would swaddle the first Christians in lion-skins and loose the animals into the Circus. Peter's needle will rise in the Borgo when Peter is dust. Lions pad through the mind of the Pope. Memories of lions circle the cringing flesh, and atop the the needle is a globe of bronze. Christians sweat and pray in the smothering skins, sun breaks over the highest tier, and the globe flares with light. The ashes of Caesar are still in their urn as the blazing globe draws in the beasts, running forward with jaws agape, and the flesh is so soft, a blood-filled sponge. The Circus rises to the unworthy disciple. Blood soaks the sand. Lions slink in the shade, and behind those first few martyrs thousands wait with bright faces and wild eyes, seeing beyond the counterfeit globe and the counterfeit sun to the illimitable sky. They know the face of God is made of light. At dawn they too will crowd the arena and press their faces to His. Claws and teeth will rip their flesh. Blood in the sand and caked about the jaws of the lion are the marks of faith. Unworthy Peter feels his head fill and throb until it must burst upon the ground. His feet point up to heaven. No lion will cut him off the cross and let him fly his agony. Faith is mortal, a weight of blood. No lion can release the Pope. His mother's dream was of a beast, and she called the beast a lion. The Pope gazes at the canopy. Blue birds, unicorns, lions, the splendid hippopotamus . . . Yes, he thinks, her dream was true. That was the portent. Yet no lion placed me on the throne of Peter; nor any lion will keep me. Some other, less gaudy beast is meant for me. More massive. More gray.

He is three years old, and the Pazzi would have his father dead. Montesecco will take Lorenzo in the cathedral; Franceschino and Bandini his brother. Lorenzo parries the dagger and runs for the sacristy with blood trickling from his throat. Brother Giuliano is flooding the floor, dead already in the tumult of the church. Poliziano bars the door, and Ridolfi sucks the wound for poison. The ruffians flee with the panicked congregation. The streets are already in uproar. An hour later, Lorenzo addresses the people from the balcony of the Medici: "My people, I commend myself to you. Hold your tempers. Let justice take its course. . . ."

"Pull them out by the ears," Petrucci directs his men. Salviati is dragged forward. Petrucci holds him by the hair to spit in his face. The soldiers kick Franceschino across the floor. He holds up broken fingers. Both men plead as the ropes are produced. Franceschino pisses in his breeches.

"The window." Petrucci points. The ropes are tied, and the conspirators struggle and scream in earnest. The blows and kicks of the soldiers seem to have no effect. Both cry out horribly as they are carried to the casement.

"Throw them out," commands Petrucci. The ropes jerk for longer than is usual, and when he peers down at the corpses he sees Salviati's teeth buried in the neck of his fellow. By the end of that week, seventy traitors are strangled and hung by the feet from the walls of the Signorial Palace. Jacopo Pazzi himself is trapped, returned, tortured, hung. Small boys dig up his corpse and drag it by the neck through the streets to the Rubiconte Bridge. The Arno carries it, floating, faceup in the water, all the way to Brozzi. It is pelted with filth from bridges as far away as Pisa—still floating, though the face is half-eaten. The Florentines say Jacopo called for the Devil but the Devil would not take him. Lorenzo sends Giovanni and Giulio to the monastery at Camaldoli. They are cousins, barely toddlers. Medicis.

And upon this rock I will build my church; and the gates of hell shall not prevail against it. Peter's blood and bone sag in their body's sack, hung by the feet in Nero's Circus.

Delfinio watches in silence from an upper window as the Abbot of Passignano and the Prior of Capua walk together in the gardens. The two are deep in conversation, solemn figures with their heads bent forward, nodding from time to time as a point is made. Delfinio views them with private satisfaction. The Abbot stops, turns, and Delfinio draws back quickly. He can hear the Prior's reedy voice, but the words are a jumble. His ears seem to age more quickly than the rest of him. The Abbot's voice is a little deeper. Perhaps they are in dispute again. Perhaps their friendship is as fast as it seems. He waits for them to continue before he looks again. The garden of the monastery abuts an orchard. Beyond that, placid cows graze a meadow that follows the slope of the hill on which the monastery stands. The two have already made their way through the gardens. Now they walk the orchard. Their conversation seems to have become a debate. Their gestures are more vigorous. As Delfinio watches, the Abbot lashes out suddenly, catching the Prior of Capua a clout about the head. Delfinio turns quickly for the stair. From the cloister he sees the two of them running between the apple trees. He shouts, but they take no notice. The Prior of Capua is fleeing with the Abbot in pursuit. Delfinio gathers up his cassock and hurries through the garden. Rotted apples crush underfoot. Cows low in the far field, and the Prior of Capua's shrieks grow louder. Suddenly they stop. Delfinio clears the orchard and sees in the field beyond it the Abbot astride the Prior. Delfinio redoubles his efforts. The Abbot's arms are caked to the elbows. Apprehensive cows watch his performance as the Abbot of Passignano rubs cowshit into the face of the Prior of Capua.

"Idiots!" Delfinio cuffs the Abbot until he howls as loudly as the Prior, then continues until he stops.

"Giulio made me!" yells the Abbot.

"Giovanni started it!" wails the Prior. Delfinio begins scraping cowshit off the boy's face. "Giovanni did it!"

"Shut up!" Delfinio tells them both sharply. The three march in silence back toward the monastery.

"Giulio said I could never be Pope. He said my head was too big. . . ." Delfinio cuffs Giulio.

"Too empty," he says, thinking. Too full. And all too soon. Piero is already in Rome, lobbying for his brother. The Abbot of Passignano is twelve years old, the Prior barely nine.

Now, outside his window, the starlings will be cheeping. The air will be still and dank with the smell of the Tiber, which only the fiercest midday heat seems to banish. The Borgo begrudges the morning its sunlight, the air is weighted down and hangs between basilicas and palaces, dripping walls and crumbling towers, until the prelates gasp and their servants cough sulfurous breath from their lungs. The city chokes on its own exhalations, and the tired *campagna* that surrounds it is dead pasture to the lush meadows of Camaldoli. The Pope remembers well enough the smell of the cowshit. Faintly sweet. In Rome the cowshit smells old as it spills from the beasts themselves. They graze old pasture, breathe old air. Their flesh sags on the bone as they wander stupidly in the Campo de' Fiori. Would Giulio remember? Delfinio? Suddenly a hand of iron grips him by the guts. He clutches his stomach as a fart burns its passage through his vitals. The private wound aches, then subsides. And of course it was true, then as now. His head is slightly too large for his body. A question of proportion. And his arms are rather thin. He was never meant to be the warrior, cloistered there with Delfinio and Justinian in the nurture of the monastery. Priest, Abbot, Bishop. Never his brother. Always, and at least, the Cardinal.

Piero!

Oh, Piero, thinks the dozing Pope, you always were a fool. Even in death. . . .

The deck of the overloaded barge seesaws in a choppy swell. An imagined Piero takes a tighter grip on the bridle of his horse. Paulo Orsini watches off the stern as their abandoned escort mills about on the banks. Cordoba and the Spanish will reach the river at sundown. The cannon strain against their ropes. The Garigliano is swollen in December. A strong current pulls the vessel downriver, timbers creaking under the shifting cannon, horses, men, and their weapons. The nose of the barge swings about, and Piero sees the far bank slide away. The boat is turning in midstream, and the men are struggling with the rudder. A wave of water slaps against the side, then another.

"Piero!"

The negotiations were protracted, official assumption of the office delayed, but Lorenzo had his way in the end.

"Piero!"

Now he has seen him, bright in the bright of earlier years, before the Garigliano took him, elder brother Piero at the head of his escort astride a massive and vicious stallion caparisoned in gold. His retinue is a loose and chattering phalanx of friends who pass rough wine amongst themselves. Giovanni waves from the bridge at Mugnone. The cardinalate was his at thirteen, with a deferral appended by Innocent—dubbed "the Reluctant Rabbit" by Lorenzo in private, later "the Persuaded," and finally "the Magnanimous." Three years have passed, and Giovanni is ready at last. Louts, thinks Delfinio as the horses draw nearer. Piero's faithful, thinks his brother. The stallion stamps the turf as Piero salutes him.

"Silence!" shouts the horseman to the rabble at his back. "Show the Cardinal your respect." He grins at his young brother. In a day of observances and process Piero's arrival is a surpassing surprise. He turns to Delfinio in delight.

"Now Pietro can ride alongside us," he tells his mentor.

"I fear not," Delfinio replies. "Your brother has more urgent appointments, Giovanni." The horsemen block the road for thirty yards or more. "The arrangements cannot be changed at this late hour." Delfinio's demeanor is humility itself. Piero's face is a storm.

"Is that so?" His voice is suddenly full of scorn, and the horse is already wheeling about, buffeting the mounts behind as Piero forces his passage through their midst. The other horsemen jostle to turn and follow their leader. The road is chaos in a moment. Giovanni calls after his brother, but the thundering hooves drown him out and Piero is lost behind his own chasing retinue.

"Today you gain the Cardinal's hat," Delfinio recalls him.

"You do not favor Piero," Giovanni challenges the old man. "Why?"

"We are already late," says Delfinio.

That evening, fireworks splutter in the dank air over Fiesole. The December air is heavy with damp. Flanked on the high table by the Abbot, who has invested him with mantle, cap, and hat, and his aging mentor Delfinio, Giovanni watches the musicians perform by the fitful light of bonfires. The investiture is complete. He turns to ask his earlier question of Delfinio and is again refused.

"I am Cardinal now," he tells his mentor. "Please answer my question." Delfinio sighs and folds his hands in his lap.

And Piero's barge rolls and yaws, all out of control, still years away. Piero clings to his horse as the river spins them around. The cannon are too heavy, and now it is too late to cut them loose. The river breaks over the wales and Piero's horse jerks loose, kicking out and falling, then sliding down the deck and over the side. Its head rises once, then sinks below the surface. The boat sits lower and lower in the water. They are sinking. Men are already jumping clear of the vessel and striking out for land, but the current is strong. He looks about for Paulo, but his companion has disappeared. Water swirls about his feet. The nose of the boat buries itself in the river and will not rise. Piero looks over the side, unbuckles his sword, and jumps.

"He is a fool," Delfinio tells his young master that night at Fiesole. "And a fool will bring down ruin on the Medici." Giovanni colors but says nothing. Delfinio knows a childish bond is being sundered. Not even a Cardinal can forgive the truth.

He stumbles to the window, rubbing his eyes, then pulling back the drapes. The river was in spate, and Piero's body never found. Peter, Piero, the whining monk in Florence: all hallowed fools. Sunlight jumps and floods into the chamber. Soon Ghiberti will come to knock softly upon the door. The Pope begins to dress. He does not yet wish to look upon the gardens of the Belvedere. Peter between the needles, the monk upon his pyre, and Piero in the waters after the fiasco at Gaeta. The ruin of which Delfinio had spoken those years before was already upon them. Lorenzo dead, Piero yet to die. Florence lost to Soderini. The days when loyalists might crowd the balconies and shout, *"Palle! Palle!"* for the Medici were an age away. He saw the last days, the ruffians breaking down the doors, their own servants looting the halls, the mob gorging on their masters. Cowled and habited, he mingled with the Beast, smelled its sweat, watched it feed in the palaces at Careggi and the Via Larga. The horses were waiting for him by the Porta San Gallo, Piero and Giuliano were already fled along the Bologna road. Half a day's ride behind his brothers, Giovanni turned his horse south to Rome.

Perhaps this too is ominous: Rome always greets him with rain. Alone but for the grooms, he enters the city by Porta del Popolo. The piazza is a sea of mud and the Via Lata a river. His own palace appears as a drab prison, lightless and forbidding in the wet. The first of his secretaries is waiting. Dovizio already knows the worst.

"They have outlawed Piero." Giovanni nods. His cloak drips steadily on the flagstones. "And you too. There are two thousand florins on your head."

Rome will protect him, Rome and his Cardinal's hat, and in return he will be the servant of the Borgia Pope. He will ignore the mules loaded with silver, the preferred nephews, the bastard son who rages through the lands of Saint Peter with a cutlass. He will nod and murmur his assent, and the Spaniard will know he is weak and no threat. He will sponsor clowns, attend carnivals, live well. He will wait.

The latest of his secretaries knocks gently, once, twice, upon the door. The Pope seems not to notice. Presently he hears the man's footsteps move away and the far door close. Only then does he quit his bedchamber for the spacious Sala di Pontifici. Raffaello's prelates gaze down on him from the ceiling and walls. The Borgia was at least adept in ornament. A table is laid for him with a single chair facing the window. The Pope reaches for bread and olives. Oil runs down his plump fingers, making them shiny and sticky. A napkin is pressed into service. The Pope reaches for water, drinks noisily, burps. Another olive follows, and more oil. The napkin again. Bread, and more water, added this time to his wine until it is a pale pink. The Pope sips and considers the cheese. Bread pumps him full of wind. Cold meats aggravate the problem and so are banned from the breakfast table. Cheeses are neutral in this respect. Olives too. His wound aches and suppurates at the very thought of cold meats. The Pope denies himself the cheese, and breakfast is over. The room is bright, with dust motes whirling in the sunlight that runs in at the windows. Empty days and waiting, dust frantic to fill the spaces after Florence. Air too has its substance, thinks the Pope. Nine olive stones sit upon his plate. Perhaps the cheese after all. Julius' face underlies his own in Raffaello's painting of the Apostles. Cardinals cluster about him: Petrucci, Riario, Bainbridge, himself. He appears twice, Cardinal and Pope, young and mature, with the face that first divided them now painted over. The glutton Borgia is absent. Always a popish Spaniard before a Spanish Pope. Alexander and, after him, Julius. There were years of nothing, years to be filled, in which not to grow dull. Distractions, diversions, drollery. Clowns.

"My cup is invaded with daylight."

"Banish it!"

The Cardinal feeds his guests with caramelized sheep's feet, sparrow beaks ground to powder, and rats roasted in honey and nutmeg. Cows' eyes shiver in jelly. Lizards fried in cinnamon fill a tureen, and black broth foams in its pot at the table's end. Cardinal Medici presides above a banquet of cavaliers and idiots. Bad poets declaim and bad singers croon. There are clowns. The waiting brings them out, draws them to him: misshapen men, clots, and vainglorious fools. He smiles, chuckles, claps, weeps with laughter, howls with mirth; he loves them, absolutely loves them. Hunchbacks and maniacs turn cartwheels down his hall while he hiccups, farts, and gulps the air as though he might eat the merriment within it. It is a hunger he never satisfies. He watches the stomachs of his guests swell and sometimes burst with his spicy curiosities. Rivers of wine disappear down their gullets, and their buffoonery is a playground of polity for him to practice lunges and feints, quick jabs and stabs to the back. The body of the Borgia blackens and swells in the pestilential airs of Rome while his Cardinal passes dishes of beech leaves pickled in wine, ginger concoctions, and pigeons' feet in aniseed.

And now? Nine olives, and bread. No cheese. No cold meats. The Borgia's face seems to stare out of his eyes in the painting of the Apostles. And behind the Borgia stands Sixtus, and behind him Innocent, and Clement, and Martin, and every Servant of the Servants of God back to Gregory and every Pope to Peter. The death of the Borgia brings Julius to the bishopric of Rome, and basilicas rise and fall about the city, domes swelling and collapsing like lungs of stone, buttresses and columns reaching up from the ground, while at the center of this monumental animal a smidgen of flesh and blood veins the whole with its passions and humors. Julius is outraged. Julius is resigned. French armies circle in the Romagna. The Emperor is hungry for Milan, or Urbino, or Rome. The Church too needs its venal armies, its warrior popes, and their creatures. The Pope joins leagues, raises armies, marches on his enemies, who are mutable creatures, by turns French, and Spanish, and Venetian, and Imperial, alike only in their rapacity and the hatred of Julius. His allies too might change from day to day, might even become one another or disappear. Good and ill hover, moving too quickly to be caught, at times too quick to be distinguished. On Easter Day, between Ravenna and the sea, two armies come to face each other across the marshy ground. A Cardinal in armor meets a Cardinal in scarlet robe and hat. Far away in Rome, Palazzo Medici is quiet and closed up. The clowns have disappeared. Fuses hiss along the line as tiny figures inch closer over the rough *macchia*. The pleasure-loving Medici stands behind the papal armies; Sanseverino with the French. Then the first of the cannon explode.

Afterward, running through the battlefield with the fugitives and mindless men, he will believe that the very air was turned to knives. The dead lie all around, cut apart, mangled, twisted. Some of the dying scream horribly, some seem merely puzzled by the guts spilling out of their bellies. He remembers a man walking dazed through the carnage, carrying, he thinks, a cudgel. He draws nearer. The man is lopsided, blood pouring from his shoulder, and the cudgel is his arm. Others appear unmarked, until they turn and reveal terrible wounds, skulls staved in, faces cut in two. Giovanni runs and runs, ignoring the hands that brush his ankles, the voices that cry out to him. It is dusk. The fighting is finished. He hardly knows where he is. The pikestaff catches him first in the stomach and, as he lies there winded, descends upon his head.

Then, as he would later understand it, because the schismatic cardinals at Pisa dawdled, accused their master the Pope of contumacy, betrayed themselves as lackeys of the hated French, took refuge in Milan, where their hootings and jeers met only the same from the faithful Milanese, and Cardinal Medici held captive there by the victors of Ravenna dispensed forgiveness to his foes, because the French army left five thousand dead in the marshes about Ravenna including their commanders and could not hold Milan and retreated and took Cardinal Medici, who escaped, and because Cardinal Medici was recaptured and rescued finally by the banks of the Po and Pisa was under the dominion of Soderini's Florence, francophile and ripe for the plucking, responsible at the last for the schismatics who so raised their master's ire, the Pope's, then it behooved the Holy See to ensure the safety of the Church by sending papal forces to take back Florence for the Medici. So it was the Cardinals at Pisa who were to blame for what followed. Not himself. Not Giovanni.

Soon, thinks the Pope, Ghiberti will appear with his ledger and deliver him from these thoughts. The day is still beginning, and already ugliness has encroached. He wanted Florence to fall in celebration, in carnivals and triumphal processions. He had thought the worst was past, that nothing could match Ravenna. His capture on the battlefield came as a blessing. Sanseverino's custody was a convalescence from the horror. He quit the marshes with the French and never looked back, but the worst was ahead. Sometimes even now it would come for him in his sleep, and he would wake in terror. Perhaps if the troops had been Romans or Swiss. If they had been fed and the promises made to them kept. Perhaps, perhaps. Cardona's Spaniards were starving, and the villages that resisted should have signaled what was in store. If Soderini had left the Bologna road open, had made his decision earlier. A desperate army of infantry and light horse moved through the valley of the Mugello, ragged and footsore, until Prato.

Thunderheads nailed themselves to the late August sky, and the air grew closer by the hour. He rode with his brother, and when he looked into the faces of the Spaniards he saw nothing. The sun had burned them the color of copper, and the hunger had hollowed their cheeks. He had looked at the walls that shut them out and wondered how such desperate beggars might scale them. Cardona gathered his captains, and the word went out. Within the walls were food and gold. Giovanni understood the contract then, that they would take this town or they would starve. The alchemy was done in an instant, and their very weariness would carry them to victory. There could be no retreat, no failure, and as the first of them broke ranks and ran for the walls, he knew that Prato would not be able to resist this hunger or match the depth of this need. And then, and then.

Because the bodies of a thousand men would not hold so much blood, and the throats of mortal men, women, and children not form such screams, nor the human frame bear such tortures—the braziers, the tools of black iron—because sinew and flesh would not form such shapes, nor the earth itself hold so many cadavers, then the sack of Prato must be a projection of the Devil, a phantasm, and though men afterward said that the sounds he heard and sights he saw truly took place, he knew that really this was but a complication of the evil, the trickery that fools the eye in a painting, not the subject itself, which is elsewhere and distant, only pretending to be there before him. The hearts of men could not be so black, and when Cardona came to him and told him that the Medici were restored and Florence was his for the taking, he counted the cost of this rightful act, the broken skulls, bleeding mouths, the horrible wounds and mutilations, the screams that he can still hear—these must all harden his conviction, armor it and protect it from the pleas of the innocent. The Medici are the masters of Florence once more, but the Cardinal cannot rest there. Behind Florence lies Prato. Behind his own soft features lie those of the Borgia. Once again he leaves the carnage behind him and turns his horse to Rome. The clowns and idiots will return; his waiting resume. The lamps blaze again in Palazzo Medici and its chambers ring with shouting voices, screams of laughter, howls, and echoes and more echoes. Under Rome lie other Romes. By January of the following year, Julius is sick. Come February, dead.

His secretary knocks at last, enters, and stands before him. Ghiberti's grayness, his flatness, his imperturbability, all these are provocation to his master. His servant glides and copes. He is effortless when the Pope wants pratfalls and commotion. These are not his functions, yet in being so unsuitable, Ghiberti tempts the Pope, almost invites the japes and practical jokes his master rehearses in his head. Chamber-pots and horses' tails wreathe Ghiberti in possible fun and games. He desists, of course. But Ghiberti is a perfect foil, the ideal candidate. The Pope rolls an olive stone between his fingers as Ghiberti opens the ledger. Upon the page his day is marked out in appointments, offices, and functions. Ghiberti coughs—he always coughs—and looks up at the Pope.

"Holiness?" His Holiness nods and Ghiberti begins to read. Tomorrow another page will turn, and another, and another. How many ledgers, he wonders, how many stacks of ledgers have the successors to Peter filled? So many years. So many popes.

With Julius' death, twenty-five cardinals march into Sixtus' Chapel. Twenty-five cramped and tetchy prelates barge the thin partitions of their cubicles, toss and turn on their narrow beds, pace the floor, argue, urinate noisily behind the curtained pissoir at the far end of the nave. Their servants scurry from cubicle to cubicle, relaying messages in hushed voices, throwing up their hands or nodding their heads. The doors are locked and the conclave is commenced. The cardinals are exasperated, barging and growing bullish. Adrian of Corneto has already been pressed by Riario's man, refused, wavered, and still wavers. Soderini plays a waiting game, his mind on his deposed kinsman, while Bainbridge appears aloof, disdainful of the politicking that hums and buzzes in the vaults of the church, sharpening, dying away, resuming. A decision must be made here, yet nothing seems clear. Slumped on a cot, Cardinal Medici feels his secret wound flare up and ache inside him. Dovizio is tireless, scampering among the doubters, pressing his cause, but all he can do is groan and turn from side to side. He regards the urinal with dread, the pot with terror. Twice a day they listen to him straining and moaning behind the curtain, but the conclave goes on.

On the sixth day, a vote is taken. Having cast their lots, the cardinals return immediately to desultory talk and their idle pastimes. Some return to their cubicles and do not trouble to emerge even when the votes are counted; others listen out of the depths of boredom. Disinterest hangs like a fog in the chapel. They are hopelessly split and know it. The returning officer announces that the ballot is scattered. None of them will be Pope just yet.

Soon the guardians of the conclave have reduced them to a single meal of vegetables each day. There is no debate now; the lines are drawn. From one side of the chapel stooped bodies and faces lined with age array themselves against the younger cardinals. Neither patience nor good counsel will bring the conclave to an end. The younger cardinals grin in the candlelight. Endurance will elect this Pope. Seconds dawdle on the way to being minutes. Minutes take on the aspect of hours. Time stretches out and yawns open before them. Nothing happens, except delay. Then, as the two sides face one another down, a loud moan is heard, and succeeding it, a vile vapor rises in the chapel, a truly horrible stink that sends all of them scurrying for their handkerchiefs. In his cot in the far cubicle, Cardinal Medici rolls in misery. His wound has disclosed its secret. All through the preceding week he felt it swelling to the size of an egg. Now the albumin is trickling between his legs, and its stench recalls him to the place he believed consigned to hell. Deep within his fundament, his cyst has burst and now engulfs him in its vapor. He moans once more. A second, more subtle torment is rising out of the stench. He sniffs and the suspicion is confirmed. Soon the surgeon will be with him, but for now he must listen as the message of his bowels is passed in whispers about the conclave. Medici is sick. Medici may not last. . . . Later that night, after the usual, humiliating probing, Dovizio murmurs in his ear that Cardinal Riario seeks a meeting. His discharge smells as Prato did.

Now he turns to his waiting secretary. "Of all the Pope's anatomy, Ghiberti, which part would you say actually joins him with the throne of Peter?"

Ghiberti looks up, startled. The Pope sits back, smiling faintly at the conundrum. His secretary is terribly dull. He will be thinking of his ledger, already worrying that the day is slipping by, time racing past. And dawn is barely risen. There is plenty of time, a hatful of hours for his diversions and pleasures.

"Come now, it is not hard. Which part?" The Pope waits.

"His faith," says Ghiberti.

Tedious, dull Ghiberti. It is a wonder he stands it, a miracle. He needs wit, not dogma, a lively sally, a joke to rouse him up. Ghiberti invariably spells gloom.

"Wrong," barks the Pope.

Suppurating, sweating on a sweat-soaked bed, he listened to Riario's drone while Dovizio stood and nodded as if he were too stricken a beast to reply for himself. He might even have wished for death. It was possible he had; he is unsure now. Riario's words were a tawdry epitaph to his ambitions as his rival talked of Peter's burden and the necessary humilities, the loneliness. Get it over, he thought in his weakness. Tell me the conclave has reached its decision. But Riario talked on and on, assuring him that he need fear nothing, his loyalty was unshakable, the others would stand at his side, young and old alike. Scant recompense, he thought, cursing his weak and leaking body. That the flesh alone should trip him in his course, no failing of the head or heart or spirit. It was unbearable. And Riario's soothing monotone sounded in his defeated ears as the victor's trumpet, hooting and crowing, deafening him to everything, all his patient hopes crashing down about him. But then his tormentor began speaking more urgently—he will not hear—his face looming nearer, which he will not see, disappearing and bending to touch the hem of his stinking robe, but the indignity of whatever he is doing will not touch him. To the vanquished, flight. Riario's watery eyes appear once more. Dovizio has stopped nodding and seems to be telling him something his ears cannot hear. Only later will he understand that his very weakness, his secret ailment and its discovery, were the keys. The cardinals did not think he would live. They thought their own opportunities would come again soon enough. His buttocks parted, and stinking air filled the chapel with his mortality, and the cardinals smelled death. He has been utterly mistaken, for he has won.

"I and my party withdraw our interest from the conclave," Riario told him. "You will be Pope, Giovanni."

Ghiberti still stands there, silent and stolid.

"Come now. Which part?" But he is dull, quite dreadfully dull. He will not answer.

"My fundament," the Pope tells his secretary in triumph. "My arse!"

Ghiberti smiles briefly, then looks to his ledger.

"The Ambassador of Aragon," he says. "I can put him off no longer."

The air in the Sala Regia is already thick with their dislike. The two rivals pace stressful tangents on the echoing floor, curt nods exchanged on introduction an hour back and since then not a word. They do not look to each other. They do not speak. Two men have come to see the Pope. Twice already, Ghiberti has appeared and disappeared. Sunlight floods by the window while lutanists practice in the adjacent chapel and the two men wait.

Through frescoed and gilt-encrusted galleries and chambers, up and down short staircases that link the Vatican's haphazard levels, moves the Pope with his secretary in tow. Perhaps it is the arched panels above which bow the flat plane of the corridor floor, some sympathetic echo, a sunk reflection nudging up against the calm marble. Or his eyes, weak and liable organs at best. Or his own slippered feet wearing a gentle groove, the merest trough as he patters over the milky slabs. Erosions and latent damage: the repeated paths of a hundred popes. Use and custom are the cambers and beaten trails of his palace. Clerics and their masters, suppliants, cardinals, and princes wash through Peter's square, scending the walls and flooding by the palace culverts into reception rooms and chambers, scouring hollows and recesses out of the architecture. The church is worn and there is only so much volume, only room for some, yet still they come to fill and drink the sump. Underneath the palace lie deep wells and cisterns that only Peter's keys unlock, and there Christ's agony slops in the darkness. The grail holds a healing sea which he may measure out and never drain. God's kingdom lies beneath a glassy skin, and this world's being is but its poor reflection: brute pigment, veined and milky marble, the body's organs throbbing in their leaking, mortal rind. He farts softly, painlessly, as Ghiberti precedes him down the staircase.

Two heads turn; two pairs of eyes fix upon his descent. He stares back. A straggly shock of black and a closer-cropped tonsure stiff with oil. Bodies: tall, and of medium height. Clothes: doublet worked with gold against a suit of plain fustian. They stand apart, both waiting for him to reach his station. The suppliants have a particular confidence. They like to touch him, reaching forward to take his hand, free hand gripping his wrist, embracing, kissing his cheek or his gown or ring. They kneel, their hands moving like crabs toward his feet. At Easter he would wash the feet of poor beggars before the Coena Domini. As he settled the arch in his palm and stroked water, over the toes, the calluses seemed to soften and disappear in the water, leaving the skin smooth and cool. When they stood, the dust would stick where the water still clung. And when he dried them, the old lesions would reappear. His movements were jerky and awkward. Christ never flinched while he bathed the feet of the disciples. Veronica's hands never wavered as she wiped Christ's brow.

"Holiness . . ." Familiar faces approach him. He glances at Ghiberti, who gazes into the floor. The whispered words, lips touched to his ring. They straighten, and he sees the ambassadors' swarthy faces pucker slightly. Their audiences should both have been in private. Is Ghiberti telling him something? Some realignment at the court of the Portuguese? The Spanish?

". . . Faria, Ambassador of Dom Manolo of Portugal, and Don Jerònimo da Vich, Baron of Llauri, Ambassador of Fernando the Catholic of the Kingdoms of Spain. . . ."

He smiles faintly, gives the merest nod.

"You have waited long, Ambassador?" The title is inflected oddly: "Am*bass*ador," as though there is some question behind it. Ghiberti sees Don Jerònimo begin to color. He looks away, then down at his own feet. The Aragonese has never, in Ghiberti's judgment, played this particular game with delicacy. A stumbler, and more so since the game turned against him. There are rumors that Vich is cleverer than he appears. As a dancing bear to an untamed one, thinks Ghiberti.

"I would ask, Holiness, why this Portingale is here, and why I have been misled, and why my master, the King of Aragon and Castile, is treated in this manner after the assistance he has . . ."

The hall clatters with the Aragonese's blunt and ill-directed arrows. Ghiberti looks deeply into the matter of the floor. The Pope's smile widens and his hands are raised, a sympathetic shrug, as though they are both victims of an inescapable muddle, a world at odds with its inhabitants and their imperfect understandings who must nevertheless bear it with good humor, as His Holiness is doing now, as Don João is doing, too, as Don Jerònimo is not. It is, Ghiberti knows, an expression designed to infuriate. And Vich, of course, is correct. He has been promised his audience in private; it has been more than a month in the arrangement. Why, then, has he, Ghiberti, not barred Don João this morning? Ghiberti watches while the trio climb slowly up the staircase, guided by the Pope toward the gardens of the Belvedere. Vich struts awkwardly beside his gliding rival. He has already lost this audience, had lost it even before he arrived. Try as he might, Ghiberti cannot fathom it. Polity, governance, good sense, and good precedents all say "yes" to Don Jerònimo and his master. But—Ghiberti's turning thought as the three men foreshorten and disappear in the stairway's weird perspective—the Pope, or the Medici, says "no."

The gardens stretch. Horizons drop and rise. The Pope's mind races after his leaping eye as the ground gallops forward and up the hill. Two great terraces are divided by a third, smaller level with linking stairs and ramps to mount the incline, and at the summit of the hill a delicate villa glows in the morning sunlight:

the Belvedere from which the gardens take their name. It is the scale that silences his companions. The first terrace is a formal garden set with mulberries and bay trees that distance shrinks to shrubs at the far end. To their left the ground falls away out of sight, while to the right a great storied arcade runs forward on three levels until the second terrace reduces it to two, the third to one, only the topmost loggia surviving unbroken to the far villa. Behind, the palace of the Vatican stands in shadow, towering above them. Wood pigeons shoot up suddenly, dive left, and disappear into the valley. The gardens appear still, perfect, empty.

"Foxes," says the Pope, motioning up the hill. The third terrace is more thickly planted, more wooded. "We suffer infestations of foxes." The ambassadors nod wisely.

All three move forward, Faria and the Pope in a broken stroll with pauses for emphasis and vague hand gestures. Vich finds himself setting off, then halting abruptly while the other two continue an extra pace, or overshooting them by the same. He turns, and the two men are behind him somehow, walking away. He follows and they stop, so he stops. The two of them continue.

"Holiness, His Majesty Dom Manolo would have me convey his keen anticipation of your gift," announces Faria. They are halted before a bed of bright peonies. "He has commissioned a fine gilt cabinet for its display which will be inscribed with his thanks. Dom Manolo wishes it known he understands the value of such a donation."

"A mere bauble," murmurs the Pope. They have crossed the terrace at a ragged diagonal. Ahead lie the sweeping curves of the steps that link the first two terraces. Faria is protesting.

"The whole of Portugal will understand your gift, and every Portuguese, whether he serves against the Saracen or loads his vessel in the Indies or works humbly in the fields, or towns, even in Rome herself. Every toiler at home, every campaigner and trader to the far shores of Afric or the Indies, will know behind their own callused hand lies a greater hand. Surrounded with the wailing of savages, they will hear your call. As their bodies fail, they will see their souls take wing. . . ."

"You are too poetic," mutters the Pope.

". . . a great enough crown to girdle an empire. A wall of gold to defend the defenders of the faith. Dom Manolo expressly commands my words to you, though their extravagance be my own. Would that our mutual grants and treaties hold good into eternity and beyond."

"Dom Manolo has hitherto sealed our compacts most generously." The Pope is gazing farther up the hill. The Ambassador nods gravely.

"The meager tokens in our gift are ever at your disposal."

"Your late token thrives, as does the compact he seals. I confess myself enamored of the beast. In eternity, you say? Or does Dom Manolo?"

"He might not ask without leave. Nor ask for leave without instruction. Nor seek instruction empty-handed."

"Dom Manolo's courtesy makes me mindful of my own. As the mason in the arts of stone, so His Majesty in generosity. In good faith, how might I instruct either?"

"Kings seek guidance as masons do, else the edifice exceeds proportion and collapses—"

"I would ask, Holiness," Vich breaks in at this point, "why it is that our late petition, lodged by us some months back, far from receiving your clerks' attention, seems only to have reached the cooks' and even there is mocked by scullions and turnspits, for my man overheard them not a week past, he said its misdirection was a matter of policy, a mark of disfavor, too. . . ." The Pope's expression is undeniably cold, growing colder as his sentence unwinds its coils and begins to stumble over its own wilder outgrowths, finally collapsing into silence, himself red-faced, his audience politely silent.

"You mentioned proportion?" the Pope prompts Don João. Their conversation continues, Faria's provocations edging forward and his counterpart's silence growing ever more furious, until a thrust at "that empty-handed type of Christian" breaks the dam of his restraint.

"Damn you, Faria!" He cannot keep silent any longer. "Damn your threadbare insolence. . . ."

"Threadbare, eh? *Baron* of Llauri, tell me, how many fishing smacks constitute the fleet of great Llauri? Remind me, please, of its paved streets and great halls, I beg you, Don Jerònimo. Describe for me its cathedrals and churches, its numberless armies, those feared men of *Llauri*. . . ."

The Pope stands between them, hands clasped before him, inclining his head to each as he speaks. Don Jerònimo grows heated under Faria's gibes, speaking faster and more vehemently until every second word is in Spanish and every other a curse. The Pope's expression is of mild surprise. Why are ambassadors so turbulent?

"Come," he commands abruptly, and begins climbing the stone steps that lead to the second terrace. His escorts fall silent and follow.

Just as the steps that lead to the second level swell in a wide semicircle from the front of the terrace, so the receding tiers of the staircase that will take them to the wilder garden are gouged from the back. The three men find themselves in a place of bare white stones where the Pope stands a little apart from Faria and Vich, as if their bickering has driven him off. His large head turns from side to side. His eyes sweep up the empty steps.

"In Llauri—" Don Jerònimo begins to speak, but stops as his voice returns louder than before, the words garbled in their ricochet off the facing steps. Faria glares at him, but the Pope seems not to hear this noise. Something holds his attention in the garden above. Set back some ten or twenty yards, a canopy of foliage clears the sight-line of the wall. A crash sounds from somewhere within it.

"Christendom has its natural enemies," the Pope says softly. "The Turk, the Saracen and Moor, all those who would blind their peoples to Christ's teaching

and domain . . . And then there are those who are born blind and must be made
to see. Are they our enemy, too? Perforce their eyes must be opened, and yet
when they resist our ministry so fiercely, when their sight is restored by extinc-
tion, I wonder what kind of enemy is this?" He turns to his companions as
though they might serve him with an answer. Sunlight skates off the blank stones.
He hears undergrowth rustling and crackling above. But the enemy is a distant
specter, more report than reality; a shape-shifter. The men who stand and wait
avoid one another's eyes. They are too alike in their petitions: Faria for a blessing
to wave in the faces of the Spanish; Vich the same for his Fernando. They are too
alike. They cannot see the real enemy.

"Come," he says again. Neither will answer his question, nor would he wish
it. He climbs the steps to the third and last of the garden's terraces, wheezes, waits
for his petitioners. Distant battles are being fought in his name. Castles fly his standard over baking plains and deltas a thousand miles distant. Pennants flutter in the
thick poisons of the air, but he is left behind to gasp in a vacuum. The war is a far-
off clangor of faceless men pulled farther away by the racing frontier. Blood flushes
the skin while the organs cool and slow their efforts within. The heart kicks sluggishly, lungs barely swell. He wanders in a shell of stone while generals spill their
lifeblood on the frontier, and he wonders how the fight might return and who
will bring the enemy to his champion. The sky is so bright that his eyes have
screwed themselves shut. Dull red spots blot the darkness of his inner eye. Faria
holds a gift in his box of manners; a second beast, by Ghiberti's estimate. The Pope
is clear. Ambassadors, their kings, their secretaries: all clowns, all tumbling after one
another and kicking each other in the backside, falling and rising, laughing and
crying about him. He looks down at the bare stones and sees the actors floating in
air, shrieking and wielding swords, limbs falling to the floor, heads rolling down
the steps, still chattering and shouting and screaming. Ribs burst and splay like the
claws of some vast bird. Bones crack in the sewers under Prato.

"Holiness?"

Stone-pines loom above the trio, and sunlight glints in the high yew hedges
as they walk deeper into the gardens. Faria is chattering of their mutual enemies.

"The proofs of his idiocy grow more blatant by the day," says the Pope
of one.

"So vast an error from so small a mind. Its birth is miraculous," replies the
Ambassador.

"You have added blasphemy to your talents, Faria. It sits well with the
others."

Vich is silent while this talk continues. From time to time, the Pope glances
at the man, who nods curtly in return. The garden grows wilder and less penetra-
ble. They walk easily enough, but it is hardly so clear where they are going. Great
crashes sound distantly, then nearer. The Spaniard looks around at these, but the
other two merely continue with their small talk. They seem oblivious of the approaching racket.

They pass by fruit trees staked with sturdy poles and collected in little groves. Fountains rush water into space. Great pines shade the men from the sun and carpet the garden in needles. They have halted beside a bank of tall shrubs with lavender flowers. Faria is smiling smugly. A joke is being enjoyed.

"I am, of course, divided by your dispute," the Pope remarks generally. He considers a pun on his "worldliness," rejects it. The day has gained an unanchored quality already. His gardens abstract him. "I am no geographer—" He raises a hand to ward off Faria's anticipated protest; he does not wish his sagacity praised just yet. "Be assured that these questions of proportions and distances lie close to my heart. I recognize their import." A crumb for Vich now? Yes. "Their complexity vexes all who delve into these matters, including my own deficient clerks, Don Jerònimo. It is appropriate care, not the concoction of jokes, which delay these matters. I have promised a settlement, and a settlement there will be, mark my words, for it pains me to repeat them."

The note of reproach is quite perfect. Both men have leaned forward intently during his discourse. Suddenly both don their masks once again. Don João is a charming courtier, Don Jerònimo a sullen child. The Pope scuffs the turf with the toe of his slipper. A dove flaps and glides until its bowed path takes it beyond the taller trees to the west. He should resume work on the wall there, although the foxes must surely discourage the rabbits. Enemies and champions: inevitably the one must become the other. Julius had at least taught him that much. They would have him draw lines around the world, across lands and oceans they had never seen, which might not even exist for all they would know. The Borgia Pope's legacy.

Now, elsewhere in the thickets of the gardens, a disturbance. Further crashes, signaling large maneuvers at a distance or smaller ones nearby. The three of them stroll forward, and there it is again, moving closer. Vich stutters to a halt, but the other two appear quite at ease, as though the gardens were silent, puzzled even at his discomfort. He can hear trees and undergrowth being shunted aside. The bushes that surround them are higher than a man. He can see nothing.

"Don Jerònimo . . . ?" The Pope prompts him, but the noise is louder and now moving toward them. He knows the scene they have inveigled him into now. He recalls the crowded balcony of six months before, the challenge laid down as the drummers of D'Acunha's embassy marched forward onto the bridge, himself left stranded and impotent as the cardinals rushed to congratulate Faria, the new Medici Pope quite obviously besotted as the Portingales' surpassing gift made its clowning obeisance below.

It is the animal. They can hardly not have heard, yet they betray no sign. Is Faria's grin a smidgen broader? The Pope is nodding at his reply. The sound of wood being splintered. They are watching him, waiting. There is an instant of silence, and then an ear-piercing shriek blows all thought away.

The trees are riven apart and it is there before him again, above him this time, its body the size of a house. He looks up and there above his head is the shrieking head of a monster. It has teeth, two huge white teeth that grow out from its face, a shoveling mouth, and in place of its nose an obscene member, a muscled intestine brandishing a tree. He steps back, and the club wavers above them. To their left a small brown wiry man dressed in ill-fitting livery emerges from the undergrowth. He is carrying, pointlessly, a short length of enormous chain. He hears the Pope's voice as it addresses, what? It can only be the beast itself.

"Hanno! Hanno! Kneel down." Don Jerònimo hears Faria's smirk break cover as laughter. The balcony, these gardens, the miserable keeper, his master, and most of all the beast: his stalled negotiations, his failure, Fernando's honor, and his own looming disgrace. The Pope is waving away the keeper. Don João turns to him in delight. Is this not absolutely priceless? The gift, its giver, and its recipient. Where is his place in this scene? The beast sways, but it will not kneel. The Pope shrugs.

"Hanno is lonely," he tells the two men. The animal swings its head from side to side, eventually following its own momentum to turn about and amble back into the undergrowth. The small tree held in its trunk is cast aside as its gray bulk disappears into a dense stand of saplings. They listen to its crashings growing fainter.

"Your Holiness's thoughts had alighted on the matter of a settlement," Faria prompts gingerly.

He feels their attentions fix on him again, or advance upon him as two masses of interest and purpose, himself denied all but the narrowest corridor between them, a sliver of room to pace in, a sliver of unreachable light above. The subtlest of his doctors have pored over the settlements of his predecessors and found only the arguments the two men flanking him have represented to him in the last months. Manolo's *Padroado* and Fernando's *Patronato*. The Portingales to the east; the Spaniards to the west; and where they met was hazardous and inequitable. They hang a war above his head and ask for judgment. *No, you may not abstain. . . .* His curialists' injunction bringing him up short in the benighted hours, the air breathed over and headachy, clogged with clauses and construals until there was no more talking to be done. And then one of them had spoken, reluctantly and to their weariness. *There is a way. . . .*

The Pope says, " 'And thou, son of man, take thee a sharp knife, take thee a barber's razor, and cause it to pass upon thine head and upon thy beard: then take thee balances to weigh and divide the hair.' Do you remember that?" He holds up his hands as two pans, his head their fulcrum, his helpless talking head. "But my razor is too blunt," he says. A little flock of small brown birds erupts from the foliage of a nearby mulberry tree, wheeling and disappearing. He thinks he sees Hanno's back, a comical gray island mooching amongst little trees and bushes below. His hands jiggle up and down. He begins to talk of equivalences and balances, of perfectly weighted claims canceling one another out, of treaties and compacts and the web of his predecessors' words, which snag and hold him fast.

"Your claims are too even," he tells them. "Ezekiel himself could not split this hair. . . ."

He talks and talks. Vich and Faria steal stony-faced glances at one another, sifting, calculating. "I cannot tip these scales, not for the love of Fernando, not for that of Manolo. Were the difference just a grain of salt, a mote of dust. . . ." Gradually it surfaces, milky and amorphous in its camouflage of watery manners, taking imaginary shape on the imaginary scales. He is in search of something, gazing over the gardens, which appear still at first, then twitch and shudder oddly as the animal's progress reveals itself; a blundering disturbance of branches snapping and startled birds beating up into the sunlight. Hanno crashes into view again, the huge head emerging foolishly from between two bushes covered with small yellow blooms, which the beast's trunk seeks out with intricate methodical curls. The three men watch in silence. Would that I were transparent, thinks the Pope.

"Holiness," says Faria, the faint note of exasperation whistling softly, not his own but his master's, not his impatience but Manolo's. "What is it that you want?"

"Plinius tells a wonderful tale in his *Natural History*," he says with sudden enthusiasm. "Every beast has its adversary, the Lion and the Tiger, the Tortoise and Eagle. . . . There are others, though I forget them now. Even Hanno has his enemy, the one he must live to destroy. Even Hanno . . ."

The beast shakes its head vigorously, flapping its ears. They can hear it, a leathery, slapping sound. The Pope beams at the animal. The animal chews. The two men chance a look between themselves.

"Have you read Plinius?" he asks the ambassadors.

Swelling tongues of steam lick upward, thin to invisible wraiths, thicken suddenly in the bars of light, a rich summery gold deepening with the afternoon beyond the linen screens of the half-shuttered windows. Sunlit swirls of fog thrust solid beams of brightness into the gloom, where, abruptly robbed of light, they continue in secret up the walls. Condensing droplets gather along the oaken joists above and presently drip in a wet echo on the rugs that cover the floor. A light mildew reappearing this autumn will need to be scrubbed off, meaning ladders and clatter, stiff brushes, elbow grease, general commotion. For the moment all is stillness. From the gloom of the far wall, a massive bed tented in fading red velvet coughs dust into a vaporous interior.

Since midday: the trudge of Arnolfo's boots between woodpile and kitchen, the lighting and stoking of the fire, drawing of water, heating of the same in a blackened copper cauldron groaning and bubbling above the blaze of the fire, the whole kitchen disappearing in bubbly boiling clouds and Emilia herself ejected choking into the courtyard, then wheeling out of the apparatus, boots banging up and down the stairs through the main *sala* and the smaller one beyond to the impromptu bagnio; jugs slopping and overspilling pots, everybody's sweat and ill temper, even imperturbable Tebaldo, even little Violetta (tears, a little after noon, put down to the general air of upset), and standing in the midst of all this one hardly seeming part of it yet directing this, reminding of that, keeping the contraption on course, waiting impassively for her own main role to begin, for, as the whole household might forget at its peril, haphazardly and frequently during the sticky months of summer, on the feasts of Saint Urban, Saint Lambert, Michael, Luke, Leonard, Barbara, Sylvester, and Peter, on Epiphany, Advent, and Halloween, the third sunday in Lent (if Easter were early) or the first day of Shrovetide (if not), and most particularly on the feast of Saints Philip and James (today), it pleased their mistress Fiametta to take what she called "a little bath."

Sploo-ooosh . . .

"Aieow!"

"Too hot?"

"You are boiling me!"

Pul-losshhh . . .

"Aaaah . . ."

"Better?"

"Mmmm."

Standing now in attendance on her mistress, she has restored her flustered and heat-sodden troupe to their respective domains—kitchen, stable, scullery, study—closed the doors at the top and bottom of the staircase, unfolded the linen liner, thrown it over the bath, and watched the water weight it in darkening patches, dragging it down to settle on the rough planks of the tub. She has added oils and petals to the steaming liquid, then watched her mistress rouse herself, rub her eyes, struggle from her shift, settle with a slow exhalation in the scented swirl of the water. The cooling bedclothes breathe a faint sourness, quickly suffocated under the thickening fug of oily, steam-borne perfumes. *Drip,* a drop from the beam above, *plop,* into the bath. The bedchamber smells of roses.

"Pumice my feet now."

"A little longer."

"They feel like hooves, like a great carthorse's hooves."

"The water will soften them."

"You think I have hooves?"

"No, mistress."

"Pumice them now."

"Patience."

At first she knew only "no," "please," "yes," "mistress," and "Roma." *Ro*-ma. Then, quickly after, "water," "straw," "good," "moment," "soon," and "patience." This shrieking city wanted to drown her in its noise: she learned first the words for the things it lacked. "Pear," "bless you." Supplied the deficiencies that gnawed at her in those first bewildering months. Her wrist had healed slowly and badly, stiffening in the damp of winter, unfreezing again in spring. Three times now. The

city had its fingers in her. She added her own barbarous accents to the cackle of
its shambalic streets, its mires and the stench rising off them—this place of waste,
muddle, and noise. "Away with you!" "A *julio*," "two," "three," "four . . ." She sep-
arates her mistress's toes between her fingers, sets to work with the pumice stone.

"Soap me now."

"A moment . . . "

"Let go. I am going to stand."

"The lemon soap? The rose?"

"He hates the smell of lemons. Rose."

Reddened forearms surface from the oily waters' depths. Fingers grip the
sides of the tub, shoulder muscles tense, arms stretched forward like an oarsman.
She will wait a second or two, gather herself, then . . . She rises suddenly, water
cascading down her breasts and belly, steadies herself on feet now planted well
apart, lungs gulping air, disappointment at her lost buoyancy, eyes focused in a vacant middle distance, the faraway look of a porter bracing himself beneath a load
and his whole world shrunk, for a moment, to weight. She had passed for a boy
once. Skinny as a rake.

"Scrub harder."

"Raise your arms, mistress."

"Slower now. . . . Yes."

She works down from the shoulders, lathering and rinsing, kneeling, leaning
forward awkwardly to lift and soap under the breasts. Her mistress's hand rests
lightly on the tight plaits of her head. The solid rounds of her buttocks. Fiametta
turns. The hand leaves her head, and thick fingers cup her chin. She looks up;
new sadnesses have swelled the face looking down at her. Accolti dead last March.
Young Chigi leaving her the next month, his parting thrust a farewell gift done
up in a case lined with black silk, a final humiliation. Black days. The household
banished themselves to the kitchen while their mistress completed her abase-
ment—long afternoons of great shouts and thuds, grunts, groans, then hours of
sobbing resounding through the house—two weeks of this before Chigi's gift is
replaced in its case. "To fill her hours," as the note had put it, the base of each im-
plement engraved with the image of its appropriate creature: a dog, a goat, a man,
a bull, and last of all—inevitably, since the procession they watched together from
the balcony of Agostino's palazzo, since its centerpiece had furnished him with
the first of his taunts—an elephant. In their case of cedarwood lined with silk,
finger-size to truncheon-size, five ivory phalluses served mute notice, and terms,
of her dismissal. Two Sundays later she sent the largest back to him, reeking,
smeared with that month's blood. Now there is only the old warhorse himself,
not so cruel as Chigi, not so rich as Accolti, and sadnesses to be masked with
gaiety until she can bury them deeper in her flesh. Interim pleasures. The upturned face is impassive, waiting for her word.

"Your dress is spotted. See the soap, here and here."

"I will rinse it tonight."

"And you are sweating."

"The steam . . ."

"Come. Take it off."

Calico, thicker than she would wish for May, crumples slowly on the floor. An underskirt of thin cotton drops, slack with damp, beside it. Sandals clatter over the rugs. This is easy for her. This has all been prefigured before; cloth castles melting about her ankles, herself naked, stepping forward. "Come. Take it off." Or a barked command in any one of half a dozen languages, or a gesture of the hand. The merchants had peered curiously at the lines scarified across her cheeks. She is turned this, that way. Often she lies, legs up in a V, while a practiced finger prods in her vagina till she yelps. Then she yawns. That is when she outwits her captors. She yawns, and the merchant backs away. The deal is off. This one he will not take. It happens eight times in succession, and her captors grow more furious every time. They are brothers, she thinks. Perhaps cousins. They slap her and spit on her but dare not bruise her badly. The caravan had wound north, always north, with nothing to mark their journey but each day's nascent and then failing heat, the wadis where they stopped, and the markets where she was rejected. The caravan begins with eighty, but in twos and threes their numbers dwindle as the goats tethered behind them do, too, until finally there is only an old man, a wheezing boy, and herself. One night they kill the old man and the boy in a ditch. She hears them quarrel over money and knows the quarrel concerns her. They hate her, cannot be rid of her. She laughs silently to herself, sitting there with her hands bound together with strips of goatskin, sitting alone in the desert, waiting to learn the outcome. The bitter *uli*-berries itch against her scalp, eight swallowed already, four remaining. Four will be enough, she thinks. They will reach the market by the water, a glare of white buildings, tiny ships on a glittering sea. The brothers will drink arrack and break her wrist, then quarrel again. She is worthless and they should kill her, but they have traveled too far north. She will conceal this injury. A Genoese merchant laughing and holding her up by the wrist, watching her body stretch, break sweat. The wrist, but she makes no sound. The brothers agreeing to a pittance. Once aboard, he sets it. He knew all along. He watches her pick the last of the bitter-tasting berries from her plaits and throw them over the side. Four blue-black stains drifting, dissolving. She mimes popping them into her mouth, one by one, market by market. . . . Understanding dawns, and the Genoese laughs; his clever little bargain. He points forward, curls his lips around the word. *"Ro-*ma." Yes, this is easy. She understands this very well. *Ro*-ma. Shrewd eyes set in a woman's laughing face, hanging on the arm of her indulgent lover, who counts the coins into her hand. The Genoese watches, collects, is gone. The woman's kisses slap wetly against her lover's gaunt cheeks, but her eyes look over the man's shoulder, stripping her. Eu-*say*-biah. Her mistress lowers herself carefully into the tub.

"Eusebia . . ."

"Mistress?" Fiametta's eyes sweep up and down her body.

"Hardly more than a girl. . . . How old are you, Eusebia?"

She shrugs ignorance.

"Turn around now. . . ." Whispered, the words sheathed in steam-laden air, in the bedchamber's watery perfumes. Custom has never smoothed the edge of this particular request.

She turns, feels the skin tauten up the backs of her legs, hears the drip-drop of water as a hand surfaces behind her. A first speculative touch, fingers stroking up the backs of her knees, her legs, fingertips brushing the skin of her buttocks. She feels the blood swelling in her sex; so easy. Think back.

"Eusebia . . ."

She has felt the late summer rains spatter on her face nineteen times and counted three more since "Eu-*say*-biah." The sky has fattened five moons since the last, and tonight, in a place very distant from here, from this *Ro*-ma, the sixth will bring three fools out to gaze at it and remember her, believing that she is dead. Leaning forward now, steamy breath, lips mouthing silently over fine-grained skin to a secret crease of darkness, parting tight-curled hair. Lips meeting melting lips. Pink-mouthed. Her legs splay slowly.

"Eusebia . . ."

She has lived through twenty-two years; traveled a desert and a sea. She is not of this place, only adapted to it. Fiametta grunts softly behind her.

"Little blackface . . ."

She waits for the fat familiar tongue.

Outside, elsewhere, heat thickens with the afternoon's passage, weighing on *Ro*-ma, lying slackly in her streets. Her inhabitants take refuge in the shade of buildings and awnings, drift unthinkingly indoors. A lull descends. In the markets of Navona and the Campo de' Fiori, matrons and their servants turn and head for home. Cows, horses, goats, unsold pigs, and sheep swelter neglected in their pens. Fish, cheeses, and meats are swept off tables and stored in boxes underneath. The tradesmen slump together in untalkative clumps. People sweat. Behind shutters, windows, and screens, in hovels, houses, and palaces, the men and women of this city lie down to wait out the stifling warmth. Nothing to do but yawn and scratch, pull cool bucketfuls of water from the well. Something of the night's ban on careless movement touches these hours. Chained in the afternoon's languor, Arnolfo and Emilia sprawl listlessly together in the kitchen. The fire burned itself out an hour ago. Tebaldo prefers the courtyard's shade. Violetta has disappeared somewhere; ears boxed when she returns, although truth to tell, Emilia would prefer her gone on these occasions. Her lazy pleasures with Arnolfo—thick-chested and hairy as a goat—somehow require these summer afternoons, not to mention the accompaniment from upstairs: vague thuds and groans, a shout or two, then moans building to a series of earsplitting shrieks, then for some minutes silence. The sounds excite her in a way actual sight of the two of them never could. Succeeding them, a puzzling coda: a succession of terrific bangs. Inexplicable these, and the evidence the mistress's overbearing Moorish whore occasionally displays in the aftermath—a split lip, a cauliflower ear—only serve to deepen the mystery. They are her signal to shake Arnolfo free or disengage his hand from its labors beneath her skirts, to dismount, to straighten from her position bent facedown over the table, wipe her mouth, spit in the dead embers of the fire . . . To stay her thoughts of the girl's dark skin against Fiametta's body. Hmm, rocking back and forth, knees clamped firmly about Arnolfo's thighs, who rocks in time and utters soft *"gn, gn, gn,"* sounds, "Aaah," as she opens the front of her dress and lifts out slack breasts one at a time. "Suck," she instructs. Arnolfo's *"Mmmmth"* is the only sound—the pair upstairs have reached their interval of silence, a shout or two from the street beyond the courtyard, perhaps, a horse's hooves somewhere. Emilia grinds a little more urgently. Hooves. She screws her eyes shut, sets to work with her fingers. Hurry now, yes, yes, yes . . . Then, *bang, bang, bang.* But now? Surely it is too soon, surely, and she is on the very point, guts boiling like jam. . . . Again, *bang, bang, bang.* Worse than she feared; suddenly she knows that these detonations come not from the floor above, but from the door. Hooves? A horse! And it is worse even than that, smoothing down her skirts, pushing disorderly hair behind her ears, gesturing in frantic silence at her late mount (dazed, still flopping heavily about on the floor), for at that moment, resounding through the ceiling from the bedchamber above, Fiametta's pleasures recommence in earnest. Great thuds from above, sharp reports from below, Emilia's feet thump up the stairs, and the house is a cacophony of banging. Tap, tap, tap, across the floor of the *sala*—*ee-eek* (a floorboard is loose), her single knuckle against the door, *tock,* quite lost amongst the battering from below, and as she turns the handle, an enormous *bang!* from within. The door swings open to show her the tub, the bed, the steam, her mistress's red flesh, the girl's black skin, two faces caught like animals. Fiametta is standing, panting, over the girl, who lies on the floor beneath her; there is a sudden silence and within that a strange complicity, as though between a predator and its prey. Emilia gasps, red-faced herself, speaks—"Your pardon, mistress"—as Fiametta's expression of inscrutable joy is exchanged for shock at the intrusion, then anger, and then panic as the knocking from below is redoubled. Emilia's quavering message is already written in her face, indeed is resounding through the timbers of the house.

"Mistress, Don Jerònimo is here."

Plinius?

Noise from Saint Peter's Square funnels down into the adjacent Courtyard of the Parrot, bouncing off the walls and casements, jumbling itself as though Babel were rebuilt in air and the air about it made stone: straw-sellers, horse-dealers, women hawking crosses and kerchiefs, pilgrims from every corner of Christendom, monks, priests, hucksters, clerks, and beggars. A donkey brays. A dog barks.

Possibly these sounds are each other, for the courtyard is deceptive on the ear. The racket is near, but baffling. An underlying plashing is the fountain next to the water-trough?

No, the fountain of the Belvedere. And somewhere amongst the babble of human voices, Antonio knows, is that of his master Don Jerònimo. And that of the Pope. And that of the Portuguese, whose monkeys lounge insolently on the opposite side of the courtyard: Bandera, secretary like himself; Don Hernando, skin burned and wrinkled from the Barbary campaigns; six of Hernando's thugs; and Venturo. His own party—Don Diego and five men-at-arms—talk casually amongst themselves. They ignore the party opposite, except for Diego, who casually eyes Hernando's horse, a powerful but strangely marked bay, as though he might walk over and take it for himself. But for this, Faria's men do not exist. The horses' hooves clop as they shift on the cobbles, and the noise echoes up and down the walls. There have been hours of this.

Suddenly, out of the vague washes of sound spilling over the rooftops, a thin trumpeting erupts. Antonio looks up, startled, expression unguarded, masked quickly but too late. The Portingales across the courtyard are already aping him, looking skyward in terror and making a great show of forced laughter, *heurgh-urgh-urgh* . . . Don Diego's hand twitches toward his sword. The bay horse neighs, and the Portingales all look up again, as one, even funnier this time, *heurgh-urgh-urgh* . . . Naturally it is Venturo's laughter that is loudest, his squeaky little voice quite perfect for this kind of thing. The elephant's blast means many things, none good, among them that their Ambassador will not be long in returning.

Soon the Switzers in their green-and-gold uniforms are beating back the crowd of petitioners that daily gathers in the courtyard of Innocent's old palazzo, opening a channel in the braying mob for the Spaniards' horses. The sun took up residence in the Courtyard of the Parrot for an hour around noon. Thereafter shadow returned. Antonio smelled damp gathering under the flagstones—the Borgo is notoriously dank. Now, outside its precincts, the sun's full force returns. A looser crowd gathers here, the more hopeless petitioners who have not gained admittance even as far as the courtyard. Antonio blinks and follows the rigid back bobbing up and down on the mount in front of his own. The audience, he knows already—knew when he saw Faria's men, when he heard the beast hooting its ridicule—has not gone well.

They cross the Ponte Sant'Angelo at an ill-tempered trot, Don Jerònimo at their head cursing a crowd of loutish halberdiers, a small boy carrying a piglet, stray monks, anyone and everyone who dares to cross his path. Behind him ride Antonio, then Don Diego and his men. The little piazza at the far side of the bridge is clear—here, above all, Antonio knows, his master will not wish to linger—and the cortege picks up speed, dodging carts with wine-barrels from Ripetta and stone-wagons bound for the kilns, sweeping aside pedestrians, ducking under awnings. The recently renamed Via dell'Elefante is left behind. They pass the bankers' houses and swing left. Ahead, a grain cart has been stopped by officials of the *stadera* a little way into the street of the jewelers. The horses close up and he draws abreast.

"Plinius!" barks Don Jerònimo at his secretary, then pulls ahead again. The road kinks toward the river hereabouts, and the stump of the Torre Sanguigni pokes its top above the pantiled roofs and chimneys. A tannery Antonio has never detected discharges its stench along this stretch, but the alternative road by the Torre di Nona hugs the bank of the river, which in this heat, and this far downstream, will stink unbearably. Just past Santa Nicola the procession turns left. Glancing over his shoulder into Navona, Antonio sees men leading strings of packhorses into pens crudely roofed with sacking, people drifting away. Everyone is doing what he is doing—although here in this city of strangers the very phrase rings false to him; another of Rome's deceptions—going home. Antonio Seròn, secretary to the Ambassador of Fernando the Catholic of Aragon, wheels his horse about and follows his master into the courtyard.

The stalls are empty. The courtyard echoes. Grooms appear and take the horses. Don Jerònimo calls over, "With me, Antonio," before ducking under the lintel and vanishing through the door. Two dozing ushers peer out, startled, to see what other surprises might follow.

Don Jerònimo's heels disappearing up the stairs, footsteps echoing along the loggia, his back vanishing as he strides through the *sala*, an unseen door flung open within. Antonio scurries after. Glancing down from the open loggia, he sees Don Diego standing alone in the courtyard below, looking up at the cloudless sky, stone-faced as ever. Once one of Cardona's favored captains, he made neither show nor secret of his indifference to his role in Rome. Ceremonial? Bodyguard? There are rumors of his "excesses" after Ravenna and Prato. The man unnerves him.

"Antonio!"

The antechamber beyond the *saletta* serves as repository and audience room. Yellowing window-screens soften the light from the courtyard to oranges and ochers, sunset colors. Even so, the rays are strong enough to brown the edges of the papers piled up in the alcoves of the far wall, those spilling from the chests beneath, and more yet carpeting a good portion of the floor: draft treaties, memoranda, copies of decrees, dispatches dating from before even Rojas's time, an enormous and aging correspondence, and buried amongst it the relevant bulls of successive popes, which Antonio has lately unearthed only by rooting through the whole of this wordy midden, stirring up old quarrels and disputes, blowing the dust off long-forgotten deceptions, squinting in the inadequate light to read, finally, *Nicholas, Calixtus, Alexander, Julius* . . . They have all had a hand in this business.

"Did you speak with our friend today, Antonio?"

"He kept himself close, Ambassador. There was no opportunity."

"But he will come?"

"If there is a gain to be had, he will come."

Don Jerònimo nods slowly. Seated here in the heat and semilight of the chamber, he looks down, his fingers toying lazily with the thin folio before him. A few irregular, dog-eared pages. Astonishing that so much should depend on so little. He knows the words before him almost by rote, Nicholas' *Romanus Pontifex* confirming his earlier *Dum Diversas* (but contradicting Eugenius' *Rex Regum*), extended by Calixtus, ratified at Alcaçovas in the year of his younger brother's birth, little Alonso. *Aeterni Regis?* That gave the Portingales more again, promulgated by Sixtus in the year of Alonso's death. Three years. . . . Alexander's *Inter Caetera*, his *Eximiae Devotionis*, his second *Inter Caetera*, then *Dudum Siquidem*, the tide turning Spain's way now, washing them west, and the Portuguese routed, it would seem, *had* seemed. At Tordesillas, their triumph. And at Tordesillas, their defeat.

Invisible lines divided unseen seas, snaked about coasts and islands whose positions seemed to shift with the whims of the popes: Cape Verde, the Canaries, Cape Bojador, Antilla. Perhaps there were no islands at all, only cloud-banks, deceptive fogs, credulous and sleepless lookouts seeing substance where there was none. Now, in the open seas three hundred and seventy leagues west of the Cape Verde isles, a frontier begins. A line is drawn. Portugal stands back to back with Spain, two foolish duelists facing east and west who will meet face-to-face again on the other side of the world. And what then?

"I will not send an army to fight in the Moluccas when one orator can win this war for me in Rome. . . ." Fernando's confident words. They too are amongst the papers in the chamber. The Indies lie to the east, and the Indies lie to the west. They may be reached by either route. So does the Pope's line bisect the globe or merely describe the starting post? Is it only a beginning or also (a hemisphere away) an end? No, Fernando had not sent an army, but the rumor of an army had set sail anyway, spectral, sails like the wings of seabirds, a squadron of portable islands blown forward on a gale of words. The Portingales had taken fright, sought confirmation of Julius, received it. He was still "Fernando's lately arrived Ambassador" then, less than two years at the post. *Ea Quae* gave them Tordesillas again, and a line still invisible and substanceless, but changed utterly. How could that be?

Don Jerònimo envisioned a shelf of land rearing out of the seas' depths, brine cascading and pouring off, the raw coast racing forward like a miracle. Colón's Indies. Cabral's New World. Geographers and astrologers should have sailed to map their precious line—successive treaties provided for this—but somehow their ships had never left port. The new coast bulged east, crossing the boundary. A gift to the Portingales. A barrier to their own pioneers, but now they are bound to it as hostages to an earlier ignorance: a ghost-line. Terms shift. Distant seas slop and spill, slap their faces with watery hands. Intentions fail and sink. Now, amongst the warren of offices of the Apostolic Chamber, in the efforts of subtle doctors and clerks behind their screens, the game is afoot once more. Dom Manolo and his creatures are in good odor with the Pope. A new bull is in prepa-

ration, that much is firm report. Thereafter all is speculation, save the general understanding that it will not favor Fernando. The Pope is a whimsical referee, his
decrees as fluid as the sea's.

"If you were to divine a singular cause of our ill favor, Antonio, what would it
be?" he asks his secretary.

Antonio shifts, considers. "The elephant."

There it is. Since the embassy of the Portingales, his world has lurched on the
back of an elephant. And now, since this morning, since the Pope's little declama-
tion, his urbane feigning of surprise—*No? Neither of you? Neither of you have read
Plinius?*—the beast has changed. *It sharpens its horn on a rock the better to gore the
belly of the elephant, is ill-tempered and untamable, but docile in the presence of virgins.*
The Pope had grown enthusiastic, all but acting out the description. Could such
an animal exist?

"He wants a companion for Hanno," Vich tells his secretary. "His favor hangs
on that."

"A companion?"

"He wants to see them fight." Vich's shrug is unsurprised, as though the
Pope's inanity passed the point of senselessness long ago.

Odd noises percolate up from the *tinello* below, pots banging, the scrape of
heavy tables being dragged out from the walls, his crédencier's barking, scraps of
the servants' backchat. Then, from somewhere behind the room in which they
wait, both men stiffen as they hear a catch click, a door open, and careful steps
climb slowly up the back stairs. The door at the far side of the room swings open
to reveal a figure swathed in hat, and cloak, his face covered by the windings of a
voluminous scarf. The figure breathes heavily. And sweats. First the cloak, then
the hat, and last of all the scarf is removed to reveal a face bright red from the
heat, which grins at the two men while the body makes slight bobbing motions,
as though ducking badly aimed stones. Antonio regards the jerky figure with ill-
concealed dislike.

"Be seated, Venturo," says Don Jerònimo.

The man sits, shifts himself forward, settles again. He fidgets, scratches, as
though the chair he perches on pains him in some way. Little rivulets of sweat
travel erratically down his forehead and run into his eyes, making him blink. He
produces a handkerchief and dabs quickly. His hat has formed his hair into a bird's
nest. Antonio and Don Jerònimo wait patiently and in silence. There was rarely
any need to actually question Venturo.

"Cursed heat. Quite stifling. Now, interesting developments, most interesting." More dabbing. "Concerning the supplication. Concerning the soon-to-be
bull. The bull, yes. No name yet, mind you, no name, though I have seen the supplication, rough sort of thing. Seen it in the chamber, it's already there, on its way,
as they say. With the clerks, anyhow, had a good old *look*, I did." Some vigorous
nodding. "They won't have your extension; no, not at all"—shaking his head—
"they'll stop it dead, so they will. In—its—tracks."

"You are speaking of the line, Venturo?" prompts Antonio.

"Three hundred and seventy leagues west of the Cape Verdes, all as before. Dom Manolo to the east, ourselves to the west. . . . Do I offend, Don Antonio?"

The mention of "ourselves" has brought Antonio's expression of distaste to a level even Venturo cannot ignore.

"Continue," says Don Jerònimo.

"To the west, that's it. Pole to pole, though, not all the way round. That's the crux, eh? Not all the way round." Venturo waves his arm in a rough circle. "Not a chance."

"That is only the supplication, Venturo. Much can change before the bull itself is issued."

"Much or nothing. Dr. Faria prefers nothing infinitely, you prefer much. Who will have his way? To whom does His Holiness lean, eh? Interesting developments, as I say. All very interesting. Faria's sister waits upon the Queen. She reports Dom Manolo to be delighted with this novel manner of diplomacy. Did you see the Medici's expression when the beast squirted the cardinals? He loves the animal more than his own blood; I heard he refused his cousin the loan of it, frightened that the walk to Florence would pain its feet. His own cousin. Did you hear that?"

Venturo's movements confine themselves now to rocking back and forth and hand wringing. His restlessness transfers itself to his speech, which stops and starts, leaping from subject to subject: the Pope's delight, his sister's gallstone, a rumor that Leno and Arminelli have fallen out, a little later that they are reconciled, that the revenues of Parma and Piacenza are to be reassigned to the Duchy of Modena, and agents of Bentivoglio of Bologna have entered into talks with Venice.

Don Jerònimo sits with his chin propped on his hands, puzzled somewhat at his own patience with this rambling knave when only an hour before he had erupted with rage at his master.

"Come to your point," Antonio snaps after some minutes. "You try my master's goodwill."

"Goodwill, eh? Well, there we are at the nub of it. There have been developments, as I say. Very interesting. Now how much am I to say, I wonder? Such hungry Spanish gentlemen as yourselves, how much will fill your stomachs today?"

It seems that Venturo is smirking, toying with their curiosity, which is too much for Antonio. Venturo cowers but makes no attempt to defend himself as Antonio strides over, draws back his arm, and cuffs him once, twice, about the head.

"Now speak, you bastard!" he barks at the man.

Antonio makes as if to strike him a third time, but a near imperceptible shake of the head from Don Jerònimo stays his hand. Venturo's fidgeting returns, worse than before. He begins speaking more urgently. Antonio hovers behind him.

"A communiqué has arrived. Albuquerque has sent word from the Indies to

Dr. Faria here in Rome. They have a compact, those two. Dom Manolo is said to favor it: a little plot to sweeten His Holiness."

"And to aid the passage of the bull," adds Antonio from behind.

"I tell you what I hear. The Ambassador is very cheerful of late. Very flowery in his manners, very sweet. Yes, well, the communiqué speaks of a shipment to be sent from Goa. A second beast; a companion for the beloved Hanno."

"Another elephant?" Antonio queries.

Venturo twists about to answer him. "I believe it is a different kind of animal. Dr. Faria said that he had never heard of its like."

"And the name of this unheard-of beast?" Don Jerònimo, mildly.

"Now that is where the store of my ignorance begins, Ambassador Vich. The name itself was not mentioned, or if it was, I was not present to hear it." Venturo laughs nervously. "I will keep my ears pricked, be assured of that."

Don Jerònimo smiles at Antonio, who smiles back.

"Ears pricked, eh?"

"A figure of speech, Ambassador. No more than that. I meant only—"

"The name of this beast, Venturo."

"As I say, I have yet to discover it. . . ."

"Ears pricked, he says, Antonio."

"I tell you both, I have yet to discover it. I swear it, gentlemen!"

It seems that Antonio is about to set to work again when Don Jerònimo raises his hand and purses his lips. He weighs the matter up.

"Don Antonio, be so good, if you will, to send for Don Diego."

"No!" shouts Venturo. Antonio makes for the door, already shouting the name, while Venturo tries to cling to his sleeve. "I tell you I know nothing!"

"Ears pricked indeed." Don Jerònimo is shaking his head regretfully.

"Please, Don Jerònimo, I have told you all I know. I have kept good faith with you, have I not? Now I beg you to believe me. I beg you!"

Venturo squirms on his chair, his face radiating earnestness as he pleads with Don Jerònimo. His eyes keep darting over the silent man's shoulder. Suddenly the door opens again. Antonio and Don Diego march in. Without seeming to break his stride, Don Diego smacks Venturo's face, bangs his head on the table, then holds the head in place with one hand, fishing with the other for his knife. Venturo begins to sob, "I do not know, I do not *know*," over and over again.

"The name, Venturo?" asks Don Jerònimo, but this only prompts a series of high wails. "Very well. Don Diego? Venturo here has promised us his ears will henceforth be pricked in our cause, now—"

"No, no, no, no, noo-ooo! Pleeaassse . . . I do not know the name. I do not!"

Don Diego bends to his task, but before he has so much as scratched his man, Venturo starts to scream.

"Enough!" Don Jerònimo orders, then slumps back in his chair. "Thank you, Don Diego. That will suffice."

Don Diego's expression has not changed since the charade began. Now he merely nods, straightens, turns about. The soldier's boots thud on the floorboards of the *sala* outside. Venturo snivels, still prostrate on the table. Antonio pulls him up and deposits him in his chair. A long minute passes while Don Jerònimo regards him thoughtfully.

"You bore it very well, Venturo," he says finally. "Very bravely." Venturo nods through his sniffles. "You must have something in your eye, I think. It is watering. Antonio? A handkerchief for Venturo here. His own is too grimy. . . . There now. Better?"

"He was to tell His Holiness of the new animal today," Venturo says, wiping his face. "He was to sound him out on it, and then you were present, so I do not know if he did or no. That is the truth of it, and I know no more."

"Naturally we believe you, Venturo. We would hardly put you through such an ordeal for nothing. You are one of our own. You will tell us when you know, will you not?" Venturo sniffs loudly and nods. "Good. Antonio will pay you. Now come here and kiss me." Don Jerònimo smells the sourness of Venturo's fear as their cheeks brush.

A minute later, Antonio has joined him on the loggia overlooking the courtyard.

"Do we believe him, Antonio?"

"He knew we dared not mark him so obviously, Excellency."

"His terror was real enough. I fear that our Pope's horn-sharpening lover of virgins and Faria's mysterious animal are one and the same. In any case, it is the fact of this beast, not its name, which must concern us now. Faria will not keep his secret long. His genius is for advertisement, as I was taught again today. And His Holiness . . . He is clever to set Faria and myself against each other in this way. And yet he craves marvels and prodigies before allies and armies. I tell you, a dragon, a gryphon, and a centaur would secure Africk, the Indies, and the New World, all three. But who was it gave Cardinal Medici his beloved Florence? Does he forget so quickly?"

"Some say that it is not a happy memory," offers Antonio.

"Oh, doubtless he would not wish to be reminded. Perhaps this explains his love of diversion, but he does not love me, Antonio. And he does not love our King." He pauses; some impasse has been reached. "I do not understand him. I do not understand this Pope of ours."

"He is simple as a woman," Antonio tells his master. "It is his whims which make him complex."

The courtyard below is silent. Its flagstones glare in the afternoon sunlight, dazzling both men. Don Jerònimo recalls the scene from that morning, the animal's sheer bulk, something crude and unfinished about it. The Pope's open delight, like a child. Perhaps because his smallest whims met no resistance, they grew out of all proportion; peas the size of pumpkins. Mice hungry as wolves. Perhaps that was it. In the gardens of the Belvedere the Pope's whims had no season, grew unchecked, became monsters. Simple as a woman. That was good. Don Jerònimo turns to his secretary.

"I have an appointment with my mistress, Antonio. I am to take her to Mass at the Colonnas. The feast of Saints Philip and James is said to be amusing, and I am in need of amusement."

"Take Don Diego, Excellency."

"Pay court to one's mistress in the company of soldiers? Absurd! She understands one weapon only, and Don Diego does not wield it."

"We are not much loved at present, Don Jerònimo. If you are caught alone, it would be an easy matter—"

"This is not Venice, Antonio. Faria would not dare. I shall go to her early, surprise her. Do you still have that minx up from the Ripa?"

Antonio nods. "A candle's worth of whatever I please for a handful of soldi. I think she must be stupid."

"I cannot say mine own is stupid. She has the reddest lips, the most golden hair, the tiniest feet, the readiest wit. She plays the lute, or so she says, sings verses. Only thinking of her stirs me up; I swear there is a part of me that loves the woman." At this point Don Jerònimo pauses in his praises, as though unsure exactly how to proceed. Antonio turns to him expectantly. There is a further aspect to be mentioned, a most encompassing particular. But is he to celebrate it or decry it? In his contemplations, true, it is a part of her he has been repelled by. Yet in the flesh, in the closeness of her chamber, in the dark, in the hours when his hands are busy on her slopes and summits, two feverish explorers roped together in his head, *then* . . . Well, she is fat. The fact is inescapable and apparent at a glance. His mistress is very fat.

Antonio watches him as the morning past and evening to come conflate and merge. The animal's bulk and his darling Fiametta's, they—as it were—*correspond.* . . . Put a horn on her nose, sheathe her in gray, and . . . ? No. He feels light and unguarded, his thoughts drifting like this under the secretary's nose. *You are a traitorous knave, Antonio, and I will cut your throat.* Under his very nose. Horns and virgins. . . .

Pitched somewhere in the gulf between outrage and admiration, the expletive bursts from him, startling his secretary, awakening slumbering servants within, sending lizards basking in the heat below scrambling for the shadows of the arcade.

"Plinius!" blurts Don Jerònimo.

It appears suddenly, a cliff of travertine and tufa rising up and running the length of the Piazza di Santissimi Apostoli. Heavy iron grilles protect tiny ground-floor windows set within deep embrasures that seem to have been hol-

lowed from solid rock. Higher up are shutters and bars. An arched gateway barred
by heavy oak doors battened with iron suggests repulse rather than entrance, and
the adjoining church only heightens the impression. Ramshackle parades of bro-
ken-down houses and stables face this architectural scowl across the piazza and
seem to cower before its bulk. Louring over the antlike denizens below, Fortress
Colonna appears as a single, enormous, impregnable block of stone.

Within, the story changes somewhat. Down the years, successive headstrong
Colonnas have indulged their passion for towers, mezzanines, balconies, walk-
ways, little blockhouses; staircases have been confidently projected through curtain walls to join bedchambers and reception rooms, grand halls envisaged by
knocking out a scullery and two kitchens. Great confidence attends the workmen's initial hammer-blows, but the business soon starts to go awry. Floor levels
are found to differ by crucial inches. Walls that should be the same wall turn out
to be quite different walls. Punching through *here* should lead to *there*. It doesn't.
Workmen poke dust-covered heads through holes to find themselves in little
studies and servants' dorters when they should be in cellars, or privies, or attics,
anywhere but here. Elderly female second cousins have turned *en deshabillé* from
their mirrors to find their quarters broken in upon by men swinging hammers.
Denizens of the *tinello* have been startled in the midst of sordid solitary practices.
It's unsettling—for the engineers not least. Shouldn't this unexpected *saletta* be
on another floor entirely? Where did this dining room come from? Their tunnel-
ing has brought them out in rooms lost for generations by some intervening "improvement," rooms that no one knew existed, impossible rooms.

Ceiling collapses are frequent. There are rumors of doors that open on nothing more substantial than the open sky and a drop of fifty feet. Passages take devi-
ous, compromised routes on their way to nowhere in particular. Behind its
massive facade, Fortress Colonna is riddled with these inexplicable gaps. Dotted
throughout the sprawling shambles are useless wedge-shaped spaces, irregular
chimneys of stale air, inaccessible "courtyards," fissures, scissures, hiccups in the
ground plan. A watercourse that no one has ever managed to find erupts periodically to turn these secret gardens swampy. Overlooking windows disgorge chamber pots and soiled rushes, dog bones and dogshit, animal guts and vegetable
peelings. Fortress Colonna abounds in malodorous defaults: accidental gaps and
wells where walls peel away from one another or meet at irreconcilable angles,
leaving scum-filled defiles and pestilential sumps. In winter, men (small boys for
the narrowest) are lowered in with buckets to clear the worst of the muck. In
summer, they stink just the same.

A small mystery: If the Church of Santissimi Apostoli truly did push itself free
of the adjoining palace to form this latest baffling space, no one can remember
exactly when. It had always been assumed that the west wall of the nave ran flush
with the east wall of the palace and the west wing of the transept intruded into
the body of the adjacent building. A number of passages at that end of the palace
have a certain blocked-off look about them. Eyeing it up from the available an-

gles, the intruding transept theory looks unassailable. Direct access from palace to church? No problem at all, a simple matter of knocking through from *here* and coming through into the upper gallery that runs all around the church. . . .

The wielders of hammers and crowbars should be inured to this sensation, but still it catches them out. Crumbling brickwork topples in, a head is poked through, and there it is, thirty or forty feet away, the wall that should have been *this* wall. It appears from the piazza that the two buildings stand side by side. It appears from here that they do not. Another of those puzzling and pointless gaps, another fault in Fortress Colonna's internal topography (some obstreperous geometry at work here). Fabrizio remembers angling his five-year-old head to peer down into this newly discovered secret space. The ground twenty feet below looked like a slice of cheese, but a hundred feet long. Anxious nursemaids had snatched him away, but thereafter he escaped at every opportunity to watch the men at work: cutting rope for the scaffold, winching up beams, emptying bags of lime, silversand, and horsehair into the plaster-vat. A man working all day at the business of splitting laths, he remembered that. A gap: the solution, to his grandfather, at least, had been obvious.

Over weeks, Fabrizio watched an outgrowth inch forward into space. The farther it extended toward the obdurate wall opposite, the more improbable it appeared, yet when it finally reached the church the apostles worked a little miracle, and suddenly it was inevitable, as though suspended between the Church of Santissimi Apostoli and the palace of the Colonna there had always been a corridor with a sprung floor, little frosted windows, its roof leaded against the weather. Had there been an opening ceremony? Fabrizio Colonna, white-haired now, stiffly erect, waiting patiently for the servants to knock the seals off the door of the same corridor, racks his brains for the memory. His mind frays between then and now. How long? Fifty years? Now the corridor is used but once a year. The procession shuffles behind him. Someone coughs. Yes! Remembered now. Files of servants had carried steaming salvers and trays of sweetmeats. The sun setting over the gable of the church had struck the frosted glass of the windows and suffused the interior with warm pink light. A chattering crowd drank wine and shifted from foot to foot as though testing the boards. The dry, resinous smell of new wood. The door closed behind the last of the celebrants. Nightfall soon; moonlight on the jumbled turrets of Fortress Colonna, on the tiles and spires of Santissimi Apostoli, two brooding masses of timber and stone. The same cold light seeped through the frosted glass of the corridor. Silence there too for a while, but then rustling, sniffing, scrabbling, and scampering as two rival hulks sent their emissaries forward. Church and palace are home to more than humans. The bridge between them made, conflict was inevitable. That night, the rat-war began.

The banging of hammers, sawing of saws, scraping of trowels, and other builderly commotions had served extended notice to the Colonna rats for some weeks before now. Slinking through cracks, flattening themselves under floorboards, whiskers twitching and senses tuned to the limit, scouts sent out from

Nest Central had monitored the corridor's construction and seen in the work-men's efforts only another pointless folly, less disruptive than some of the others and—the obvious function of providing some unneeded peripheral nest-space apart—pretty much of no account. The advice offered to Nest Central was "Disregard."

Wrong.

The first raiding party is encountered, confusingly enough, way over on the west side of the palace: two females returning from a forage find themselves con-fronted by strange-smelling rats who set upon them, killing one, impregnating the other. That same night a nest is despoiled behind the wainscoting of the kitchens, three males are found with their heads bitten off beneath the steps lead-ing down to the cellars, and several traumatized females are come upon, cowering in a crack in the exterior wall, their exposed tails chewed down to stumps. Clearly these are more than mating kerfuffles. Urgent meetings in Nest Central result in more scouts being sent out and a first, hesitant call to arms.

Sniggering Apostolic rats ambush the corridor scouts, killing all but one, who reports back on the source of the trouble. It is worse than Nest Central first feared: a rival colony, as big as their own (?), as ferocious, perhaps, acquisitive, ex-pansionist. . . . More meetings then, although there is only one course of action. The culverts and roof-spaces of Fortress Colonna grow thick with rat-secretions as the colony twitches itself into action: attack-posture, submit-posture, win-posture, lose-posture. . . . Mock battles break out and rat-squeals sound in regis-ters reserved for threat, rage, distress. In a chamber buried deep within the labyrinth of Nest Central, nine males breathe the colony's heady chemicals, bod-ies shaking in resonance, tails thrashing, and snarling, pulling tighter and tighter until they are fused together, become one central symbol, an overwhelming mes-sage to attack.

The Apostolic-Colonna rat-war would be fought tooth and nail through the darkness of the next three nights, a desperate hole-and-corner affair of chance encounters in confined spaces, ferocious skirmishes, raids, repulses, even one-on-one trials of strength fought out on open floors in full view of the giants. There are atrocities, too. The second night a stricken Apostolic female, her legs bitten off, is left as bait for the mercy-killing party, which advances cautiously, noses sniffing, whiskers twitching, looking all about for the enemy they know is near, somewhere in the vicinity, careful now . . . But those screams! Those wounds! Proper procedure is abandoned as they rush forward to nip her jugular, and Colonna rats—lying motionless all this time, unseen, unheard, simply observing up till now—drop from the rafters above and fall on the mercy-killers, cracking spines and gouging eyes, leaving nine dead on the floor of the corridor before scampering off in jubilation to lick the enemy's blood off one another's fur.

Neighboring colonies lodged beneath churches and chapels along the Via Lata relay the strife, feeding it north to country cousins scraping an existence from the vineyards and pastures of the Pincio, south into the metropolitan precincts. Socketed in their holes, tongues slippery with acidic secretions, gray-pink gums peeled to show sharp yellow incisors, Rome rats the city over twitch, scrabble, shudder at the slaughter. Commotive pheromones come reeking down the tunnels. . . . Feral cats and rat-catchers are accepted hazards, but a rat-war! Claws scrape and scratch in agitation; only the River colonies keep their cool, stationed down by the Tiber, ears tuned tight to the upper registers, the frequencies of distress, noses jabbing as ever across the dark flood toward the Borgo. Faint alarm signals from the north provoke no reaction here. To them, the war is but a local squabble, a rehearsal of apocalypse. The real danger will come from the west: monsters lurk across the river. They've seen bodies float across the size of small foxes, scabbed with disease, bristly and powerful, maladapted for anything but slaughter. . . . One day the rats of the Borgo will cross in search of nest-space—they know this, these legions of the Roman *limes*—and then the real war will begin. So they listen, and wait, and sniff, and wait. . . . There are rumors, only rumors, that the Borgo rats eat dogs.

Meanwhile, from the deepest cellars to the highest garrets, along passageways and ceilings, the human inhabitants of Fortress Colonna are kept awake by the scrabbling and squealing. A pot-boy slumbering in the *tinello* awakens to find himself the chosen battleground of crazed furry bodies. Fabrizio himself recalls a brute the size of a cat flying past his shoulder as it leaped from balustrade to floor, three balls of black terror in hot pursuit. Six hundred and twenty-seven rats lose their lives in these internecine nights. Come morning, servants stumble over piles of the dead. By the third night, the last of the Apostolic invaders has been chased down, killed, and Fortress Colonna is at peace once again. The corridor that began the slaughter is the focus of an obscure dread, held in terror by Colonna and Apostolic rats alike. Forbidden territory to begin with. Later, something more complex.

A servant has dropped the keys. A jangling, a crashing. Dust dislodged from the lintel trickles onto his head as he bends to pick them up. Try again. The lock is stiff, creaking in protest as the key grates inside. Seal wax crunches under his boot. Colonna stands still as a statue. The servant grunts, puts his shoulder to the door, which comes free, swinging open. . . . Droppings litter the floor like gravel, loose boards stick up, and the floor itself twists and rises in the middle. The raddled walls are scarred and eaten away to expose the bare laths beneath. Frosted windows and moonlight. Candlelight. He advances into the corridor, and his guests follow. Before him, studding the floor, double-shadowed in the different lights, bodies stir and drag themselves to safety. Others remain inert. Behind the walls a mad scrabbling starts up, and a strange crunching sound.

After the rat-war, memories of the slaughter kept an uneasy peace in the corridor. Occasional encounters were played down, discouraged by Nest Central and its Apostolic counterpart alike. Killing of intruders on either side was understood as a basic condition of the truce. Who knows the crime of the first miscreant rat to venture here and find asylum? Looking back to see his pursuers stalled by the nameless prohibition hanging over this place, barred absolutely from return or advance, did he regard this place as haven or dungeon? Which side did he come from? It hardly matters, for word spreads fast, and soon this corridor plays host to a stateless colony of outcasts: nest-foulers, young-gobblers, psychotics, thieves, defeated pretenders . . . The unwanted of both camps flock to the corridor, sniff the air, squeal their presence, note the strange behavior going on around them, forage for something to eat, and find, well, plaster.

A stateless rat is a hungry rat. Plaster is better than nothing. The outcasts feed, breed, suckle their young, clamber about beneath the floorboards, build nests behind the walls. They tend to sleep a lot, although frantic outbursts of activity are also typical. It's the diet: sand, lime, horsehair—plaster—which sharp incisors make short work of as the hungry outcasts chase their stomachs up the walls. But hair is tough, fibrous stuff, hard on the digestion, and the story of those early colonists is a tale of internal dilations and spasms, hemorrhages and hemorrhoids, all kinds of gastric hell. Torpid rats lie motionless while determined bowel movements wrestle this stringy sustenance past pancreatic cysts, ulcers, reservoirs of catarrh, bodies hunched, guts concertinaed, all effort directed inward to strain nourishment from the monotonous diet. It's exhausting—hence the sloth.

The lime is just the opposite, winding up their metabolisms, setting tiny hearts racing, appetites quickening, strange enzymes pumping through the system to send their bodies crazy. The hair slows them down and the lime speeds them up: the corridor rats alternate between mania and torpor, snapping between states with no more warning than a spring thunderstorm falling out of the unseen sky above. And now, as ever, unseen lime-crazed guzzlers scrape madly in the invisible recesses while helpless sluggards drag their hair-bloated stomachs across the floor in full view of the advancing party. Servants pick up these unfortunates by the tail and dash their heads against the crumbling walls. Rat-blood trickles down the laths, and rat-bodies are tossed down to their fellow outcasts below. The scrabbling and crunching grows muted and quickly cedes to a few barely audible ripping sounds. After an unrelieved diet of plaster, freshly killed rat-flesh is delicious.

Onward Colonna, stiff-legged, into the ramshackle conduit's gloom. He wears a hat, a strange affair of banded velvet shaped like a chimney pot. His jerkin is a carapace of hard black leather studded with buttons and sewn in diamonds. Since his wounding at Ravenna, it has hung loosely on his frame. Standing naked in his chamber some hours ago, he counted the emergent outlines of his ribs pressing from beneath his skin. His flesh is wasting. His staff bangs solidly on the sandy shit-strewn floor. Ratnoise. Moonlight. The statues raised to him will be splendid when he is dead.

"Door!"

The servants fiddle and fumble, hunched ahead like thieves about the lock. Colonna notes the position of planks warped to trippable height; difficult terrain. At his back the column ripples, wanting him to move forward: Ascanio and his bastard brother, Umberto, their whores, their sister Vittoria, her page, his higher-placed familiars. Behind them, the orators: beloved Naples and his train, Aragon and his train. Behind them, his companions: Don Geraldo, Villefranche, Cesare, the loyal Gersault, and others, solid Colonna men, old now and faltering where once they clung one-handed to the barricades and broke Orsini heads with the other. Great days. . . . From somewhere at the back of these known and unknown faces come birdish twitterings, whinnies and squeals, the scrape of over-filled churns. He has a secret buried in his head.

The far door is open at last; beyond it the gallery of Santissimi Apostoli continues at a slight angle to the line of the corridor. He advances, ducks, emerges, turns. Ascanio follows, kisses his hand, murmurs something, moves on. Umberto next. Their sluts blush and curtsy. A crash booms dully. Someone has stumbled on a floorboard; a delay, another face. Vittoria's, furious at him for some reason he cannot recall or has yet to be told. A killing undoubtedly. She bobs, disappears. Other faces waver in front of his own before shuffling along the gallery, faces he loves, or has loved, faces he has reviled. He is glacial. Faces blur with the years, merge, combine. Finally they are all the same. Best to show nothing.

The servants follow, wheezing beneath their loads. His appointed place awaits him in the center of the gallery, but something is missing. He looks again into the corridor, peering over greasy heads and hoods . . . there. An enormous gilt-encrusted chair is wobbling toward him. Other servants are pressing themselves against the walls to allow it passage. It is upside-down. Legs are visible beneath.

"Chair!" barks Colonna as it passes. The chair halts. He hits it with his staff. It continues, only now it is his guests being asked to stand aside, and the gallery is already crowded, somewhat sweaty, too, no one is too pleased at deferring to a piece of furniture. The chair's progress slows. And slows. And stops. A mountainous woman has flattened herself against the rail of the balcony and is trying to pretend that really there is no problem, if the chair would merely continue, then she could do the same, engaged there in flirtatious conversation with—who? Colonna squints—the Spaniard. Vich. The chair is making little charges, rebounding off the woman's stomach. The width of the gallery; the width of the chair; the width of Vich's mistress: these dimensions are in basic disagreement, and now Ascanio and Umberto are laughing openly, his old comrades smirking discreetly. Even Vittoria's lips are pursed. The chair grows more frantic, the woman's expression appearing by turns poised and toadlike as the contraption buffets her, until one of Vich's party steps forward and solves the problem by kicking out the unsteady legs beneath. The chair collapses, Vich offers his hand, and Colonna watches the flesh-mountain step daintily over.

For a moment he is enraged, but several of his guests are applauding the maneuver. He wavers, undecided. He stares, unconvinced. And then the mists in his mind seem to thin and clear.

"You!" He points.

Don Jerònimo approaches, already gesuring to the woman.

"Lord Colonna, allow me to present my companion, the lady Fiamm—"

He points again. "The mulish one. The kicker." He stares harder as the man steps over outstretched legs and squeezes past the plump, soft bodies. Dark hard face . . . is it? Yes, he is right. A face he knows from a cloudless place, the one time spared him by his wound.

"Ravenna," Colonna says, as the soldier's face draws near. "You fought at Ravenna."

"Yes, my lord," answers Don Diego.

The other battles drift by him in watery confusion, their clangor and stench all mingled and mazed, but this place remains. The secret sanctuary of his wound—Diego would understand. Ravenna's lesson would be written on him, too. The chattering heads to his left and right puffed and blew off, filling the air with their noise. What could they know unless they too had flattened themselves in Ravenna's cold mud, had jerked and shivered, fouling themselves beneath the French cannon-fire? He remembered men standing witlessly in the midst of it all. Cardona's companies were routed or fled and, not about to silence those guns, they were trapped in the marsh with no cover for retreat. He'd ordered the horses brought up, and they had charged. The cannon had plucked men from their horses, scything through flesh and bone. Riders had vanished entire in sprays of red and white. Hillocks rising out of the marsh's black mud had snapped the horses' legs like twigs. He had fallen heavily, stunned, and come to surrounded by boys. His drummers had found him and were looking to him, waiting for his word. Something was wrong with his ears; he could hear only deep rumbles and thuds. He'd looked about and seen the ground rising to their left, drifting smoke. "This way," he'd directed them. They must not panic, must not break now. "This way, men."

But they were boys. Untried children. He had lost his bearings, and the cannon-noise had seemed to surround them. "This is the way. . . ." They would be safe now, safe with their commander, who had fought these battles for thirty years from Naples to the Alps, who had survived a belly-wound at Gaeta, who had killed a hundred men with the knife they could see at his side, who had walked from the killing-ground too many times to fall here. Why should Ravenna prove different?

"My captors told me your company fought like devils," he tells Diego.

"We fought as Aragonese, my lord," replies the man in blunt tones. Behind him, Colonna can see Don Jerònimo and his consort—has he seen her somewhere before?—stranded awkwardly, waiting to speak or be spoken to.

"I would keep your Colonel Diego about me tonight, Don Jerònimo." The Ambassador nods graciously. Colonna nods his thanks. The Ambassador makes a little bow and begins shuffling back along the crowded gallery, his woman in tow. A hothead by many accounts, Vich. A cold and clever one by others.

"No longer 'Colonel,' my lord," Diego says.

"Peace has always made fools of men like us," replies Colonna. He does not wish to hear more. Complex clouds of rumor hang about Diego. Something happened at Prato; some ineradicable stain colors the man attending him now. He was not there and saw nothing. He does not wish to know. He wishes to know less and less of the days since Ravenna.

He remembered that crossbowmen had come into view on their flank. He turned his little company about, but more appeared ahead. The battle was all but over. The crossbowmen were a ragged lot, grinning as they strolled forward, swinging their weapons casually, calling to one another. "Hold fast," he called. They were only drummer boys. The crossbowmen moved nearer, and he could see puzzlement wash over the nearest faces. Only drummer boys, but he could not lay down his sword for them. He called again, "Choose your man," and when he said it he saw incredulity even as the soldiers raised their arms. The boys were whimpering about him. He shouted, "Colonna!" and ran forward. He saw them shoulder arms. He heard the tock and thud of the loosed bolts finding targets and the high screams start up behind him. His shoulder first, then a second later his leg, low down somewhere and knocking him to the floor. He lay flat and looked back to see his boys had not moved, only bunched tighter together in their terror. They were shrieking now. The crossbows were reloading almost casually. Some were trying to crawl forward, and the men were kicking them back to their fellows, heavy kicks that lifted them off the ground like sacks. He prayed to a blade of grass. He saw them walk toward him. Knees in the small of his back pinning him down, a thrashing metal spider. Fingers busy at his throat and the gush of air and light as they stripped his helmet. A foot bearing down hard on his neck, he felt the instrument's blunt nose butt his skull, the finger squeezing the trigger, hearing the moment explode and crumble like a stone smashed on an anvil and just before it a word whispered in his ear that he had not understood. Meurtrier. They had pressed the crossbow to his head and fired a bolt into his skull. The French surgeons had sawed off the shaft and left the barbed head in his brain. *Merr*-tree-aye. It was still there. He lived.

Below, in the nave of Santissimi Apostoli, a pig is being strung by the hocks and hoisted up to swing twenty feet above the floor. A thurible soon joins it, belching thick smoky arcs that the pig's wilder trajectories intersect and cut, sending fragrant wafts of olibanum forward to do battle with the noxious airs of the crypt. Servants carrying brimming churns have bunched together at the far end of the gallery. "Deploy yourselves evenly!" bellows a barrel-chested major-domo into uncomprehending faces. One or two begin to pluck at the drawstrings of their hoses. "Spread out! There!" He points across the nave to the opposite side. They lug the slopping churns by their handles. Chicken-carriers follow. "Not you!" Chicken-carriers stop. Vich's mistress is proving something of a problem again. Ascanio is essaying a handstand, and Vittoria seems to be, perhaps, praying?

Below, flanked by his deacon and subdeacon and surrounded by a gaggle of grubbily smocked urchins, a bearlike man strides powerfully down the nave. Behind the rood-screen he deposits a chalice with a bang on the altar. A Bible follows. The urchins form lines to either side of the chancel and begin limbering up, drawing deep breaths and emitting piercing squawks. Ushers stand at the doors through which dim sounds can now be heard, muffled shouting, wolf-whistles, the odd thud. Father Tommaso cracks his knuckles and looks to his choir, his ushers, up to the gallery, where the majordomo nods solemnly back at him. His deacons have disappeared through a small door in the transept. He follows.

The sacristy is somewhat cramped: the corner of some other building seems to have broken through the facing wall and beached itself here like the prow of an unpiloted vessel, effectively dividing the once square room into two triangular ones. With the help of his deacon he pulls on alb, chasuble, amice, stole, rummaging amid the layers of linen to girdle himself with the cingulum, held out by Brother Bruno, a tough, wiry-haired native of Ripetta. Brother Fulvio busies himself with tapers and tablets of incense, whose cloying smoke quickly fills the cubbyhole. Bruno and Father Tommaso exchange glances. Brother Fulvio is tall and willowy, fair-haired and blue-eyed, a Perugian, in Rome for three weeks now and lodging with Tommaso on the orders of his Bishop, who had been charmed by letters of introduction mentioning "the humility of Saint Francis." Well, taming wolves was one thing; Tommaso would have liked to see Saint Francis celebrate Mass for the Colonnas.

"There will be incidents," he begins, "but so long as the tanners don't turn up . . ." At that moment a piercing whine reaches all three pairs of ears, modulating into a soprano squeal, resolving itself as a kind of screech coming from the main body of the church: *"Ex-cla-ma-ve-runt ad te"*—a pause—*"domin-aaayy . . ."* The choir has begun singing.

"Idiots!" barks Father Tommaso as a louder din begins to echo down the nave, bangs and shouts, hammerings, the sound of the faithful called to prayer. Bruno hands him the maniple, lights candles, as a first *"Alleluia-aaa!"* drifts in from the chancel, then a second one, longer, its jubilus more drawn out still, and more bangs and thuds and shouts, the swinging pig squealing. Fulvio closes the lid of the thurible, crosses himself, and precedes them both into the church. *"Exultate iusti. . . ,"* quavers the choir. *"Introiboadaltaredei-eee,"* hums Father Tommaso. *"Ad deum quiletificatinventutam me-am,"* descants Bruno. *"Iudica me deus"*—rattling along quite nicely here—*"to-oo-tum"*—a glare at the choir in passing. They go through the routine again. He murmurs, *"Deus tu conversus vivificabis nos . . ."* Gets, *"Et plebs tua letabitur in te,"* in response. The church is lit with candles set into the pillars upholding the gallery. Aloft, the thurible appears to have ensnared itself with the pig, for both are being untangled *("Domine exaudi orationem meam . . .")* by serving men who lean out over the nave. Faces peer down at him: Vittoria's (rapt), Ascanio's (bored), Don Geraldo's, and Villefranche's. The old man stares stonily ahead. Behind him a soldier is toying with his helmet and three identically dressed women are . . . no, in fact, they are not. There is only one after all. Very fat. Suddenly the pig and thurible are set to swinging once again; smoke and squealing as the choir reaches its twelfth Alleluia, the door begins to shudder as though being battered from without, and Father Tommaso shouts, "Ready?" down the nave to his ushers, who nod and move to unbar the doors. *"Dominus vobiscum,"* he intones as the little procession reaches the rood-screen. Tommaso turns, flexes his shoulders, takes up a position in front of the screen. Bruno mumbles, *"Et cum spiritu tuo . . ."* in reply. They glance at each other, old comrades and veterans. Fulvio has continued on to disappear somewhere behind the screen.

"What?" murmurs Colonna, lost for the moment in a quite different thought. "Have we begun yet?"

"Right," the priest commands his ushers. "Let the bastards in."

Don Diego watches the heavy crossbars slide back, jam momentarily as the doors are pressed from without, then jerk free. The ushers stagger, suddenly encumbered with the oaken rails' full weight, the doors just as suddenly weightless, it seems, for they shiver, clatter, spring lightly open to reveal the faithful stilled in the doorway, mouths agape, silent and cowed, stopped dead in their already stopped tracks. A couple look half-wonderingly back at the bobbing heads behind. Impossible, this moment. No one quite believes it. The line of pressed and waiting bodies swells for a second, then breaks, outriders and vanguards forming to make the breach in the undefended church's skin.

Its defenders take their stand a little behind the ambo, Bruno at their center, legs braced, arms hung loose and at the ready. He eyeballs the advancing congregation. "Hold it . . . Hold it!" Face them down at the start. He singles out a beefy individual leading a mastiff by the collar whom several more timorous rogues are nudging forward. "You! Yes, you. No dogs!" He is ignored. A flanking movement is creeping around to his left. Diego nods approvingly to himself. Delay them, thinks Bruno. Take their brunt here. A right-hand movement has joined the left—the inevitable pincer-maneuver—and now the center is edging up the middle of the nave, shunted forward by the press of bodies behind, drawn on by the luxuriant unoccupied space before. Bruno's retreat is inevitable. It must be measured, unforced. One step at a time. Good God, one of them's brought a brace of chickens! Bruno glances heavenward to where the pig still swings, momentarily silenced by the sweaty surge of bodies below. Ignore the pig.

Those already in the church are coming to rest, or something approaching rest—a lot of scratching, nudging, and toe-treading is still going on. The ingress of bodies outside is slowing, ineffective shunts and squirmings to get in proving less and less effective, some kind of equilibrium is reached. The field is taken, thinks Don Diego above. Raise standards.

But the congregation gathered to celebrate the feast of Phillip and James possesses no standard, knows no victorious cry beyond the rumbling of stomachs, so they stand there and jostle stupidly amongst themselves. What now?

Like Prato, thinks Don Diego. Like the horrible quiet of Prato in the dumb moments before the nails and hammers were produced, the fires lit and dice rolled. The aimless yawning hiatus, the gluey bog of the Pratesi's nonresistance. Clambering over the low turret to the breach their laborious cannonade had at last opened—it was already late in the afternoon—Diego saw Prato's defenders either fleeing or mooning in half-embarrassed fashion by the Porta del Serraglio like children caught in a game of hide-and-seek, knowing they are too old for this silliness. His halberdiers were pushing at them, nudging them back, but it was too desultory, and when challenged, the Pratesi simply dropped their weapons with a shrugging gesture. His own sword was tight in his hand, its hilt seeming to pierce the heel of his hand and weld itself to the bones in his arm, so indivisible were they. He did not understand this soft yielding of theirs, this nothingness, like a fawning dog that no matter how many times you kick at it will drift back and nuzzle to be fed, this cloying passivity. It enraged him. He understood his halberdier singling one of them out, cursing and shouting—this being somehow ludicrous, forced, goading at a different level—pushing the unprotesting man back against the wall he should have been defending, using the butt of his pike to drop him, the point to stick him. Then his turning from this miserable execution still unsatisfied, the same question still written in his bafflement. What next? What now?

"... eh? Eh, Colonel Diego?" The service is under way below, a beardless deacon swinging the thurible over the altar, the unsighted mass of the congregation already bored and talking amongst themselves, bareheaded journeymen, some monks at the back, a dog on its hind legs, barking. . . . "Don Diego!"

He comes to, Colonna's voice jerking him out of this. A tall, elderly man has entered and stands on the other side of Colonna's chair. Colonna looks up at him, raises a hand, which the other brushes with his lips, glancing at Diego as he does so.

"Vitelli, dear old Misha . . ." They are friends, or more than friends, it seems. Vitelli wants to smile his affection but glances again at Diego instead, his mouth twitching slightly. "Vitelli, this is Colonel Diego here. I am keeping him with me tonight."

Vitelli nods his head. "I know of Colonel Diego, naturally."

Behind him stands a young woman who looks up quickly at his name, gazing steadily across the two older men, weighing him up. Her nose is thin and hawkish, set in a strong face, too strong to be truly beautiful, her eyes brown, perhaps, but seeming almost red from the great cascade of coppery hair spilling over her shoulders. Diego notes her face with a start, another as he realizes she is costumed like a man.

"Signora Maria Francesca d'Aste," Vitelli announces. "My wife."

The woman offers her hand to Colonna, who kisses it. Then she thrusts it at Diego himself. He hesitates. Vitelli growls, "Keep your place," but she remains there, arm outstretched. He looks between them, feels himself color. She simply waits, staring into his face, challenging him. Abruptly she laughs, withdraws with a little flourish of her hand. Another latecomer has entered. She turns away from all three.

"Will *you* kiss my hand, Cardinal Serra?" she asks of the red-smocked man bustling through the press of the passage.

"Will you kiss my ring?" retorts the Cardinal, squeezing past her. "Vitelli. M'lord Colonna." He makes little bows to both. "Captain Diego. Is our Ambassador . . . ? Ah-ha! No need to answer. I see his marker. Lord, she is even fatter. . . ." He moves on and is presently swallowed in the crush.

"I still think of Paulo from time to time. . . ." Colonna is speaking absently, gazing out into the noisy maw of the nave. "I mean your cousin, Misha. I think, sometimes, that he was the best of us, in his way."

"Paulo cared for nothing and nobody. Least of all himself," Vitelli replies. Colonna nods sadly. Their eyes drift back to the spectacle below, or are drawn down there.

Below, the swollen mystery of the mass is throbbing, growing tight and bloated as the stomachs of drowned pigs swept down the Tiber by spring floods, unfurling fillets of itself in the long, drawn-out Alleluias of the choir that are sometimes audible above the racket of the worshipers' yacking, a dog barking, pig squealing (still swinging overhead), several chickens, *"Alleluia-aaaa. . . . Alleluia-aaaaaahhh . . ."* Angels ride in on tongues of sound that flap through the church's toothless gums, and Bruno prays that he will read well: the ambo is well inside enemy territory. Silently, invisibly behind the screen, Father Tommaso prays with him. Subdeacons and ushers gather together, bearing candles and little thuribles. Slowly the procession forms up.

"Should not the choir be silent now?" inquires Fulvio of Father Tommaso.

"Shut up," responds Father Tommaso.

Above, idle pot-boys are leaning over the balustrade to let thin strings of drool dangle from their mouths, then, just as it seems they must break, sucking them safely back up. Or not. It is a contest—longest string wins—somewhat vexing to those below. Trays of sweetmeats circulate perilously: pork in cider, beef in radish sauce, borne by sweating serving women who edge their way in difficult procession through the clumps and clusters of the guests. It is hot up here. And sliced tongue! Mmmmm. Fiametta *loves* a slice of tongue, signaling, waving, ignored, finally shouting, "You! Over here!" which attracts pained expressions from those around her, a smirk from Ascanio, but nothing at all from Don Jerònimo da Vich and Cardinal Serra, who, it would appear, are leaning out over the rail to watch and pass comment on the gobbing contest going on opposite—"Not bad, that one" and "More phlegm needed" and "Ooops! Overextended himself"—until the serving woman continues on, other attentions drift away, a kind of privacy is regained, and their real conversation resumes.

". . . so I had Diego there tickle his ear."

"And?"

"And nothing. He does not know, nor does it matter. I meet our friend again tonight. Venturo is only for appearance. What is the word from His Holiness?"

"I believe he is rather delighted. Ghiberti sought me out this afternoon, seemingly to demand sureties against the resurgence of 'your monstrous conduct and temper,' which I gave willingly"—Serra chuckles—"after which he let me know that His Holiness is retelling the episode with his customary brio to all who will listen. The role of the elephant in particular is growing . . ."

"Monstrous?"

"Monstrous. Yes, absolutely monstrous; look there now—" Serra points across to the pot-boys again, one of whom is jiggling a veritable stalactite of saliva, eyes narrowed in concentration, sucking now, up it comes. Vich turns at this hint to find a man standing behind him and to his right. He nods and the stranger nods back, moves off once again.

"Do you know him?"

"No. Faria's creature, most likely. Yes, look. He is leaving now we have seen him. Enough of all that. Tell me of our King."

"The court was at Toledo when last I heard, but he is aloof from this affair. The negotiation between our ministers and Manolo's proceeds. I take my instruction from there, and King Fernando his intelligence. We are players here in Rome, merely players. . . . Good God, look at that one!"

And this time it is Serra's turn to look about him in vague alarm, but, finding only Fiametta busy with her sliced meats in place of the expected eavesdropper, he redirects his gaze across the nave to the pot-boys, one of whom has unleashed a truly colossal pendant of drool, a glistening column that stretches down, little pearls of quicksilver gloop running down its sides to thicken and strengthen, farther, farther, more and more, until it seems it must wet the unsuspecting head below, but no! No, it is being retracted, its lithe tongue quivering as the Gob Maestro's own winds the excrescence back, spooling and spooning, cheek, jaw, throat, even stomach muscles all pumping in concert, the last foot of phlegm whipping back up into the gullet that spawned it with a slap, swallow, and gulp.

"Remember me in your next dispatch," says Serra, moving off. Pot-boys are slapping the victor on the back, making him choke a little.

"You are leaving?"

"I will attend our host for a while. An uncle of mine once fought with the Colonnas at, I think, Parma. Or Piacenza. Against the French, at any rate."

Vich looks into the pit of the church, where a deacon seems to be conducting the reading while ushers and subdeacons defend the ambo with shoves and curses against the surges of the crowd. The priest directly beneath him appears oblivious of all this commotion farther up the nave, fiddling about with thuribles and pyxes, mouthing inaudibly, now what would it be . . . the Creed?

It occurs to Father Tommaso, indeed intoning, *"Credo in unum deum,"* that soon the halfway point will be reached and the so-called Mass of the Catechumens will be over. Such markers keep the spirits up. The choir sings: *"Confitebuntur celi mirabilia tua domine. . . ."* Fulvio inquires whether they should not be forming the offertory procession now and is answered in the negative. It also occurs to Father Tommaso that if the sainted Fulvio should open his mouth one more time, and words issue from that mouth not contained in either the missal or the psalter, Father Tommaso will close said mouth with his fist. The choir sings: *". . . et veritatem tuam in ecclesia sanctorum. . . ."* Father Tommaso repents of said thought. *"Alleluia, alleluiaaa-aaahh!"* It being unworthy in the presence of the host that lies before him on the altar, inanimate for the nonce. Elaborately farced neumes blend their warbling trebles in the barrel of the roof, inviting angels to the feast. They have arrived invisibly and cling to the ceiling like bats: there are just over twenty-seven thousand of them at the moment. Christ is as yet absent.

But sometimes he comes—even here, even now. Sometimes he flickers in the host, or in the quiet that the host might sometimes command before the faithful bray out their smirched faith and sup on cleanliness again. For Christ is like the coldest cold air, skin-pricking and lung-burning. He may be here tonight, thinks Tommaso, clearing this space in his thoughts, Christ who was sown in the Virgin and rinsed at the Passion, reaped by enemies, threshed at the scouring, winnowed in foul words, ground in the mill of the gentiles, and made into pure flour and blood and cooked in the sepulcher for three days—from which a loaf came forth. This loaf: the host. He incenses it and the altar again. He washes his hands. He prays.

His deacon and subdeacon will pray with him, for they are no longer simply Bruno, his old comrade who has rejoined him in the interval, and Fulvio, the pious whelp whom he will punch in the teeth. They are his ministers and officers, and he is their ministry and office, mill and press of the bread and the wine. They pray, and the choir chants. He says to the two of them: *"Dominus vobiscum"* and *"Sursum corda"* and *"Gratias agamus domino deo nostro."* They give back to him *"Et cum spiritu tuo"* and *"Habemus ad dominum"* and *"Dignum et iustum est."* Somewhere in the church the sacring bell rings, and the din beyond the screen begins to subside. The choir falls silent. He remembers their father the Pope, then the living, then the saints who are dead. He stretches his hands over the wheaten disk, hands like rolls of meat, heavy and black-haired. He says the words.

Flanking him, Bruno and Fulvio turn face-to-face, Father Tommaso's profile—broken nose, chin-stubble—dividing them as Fulvio gazes rapt and vacant into the host's mystery, as Bruno darts glances through the rood-screen's tracery to the congregation beyond: heavy, weather-tanned faces staring up dumbly, silent at last, waiting. More angels arrive. Rats scamper over the floors, inaudibly. The first bell sounds high above, then the second, reaching the sounding chamber of the church in shuddering concussions of sound that hammer the air, and Father Tommaso reaches for the host, murmuring, holds it, murmuring, lifts it chest-high, pauses, higher, and Bruno sees Him mirrored in the faces of the faithful, in their crumpled mouths and snot-streaked noses, higher, their widening eyes and bobbing Adam's apples, all waiting for Christ. . . .

Now.

HOC EST ENIM MEUM CORPUM

"Jesu! Jesu!" "Wash me, Christ!" "Here! Over here!"

A single instant, and the church's silence is a cacophony of bellowed prayers, holy roarings, a din of supplications, orisons, petitions. Christ is not gradual, he is sudden. Rosaries swing about and tangle with wooden crosses. People get hit in the face by other people's amulets. This is not enough, so there is jumping, too— a good sight of the host being prophylactic against blindness, impotence, and death until sundown tomorrow—while the sick are lifted head-high to likewise receive full benefit: a one-legged woman, a badly mangled fighting cock, the dog (though it is healthy and escapes), coughing infants, somebody's grandmother. Even the pig joins in, squealing away up there, while from the gallery churns of milk are poured downward over the celebrants below. Cabbages are thrown. As-canio has one held by his page while he pisses into its leaves, then hurls it out, sailing high over the celebrants' heads, glancing off a pillar, finally impaling itself on a candle-spike jutting from the back wall. Boys release chickens, which try to fly, fail, and have their necks wrung. The pig is lowered into a waiting scrum of pig-fanciers who tear it limb from limb—prayerfully—spraying themselves with bright red pig-blood. The dog gets tangled in the pig-guts. There is vomiting, too; the victorious pot-boy, having been patted, thumped, and shaken all to no avail, is finally swung upside-down by the heels until his recalcitrant mucal stomach contents spray out. . . .

In the midst of these devotions, the demon Tutivullus arrives with pen and parchment to take notes from the rafters, said notes to later be collated and later still presented to the loose-mouthed sinner him- or herself at either the Pearly Gates or the Mouth of Hell, whichever should prove appropriate. He primes his pen and cocks an ear: lot of gossiping going on, lot of yelling, too, use block capitals for that, some more or less amiable scuffles, bit of fighting near the back— not his department—howling infants, note it, a barking dog, forget it. Dogs have no soul. Now, have all these infants been baptized? . . . Angels (a little over twenty-seven thousand) whirr and pout. More vegetables rain down. A Bologna sausage. That fight, though, near the back. Seems to be spreading, is it? Yes. Getting worse, is it? No. It's the monks. Odd.

Colonna squints into a nether gloom that even two hundred giulios' worth of beeswax candles has not fully dispelled. A gray stain is spreading there, outward from the back left corner, its leading edge all aggression and thumps on the head—Colonna does not object to this; the reputation of the feast of Philip and James rests largely on its rowdiness—but within this aggressive cordon sanitaire, a weird calm seems to be descending. Within, it seems, people are not fighting.

They are, in fact, kneeling. They are, in fact, praying. And they are kneeling and praying because whenever they try to rise, or stop praying, one of the gray-habited monks is beating them over the head. Not just monks, either. They have helpers, unmonkish ones, and the gray stain of prayer is spreading farther up the nave. He has been calm till now. The presence of Diego and Vitelli have cheered him somewhat; even Vitelli's little vixen has proved amusing, the rumors notwithstanding, useful in keeping Serra, who bores him, at bay. His wound has throbbed no more than usual. But this, this . . .

"Monks!" barks Colonna. Nearby sycophants grunt their disfavor; just what they were thinking, too. Don Diego abandons his musings on the pig-gut-entangled dog and peers forward. Monks, yes. Others, too, taken in with a glance that sweeps across the nave. Two men: one big, one small. He feels a shudder run through him. It was cold in the marsh, the marsh outside Prato. He shouts, but it comes out as a kind of croak. He senses the amused attention of those around him in which his own sudden hunger is wolfish and jarring. He doesn't care. He points, eyes fixed forward, still scarcely believing. Them. The order comes sharp and unbidden, the tone of the very command they stripped from him. "Get them!"

"Get them?" Colonna looks up, half-vexed, half-amused, at this little usurpation. "Yes, why not." To his men, then, sweating in their much-complained-of breastplates and helmets, "Bring them here!"

"An arrest?" inquires Cardinal Serra, all elevated whimsy.

"Yes, drag them up," says the flame-haired signora to the little conclave about Colonna. She appears flushed, though this may be another effect of the hair. "Drag them up and cut their cocks off." Vitelli raises an eyebrow at his wife. Someone coughs uncomfortably. The soldiers have disappeared downstairs.

Presently they reappear in the cross-waving, poultry-slaughtering tumult below: communion with Christ by proxy and other mass-appropriate activities grant precedence to the minimilitia's toe-stamping beeline through the pig-guts, cabbage leaves, ambiences of abbatoir and dairy, the whole squawking carnival of faith. . . . Shins get barked, the lame and the halt are shoved brusquely aside, though most step smartly sideways to let them pass. Thus the snatch-squad advances, diagonally across the floors of the Church of the Most Holy Apostles on the feast of Philip and James in the year of Our Lord fifteen hundred and fourteen, until they reach the monks.

Violence.

Light radiating through the smoke-striated air from the girandoles of the candleholders, striking the blistered plaster, blending one barely illuminated body with the next, makes the demon Tutivullus's already difficult job no easier. These monks all look rather similar; the soldiers, too, whose status at this Mass is rather ambiguous anyway. Would they be counted as "congregation" or not? They weren't here earlier. They're certainly here now, toting with difficulty one monk and two (secular) aiders and abettors back across the church, fighting a desultory rearguard action against the rest of the monks, who seem to be objecting to this. Well? He sighs, picks up his invisible pen once again, and starts scribbling:

"Oof! You little bastard!" "Grab his leg," "Eh?" "This one, grab it!" "Aaaaagh!" "Not his balls, his leg!" "This is unnecessary." "Shut your mouth!" "I am perfectly willing to walk." "One more word from you and I'll . . ." "Let him walk." "Uh?" "Gnnaaarrgh!!" "Let him bloody walk and give us a hand with this big bastard!" "Ooof!" "Shit!"

First it seems that the crowded gallery is moving en masse toward the group about Colonna, Fiametta being shunted forward like the blunted prow of a ship; but then the prow splits open, becomes a disgorging mouth, as a struggling bunch of soldiers is launched forward, nine or ten of them hanging on grimly to something that thrashes energetically within, something loud, something big. A smaller bundle follows, and then, more calmly, a monk escorted by Colonna's sergeant, the hem of his habit stained pink with the milk-and-pig-blood mixture, the whole garment spotted with mud.

"Beat them!" orders Colonna, at which the remainder of the soldiers, forcing a likewise difficult passage through the crowd, fall to punching and kicking of the normal-sized one, who responds with encouraging grunts and curses. The larger one merely roars, though in truth few blows are landed; it taking a minimum of eight soldiers to hold him still, very little of him is available for either punches or kicks. As to the monk, he stands erect and in silence, looking on with an expression of contempt. A soldier approaching with raised fist finds himself stilled by the very lack of resistance, arm up and ready but feeling oddly foolish. . . . The monk looks past him to the scarlet of Cardinal Serra.

"Punch him!" shouts Colonna, enraged by this hesitation.

But the monk begins to speak: *"Misere mei Deus secundum misericordiam tuam, iuxto multitudinem miserationum dele iniquitates meas"*—a pause—*"legit?"* This last is directed at Cardinal Serra, who has been avoiding his eye, rather fearing that this might be coming.

"Legit," Serra confirms reluctantly, then turns to Colonna. "He reads, my lord. He is a clerk of the Church. You may not touch him." Colonna looks irritated. "Then punch the others!" he shouts at the soldier, who turns to do just that.

"Stop!" commands the monk. The soldier stops, confused again. Several of the others stop, too. "Touch not mine anointed, and do my prophets no harm!" says the monk.

"What!" erupts Colonna.

"These are not prophets!" shouts Cardinal Serra. "And you are not David, monk!"

"I am Father Jörg of Usedom," retorts the other, "and I claim—"

"Very interesting. Beat them!" Beating resumes.

"And I claim the *privilegium clerici* for these my servants just as for myself," continues the monk.

"Claim it, then," answers Cardinal Serra, eyes fixed on the writhing mounds before him. "In the meantime, we continue with beating. Go on! Harder, you lackeys! Work up a sweat!"

"That's it, Serra," grumps Colonna.

"I protest my claim!"

"Not to me you don't. Go on, kick them, too!"

"Usedom falling within the diocese of Stettin, and Stettin being both peculiar and currently *sede vacante,* I protest *omisso medio.*"

"Don't you quote the canon at me, you miserable cur!" Serra is growing vexed. "How dare you pit your learning against a cardinal's! Besides"—he calms himself—"protests *omisso medio* were revoked by the Council of Basel three decades ago." A soldier is trying to angle his foot through the armpit of one of his fellows to stamp on Salvestro's face.

"In that case I would lodge a writ of *significavit,* and Stettin being *sede vacante,* as I said, I would lodge it with myself as both ordinary and metropolitan."

This gives Serra pause for thought. Suddenly he brightens. *"Significavit,* you said?"

"And I would lodge it *doubly,"* Jörg clarifies. Serra's face falls.

"I am judge here!" shouts Colonna, anger mounting at this presumptous quibbling.

"It is Justinian who says, If the cause be ecclesiastical, the civil judges shall take no part. Novella the one hundred and twenty-third, if memory serves," Jörg offers coolly.

Several of the soldiers have once again slowed beating to follow this exchange. The foot-angler is hopping up and down on his free leg, the other having been trapped in some unexpected convolution of the morass on the floor. This time it is the red-haired signora who steps in—literally—planting one leather-booted foot in the exposed side of the smaller of the two, *thunk!* followed by her own excited gasp. The soldiers take the hint and set to work again.

"An excellent point," rejoins the Cardinal. "Is the cause indeed ecclesiastical? For it seems to me that—"

"Common brawlers!" bellows Colonna. "What's so ecclesiastical about that? The offense is brawling!"

Cardinal Serra sighs. "Brawling . . ."

"In church," completes Jörg. "An ecclesiastical offense." Serra is downcast, Colonna only confused.

"But," Serra comes back suddenly, "are they actually clerks? Are they literate? I have yet to hear the verse you earlier recited so prettily issue from either one of them. What are they, monk?" Some great roars sound about now.

It is Jörg's turn to pause. What are they indeed? "They came to us as vagrants and ruffians," he begins. A grin begins to spread over Serra's face. "And yet they turned out to be our salvation, even if unwittingly, our church being imperiled by . . . by certain perils. We are very precarious on Usedom. So we have come to petition His Holiness. Being ignorant of Rome and the way by which she is reached, it was these men who aided us in our travels, travels which have ended only today."

"They are guides!" crows Serra. "Guides are not clerks! Guides are temporal, out of bounds. . . ."

"Guides, yes. And protectors, too, on occasion—"

"Temporal!"

"—and foragers, and cooks, and lookouts—"

"Temporal! Temporal! Temporal!"

"—typically sitting a little way off from our camp when we would stop for the night, their function then being, as it were, regulatory, concerned principally with ingress and egress . . ." Serra's grin disappears suddenly. He frowns, a dawning comprehension at what is coming next. "And thus, in that capacity, I must describe them as—"

"No!" Serra breaks in, to no avail.

"—doorkeepers. Who are commonly, I believe, counted as clerks."

It is apparent from Serra's dismay that something important has been reached. Colonna's "Beat them anyway!" has a formulaic quality to it, and Serra's invocation of the Council of Vannes to sanction this is met, predictably enough, with Jörg's of the Twenty-eighth Apostolic Canon.

"Not even God will judge the same thing twice," he adds, quoting Nahum, and carries on with the *At si clerici* of Alexander III for good measure.

"Reversed by Innocent the Third," counters Serra, still rather reeling from the "doorkeeper" setback. "In the decretal *Novimus*, I believe. And in fact"—rallying somewhat—"I believe the first Pius provided that disobedient clerics might be handed over to the temporal courts. Yes, I'm sure of it, *curiae tradantur,* that's the phrase. . . ."

"*Suo episcopo inobediens.* If, and only if, disobeying his Bishop. *That's* the phrase," Jörg rejoins. "And even then only *cum consensu episcopi sui,* which is to say only with the consent of his bishop—this is according to Fabianus—which is to say, *sede vacante,* as we have established, said Bishop being for want of another represented by myself, only if I give my consent. And I do not."

"No, of course you do not," Serra answers calmly, "and why should you, indeed? For unless you were acquainted with Innocent the Third's decretal, how would such an act be sanctioned? Then again, if you were to be acquainted—"

"Come to the point, priest," barks Colonna, losing patience.

"The point is that my monkish friend does possess jurisdiction in this case, and is bound to exercise it, too. Immediately, let me add. And then these scum are yours. *Saecula potestati tradantur,* which I construe to mean, 'They are to be handed over to the temporal court.' Eh? Ha!" Serra's jaw juts as he turns from Jörg to Colonna. "They're as good as yours, m'lord." Colonna nods, mollified. Vitelli nods. His wife grins. Jörg grins, too, though inwardly.

"*Saecula potestati tradantur?* Is that what you said? Innocent the Third? Now let me see . . . We have established that they cannot read, have we not?"

"No backtracking, monk."

"Of course, of course. This decretal of Innocent's, now. I seem to remember it from the *Tertia Compilatio*. It would be the seventh canon of that collection? The tenth distinction of that canon?"

Serra is blasé on the point.

"I thought as much. Cardinal, that decretal certainly allows for the handing-over of clerics. But only for the offense of forging papal letters, and if they cannot read, it would seem unlikely that they can write, and more unlikely still that they should forge the words of His Holiness—"

"Quibbles and quarrels!" shouts Colonna. "I'll do with them as I wish," picking up his staff and jabbing at the nearest of the the two. "There!" He jabs. "And there!" The soldiers shrug off their fatigue at these encouragements and set to. Soon the gallery is loud once more with curses, groans, and effortful grunts. Vitelli watches impassively. His wife twitches beside him, echoing and egging on the punching militiamen. Beside her stands Don Diego, who says nothing and whose face betrays no sign.

"Unhand them." It is the voice that is unexpected, issuing as it does from the Cardinal.

"I am the master here, priest," Colonna dismisses him.

"The monk has proved his case. You will unhand them."

Serra is different somehow, more robe than man. He looks glassy, oddly mechanical. "They are of the Church. Strike them, and you strike at Christendom!" His voice is different, too, disembodied, strengthened with new authority. Colonna stares up, amazed, then aghast at the betrayal. "It is not I who command you, Lord Colonna," Serra continues implacably, "it is the Church herself, every stone, every saint, every Pope. You shall lay no hand on her servants, nor touch her anointed. No hand, do you hear! No hand!"

Colonna is muttering, "Church be damned, damn you, damn you all," under his breath, rocking back and forth in his chair.

"Father!" It is Vittoria, who has forced her way through the crush of the gallery, through the now silenced audience, and stands now before him, accusing, furious, flushed with anger. Vitelli's wife eyes her coolly. "Father, how could you!" His men look to him.

The gallery is silenced. The whole church is quieter, less populous, people drifting out in ones and twos. The postcommunion is always rather boring. A few men and women are sitting against the walls. The flagstones are smeared with scraps and scrapings, cabbage leaves, chicken feathers, milk, blood. The dog is gone and the pig-guts, too: eaten. Behind the rood-screen, Father Tommaso murmurs, *"Per Christum Dominum Nostrum,"* and Fulvio and Bruno supply a final, "Amen." The monks too are silent, gazing up at the wordless scene above. Two battered men are being lifted to their feet. One, the greater, shakes off his would-be helpers impatiently. The other leans heavily on a proffered arm, clutches his ribs, winces rather theatrically. His face is swollen with bruises. One eye is closed. Through the other he sees an old man wearing a strange conical hat seated in an ornate chair, the red robes of the Cardinal, the gray of Father Jörg, faces behind these blurring in the gloom, a red-haired woman, her elderly escort. And then a face somewhat darker than the others, a face that since its first outburst has remained unmoved throughout all this, waiting patiently for this moment, certain that it will come, whose eyes fix themselves on his and will not let him look away. It is a face he knows.

"Welcome to Rome, Salvestro," says Don Diego.

"Turn over."

They traveled back in silence from the church, crossing Navona, moonlit and deserted but for drunks, the back streets mostly shuttered up, a few dim lights visible, some angels stacked in a mason's yard, nothing much. Nothing for Fiametta to catch hold of and wring out a conversation, something light and witty, to excite his mood, perhaps. The Aragonese are so wooden, she thought then, and thinks again now as she complies, rolling over on her stomach, stifling a soft belch, raising herself on all fours. She feels his hands grip her by the ankles. A little farther apart? She complies. A thumb appears in front of her face. She sucks on it.

"More."

Fiametta arches her back experimentally—more what?—imagining how her upturned buttocks must look, yellowed ivory in the candlelight. An approving hand grips the nape of her neck. The thumb is withdrawn and presently is felt once again. She feels hot there, ready. He likes this, likes the waiting. Ambassador Vich. She squeezes on the thumb, signaling her impatience with little twitches and grunts. Her hands reach back to try and grasp him—impossible, of course. He likes this, too. He was cold to her at the Mass, preoccupied. Now he is all attention. His member brushes her lips—up, slowly, slowly—down. She pushes back, but he withdraws. Not yet.

"This afternoon . . ."

Ah, that game. This afternoon . . . What to give him? This afternoon, the two of them standing there in their shifts, little blackface still shuddering as he burst into the room. . . . He wants more of that. The bath? Yes, give him the bath, the rose-scented steam, the girl's body, and the sweat running down it. He wants the girl, too, of course, her stony-faced silence, her darkness, but he dares not. . . . So she spins it out for him, little gasps and sighs punctuating her "And then"s and

"So I"s, her own excitement rising at the half-concocted memory, her voice now languid, now catching in her throat, as the girl does *this* to her and she does *that* to her. . . .

He goes into her suddenly. She catches her breath, silenced, cut off in mid-sentence. He is rigid, quite still in the moment before withdrawing—slowly and tautly, a bowstring being drawn back, a chicken eased off the spit—and she softens, drifts. She abandons him and recalls, or imagines—it is jumbled up and senseless, part of her abandonment—linen swinging in a soft breeze, two tethered horses rutting, laughter from somewhere, a tiny spoon tinkling in a silver goblet, bells ringing, Christ's face, the smell of red and yellow roses, Colonna's chair bobbing along and the people laughing at her, a slap on the rump, the girl's coal black eye glued to a crack in the floor of the attic room above, watching her bend to his pleasure, grunt for him, cry out. He works steadily, his flesh slapping against hers. She feels him buck and shiver. He is done.

A draft from somewhere plays irregularly on the candle at their bedside, the flame lurching over, then righting itself, until the wax gutters and spills, pooling in the reservoir. Too late, she thinks, and turns to her lover. He has dozed, sliding in and out of sleep. She toys with her pubic hair, watching him, idly pulling out the slick strands and winding them about her little finger, his semen trickling uncomfortably between her legs. He looks back at her. She sees he is still half-erect.

"Who was the red-haired girl?" he asks, breaking the drowsy silence.

"Vitelli's wife?"

He does not answer, simply continues looking at her. A new feature in his conversation.

"She was his brother's ward, or his cousin's. Vitelli married her the day she came of age."

"People were talking about her. . . ."

"People are indiscreet. So is she. Vitelli indulges her."

The questioning silence again.

"Prefers the *stufe* to her bed, the lower the better so far as she's concerned. There are those who call her a whore, and a few who say it is the cuckold who really calls the tune."

"Vitelli?"

"Perhaps he takes as much pleasure in her amours as she does. She's young, he's old. . . . Though I am not sure I would call them amours," she adds artfully, catching on to his mood.

"How not?" He is wide awake now, all ears. She looks down. Stiff as a post.

"You know her nickname? In certain circles, here and in Bologna where Vitelli serves, Signora Vitelli is known as *La Cavallerizza.* Or sometimes *La Cavallerizza Sanguinosa.* . . ."

"I do not follow." She is stroking him, gripping him about the shaft and working him slowly up and down. *I do not follow.* . . . Well indeed, let me tell you, thinks Fiametta to herself. Let me tell you since you want to know so much.

"She takes her pleasure wearing spurs." It catches her by surprise, a high strangled yelp her only warning before the sudden spurt spatters them both. Vich twists and groans. "Well, well," she murmurs, sliding the soft slab of her tongue down his chest and belly, half-remembering a joke she heard once about Spanish horsemen, something about mounting and spending whole days in the saddle. Little molten pearls, vinegar and sugar. She licks, leaving a broad wet stripe, a hot-and-cold arrow pointing to his crotch. She blows on it softly, feels his hips shift. Her hair brushes over the head of his member, hardly softer than before.

"Spurs, my Ambassador, the spurs are one version, anyway. . . ."

She turns to take him in her mouth. His voice comes thickly: "One version? What do you mean?" But when she tries to rise to answer him, his hand pushes her down again. She almost gags, then resumes her labors, patiently, artfully. Somewhere outside, a churchbell chimes a late Mass. A horse clops on the cobbles outside. They have found a rhythm now, her head resting on his stomach, pumping lazily together. Then the hooves stop. And, an instant later, so does her Ambassador. She raises her head in inquiry, and this time he does not reach to push her down again. He sits up, the two of them listening. The horse snorts. They hear its rider dismount. Suddenly he is sliding out from under her, her own realization dawning, unable to suppress the note of complaint that creeps into her voice.

"Him again? Tonight?" He nods, struggling into his hose, prick stiff but forgotten. "Make him wait," she urges.

"Impossible."

"Then tell me—"

"I may not," he cuts her short. "Not yet." He is at the door. "Sleep. I will wake you when we are done."

She hears his stockinged feet pad softly down the stairs, the bolts on the door being drawn, the scraping of the key, a murmured greeting in the hallway.

They will proceed to the scullery, that much she knows. There have been five or six such nocturnal meetings since the turn of the year. Her house is at his disposal, she has told him that. Vich has been more attentive of late, more solicitous, inquiring after her debts, even settling them on occasion. He has escorted her in public where before he would rarely be seen with her, allowed himself whole nights in her bed where before he would leap up theatrically after having her, pretending some urgent business at the embassy. Even his lovemaking has grown more urbane. Yet somehow, in some way, he has grown remote.

To begin with, she would yawn and grow conspicuously bored as he prattled freely of his work. It only encouraged him to disburden himself further: his dislike of his slippery secretary, Antonio, his anxieties at Diego, the resentful soldier billeted on him the previous year, the dishonesty of his servants, the petty humiliations visited upon him by cardinals, the other orators, apostolic bureaucrats, even their master, the Pope. Careworn, flustered, inept, he would take out his frustrations in fits of pique or sudden meaningless rages. But he was not remote.

It was new, or recent, noticeable only in the last few months and then only in the pretty turns of phrase with which he placated her. He knew she knew.

And so, stripping the sheet from the bed to wind about her, tiptoeing across to the door, it is not curiosity which drives her downstairs, for she could hardly care less what they might be discussing. Nor is it any sense of grievance that leads her past the wood stacked in the hallway, the least used pans hung high on the walls there, scrubbed and sanded to a dull sheen in the moonlight streaming through the barred transom above the door. Never, in the months leading up to this night, did she feel a slight in his reticence. Instead she recalled the unmannered petty nobles who would flood into the city from the Romagna in Easter week, bighearted red-faced simpletons whom she would escort safely through Rome's invisible labyrinths and unspoken riddles. Signor Shit-in-the-Woods, Count Open-Purse. Greenhorns, easy prey to the Ripetta whores, their pimps, the pickpockets in Navona, or the hucksters at Saint Peter's, she would shepherd them safely from church, to inn, to bed. Performing mightily in each, engorging soul, stomach, and prick, she would dispatch them finally as Rome's conquerors, waving pretty farewells. They were innocents, her lovers. That Vich should know more than his mistress marked him for a fool. He has grown worldly, she tells herself. Or thinks he has.

She moves barefoot over the cool flagstones. They have been lovers for almost a year now: she was reeling still from Chigi's petty cruelties, from Accolti's death. At least his widow still rented her the house. Vich too was unanchored, charging about Rome like a little baron, brandishing his temper like a club, snubbed, laughed at. Fernando's new orator was a furious clown. She knew of him long before they met. She taught him manners, Rome's manners, the manners that he wore at first like ill-fitting armor, latterly like the smoothest clerk. And latterly the jokes about the hothead have stopped altogether. Her work. She knows him better than any of them, better even than he knows himself. He has no secrets from her. So she will press her ear to the door, fix an eye to the keyhole. She will read him like a book. He will have no secrets. . . . Then she starts and almost cries out, all these thoughts forgotten at the sight before her. At the end of the hallway Eusebia is kneeling at the door.

Strangely silhouetted by the slivers of light escaping through the door's shoddy planking, the girl's shape seems rather to collapse than turn at her mistress's approach. She looks up quickly, then presses her face to the door once again, seemingly unperturbed at her discovery. Shocked, then suspicious, then complicit in her eavesdropping, not daring to whisper her admonishment, Fiametta drops beside her. They kneel there together, motionless and silent, peering through the cracks in the door.

". . . yes, very amusing, very funny indeed," Vich is saying sourly, poking at the embers in the hearth. The other chuckles. Fiametta wonders, irrelevantly, if he is still stiff. If the other man should see it, would he make a joke? Are they close like that? The women see him seated at the table, where Vich joins him.

"There will be plenty more such farces before we see this through. Did Venturo tell you the latest?" The other's accents are foreign, different from Vich's. His face is not unknown to Fiametta, but she cannot place him. A meal somewhere.

"I would rather have heard it from yourself, and wonder why I did not?"

"Your correspondence did not mention it?" The other's voice is sharper.

"It has not yet arrived."

"Ah." The voice relaxes. "Well, we received word only yesterday ourselves. When your own does arrive it will contain few surprises. A second beast has been procured, or rather chanced upon. . . ."

"Already got? Why have I not been told of this? Venturo mentioned a notion. An intention. Now it seems the beast is all but in the Belvedere. Do they know about this at Ayamonte?"

"Calm yourself. From where else would I learn of it? Read the dispatch for yourself if you wish." He reaches into his coat and passes a small packet across the table. Vich takes it unhurriedly, unfolding the pages one by one and flattening them on the table before him.

"'Alfonso d'Albuquerque, Governor of the Indies, sends greetings,'" Vich reads aloud. He scans most of the first page in silence, then begins to read again. "'And in pursuit of Your Highness's wish that these seas be made safe for our ships, I sent an embassy north from Goa. Diego Fernandes of Beja was my Ambassador, assisted by James Teixeira and Francisco Pais and others, including Duarte Vaz, who was interpreter. With them I sent some items of silver, others of brocade, and a quantity of velvet to be given to Muzzafar, who is King of the country of Cambaia, or Gujarat, where I would build a fort at Diu. They arrived first at Surrate, then Champanel, where they were told that the King was at Mandoval.' Something of a chase, it seems. What does this have to do with the beast?"

"As I said, the embassy was unrelated. The animal was pure fortune."

Vich begins to read more quickly, mumbling comments to himself.

"No luck with Muzzafar . . . no fort at Diu . . . exchange of gifts . . . Ah, here we are. 'The King offered my ambassadors expressions of his friendship, guarantees of safe passage, a quantity of gold plate, a richly carved chair inlaid with mother-of-pearl, many other ornaments, and *a monstrous beast.*' This is it?" The other nods. "'It is the height of a man, with rather a low body. It stands on four legs, its head longish and elongated like a pig's, the eyes near the front. It has the ears of a mouse, the tail of a rat, and a horn on the end of its nose. In the country of Cambay, it is called a *Ganda.* It is ill-tempered and is said to hate elephants. For nourishment it takes grass, straw, and boiled rice.' I imagine the Governor of the Indies was unamused."

"Albuquerque will get his fort in the end, but for the moment, yes, he has only pretty words, a dinner service, and . . ."

"And the animal," supplies Vich.

"Two oceans and a sea away in Goa as we speak. It will be some little while yet before it sees the inside of the Belvedere. I presume your dispatch will advise you."

"When it arrives," Vich responds. He sounds gloomy. "I distrust the irregularity of these communications. We are a long way from home, you and I. . . ."

"But what do you mean?" rallies the other. "We are at the center of the world. We are at Rome!" Both men laugh.

"How will you make the arrangements? A ship, crew, some worthy-seeming fool to play Columbus . . . My instructions are to aid you in this business. For all his foolery, our Pope is not a fool. One whiff of complicity . . . " He shrugs. "We would be embarrassed, at least. There would be repercussions. The negotiation at Ayamonte is delicate at the moment. There are those who would rather see it fail altogether."

"Serra mentioned it earlier tonight. I spoke with him at Colonna's. Simply dropped the name as though it were nothing. I do not know how he learned of it, but we must presume his inquiries will continue."

"What does he know?"

"Nothing, or he would not have tested me so crudely. I was casual, and there was an altercation with some monks which distracted him. He would have liked to question me further. If Serra knows of Ayamonte, then others will, too. We cannot rely on discretion; the truth will out. Once the expedition leaves we are undiscoverable. We must reach that point."

"Outrun the truth. Problems, difficulties," murmurs the other.

"All of them soluble," Vich declares, smiling. "For my part, I intend to delegate."

"Delegate?" The other's voice is shocked, a note of alarm creeping into it. "Delegate to whom?"

"You know him very well. He is clever, resourceful, adept at disguise; above all"—Vich is grinning—"he is the soul of discretion. My secretary. Signor Antonio Seròn."

The name seems at first to strike the other dumb. His face is incredulous. Then comprehension dawns, a smile spreads from ear to ear, and when he speaks his tone is admiring. "Don Jerònimo, you were born to this business."

Behind the door, the girl is motionless and silent. Her mistress, however, begins, after a minute or two, to exhale heavily, to sigh, to shift about awkwardly. There is a problem.

When, at Easter, a bathed Fiametta crosses the brook of the Marrana by the footbridge at the Church of the Greek School, swaps its stench for that of the noisy wharves between the Tiber and the Aventine, and picks her way through the ruins of the Savelli Keep to go to Mass at Santa Sabina, she takes with her a little cushion. The frescoes of the saints in the roundels are very fine and those of the holy cities marvelously detailed. The different-colored marbles adorning the clerestory usually claim her for a minute or two, the mosaics above the door and on Zamora's tomb also while away the time, but of most importance is the floor.

The floor is neither beautiful nor richly worked, no different in effect from the one she kneels on now. With the cushion, Fiametta may direct her thoughts to the Passion, to the Savior's suffering, his pain, or even try to follow the Epistle. Without the cushion, though . . . The floor of Santa Sabina is laid with unyielding flagstones, like her hallway. Almost from the moment that she took up her station there, in the hall, on the unforgiving floor, Fiametta's knees began to hurt.

She begins by kneeling on both, sitting back on her heels and craning her neck to peer through the crack. After less than a minute of this she gets cramp. She shifts position slightly, then alternates from one knee to the other, swapping regularly to begin with, then with increasing frequency until both knees are in equal agony from the hateful flagstones, on which she finally squats, all her weight bearing down on the balls of her feet, her arches straining, knees splayed in an effort to press her face to the door. . . . Hopeless. She is too fat to be a spy. Finally she sits back, resigned, propped on her arms, to listen but see nothing.

But the girl does not move, seems not to stir a muscle. The men's talk drifts through the door. A beast, somewhere. A negotiation, somewhere else. They do not really trust each other; Fiametta, stretching out her legs, idly catches the undertone. She does not care, wiggling her toes. And again, the girl does not move. But then there is a shift, a sudden change, and Fiametta almost scrambles to her feet, sure that the men must have heard, seen, sensed . . .

Eusebia is soundless as before, just as invisible. Her Ambassador is describing the beast, or reading a letter, something. But the girl is rapt, the air prickling with her attention, its abrupt focus stabbing through the door. Something they have said has provoked this in her. Her excitement is palpable. How can they not feel it?

". . . it takes grass, straw, and boiled rice. I imagine the Governor of the Indies was unamused," Vich is saying. She *knows*, thinks Fiametta, eyeing the girl, she knows what they are talking about. A beast, a Governor, the Indies . . . Which of these has galvanized her? The two men talk on, the candle burns lower, or redder, the cracks in the door glow like embers now. Eusebia is blank again, a silhouette of nothing. What do you know? Fiametta wonders to herself. As if in response, the girl rises to her feet. The voices within have fallen silent for a moment. They are bidding their farewells.

Fiametta struggles up. Together they hurry back down the hallway, climb the stairs in silence. Outside the door to the main *sala,* she turns to her maid, pinching her arm and hissing in her ear, "Never again, do you understand? Never again." She jerks her thumb back down the stairs. "What did you think you were doing?"

Fiametta expects the girl to hang her head, adopt her habitual cringe, to remain silent. Instead Eusebia faces her squarely, and when she speaks her voice is unguarded.

"I was thinking of the country whence I came," she tells her mistress. "I was remembering the great river which divides it and the forests which grow along its banks. I was remembering a village there, where my father's brother took me, and I was watching a boy who was fishing in a pool beside it."

These words mean nothing to the woman gripping her by the arm. It is her voice that silences Fiametta, for it is neither wistful, nor sad, nor apologetic. None of the tones she would expect. Even unknowing, the two men have sparked something in her servant. She looks into the girl's face, searching for whatever she is hiding there, but the barbarous markings that run in lines across her cheeks are like a mask; her passivity is impenetrable. The sound of chairs scraping comes from below. Eusebia turns away then, and Fiametta watches as she continues upstairs. She waits until she hears the men open the scullery door and pad through the hallway before she makes her own way back to the bedchamber. The sheet clings to her, damp with sweat. She hears the bolt drawn back, the door opened and closed. Hooves clop loudly in the courtyard, are silenced abruptly as the horse turns into the street. Vich's careful quiet footsteps on the stairs. He is considerate, she thinks, feigning sleep. Kind, as the door is opened. Warm, as he slips into the bed. He plants a line of chaste, deceitful kisses down the nape of her neck. Vague *mmm-mm*s from Fiametta, as though dreaming of him.

"*In*-dia-aah," he murmurs, half-mocking, leaning over her to kiss her breast. She rolls onto her back, stretching, wanting him. "Where the King"—he has her nipple between thumb and forefinger—"lives in a volcano." Her other breast flops lazily over to join the first and partially bury it. "Ah-ha! *Af*-rica-aaah." He sucks busily for a second, then licks around the underside.

"Is he gone?" she asks, yawning, reaching for him. Vich does not answer. His tongue moves down, darting into her navel, his teeth nipping at her, farther down. She raises her head to look down in surprise—he has never done this before. Vich carefully parts her lips with his fingers, flicks his tongue experimentally. He is improvising, different from the man of a few months ago. She lets her head fall back. His weight shifts on the bed. She breathes in, waiting, her hand tightening in his hair. She feels his breath on her, his head poised in the gulf between her thighs.

"*Ro*-ma," he murmurs as she pushes his head down.

Ro-ma, it would seem, is humid tonight. There is water in the air, or vice versa; indoors and out, commingled promiscuously in the troughs and sloughs of the city's contours. In the damp folds of the Velabrum, the wet crease of the Subura, rank vapors and steaminess imply spatterings, localized downpours, short-lived but drastic squalls. Heavy dust-laden fogs lumber into town. *Ro*-ma drips tears and oozes sweat, secretes and releases drool. Lips pucker or slaver, tongues loll or stiffen. The Caput Mundi grows hydra-headed and thirsty, these mouth-to-mouth exchanges marking junctions, short-lived intersections in the commerce that the city carries on with itself, a new and fluid topography. Its creatures seek each other out in damp-ridden bedchambers and musty attics, in doorways, against the walls of lightless alleys, blind grindings and gropings, mouths crammed with spit, throats gagging on innards, swilling and swallowing and gasping and grunting. . . . On the piano nobile, in a tangle of come-flecked sweat-soaked sheets, Vich is a muscled darting fish feeding on the water-bleached carrion of his mistress. Beneath a wharf in Trastevere, some Corsican bravo bruises the slack tonsils of his sweetheart. Elsewhere a barge captain licks the plump cheeks of his "Roman heart's desire" (he calls her that) in a manner practiced on his Magliana, Vicinia, and Ostia "Heart's desires." An elderly banker's wife snacks on her page's downless upper lip; a tart pulls up her shift. Amongst jangling bits and bridles a saddler plants his laughing mouth over that of his partner's laughing daughter. A consumptive shoemaker hacks midkiss and coughs a gobbet of gray phlegm down the throat of his perfectly lovely wife. It is a detail: they are in love and have no money. It doesn't matter that the tart will go unpaid, nor that the page will, that three dogs are fellating themselves in Pescheria, inspiring a baker's boy who will later try the same in Ponte and find he cannot reach. Think supple, he thinks. . . . Then again, a stone's throw away, the Albergo d'Orso, top-floor, east-facing window: An ex-functionary of the Apostolic Camera stands motionless, his bronzed body muscled and naked as a god, eyes searching the anterior darkness while minions tongue him from below, all three waiting for sunrise and ejaculation. Dawn is hours off.

How about nice little dry kisses? Grandpa to granddaughter's soft white forehead, or tearful mother to departing son, or like Vittoria Colonna's on the hard dry wood of her crucifix with its little carved Christ, the thorns so well-realized that she has sometimes bloodied her lips, so salty-sharp, mmm-mm, while Papa bites the heads off rats (an untruth, Vittoria's single sin today) and howls in the dusty gallery where the servants finally abandoned him, alone but for the drummer boys of Ravenna whose tattoo throbs within his skull, stamping madly on the broken boards. . . . Shall we continue? Cardinal Serra is slumming it on a pallet in Ripa with an unwashed girl from the docks who kisses his "wound," or sucks out the "lance," or swabs his face with her vinegary juices, or something equally banal, while downstairs (these events are unrelated), Ascanio and "friend" pour wine down each other's throats: from the cup, from the jug, from the mouth, from the . . . And upriver, in the malarial dankness of the Borgo, in the inky darkness of the back hall of the Pilgrim's Staff, lying together on the straw mattress acquired that afternoon in Peter's Square, Wolf is kissing Wulf.

Wulf cried earlier, on the way back from the church, but now he has cheered up somewhat and is surreptitiously masturbating under his habit, hoping Wolf will not notice. To one side of him the bulky outline of Bernardo masks the slighter one of Salvestro, who groans softly from time to time. To the other lies Father Jörg. The faint tinkling of sheep bells sounds loud in the night's stillness, *ting, ting, ting,* a flock being driven up to the pastures of the Pincio, *ting, ting, ting,* through the backstreets of the Borgo, across the bridge of Sant'Angelo, silly directionless sheep bumping into one another, bumbling along the Via Lata, fading in and out of earshot, a familiar sound to Rome's tireless lovers, the smoochers and snoggers, the wives of snorers and grinders of teeth, to the earliest of early risers and latest of late sleepers, to the sleep-abandoned. A familiar sound, too—recognized, discounted—to Don Diego, who kisses the pommel of his sword. Lying on his cot, staring into the insomniac darkness, he sees the shapes of enemies: a great gallery of backbiters, suave liars, two-faced placemen, soft-skinned smooth-faced back-stabbers . . . *Ting, ting, ting* . . . Gone.

If I am to be thought a monster, he thinks, sword rising above the first bowed head, why should I not slaughter them all?

The blade quivers and Diego imagines how it will bite the bone of the skull. Or slice the soft flesh of the face. Yes, but whose face? Who, if this scene were actually played, would he drag forward to be the first? The tip of his sword taps the fat chin of Ramon de Cardona, and obediently, slowly (so Diego can savor it—this ritual has been refined in repetition), the fat-faced Viceroy of Naples looks up at his accuser. The moment of recognition. Fear. Excellent, thinks Don Diego.

"Forgive me, Don Diego."

"*Colonel* Diego," Diego corrects him.

"Colonel Diego, forgive me my cowardice at Ravenna, where I—"

But Don Diego, faced with his former commander, cannot restrain himself at the sound of his voice, even imagined. He stabs forward and the tip of his sword disappears into the Viceroy's throat, abruptly cutting off the confession. Blood runs along the flat of his sword. The Viceroy gurgles and chokes. On his bed, Diego sighs. Patience, he tells himself. Try again. He stares into the teeming darkness, and once again Ramon de Cardona shuffles forward, fat frightened face upturned to his own.

"Forgive me, Colonel Diego. I am a coward. I left my men at Ravenna. I betrayed you at Prato, and afterward . . ." Don Diego signals for him to pause, then cuts off one of his hands. The Viceroy howls, then continues. "Together with Cardinal Giovanni di Medici, now our Pope, I conspired to place the disgrace of Prato on your shoulders when it was rightfully our own. It is our filth which stains you"—Cardona fouls himself at this point; he seems to be naked now— "mine and the Cardinal's."

"How?" demands Diego. "How did you do it?" But Cardona only stammers and sobs. The real Cardona could answer, thinks Don Diego, running him through. He is growing tired of Cardona's presence in these nightly parades and beckons impatiently to the next witness. Another pudgy body hurries to take the corpse's place. "Forgive me, Colonel Diego," begins Cardinal Giovanni di Medici himself, bug-eyed with fear. "I am scum, I am traitorous and mendacious, I—"

"How? How did you do it?" barks Diego. Medici's stammering. His disgusting sobbing, but no answer. Diego thrusts quickly at his stomach, then slashes sideways. "If not how, why?" he shouts. The prelate looks down in amazement at the innards spilling out of his belly. He tries to gather them in his hands and stuff them back in. Diego cuts his throat. Boring. Who next?

In his mind's eye a whole crowd of panicky preening courtiers whirls up. Diego scans their faces as they mill about and chatter. They are interchangeable, copies of one another. That was how I missed him, thinks Diego. But the face he seeks soon comes into view, there, at the very edge of this shrieking flock, and there, in its midst, and at its rear, moving smoothly about amongst them. "You!" he commands. "Come here."

A man in his late thirties steps forward confidently. He is dressed like a courtier, in French silks, sleeves slashed, ostrich feather in his hat. His sword, though, is a heavy steel affair, not the useless brittle rapier affected at court, and his gait is vaguely military, a gentle swagger. His face gives away nothing, and that too is as Don Diego remembers, for the first time he set eyes on the man he saw only that: a face poked through the flaps of a tent.

It had been evening and they were gathered in Cardona's marquee: he, the Viceroy, five or six of the other commanders. They were arguing about supplies, as they had been the night before and the night before that. They were on the march to Prato.

The army that had left Bologna two weeks before was almost ten thousand strong. They had all but exhausted their own provisions in a week, and the chests loaded with Bolognese ducats were now in the possession of the victuallers who had followed the baggage train, sold their wormy meal and rancid bacon, and turned tail. They were camped near the headwaters of the Savena. A little village had been ransacked the night before while the sergeants stood by, either helpless or cheering on the men. The next day had seen the first attack on the baggage train, and when they'd pitched camp three men, the ringleaders, had been hung. There would be nothing more until Barberino, and even there they might have to fight before they filled their bellies. None of that had been settled yet.

Suddenly there had been horses and shouting outside the tent. They got up quickly, though no alarm had been sounded. It was Medici and a party of horsemen, a dozen or so, who acted as his escort. He came in alone and the talk went on, Medici saying little or nothing, until the talk turned to Prato, which was ruled by an old condottiere called Aldo Tedaldi, according to Cardona, who might or might not resist them.

"Tedaldi? Tedaldi put us to the bother of a siege?" Medici had spoken up abruptly. "Aldo and I all but grew up together. No, no, no. . . ."

They had accepted that. Medici seemed untroubled, content to leave the situation in their hands. He took a cup of wine or two, listened carefully. A short time later a face poked itself through the flaps of the marquee. Medici looked around, nodded to the man, and bade them all good night. Diego left shortly after, walking the short distance to his tent flanked by Don Luis and Don Alonso, two of his more trusted men-at-arms. Outside, all about them, the darkness seethed with movement. Heads turned toward them and followed them as they passed. In the dark, the men were not bombardiers and pikemen, harquebusiers and crossbowmen, not captains and sergeants, companies and battalions, not Spaniards and Germans, not *stradiots, avventureros,* and *lanze spezzate.* They were sloping animals, hungry patches of darkness. By night, the camp was theirs.

"It was you, the face in the tent," Diego tells the phantom now.

"It was."

He had seen him throughout the days that followed, but without ever truly taking note. He seemed to move freely and without fear between the various Free Companies, which contained the real rabble, lawless cutthroats and fugitives who had attached themselves to the regular army at Bologna. The whole force moved through the Mugello valley, herded like cattle by their sergeants and captains. When the smoke from a village was sighted ahead, the pace would pick up. The horses dragging the carts and cannon would be whipped to a reluctant trot; eventually the whole army would be charging a cluster of miserable hovels. The villagers had long since fled, taking all they could carry, driving their livestock before them into the hills. They could be seen sometimes on the higher crags overlooking the valley. They were small as flies, watching the straggling carcass that dragged itself along the valley floor far below. The men were racked by dysentery and fevers. Every morning another group of the sickest was left behind, wailing to their comrades not to abandon them. The peasants would sometimes not even wait until the tail end of the army was out of sight before descending to cut their throats.

Diego organized forage parties and vanguards, sent out scouts. Medici himself seemed serene while the force that was to oust the Podesta and return him to Florence degenerated into a starving mob. The nights were broken with shrieks and cries as suspected thieves were beaten to death by their comrades. Patrolling the column of carts and cannons with his men-at-arms, Diego saw a blankness in the men's faces. Their eyes would fix on a distant outcrop of rock and not see a man an arm's length away. The attacks on the baggage carts were desperate skirmishes, the looters almost oblivious of their own injuries. It was Florence that drew them on; *La Crasa Puta,* they called her. They would rip her open and feed on her like wolves. Prato was nothing more than a name.

As the army crawled down the valley of the Mugello, the common soldiers seemed to detach themselves from the spine of carts and cannons and spread out to fill the broadening floor of the valley. They moved like cattle, stumbling forward aimlessly. Riding high on the right-hand slope, Diego looked down at the horde strung out below. He saw a beaten army; within it, an army of murderers. Medici's sergeant moved through all this unscathed.

"There was a meeting before we reached Prato, was there not, between Cardinal Medici and an envoy from Florence?" Diego inquires now of the foppish sergeant. He thinks of hauling up Medici by the ears again and tickling between his legs with the point of a dagger, but the sergeant will do as well. "I would run you through if I found you alone," he adds before the man can answer.

"I do not doubt it. And yes, there was a meeting, but I can say no more than that."

In the darkness of his bedchamber, Don Diego conceives the sergeant standing before him awkwardly, staring at the ground between them, discomfited by the interrogation. But pleading for a hearing? Pressing his case? Begging for his life? That he cannot imagine. "You were not at the center of this business, I know," he tells the man. "But you were its functionary. Without you, or another like you, I would not have been entrapped. . . ."

He stops. The man is laughing at him.

"Entrapped? Don't you understand that you were the factotum all along? Without you, none of it was possible. Without *you,* Captain Diego."

"Colonel," grumbles Diego, thinking, True, true, but how? He jabs at the sergeant with his sword, which disappears into the man's chest to no obvious effect and reemerges bloodless.

There were clues, if he could scratch them up: it being Medici who had ridden ahead to parley with Tedaldi and Prato's "defenders," who had returned with a tale of being driven off a mile or two short of the city. "No cause for concern, though," he said lightly. "They will talk—when the time comes." The army was three days' march away then. Cardona nodded complaisantly. There was a studied quickness to their exchanges.

Rehearsed, thinks Diego in the night-silenced embassy. The silky sergeant has disappeared, just as he had in fact disappeared somewhere along the march. He has no memory of him until Prato, where he is spied again here and there amongst the very worst of the militias, sauntering about, at once purposeless and purposive, *at large.* . . . They called him Rufo. Sergeant Rufo; was that his name? He never knew what the man did, nor Medici—precisely. Nor Cardona. Prato surrendered and yet was sacked. And Tedaldi died. And his family was killed.

Not by me, thinks Diego. And that was not how it appeared at the time. His disgrace had been carefully prepared. With the army bivouacked in the lush fields about the town, the town itself resting in the soft earth, on a river that, though it swamped land a little upstream of the city walls, never flooded, in the soft warmth of late August. They carded wool—the Pratesi—the town was built on it. Softness, warmth. . . . He is reaching for something, in the unconnectedness of the two, army and town, the horrendous implausibility of what was to happen the next day. He must have been already marked and as ignorant of his fate as the Pratesi were of their own.

And now in the dark and its gripless substance, in his dark keep, he reaches again for his sword. Tonight has changed everything. Cardona, Medici, his "Sergeant Rufo . . ." Now, though? "Now the fourth player." *Drag him up. . . .* The sword wavers over a white neck, the waxy flesh. Pull him out from under Colonna's trained apes and stand him on his feet, this *Salvestro.* He had thought him lost, escaped. Here he was. *Peace has always made fools of men like us. . . .* But not always. Come now, lift him up and look him in the eye, the one not swollen shut. Regard, a pawn even more miserable than himself. Watch him run away through the streets of Prato with his tame giant in tow. There are horsemen chasing him; himself among them—how foolish he was. Letting him hide in a bog and letting him escape. He knows the rest, this golden pawn—the how of it, if not the why. Was it Salvestro who actually held the knife? Who actually did the cutting? It does not matter. An enormous calm wraps itself about him.

The vagabond is still standing there, waiting apprehensively. I place great faith in you, he tells the wretch. You seem a resourceful fellow, the sort to survive. You will find me again when I need you. Diego is a magnanimous warlord, his sword cradled in his arms. You may go now. . . . You will find your way back, he calls after the man, who has turned tail and is fleeing into the distance; there's no escaping me. . . . Footsteps downstairs; His Excellency's return. How much longer now will he be His Ladyship's mastiff? The secretary is ambitious. He will help. Almost asleep now. Almost at rest. . . . Come back! Does he shout this? Perhaps, for the footsteps stop, above him now, Vich's apartment. Silence: the sound that listening makes. A kind of chuckling—his own. But look at the wretch come back! Bounding and sprinting and racing to the rescue, just look at him . . . scrawny, tousled, unwashed, unfed. Look at him run, with his swollen eye and filth-stained rags. Look at his surprise, being pulled to his feet, noticing Diego for the first time.

Welcome to Ro-ma, Salvestro. . . .

My savior, thinks Diego, laughing to himself. My savior, the throat-cutter. He will have the truth cried in the streets, present his case, appeal to the King. He will restore himself.

Darkness again, although different in kind—more absolute—the eyeless blackness of a mine-shaft or a ship under fifty fathoms of pitch; this rearmost chamber is an inky pit stirred only, now, by whispering.

"It wasn't."

"It was."

"It wasn't."

Asking after the Pilgrim's Staff earlier that afternoon, Father Jörg, Salvestro, Bernardo, HansJürgen, and rest of the monks were directed from the piazza to turn left into the "dismal rat-hole at the side of the Albergo del Sol," left again down "the open sewer of the Via dell'Elefante," to "follow the most depressing of the three alleys running east until you feel like killing yourself" and eventually find themselves in front of "something that looks like Sodom after Lot left— you'll know it by the gloom." This soon revealed itself as flattery.

Apart from a few of the most inaccessible attic rooms, the hostel is windowless. By day the main door is left open—this helps—but the tenement opposite stands a full story taller, the doorway itself is prefaced by a porch, and the building faces north. Drizzles, downpours, and damps find a welcoming home in the cracked roof-slates and disintegrating pointing: the crumbling fabric of the shambles squatting in the Via dei Sinibaldi is permeable to most kinds of weather. . . . But illumination? Its passageways and drafty stone staircases are black with candle-smoke, its ceilings gluey with tarry fumes from oil-lamps carried by the denizens who stumble from room to room, dragging immense shadows behind them, skewed *brockenspecters* that stalk their owners through the corridors and enfilades, sliding along the soot-streaked walls like murderers. The Borgo is the dankest quarter in the city, the Via dei Sinibaldi the dingiest street in the quarter, the Pilgrim's Staff the most dismal building in the street, and the rearmost chamber the darkest in the whole building. Well-known poets have spent nights here in search of the authentically "Stygian." Sunlight staggers in only to die.

"Had the windows walled up," the proprietor explained. He pointed to some patches of brickwork. "Stop the bastards who won't pay crawling out and not paying. I'm Lappi. There's a big place at the back, get you all in no trouble. Good lock on it, too. Got straw?" The dormitory room would cost them twenty-three guilii a week, in advance. "Bit gloomy back there, but then you're Germans. You'll be used to gloom." Lappi was squat, wiry-haired, long-armed. His face resembled a cowhide stuffed with violence into a sack. It uncrumpled, briefly, when Father Jörg threw open the chest, handed the man a heavy silver goblet, and asked how many weeks would it buy? "Where'd you get that lot!" he blurted out at the sight of the silver and gold plate.

"So *that's* what was in it," said Bernardo, who had carried the chest for the greater part of the journey.

Holding aloft a single candle, Lappi escorted them into the bowels of the building. A cavernous chamber yawned before them. Volker, Henning, and some of the others were sent out for the cheapest palliasses to be had; these were set down on the floor, and then Signor Lappi was sent for again.

"I wish to know where we might give thanks," asked Father Jörg of the hosteler.

Lappi's earlier astonishment had already given way to suspicion. "Oh, you do, do you?" he retorted swiftly, eyeing his latest guests. Then he remembered the chest. "Well, that's reasonable. Thanks is a fine thing, very fine. Given a few myself over the years, off and on. Can't say as I have a specific place for it, though. . . ." He limped on through a few more improvisations. "Why don't you give thanks here? Bit dark at the moment, but there's a few candles in the store. I could spare a couple, on the cheap. Got candles, have you?"

"We wish to celebrate Mass," said Father Jörg, at which light dawned in Lappi's face and something else too, perhaps, in Salvestro's view. He was eyeing Lappi, as he had eyed the innkeepers throughout their journey, from Stettin down the valleys of the Oder and Neisse to Gölitz, to Dresden, through Chemnitz and Zwickau to Plauen, on to Nuremberg, and Regensburg, the Alps rising above them, then under them, then behind them, the country changing almost from day to day, the little and greater towns that led them south, Piacenza, Carrara, Viterbo . . . Rome, eventually. Innkeepers in all of them.

"Mass!" exclaimed Lappi. "Well, you're in luck! It's Philip and James tonight. Used to go to it myself. . . ." He began to give directions. "The first thing is to put this gloomy shambles behind you and get yourselves across the river. . . ."

Salvestro watched Lappi point this way and that. Innkeepers, he had decided, fell into either of two categories. There were the brutish, near silent ones, prone to rare but spectacular rages, public displays of wife-beating, and insolence. They were usually huge and red-faced. Then there were the helpful ones, overflowing with suggestions, tips for the route, attentive at the table, happy to turn their own staff out of their beds to make room for late-coming weary travelers. These were the ones who swindled their guests, pilfered their possessions, and organized surprise ambushes an hour or two farther up the road. To Salvestro's way of thinking, Lappi was probably one of these.

". . . so, you're across the river. Go north past the Sanguigni Tower. It's fairly tall and square, but don't confuse it with any of the other fairly tall square towers, Sanguigni's the one you want. Keep Citorio on your left then swing east past the Mitre; there's no sign, but you'll know it from the smell of cabbage—never did understand that—bear right, across the Via Lata by Saint Mary's, right again, and you're in Piazza Colonna. Santissimi Apostoli is smack in front of you. Get there early, mind you. Usually a bit of a crush."

"Thank you," said Father Jörg.

"That's a real Mass, that is," Lappi reminisced fondly. "Not many like that nowadays. Anything else before you go?" Father Jörg shook his head. "Well, the Church is a whore, as they say," said their host. "Enjoy her."

"It *was.*"

"It *wasn't.*"

Salvestro and Bernardo are whispering. It is a whisper-inducing darkness.

The monks who had stridden confidently out of the hostel earlier that evening reentered it demoralized, bewildered, jarred. Wulf had cried. Father Jörg had rebuked him, "We set out to give thanks. We gave thanks. Now be silent." He should have said more, rallied them somehow, Salvestro thought. In the melee of the church, Jörg had retreated into himself, gazing sightlessly forward in prayer. He was untouched and untouchable. Salvestro had looked to him for some sign, a command, but there was nothing. It was Gerhardt who had given the lead, striking out fearlessly, forcing the brawling celebrants to their knees. Now he wore an air of silent contempt, and Salvestro himself was preoccupied with quite different concerns, his bruises throbbing. They were all locked in their own thoughts, and, preparing for bed in self-reproachful silence, the monks avoided one another's eyes as though they had failed some collective trial and were consequently set apart from one another, each to ponder his failing alone. The silence was heavy with private bafflements and shock. They were unprepared for Rome.

When they finally walked out of the church it was Gerhardt who led the way, as though Jörg had exhausted himself and lost his argument with the Cardinal, instead of winning as he had. Bernardo lingered near the back and was the last to join the huddle that regrouped outside, muttering, "Look what I got," in a pleased-furtive manner and drawing back the flap of his coat to reveal a large cabbage. "Got itself stuck on a candlestick. . . ." Salvestro was looking at the cabbage, wondering why it was so wet, when a sharp burst of laughter sounded, nervous and high-pitched. Jörg had wandered a few yards away from them and tripped on the rough ground. Someone had laughed, that was all.

With the candles doused, the sound of wakeful breathing filled the dormitory. Now that he was lying down, Salvestro's ribs gave him no peace. One side of his face felt tight and huge with swelling. But the blows and kicks were as nothing to their aftermath. *Him,* he thought over and over, but without advancing beyond the quick blow of the recognition itself, which felled him each time he approached. Gradually, the breathing around him changed character. Inhalations grew deeper, exhalations longer, the first snores sounded. Some rustling on the other side of Bernardo ended with a stifled half-yelp; someone sleep-talking nonsensically on the far side of the room ceased finally or was silenced by his neighbor. Private nervous exhaustions slackened and loosened, sinews relaxing and unknotting, cordage unwinding and racing off the spindle, the bucket plunging down the well-shaft into oblivion. Salvestro waited in wakeful silence for the last of them to sink into sleep before reaching over painfully to shake Bernardo.

"It was him," he whispers.

The giant stirs, comes more fully awake. "Who?"

"The Colonel. At the church." His mouth is swollen. It hurts to whisper.

There is a short silence while Bernardo thinks about this. "It was not," he says.

"It was."

"It wasn't."

"It *was.*"

"It *wasn't.*"

Someone stirs then, someone who might be the Prior, and both of them fall silent. Salvestro waits, counting interminable minutes before reaching over again, more painful still this time—the flesh around his ribs seems to be stiffening—to shake Bernardo. But Bernardo has fallen asleep and a little later begins to snore, and Salvestro realizes from past experience of Bernardo's snoring that he will not be wakened easily, at least not without violence. He is far from sleep, alone but for the head that rears up like a grizzled monster out of the depths. Hobbling back to the Borgo, he'd kept glancing over his shoulder to see if they had been followed. When his companion had asked him whom he sought, he'd said nothing. Bernardo had not recognized him.

He was unsurprised—Bernardo was ignorant. He was ignorant himself, though his ignorance was different in kind. Colonel Diego was a familiar sight to any who had survived the march from Bologna to Prato that summer. Unlike most of the commanders, he traveled light. His tent, bedding, and armor went with the baggage, the rest with himself. He rode back and forth on a powerful roan, dressed plainly, always helmeted, his saddlebags bulging with kit; a point of reference in the bland contours of the Mugello, his comings and goings monitored almost instinctively. Even the Sicilians, if asked where one of their compatriots was that day, might answer without looking up that he was farther up the column, "about a stone's throw past the Colonel" or "pretty much where the Colonel crossed the column this morning, just behind the cannon." He hung on the valley's lower slopes, this side, that side. He might disappear for most of the day, and the men would begin to ask casually if anyone had seen the Colonel, or angrily, "Where the hell has that damn Colonel got to," as though he were late to a wedding. He was outside the stench and viciousness of the camp. In the days before they reached Barberino, the very worst, when Salvestro, Bernardo, and Groot slept sitting up, back to back, to ward off the throat-slitters, when even the Sicilians briefly stopped knifing each other in some show of self-preservative solidarity, the Colonel appeared unchanged and unchangeable, like an image struck for a medal.

But his face, the human business of eyes, nose, mouth, hair, the flesh on the frame, that was lesser and unnoted. A recognizable man hid behind "The Colonel," but for all their familiarity with the horseman who moved with such assurance about them, the man went unremarked. He was irrelevant to the soldiers who stumbled through the Mugello. He moved in their middle distance. The armature of his trappings fended them off, and without it the soldiers would not have known him. I saw him stripped of that, thinks Salvestro, once.

But the clamor surrounding that moment seemed a far-off noise, someone else's exhilarations and terrors. Their flight that night and the Colonel's shocking naked face as he'd reached for them appears to him in the breathing darkness as a dream of escaping-without-escaping, the pursuer's swipe missing by a fraction again and again. If not the Colonel, it was the islanders; if not them, then the villagers who had chased the Christian Free Company across darkened countrysides, the dogs that bared their teeth at the sight of him. . . . The forest was a kind of oblivion, a willed forgetting of them all. Always there is a man—himself—running at the limit of his strength. At his back are his pursuers, whose hardened fingers scrape at his spine, driving him forward, drawing them after him. He runs toward nothing. Here is the Colonel again, naturally, *Welcome to Rome.* . . . There are cold waters where he is safe—tideless waters or nearly so—but they are far, far away. He will not reach them before the fingers close about his neck.

Then there is the moment that stands adjacent to that of his capture, its only alternative, the possible moment when he stops. Imagine the doe turning on the dogs and charging forward, reckless and fateful. Or himself rising back out of the water or hurling himself on the mob. Imagine their surprise! Imagine the jolting stop, the body turning, the heart's aghast pumping. Turn back, when turning back, in this instance, on this night of the Colonel's reappearance, means the starving scramble that carried them into Prato. Turn on *them*.

But the moment is futureless. Bernardo's snores continue, broken by odd gulps and constricted swallowings. There had been a man on the march—a harquebusier called Jaggetto—who carried a canvas bag slung over his shoulder. Every night he would disappear, reappearing the next morning with his bag replenished, its new contents bulging through the thin material. When the weather turned warm, the bag stank. No one spoke to him or offered him violence. He was shunned, outside them. That a man should, that men in general, that they themselves might, if . . . It is the moment when the drawstring is loosened, the mouth opened, when something unfaceable is faced. A possible moment, but possible only because remaining undone, conceded as unthinkable. Unfutured. The three of them, himself, Bernardo, and Groot, stood with their pikes at the ready, the whole company drawn up, the whole army on the plain before the walls of the town, waiting there in the sticky heat. For most of the morning, cannon popped and puffed from a position way over to their left, and sometimes a ball would strike a gate-tower. They cheered then, but the cannonade was desultory and formal. They had been told nothing.

The sergeants stood in a little group in front of their men. Salvestro thought of the hours before Ravenna; but there was little enough of Ravenna in what lay ahead. The walls before them were deserted, and although a breach gradually opened under the cannon's peppering, no one appeared behind it. There was a company of men set forward of the others who called themselves "the Tifatani" after a desperate skirmish some years before in the pass north of Caserta. They had grown restive in the heat and boredom of the wait, nervous too, perhaps: it was waiting for relief that had decimated them in the col that split Mount Tifata, their cowering and waiting for the crossbows above to find them, the bite and the shudder as their flesh puckered about the shank. Then the pain, which came seconds later, and the screams of those who could not bear the pain. The survivors wore long scars on their right-hand cheeks in remembrance. And the hunger was there amongst them all, eating them from the inside and accepted now only on the promise of its satisfaction. Waiting then, like a breath gulped and held down, swelling until the lungs would burst. . . .

So they stood there, filthy and ragged, eyes staring out of scabbed faces, the very teeth loose in their gums. But the lines trembled, edging forward and being shouted back by the sergeants, who now strode up and down, watching for the first toe to step out of rank, exchanging curt questions as they passed one another. And there were no orders. And it could not last. The battle the army had fought with itself almost from Bologna was lost sometime in those hours, and then it was only a matter of waiting. There was a scuffle somewhere near the back, a few shouts. It was a little after midday. The shouting reached the Tifatani and fell on them like a storm of arrows. They broke ranks and ran toward the breach. Others followed, then them all. That was how it began.

A cliff of bodies fissuring and crumbling, tumbling and cracking into shards, clods, atomized crumbs, until what was solid and whole reaches the hungry waters as a fiberless chaos of fragments, sops dissolving into mud. The breach sucked them in. There was the Colonel, poised briefly atop the cannon-smashed masonry. A press of bodies surged up to the narrow opening, jostling like grains of sand in an hourglass to force their way through the waist. A gate opened to the right of the breach, and strings of men peeled off to make for it. Men-at-arms gathered their reins and drove forward through the crush, spurring their mounts to buffet aside the common troops. Not an arrow, not a bolt, not a charge was fired from the walls. The men poured in. Winter chains glaciers to the crags and faces overlooking the lake they cannot reach. Then spring, and release, and the lake can only wait for the frustrated acreage of slabs and strata to collapse and reemerge as boiling torrents that roil down the ravines to spear its placid waters, to make them foam. . . . But, in the dark of the dormitory, Salvestro thinks of Jörg's implacable calm as the soldier raised his fist, the soldier's bafflement in the face of this, his defeat. Had the Pratesi thought they could save themselves like that?

The three of them found themselves amongst men they did not know, running past the great turret of the gatehouse, where some troops were struggling with the crossbar against the unwitting pressure on the gates from without, past others holding some local men at swordpoint, running into an open cobbled area, which narrowed, becoming a street, then streets, with low houses of brick and wood, the lower stories arched but boarded shut, across little wooden bridges that traversed narrow stagnant canals when their feet would thunder like hooves for a second or two, a few of them turning into streets that split away every so often, until, eventually, the three of them halted to catch their breath in a street the width of a cart, Salvestro and Bernardo leaning on their pikes, Groot bent double and wheezing. Except for their own panting and the soldiers whose shouts they heard only distantly, they were alone. The town was silent. Empty. They looked up and down the street.

"Let's head back," said Groot.

They turned and retraced their steps carefully. In response to the town's compulsive silence, their voices dropped to near whispers, then they themselves were silent, walking slowly through deserted lanes. They rounded a corner and crossed a ramshackle footbridge. Salvestro kept glancing up at the upper-floor windows and stumbling slightly. The ground was rutted. No faces appeared. Then he felt Groot's hand on his arm. He looked ahead.

There was a group of soldiers, a score or more who filled the narrow street. They stood in a tight ring with their backs to the trio, looking down at something within. One or two glanced around blankly as they approached, nudged a neighbor, who glanced, too, then turned back to whatever was going on inside the circle. The men were silent as the streets, as the whole town. The three of them came up, Groot nodding a curt greeting, which was returned. The men shifted grudgingly aside for Salvestro, then looked down again. On the ground before them a woman was being raped.

Two men knelt to either side of her lower half, holding her legs. They frowned in concentration, grimacing quickly when the woman's spasmodic struggling prompted them to renew their grips and lean back to splay her legs farther apart. A third man sat on his heels, the woman's head tilted back and trapped between his legs. He wore thick leather gauntlets and the woman was silent, for he used one gloved hand to press down on her nose and mouth. Strangely framed by the leather gauntlet and the cloth of the man's hose, her eyes rolled about in their sockets. Her arms seemed to be pinioned somehow behind her back. A soldier with black curly hair cropped short was lying on top of her, arching awkwardly while his arm fumbled beneath him, at his crotch.

"That's it, lad. Take your time," said the man holding her head. The woman struggled again, and he pressed harder on her face.

"Watch her breathing, Cippi," said one of the men holding her legs.

"I've got her," Cippi said. Then, "That's it, lad, that's it," as the soldier pulled his arm out from under him and his hips jerked quickly. His head was turned sideways, away from the woman's, so that Salvestro saw that he was young, not much more than a boy. When he was done, Cippi looked up again, his glance taking in the three of them before passing on around the ring of impassive faces. "Who's next?"

Two others of them took her. A nod to the one called Cippi as they stepped carefully around the woman. Then they knelt, spat on their palms, went into her. She seemed to suffer most in the intervals between them, her torso twisting ineffectually and her breathing coming very fast. The last of them was more brutal than his predecessors. "That's it. *That's* it," Cippi urged him as his hips rose and fell.

His voice and the quick impacts of the bodies were the only sounds in the street. The three men were silent as they performed the act. The others were silent as they watched. The last of them raised himself carefully off the body on the ground. Cippi looked about him. Salvestro's face felt to him oddly stony, like bags of gravel hung there. And the woman's white legs were like clubs somehow, heavy and brutal. The men holding them were too drained, too lifeless, to pull them free. It was like that. He was too weak. The hush was a hand clamped over his mouth a long time ago.

"All right, where is he?" Where's our little fairy, eh?" Cippi was saying. A few men grinned. The last soldier was using a handful of grass to wipe the blood from his member. The ground between the woman's legs was wet where she had stained it. She urinated now, prompting Cippi to shove down on her face once again. He turned his head the other way, and Salvestro saw that his right-hand cheek was scarred, the Tifatani scar.

"Here he is!" exclaimed Cippi in a parody of welcome as a fair-haired boy was pushed forward, white-faced, staring down at the ground between his feet.

"Careful," warned the same man as before. The woman's struggles were growing faint.

"Don't tell me my business, Pietro," Cippi warned him back, but his hand came up a fraction and the woman's body jerked as she fought for a lungful of air. The blond boy was on his knees between her legs, his hands fumbling at his crotch, head bent forward. Salvestro noticed that the woman's heels were grazed, the skin there all torn and bloody. It struck him that this was strange. The ground was of packed earth, hard but unabrasive. How had her heels been cut about like that? Then he saw the boy's hands fall away from their labors and hang loosely at his sides. His head remained bent forward. He had begun to cry.

"You bollockless fairy," Cippi growled in disgust. "Go on, get up. Wipe the snot off your face." The boy got up, still crying, and pushed his way out of the circle. "Anyone else?" Cippi scanned the faces around him. The woman was almost still now, her uncovered legs slack in the grip of Pietro and his counterpart. "Visitors, eh?" said Cippi as his eye found them again. "You want to take a turn?" He was talking to Bernardo, who recoiled slightly, embarrassed, with a foolish grin on his face. "Well, big fellow? She's still got a couple of goes in her. A pole the size of yours'd wake her up a bit." Bernardo was shaking his head. "No?" He turned to Groot. "How about you?" The soldiers were watching them now, a faint contempt in their grins.

"I'm getting a bit old for all that," Groot replied levelly. Cippi stared at him, then quickly at Salvestro, then down at the woman. The men were silent.

"No one else?" said Cippi, head bent down. "Anyone?" No one answered. "Well, you're not much use, then, are you?" he said to the woman. Then he looked up and his eyes found Salvestro's. "Not much use, then, is she?" he demanded. Salvestro said nothing. "I *said,* not much use, eh?" he repeated, more aggressively this time. A long moment passed. Then Salvestro shook his head. Cippi scowled and looked away. "Steady, lads," he warned the men on her legs, then pressed his weight down on her face.

At first there was no reaction. The woman lay there, limp and inert, even her eyes hardly moving. Salvestro realized that he was counting, silently, one, two, three . . . Cippi looked up at him again. Eleven, twelve. Her struggling began very suddenly, her shoulders twisting, her head twitching in Cippi's grip. "Bit of life in her yet," murmured Cippi, looking away, pressing down. "That's it," he encouraged the other two, for her legs were thrashing now, or trying to, and the men were sweating. "Ever had a dead one?" Cippi asked Pietro at one point, but no one smiled now. Pietro shook his head without looking up, brow furrowed with effort. "It's not so bad." He pressed down harder. Gradually the woman's movements grew spasmodic: no less violent, but more infrequent. She was twitching, and lying still for a moment, then shaking, and lying still for a moment. Cippi was muttering instructions to the other two: "Hold on now, they kick out at the end, not long now, keep at it . . ." The woman was hardly moving.

"What about me?"

I said that, thinks Salvestro in the dormitory's darkness.

His voice sounded strange as it broke into the circle of their grim concentration, hollow and reedy. Cippi's expression dared him to continue. Some words went back and forward, something. They didn't like it. He handed his pike to Bernardo, and then he was kneeling where the others had knelt before him. The compounded silence fell on him and he was water, not flesh. Her dress had slipped down. He pushed it up to expose her. She was bloody, her pubic hair matted where the blood had dried. The insides of her thighs were brown with it. He had the sensation of hearing her screaming—impossible—which thudded and slammed him all the worse for being stifled, for being part of the men's silence. "I'll have her," he had said. "If you're finished with her." He saw Cippi's expression modulate into something else, something narrow-eyed and shrewd. "Always heard the Tifatani were an open-handed lot," he added, meeting Cippi's gaze. Then he slapped the woman's thigh. "To work, eh?"

She smelled of urine and sour sweat. He had expected that, but as he laid his length over hers, he felt the coldness of her flesh, its clamminess. He entered her quickly and turned his head away from hers, as the curly-haired boy had done, feeling himself shrink from her. She was formless. He felt nothing as he pumped and jerked about inside her. With his eyes screwed tight he imagined their positions reversed or himself somehow looking down on the act being committed, her legs spread apart and her back tensing, the ring of blood and then her screaming, the whiteness of her flesh, a kind of deadness . . . And the darkness that was the water in the cask, or only his eyes shut tight. Or the dormitory, here, now. . . . Or a long time ago, and there. And her.

Groot told him afterward that the one called Pietro had crooked his little finger suggestively, then winked, and the one called Cippi had given the signal for them all to let go, hoping that the woman would buck and struggle beneath him, throw him off, perhaps. But she had only flopped about like a drunkard and he had pumped away, eyes shut and unaware, his grunts so low that one of the men had had to cock his ear to his lips to make them out, then report derisively, "Misses his mother, this one." Imitating his mewling, *"Mama, mama, mama, mama . . ."* A few of them had laughed. Then they had drifted away.

Bernardo had pulled him off, or lifted him clear. He remembered being propped against a wall and Bernardo shouting at him, "Why'd you do *that?*" The sun was lower now, casting a shadow down the center of the street that cut the woman in two. Groot said, "She's stopped bleeding," then pulled her dress down to cover her. They would have dragged her here, Salvestro thought to himself. That's why her heels were cut. Groot said, "She's not really breathing."

He crawled over to the woman. Without Cippi's hand over her face he could see that she was young and rather plain. Some brown hair had escaped from under the bonnet that was still tied under her chin. Her eyes would roll up into her head, then drop, then roll again, more slowly each time. Salvestro wondered where her shoes were or how she had lost them.

"We should keep her warm," said Groot. "It's the cold that'll kill her." She was like ice. The three of them took off their tunics and wrapped her in them. Then they stood about, looking down at her, not knowing what else they should do. She took quick, shallow breaths, which grew quicker and shallower until they amounted to no more than a shivering of her chest. Salvestro knelt and held her head off the ground. Her face was slack and her eyes saw nothing. The three of them waited, feeling awkward gathered together over her. They did not look at one another. Groot kept reaching across to pull down her dress, but it already reached her ankles. There was the faint rattle of her breath, growing fainter, failing. Slowly the shiver shrank to a tremor, then nothing. And then, once again, there was silence. The girl was dead.

The same silence? Salvestro asks himself, wakeful, benighted.

No.

They picked up their pikes and trudged back. Bands of soldiers were roaming through the town, kicking in doors and dragging those inside out into the street. "Why did you do that?" Bernardo kept asking, although he was mumbling it to himself, wide-eyed at what was taking place around them, not expecting an answer. He repeated it over and over until Groot burst out angrily, "He was trying to spare her. Now shut up!" It made no difference. Salvestro was silent.

In front of the Pieve da San Stefano they were preparing to burn a man. "The Moor called Nana has despoiled the shrine of San Pietro and violated a woman in defiance of guarantees of safe conduct given here. . . ." The Moor grinned stupidly as the charges were read out. Groups of soldiers were walking about in front of the church, mostly drunk. On the other side of the square, the Palazzo Pretorio was guarded by men who Groot said were the Colonel's. It was almost evening.

They slept in the square that night and went hungry. The next day Salvestro woke early and roused the other two. They walked by the Via dei Cimatori into the quarter of the town called Gualdimare. The same scum-covered canals. The same streets. Yesterday's silence. Two fortresses raised themselves clear of the surrounding buildings. Medici's men stood outside one, Cardona's outside the other. The two groups were waking up as they passed them. They moved deeper into the quarter, and the stone houses were replaced by brick ones, exposed stairways running up their fronts, all just as yesterday. Funny little mills backed onto the little canals. Between each house and the next, the narrow *quintani* were filled with stinking refuse. Again Salvestro kept looking up at the windows on the raised floors. Again no faces appeared. "Why did they not come out?" he muttered to himself. Then, "Not a sound." The other two looked at each other. "Just let them take her."

The day was already warm. Groot and Bernardo followed Salvestro, who had the air of searching for something, peering about him as he strode along, and even twirling his pike.

"I think I will die unless I eat," Bernardo said presently.

"Well then, we must eat," Salvestro answered brightly, and ran up the next stairway to the door at its top. He knocked politely. "No one home?" he inquired of himself. "Oh well . . ." And with that he began swinging at the door's planking with his pike. The street resounded with the din as the other two stared up open-mouthed. A voice within shouted something. "Come on, come on! Open up!" Salvestro bellowed back. The door flew open suddenly and he charged in. Some screaming followed, and then several great crashes, and then a man's voice begging or pleading for something.

Bernardo and Groot climbed slowly up the same stairs and peered in the door.

"Ah, there you are!" Salvestro greeted them. "We're about to have breakfast."

He was sitting on a chair in the center of the low-ceilinged room. At the other end, two women, one old, the other middle-aged, were trying to cower each behind the other. A man was on his knees, somewhat tearful, murmuring, "Anything, anything. We have nothing. Take it," and suchlike. Most of the furniture appeared to be in the fireplace, which was unlit.

"Didn't I rape your daughter yesterday?" Salvestro asked the man, who shook his head, bewildered. "Are you sure?" he persisted. "She looked very much like you—ugly, I mean. These streets are all the same to me." The man only shook his head.

"It was another street," Groot said quietly.

"Everything we have is yours," said one of the women.

"Or maybe it was your mother?" Salvestro went on.

"He means to . . . Oh, Jesu, gather me now!" the old woman cried out.

"It was not here, Salvestro," said Groot.

"How did it feel?" asked Salvestro, getting up to take the man by the neck and drag him to the window. "How did it feel!" He began cuffing the man about the head. "How was it, watching her die down there! Watching me finish her, eh! How was that!"

The man began to cry out that he had no daughter, but Salvestro only grew more furious at that, shouting, "Why don't you fight! Why don't any of you fight!" beating the man with his fists now, the two women howling and not daring to move. Groot pulled him off and wrestled him to the floor, holding him down until he calmed himself. "Silence," Salvestro said softly.

"I'm still hungry," said Bernardo. "I think I'm going to die."

They ate everything in the house. Salvestro did not speak again that day.

He remembered sleeping in odd snatches, a few minutes on the steps of San Giovanni and waking to dazzling sunshine or propped in the corner of a high barn somewhere while men rolled barrels around him, a sound such as wooden bells might make, a silvery rumble. Someone said, "That's nothing. Look here," throwing up a trapdoor and faces staring up at him out of the darkness, then the screaming that started up when the trapdoor was closed. Braziers were set up in some of the squares, the instruments stacked against the walls. The worst of it happened out of sight, in the dyeing sheds that backed onto the river. The Pratesi were marched down in little groups. Some of them vomited as they were led down there. The smell stayed in his nostrils: scorched hair and skin. Once Bernardo was chasing some children about and Groot grasped him by the arm. "Watch him. Don't let him . . . You know what I'm talking about." He nodded dumbly, not knowing. Groot went off somewhere.

The days fell into each other. He could not stay awake. Someone took his pike while he dozed one day, and Bernardo grew worried about it, repeating the tag that had been dinned into their brains by the sergeants at Bologna, "A good pikeman is never without his pike," and drilling himself there in the street: One, lower the pike; two, step forward; three, thrust. . . . One, two, *three*. One, two, *three*. He turned away from his friend's display and tried to go back to sleep. The other two marched him about, brought him food, or perhaps he found it for himself. The other soldiers looked at him curiously. He ignored them. They spent some time with the Sicilians, but he unnerved them somehow, breaking into laughter for no reason or drumming on a tabletop for hour after hour, talking in his for-est-language or what he thought of as that. Bernardo turned up with a tiny corpse in his arms, exclaiming, "I didn't do *anything!*" when Groot began shout-ing at him, then wandering off again to get rid of it. "I told you!" Groot hissed in his ear, but he didn't understand. "Remember the boy at Marne? Remember Proztorf? I told you to watch him!" And then the day came when Groot returned and shook him awake to tell him, "Come on, come with me. I've got us a way out. Come on, we have to talk to him. . . ."

He was led around the back of San Stefano, through a little door, across a courtyard, through a long succession of empty rooms. A finely dressed sergeant eyed them from behind a table. "Are you the Colonel's men? I have a task for you. . . ."

An unfamiliar sound now, here in Rome. His memories are silent, or overlaid with silence. The voices rumbling together in Prato are not distant but smoth-ered, and the noise that takes their place is cloistered and pent-up as a madman swinging at phantoms that dissolve beneath his frustrated fists. He dangles above the silenced street, a hapless stage-angel clawing at the ground where Cippi kneels, his hand tightening over the girl's mouth. His disowned carcass couples with hers, and the quiet of the scene is cankered. The Pratesi cowering behind their doors choke back their shouts of outrage, the watching men chew on their tongues, the hand over the girl's face forces her cries back down her throat. . . .

All tears come too late. It was a saltless sea that carried him away, watching a thin white ghost as she wrestled with her tormentors. *Hold her now.* . . . Her weirdly framed eyes roll in her head, or did he imagine that later? The boat pulls away from the shore, but not quickly enough, no, never quickly enough. Her bent body jerks about like a puppet's—did he see that? The water folded her shrieks in its custodial silence. The dulled drumbeat of his blood drowned her out as the weight of the Achter-Wasser pushed in on him. Is that what she heard, too? As they picked her up, one on each side, as they pushed her head forward? As they drowned her there, that night, in a barrel of rainwater?

Silence upon soiled silence; Prato's smothered quiet upon that night's complicit hush. Bernardo pulls him whimpering off the dying woman. He lies bruised and wakeful amidst the softly breathing bodies. Some rustling, the odd cough. Anything else?

It begins quietly, growing slowly in definition: a mucal mewling or snorty-snuffly sound. The monks sleep soundly. Bernardo snores on. Only Salvestro is awake, alone in the chamber, in the hostel, in the Borgo. In *Ro*-ma. No one hears and no one cares. Little liquid hiccups and half-stifled sobs erupt unvigorously and sink swiftly in the night's tarry silence. It's too late. It always is. Salvestro is crying for his mother.

Reveille, breakfast, the pot, a Mass.

"*Otium, negotium,*" hums the Pope, sweeping briskly out of the chapel into the *sala* beyond, farcing the *o*'s into antiphonal neumes, *o-oo-o*, stopping to glance out of a window at the loggia overlooking the courtyard, deeply shaded, noisy with the shouts of today's jostling petitioners. He considers showing himself, taking a turn around the gallery.

"Holiness, the Bishop of Spezia has been waiting three days already," murmurs Ghiberti. "There is an audience after that. . . ."

The Sala di Constantino is loud with chatter that falls silent as he passes through, the painters and paint-mixers high on their scaffolds peering down at him, the air heavy with oily and metallic vapors. Chatter again as he exits and finds himself in the Eliodoro. Through the windows to his right the Belvedere gardens sweep up the hill, part-shadowed by the palace, then glorious in the morning's sunshine beyond. The Vatican hogs the Borgo's light. Ghiberti coughs, or sniffs, prompting him again. The ledger is clasped to his chest. Leo sees the Bishop standing alone in the Sala di Segnatura. "*Otium, negotium . . .*"

A dolphin, he thinks a few minutes later, because of the lips. The gulping, too, great roomfuls of air swallowed and belched up in droning periods. The dolphin-like Bishop of Spezia squints inflexibly at a point three feet in front of his nose, turning his head from side to side in slow quarter rotations as Leo paces before him. The monologue began as he entered.

And continues now, interspersed with ill-rehearsed urbanities, each of these prefaced alternately by "If I might be so bold" or "How should I put it to Your Holiness?": locutions Leo detests, and three of each so far. He listens with diminishing attention, recalling Spezia as swampy and uninteresting; by the sea. A softly spewed fog of rhetoric is clouding his cloudless morning. Bulky entities float shapelessly within it: the objects of the Bishop's lament. Pay attention, he upbraids himself. Ask a question. Concern yourself with the sadnesses of Spezia. He could inquire if Turkish corsairs were a danger, baffling the thick-lipped Bishop. Or ask after the quality of the hunting.

". . . and as to her origins, all profess the completest ignorance; she herself will say nothing except that she was saved and brought to Spezia by one who came and left in the night, who will come back one day to take her away—you can imagine what the simpler folk make of that—that she is waiting now, and any who wish to wait with her may do so. . . ." The Bishop has a minor saliva problem and sucks noisily from time to time, perhaps for emphasis.

Certain facts begin recurring, sifted dutifully by the Pope. It seems an eight-year-old child arrived in Spezia two years ago. It seems a prayer-house has since gathered about her. It seems grants of money have been removed from the diocese and reassigned to said prayer-house. The benefice of Spezia is not a rich one. It seems its Bishop is in Rome. The Pope arranges and rearranges these bland counters. He smiles placidly at the Bishop from time to time, encouraging him to go on. It is useful to be thought stupid.

Ghiberti, standing quietly near the back wall of the *sala,* steps forward discreetly, looking sideways with the odd nose-wiping gesture he has adopted lately. A hum of conversation penetrates from the Sala d'Incendio next door, rises and falls in the high spaces of the ceiling.

"Her influence, you see, is spreading," the Bishop says. "There are women amongst her followers who are, how should I put it to your Holiness, who are *ill thought of* in Spezia. And it is not only the common people. The diocese relies on its patrons, who have fallen under her influence, my own sister amongst them, Violetta. She has taken an interest in this Amalia, the girl, I mean. And, Your Holiness will understand, it is difficult for me to move against the sect directly, my sister, you understand. . . . She owns much of the land in Spezia, and two other estates besides. She can be very headstrong, my sister."

Leo nods sympathetically. He has sisters himself.

"Since she abandoned the Church, we hardly have two cantors to rub together, if I might be so bold. . . ."

Two cantors to rub together? Julius appointed this weak and stupid man. Perhaps because of his sister. There would have been a reason; there always was with Julius. To do with the Genoese to the north, or the marble quarries at Carrara, or even the French. Julius couldn't belch without thinking of the French. His appointment would have been calculated, weighed. Perhaps not today, not this morning, but Spezia must once have been of interest. It is a place, by the Bishop's account, where churches teeter on the brink of collapse and the host molders in its pyx. Where priests go hungry and their bishops starve. The Prelate is coming to the meat of the matter, although Leo is there already, and already weary of understanding this Bishop of Spezia, and why he is here, and what he will ask for in the next minute, and why he has heard this particular complaint amongst all the thousands of others that he will never hear.

"And for all these reasons, and others I have not said in deference to my sister, I petition Your Holiness to examine the child Amalia for heresy here in Rome, for I believe she is as injurious to the church in Spezia as Savonarola was in Florence, the very town where you were born." The Bishop delivers this sentence in one breath and falls silent. There is a long pause. Ghiberti moves toward the far door.

"When you say 'examine this child for heresy here in Rome,' do you mean that she should be examined here in Rome, or that her heresy was committed here in Rome, or both?" asks the Pope.

The question travels slowly to the Bishop, extending tendrils that wrap themselves about him. His head wobbles gently. The face remains complacent, telling Leo that his ire remains unnoticed. But he would like a little more time. To mention Savonarola, to *him*. To bandy that name about in here, before himself, before a Medici. The man's clumsiness. And then, *the very town where you were born. . . .* The insolence! This must not cloud his judgment; he needs to be calm. "I presume you mean her to be examined here in Rome?" he hazards. The Bishop nods gratefully. "Let us walk," he suggests, and takes the Bishop by the arm, leading him toward the door Ghiberti has now opened to reveal the *sala* beyond, crowded with gowned and robed figures. Suddenly hushed.

The two men pause, standing arm in arm. Leo's smile administers a vacant balm to the attentive assemblage. One of his minor talents is finding usefulness in the apparently useless. The Bishop at his side has a function now, though he is ignorant of it. They advance into the Sala d'Incendio, Leo nodding slowly, head turning about, conferring silent benediction over the heads whose bodies move backward before his own. The Bishop of Spezia smiles broadly. A little circle forms about them.

"I think it would be best," the Pope says pleasantly, "if I deprived you of your benefice." The Bishop stops smiling.

Minor princes, their manservants, priests, hangers-on, higher-placed members of his *famiglia,* clerks of the Camera, bureaucrats and functionaries of Rome's communes, pay polite attention. A discreet cluster forms about the scarlet of his mozzetta, emanating hope. They are here to be noticed.

To be witnesses, thinks Leo, then corrects himself. Gossips.

He says, "A young orphan is taken in by your sister, whose charity extends to reforming the Magdalens of Spezia, but not so far as lining her brother's pockets. In return, her brother neglects his offices, allows his churches to tumble into ruin, squanders the scant revenues of his diocese, and mismanages its lands; then, finding the cup half-empty instead of half-full, he comes to Rome and asks the Pope to have the orphan girl burned in the Campo de' Fiori. Now tell me: what am I to think of this?"

By tonight there will be so many chastised bishops being sent back to Spezia: on the back of a mule; impoverished; struck to the floor and tongue-lashed till they miraculously bled; clapped in chains and hauled off for questioning in Sant'Angelo. A cloud of little orphans will attend them, and a whole gallery of elder sisters. Mugs will be raised to him in the inns of Rome. Jokes cracked. He looks about him as though helplessly, as though he takes no pleasure in these displays. Concerned faces peer back at him. The Bishop has started gulping again but says nothing, which is wise. "I hardly know *what* to think," says the Pope.

A minute later Ghiberti is hurrying along beside him, back through the Segnatura. He stops abruptly in the Sala d'Eliodoro.

"What are the revenues of Spezia?" Leo demands.

"Small. Around four hundred ducats. He holds Pontano, too, though, which yields a further three."

"Have him know my pleasure consists in his granting the latter to his sister's hospice."

"The revenue or the sum?" asks Ghiberti.

"The sum! I am not about to assign church revenues to a houseful of retired whores. And hint at a legate to check that he complies. His sister and this barefoot child of heaven can wait for a stranger from Rome alongside their 'stranger from the sea.' Why not?" Ghiberti makes a note in his ledger. "And now? Whom else must I see?"

"The common petitioners. At least four or five of them. . . ." Ghiberti begins to read from his ledger, "'Marten of Bisenzio, Iacopo of Trastevere, Joanna of Citatorio, a Johannes Tiburtinus, Giancarlo of Pontormo, Giancarlo of Volterra . . . '"

The names soothe him, gazing out of the casement over the gardens below. The curtain of shade has drawn closer to the palace, a mere strip now. From far over on the west side come vague crashings. Hanno is destroying trees again. The garden is wilder over there, invisible from here. He thinks of yesterday's antics, Vich's histrionic fury, Faria's marble calm. They do not fool him, either one. He turns away.

"'. . . Matthaus of Roos, three women—unnamed—Robert Marck, gentleman, Paulo of Viterbo, Brother Jörg of Joosdom, Aldo of Pisa, Antonio of Parione, Hubertus of Parione, Salvatore of Parione—they are together, I believe—Philip of Savoy, the Prior of Minervino—'"

"He is not," Leo breaks in sharply. "I deprived him, and refuse leave to appeal. He knows why. Continue."

"'Father Pietro of Gravina, Cosmas of Melfi, Bartolomeo of San Bartolomeo in Galdo, Rodolfo of Fiefencastel, Maximilian of Chur, Signora Jadranka of Sebenico, Jacob of Ragusa, Adolphus of Freiburg . . .' Ah, greetings, Cardinal Bibbiena."

A bearlike man capped in green and cloaked in red is striding briskly toward them—albeit backward—through the Sala di Constantino. "Good day, Gian Matteo Ghiberti!" he replies, head angled up at the green-and-yellow splotches on the ceiling. He makes a half pirouette as he enters, smiling at Leo, who embraces him. "Holiness"—he steps back to make an elaborate bow—"*Optimus et Maximus.*" Two more bows follow, increasingly elaborate. Leo smiles.

"Dovizio is downstairs; I saw him as—"

"Dovizio! Then why is he not here?" Leo exclaims. The clouds are beginning to lift.

"He has no invitation," replies Bibbiena.

"But neither do you!"

"Sack the guards!" shouts Bibbiena. "Then promote them! We were talking, Dovizio and I, making jokes about you behind your back. It is so much more interesting than talking to you in person."

"Why? Have I grown dull?" This day needed Bibbiena.

"Deadly. But you are Pope and can be as dull as you please. I saw Leno as I came in, in a state of most oily excitement. He has news from the Colonna Mass for you." Leo's light spirits evaporate at the mention of Leno. "Cheer up," Bibbiena admonishes, "it could be much worse. His master, for instance."

"Now, now!" Leo protests. "Cardinal Armellini is my loyal and obliging servant."

"Agreed, and a hypocritical extortionist. . . ."

"You cannot use such language!" Leo is laughing.

"Agreed again. The last time I described him as such, a mob of true hypocritical extortionists laid siege to my palazzo, demanding my head for the slander. Granted, a mob of four men and a dog more or less fills the current Palazzo Bibbiena, but even so. . . . My hands still shake to think of it. Look." Leo takes the proffered hand. "Come," says Bibbiena.

"The petitioners?" says Ghiberti.

Otium, negotium . . .

"Very restive as I came in," says Bibbiena. "They want their Pope."

"Do this for me, Gian Matteo," Leo asks his secretary. "Take four or five. Hear them out and . . . Do as you think best. On my authority." Ghiberti nods impassively. "And give my blessing to my brother when you see him."

He is turning away, walking back through the Sala di Constantino with Bibbiena on his arm. Bibbiena is saying, "Now there is a dreadful slander running through the corridors of your palace, and it is not one of mine. I heard it as I came in. Now tell me, is it true or is it not that you forced the Bishop of Spezia to eat a toad this morning?" Ghiberti listens to the Pope's silvery laughter, rising and falling, until the two men glide away and the sound is replaced by another. A murmuring or whispering, a rumbling susurration. It never stops, this sound, which is of hushed voices behind doors, of anxieties in rooms other than this one, in places other than here. Ghiberti closes the ledger.

On the floor below, Leno hears it, too. He ignores it—and most sensibly, for it tells him nothing, cannot be sold, is valueless. Rough-cut marble is twenty-three giulii the toise. That's a fact. He employs two hundred and five men and women: another fact. One hundred and thirty-two of them in workshops owned by him outright behind the Via delle Botteghe Oscure. One hundred and four of them Jews. Fact, fact. He is waiting for the Pope in the anteroom of the Sala Regia. A fact? What if His Holiness does not come? An abstract fact. Useless.

Further: There are a hundred giulii to the scudo, and twenty soldi to a Genoese lira, fifteen of those to the English pound. The florin and Venetian zecchino are firm at one to one. There are four soldi to a cavalotto, six quatrines to a soldo, one of those to two Genoese denarii, four to a baiocco, ten of those to the giulio, or paolino, or carlino, though you don't see many of those nowadays. No one in his right mind accepts dalers, and the same goes for stivers, batzen, and copstucks. This is all very diverting. One hundred and fourteen Milanese soldi buy a single silver crown, which equals three Genoese lira plus a number of Roman soldi fluctuating between twelve and twenty. Four bagatini make a quatrino. Fact, fact, fact.

A riddle: If one Venetian ducat is a little under two and a half livres tournois, and a toise of rough-cut marble is sold at five and a quarter livres, how many toises will fill his largest purse—capacity: one foglietto, usual weight: one libbra— with Venetian ducats? Answer: Not all the quarries in Christendom. Ha ha. The Republic's ducat is money of account, a figure in the ledger, a handshake and settle up next year at Besançon. Hurry up, he thinks, fidgeting on the bench.

From time to time members of Leo's *famiglia* poke their heads around the door, stare at him, then withdraw. An official he knows from the Camera nods to him. Some young men leapfrog each other down the corridor, then run away. It is warm, waiting in the antechamber. He is sweating. Bibbiena wouldn't have forgotten him, would he? Or decided to forget him? It wouldn't be the first time; a good laugh at the expense of Signor Giuliano Leno, left waiting for the day. Price each guffaw at a giulio, how much would that come to per annum? Last year someone tallied up the number of pasquinades against each of those lampooned, then chalked the results on Pasquino's chest. Amongst the most reviled inhabitants of Rome, Giuliano Leno ranked second.

Muffled shouting reaches him then, rolling down the corridor from the courtyard of San Damaso. The noise increases, becomes part groan, a strange mix of applause and disappointment. It begins to subside. The noise the petitioners make, thinks Leno. Petitioners imply the Pope, thus more waiting for himself, and—two lira to the justino—the hardening conviction that Bibbiena has decided to add a giulio or two to the mockery-account. Or a soldo, a full scudo. . . . Then, as if to confirm his fears, the sound of laughter assails him. And then, as if to allay them, the Pope appears, flanked by Bibbiena and Dovizio at the far end of the corridor.

The three of them pause. More laughter, some embracing. Bibbiena's green-trimmed hat bobs up and down. Leno stands up to be noticed and organizes his thoughts: Vich and Serra, that's good, though his man caught nothing of their conversation. The monks, too, it will amuse His Holiness, and while he is still chuckling, ask him about the bill. The Camera has delayed his payment again, and he is down to a skeleton crew. Dovizio takes the big man by the arm; Bibbiena catches sight of him standing there and raises a hand before he is led away. Leno waves back quickly. The Pope composes himself, then marches quickly toward him, hardly stopping to take his arm, sweeping him up and continuing.

"What news, Leno?" he asks briskly, propelling him forward, releasing him to take a narrow spiral staircase whose wooden steps become stone ones halfway down, then give out onto a broad, high-ceilinged corridor echoing the one above. Barred vents set high on one side admit vivid shafts of light. On the other, arched openings in the brickwork hung with sackcloth disgorge a clangor of pots and pans, cooking smells, and aproned scullions who shoot in and out the doorways while being shouted at from within. Men balance trays on their head and stagger about, trying not to collide with others carrying firewood, fish-barrels, huge steaming tureens. A barrowload of calves' heads is wheeled past. A second is filled with eels. It is hotter down here, Leno realizes as he relays to the Pope what was relayed to him the previous night sometime after midnight and wipes furtively at the sweat trickling stickily from his armpits.

"Vich and Serra?" Leo queries at one point, but otherwise he is silent, content to watch the whirl of *sauciers* and sous-chefs, bloodied butcher's boys and pot-scrubbers, their swervings, near-collisions, and hops over the gutterful of rancid water that runs down the center of the passageway. From time to time, billowing clouds of steam and smoke lift the greasy sacking. Within, the two men glimpse fires and huge red-faced men wielding meat cleavers.

"Go on," says the Pope. Leno is telling him about the fracas. His Holiness repeats the choicer morsels in absentminded good humor: "Monks? German monks?" And then, "Quoting Gratianus? Poor Serra. . . ." Mention of Signora Vitelli brings an arch expression to Leo's face and a comment in Latin about backward-facing horsemen, Parthians or something, Leno doesn't catch it. "Well, Colonna was mad even before Ravenna," says the Pope a few minutes later. "Presumably even more so now."

"Oh yes," Leno agrees happily, but then remembers his man's report, which had grown garbled toward its conclusion—had he truly seen the evening out as promised?—difficult to disentangle. A dull crash sounds above the din of the kitchen, followed by anguished cursing. "Actually, no," he corrects himself. "It turned out that two of the monks' men had seen action at Ravenna. He was happy enough to release them."

"The monks?"

"No, their men. Vich's captain vouched for them." The Pope gazes blandly at the sacking over the nearest doorway. The bellowing within has reached a new pitch. He turns to Leno as the other continues, "Your name was mentioned. They claimed to have fought for you, too. . . ."

More bellowing. A crisis in the kitchens? Leno stops.

"Continue," says the Pope.

An eel appears. Its head peeks out from under the sacking and waves from side to side, sniffing for water. The eel distracts Leno, and the amusing tale he has brought along to tell grows messy, slippery. He cannot remember the name of the captain. The eel makes a dart for the gutter, slithers in, and starts swimming. Two others appear, and three more behind them. And their former captain, had he been delighted to see them or displeased? It was one or the other, and he had called them something. . . . It is all suddenly snarled in itself, and awkward, and the Pope seems unamused.

"They were Diego's men," Leo says abruptly. "They acted under his orders."

That was the name—Diego—floating free of some weighty introspection that seems to have seized the Pope and now carries him away. Leno cannot keep up with it. Ragged pot-boys are leaping into the passageway armed with brushes and short-handled rakes to drive back the advancing flood of eels—several dozen of them now. Why is His Holiness not doubled up with laughter at this? He observes coldly as eels curl themselves about ankles, slither into the gutter, are picked up by the tail and thrown into pots and buckets. Leo does not smile at the eely japes and wiles. One is attempting the stairs. A private cargo carried on a private current of thought. Leno flounders in its wake.

"If it would please Your Holiness to know more of these two, or the monks . . ."

That rouses him. "Do not give it a second thought, dear Giuliano. It was the mention of Vich's creature, that is all." An expression of world-weary regret sinks furrows in his countenance. "Prato still pains me, even now. . . ." He is briefly noble in his melancholy.

Leno nods sympathetically, feigning comprehension: Prato means the wool trade, dyeing and weaving, a fair in the autumn switched to Florence (unsuccessfully) during the occupation a couple of years ago, or was it three? He is given no time to reflect on these various possibilities. Eel-anguish has become eel-irritation: biting and general slitheriness have replaced earlier thoughts of escape. The beslimed and bloody-fingered pot-boys scrabble bravely for their tails, and the Pope at last acknowledges the spillage of torrid kitchen-chaos that assaults them now from all sides.

"These eels!" he exclaims. "Should we give the boys a hand, Giuliano? Or shall we take the side of the eels?" Leno laughs along, uncertain how, or if, to answer. The Pope turns for the staircase.

They talk of the relentless steaming that Rome will soon receive at the hands of the punitive Roman sun, the worsening rat-problem, Leo's longed-for *villegiatura* (still months away), and the stables under construction for La Magliana, a blockish mausoleum for horses and their keepers. But the time to mention the balance on the excavations at Saint Peter's seems in perpetual deferment, inappropriate when the Pope is talking so wittily of yesterday's lumpish orators and their rendezvous with his elephant, ill-advised while the Pope kindly praises his decorative crenellation atop the Torre degli Anguillara, unmentionable amongst mild complaints about the recementing of the loggia in the Belvedere, and unpaid on his dismissal.

Thirteen hundred scudi d'oro. But he has been paid the compliment of a private audience seven times since the Pope's accession: in the vestry of the Chapel of Nicholas V, in the room off the *tinello* where the serving trays were stored; a part-demolished pavilion in the gardens to the west of the palace; very briefly at the rear door of Leo's palazzo in Ponte, when he had been told to come back the next day, so twice there; once outside the closet while His Holiness evacuated his bowels within. They conversed through the door. Today, of course, in a passageway by the kitchens. Most cherished moments, all. Leo glides away, waving. Leno turns for the door.

The unlucky petitioners are drifting out of the arched doorway from the courtyard of San Damaso, a morose herd whose disappointment engulfs him as he waits for his horse. He feels inviolable, anointed amongst the unanointed. Thirteen hundred is not so much. He mounts and rides through the crowd, past the steps to the old basilica, taking the street running along its south side. The shadow of the obelisk falls on the wreckage of Santa Petronilla, still piled against the dwarfed turret of Santa Maria della Febbre. A few wagons are lined up against the wall, with men sitting idly beside them. The rutted ground makes his horse stumble. He halts there and looks up.

Out of ground scarred with trenches and pits, a huge ruin looms above him. Four brutish piers of stone reduce the surrounding houses, chapels, and inns to a scattering of hutches and hovels, the shards and splinters shed by these hulking blockhouses in their eruption out of the ground. Their formless tonnage heaves skyward, where, gaining height, they become the bell towers of a race of titans, vast and impossible, and then . . .

And then nothing. Precarious vaulting links two of them. Below, figures the size of insects pick their way through piles of unused masonry and wood to inspect dilapidated bits of stonework. Some friars are laughing amongst themselves on the other side of the site; two fastidious mules have stopped in front of a shallow pool of water; some children throw stones at the nearest of the piers. Leno looks back over his shoulder. Towers of white smoke fatten and rise in the sky a mile or two to the east as though in mockery of these behemoths' bulk. The lime kilns are working full tilt. When he looks back, he sees that one of his workmen is pointing across the broken ground toward him. One of the friars is with him, peering over with a hand raised against the sunlight. His happy rosary starts up again: a hundred giulii to the scudo, and twenty soldi to a Genoese lira, fifteen of those to the English pound. Cloth and stone, he thinks, turning his horse about. Rome shucks its shift fifteen times a day, but the body beneath is stretched and scabbed. The old sow peers at her litter and sees faces of old men. Peter's basilica is barely conceived and ruinous already. Four soldi to a cavalotto, six quatrines to a soldo, one of those to two Genoese denarii, four to a baiocco . . .

"Are you Leno?"

He looks down, startled. A rough face stares back up at him evenly.

"I said, Are you Leno?" the fellow demands again. "Because if you are, I have a proposition for you."

Proposition? The ruffian has taken his horse by the bit. The presumption! But a proposition. A proposition comes without charge. Propositions have served him well in the past. The ruffian waits. He looks more closely and sees that the rags twined about the man's body are actually a habit. A proposition from a monk?

"What?" he says.

His own face stared up at him, wavering, its bony angles rendered more severe in the cool dawn light. He plunged his hands through the cheeks and scooped freezing water to splash on his forehead, feeling it trickle down over his eyes and mouth to his throat, where he brushed it off. A few strands of straw floated in the bucket. The water was black and ill-tempered now, slopping at the sides.

He led them in silent prayer before they set out, though the shouts and thudding footsteps of the Pilgrim's Staff's other inhabitants broke in on their devotions and he found the stillness he sought elusive. Their chamber abutted the passageway, which led to a tiny courtyard where the sky was a small square of light high above framed by the sheer walls of the hostel. Men and women crowded about the well here each morning to fill their buckets before tramping back through the passageway to their quarters elsewhere in the hostel. The footsteps seemed so loud, almost deafening. Jörg opened his eyes and saw in the candlelight the other monks on their knees, each beside his pallet, hands brought together beneath the chin. Pray with me, he thought. Not against me.

But he felt easy in himself, addressing them. The terrors and hardships of their journey were behind them. This was their moment of ease, too. Besieged in ignorance, they had fought their way out to reach the safety of their commander's citadel. His largesse was their salvation. He told them this. Their habits were like gray stones, like monuments to themselves. He felt their attentions gather and turn on him.

On waking and lighting the first candle hours before, he had seen the giant lying on his mattress, gnawing on something. A cabbage-stalk? Salvestro had been asleep, but tossing and turning as though in the grip of a nightmare. The bruising on his face was a vague mass of blues and purples. For whose sins? wondered Father Jörg. The two of them had left before the other monks had woken, although Wolf had stirred, or was it Wilf, asking them anxiously where they were going. He had reassured the novice that the two of them would return, but why should that be true?

The question returned to him unbidden as the monks finished their private prayers. During the journey, the two men had camped apart from the brothers, had walked on ahead for much of the time. Nothing had passed between them and Gerhardt as he had feared it might. Their duties were done now. Why should they stay?

Then he heard HansJürgen chivying the others, little flurries of action and commotion stirring him and breaking in on these thoughts. His heart began to sing. So many days had had to pass before this one, days like quicksand and unbridged ravines, like undertows and blizzards, days to be struggled through and broken down, their shards left strewn behind them. Days like ice. If he closed his eyes, he could remember the first of them, the sound the tiles had made as they shattered on the floor of the church, itself buckling, its flagstones snapping like cakes of powder. Today was the day they all folded into, which would gather them and lay them end to end, making of them a bridge or passage to this place, which was Rome. And to Rome's master, for today they would petition His Holiness.

"No," said the first of the *bancherotti*. "Can't help you with this." He was slightly built, with a neatly trimmed red beard whose point waggled from side to side as he shook his head. "Nice piece, though."

The next one weighed it in one hand, held it up to the sunlight, commented appreciatively on the quality of the silver, but then said, "Don't really handle this stuff," and nodded them farther down the piazza.

The morning's pilgrimage was beginning in earnest: the flow of men, horses, asses, and wagons streaming across the Ponte Sant'Angelo already filled the Borgo Vecchio and Via Alessandrina, debouching into the piazza, where the current grew turbid and contradictory, little eddies forming about the hawkers of food, water, straw, bad wine, copies of Veronica's handkerchief, and plaster heads of Saint John. The river split there, throwing out an arm to the stalls of the *bancherotti* that lined the side nearest the Via dell'Elefante. Pilgrims carried thence would throw down their bags of coins with a thump on the long tables, demand the day's rate for groats, or stivers, or gulden, or Lübeck shillings, then howl robbery, haggle, curse, claim to have been offered a rate twice the one offered now only two minutes ago, at which the *bancherotto*, having been summoned by the dawn carillon of Santo Spirito's bells to the daily bleary-eyed money changers' meeting in the lower room of the Inn of the Horn of Plenty, having greeted there his sleep-befuddled competitors and then fixed with them the day's rate for upward of twenty different currencies, and feeling some hours later that anything agreed at so ungodly an hour should be stuck to even if only to justify getting out of bed so early, would advise the pilgrim to take the earlier rate or otherwise send him packing, and then the pilgrim would mutter, groan, plead, but eventually accept and walk away with a bulging bag of Roman soldi and scudi d'oro. It was business as usual in the piazza.

But Bernardo's and Salvestro's business was not usual, or not usual enough.

They trooped from one bench to the next, collecting suspicious glances at the spectacular purple-blue bruises adorning one side of Salvestro's face and comments like "Interesting," or "Beautiful filigree," or "Haven't seen the likes of this before" from a succession of men who weighed the heavy scabbard in their scales, scraped at the oily patina with their fingernails, or held it up to the sunlight, then continued, "But I'm afraid . . ." or "Unfortunately . . ." or, most frequently, "No."

"There's three things I won't touch with the end of a pole," the last told them bluntly. "One's Swedish dalers, and the other's raw metal." Bernardo was already turning away.

"Well, where *can* we sell it?" Salvestro burst out in exasperation.

"Something like that? I'd hammer it down and sell it in Ripetta if I were you, and I'd keep it wrapped up in the meantime."

Salvestro digested this. "We didn't steal it," he said.

"And we haven't got a hammer," added Bernardo.

The man eyed them steadily. "It's yours by right, so you say?" They nodded. "Well, if it is, you could try Lucullo." He pointed a little way down the Via dell'Elefante where a large crowd engulfed a number of benches, behind which three or four young men scampered about, weighing and counting out coins at extraordinary speed.

"What's the third thing you wouldn't touch?" asked Salvestro as two men approached carrying between them a large weighty sack.

"The French," the man said, turning to serve his customers.

Howls of outrage, followed by claims of a rate twice as good and offered only minutes earlier, pursued them across and then down the street.

In contrast with the other customers in the piazza, the crowd about Lucullo's pitch seemed calm and good-humored, jovial even, with bags changing hands every few seconds rather than every few minutes, no haggling, and one man who feigned outrage at the offered rate was quickly frowned into silence by his neighbors as if this were the height of ill manners. Little flows of geniality and goodwill darted back and forth across the benches. Pilgrims were passing the wait comparing flea-bites and rolling down their stockings to show off knees scabbed from the crawl up the Holy Stairs of the Lateran. Salvestro waved the scabbard about until one of the young men turned from serving another satisfied customer.

"We're looking for Lucullo," announced Salvestro. "Are you him?"

The young man shook his head. "I'm Lucillo, his son. We all are," indicating the others. "His sons, I mean. Unusual piece." He took the scabbard. "I'm afraid we cannot offer a price on raw metal until Father returns. That will be late this afternoon. Can you wait?"

"This is all we have," Salvestro confessed. "What do we do in the meantime?"

"And what do we eat?" Bernardo added.

"Well, you could look for him at the Broken Spur; if not there, then the Sly

Batavian, or perhaps the Golden Shower." He thought for a second, then called out, "Where else might he be?" to his brothers.

"It's Tuesday. He'll be at Rodolfo's," one of them shouted back.

"Of course. He'll be there, gentlemen. That's the tavern of the Broken Wheel in Ripa, a little way past Santa Caterina's. Is there anything else I can help you with?"

Salvestro looked about at the smiling faces pressing in on the benches to either side of him. "You must give very good rates here," he said.

"Actually, taken as a mean of all our rates, the rate here is marginally worse than everyone else's," said Lucillo. "We do however offer exchange rates on several low-rated currencies unexchangeable elsewhere in Rome, and these anomalous rates drag down the mean."

"Swedish dalers, for instance?"

"A good example," Lucillo replied gravely. "We will exchange copper dalers, but only on a raw metal basis. The current rate is four thousand two hundred and fifty-eight dalers, or a little more than a bucketful, to the soldo. Our strong advice to daler clients is to spend their dalers where they are accepted as coin, the northernmost parts of the kingdom of Sweden, for instance."

"And what about the French?" continued Salvestro. Customers on either side of him shook their heads at this, but, a brief expression of startlement aside, Lucillo retained his poise.

"Lucullo and Sons has an active policy which is reviewed on the basis of events as they become apparent and implemented at our discretion in regard to ad hoc transactions presented to us by individual livre clients. At times we have conducted French livre transactions, and at other times we have dealt directly with clients whom we believed at *that* time to be French, but never the two together."

"And now?"

"At the present time, our policy regarding the French is not to touch them even with the end of a long pole."

The pilgrims were streaming up the Via dell'Elefante now, the other thoroughfares already choked. Eager, trepidant faces bobbed in and out of view, trying to get a look at whatever lay ahead. One or two stopped for a moment to gawp at Bernardo, and then Salvestro, before they were carried along on the flood. A few inns had opened their shutters and put up awnings of faded sacking against the sunlight. The first of the day's drinkers were installing themselves at the best tables to watch the jostling throng, tankards in hand. Standing a head or so higher than even the tallest pilgrims, Bernardo looked down the street, then back into the piazza. "I can see the monks," he said, shading his eyes. "I think it's them."

"Come on," said Salvestro. "Let's find this Lucullo."

A large crowd ballooned from the archway leading into the courtyard of San Damaso, packed elbow to elbow at the front, loosening as it swelled and swung back into the northwest corner of the piazza but growing more anxious and ill-tempered there. HansJürgen felt sharp elbows dig at his ribs and smelled his neighbors' sour sweat. Every few seconds he would rise on the balls of his feet to see if they had made any more progress. Two soldiers armed with pikes and dressed in gaudy pink-and-green uniforms flanked a cleric who questioned each of the petitioners and recorded their names in a ledger before admitting them to the courtyard. "No one gets in after midday," someone said in a worried tone. Similar comments followed. Tensions whipped themselves into minor panics, subsided, returned in the form of anxious questions and outbursts of temper. It was hot, jammed together. They had been there two hours.

A long row of benches extended along one side of the piazza almost to the rearmost part of the crowd. The money changers behind them barely glanced at the petitioners, the pilgrims doing business there likewise. HansJürgen looked about him to try once again to count the brothers. The crowd's internal shufflings and drifts had spread them in a long straggling line, but they seemed not to have moved forward since they'd arrived. A sharp yelp sounded, a voice he knew. He looked forward; someone had trod on Brother Matthias's toe.

More time passed, dawdling seconds, lumpish minutes. He tried to retreat within himself, to direct his attentions there, but the archway pulled and tugged at him. They were none of them any nearer. The sun rose steadily higher. Men and women passed through the archway in an excruciating trickle. He glanced around him and saw faces stamped with his own muted worry. Wulf, Wolf, and Wilf were behind him. It was when Wolf was asking him how they should address the Pope that the shouting started.

It was up ahead, nearer the doorway. Angry faces were turned toward a flurry of movement, a gray robe like his own flapping about, entangled with someone's cloak, perhaps. Then the cloak, or its owner, suddenly disappeared, and HansJürgen saw that the habit was Gerhardt's and he was shoving forcefully at the petitioners around him, forcing a way through to the front. The whole crowd seemed to be shouting in protest when Hanno reached back a hand, pulling him forward, and he hardly had time to grasp Wolf by the cowl of his habit before the monks were all moving forward in a line, cutting brusquely through the crowd to the gate, where Gerhardt was shouting angrily at the two guards, then the cleric, who nodded and stood aside. HansJürgen kept hold of Wolf. Florian seemed to have the other two and was following. But the crowd understood what was happening now. An old woman screamed abuse into his face. Someone shoved him violently between the shoulder blades, and he almost lost his footing. When they too passed beneath the archway, Father Jörg was pronouncing his name for the benefit of the cleric, "Jo-*urg* of *Yoos*-edom," the two guards were pushing back the other petitioners with the butt-ends of their pikes, and Gerhardt was explaining with satisfaction to Georg, "Well, *someone* had to do it, else we'd have been standing there all day. . . ." Someone had spat on Wilf, and he was crying. "We'll tell the Pope when we see him," Wolf promised vengefully.

There were scarcely fewer people in the courtyard than outside, but they were calmer, wandering about in little groups, looking up at the loggia, or resting in the shade of the colonnades that echoed it on two sides of their own level. A few were asleep. The sound and smell of horses wafted through a wide, high passage on the south side of the quadrangle, and from time to time someone's mount would be led out, already saddled, by ostlers dressed in livery similar to that of the guards. There was this and the clamor from the piazza, which sharpened in pitch a little after their entry. The cleric with the ledger had disappeared, and the guards were shaking their heads, barring the entrance with their pikes.

Most of the courtyard was in shade when they entered, but as the time passed and the sun crept higher, the shade began to ebb. The entrance to the palace was a pair of heavy and fantastically carved doors. They remained closed. HansJürgen restrained the urge to pace the courtyard. His stomach felt light and quivery. Jörg stood a little apart from the others in the full glare of the sunlight. The other petitioners watched him curiously. He seemed to be looking at nothing, his face calm and composed. HansJürgen thought back to the times he had seen that same expression, on the night of the church's destruction, on that of the Abbot's death. The day that followed it, too. How had he doubted the man? Was his own faith so weak? And now the impossible pinprick of light their Prior had glimpsed was a whole blazing sun. Soon they would be ushered into the cool of the palace and he would be waiting there to receive them: the Pope himself.

"Man of the cloth, eh?" The voice startled him. He turned to find an old man addressing him, his face wrinkled and creased from the sun. HansJürgen nodded. "How'd you get in, then?" the man continued, "Don't usually let monks in here. Not often, anyway."

"We have come all the way from Usedom to petition His Holiness," HansJürgen replied, smiling benevolently at the man. "I'm sure he will at least see us."

"See you?" exclaimed the man, and began laughing. "That's another tale entirely. I was wondering how you got in *here.*"

"We are here to present our petition," said HansJürgen, more stiffly.

"Ah! *Single* petition. That'd be how you got in. Why let thirty petitioners in when you can get one and twenty-nine of his friends? Yes, that'd be it. Clever, these clerks. I'm Batista, in case you're interested, or even if you're not."

At that moment there was a sudden shout, and almost as a man the men and women leaning against the walls and columns, laid out on the ground, or standing together in little groups began to call up to the empty loggia above. A dozen or so ran to the palace doors.

Batista looked around casually. "False alarm," he said. "You get used to them after a while."

The noise died down as quickly as it had started. Batista ambled away. Beneath the colonnades, three women had surrounded a man dressed in strange purple robes and were taunting him, "What, *the* Prior of Minervino? The famous one? Well, your Minervino-ness, let me kiss your arse unless you want to kiss mine. . . ." The man was swatting at them furiously but without effect. HansJürgen looked again at the Prior. He was standing alone, quite motionless. Most of the monks were sitting on the flagstones, backs leaning against the wall, fanning themselves in the heat. Wulf, Wolf, and Wilf were playing a game that involved hopping and jumping. Two men were throwing small coins against a wall and gambling on the outcome. There was a current of controlled impatience. The recalcitrant minutes dripped and pooled in the courtyard, he did not know how many.

He walked slowly up and down one side of the courtyard, up to the wall of the palace, turn, back toward the piazza. Gerhardt, Hanno, and Georg sat together in silence, and each time he passed them he felt their attention as a kind of prickling in the air. Since his defeat in the chapter-house, Gerhardt's demeanor had changed. Through all the hardships of their journey, the constant wet and cold, the terrible emptiness of the mountains, he had affected a steadfast simplicity, answering all but the most matter-of-fact questions by saying, "I am a builder, that is all," or, "I know stone and wood and nothing else," or merely holding out his hands as though their scars and calluses were stigmata exempting him from inquiry. It was a retreat only, as HansJürgen understood it. There had been no recanting or any sign of remorse. He had doubted, and conspired, and been proved wrong, for here they were in Rome itself, and if he should let his thoughts run only a little ahead, then they would be ushered into the audience hall, within it a throne, upon it a man, and a man like no other in Christendom. A Pope, HansJürgen told himself, rolling the enormity of it over in his mind, daydreaming, paying no attention, or not enough, when it happened.

Afterward he would recall the sequence of sounds more exactly, as a rustling and scraping, as quick footsteps and the bang of the doors, then the great clamor that started up and at which he looked around to see that the doors were open and a man in dark robes was standing in them, surrounded by the same Switzer guards, holding open the same ledger, his mouth opening and closing but the words quite inaudible beneath the shouting, something quickly passed through the door not once, but five, six times, and the petitioners all scrambling and flailing at one another to get nearer. Then the note changed to anger, and then it was a groan of disappointment, shouts of "No! No!" but the doors were closing, and succeeding the dull boom of their slamming shut, an abrupt silence. There was a moment only of this before the mass of bodies seemed to come apart, murmuring and grumbling. He saw one man crying.

They began to wander toward the archway that led back into the piazza, and HansJürgen had to push his way through them to reach the Prior. The brothers were clustered about him, looking from Jörg, to the closed door, to the petitioners streaming past them, and back to Jörg again. But their Prior was silent and seemed as bewildered as they. HansJürgen felt a hand on his arm, Batista's.

"No luck, eh? You've got to be sharper than that."

"But, His Holiness . . . ?" began HansJürgen.

"That was his secretary," snorted Batista. "It's a rare day His High-and-Mightiness drags himself down here." He held up a small chinking bag. "Still, twenty soldi, not bad."

HansJürgen turned and pushed his way through the men and women who now moved dully across his path. Jörg was turning his head this way and that as though searching for something in the blank wall. He grasped HansJürgen's arm.

"What has happened?" he asked. "I heard shouting."

"There will be no audience today," HansJürgen said bluntly.

"No audience?" echoed Wolf. They had given up their game and drawn nearer.

"When do we see the Pope, then?" asked Wilf.

"Tomorrow?" ventured Wulf.

The same questions wrote themselves in different hands over other faces: bewilderment in Joachim-Heinz's, amazement in Heinz-Joachim's, disappointment in Gundolf's and Florian's, mixtures of these in the others ranked behind them. At the very back stood Gerhardt, Hanno, and Georg. Their faces showed only skepticism, and HansJürgen felt the noiseless hum of uncertainty, indecision, a reverberation from the distant monastery, a stirring of the monks' discontents. It cannot happen again, he thought. He cannot lose them again. But then the Prior's voice sounded.

"Well," said Father Jörg, looking into the faces about him, "if His Holiness cannot see us, I am sure he will not object if we worship in his chapel." His tone was unconcerned, even jocular. The monks looked at one another. The Pope's chapel? What was this? "Today he tests us. Tomorrow he rewards us. We shall sing a Mass for our benefactor," Jörg continued, "and we shall sing it in the greatest church in Christendom."

He turned and began to walk toward the archway. For a moment they did not move, and HansJürgen held his breath. "In Saint Peter's!" Jörg called out. Peter's name jolted them, or the confidence of his invoking. Florian was the first, then Volker. They shuffled forward, then hurried to catch up, and the others followed. Bringing up the rear, HansJürgen released his breath slowly, silently, so that none of them might notice.

They had seen signs painted with blue-, black-, and rust-colored cats, crossed and uncrossed miters, smiling suns, headless sailors, drums, compasses, a portcullis, several fish, but not as yet a Broken Wheel. They had been around Santa Cate-

rina's three times, halfway down the Via delle Botteghe Oscure, then back, up and
down between the river twice, and had viewed the Melingulo Tower from seven
of its eight possible angles before Bernardo noticed a narrow alley running between a large stables and a crumbling granary. Projecting out of a wall at the far
end of the alley was a pole from which a sign, perhaps the one they sought, might
once have hung. The two of them moved forward.

Beneath the pole was a low and narrow doorway. Bent double to peer in,
they were able to make out a sunken floor, some chairs and rough tables, and a
counter running down one wall, behind which stood a man who viewed them
over the top of a glass tilted to his lips and seemingly frozen there.

"Is this the tavern called the Broken Wheel?" asked Salvestro, at which the
man threw the glass's contents down his throat, gasped, coughed, belched, and
nodded. The hum of raised voices sounded from somewhere in the building's
depths. A dog joined the two of them briefly at the door. The man ignored them
steadily. Salvestro looked up the bare signpole. "Where's the wheel, then?" he demanded.

"Broken," said the man, intent on pouring himself another tot. "Are you
looking for someone?"

"Lucullo." The man looked at them sharply, spilling a little of the liquid on
the counter. "His son sent us. Lucillo." The dog left at this point.

"In the back." The second tot followed the first, and he gestured with the
empty glance toward a thickening of the gloom in the back wall. "Follow the
corridor, and don't open any doors that aren't already open."

The noise grew louder and more distinct as they stumbled down the corridor, registering as loud competitive talking mixed with odd shouts and interjec-
tions, until the two of them emerged at the top of three steps and found
themselves surveying a spacious rectangular room, almost a hall. Large candles
blazed from every table, for the place was windowless, throwing a strong yellow
light over the faces that turned from their conversations and tankards to stare at
them now in silence. Two pillars emerged from the stone floor and continued up
into a wooden ceiling. The floor itself was filled with tables and chairs and surrounded by raised wooden booths, seven or eight on each side. Cooking smells
wafted in from somewhere.

Salvestro cleared his throat. "We're looking for Lucullo."

More silence. Then, when they were about to turn tail and go back the way
they'd come, a voice called from one of the booths, "Here. In here," and at that
the rest of the Broken Wheel's patrons turned away from them as one and resumed their earlier conversations. Salvestro and Bernardo threaded a path among
the tables to the source of the voice. A head peeked out, followed by a large hand
that beckoned them to sit down.

He was a big man, richly dressed, broad-chested, and gray-haired. A strong
brow jutted over steady eyes that watched their scramble onto the bench across

the table from his own. A number of pies sat before him, hot and meaty smelling. Bernardo watched the pies carefully.

"You know me?" asked Lucullo, putting down the spoon that he had been about to plunge into the nearest of the pies. Salvestro shook his head, but as he did so a strange sensation began to creep over him, as if he did know Lucullo, had known him for years, in fact, always enjoying his company, sad when they parted, delighted at their meeting once again: an enveloping pleased-to-be-there well-being. It seemed to radiate out of Lucullo in warm, irresistible waves while Salvestro explained how they came to be there. "Shall we take a look?" Lucullo suggested. Salvestro passed the scabbard across the table. Bernardo continued to monitor the pies.

"Bit of copper in it, that's normal enough," Lucullo began. "The wire fused in this pattern round the top, that's almost pure. Nice design, too; unusual." He balanced it on two fingers—"Just over a pound in weight"—then thought for a moment. "I can give you one hundred and eighty-five soldi for it."

Salvestro was already reaching across the table to shake on the deal when Lucullo raised his hand. "Wait. As the founder of Lucullo and Sons, I must advise you of certain facts. First, the value of the silver in this scabbard is probably a little over three hundred soldi by weight; thus in choosing to deal with me, you are accepting a loss of more than a scudo. Were you, take this to the Zecca, you would be offered something close to that sum, minus fees, which are commonly a tenth on small articles. Lucullo and Sons would urge this course of action. You would need to produce some form of provenance, of course, and then wait ten days for the dividend."

"Ten days!" Salvestro exclaimed. "We need to eat now, not in ten days."

"Ah." Lucullo's brow furrowed. "I rather feared that might be the case. Your friend here, I couldn't help but notice, has the look of a man eager for sustenance, and that being the case, I'm afraid that I have to insist on a prior condition. Before we make the exchange, you will have to eat. In the current situation, it's only proper."

"Only proper," Bernardo agreed happily. The pies, four of them, were beginning to get cold.

"Proper?" Salvestro burst out. "What on earth . . . I mean, we can't eat because we can't pay. And we can't pay because we can't eat . . . ?" He felt he should feel more outraged by this twist, but again some strange benevolence from Lucullo seemed to sap his belligerence. His resistance ended when Lucullo pushed the four pies across the table and Bernardo took the first of them and simply swallowed it. Salvestro reached for the spoon.

The bruises on his face began to throb as he ladled lumps of meat and pastry into his mouth, trying at the same time to pay attention to Lucullo, who explained that these pies were in the nature of gifts and implied no contract between them, that had he exchanged the scabbard while they were hungry, it might have been said that the deal had been done under passive duress, while if he had loaned them the money for the meal, he might then have demanded its immediate repayment and set the price as he liked, and that to protect the probity of Lucullo and Sons, he was thus forced to either forgo the business or buy them lunch, and in the meantime how were the pies?

"Good," answered Bernardo, who had finished his two already.

"Now leth make the eckthange," said Salvestro, who was still chewing.

Again the hand came up. "One more thing. It is a slippery matter, but as necessary in its way as the pies. Your respective dispositions, here, at this moment. Would you be so good as to describe them to me?" Salvestro translated this for Bernardo, and then both men indicated that their dispositions at that moment were exceptionally good. "You feel well in yourselves?" They nodded. "Agreeable toward others?" They nodded again. "In particular toward me?" Salvestro hesitated then, suddenly and briefly wary. He swallowed the last of the pie and gave a slow nod. An expression of resignation appeared on Lucullo's face. "As I thought," he said. "It is an entirely spurious sensation, which I must urge you to ignore. It's me. Since I was a child, people have liked me, agreed with me, found me *agreeable,* been *agreeable* around me. My whole life, all I have ever heard is the sound of concord. Can you imagine that?"

"No," said Salvestro, but really feeling that, yes, it made perfect sense. Why not agree with a man like Lucullo?

"We get chased a lot by dogs," said Bernardo.

"My sons suffer the same affliction, though to a lesser degree than their father. You noted yourselves the nature of our trade in the piazza. I mention it because I would like you to discount it from your decision on the exchange. You could leave now, having gained a lunch, and try your luck at a pawnshop. No obligation. Now dismiss your feelings and decide."

"Done," said Salvestro, and reached across to shake on it. Lucullo began counting out coins from a large satchel resting on the seat beside him and stacking them in columns of ten.

"We get chased a lot by dogs," Bernardo said again.

"I have never been chased by a dog," replied Lucullo.

"You're lucky, then," said Bernardo.

Lucullo said nothing to that but after a moment or two murmured, "It's a curse."

Salvestro and Bernardo looked at each other, Salvestro wanting to nod happily at this, but both of them feeling at the same time that immunity from dogs was most emphatically not a curse. "Why?" asked Salvestro.

"Imagine what life would be like if everyone always agreed with you," said Lucullo then. "I mean *everyone,* and *always.* You're with a woman, your first love, for instance, and you say to her, Shall we take a walk together in the orchard? Of course she agrees, so off you go. You tell her that you love her and ask does she love you? Of course she does, and a little later, when you ask her for a kiss, she yields. And yields further, too, naturally, if you suggest it, and says yes when you ask for her hand in marriage, and yes again when you ask that she forgive your infidelities, which are numerous and sometimes monstrous—why should her sister prove any less compliant than she?—and when you tire of her off she trots to the dower-house, or the nunnery, or the stew. . . . Take a tavern, another instance. There you sit with your old drinking partners. Another drink? Of course. And another? Why not! You decide you've had enough. So have they. But a tiny glass of rum, perhaps? Capital idea! And then a gallon of brine? Very well. And then round the evening off with a pint of pig's blood? Everyone hurries to knock it back, and anything else you want to suggest. Do you see? Do you see what it would be like?" Salvestro was nodding sympathetically.

"Perhaps you do," Lucullo continued more quietly. "And perhaps my wife does indeed love me, and my friends do truly live only to drink with me. But perhaps you are all merely agreeing with me, with Lucullo, the most *agreeable* man in Rome. I will never know." He was silent for a moment. "Anyway"—Lucullo roused himself—"this is all very gloomy, and as your friend here says, there are indeed patches of sunlight in it." Bernardo looked blank. "The dogs," Lucullo reminded him. Bernardo shrugged. There was a short silence.

"And your line of business," Salvestro ventured. "It must be helpful there."

"Money? Well, what is money but agreement? Silver is a pretty metal, as everyone agrees. But if they did not, would it still be pretty? Perhaps it is a little more beautiful in Venice today, or the Hansa ports, or Constantinople, or less. How many ducats to the dinar? How many dinars make a Reich dollar? Scudi, zecchini, gulden, and groshen. . . . Their little quarrels are a noise the world cannot bear to hear, and their makings-up are how we *bancherotti* make our fortunes. Since Adam covered his privates, our sadnesses and joys have been theirs. What can we agree upon when we cannot agree upon that? Money is the most agreeable thing in the world."

As an archer sure of his target will look to his quiver rather than follow the shaft's inevitable path to its target, Lucullo looked away when this little speech was ended, and sure enough, Salvestro found himself agreeing, nodding, hardly understanding more than the gist of what had been said yet still convinced that whatever it was, it was so. Lucullo sighed heavily. Bernardo was silent.

The back room of the Broken Wheel had grown more crowded. A few men had entered by the passage that the two of them had taken earlier and been greeted by receptions similar to their own. More frequently, though, a door in the wall opposite swung open and disclosed glimpses of a staircase as men walked in and out with oily-skinned young women dressed in gaudy-colored satins and muslins. Two young men came and went through a curtained doorway next to it, carrying trays of food and drink. Then Bernardo spoke.

"No, it's not," he said.

Lucullo turned to look at him, his astonishment all the stranger for registering on a face so unused to astonishment. Then, as if in sympathy, Bernardo's own face began to move. First his brow furrowed, then wrinkled, his lower jaw began to jut, and his eyes narrowed, anchoring themselves to a point just beyond the end of his nose. Salvestro's own surprised face mirrored Lucullo's. The two men watched as Bernardo's jaw began to work, his cheeks contorted, the muscles there flexing left and right as though two fat men were fighting for sole possession of his mouth. His Adam's apple pumped steadily, then quicker. He chewed on his tongue. Salvestro's astonishment became amazed recognition at what was taking place. He's thinking, he thought. Then Bernardo spoke again.

"Money," he said. "It's not agreeable. It's not agreeable at all because . . ." A pause then as his face heaved in the grip of a final contortion—part gulp, part spasm—which unfurrowed his brow, retracted his jaw, and sent both fat men tumbling down his gullet. "Because there's not enough of it."

An hour later—no, two or three, sitting on the edge of the bed and pulling his shirt back over his head, Salvestro reflected on Lucullo's reaction. He felt the bed move slightly as the woman rolled over behind him. A dim clangor of banging doors and raised voices reached him from below. It was precipitate, in his opinion. Precipitate, and even unconsidered.

Lucullo had sat bolt upright at Bernardo's contradiction, and for a few seconds he had said nothing, only stared incredulously across the table. But then he had risen to his feet, slowly, and even before he'd opened his mouth Salvestro had felt it—great waves of it rolling out and engulfing the room, flooding it in an instant: bonhomie, or good cheer, or a vast and irresistible happiness. When Lucullo spoke, calling for drinks, more food, for general celebration, it seemed to Salvestro that the light brightened about their corner of the room, shining in the faces that turned toward them, already calling for food themselves, drink, too, for a general celebration.

"In a *barrel,* you say?" Lucullo's fascinated face drew the other patrons like a beacon, agog, shaking their heads in wonderment, exclaiming along with him as the two of them spun the yarn of their undersea voyage to Vineta. The customers of the Broken Wheel were a shabby and ill-dressed crowd beside Lucullo, peering over the backs of the adjoining booths, clustered on stools about the end of the table, and standing room only behind, all nodding away with Lucullo.

"And this would be where you acquired the scabbard, I imagine." It seemed that Lucullo was breathless to hear more, so it was breathlessness that the other patrons aped then, and Salvestro heard himself agreeing that yes, it was indeed, wondering at the same time how it might have been possible to pick something from the bottom of the sea while sealed in a barrel. Then it was Bernardo who would say, "No, actually. You see, he was in the barrel. . . ." And Lucullo would throw up his hands in delight, exclaiming, "There's a man who speaks his mind," or, "He certainly tells it like it is." He proposed a toast to "the explorers," and the Broken Wheel drank to their health as a single Lucullo-like entity. Food arrived, pots of steaming soup in which to dip the hard, flat bread that was the best the Broken Wheel offered. Pots of beer and cups of rough wine were ordered in a constant stream, but even as he nodded and smiled with the others, Salvestro felt a second disposition underlying the general merriment. The talk drifted casually, but only when Lucullo spoke, and when he did not a vague panic seemed to take hold of his court, which they assuaged with drink. The faces about him glowed and shone with Lucullo's excitements, his own, too, he realized at one point, and he wondered if the others sensed something beneath their own reflected agitations and excitements. For it was fun, and good-humored, and underneath that were imperturbable depths that cared nothing for laughter and delight in the Broken Wheel. Underneath was a yawning emptiness, and this too was Lucullo's.

Now a single yelp pierced the wall of the upstairs chamber, a woman's voice. It was followed by another, then a succession of deep grunts. Something on the other side of the partition began to knock rhythmically. The bed, he thought. It roused the girl, who cocked an ear. "That's Anjelica. Your friend must be . . ." She stopped in midsentence.

"The Pilgrim's Staff? You mean to tell me that you're staying at the Stick, the worst doss-hole in the city? Stay with me!" Lucullo had burst out. Salvestro was already accepting, the press of their audience closing on him, urging him on, for only a fool would refuse, and what an offer, and *yes, yes, yes.* . . .

"No," said Bernardo. Was it the brief stilling of his deeper disquiet that he felt then? "We can't. We have to stay with the monks," Bernardo went on, and for a second it seemed as if Lucullo might protest before he clapped his hands together, saying, "Well, that's a 'no,' no question. Certainly knows his own mind, this one, eh?" *Yes, yes, yes.* . . . Respectful comments on the quality of Bernardo's mind followed, and then the talk ranged wider, to the time that Lucullo had once spent in a madhouse, then back again to Bernardo and himself and their journey from Usedom far to the north. When it was time for Lucullo to meet his sons in the piazza, he exacted promises from them that they would return and drink with him again. He left, waving, and the gathering faltered as suddenly as it began. Their audience drifted away, rubbing their eyes and looking about them in vague bewilderment as though just awakened from sleep. They were left alone with the last of the celebrants, a man of about their own age who introduced himself as Pierino, a scholar who seemed to have found himself marooned in Rome for want of funds to leave. "Just get out, just get yourselves out," he kept muttering, for he was quite drunk, then would apologize for his rudeness: "I mean Rome, not this place."

They left him eventually, Salvestro demolishing Lucullo's colonnade of soldi and scooping them into a ragged triangle of cloth torn from his shirt, which he tied carefully. The other drinkers nodded perfunctory farewells as they weaved through the tables to the door opposite the one they had entered. At the bottom of the stairs, one of the women he had seen earlier barred their way. "Anjelica!" she shouted up the stairwell.

"What?" Salvestro had asked.

"Lucullo left you a gift," she said, then shouted again. Anjelica appeared and looked down at them both over the balustrade.

"So which one of you is the famous Bernardo?" she asked, and when Bernardo indicated himself he was told, "Come on up."

The bed next door was silent now. Salvestro pulled on his boots. The woman was quiet, dressing herself quickly on the other side of the bed. She stood and dusted herself with a powder that smelled of roses. Salvestro felt her hand trail over his shoulder as she walked past him to the door. "Why so quiet, Master Explorer?" she asked. "It happens to everyone one time or another."

As he waited for Bernardo to emerge, Salvestro heard heavy footsteps coming down the stairs. A man with thinning hair poked his head around the door. "You Bernardo or the other one?" he asked.

"I'm the other one," Salvestro replied.

"Well, you'll do." He was unwrapping something from a length of cloth. "Lucullo left you this." He weighed the scabbard in his hand. "Nice story, that business with the barrel. We can always use a good story here at the Broken Wheel. You'll have met Simon out the back. He's there to scare off the pilgrims. Next time, come in from the other side, through the yard. I'm Rodolfo, the most *disagreeable* man in Rome." He laughed then at Salvestro's continuing bafflement. "I own the place. Anyway, there you are." He handed over the scabbard. "Where'd you get it?"

He recalled coming blearily awake that morning from a dream in which his teeth had clamped themselves to tree-trunks and would not let go. He swallowed twists and slivers of bark, and his incisors gouged shallow grooves in the tree-flesh beneath. The sour sap seemed still to fill his mouth as he opened his eyes. Bernardo was already awake, gnawing on a cabbage-stalk. He motioned to him silently and put a finger to his lips. They rose, and it was only then that he noticed the Prior, wakeful like themselves amongst the other sleeping bodies.

"This is for your labors," Jörg said, speaking softly, his hand emerging from the chest. He placed the scabbard in Salvestro's hand. There was a furtive air to the transaction, as though the other monks might protest their Prior's extravagance. There had been other such moments, when Salvestro had resisted the urge to engage one or other of the monks in conversation, or had overheard their talk and wanted to burst in with some insight of his own. Above Bolzano, still in the mountains, they had walked until nightfall without encountering another soul and had to make their beds as best they could amongst the trunks of a pine forest. The near blackness beneath the trees' canopy, the windless silence, these had unnerved the novices. Shivering in the cold air, Salvestro listened as Jörg told them, "But there is no silence. God breathes everywhere. Can you not hear?" And when they shook their heads he went on, "No? Are you sure?" He had breathed louder himself, then cocked an ear to each of their chests in turn, saying, "I think that I hear it," then, when they had finally understood, "It is God's breath, do you hear? Only lent to us. Listen. . . ."

And listening himself, Salvestro had thought of the street in Prato where they had left the girl, where the silence was a pent-up pounding from which he had fled, diving within himself to escape it. Before he could stop himself he had said something, something about the worst silences being the loudest, something stupid, but Jörg had turned to him in surprise and said, "There now, you see? Salvestro here understands," and he would have said more, but at that point two of the older monks approached and the Prior turned away from him as though this endorsement had exceeded some fixed, invisible limit in their dealings with one another. There had been other such incidents, too—unguarded slaps on the back as an inn hove into view, brief words of encouragement, fleeting exchanges of words on the road—and each time Jörg had pulled back, stopped himself, as though to acknowledge him in that way were too flagrant a breach of his reserve or implied too intimate an acceptance of what he was. The scabbard was given in a like manner, for as he'd murmured his thanks Jörg had turned away impatiently, and he'd felt vaguely baffled and ill-placed, as he had before. He and Bernardo existed in a limbo between the monks and their Prior, as if they were the wedge that split them apart. He tucked the scabbard in the drawstring of his hose.

"The Prior gave it to me," he said to Rodolfo.

"A gift from a clerk! Good God, we should put it on a plinth," Rodolfo retorted. At that moment, a large hand appeared around the door opposite and Bernardo tiptoed out, clothes tucked under one arm. He dropped them on the floor and began to dress quickly, glancing up at Salvestro and Rodolfo, who watched curiously. The big man nodded toward the stairs as he pulled on his boots.

"Time to go," said Salvestro.

At first they had not understood. Their Prior stood before them, his arm bent back behind him like Moses pointing down to the Promised Land. They looked forward obediently, then looked to each other. Before them was a field stripped bare of grass, a part-dried sea of mud, a desert.

"Saint Peter's!" proclaimed Father Jörg.

The monks stayed silent, dumbfounded by the conundrum. They looked again, but what more was there to see? Four great stumps of stone standing on ground cut with a few trenches and dotted with puddles of stagnant water, a row of tumbrels, people wandering about among little depots of timber, stone, and gravel. Ruins.

The silence gathered weight. Jörg looked back and forth, confused and suddenly uncertain. Then someone said, "Doesn't look like His Holiness can keep his churches any better than us."

It began as something that might have been a sneeze, then a wheezing escape of breath, then a hiccup, but a hiccup of laughter. Another followed, then another, as their stifled laughter broke out, and then they were laughing at him without restraint, some bent double, others slapping their sides at the sight of their Prior, who kept looking back and forth as though in disbelief that the muddy wreckage behind him did not awe them to silence. They guffawed, and giggled, and whooped, and chuckled, and standing at the back, HansJürgen too found himself unable to quell his own rising mirth and laughed heartily along with the rest of them at the absurdity of it. Jörg let his arms fall to his sides and stood before them helplessly. HansJürgen saw the bewilderment on his face, his utter incomprehension, and at that or what it meant, his mirth evaporated as suddenly as it had begun. Of course! he thought. How else could his Prior have blundered so? The fact had been there before him in Jörg's stumbles and pratfalls, his artless gazings into space, and seeing now the blank shock scrawled across the Prior's face, he suddenly understood, and it sobered him in an instant. He cannot see, thought HansJürgen.

A door behind the staircase led them up a flight of steps to the back of a storeroom filled with oddly shaped blocks of stone and incomprehensible machinery: wooden frames, wooden-toothed wheels, rope, an oversize funnel. They picked their way past hoppers of stone dust and racks of chisels to a door opening onto a deserted yard. The street beyond the archway opposite was crowded with men carrying sacks, pushing covered barrows, leading reluctant mules laden with cages and crates. One pulled a sled upon which clods of earth had been piled; as he passed they saw that the clods were vegetables of some kind. Swedes? A ragged old woman asked if they wanted to buy a flower for their sweethearts. They did not.

"We should be getting back to the Stick," said Bernardo. "It's almost dark."

Salvestro looked up at a sky tinged with pink to the west and otherwise bright blue. "It won't be dark for hours," he retorted. "What's the matter with you?"

"We'll be late," Bernardo went on. He seemed perturbed. "I don't like it."

"What? Don't like what?" Salvestro was growing exasperated.

Bernardo shifted uncomfortably and jerked a thumb back at the courtyard. "All that. I didn't like it before. I don't like it now." He had colored slightly. Salvestro realized that he was talking about the women.

"Well, Anjelica certainly seemed to like it," he said, "from what I heard."

"Oh, she liked it all right," said Bernardo with some emphasis. "Just like that other one. But I didn't like it." He squirmed and fell silent.

"What other one? Since when did you—"

"That one with all the sisters, when we were still with Groot and the others." He touched his head. "Red hair."

Salvestro sighed. "That was me, not you. And she didn't have any sisters."

"It was you first," Bernardo retorted. "Then it was me. Then after she'd done it she brought all her sisters and they did it too. She had four sisters. I counted. . . . What? What's so funny?" Salvestro had begun to laugh. "Anyway, I didn't like it."

"Let's go up here," said Salvestro. "Don't worry, we'll be back at the Stick soon enough. In the meantime we've a bag of silver and the whole of Rome before us. You liked Lucullo, didn't you?"

"Don't treat me like a fool," Bernardo snapped. Then, as they set off up the street, he added, "I'm not a horse, you know." Salvestro lengthened his stride and pulled a pace or two ahead. He remained silent.

The two of them weaved a path through the oncoming porters and small tradesmen. Little workshops and stalls were set into a row of crumbling arches. Opposite these stood clusters of wooden shacks, each one flying a mixture of tattered clothing and rags from a pole projecting through the roof. A weak southerly breeze stirred these pennants, carrying before it dust lifted from the dry slopes of the Capitoline visible behind them, scents of horse and cow dung, the odd fishy whiff from the market about the Pantheon, and something else, something acrid. Salvestro sniffed cautiously.

"Lime," he said.

They turned the corner at the Church of Saint Nicholas and a new vista opened before them. The shacks gave way to little windowless brick huts, a few larger ones amongst them, each topped with a chimney from which opaque white smoke issued up into the sky. The street dissolved into myriad little paths that wound their ways among them. Looking in the open doorway of the first, the two of them saw a red eye of fire in the darkness, winking as a blackened figure moved back and forth to feed logs into the flames. Heat shimmered on the bricks, and the smell of lime grew stronger. He stopped abruptly.

"What?" demanded Bernardo. "What is it now?"

After the first week, after the dye-houses and basements where the Pratesi were tortured began to excrete the cadavers of the more stubborn or penniless in greater numbers, after the outlying wells into which those cadavers were tossed had been filled and rats were feeding in packs on the corpses left in the streets, a company of pikemen was ordered to dig pits. They were deeper than the height of a man, six or seven of them. For the bodies. He had come across one in his wanderings around the city, stood over by three men carrying shovels who had hailed him and shared a flask of fiery liquor. A fourth was in the pit, methodically raising his shovel and bringing it down on the topmost skulls of the dead. Salvestro had looked down at the heads and tangled limbs: a hand, a foot, another hand. There was part of a crotch, a man's crotch; there a shock of red hair. His eye wandered over limbs and fragments of limbs. Then something moved at the edge of his vision, something twitched. He watched carefully, and the next time he saw it plain. A hand was lodged between a head and part of an arm; the fingers grasped feebly. One of the three began shoveling a pile of light gray powder over the corpses. The air grew acrid with it. He sat with them and drank. After a while, one of the men cocked an ear. A faint rustling or scrabbling sound was audible in the pit behind them, then another, and perhaps a third. "Lime's beginning to bite," said the man.

"Come on," Bernardo said now.

Salvestro shook his head to clear it. He hawked and spat a gobbet of thick white phlegm. Beyond the lime kilns, the ground fell away to one side. On the other, a barnlike brick building extended two windowless wings, defining a courtyard in which sacks were piled in large depots. Men were wheeling hand-carts filled with powdery gray rock to an entrance somewhere at the back. A dull pounding boomed behind the barn doors at the front. As they listened, a shrill whistle sounded and the pounding quickly became irregular, then stopped entirely. A few seconds later the doors were thrown open.

At first it seemed that the manufactory's interior was not so much dark as opaque. A cloud of gray-white dust bulged in the gaping doorway, swelled there, became a falling wall of fog that billowed forward across the courtyard toward them. Then Salvestro saw that there were figures moving within it, white as wraiths, and out of the cloud the men began to emerge. They staggered forward coughing, their eyes screwed tight against the burning powder, dozens of them stumbling out of the lime as white as ghosts.

"Who's that?" Bernardo said.

The lime-workers seemed not to see them as they stumbled past. Salvestro looked into one or two of the ashen faces, but they did not look into his. "No one," he said.

"What? No, over there." Bernardo pointed. Beside a stand of strange white trees perhaps fifty yards away, a man on horseback was visible, his back turned to them. He seemed to be talking to the figure standing beside him and gesturing forward from time to time at something lower down the slope. The figure on foot wore a habit.

"It looks like Gerhardt," said Bernardo. The habited figure turned obligingly.

"Yes," said Salvestro. "It does." As they watched, the horseman nudged his mount forward and disappeared down the slope. The monk followed.

They walked forward until they stood beside the same trees, not white but covered with lime dust. The ground dipped before them, becoming an immense bowl scooped out of the earth. Within, it appeared to Salvestro, a whole city had been built, then razed a foot from the ground. Foundations, little stone piers, broken columns, and toppled arches lay scattered about, and amongst them swarmed a locust-army of pick-swingers, hammerers, and barrowmen. Gerhardt and the horseman were visible moving amongst them far below. The bowl echoed with the workers' shouts and rang with the sound of metal on stone.

"What's he doing here?" Bernardo asked.

Salvestro shook his head. What indeed? All he knew or wished to know of Gerhardt was contained in the desperate minutes he had endured on the shore of the distant island. Under the islanders' kicks and blows, he had glimpsed the monk's cowled head, then his eyes, just visible outside the circle of his pain, watching him calmly and without excitement until panic had flashed across his face, he had turned to flee, and an instant later Bernardo had fallen on the is-landers like a huge, implacable animal. Bernardo had not seen Gerhardt that night, and Salvestro had not told him of the monk's part. Now, receiving no an-swer to his question, Bernardo lost interest in the scene before him. "We should get back now," he said.

Gerhardt had got down on his knees. He was peering at the ground, then gesturing up at the horseman, then looking down again. Salvestro's eye wandered across the scene. Lines of men pushing barrows snaked through the ruins to the west side of the bowl, upending their loads onto piles that rose like anthills at the foot of the slope. Steps had been cut into earth, but steps for a giant, each one eight or ten feet high. The lime-workers toted sacks that they balanced on their backs, and thus bent double, they scrambled from one platform to the next on ladders set side by side, so close that they appeared as the ratlines of a ship's rig-ging or a huge mesh in which the porters struggled blindly, crawling up and down, up and down. . . . Below were depots of sacks, and sacks being filled, and sacks being lifted onto backs, and on the floor of the great crater the ant-army hammered, swung, scurried about, and the work of destruction went on. Salvestro thought of the shovel's rising and the gristly thud as it fell, of the cadaver's imper-turbable grin. Only fill this sump with water, he thought. The dead give up their flesh; the drowned not even that. Was this what had awaited him, down there, in the black fathoms? Did the scavengers below know the builders whose arches and walls they tore down to feed their kilns, whose flesh they flayed to the irre-ducible bones? *Lime's beginning to bite.* . . . The grin was in the skull, he knew that, and even lime had not dissolved their skulls.

"We have to go," Bernardo broke in again. "Have to get back to the Stick."

Salvestro nodded. "We'll go back now," he said.

"How long has this been going on?" he hissed, but Jörg only pursed his lips and looked away. HansJürgen looked around the chamber at the monks who had returned so far. He would have to go out again soon. "How long?" he demanded.

"It is unimportant," Jörg said. "I see well enough to pray."

But not well enough to tell a church from a mason's yard, thought HansJür-gen. The gale of helpless laughter had blown over the Prior while he had turned this way and that, blinking stupidly in the sunlight, stamping off abruptly in a baf-fled rage. HansJürgen found him seated against a water-trough amongst the cat-tle-drovers and hawkers waiting to pay their dues to the officers at the Porta Pertusa. He had given him his arm and guided him back, but when the two men reached the site of his humiliation the monks had scattered. A few were wander-

ing about the stone piers of the "church"; more were found in the piazza. Henning, Volker, and a few others had returned directly to the hostel. Florian arrived
shortly after they did with the news that Wulf, Wolf, and Wilf had run off in the
direction of Santo Spirito. Jörg seemed to have grown weary and spiritless.
HansJürgen guided him to his pallet and went out with Florian to search for the
others. As the afternoon wore on, they drifted in of their own accord in ones and
twos. Now only the three novices, Joachim-Heinz and Heinz-Joachim, Matthias,
Georg, and Gerhardt were unaccounted for. The silence of those already returned
was an oppressive weight bearing down on the chamber. Their eyes followed him
as he rose to continue his search.

I see well enough to pray. . . . But was prayer enough, here, in Ro-ma? The
monks already looked to him for a sign, an indication as to what they should do,
but he had nothing to tell them. Their faces were apprehensive and questioning.
Henning had asked him if they would be returning to Usedom soon.

The sun was falling behind one of the low hills in the westernmost quarter of
the city as he walked down to the Ponte Sant'Angelo. The pilgrims and tradesmen seemed to carry him along in a great noisy flood of bodies. He gave himself
up to it, the alien jabbering, the smell of sweat, the cheap wine on their breath.
Tonight the Prior would have to address them, present himself again as their
shepherd. They would follow, if led. They would follow. He clung to that as the
crowd jostled in the little square before the crowded bridge. He craned his neck
to look ahead and saw a sea of bobbing hats. The crowd inched forward through
the square, slowing further as it squeezed onto the bridge. He had made only a
few stuttering steps when a voice at his elbow said his name.

Salvestro was leaning over the parapet. An expression of mild confusion
passed over his blotched face. "We didn't know you were with them," he said
defensively.

The same confusion surfaced amongst his own features. Them?

"Who?" he asked, at which the other pointed down to the riverbank where
pilgrims and boatmen were crowded together, arguing fiercely about the price of
the passage downriver, then holding up the hems of their cloaks as they minced
down narrow planks laid over the river mud and boarded the nearest of a fleet of
jostling pirogues. The boats swayed wildly, knocking against one another as they
darted in and out from the bank to take on their passengers. The boatmen cursed
and shoved, wielding their oars like barge poles to get clear, then they disappeared
under the bridge and were off down the river.

HansJürgen overlooked this scene, uncomprehending, and was about to demand some further explanation when outraged shouts echoed from beneath the
bridge and Wulf, Wolf, and Wilf shot out, tearing hell-for-leather along the bank,
weaving a deft and mud-defying path through the startled pilgrims, who swayed
and waved their arms for balance. The shouting beneath the bridge increased in
volume, and a second later Bernardo erupted into view.

It seemed to the two observers that a maddened and mud-bespattered water buffalo had burst among the unsuspecting crowd, upending pilgrims by the plankful as it cut a swath of chaos in pursuit of the absconding trio. All four disappeared around a bend in the embankment while men and women picked themselves up out of the mud, gazed about in baleful shock, and then began to brush at patches of filth on their clothes, making them worse.

"That's the second time," said Salvestro. "They'll be back again in a minute." They were.

"Stop!" barked HansJürgen, and the three novices skidded to a halt, looking up wild-eyed with their shouts and laughter dying on their lips, suddenly the still point amongst the lurching pilgrims about them. "Come here!"

Bernardo reappeared, charging around the corner, heedless of the various pilgrim-shaped obstructions that melted magically at his approach or found themselves facedown in the mud. He ground to a halt at the sight of the three of them, momentarily baffled by this conclusion to the pursuit.

"Up here!" Salvestro called, then turned to HansJürgen. "We saw them down there and thought they were lost," he explained, "so Bernardo volunteered to, er, collect them. We thought . . ."

"Quite," replied HansJürgen. "That was the right thing to do. I was in search of them myself." He eyed the trio sternly as they trudged up the stairs from the river and waited at the end of the bridge. Wilf looked back at their late pursuer who was trudging up the steps after them. All three began once again to giggle. "Silence!" HansJürgen shouted, then turned back to Salvestro. "Thank you," he said, and hesitated as if he might say more. He felt awkward, beholden somehow. He is a hired lance, and faithless, HansJürgen reminded himself. He had avoided the two of them since they had found him on the beach, as though his helplessness then were shaming. A few words had passed between them on the journey. That was all.

They walked back against the flow of the crowd with Bernardo at their head, Salvestro and HansJürgen bringing up the rear. The three youngsters chattered in guarded voices between them.

"Did you see the Pope?" Salvestro asked at one point.

"No," HansJürgen replied shortly.

Dusk was falling as they took an alley off the Via Alessandrina. The streets narrowed and darkened until it seemed to HansJürgen that night had fallen, though when he paused outside the entrance to the Stick and looked up, the sky was still luminous. Joachim-Heinz and Heinz-Joachim had returned in their absence. They had decided to divide and scout out the river from opposite banks, switching over by the bridges at Tiber island. Joachim-Heinz had observed the latter part of Bernardo's pursuit of the three novices until he had lost sight of them under the bridge at Sant'Angelo. Matthias limped in a little later, helped by Georg. A horse had kicked him. Only Gerhardt was still missing.

Father Jörg lay on his pallet, his lips moving almost imperceptibly in prayer. The other monks gathered in twos and threes to talk in undertones HansJürgen could not hear. Wulf, Wolf, and Wilf fidgeted and jabbered together in whispers. Only their two guides seemed at ease, Salvestro dozing, Bernardo picking the mud from his clothes as it dried. HansJürgen thought to join the Prior in his devotions, but he could not settle. Blind, or almost blind. . . . He marveled again at his own stupidity. How many of the others had understood the weakness revealed that afternoon? It hardly mattered; they would learn it soon enough. Such a thing could not be concealed. Bring this day to a close, he thought.

He might have fallen asleep, though it was brief and troubled. A sudden commotion had him stirring, looking about him. What? The brothers were getting to their feet. Where was Jörg?

"Brothers, today we have been tested. Our hardships have changed their natures. . . ."

To what? HansJürgen found himself asking. He struggled to his feet as Jörg spoke of their mishaps, recasting them as tests and trials, necessities on the path to reward. He spoke forcefully at first, and the monks hung on his words. They want to believe, HansJürgen thought, or wished. Soon, though, he began to drift and ramble, to repeat himself, and HansJürgen felt the same drift move through his audience. Then, in the midst of this address, the door banged open.

Jörg stopped and turned to the source of the noise. Gerhardt stood in the doorway. There was a short awkward silence before Jörg said, "You are late, Brother." Gerhardt was white with dust from the crown of his head to the soles of his sandals, his appearance made even stranger by Jörg's failure to mention it. He made a casual apology, and Jörg returned to his theme, which had become an analogy between their own misfortunes and the Pope's; but the monks were no longer listening. They glanced about at Gerhardt, who stood in their midst pulling their attention to himself while outwardly hanging rapt on the words of his Prior. When Jörg was finished it was Gerhardt they watched as he strode to his pallet on the far side of the chamber. Hanno and Georg followed.

The monks settled slowly that night, carefully picking at the lumps that had formed in their mattresses, going out in ones and twos to splash water on their faces. New rituals, thought HansJürgen. His unease ballooned inside him.

Father Jörg had taken out his quill and was writing with painstaking slowness, his face only inches from the parchment.

"*The Devil conjured cities for Christ in the wilderness, to test him, and to test his worthiness. Just so do the monks of Usedom face this city called Roma. Some see a city of churches and pilgrims. Others see only difficulties and tasks which they would rather leave to others. Some will persevere, and others will not. The monks of Usedom will be winnowed here, as Christ was, and the chaff will be threshed away. Already the husks are peeling off the corn. . . .*"

Jörg paused there, not quite sure how to proceed. There were matters he wished to treat of and yet no manner in which to treat them. He listened to the sounds in the chamber: low murmurs, straw-rustles, the odd cough or sneeze . . . Then the scratch of his nib as he resumed.

"Their Prior led the monks of Usedom to Roma, but some came only against their will. . . ."

He stopped again. He heard the same sounds as before. Other than these, there was silence. Gerhardt, Hanno, and Georg were still huddled together on the far side of the room, the latter two nodding from time to time. Jörg bent over his parchment and began scribbling more quickly than before, his earlier reservations brushed aside.

"Their Prior found in Rome that his enemies had not changed. Brother Gerhardt plotted against him on the island and undermined him in Rome. He mocked his Prior, and the monks of Usedom ignored his authority, mocking him, too. To begin with, he would disappear for the best part of the day in order to raise speculation about his true activities. Thus were the monks of Usedom distracted from the proper object of their attention, namely their Prior. After that he would gather select groups of malcontents and instill in their breasts the selfsame bile which poisoned his own, namely envy, for he once believed that he would be Prior himself, but Our Lord directed otherwise. . . ."

He continued in this vein for the remainder of the page, then stopped and began to read through what he had written.

HansJürgen lay back on his pallet, watching Gerhardt out of the corner of his eye and listening to the sound of Jörg's writing. Gradually the tiny noises ceased: the nib stopped scratching as Jörg ceased his account, the rustling quietened, only a few low voices disturbed the hush. The Prior was still bent over his parchment when he motioned with his hand for the lights to be put out. The smell of candle-smoke drifted around the chamber. He heard the Prior shift and guessed that he had taken up his quill once again. Its point scratched across the parchment, but more harshly than before and the same motion over and over again. *He is scratching it out,* HansJürgen realized belatedly, *whatever he had been writing. . . .* He was asleep, or on the brink of sleep, when the voice sounded in his ear.

"It was lime dust. We saw him at the quarry."

He could not rouse himself in time. He raised his head, but there was no one. Lime dust. Quarry. . . . Was there more? The voice had been Salvestro's.

"Ghiberti."

"Holiness?"

"Where is Sergeant Rufo?"

A serving man bearing a candle-snuffer maneuvers himself gingerly through the panel door in the far chamber, catches sight of the two men, and stops, legs straddling the sill. Leo gestures impatiently for him to get on with his business. Soon candle-smoke wafts toward them from within the darkening room. Minatory rumblings gurgle in the softness of his bowels; tomorrow's turd promises much pain. It is possible, he thinks, that Leno's intelligence will prove baseless. And it is possible, he thinks, that it will not. Only Rufo will know with certainty, for only Rufo came face-to-face with them. They listen to the man pad about in the adjacent room. Rufo and, perhaps, the Colonel. At length, the far door closes.

Ghiberti says, "I believe he is in the service of the Republic of Venice, Holiness."

Is it foolish of him to reconvene Prato's combatants here in Rome? Would it not be more foolish for him to do nothing while they maneuver about him? Undirected, men err. Misdirected, they sin. Misfortunes follow, and gluttonous categories yawn open: the cavernous "Unforeseen," the engulfing "Unexpected," dimensionless as the adjacent darkened *sala* with spongy Bishop-of-Spezia lips. The future almost always exceeds expectation. . . . Is this wise?

Yes, he thinks, weighing, pondering, best to err on the side of caution. Better to have their throats cut.

"Send for him," he says.

". . . ?"
". . . !"

It takes a week. Premasticated by clerkly molars and part dissolved in the mouth-juices of garrulous papal *fonctionnaires,* this juicy morsel of gossip is passed mouth-to-mouth Tiber-ward, west across the bridge, then coughed up in the city proper: a sickly information-slick to be sniffed as cautious dogs sniff the acidic foam on one another's vomit. What's His Roly-Poly Holiness up to now?

"The Bishop of Spezia?"

"That was *months* ago. . . ."

"It was last week."

But it isn't the Bishop of Spezia, and it isn't the escalating rat-problem, and it isn't the eels, either. Disrobed women and semipublic copulation? Buggery? The French? No, no, no, no. . . . Well-placed sources from the kitchens to the Apostolic Camera report a *conversation.* . . .

"Bor—and may I add—*ing.*"

"No, wait, listen to this. . . ."

There follows, "Mmm-hmmm," and "Uh-huh," and "So what?"

So this is not exactly Rome's staple rumor-fare; no pratfalls, pranks, or pox. No precipitous falls from grace or richly deserved comeuppance, not a mention of the ever-unpopular Cardinal Armellini. The city's ticklish collective cortex sweats in its travertine-and-tufa brainpan. The gossip meanwhile mutates, sprouts odd prehensile limbs, gradually becoming something Rome can recognize. . . . Enter the Rumor-Beast, sporting a pelt of voided velvet with a pomegranate design, seven legs, a single head, and three tails (two more than the average Englishman). Iberia-on-Tiber is at odds with itself, bruits the Beast, extending a number of lobster-like antennae. Ambassadorial discontent is hardly enthralling but at least offers a point of purchase on this nebulous and somewhat abstract anecdote.

"Well, what would you expect from the Portingales?"

"And the Spaniards."

"Hmmm. . . . Do they really brush their teeth in piss?"

The Rumor-Beast gallops about, evolving and disintegrating, shedding a pair of udders in Pescheria; growing gills in Ponte; in next-door Parione excreting a bubble of quivering mucus within which movement becomes more labored, notwithstanding the addition of fifteen virile tentacles. A last sad schlepp down the Via delle Botteghe Oscure, a slimy southward sashay for the salving river. . . . Too late. Fate decrees suffocation within an exoskeletal carapace of its own sun-hardened snot. The Beast is dead. The Rumor lives on. A gravelly tongue slaps and slobbers in the ears of hemispherical friars, demimondaines, quavering, crotchety semirecluses . . .

"They're as bad as each other, arrogant bastards."

"Haughty, I'd say."

"Right, haughty *bastards*. . . ."

Proud, too, and overbearing, and . . . Well, the Rumor finds its first and easiest handhold in Rome's multiple xenophobias, for just as Bohemians are heretics and all Poles are thieves, so Florentines are grasping sodomites, Venetians uppity, and Neapolitans fit only for simple agricultural tasks. The Hungarians? They flap their arms while drinking and wear strangely formless hats. The English are foul-mouthed, avaricious, insular, reeking, tailed toads, while Germans eat like pigs and make boring conversation. The second-best feature of the French is their singing, which sounds like a nanny goat giving birth to a cathedral. The best is their departure back over the Alps two years ago. A few toothless relics of the Borgia's tenure rattle around in the wings of decayed palazzi, jealous guardians of the *limpieza di sangre* clotting in their veins, geriatric boosters of the Black Legend, who can't for the dwindling life of them see how chasing about the Indies for weird animals accords with the hard-won Spanish reputation for extreme military cruelty. The contest finds more cheerful acceptance in Rome's stables and cheaper bordellos, amongst the grooms, whores, and soldiers on secondment from Cardona's army in Naples who swagger and strut about, propping their stubbly chins on the counters of Ripa's taverns while affecting a complaisant impartiality and placing bets on the outcome.

"Gambling! Another unattractive Iberian vice."

"Gambling on what?"

This is far from clear. Further Rumor-modulations play on the city's taste for exotica. Dear old Hanno is implicated in the odd tripartite contract hammered out in the gardens of the Belvedere (this meeting now being reported as "ill-tempered" and even "stormy"), the elephant's popularity feeding a burgeoning Roman curiosity as to the identity of the beast to be procured, the more bizarre the better. The Camelopardis is a strong contender, also the fearsome Scaly Boar, various dragons . . . Kite-flying is the very lifeblood of a vigorous and rude-limbed Rumor, it being closely akin to appetite and metaphor.

"It has"—Colonna pauses, sighs, exhales, ponders, heaves himself upright, begins taking off his shirt—"a most *impervious* armored hide." Vittoria tsks and
clucks as her father repeats this bon mot, watched by one hundred and twenty-
seven pairs of eyes. Off come his shoes. Soon he is stark naked, hat excepted. Vittoria leads him out quietly. Why must he always do this during Mass? Does he
not love God? The arrow digs a little deeper into his skull.

"Hooves." A dwarf says this to his dwarfish wife in a sweltering attic-room of
the Vatican. (Rumor thrives on feedback.) "Hooves," she repeats. It becomes a
password between them. A troupe of their relatives is planning to descend on
them from Magdeburg sometime in the late summer and try their luck with the
Pope, who is said to like dwarfs. "Hooves," he says again.

"Hooves," says his wife.

"Tail like a rat," mutters Cardinal Serra in his apartment a quarter of a mile
away. "Perhaps it *is* a rat." He is grumpy because Vich will not take him into his
confidence and has refused three successive invitations to dinner in the past
month alone. Something's in the air, he smells it, something to do with Ayamonte. A rat.

". . . and it sleeps by leaning against a tree, for, lacking joints in its knees, once
toppled it may not right itself. A large saw and a larger store of patience are all
that is required. The beast is yours. Alternatively it may be lured out and tamed
using virgins. It is very partial to virgins, this beast. . . ." They nod.

In the locked basement of a farmhouse on the Pincio, isolated, carefully chosen, stinking of mildewed plaster and cowshit, La Cavallerizza throws red hair
over her naked shoulders and clamps her thighs tight about the boy's face. A
threatening flick from one pointed fingernail to the bobbing member draws the
reluctant tongue upward into her innards. She settles herself more firmly in the
saddle. "What *(oof)* I want to know *(unnnk)* . . ." Vitelli looks at his wife in mild
surprise as the boy begins to struggle. She reaches for his testicles. ". . . is how big
(uurgh) is this horn *(aaagh)* on the end *(aaargh!)* of its nose?" *Eeeurgh-aaAARGHH!*

"But most important of all . . ." They lean across the table, politely agog.
". . . really, of the utmost significance . . ." They incline their heads to become
mirror-images of each other's rapt and patient fascination. ". . . absolutely key to
an understanding of this beast. . . ." Their heads touch, their attentions being that
undivided. ". . . is that it *absolutely loathes elephants.*"

Thank you.

The animal swells like a bladder puffed with boozy breath and collapses
like a lung. Printers around the city sell out their editions of Pliny's *Natural History* and print more, which sell out, too. Informal factions coalesce about the
Spanish and Portuguese, whose contest becomes heroic, or fierce, or faintly ludicrous, depending upon the circumstance. The Pope is generally applauded,
though for what remains unclear. Grooms groom, menders mend, diggers dig,
drunks drink. . . . Everyone talks. Rome's gossipmongers find their calling in-
fested with rank amateurs who prove alarmingly adept at the Confiding Whisper,

the Wild Claim, and the Vague and Unfounded Assertion. They take refuge in hyperbole and lying.

"Why?" asked Salvestro.

"Why indeed?" replied Pierino. "It is an enigma."

"So the Elephant and the Enigma, they would be old enemies," offered Bernardo. The onlookers who gathered about their table attended the conversation more closely as he spoke. "This is very simple. It's like Christians and Turks, or cats and dogs, or the French and, er . . ."

"Everyone else?" supplied Lucullo.

"Yes," agreed Bernardo. "The Enigma is like Everyone Else."

"And Everyone Else is the Enigma?"

Everyone else nodded.

At first, as talk of this latest Hispano-Lusitanian spat scended and breasted the abutments of Rome's inert attention, the Broken Wheel maintained a lofty disdain, a faintly self-conscious insouciance compounded of genuine ignorance and the patrons' clubbish resistance to whatever the rest of the city finds noteworthy. The tavern's bordelloish light suggests a perpetual "just before midnight": opaque mustards grounded on candlelight-through-cheap-wine crimsons and pinks. Who cares about diplomacy when disinterest is so sublime? For three weeks this was the party line, which the recently dubbed "Enigma" dispensed with in three minutes flat, busting horn-first through the wall with a buffoonish butt of its head and setting the wagging tongues of the Broken Wheel's topers flip-flopping with talk of its improbable anatomy. The tavern's idiolect quickly gained mastery of the word "perissodactyl," and Salvestro and Bernardo found themselves coopted as resident weird beast experts. The "Master Explorers" tag has stuck.

"But what I want to know," Pierino continued, "if our Pope loves his elephant so passionately, is what does he want with its most fearsome enemy, this . . . enigma?"

"Popes want whatever they cannot have," a voice piped up near the back of those gathered about their table. The speaker was a man whose features crowded together near the center of his face, giving his head a deceptively swollen look. "Usually it's the revenues of the Duchy of Modena. I was a copyist in the Camera under Julius. He wanted to build the greatest church in Christendom for three and a half *soldi.* . . ."

"That would be it," said Salvestro, and was about to develop the point when a second voice broke in.

"It would be better to ask why the Spaniards or the Portingales are so eager to give it to him." A tall man with a high shiny forehead; those around him peered up in mild indignation. Who was this lanky oddball to offer unwanted advice to the master explorers? "And where are they going to get this animal, anyway?" he went on.

A few of the more belligerent listeners muttered, "Shut up," or, "Mind your mouth, beanpole," but Salvestro held up his hand to quell them.

"Fair questions both. I myself have yet to see an Enigma for sale in Navona," he answered genially. "Where indeed? And why?" He contemplated both questions for a moment. "Bernardo?"

Bernardo had been nodding along sagely. Now he looked up, startled, to find the eyes of their audience upon him. From across the table, Lucullo and Pierino watched expectantly.

"Right," he said. "Well, not here. So, somewhere else. When I think of where such a beast would be found, I don't think of anywhere in particular. I'd start by going somewhere I've never been before to see if that's where it is. If it isn't, I'd go somewhere else, like, uh . . ." He floundered for a few seconds.

"Good God, the man's a marvel!" Lucullo burst out then, and the crowd, which felt perhaps the first uneasy stirrings of skepticism at Bernardo's answer, performed a swift volte-face. Warm agreement prevailed as Lucullo continued, "Where and why? Nonsense! Bernardo here leaps straight to the crux. It's the 'how' that matters, that's what he's telling us. That's real independent thinking for you!"

"Exactly!" Bernardo exclaimed, deciding to join the sudden consensus. He scanned the complaisant faces and nodding heads before him for that of their interrogator, but the lanky man had disappeared.

Looking at the same beaming and amicable countenances of their adoring audience, Salvestro thought to himself, We should have come to Rome a long time ago. Then, following close on its heels, the accompanying thought came to him, as it had the day before and the day before that: We should have fled this place the very day we arrived. For there was still the Colonel. Somewhere within the same city that clasped him so fondly to its breast, the Colonel awaited him. Welcome to Rome. . . . They had been there twenty-five days. The face would come at him in the pitch-dark of his waking and would not be dispelled until he rose, stumbled over the sleeping bodies of the monks, and splashed a little water on his face from the well in the yard. Twenty-five such thoughts and twenty-five reprieves to match them. When he returned to rouse Bernardo, the soldier would start to fade from his thoughts. Then, and only then, their days in Rome could begin.

At first they fell into step with the successive bands of pilgrims whose circuits looped between Rome's churches. Huge hymn-singing crowds of them would gather in the Piazza of Saint Peter's early in the morning, then set out in groups of thirty or forty for the first of their stations. Most would march off briskly to take boats from the Ponte Sant'Angelo or stride along the riverbank as far as Santa Sabina, where they left the towpath for the Porta Pauli, passing by the pyramid to begin the dusty trek to San Paolo fuori le Mura. Others, however, would forsake this farthest-flung of Rome's stations and begin directly with the Lateran, which was a twenty-minute dawdle through Ponte and then a stroll through the ruins, rather than the hour-long forced march along the Ostia road. Accordingly, Salvestro and Bernardo preferred the Lateran and visited it four times in as many days.

After clambering up and down the Holy Stairs, the pilgrims would amble toward the squat towers of the Porta Asinara and thence to San Croce in Gerusalemme, Salvestro and Bernardo still in tow; there both men dutifully peered at the fishes carved inside the newly installed water stoup. A few prayers and they were all off again, up the little hill and through the Porta Maggiore to San Lorenzo fuori le Mura, which stood alone on rough pastureland and was linked to the city only by the ant-column of supplicants who trudged toward it carrying their staves, crosses, and occasionally each other, for a bustling tavern stood just outside the gatehouse. Once around the cloister and it was time for Santa Maria Maggiore. The pilgrims' pace had slackened by now, and the crowds of ragged hawkers who followed them about selling everything from caged birds to water met with greater success as the marchers sought excuses to rest their feet.

They took the Aventine road, keeping the city on their left, while to the right the dwellings and outbuildings quickly gave out and beyond there was nothing but fields, a few gardens, the odd ruin. The pilgrims strung themselves out along the road, the slowest and most weary slipping off to the left on one pretext or another and disappearing back into the city. Leading up to the church was a long, gentle slope, which the pilgrims would negotiate with loud shouts and theatrical flourishes of their staves as though they were scaling the Alps rather than the low hump of the Esquiline. The "climb" was an excuse to pass the wineskin, or slap one another on the back, or offer extravagant prayers for their survival. But there was no hymn-singing now, and for that Salvestro, at least, was glad. On the top of the hill stood the church of Santa Maria Maggiore.

It might have been the Lateran, or Santa Croce, or even one of the little chapels that clustered about the greater churches as though an earlier cathedral had exploded and left its wrecked oratories scattered about the church that would replace it. It might have been one of the little wooden structures at which the monks had stopped to give thanks on their journey. Bernardo always went in. Salvestro looked at the massive walls, the dark interior, heard on occasion the warbling and wailing of a choir. . . . At Santi Apostoli he had been swept in by the press of the crowd and found himself in an ill-tempered carnival rather than a church. Throughout these latter tours he waited outside, his curiosity mounting, until, striding up the Esquiline, he told Bernardo that they might as well peer inside this one together if it was all the same to him, which it was.

A huge bell tower dropped from the sky like a stone battering ram driven down into the nave. When the bells rang, their clangor thundered down the shaft and exploded within the body of the church. The pilgrims covered their ears and shouted to one another, but Salvestro stood in silence next to Bernardo, looking not at the great colonnades that ran down either side of the nave, nor at the mosaics inlaid within the walls, nor at the different marbles of the floor. When everyone else had drifted out to view the treasures of the oratory of the *presepio,* Salvestro found himself standing there alone but for Bernardo, gazing up into the gloom of the roof. Subaqueous light filtered through the tracery of the carved marble windows and struggled up into cavernous spaces high above his head. Then, when it reached the ceiling, the light seemed to come alive, drawing new energies from what it struck there, for the ceiling was made of gold.

Salvestro drifted, turning slowly on his heels while a sheet of light wheeled above him. Vaults tessellated the curves and contours, forming diamonds and swooping scimitarlike insets. Glaring sunlight fattened in the heat of early afternoon and broke apart against the hard marble. The rays that struggled through beat weakly on the garish panels overhead, as though the air itself were an impedance. Salvestro saw the metallic scales of a massive armature and, at once held by the vista and lost within it, felt that he was suspended within the nave, not looking up but strung by the heels and falling headfirst down to the dim glister sunk deep below him. The interior was viscous, inescapable. A great gold animal heaved itself over the bed of its domain. He was in the barrel, trapped again, falling into Vineta. . . .

When they emerged, a friar standing by the door told them that the ceiling was gilded with the first gold to be brought back from the New World, but Salvestro did not care about that and thereafter he avoided Rome's churches whenever possible, preferring to wander up and down the bustling riverfront, where watermen took on their passengers and cargoes, shouted at each other, and battled the caprices of the Tiber's currents and eddies. They saw a mule drown and below the Ponte Cestio a boatload of bottles capsize its craft and sink in an instant. A few men stopped to watch the dark shapes tumble down into the white sand of the riverbed and then disappear as though the water there flowed over a bed of thick cream. One spectator told his companion that he had seen whole bargeloads of stone vanish as quickly. The Tiber's sandbeds were deep enough to swallow Rome.

Salvestro's store of soldi transferred itself in steady installments to the pockets of the innkeepers whose taverns fronted the wharves and who gave them in return fat fillets of sturgeon, stringy chickens, heavy Campanian wines that tasted of black currants, and plates of steaming swedes and carrots, whose combined effect was to turn their bowels to water and their heads to cauldrons of blood. They squatted miserably in the grip of their quivering guts and shivered as though they had the fever. When Salvestro's haphazard calculations revealed that eating like kings would soon render them penniless as peasants, they reverted to doughy biscuits soaked in thin vegetable broth, unsalted porridges made from meal, or mashed beans and chickpeas and drank beer until they pissed like horses. The sun seemed to rise higher by the day. The afternoons were yawning wastes of heat.

The streets emptied as pilgrims, priests, and the city's natives alike denned themselves in palazzi, stables, huts, hovels, and makeshift bivouacs of poles and sacking. Salvestro and Bernardo sought refuge in Rome's ruins. To the south and east, the clotted precincts loosened and liquefied; granaries, stables, and high-walled houses drifted on independent currents and beached themselves on isolated plots of land. The streets unraveled and a strange detritus took their place: great blocks of stone, massive buckled walls, toppled columns and arches. Farther and the ruins began to gather themselves into bare blockhouses, little amphitheaters, roofless temples. Ivy and scrubby bushes gouged footholds in the mortar. Goats clambered about, and, Salvestro and Bernardo slowly realized as they stumbled dull-witted from drink in search of shade, the most massive of these survivors of time's slow violence were the refuge of others besides themselves.

Salvestro sensed that they were watched long before their observers showed themselves. Bernardo trudged beside him, oblivious of the faint rustles and near noiseless footfalls that pricked his ears always from behind or above. He remembered his time in the forest when he had tracked his own kind for long hours, watching their anxiety mount as the invisible fact of his presence had dawned on them, feeling their reaction as a kind of pleasure, the fact that he existed and was not nothing. Now the roles were reversed. It was their fifth or sixth foray into this deserted-seeming world, a late afternoon of blazing heat in which they had slumped, Bernardo falling fast asleep in the shade of a great curving colonnade, himself dulled and drowsy. Their spy was simply and suddenly there, had neither approached, nor emerged, nor dropped from some hiding place.

He was clothed only in scraps of cloth wound about his waist, his body streaked with filth and his hair matted in stiff plaits that reached his shoulders. His face was expressionless. He made no sound. Then, when Salvestro struggled to his feet, he skipped backward, turned, and was gone. Salvestro rubbed his eyes and reached down to shake Bernardo. Hard white light glared off the dust, bleached earth, and stone. Archways stretched and curved away to either side of them and rose in tiers above. Within, the shade was blacker than tar. He could look within and be dazzled when he turned his gaze outside, or look without and find himself blind amongst the shadows of massive piers and porticoes. Cicadas rasped and fell silent and rasped again. The heat seemed to gather weight and press on him. He squinted and listened and heard nothing, and then the man was back.

This time with three of his fellows, appearing as suddenly as before. Two more strolled up from the left, then a small group appeared on his right. Soon there were twenty or more of them, standing casually and in silence before the two men, ragged men and women dressed in a motley of rags and ill-fitting garments. A few squatted on their haunches, planting heavy clubs in the sandy ground before them and staring directly at the two of them with blank expressions on their faces. Several had crudely bandaged stumps in place of hands. Others carried yellowish sores, which they would brush at as the flies tried to settle. No one spoke. Bernardo stood up slowly. Salvestro looked about him and thought of flight. Then the crowd before them stirred and parted. One of their number strode to the front: a woman.

She wore a leather coat and tattered skirts cut below the knee. Heavy silver earrings hung from her ears, and a few locks of thick black hair escaped from beneath a battered cap. Her face was burned to a deep brown by the sun, the skin creased about her eyes. The fingers of her right hand were decorated with rings of some plain metal that clicked and clacked together dully as she toyed with the handle of a short knife. She planted herself between Salvestro and Bernardo and the crowd, looking the two men over. Someone behind her made a sound. Her head twitched almost imperceptibly to one side, and her shoulders stiffened. The exclamation was stifled abruptly; her eyes never left the two of them. Salvestro stared back and found he could not match her gaze. The silence was a key winding in his bowels, urging other such silences upon him.

"You do not belong here," she said; then, treating Bernardo as though he did not exist, she marched up to Salvestro and thrust out her arm. "Whatever you have. Now." When he hesitated, the men and women behind her growled and began to shuffle forward. Bernardo shifted beside him. Salvestro thought again of flight. Stupid, he told himself, thinking of the huge ruin at his back, colonnades, shadows, hiding places . . . Stupid. He reached for the bundle inside his shirt, fumbling with the knots, then placing it in her outstretched palm. She clenched her hand and unclenched her hand, watching him with frank dislike. "Not much, and not much good in any case." Her other arm moved in a blur, the little knife flashing as though the bag might as likely have been his face. Coins spilled onto the ground.

"You could buy food," Salvestro said weakly.

The woman made a play of looking about. "How strange! There don't seem to be any markets around here. Wonder where they disappeared to. . . ." A few men chuckled behind her. She pointed to the coins scattered about her feet. "Pick them up."

"There's a market." His voice sounded thin and unconvincing to him, though what he said was true. He pointed vaguely. "You could—"

"In the city? Well, we'd get a warm welcome there now, wouldn't we?" Underneath the mockery, her tone grew more threatening. She pointed again. "Get on your knees and pick them up."

She will not stab me in the neck, Salvestro told himself. She wants to prove herself master, that is all. He dropped to his knees and began to pick up the coins. Bernardo fidgeted behind him. The woman remained stock-still, even as he picked the last of the soldi from between her bare feet. He stood up warily. There was another silence. "We could buy food for you," he offered. She stared incredulously for a second, then burst into harsh laughter. Bernardo smiled uneasily.

"Break their heads," said a voice.

"Shut up," the woman said sharply. Salvestro noticed for the first time that she was barely older than him. She put her arm out again, but this time to gently cup his cheek. Her fingers curled about his ear. He saw her throat work, her neck stiffen, he tried to pull away, but too late. The woman spat full in his face. The little mob behind her erupted into laughter. "You don't belong here," she hissed. "If we find you here again . . ." Her fingers stroked across his throat.

After that they took refuge from the afternoon sun in abandoned outhouses and tumbledown cottages that they sought out on the margins of the city. Noisy crowded streets would suddenly give out and be replaced by pasture. Bustling squares and plazas turned into open fields, or vineyards, or vegetable plots. Farms backed onto churches and ruined houses rose in the midst of orange groves like deserted vanguards of a main force that never arrived. Broken by imposing gate-houses, Rome's walls rose and fell with the lie of the surrounding land, but the city itself never seemed to reach them, as though the sun had shrunk its flesh to a pellet rattling dryly in a hollow rind. The two men wandered a region that was neither city nor country, being themselves not quite of one or the other.

Nevertheless, sundials cast shadows that lengthened and crept about their ste-lae; bell towers and obelisks aped them. By late afternoon the Roman air was a balloon of heat pumped to bursting point and awaiting the needles of dusk. Days passed in this manner. The two men would make their way back into the thick of the city, then rousing itself for nocturnal sports such as wasting money, drinking gut-rot wine, and pissing out of upper-floor windows. By early evening small and sportive carnivals would begin to erupt out of Ripa and advance along the east bank of the Tiber as far as Scrofa: a riverine crescent of fun and games involving plump acrobats, rigged dogfights, and gambling by torchlight. The more devout pilgrims pursed their lips—an expression known locally as "the donkey's bum-hole"—passing through the siesta-charged throng on their way to lodgings in the Borgo and an evening of consoling dullness. Salvestro and Bernardo joined them of necessity. Of their original one hundred and eighty-five soldi, twenty-three remained.

Past the bridge, the crowd began to thin and Salvestro would consider their route from Sant'Angelo to the Stick. Sometimes they would stride boldly down the center of the Via Alessandrina, through the square in front of San Giacomo Scossacavalli, past the palace of the Cardinal d'Aragona, reaching the Via dei Sini-baldi by one of the Borgo's cross streets. More often they used the shambles that clung to the back of the hospital of Santo Spirito like flotsam washed against a cliff by some ancient storm, threading a path through the makeshift shacks and skirting the cooking fires of the squatters who made their homes there. There was the towpath, too, which took them almost around the bend of the river before a drover's path skirting the foot of the Janiculum led them back. If they took the arched passage past the Palazzo della Rovere, they could approach the Via dei Sinibaldi from the south. Continuing in the direction of the Porta Pertusa al-lowed them to enter the same street from its westernmost end.

Salvestro invariably grew silent as they neared their nightly destination. Bernardo prattled freely, and then he too fell silent. They paused and waited a minute or two, watching the few passersby as they moved up and down the street. Salvestro eyed the various patches of black shadow whose shape and size gradually became as familiar to him as the street's daytime aspect, watching for a movement, a change, the slightest and least noticeable of shifts. There was a partly collapsed wall almost opposite the Stick. A little farther was something that had once been an elaborate drinking fountain. There were doorways, niches, corners . . . He waited and Bernardo waited, too. Only when the street was empty and silent, when the slightest intake of breath, or footfall, the slither of metal in a scabbard, could be depended on to betray the presence he awaited would the two men walk forward, into view, and seek the safety of the hostel. For, as Salvestro could not help but repeat to himself, there was still the Colonel. It would be here that he would spring, if he chose. Every evening, as they gained the safety of the hostel's dark interior, Salvestro would turn, see nothing, loose a long, pent-up breath, and hear Bernardo do the same. When challenged on this, his companion denied the man's existence nevertheless.

By night the Stick seemed to grow half as big again, adding staircases and new overhanging stories imperceptible in daylight. Lappi lurked within, shouting obscene challenges at all who crossed his path and only conceding the right of entry with a grudging, "Well, that's as may be!" after elaborate identifications. Sometimes he stalked the corridors or concealed himself around corners to bellow threats in the ears of elderly women. In the rear chamber the monks squatted on their mattresses as though from dawn, when the two men had risen and stepped carefully over their sleeping bodies, to dusk, when they returned, the monks had done nothing more than sit up. Salvestro thought vaguely of "special devotions" and "audiences with bishops," or the Pope. The monks did not speak to them. Gerhardt and his claque whispered together in their corner. Father Jörg scribbled jagged lines that wandered over the parchment in accordance with the humped lid of the chest he employed for a desk. Brother HansJürgen watched in silence.

As they stumbled down the passageway, Bernardo would resume prattling of the onions they had eaten in place of supper or reminiscing on a succulent fennel of the day before, Salvestro grunting perfunctorily in response. Their talk died again at the door. The monk's eyes followed them across the chamber as they settled on their mattresses. If he glanced across, HansJürgen would look away. He remembered their second night, when he had crept across the chamber to whisper a warning in the monk's ear, found himself kneeling there in the dark at a loss as to what he was warning against, had mumbled something about Gerhardt, something about lime. His misgivings had intensified but grown no more defined since then. Why should I care? he thought angrily to himself. Jörg was all but blind; he had known it before any of them. Now it seemed that they had fallen from the Prior's awareness as through a trapdoor. The nights spent facing one another across the paper-strewn table in Jörg's cell belonged to someone else's life, not his. The grievance gnawed at him like a known but unprovable theft. He thought of the wretches who sheltered in the ruins with their bandages and stumps. Wiping the woman's spit from his face, he'd choked back the urge to ask her, If they did not belong "here," where then did they belong?

Not there, he thought, and not here, either. The chamber stank. The straw in the palliasses was unchanged since their arrival, and many of the monks' habits were crusted with filth, although Gerhardt and those who gathered about him went better-kempt. He did not know how they filled their days. It was Gerhardt who now led the evening prayers, which were brief and concerned principally and successively with their "plight," their "trial," their "error," and finally the "error into which they had been led." Jörg remained silent, sitting isolated on his palliasse. HansJürgen moved among Florian, Joachim-Heinz, Heinz-Joachim, and a few others, whose numbers slowly dwindled with the passing of the days.

Wulf, Wolf, and Wilf came and went as they pleased. Their habits were skirts of rags caked with river mud, for they spent most of their time amongst the beggars and ruffians below the Ponte Sant'Angelo. Salvestro and Bernardo had twice seen them as they passed above, for the three would shout up, "Bernardo! Bernardo!" in unison, drawing curious glances from the pilgrims waiting to board the lighters, small rowboats, and pirogues. They would raise their arms and hold them there in a mute acclamation that was only part mockery. When Salvestro called for them to come up and return with them to the Stick, they ignored him. When Bernardo himself called they ran away. In the chamber they acted as though none of this had ever taken place, ignoring the two men along with the rest of the monks. The hour or two before the lights were dowsed was a time of intercepted glances and constrained silence.

Only Jörg seemed oblivious. Night by night, the monks sleeping closest to him would shift their mattresses away from his until his sightless figure became the center of an island eroded to himself, HansJürgen, Salvestro, and Bernardo. On the other side of the chamber, Gerhardt's territory swelled. Still the Prior said nothing and offered no challenge. He woke, prayed, slept, and scribbled. Salvestro lay back on his mattress and stared into the darkness. The scabbard concealed in the straw of his palliasse dug into his back. He thought idly of telling Bernardo that it was Gerhardt who had formed the islanders into a lynch-party. The thought of the man's neck snapping like a wax candle as Bernardo dangled him from one hand was a pleasant fantasy. Why did the Prior not expel the malcontent? The question was plausible only in darkness. To look on Father Jörg now was to know that he would do no such thing.

Having taken the westernmost alley that led from the Via Alessandrina one evening, they had waited and watched from the safety of the passageway as a group of men carrying bales of straw, then a man with a laughing woman on his arm, then someone being pulled along by two yapping dogs disturbed the Via dei Sinibaldi's darkness. It was the dogs that gave him pause, for they had seen them that morning, leading the same man down the Via dell'Elefante, when they had barked furiously at Bernardo, prompting the latter's usual disquisition against the hatefulness of dogs. "The ones I don't mind are small, or asleep," Bernardo had begun, and Salvestro had half-listened to the remainder of the familiar meander through the different breeds and their relative hatefulness, which boiled down finally, as it always did, to the observation that "the bigger the dog, the worse it is." Those now disappearing around the bend the Via dei Sinibaldi took about the Chapel of Santa Simonetta were medium-size dogs. He waited until their barking had subsided into silence, and then he noticed the shadow.

A little way past the entrance to the Stick, amongst the jumble of dim shapes that were the broken wall, an oddly shaped patch of dark added its outline to those of the toppling masonry. He raised his finger to his lips, then whispered in the man's ear. Bernardo crept back into the alley. Salvestro waited. He was already thinking of tomorrow's dawn, when the ghostly face that haunted his waking would appear to him as usual, say the same words—*Welcome to Rome. . . .* —and be banished for good with the thought of what they were about to do: *Last night we rubbed you out for keeps. . . .* When he judged a sufficient time had passed, he stepped boldly into the center of the street and ambled toward the Stick. The saliva pooling in his mouth was salty and thick. He thought of Bernardo skipping forward silently, at his best now, a silent phantom, big in the darkness, his hands big and quick. What if instead of doing as instructed, he simply launched himself at his target? He moved forward. The shadow did not move, though he knew it for a man now, crouching, perhaps, or sitting. A man can assume a lot of shapes, he thought, or was thinking as he moved forward, and he barely had time, the split second it took to open his mouth and shout, as it seemed a silent cannon fired two bodies into the street and Bernardo raised his arm above the skull, which will split open like ripe fruit in another instant—no, no, no, "No!" he shouted out, for it was not the figure he feared. The man was winded, lying on his back and waving his arms and legs feebly. He was not the Colonel at all.

"Just like on the beach," said Bernardo. They both looked at him, confounded for a second, Salvestro bending to offer his hand, the other struggling to rise. It was HansJürgen. "When we found him on the beach," Bernardo went on, addressing Salvestro now. He laughed briefly and nervously.

The monk gathered himself slowly, standing in the darkened street, taking deep breaths of the warm night air. He cleared his throat noisily. "I wished to speak with you, Salvestro," he said.

They walked in silence together, with Bernardo trailing ten paces behind. They took an alley that led north, crossing the Via Alessandrina a little way short of the piazza. The silence soon grew oppressive, and Salvestro, certain that this strangely contrived meeting concerned his whispered warning, cast about for some way to broach the subject of Gerhardt. They wove a path through the pedestrians in the Via Hadriani and emerged on the Via dell'Elefante. Here HansJürgen stopped and indicated the far side of the street as it led up toward the piazza.

"There are benches here in the day," he said. "The money changers work here."

Salvestro nodded, wondering what this had to do with Gerhardt. The monk's red-rimmed eyes cast up and down the street. Torches clustered and flared in the great square farther up. He looked bewildered.

"You have coins," he said. It might have been a question. Salvestro waited. "I have tried to exchange our silver here, but they will not."

"Raw metal," Salvestro said. "The *bancherotti* only deal in coin."

"And you have coin." HansJürgen nodded to himself as he said this. He seemed uneasy, unsure how to proceed. "How might we, I wonder, exchange silver here if these *bancherotti* will not . . . I wonder how you, Salvestro, were able to. If you could . . ."

A horse came to a stubborn halt in the midst of the passersby before them, its hooves scraping on the cobbles. The rider dismounted and tried to pull it forward by the bridle. Eventually he tied a scarf about its head, and thus blindfolded, the animal suffered itself to be led into the piazza, where it quickly disappeared from their view in the sluggish and swirling crowds. Salvestro was about to say that he could exchange the monks' silver for Roman soldi on the morrow.

"Do you know how we spend our days?" HansJürgen asked, still peering after the horse, though it was nowhere in sight. The palace rose on the far side of the square, black against a black sky. "There—" He pointed to the jumble of towers and rooflines. "We sit in the courtyard in there." He made a sound that sounded to Salvestro like a stifled hiccup. It came again and was again choked back. Then HansJürgen began to laugh helplessly, a bitter, mocking noise. The people walking past looked at him curiously as he gasped and wheezed. "We sit in a courtyard. That is what we do, I and my Prior. We sit in a courtyard and wait for the Pope!"

"It wasn't." Bernardo had approached and now spoke to Salvestro as though HansJürgen were not there. "I told you."

Struggling with his astonishment, Salvestro turned to his companion in bafflement. "Told me what?"

"I told you it wasn't, but you didn't believe me. It wasn't the Colonel."

"It was," said Salvestro, turning back to the monk, whose laughter had become a rasping cough. "We will go tomorrow," he told HansJürgen. Then he added, "You can count on us," which started the monk laughing once again, more harshly than before.

The next day they walked into the Broken Wheel with two thick silver bracelets set with milky green stones and, after the same procedure as before, were given three hundred and seven Roman soldi by Lucullo, who after counting out the coins declared that he was a happier man for seeing them, and as before, the rest of the patrons agreed with him. Would they take a drink? They would. So would everyone else.

"Now," said Lucullo, "I've been talking about this with Pierino here, but you're the men to ask. What do you make of the latest tomfoolery of this Pope of ours?"

Salvestro looked at Bernardo.

"The Spaniards are already hot under the collar, eh?"

"And the Portingales," added Pierino.

Bernardo looked back at Salvestro.

"So what do you make of it?" Lucullo pressed on.

"Of what?" asked Salvestro.

"This business about the beast."

There was a short silence.

"What beast?" asked Bernardo.

Pierino began waving about a small leather-bound book. "One of the few I haven't pawned," he said. "Yet. It's all in here. Plinius." He began skipping through the pages. Salvestro and Bernardo drank, and grunted agreement whenever it seemed appropriate. "Alternatively it may be lured out and tamed using virgins. It is very partial to virgins, this beast. . . ." Pierino was explaining some minutes later. They nodded. Later a disagreeable oaf appeared to challenge their competence on the subject and was rightly shouted down. Later still they left, gazing about them in mild surprise once outside, for they had entered in daylight and now it was night. The happy ambience of the Broken Wheel seemed to blur the distinction between them. They stared up as though in search of a solution to this vague mystery, but the sky, being dark, was of no help.

Brother HansJürgen accepted gravely and without demur the two hundred sixty-five soldi they presented to him that night. Hanno and Georg gaped in open curiosity until a muttered word from Gerhardt reined them in, but Father Jörg said nothing. Salvestro watched and waited as HansJürgen murmured in his ear, but the Prior only nodded. It was later, when the lights had been dowsed and the denizens of the chamber were no more than the sound of their own breathing, the sour scent of their unwashed bodies, and the private anticipation of sleep, that Salvestro heard the man shift on his palliasse and say, distinctly, "Our thanks to you, Salvestro." Someone on the far side of the chamber laughed.

When they had added what Salvestro called "their commission" to what Bernardo called "their money," the two men found themselves, according to their respective calculations, in possession of either "a lot" or "fifty-seven" soldi. In the darkness of the chamber, Salvestro quietly tore a second square of cloth from his tattered shirt and tied the coins within it, resolving at the same time that they should buy themselves some new clothes, for even by the flexible standards of the Broken Wheel, they were coming to resemble scarecrows. The next morning, and every morning thereafter, they made their breakfast from hot bread purchased at a bakery in a side street a little way south of the Pescheria, for the bread at the Broken Wheel, though very cheap, was invariably hard and sometimes wormy. The tavern's pies, however, were without peer, and they took their other meals there while they held court along with Lucullo and Pierino. Lucullo's enthusiasm for the independence of Bernardo's thinking remained undiminished, and with it the enthusiasm of the establishment. Two things only disturbed this happy arrangement: "the oaf" and "their money."

The oaf reappeared twice in the fortnight that followed. Salvestro had been speaking of their preparations for the voyage to Vineta: the barrel, the rope, problems with the boat. Bernardo had digressed enthusiastically on the rowing: "One, two"—he pumped vigorously on imaginary oars—"one, two, one, two. . . Like that."

"Fascinating," said Lucullo.

Then he was there. The oaf, with a supercilious sneer on his face. He was standing near the back as before, passing comments along the lines of "One, two, one, two? What happened to three?" until someone told him loudly to pipe down. Later, when Salvestro went in search of him, he seemed to have disappeared. None of the regulars had the faintest idea of his identity.

The second time he was more brazen. "Insolent," was how Lucullo described the tone later. They had come back to the subject of the enigma, as Bernardo persisted in terming it. "I've been thinking," Bernardo began. "This business with the virgins and the knees can't be right. If all you really needed was a virgin, or a sawblade, then they'd be so easy to capture. . . ." He stopped for a moment to consider the position this opinion had brought him to. Those nearest craned forward to catch whatever might follow, echoing Lucullo's inclination from across the table. "Well," Bernardo finally continued, "we'd be overrun with the things. . . ." Lucullo was nodding. "There'd be herds of them. . . ." Everyone else was nodding, too. "Whole flocks of them. . . ."

Then the oaf popped up, near the back inevitably. Up came his head with its high forehead and thinning hair. He snorted.

"Not only insolent, but derisive," was how Pierino described the tone later.

It was not a loud snort, nor particularly prolonged. There was little that was truly horselike about it. Nevertheless, heads turned, lips curled, scowls appeared. It was a nigglingly sarcastic flap of the gums, a plosive "Pah!" a nastily calculated aural fart wherein insolence, derision, and rank disbelief cohabited in an irritatingly smug ménage à trois. "I should have plugged his mouth with this bottle," was how Salvestro put it later, swiftly plugging his own.

"You should," Lucullo urged.

"You should," the whole tavern agreed. But, scanning the tavern, they noticed the oaf had disappeared once again. A few days later, their money had, too.

"Pies, bread, and beer," Salvestro explained tersely to Bernardo. The two men peered anxiously at a scrap of stained cloth on which rested a solitary soldo. They had tried, in the days preceding their inevitable bankruptcy, to eat the Broken Wheel's bread. But the bread was hard to countenance when there remained, wafting temptingly out of the kitchen, steaming enticingly on tables all around them, being guzzled and served up a second time in the guise of loud and happy belches, the possibility of pies. They ate the pies. They were broke. "There were times we would have counted ourselves kings just to eat the bread," Salvestro complained. "Remember Vühl?" They had eaten raw millet at Vühl. "Or Barr?" They had eaten a mole at Barr. "What about after Marne?"

Bernardo's distress increased sharply. The Christian Free Company had spent five days camped in a stony valley while the villagers of Marne and their neighbors had scoured the countryside for them, carrying pitchforks, mattocks, and scythes. Marne was where the boy had been killed, or worse than killed. "Why'd you bring all that up?" Bernardo whined.

Salvestro looked away. "I meant, after Marne, we didn't eat anything at all," he said. Bernardo was shaking his head, not listening. Salvestro reeled off the names of other villages and other dishes they had eaten only with the greatest reluctance: corn husks at Hummingen, raw sheep's trotters at Wöhlfart, and, at a particularly miserable place whose name for the moment escaped him, a dog. "And what about the herring?" he appealed finally. None of this made any difference. They could not bring themselves to eat the bread.

Pierino was the first to notice their predicament. Nursing their mugs of beer for hours on end, they looked up more than once to find him glancing at them curiously. He stood them rounds and bought them food, shielding his purse with his hand as he counted out the coins to conceal the paucity of those remaining. Even Bernardo quickly came to feel that this was unendurable. Lucullo too inquired discreetly after their means, but Salvestro brushed him off airily by saying that the situation would soon put itself right and winking in a conspiratorial manner. Inwardly he berated his stupidity. He had planned to exchange the scabbard the next day, which, being a gift from Lucullo to themselves, was awkward enough in the first place. Now it was impossible. The greetings that heralded their arrival each day at the Broken Wheel remained as hearty as before, but the two men found themselves more and more ill at ease as mugs and platters were ordered and consumed. One night, one of their intermittent drinking partners, a horse-dealer in Navona called Rosso on account of his carrot red hair, leaned back in his chair and asked in a loud voice, since everyone else had bought a round that night, and the same the night before, if they were planning to do the same anytime soon. He was instantly shouted down by the others, yet after that they began to be regarded differently. Lucullo and Pierino continued as friendly as before, but other tables at which they sat would mysteriously break up a few minutes after their arrival and reconvene, without them, across the room. Other patrons would sit in stubborn silence with empty mugs before them until Salvestro rose, tapping Bernardo on the shoulder to follow him. They began to run up debts, and Rodolfo, although he said nothing, regarded them archly from his station by the door to the kitchens. Salvestro watched Bernardo. Fear of a catastrophic outburst of temper from his friend joined the list of his worries as Bernardo grew vaguely but increasingly bewildered at the various cold shoulders offered them by the tavern's patrons. He remembered the parting comment of the leader of the brigands who made their home in the Ruins. We don't belong here, either, he thought.

But it was neither Rodolfo nor any of their erstwhile drinking partners, not Pierino, and not Lucullo, either, who finally made their situation clear to them. They had stayed away for several days until, sick of their own company, bored and aimless, above all hungry, they had been driven by the tedium of the streets back to the warm bunker and welcoming fug of the tavern.

Rodolfo was nowhere in sight. They slipped past the kitchens and installed themselves at an empty table. A few men sitting at a neighboring table glanced around to look at them. One nodded. Salvestro nodded back. Anjelica and a girl he had not seen there before drifted in and out of the kitchen carrying large trays of food and drink. Salvestro raised his arm to catch her eye a number of times, but she seemed not to notice.

"Bread today, Bernardo," he said. Bernardo said nothing.

Eventually the men at the table next to their own ordered another round of beer, and Anjelica was forced to acknowledge their presence.

"We'll take a loaf of the bread," said Salvestro.

Anjelica eyed them blankly.

"No beer today," Salvestro continued in a jovial tone. "Just plain old bread."

"Rodolfo wants to see you," said Anjelica.

"Well, that's as may be," Salvestro replied, feeling himself color. "That's fine. Always good to see Rodolfo. In the meantime we'll take some bread."

"He saw us last week," said Bernardo. "Why does he want to see us now?"

Anjelica put down her tray. "That's between you and him," she said evenly.

"So," Salvestro plowed on, sensing himself sink deeper into his own furrow, "some bread."

Anjelica stared at him. There was a long silence. "People are getting tired of your sponging," she said flatly. "They're getting tired of you, too."

There was a second, longer silence. Salvestro stood up suddenly. "Right. Come on, Bernardo. We'll have a word with Rodolfo about this." Anjelica's expression did not change. She watched as Salvestro walked stiffly across the tavern, followed by Bernardo. At the neighboring table, the man who had earlier nodded now muttered, "Good riddance."

"What about Rodolfo?" asked Bernardo as they reached the courtyard outside.

Salvestro did not reply. He breathed deeply and slowly, sucking in great lungfuls of the night air, standing with his back to the big man, who asked again in his bafflement, "We were going to see Rodolfo, weren't we?" A deep breath in, a deep breath out. Like rowing, he thought to himself. Just like Bernardo's beloved rowing.

"I do not think we'll be seeing Rodolfo again," Salvestro finally answered.

Someone coughed.

Someone who was neither Salvestro nor Bernardo, who was half sitting, half standing, leaning against the sill of a bricked-in window, arms folded, unnoticed up till now behind them, the same supercilious expression as ever plastered across his face, at once infuriating and apt, a smirk that sent Salvestro's thoughts scuttling back into the mason's shop-cum-tavern entrance, where resided such articles as rusty saws, lump hammers, and large jagged-edged chisels, ideal for inflicting serious and lasting damage on human flesh and bone, for the cough, a mock polite attention-seeking throat-clearance, was emitted by a tall man with a high forehead and thinning hair, hatless, otherwise dressed in drab but generously cut clothes, who now moved forward with hand disarmingly outstretched, saying, "Rodolfo gave you my message? Thank you, gentlemen, for agreeing to meet me in these circumstances, and let me apologize for my earlier conduct, although as you will shortly see there was a reason behind it. I have a proposition for you," in such friendly and conciliatory tones that Salvestro was brought up short, undecided as to whether he should forthwith break the man's nose, take the proffered hand, or simply turn away and leave him standing there: the oaf.

"Perhaps we might speak somewhere in private? Perhaps," he continued suavely, "I might be so bold as to offer the two of you . . . supper?"

It was, Rodolfo reflected four days later, not the kind of thing that would be talked about for years. It was more the kind of thing that would be talked about for months. His patrons, after all, were a various and independently minded bunch—he cultivated them as such—thus not easily surprised and inured to reversals of fortune both upward and downward by virtue of having undergone or engineered so many themselves. Nevertheless, he conceded privately, the reappearance, not to say transformation, of the two most recent and wayward of the Broken Wheel's regulars was more than merely surprising. It was—and he was not a man given to hyperbole or even speech unless absolutely necessary— startling.

It was midevening and the tavern was filled to bursting, men sitting six to a bench, two to a chair, any number to a table. The women rushed about with pint-pots and plates, barging through the knots of drinkers who always seemed to cluster near the door to the kitchens. In the kitchens themselves the cooks were a blur of food-stained aprons and bad temper. They had given up speaking and resorted to growls. Things bubbled, then boiled, then boiled dry, then burned.

"Good God!"

"What?"

"Oh, my. . . ."

Salvestro first, followed by Bernardo, had entered the Broken Wheel by the main staircase and now stood at the top of the three steps leading down to the main floor. Over the dazzling white cotton of their shirts, they wore tight-fitting doublets of ciselé velvet, its pile cut in intricate designs of curling roses and other ornamental plant life. Gold-braided laces ran up the front, and silver ones secured the sleeves. *Cioppas* of *velluto ricamo* jacketed them in rich blues that shifted as the candlelight caught the warp and weft of the pile. Belts, buttons, and brooches dotted their ensembles with little gleams of bronze and silver. Their birretas were each set off with a *fermaglio* in the shape of a silver scimitar. Salvestro wore a neck chain.

"What the . . . ?"

"Incredible!"

". . . believe it."

The first spluttering reactions set off a chain of little sprays and showers of food-bits. Brief drizzles of beer arced gently from the amazed and gaping mouths of the tavern's patrons. Truncated exclamations succeeded them, and, standing behind the two men, even Rodolfo looked surprised.

"If it ain't . . . ?"

"It is."

"It is?"

"It *is!*"

Pie-munching mouths concealed themselves behind napkins. Eyes peered over the top and widened to take in the dandyish transformation.

"Friends," began Salvestro to the agog assembly. "Friends and fellow patrons of the Broken Wheel . . ." Then he stopped.

He had wanted to say something about their welcome, about belonging, or not belonging, and the places that had evicted them or the bruising chain of bad luck and circumstance that had dragged them to this point. But, as he stood there rocking on his heels with the whole tavern waiting on his words, all he could see outside the ranks of faces turned to his, outside the cocoon of overbreathed air and candlelight that was the tavern, his haven . . . It was black out there, the outer dark he had emerged from. An endless forest. A bottomless sea. He stood with his mouth open, wondering how to say this.

Bernardo nudged him from his confusion. The faces were turning curious and impatient at his silence. Reaching into the purse attached to his belt, he held up a fistful of coins and said simply, "For the last weeks we have drunk your beer and eaten your food. Tonight Bernardo and I ask you all to eat and drink ours." He turned to find Rodolfo and poured the coins into the man's cupped hands. For a moment the Broken Wheel was quiet, then a voice shouted, "A cheer for the Master Explorers!" and, the voice being Lucullo's, the Broken Wheel cheered.

"Well, you two are full of surprises," said Rodolfo, still fumbling with the coins. "Hardly expected to see you again. Did the fellow looking for you find you?"

But Salvestro's eye was roving around the room, spying out Lucullo and Pierino at the far end. "Looking for us?" he answered absently. "Oh. Yes."

Rodolfo's eyes followed the trajectory of Salvestro's thumb back over his shoulder to the foot of the stairs, where a tall, balding man he vaguely recognized lounged against the wall with his arms folded across his chest. Bafflement passed across his face. "But . . . ?" he began to say.

But Salvestro and Bernardo were already halfway across the floor and busy picking up handshakes, backslaps, and informal salutes. After clearing the forest of raised arms and beer mugs, they took their seats with Lucullo and Pierino, turning to take in the grinning goodwill still flowing their way from all parts of the tavern. A long procession of beer-filled jugs began marching out of the kitchen.

There was a brief pause as Lucullo and Pierino took in the full measure of the pair's transformation.

"Well?" asked Pierino.

"Well indeed," Salvestro replied calmly. Then he leaned forward and spoke in an urgent whisper. "We have to keep it under our hats." The other two nodded. "Delicate business, but we've fallen on our feet this time." They nodded again.

Then, before he could say more, a man appeared beside the table whom Pierino and Lucullo recognized as the ill-mannered scoffer of a few weeks ago. Lucullo raised an eyebrow as the man pulled up a chair. Salvestro and Bernardo shunted sideways to make room for him.

"Allow me to introduce myself," he said quietly. "I am Don Antonio Seròn."

Then Bernardo, who had begun fidgeting on his seat from the moment of sitting on it, blurted out, "We're going to get an Enigma." He looked about him excitedly and dropped his voice a fraction. "Me and Salvestro. We're going to catch one for him"—he indicated Antonio—"and give it to the Pope."

It was past midnight, Salvestro remembered later. The warm bodies sweating in the Broken Wheel had left their stale and cooling odors to drift about the jumble of pushed-back chairs. Slurred farewells had been exchanged. Antonio had stayed only a few minutes, and thereafter they had added their own voices to the racket. To the Master Explorers! The Beast! The Enigma! And now the soft scraping of brooms, water splashing into a bucket from somewhere within the kitchens, the thud of a head as it rose, focused blearily, then fell once again on the table. The tavern was almost empty. They rose heavily and ambled stiff-legged for the stairs. Rodolfo stopped them there.

"It wasn't him," he said.

"What?" Salvestro screwed up his face and rubbed his eyes.

"The fellow here a week ago, the one looking for you. It wasn't Don Antonio, or whatever his name was."

"Who, then?" Salvestro felt the beer all cold in his veins. He wanted to piss, get outside.

"Didn't leave a name, just said he'd be back," said Rodolfo.

"Well, what did he look like?" Salvestro persisted. He felt suddenly wide awake.

Rodolfo thought for a moment. "Didn't get much of a look at him," he said. "A gentleman, from his clothes. But from the way he carried himself, and the way he spoke, I'd say he was a soldier."

Imagine . . . Ambassador Seròn.

Or, *Don Antonio Seròn,* Orator of Fernando the Catholic of Aragon and Castile. Don Antonio this and Don Antonio that. His Excellency. . . . Early morning favors such contemplations, with its steely blues and abated sunlight, the inevitability of sunrise. Few birds twitter in the vicinity of the palazzo (Palazzo Seròn?); a cautionary silence prefaces the loose-tongued and beady-eyed day to come. Settle, he tells himself, ensconced in his cot, ancillary panic-flutters rising about him in scalloped wavelets, sucker-mouthed fish contained therein. The future gives him gooseflesh.

Two ships, two beasts, a contest—of sorts.

"And so I devolve this duty to you, my trusted secretary. I need hardly stress its importance, nor its difficulty. Our Pope will have his way. . . ." And so on. Don Jerònimo, Idiot of Vich. That was weeks ago, and what since? Polite inquiries about the enterprise and complaints about his mistress, who sweats "like a horse" and whines for money "like a stuck pig." But he keeps going back. Why?

More flutters at that, foamy-fringed and rhipidate, tortile as eels or conscience. No one else is up. He is alone in a rowboat straked with sapwood, tossed lightly by the surging currents beneath. There are no "friends at court" for Antonio Seròn. There would be no appeals, no judicial messiness in the cellars, as they cut his guts out for the confession. Something at the point of a knife in an alley, and here in Rome, without warning if his allegiance were known. And the hand on the haft would be Diego's. . . .

The fluttering subsides at that thought, becomes winglike and unliquid: Seròn rising. Below, little ambassadors confer in roofless buildings, little secretaries attend them, little soldiers march up and down. Secrets are represented by yellow envelopes and whispering; policy by an empty scabbard. The order is being given to dispose of himself, of Seròn. The soldiers draw their swords and run about under the orders of their commander, although their victim has already fled, forewarned, it seems. But by whom?

Let it rain powder, a fine volcanic ash to a depth of three inches, in which the tailored shoes and boots of the players make fine, crisp prints. Here—these tiptoed heelless ones—these are Venturo's as he creeps in the back door of the palazzo. Hoofprints record the Orator's cortege as it plods from stable to stable, and these more martial impressions signal a militia of some kind. There are indecipherable scuffs and skids, meaning violence, perhaps, and then there are the looping and overlapping tracks that lead from the palazzo, swerving south of Navona, north of the Campo de' Fiori, taking alleys and backstreets westward to where the Tiber bumps up against the city. A little way north once more—here the trail grows circular—in the back and out the front of a discreet and well-known stew, back down toward Tiber island, where a top-floor room at the Sign of the Portcullis appears as just another point on the route, for footprints in volcanic ash are mute on their own relative importance, assigning no more significance to the heels that will drum on the boards in this cramped room overlooking the Tiber wharves than the boot-marks that later lead back to the stew, in the front and out the back, and then, a little more deliberate, a little foot-sore, perhaps, retread the path back to the palazzo. That path is his. He has trod-den it seven times now. Today will be the eighth.

It had been the day he'd found the ship—the *Santa Lucia,* a tub impounded at Ostia for her drunkard captain's debts. A thunderstorm rumbled and threatened on the ride back to the city but finally came to nothing. Vich was squinting over his papers, politely interested in his progress. A ship? Well done. And a crew? Not yet. But the crew Seròn sought could be found in any tavern in Ripetta; the crew did not trouble him, nor his Ambassador. They sat across from one another, the light outside falling, cartwheels rumbling faintly as they passed over the paving about San Simeon's.

"I wonder, Don Jerònimo, have you remarked a change in our Captain Diego's disposition?"

Should his curiosity have been so naked? Should he not instead have waited for Vich to remark the change himself or exercise his wits about the question of why he had not? Too late to worry now, and his fears were groundless, for Vich was happy to nod his puzzlement. The soldier's sullenness had evaporated in re-cent days and been replaced by a lofty and private amusement.

"We may even see a smile," Vich speculated, "by next Easter." Seròn laughed politely. They called for wine and began drinking, matching each other cup for cup. It was after the fourth or fifth that Seròn began to muse aloud about Diego, to wonder at his aptness for his duties in Rome. He felt his curiosity grow like an appetite, sitting there as an equal, throwing out casts into his ignorance. Diego's disgrace hovered like an omen between them, and Vich became untalkative, awk-ward. Eventually there was silence. He realized that he was drunk, in danger. He could not remember what he had said. In his sudden anxiety he got up to light the candles, and that seemed to rouse Vich, who said, "You know most of it al-ready, Antonio. Why is he here? A favor to Cardona. What else was he to do with him after Prato? The smoke still lies thick over that business."

More drinking. More nods and nudges. Were they both pretending to be drunk? More disclosures.

"It turned on Tedaldi's surrender, whether given or not, and to whom. . . . Or not. Tedaldi's wife was killed in a cellar with the children, as hostages to his si-lence, perhaps. Or perhaps they knew as much as he. . . . Someone took Tedaldi's surrender, and then someone lied. Prato was sacked. Tedaldi's family were killed. These acts were the offense, the lie was its cause."

He stopped there, as though he had reached the limit of his discretion. Seròn watched him toy with his glass, hold it up to the candlelight. It was quite dark outside. He refilled the Ambassador's cup.

Vich spoke again, but now he was unguarded, speculating as though to him-self. "Who, though? Who accepted Aldo's terms? Somewhere between the square of San Stefano and the camp outside the walls, the surrender became a defiance. I passed through that square once, it is a short ride out of town. It was Diego who parleyed with Aldo, he who carried the challenge back to Cardona. . . ." Vich was almost unaware of him now, swimming alone in a current of wine and confused memory.

Seròn pushed a different piece of the puzzle forward. "But he believes himself innocent, and maligned."

"He was not the only one to speak with Tedaldi. I do not know all the comings and goings. He claimed to Cardona that he was not privy to the terms of the agreement. He never challenged the fact that Aldo gave up the town. The men who put the knife to his family were never found, and without them his accusations were baseless, futile. . . ."

"Accusations?"

"Who knows what took place, or who in fact spoke with Aldo that day, or what was said. . . . One man entered, another waited outside. Who knows?" Vich shrugged and swallowed more wine. Seròn watched him slump in his chair.

"But the other man," he said. *"He* would know, whoever he was."

"Whoever he was? You need not pretend, Don Antonio. We both know the other man was Cardinal Medici as he was then. Our beloved Pope as he is now. Yes, he would know." Seròn looked down into his lap. Tiny flies flew in noiseless circles about the candle. Warm air rising out of the courtyard carried the smell of the stables into the room. Then Vich spoke more crisply, rising from his chair. "But as to his new cheerfulness, I have no idea. Perhaps His Holiness would know?"

No, thinks the secretary, rising now, dressing. His Holiness does not know. There is a picture to be painted, beginning in darkness of the cellar where Tedaldi's family offer their throats to the murderers, whose other hands stretch, palm held out for payment by one whom the frame has yet to capture. His hand is visible, for the cutthroats must have been paid. Part of his sleeve, too, and bright sunlight. . . . Diego's joy would be to wrestle him into view, but it is the cutthroats who will do that. The soldier's face comes to him now, pressed close to his own—he had been intimidated, felt encroached upon, as Diego had accosted him—the man's mouth moving clumsily to relate the tissue of acts that made him clean, graced and favored once again. Why had the soldier come to him? "They are something he cannot deny, do you see, Don Antonio? Ally yourself with me, be ready when the time is right. He would rather give up his tiara than let the truth of this be known. . . ." It seems His Holiness's hirelings are in Rome.

It seems that they are once again for hire.

It is another game, anterior to his own. Diego must be placated, humored, eventually thwarted. It will be to the soldier to whom Vich will go, if his secretary should be unmasked. And now Seròn has that. For the moment, Diego is his. Whatever else it may cost him, his own business will not cost him his life. Diego's loyalty was stitched into his very sinews. Betrayal would always destroy a man like that. And then he thought of Cardona, Medici, even Vich, who appeared to him

as infinitely calculating giants, slow-moving and implacable as thunderheads. If
the heavens opened above him, if the rain scoured him of his subterfuge, the two
men would be much more than figureheads nailed to the *Santa Lucia's* prow,
more useful here in Rome than afloat in a leaky ship. Without the giant and his
keeper, Diego's claims were nothing. If the rains were to be brought down on
him, then Diego's impotence, or the promise of that (the unspoken threat of its
opposite?), might stay the heavy hands raised against him: the Pope's, Vich's . . .
He trussed the two men in gaudy new clothes, gave them money. Fed them and
drank with them at the tavern. Fattened them up for sacrifice. When the storm
broke, who demanded justice of the weather?

Outside now, the shadow-city is being folded into the cracks and recesses of
the City of the Sun. The spectral casts of Rome's eaves and overhangs, the lightless juts of her churches and towers, are yielding to the sun's corrosion: dark diagonals steepen on the stained plaster of the walls, stunted silhouettes swing slowly
into coincidence with their templates. A night-city echoes the arc of a climbing
sun and creeps toward its vanishing-point, shrinking, foreshortening, triangulating
itself out of existence. By midday there will be nothing. A minute past and the
cycle begins again. Don Antonio quits the palazzo and heads west, a horseless
gentleman with a high forehead and thinning hair hurrying past the sleep-caked
early risers, smooth-faced himself, head down, unremarkable and unremarked.

The walking calms him—he cannot eat before these assignations—the steady
thudding of his feet on the hard-packed dirt. He waits for a train of carts loaded
with barrels of fish on the way up to Pescheria, looking left and right before
crossing and ducking into the alley running along the side of the Chapel of Am-
brosio. The ropemakers are stringing lines in the Via di Funari. They barely glance
up as he hurries past. Another look about at the entrance to the courtyard, in the
door at the old stonemason's place, always unlocked, long abandoned, down the
steps. He finds himself in front of the kitchens, another staircase rising above him.

Rumors of two loudmouthed tellers of tall tales, of two buffoon-explorers,
had first drawn him to this place. He had found them ragged and penniless. Two
days in the tailors' shops, an hour with the barbers in Navona, the pair of them
being shaved side by side with apples in their mouths. Pigs for the oven. Since
then he has been back here only to ensure that they remain in Rome, to drink
with them and celebrate their good fortune and, on three mornings since the
night of their peacock reappearance, to perform on himself the same transformation in reverse. The tavern is deserted at this hour, except for Rodolfo, who
seemed so wedded to the place as to be unimaginable anywhere else.

"We never see you except at the crack of dawn, Don Antonio," the
innkeeper's voice addresses him from above. "Are you still in search of a ship? A
Genoese passed through a few days ago. . . ."

But the ship is already got, or as good as, and Antonio is in no mood to swap
pleasantries this morning. Rodolfo slaps him on the shoulder as he passes, and his

voice pursues him up the next flight of stairs. "Anjelica and Isabella have been asking after you, say they miss the smallest tip in the city," he shouts up, laughing, disappearing into the kitchen.

Minutes later he is out by the "front" entrance, under the signless signpole, down the alley toward Santa Caterina's. Strings of horses are being led into the stables, the streets more crowded here. Now he wears a stained apron, heavy boots, a scarf tied about his head. Faint river-vapors taint the air with fetid watery whiffs as he strides toward the wharves. He is a porter at the docks, or some such. It is a loosely themed disguise.

Pressed and swollen by the narrowing of its channels, the current quickens to either side of Tiber island so the rowboats and small barges ferrying sacks of wheat or wine barrels from the larger wharves of the Ripa Grande battle against the flow until the forks rejoin and the flood calms itself once again. Seròn weaves a path along the waterfront between sweating sack-toting men and barrows piled with crates. Someone leads a string of goats toward the wharf, where a bargeman waves him off. "No, no goats. I won't take goats. . . ." Bloodshot eyes peering over their drinks accord him less importance than the view (river, boats, cows grazing across the river, the dome of San Pietro in Montorio), the view less importance again than the beer foaming in their tankards, a liquid lower horizon. The man he is here to meet will have marked him by now, will be watching him as he strides past the taverns lining the waterfront, entering at the Sign of the Portcullis, almost the last. A small, nervous-looking boy is wandering about inside, trying to sell— no, give away bread, but bread so flat and hard that it might have been cut from leather. No takers. A moment now to compose himself, though the danger is behind him, not before, unless . . . Reject that thought. The ship is got, tell him that. Salvestro and Bernardo? No. Keep that close. He will ask too about the bull, about the sheaves of charts, the depositions and supplications, but there is nothing to report on that. Summer is unkind to the busy-brained clerks of the Camera; many have already left to ape their Pope in his forthcoming *villegiatura*. The bull is stalled and will remain so until one or other ship hoves into view, aboard her decks a living, bellowing, stamping monster. . . . His Holiness's decision hangs on that.

But it will not be my ship, thinks Seròn. Nor Fernando's ship, either. And not my beast. The knife in the alley is very distant now. Corridors run off to either side of the stairs, once, twice, another shorter flight. There will be two ships, one of wood and canvas, loud with the shouts of its victorious crew. . . . And there will be a second vessel, a spectral nonship, the ship that does not return. That one will be Vich's, and though its wreck be a thousand leagues away, unseen by the Ambassador or anyone else, he will sink in it nonetheless. The steps stop.

There is a small room beyond, its ceiling sloping with the outer roof. In winter it is very cold, but it has a fine view of the bustling wharves below. The man he meets here will be standing in front of the casement, looking down. This is not what he is, but only the necessary interim between what he was and what he will become. Ambassador Seròn. He is not traitorous, he tells himself, opening the door and ducking his head beneath the lintel.

"You are late, Don Antonio," says Faria, turning from the window to face him. "What do you have for me today?"

They light bonfires at dusk and carry furniture into the courtyard. The Pope's impedimenta are piled onto horseless carts that the ostlers manhandle about the yard in a complicated game of checkers, shunting four or five of the already loaded tumbrels to extricate those remaining empty. Slow processions of favorite chairs, sets of knives and glasses, chests of linen and pewter, and the books of his clerks arrive in the red light below and are stacked on sacks of oats and flour. Dry hams are wrapped in muslin and the muslin soaked in oil. Oil is brought, too.

Tomorrow a fragmented column of three dozen carthorses and oxen will sweat and foam in the late July sun. Outriders will flank them. The Romagna villagers will turn out and kneel for his blessing at the side of the road. He will give it. They will reach the hunting lodge at La Magliana by nightfall, with luck.

Awkward bundles are lashed on with fraying ropes and a prayer: the translation of his relics-to-be. This has taken the better part of a day already and will surely continue beyond midnight. When he dies, they will strip his apartments in ten minutes flat.

Two men emerge, struggling at either end of the barrel of a small cannon. Their silhouettes pass before the red firelight like crabs locked in slow, confused conflict. The cannon will be for announcing things. If he should kill a stag, for instance. His feelings for the man standing quietly behind him are complicated, involving neediness and distaste. He watches incuriously now. A muddy excitement, too? Cooking pans and firewood. What do crabs think of, dismembering one another? The cannon is leaned against a wall and left there.

"You understand why I have summoned you?" says Leo without turning from the window.

"They are here."

Leo nods.

"Where? It can be done tonight."

Where indeed? They have been seen in the Borgo; one or two of the *bancherotti* have mentioned "a huge simpleton" and his companion. Snippets of similar information have filtered through from Leno's informants about the Via delle Botteghe Oscure. Is it truly they? Diego had recognized them according to Leno, or Leno's man, and had done nothing more. It proved nothing, for Diego would know that he was watched. *He attends to his duties, is regular in his habits.* . . . *He does not confide in his subordinates.* . . . (Or has nothing to confide?) Two weeks ago, *He has taken a woman who visits him at night.* . . . If Diego knew where they were to be found, he would avoid them: a dog leading his huntsman astray. He tells the man these things, then turns to face him.

A wide smooth face watches his own. A smile that never surfaces lurks in the shape of Rufo's mouth. "I will begin with the taverns here and around Santa Caterina's," he says. "And then I will pay a call on a certain tradesman of our acquaintance. He will be happy, I am certain, to renew our old compact."

"Yes, yes," Leo mutters. Rufo's skin is like wax, his expression immobile. The man's tasteful finery jars vaguely with what he knows of him. At Ferrara, Ghiberti has informed him, he was acknowledged as the Duke's torturer. "Ghiberti has made arrangements for you here. It is a short ride to La Magliana, when you have news."

"I know their faces," says Rufo. Is this a boast? A threat?

"You, and Diego, too," Leo counters. The two men look at one another. He turns back to the window as Rufo bows and withdraws.

Below, the crackling of the bonfires, the thuds and scrapes of the baggage, and the fatigued grunts of the men mingle and echo in the courtyard. There are women holding up torches, three of them. Some of the carts are still empty. He will be happy to leave the Rome that has a Rufo in it. A thin trumpet reaches his ears, and his eyes rove briefly over the servants below before he realizes that they cannot hear this sound. It comes from the gardens at the back, a feeble hoot. Hanno is sick again.

It is the heat, the animal's keeper tells him. Too much for the beast's constitution or not enough? He wallows away whole baking afternoons in a pool dug for him on the western edge of the gardens, now reeking from his own feces. There is a plan to soften his skin with lanolin. Leo thinks of the animal's solitude, entertains the fantasy of their roles being reversed. As he scurries about, curly gray elephant trunks point to him and hoot softly in elephant-language: Look, a Pope. Observe his funny hat. Pay attention now, he is saying a Mass for the souls of the soon-to-be dead. Look how wicked he is; no wonder his turds cause him more pain than molten lead. . . .

Rufo will dispose of them, and then the business will be finished.

Now the servants in the courtyard move to and fro among the various entrances and carts carrying large meshed boxes. He realizes he was waiting for these to appear, or their contents. The boxes are stacked in piles beside the last two unloaded carts and left there. The men dawdle for a few minutes, then disappear within the surrounding buildings in twos and threes. For a moment he is puzzled by this, then disappointed. The yapping chaos of paws and tongues he has half-consciously been awaiting will take place not tonight, but, as it always does, on the morrow. He is distracted. Distraction accounts for many of his smaller mistakes. The dogs will be loaded in the morning.

He did not have the air of a man with something to sell.

"Not wool itself. The promise of wool," the merchant explained.

Diego nodded, listening to the faint note of exasperation as it swelled periodically in the man's voice, was apprehended and camouflaged, then swelled again. His horse was short and heavy-boned, bred off a jennet by the look of its head. He remembered dark-skinned men driving small herds of mountain ponies down from the Sierra de Segura for the fairs outside Lorca and Murcia. The merchant's animal was slope-backed like them. It stood patiently outside while the two of them talked in the shade of the stables. Don Antonio usually dealt with these men, listening to the snippets of intelligence they gathered as they swung between Venice and Genoa, then descended through Florence to Rome. In return he supplied them with introductions and (near worthless) passports for the Kingdom of the Two Sicilies. They usually demanded the Ambassador. This one asked for Antonio by name as though he knew that the route to Don Jerònimo da Vich passed unavoidably through his secretary.

"He is not here," Diego replied. The wool-merchant sighed.

Don Antonio was at Ostia. Repairs to the ship and repayments to its captain's creditors would keep him there for the best part of the week. Vich himself had left unescorted only minutes before the merchant's arrival and given no indication of his destination, which meant that he was with his mistress. It was almost sunset. The man before him was dusty and sweat-streaked from the journey and yet had not been able to wait until the next morning. He spoke in courtly, old-fashioned Spanish about the state of the roads through the Romagna, about his business in Italy, which involved sales of English wool to Italian cloth-makers. He was a broker of some kind.

"I am called Don Alvaro Hurtado of Ayamonte," he said for the second time. "Perhaps word could be got to Don Jerònimo tonight." He talked on, returning to his request every few minutes and accepting Don Diego's watchful silence as neither refusal nor assent. He knew better than to bluster or cajole, and Diego knew better than to inquire after the intelligence that urged its importance through the screen of the man's inexhaustible patience. The imperceptible cooling of the courtyard drew warm air suffused with hay and horse-smells from the open stables.

At length Diego said, "If I am able to reach Don Jerònimo tonight, where can you be found?" The merchant gave him the name of an inn and assured him that he would available at any hour that night.

"I will leave word with the doorkeepers to wake me," he said.

"Pay them, too," counseled Diego.

The merchant grinned in agreement, then bade his farewells. Diego watched him mount and ride slowly out of the courtyard, already calculating the least inopportune moment to rouse the Ambassador from Fiametta's bed. Late, he thought. Late would be best. Better to pull a man from his sleep than from the act itself. He heard the man's horse break into a lazy trot. You are no wool-merchant, he thought.

His mind's eye followed horse and rider down the street. A little way down and both would pass a semiderelict tavern whose weather-defaced sign bore traces of paint that had once depicted a lion holding a scepter. From his vantage point within, a man sitting in the window seat would carefully note the appearance of horse and rider, the times of their arrival and departure. Sometimes he was a small, sharp-faced fellow; sometimes fatter, red-faced, and wheezy. Sometimes neither, but he was there whatever the hour of the day. At night he roamed about the palazzo and remained mysteriously immune from the attentions of the watch-patrols.

The men who shadowed him about the city were less obvious. Sometimes whole days would go by without his catching sight of them. It made no difference: they were inevitable, assumed by him as such. Whether their presence was to prevent him reaching after the two men or to discover them by trailing him, he did not know. Perhaps he should have gone after them the night of Colonna's Mass. Passing opposite the Castel Sant'Angelo, or catching sight of the Palace of the Vatican, he would think of the ermined figure scurrying through their corridors to hear his agents' reports: *Accompanied Don Jerònimo da Vich to the Chapel of Saint Cecilia but did not enter. . . . Engaged in dispute with carter who blocked the road through Ripetta. Carter withdrew. . . . Pursued his duties in a normal manner, ate as per usual, drank unexceptionably, pissed the same, slept well. . . .* And the cutthroats themselves? *No sign. . . .*

His dreams had grown strangely bloodless: robed figures twisting their pudgy fingers, sweating functionaries swapping secrets, quick commotions and anxieties, nothing in earshot. There was a weightlessness to this time. The days deferred their import to other days, which deferred it in turn. The future built its inevitable castle. When he felt his nerves tighten and relax, his stomach knot and unknot, he was drawn back to the minutes before battle when he would submerge his fear beneath the certainty of what was soon to take place: the rush forward, the vast volume of noise, the division of men into victors and vanquished. . . . This *must* happen. A deep calm lay in it. His Holiness watched him across a battlefield of churches, stables, houses, hostels, and shops, across the clutter of Rome, waiting for him to break as his own men had cracked under the bombardment and run forward across the broken ground at Ravenna. And were cut to pieces there while Cardona fled in panic and the maggotlike Medici left the field unscratched.

But I have the cutthroats, he thought.

Or Don Antonio does. Wrapped safely in stiff new bright white linen and right under the soft priest's nose. . . . The secretary's account of their "recruitment" to the expedition had been delivered to him as a cautious gift. He had accepted it, with caution. "They are yours, when the time is right," the secretary had said. "They believe they are to lead our efforts to procure Leo his beast, as if two unlettered simpletons would have the slightest chance of success in such an enterprise. . . ." Antonio had laughed. Diego laughed along. He did not trust Don Jerònimo's secretary.

When the bells of San Simeon's had rung the hour before midnight, Diego gave orders to the servants that he was not to be disturbed. Leo would have a man amongst them, too. He locked the door to his quarters and trod softly through Vich's rooms to reach the stairs running from the Ambassador's private study to the street below. Sometimes there was a mounted man who patrolled in desultory fashion around the backstreets between Scrofa and San Appollinaris. The moon was sunk; that was good. He was soon slipping down one of the side streets that ran south from Navona. He settled into a long stride and followed the same street almost to the river, then dove into the clot of taverns and storehouses behind the waterfront, taking narrow alleys west into Ponte.

He found himself approaching the gate to Fiametta's house from the north. He walked quickly down the street. He was wondering whether he would have to wake the entire household to extricate the Ambassador. He could not remember a doorkeeper. Perhaps the main gates would be unlocked and he would be able to knock softly on the door. Vich was a light sleeper. They would return together or perhaps go directly to Don Alvaro. Leo's spies were lowborn oafs. They would not dare report his evasion without adding where he had been. He was turning these matters over in his mind, moving quickly and quietly but not watching. He saw the angular collection of shadows standing quietly opposite the gates only when he was almost upon them.

A man and a horse.

He almost stopped. He almost reached inside his doublet for his knife. But his instincts were better than he was, so he did not stop. He did not reach for his knife. The shadows shifted slightly. The horse snorted. He passed by as though unaware of their existence. The man he did not see. The horse he knew.

It took him the best part of half an hour to work his way around to the back of Fiametta's residence. The shutters were closed and no lights showed. His head was clear now. It was still possible that Vich was in no danger.

The ground fell away at the back of the house and the wall was higher, but a stepped buttress pressed against the bulge of the masonry. He began to climb, feeling forward for cracks in the crumbling mortar. Twice he lost his footing, and the second time he clung on only by driving in a hand and clenching it there until his foot again found a purchase. The rough stone peeled the skin from his knuckles. Concentrate, he told himself. Rome had softened him.

The roof was tiled, the tiles held in place with little strips of lead. He looked back at the night sky, which was lightless and would reveal no silhouette. Peering over the gable, he saw the courtyard, a woodshed within it, a run-down stable, a well. Then the wall that curtained off the street, its gate barred. He could make out the shape that was the horse, a big animal, its markings invisible from his vantage point. He had known it at a glance in the street. The horse was the mount of his own counterpart at the embassy of the Portingales. The man he could not see but knew was there was Don Hernando, Faria's man.

He began bending back the lead ties and lifting off the tiles. Fiametta employed a cook, a man who did the heavier work, a young scullery maid, and the Moorish girl. Only the last two slept on the premises. He stacked the tiles on the parapet and peered down into the hole they left. The room below was a pool of darkness. He swung his legs down and let himself fall.

More men died in the aftermath than in the battle itself. The certainties of the fight gripped men for good or ill, but when the fight turned and was won or lost the lines would break, the companies drift apart, and men drift through the cannon-smoke like ghosts. Some lost their heads in it, running over open ground, shouting the names of their lost comrades. A void of unknowing lay beneath the combat, and men would fall endlessly within it. Diego dropped less than a foot before his feet touched the floor. He landed soundlessly and crouched there, his nerves twitching and tensing.

He told his men, the untried ones and the veterans alike, to be still in these moments, to move slowly if at all, to crawl along ditches, to hide and watch. "If you do not know where you are, why would you move?" he would bellow at them. "Where to? This in the fight—" He raised his right arm. "This after it—" He slapped his forehead. He felt blindly about him, waiting for his eyes to make sense of the darkness about him. A bed. Empty. A chair. Some chests, perhaps, stacked in the corner. The door.

He realized that he was able to make out these things because of a faint illumination. At one end of the bedchamber the floorboards were cracked and separated by slivers of yellowish light. He lowered himself carefully to press his eye to the widest gap. The room below was a bedchamber, too. Two candles stood to either side of a canopied four-poster. Two large fleshy legs were visible upon it. Fiametta's legs. No sign of Vich. And the bed here was empty, meaning its occupant was elsewhere in the house. Had the bedclothes been warm? Remember Hernando outside, he told himself.

He raised himself from the floor, opened the door, and felt for the first step with the tip of his toe. So intent was he on his noiseless descent that it was not until he reached the landing of the piano nobile that he heard voices. They came from downstairs and grew more distinct as he negotiated the second flight. Men's voices, unguarded, careless of being overheard. One of them was Vich's. The other? The other he knew too and, taking the last step from the wood of the staircase to the stone of the hallway, would have put a name to in the next instant. Instead he stopped in his tracks. The mystery of the empty bed revealed itself to him in the shape of the girl silhouetted and stationed at the door, but it was not at her that he started. Hernando's presence at the gate was suddenly obvious, self-evident.

"And what shall be done with Venturo?" Vich's voice reached him through the door.

"Leave him to us," answered the voice, which he recognized now as Faria's.

She saw her future one time in an inlet of the river. A grove of thick-trunked iroko-trees grew along the bank, clinging to the loose clay with roots that stuck out of the ground like knobbly elbows. The river had found a way through them farther upstream, and a little cascade of water spilled down over some rocks, then fell into a long still canal. It was cool and shaded beneath the high canopy of the trees. The sunlight was hard and white as it struck the surface of the river, a great restless glare. Here it prickled the dark gloss of the leaves a hundred feet above her head and fell in shafts onto the forest floor. The earth was cool on the soles of her feet. It crumbled between her toes.

A boy was fishing. He stood very still, only his arm moving in a deliberate arc as he drew a long fishing-pole over the still surface of the water. He was on the other side of the pool, a little way down from her. He looked up when he noticed her presence and smiled. His teeth were a flash of brilliant white. A heron crashed about in the undergrowth farther within the forest but did not dare to come closer. She sat down, clasped her legs to her chest, and watched him fish, only her eyes visible above her knees. His arms had a nice shape, and his movements were calm and graceful. The rains had come twice since she had become a woman and none of the boys at home had touched her.

From time to time, men's voices reached her from their canoes on the river. They were from Atani, a half mile or so upstream. Namoke, her father's brother, was there now talking with the elders about their yam harvest. The yams at Atani were no bigger than alligator peppers, shriveled little things. Namoke thought the villagers' quarreling had soured the earth in the yam-plots, and he was there to draw the sourness out and throw it into the River. She had helped him tie on his headdress, and then he had started the talking. It was still going on. She had slipped away because the Atani people seemed to do nothing but whine and Namoke seemed to do nothing but nod, very slowly and very gravely. Atani was two days' walk from Nri. She had never seen this boy before. He was self-conscious now, knowing that she watched him. His movements were stiffer.

The pole twitched. The boy flicked. The pole bent and shuddered. He drew his arm back slowly, its tip passing over his head, the line rising out of the still pool and shedding little beads of water. A fat brown fish broke the surface. The boy drew it slowly toward him and reached for it, his arms stretched wide apart. He fumbled in its mouth for the hook, and when he drew it out, she saw that a tiny silver bait-fish was still fixed to it. It wriggled and glittered. When the boy cast again, he did not use the pole but set the tiny fish gently in the water and watched as it swam into the center of the pool, drawing the line behind it. The forest smelled of earth and ferns. She hugged her knees hard so her legs pressed against her breasts. The boy caught two more fish in the same manner, extricating the bait-fish alive both times and letting it pull out the line.

That was me, she thought, alone, in the dark of her room. The little fish wrestled with the weight of the line, darting forward and being pulled back, swimming vigorously toward the dark water where the pool deepened and the larger fish waited. What did it think when the jaws closed about it? What when they opened again and it found itself alive? The big fish were gathering about her now. From the bedchamber below, Fiametta's token protest sounded: a wheezy "Make him wait. . . ." Vich strode toward the door. She heard the other man's voice as they greeted one another downstairs, the creak of the door to the kitchen. She slipped on her shift and pressed her face to the floorboards.

Fiametta flopped in sweaty disarray on the bed. She rolled over and reached for the chamber-pot, squatted, pissed lengthily. Eusebia watched as her mistress emptied the last of a wine-jug into a glass and drained it in one swallow. There was some blood on the sheets, though whose she could not tell. Their lovemaking had sounded no more violent than usual. She would wash them in the morning. Violetta would have to face the wine-merchant. Fiametta had taken to drinking rough wine when Vich was absent. A glass or two in the afternoon had increased to a bottle or more in the last weeks. She complained of strange aches and pains and ordered Eusebia to massage her shoulders and legs for hours on end until she fell into a stupor sometime in the evening. She would sleep then, though badly, and wake the next morning with the wine still on her breath, her face blotched and puffy. She fell back now amongst the pillows and sheets, grunting softly in her drunken discomfort. Presently she was snoring. Eusebia rose silently from the floor and crept downstairs.

". . . wonderful, apparently." That was Vich's voice. She put her eye to the door.

"He will be there for the rest of the summer, if left at the mercy of his whims. Who would have guessed our Pope such a huntsman?" the other replied.

"He bags nothing but rabbits, even hunting in the French manner. He took to his bed for a day after the ride, and La Magliana is less than a day's easy riding."

"He might be sick."

Both men fell silent at that.

"Sick or not, he will be at Ostia. He must see the ship leave, and be seen to do so." Vich's tone was inflexible.

The other murmured his agreement. There were glasses of wine before both men. He took a swallow, then said, "I have heard nothing from Ayamonte in over a month."

Vich raised his own glass. "Nor I."

"My last dispatch was from Fernão de Peres. It spoke only of problems and delays. . . ."

"Their problems. Their delays," Vich retorted. "My beloved secretary tells me that our own vessel will be ready to sail in three weeks. He has a crew, a captain, two men who will wave prettily to His Holiness from the deck and, according to Don Antonio, will be capable of holding a rutter the right way up and even drawing lines upon it. . . ."

"What of the animal itself?"

"What of it? They need only know that their Pope would have it and, as good Christians, that they will fetch it."

Kneeling behind the door, Eusebia thought of the big fish waiting in the dark water, of herself swimming directly into their mouths. It would be easy to stand, open the door, walk coolly into their openmouthed amazement. . . . *Bite, and I will pull you home with me.* . . . The boy jerked suddenly. Again the pole bent. And bent further, the line taut and straining. The boy looked up at her and grinned his embarrassment. The hook was snagged. He angled the pole about, trying to free the line. She smiled back, but he could not see this with her knees drawn up close to her mouth. The earth was black and soft, good for sitting on.

Yes, she thought, the big fish bite when they like. And then they are brought to shore. Vich was talking in scathing tones of his secretary, who thought he had made a fool of his master. "A particular pleasure of this business will be dealing with Don Antonio Seròn," he was saying. She felt the line tautening, the hook tugging, the arm tensing like the great brown muscle of the river itself and pulling her back to Nri with her prizes. . . .

Eventually the boy gave up and waded into the pool, running his hand down the line but watching only her and moving toward her through the water. She did not stir, thinking only that he would be wet and his flesh cool. His eyes narrowed as he found the hook. She watched the water run over his skin when he straightened. She rose, too, thinking that he would have her here, on the soft earth that she was brushing from her feet. She was not frightened. She had seen two of her brothers do it. When she looked up, though, everything had changed.

The boy was staring at her face, not her eyes, which followed his, not her mouth, which wanted to press itself against him, but her cheeks, and the *ichi*-scars that ran in neat lines down each side of her face. She took a step forward, but his face had already dropped. He was making odd little bows and backing away from her across the pool. He was frightened. When he reached the far side, he picked up his pole, drew his creel from the water, turned, and jogged away through the trees.

Somewhere above her head, the floor creaked. Her head came up. Fiametta turning over, she thought. She and Namoke had stayed in Atani another three days, and she had not seen the boy again. But his *chi* came and made love with hers underneath her bed that night. If she closed her eyes, she could feel his hand against her cheek.

"And what shall be done with Venturo?" Vich's voice came through the door.

"Leave him to us," answered the other.

The ship, the beast, these clumsy men with their clumsy dreams. She was the tiny silver fish and the girl who saw the tiny silver fish, which was the future.

She closed her eyes.

She felt a hand against her cheek.

When Faria had bade his farewells, Vich had gone upstairs and had her again. She was bleary and protesting as he roused her. He held her by the ankles and took her briskly while the woman rolled and flopped beneath him. She sweated sour wine, and when he woke at daybreak the next morning the air in the room was foul with the smell of her. She had begun to irritate him, offering foolish pieces of advice in a hectoring tone. He did not need her to tell him how to behave as Fernando's orator in Rome. The sheets were smeared with her facepaint. She disgusted him.

Yet she drew him to her, too. The thick flaps of her flesh folded him in. He pressed his face between her breasts. Sometimes, sweating and bucking between her thighs, he felt himself sinking as though into a bath of soft fat. In the dark her hands were soft bolsters of human meat tipped with porcelain nails. He shuddered and pressed his mouth against her to keep himself from shouting out at the moment of climax. Her own pleasure arrived in the form of drawn-out sighs broken by little grunts and groans. Flecks of rheum had clotted on her eyelashes. A tiny bubble of spit ballooned and burst at the corner of her mouth. She leaks, he thought, dressing. Washed-out yellows stained the eastern sky, promising another day of heat. He closed the door behind him softly so as not to wake her.

An unfamiliar horse stood in the courtyard of the palazzo. Diego was giving instructions to one of the stableboys. The soldier looked up as his own mount entered.

"There is a merchant," he said.

"Here?" He glanced down at Diego's hand, which was bandaged. "Trouble at the tavern?"

"Trouble with a wall," said Diego. "He arrived yesterday. I told him you could not be found." The other stableboy had roused himself and now approached, coughing into his sleeve.

Vich dismounted and handed him the reins. "Where is he? What does he want? Don Antonio should be . . ." He let the sentence fall silent.

Diego gestured inside the palazzo. "I do not know what he wants. He calls himself Don Alvaro Hurtado of . . ." The soldier paused and thought. "A town called Aya-something."

"Ayamonte?" Vich questioned the soldier, whose expression did not change.

"You have heard of it, Excellency. I supposed it unimportant. Ayamonte." He rolled the syllables around his mouth. Vich watched impatiently. "I believe it was

Ayamonte," he agreed. The Ambassador was already disappearing inside the door to the palazzo.

Vich found the merchant sitting on a short bench that stood before the fireplace in the *tinello*. He rose and nodded as the ambassador approached.

"You know me?" he asked.

"I have been waiting for you," replied Vich.

They moved through the palazzo, still cool and quiet at this hour, upstairs to Vich's study. Vich closed the door carefully. The two men watched each other for a moment, then both broke into broad smiles and embraced warmly.

"When I saw the horse, it was all I could do to keep from laughing," Don Jerònimo said, chuckling. "I knew it was you then and there."

"Best-bred horse in the world," Alvaro replied in mock gruff tones. "It goes up . . ." He indicated with his hand.

"And it goes down." Vich joined in the recitation, and both men laughed. "Is Tendilla still alive?"

Tendilla was the master of horse to the counts of Burgos, the author of the phrase that had first bound them together in laughter more than twenty years before, and the passionate advocate of mountain ponies as the only animal both native and suited to the kingdoms of Spain. They began to chatter freely of their service at Burgos, the cold in the winter, the burning summers, their escapades.

"We were boys, mere boys," Vich said, wiping his eyes at a memory of the Countess, a woman even larger than Fiametta who had recommended clemency to her husband when they had been caught amongst her ladies-in-waiting.

"Your head is to be found on your shoulders, not between your legs," Alvaro imitated the Countess. "She spoke like a peasant," he said.

"Fine woman," Vich added.

Don Alvaro agreed. "And where was your head last night?" he asked, still smiling.

"Going up . . . ," Vich began.

"And going down."

In chorus again. More arm movements. More laughter.

They called for breakfast, and a tray of bread, oil, and cold meats arrived. The two men fell silent as they ate.

"The soldier, your Captain Diego," said Don Alvaro, wiping his mouth, "knows I am not a wool-broker. Or suspects as much."

"Is that your story? Diego can be trusted to keep silent. Tell me your news now. How did you engineer this journey, my dear Alvaro?"

In answer, the other merely spread his arms wide and shrugged helplessly. "The drying of fish and the drawing of lines on maps. That is all that happens at Ayamonte; that and the plague spreading up from the Marismos. The agreement is all but complete. Don Joao will approve it, the Portingales believe. Our King Fernando still keeps his counsel."

"He is unfathomable," said Vich. "The policy suits him well."

"We must proceed on the assumption of his favor if our efforts are to harmonize with those of the Portingales. How do the preparations go?"

It was Vich's turn to shrug. "Don Antonio has the business in hand."

"Can he be trusted? I mean, is he competent in this subterfuge?"

"No one is more suited," Vich said smoothly.

"Of course. I intended no slur. . . . The Portingales are all but ready. A month, I am told."

"The ship and crew will be ready by then," said Vich. "Faria has proved a faithful ally. It is right that we find common cause with the Portingales, in this matter, at least."

"It has not been so amicable at Ayamonte. Does Faria talk of Fernão de Peres?" Vich nodded. "Face like a bag of nails, tongue like a rasp. If I see him again, I will spit. The architect of their parley," he explained at the sight of Vich's raised eyebrow. "Very clever, tireless, precise. And facing him across the table, the dullard of Burgos!" Don Alvaro laughed aloud.

"Has this business not gone well for you, my old friend?" Vich asked quietly.

"Well enough. An equal mixture of sugar and poison is being poured into Fernando's ear on the subject of Don Alvaro. . . ." He paused, and when he looked up Vich saw that his face was strained. "There will be no mishaps, will there? No mistakes made here in Rome?"

"There will be no mistakes," said Vich.

Alvaro glanced about the room. His gaze fell on the sheaves of papers and charts stacked on shelves against the wall. "It is a thankless task," he said. Vich said nothing. "And will remain so, Jerònimo. When it is over, there will be a reckoning, do you understand me?"

Vich said, "Go on."

"Distance yourself. To the vulgar eye there will be only a shipwreck, a failure, and the crowing of the Portingales. Fernando moves his court to Seville in autumn. You have enemies there whose intrigues will demand an object." He paused to weigh his next words. "Do not allow yourself to be made the scapegoat. I do not know if I will be able to protect you then." Alvaro's voice had dropped. "I am ashamed to say this," he said.

"There is no shame in it," Vich replied briskly. "Do not trouble yourself with these things. My honor is spotless and will remain so." Then, when he saw the anxiety undiminished on Alvaro's face, he went on, "Your intelligence is welcome but anticipated, my friend. Whether he and the gossips of Seville know it yet or not, the scapegoat is already chosen."

They talked then of their time together at Burgos, of the country about Valencia. Vich inveighed against the Italians and their manners until Don Alvaro laughed aloud. It was almost midday before he looked down from his window to watch Don Alvaro saddle his horse and ride slowly out of the courtyard. He stood there for some time after man and horse had both disappeared, turning his old friend's reappearance over in his mind. Malice was to be expected. Fernando's ear had had enough poison poured into it to fill an ocean. His eye wandered idly over the jumble of rooftops and chimneys. The sun beat down, bleaching the clay pantiles to pale orange and glaring off the walls. Something nagged at him, but he could not grasp it. Something unaccounted. . . . He wrestled to discover it amongst their sentimentalities, the man's patent worry (as if he would not know to guard his back), the talk of scapegoats and gossips. *I am ashamed to say this. . . .* Why shame?

But whatever it was that bothered him eluded him, too, and finally Don Jerònimo shrugged the thought aside. At Burgos, Alvaro had been clever and useful, and weak.

He remains so, Vich told himself then. There was no mystery. Nothing had changed.

A soldier, by his bearing. . . . Who else could it be?

There were all kinds of soldiers, Salvestro told himself. And their bearing? A strut, a swagger. A feathered hat on a tousled head. Sword-hilt upmost and codpiece outmost. The best soldiers, as everyone knew, were Walloons, Savoyards, Gascons, Croats, and Corsicans. And Dalmatians, who were insane. Harquebusiers went about with gloomy faces pitted and blotchily tattooed with greenish-blue gunpowder-specks. They fiddled about with swabs and bits of wadding, and on the march to Prato, one of them had confided to Salvestro that he kept a store of waxed matches up his rear to guard against sudden downpours. Swiss *Reisläufer* and *Freiharste* did everything in formation except fight, and Breton companies could be identified by the black crosses they painted on their foreheads. There were fat soldiers, who waddled. And thin ones, who did not. A good pikeman wore his corselet at all times (he had never managed to acquire one himself). Virtuous men-at-arms slept in their cuirasses and took the field in suits of Missaglia armor topped with brightly colored banderoles astride horses the size of houses. Little bands of squires and crossbowmen trailed them on ponies. Field-masters and *Trossmeisters* were large with red faces and shouted a lot. Bombardiers spoke a numerical language that nobody else understood, and practitioners of the arme blanche talked to nobody at all unless able to trace their family back fourteen generations. . . . He thought also of the still figures, scattered over the fields after Ravenna, that looked like dark grave-mounds as the dusk fell. Did the dead have a bearing, too? Rodolfo was of little help on the question that had dug its barb in him a week ago and would not be drawn out farther.

"I told you, I hardly saw him. He was standing down here, and I was going up the stairs. Told him I'd never come across either of you, but I'd pass on a message if I did."

"And he asked for us by name?" Salvestro pressed.

Rodolfo nodded. "Then he walked out. Got a perfect view of his hat, if that's any help."

Salvestro walked back to Bernardo, shaking his head.

"Told you it wasn't him," the big man said without conviction.

News of the "soldier's" inquiry had galloped after him that night, its shadow cast forward to swallow him up. They had not dared return to the tavern since, and did so now only for Don Antonio's sake. He was to return from Ostia that day with news of their ship and shipmates. It crossed Salvestro's mind that they might have accompanied the secretary, but Don Antonio had not raised the possibility, and curiosity aside, he had no real reason to bring up the matter himself. In place of Ostia, the two men had endured a week of nervousness and boredom in Rome. Salvestro had struggled to find some other explanation, but the fact was finally unavoidable. Somehow the Colonel had found them.

"Anyway," Bernardo said, "Rodolfo told him we weren't here."

Two nights before Salvestro had awoken, skin greasy with sweat, the wavering image of the Colonel's face imprinted in the darkness. Next, with rot-fringed clarity: *Time to leave.* He considered: *Get out. . . .* Heard, *Run, run, run for the sea. . . .*

He had sat up and felt for the hole in his palliasse. The scabbard was still there. With care, and converted into coin, it would see him safely north of the Alps. Alone, he was indistinguishable from any other out-of-work footpad. Bernardo snored softly to one side of him. Jörg's breath rasped on the other. He sat upright for a long time.

"He knew to look here in the first place," Salvestro replied. A large sack had descended the stairs and now seemed to be walking unaided into the kitchen. A groan—Rodolfo's—greeted its arrival. Stubby legs appeared and disappeared as it squeezed itself through the doorway. No sign of Antonio yet. Today, he had promised, they would fix the day of the expedition's departure. Time to go. *Time to go. Time to go. Time to go. . . .* He had sat upright and stared ahead into the darkness. He imagined the first candle to be lit next morning, Bernardo turning over to find him gone. What would he do then? Quietly, he reached for his clothes.

"Should we have some food?" Bernardo suggested.

"It's too early," replied Salvestro.

They were the Broken Wheel's only patrons at that hour. Rodolfo's voice sounded from within the kitchen, "No. That's final." Some mumbling followed from whomever he was talking to. "I said no. It's inedible. I cannot even give it away."

"Perhaps some bread," Bernardo countered, overhearing the exchange.

Salvestro's face was blank. He was thinking of his hand running over the fabric of his new clothes, thick velvets and cottons, laces and buttons. The monks had stared in open amazement at their transformed appearance, but not one had asked how this transformation had been wrought. Only Jörg had not stared. He saw nothing now. Salvestro had come upon HansJurgen passing a candle back and forth across his face, the Prior telling him, "No, nothing. Nothing at all. It is unimportant. . . ." He would have to abandon his finery, dress like a vagrant again. He weighed this up, already knowing that he would not leave, not that night. Soft snoring and the rattle of the Prior's breath lulled him and pressed him down. He slept.

"Bread? Yes, why not?"

The sack reappeared, a burlap bulger encircled by hands and supported by feet. It moved unsteadily toward the stairs. Salvestro pushed back his chair and made for the kitchen. The sack staggered up the stairs. A stocky man dressed in soiled baker's whites was attached to it, his back straining as though the sack were attempting to push him down the steps. Salvestro glanced indifferently at the un-equal struggle, then poked his head into the kitchen. Rodolfo was muttering to himself and shaking his head. He looked up at Salvestro. "If you want feeding, you're out of luck," he said. Salvestro looked at him blankly. The door at the top of the stairs slammed shut. "Well?" said Rodolfo. The sound of the outer door fol-lowed, fainter. Rodolfo looked at him quizzically. Still Salvestro did not reply. He seemed to have forgotten why he was there. "What is it?" asked Rodolfo, curious now.

Salvestro looked down at his shoes, then turned and eyed the staircase. He glanced back at Rodolfo, an absent expression on his face. Then, swiftly succeed-ing one another, Rodolfo saw bewilderment, puzzlement, disbelief. He was about to ask what troubled him when Salvestro turned away abruptly and began to climb the stairs.

A man was unloading fresh straw from a high-sided cart in the courtyard. Sal-vestro walked out into the street, looked up—two carts like the one inside, a sea of bobbing caps and bonnets, a man on a horse—then down—more heads, their hats, other horses, two men selling apples from a barrow, three women eating them. The sack.

He began to thread his way through the crowd, slowly at first, but then, as his quarry was lost to view, he became more forceful, breaking into a half-run and elbowing people out of his path. Stifled curses pursued him down the street as men and women stepped out of his way or were jostled aside. At the end of the street he stopped. A line of horses was being led out of a stables. Deep blue sky framed the bells in the open campanile of Santa Caterina's. Salvestro looked left and right: more carts and crowds, more barrows and bales. No sack.

He chose left, hurrying up the broader thoroughfare, dodging the piles of horseshit. He heard cowbells somewhere, human voices, the creak of cartwheels. Narrow shaded alleys opened between the buildings every few yards or so. He peered into them as he passed, squinting to squeeze the glaring sunlight from his eyes. The sack reappeared, bulbous as before, a monstrous goiter of its human ap-pendage, which staggered with alacrity through the washing lines strung between the windows. Salvestro ran after it, gaining half the length of the alley before man and sack reached the end, turned right, and again were lost to view.

A small courtyard: ramshackle balconies, more washing, silence, and a penetrating smell that Salvestro recognized. He stepped out of the alley, sniffing. A low arcade ran along two sides of the yard, its arches planked over but punctured with little doors. Salvestro moved from one to the next, still sniffing, the odor growing stronger: damp clothes and boiled millet. He pushed at a door and found himself in a low cellarlike room dominated by an enormous brick oven. A pile of wood lay in one corner; sacks filled another. Two large tables were strewn with odd, long-handled implements, spatulalike and vaguely gruesome. Flour spotted the floor. From the room beyond came the sound of a sharp slap followed by a thin cry of protest. Salvestro closed the door carefully behind him and moved toward the noise.

He was standing with his back turned, arm raised over a boy of nine or ten whose own arm was raised in a cowering defense. For a moment Salvestro thought that his hands were oddly discolored or burned, for he wore stained cotton gloves. In his hand he held an object that Salvestro could recognize by sight, taste, smell, touch, and—now—sound: a flaccid, gray, leathery, oval loaf of inedible, unsalable bread that slapped with dull force on the boy's head. The boy squawked. Then he noticed Salvestro.

In a moment the man will turn at the boy's prompting and show a face prickly with black stubble, red cheeks, a mountainous ridge of bone across the brow; but the squat legs, broad back, wiry black hair, these alone are enough, as they were at the tavern. The sack has disappeared or, more accurately, is indistinguishable from the scores of identical sacks tossed in a mound against the far wall.

The man froze, gloved hand holding punitive loaf forgotten and left suspended over the boy. He turned to face his old comrade.

"Hello, Groot," said Salvestro.

Assume disparity: dogs on a chained bear, crows mobbing the solitary hawk, metal colossi leaking yellow lubricant into the wavy yellow-beige sand. Grit, mangy fur, feathers, and lousy down. Pain-noise, exhaustion, unsweet inglorious death. To be Bernardo is to cling on, to brace oneself against desertions of what is familiar, to find things that are orderly and imitate them. His unremembered dreams are sculpted, geometric, filled with wistful icons. Why is wakefulness not like this? Why is wakefulness crowded with dogs, and what are they for? Dog-pelts are uncoveted. Few cuisines make use of dog-meat. A necklace of dog-claws remains untalismanic. So dogs (understood broadly here) are for tormenting Bernardo: the big man, the simpleton, and the present dog, worrying and snapping at chained and anxious Bernardo, is Antonio.

"Just left? Just walked out and left you here?"

"It's happened before."

"Before" is a storehouse of old resentments and the resignations foisted upon them. At best, the dogs slink off and live to fight another day. "Before" is where they kennel themselves. No one is sympathetic to Bernardo's private plights, and when they are it is because they want him to do something terrible, an act that is unspeakable. The stones that fit his hand are the size of skulls. Antonio wants him to betray Salvestro, so he is being nice to him, deploying a tactful concern to make him do this, the latest of his unspeakable things. The secretary sits opposite, an untouched mug of beer between them.

"I cannot believe he would just walk away without a word. Not without a reason. After all, he knew that we were to meet here today, unless he is trying to avoid me. An unintended offense, perhaps? I am racking my brains, but. . . ."

Here they come, on their springy legs with their full-sail tails and fish-flesh tongues, a-bristle and befanged, jaunty for the mauling.

"What would cause him to run off like that? It really is very worrying, for you not least, Bernardo. What does he fear so much that, well"—and here Antonio's hands come up, fingers splayed loosely in priestly helplessness, the promise of absolution when, oysterlike, Bernardo should decide to yield his pearl—"it is his own secret to take to the grave as he wants. I must presume."

Hints of questions, raised eyebrows, quizzicalities, a weaseling miasma of offer balanced against vaguely sketched Salvestro-dooms: Antonio's game, his area of expertise.

"For instance, he might have . . ."

Or, "I only hope that whatever it is . . ."

And, "But I'm sure that . . ."

Dogs.

Bernardo's eye sidles around the steady and reasonable eyes opposite. This is how it always starts, these smooth tones and unanswerable arguments. The patent and patient *concern*. . . . Remember Marne now, "Bernardo . . ." Remember Proztorf. "And if you don't, well . . ." Well what? It gets worse. Because the accumulation of his past errors and stupidities is by now a cliff of granite, an overhang of wrongness, and a fat rock-slab of getting it wrong again. Antonio toes some more shingle over the edge, which dwindles to dust as it speeds down in individual arcs and tumbles to rematerialize as rocks bouncing off his head. The bad things happen now. Dogs or rocks is the choice.

"I'm not supposed to say," he began. Then, "It wasn't him, anyway."

Then he rambled forward blindly, into the stones and dogs that cracked against his skull and stripped the flesh off his hands, into Prato and the Colonel, who was killing Salvestro now, somewhere outside, for what else was there to flee from? Why else would Salvestro leave him here, on his own?

"He is a Spaniard like you. Here in Rome, Salvestro says, but it wasn't him. I told him that."

The morning advanced uncharitably. The Broken Wheel's patrons began to drift in and take up positions in a respectfully distanced semicircle around the

Master Explorer and his interlocutor. Nobody at the Broken Wheel liked Antonio much. Bernardo stared about him between sentences to measure their effect. The cliffs of black and rotted compacted sin grew blacker and more compact and did not fall. Dogs squatted to spatter the ground with dog-mess and did not chew on his hands. There was Groot first, then Salvestro, now Antonio. He had to do this. He was not supposed to; it was one of that vast set of things, bad things, all of them. He had to do it, and afterward Antonio would tell him what he should do next, now Salvestro was gone.

"I have not come across this Colonel Diego," said Antonio. "Tell me about him."

They walked in twos, Groot and the sergeant ahead, Salvestro and Bernardo behind. Rounding the Pieve di San Stefano, they seemed to be heading toward the Palazzo Pretorio, and Salvestro remembered dully that this was where the Colonel had set up his headquarters. It was almost dusk, and on every corner soldiers were struggling to light braziers, or torches, or chaotic bonfires of smashed furniture. At night the town came alive with flames and sparks. No one seemed to sleep. Nothing stopped.

They passed in front of the Pretorio but did not enter, Groot and the sergeant swapping commonplaces about the warmth of the season and the fear of disease. There were no cadavers in this precinct, for the Colonel had put a price on the head of any man caught leaving a body unburied. The edict's force exhausted itself gradually as they moved into narrower, darker streets. The smell of putrefaction came in thick waves, strangely regular until Salvestro realized that the *quintanas* between the houses were their source. They passed a little orchard in which invisible dogs could be heard snarling at one another. Two shapes hung like sacks from the branches of an apple tree, black outlines in the failing light. They wore signs about their neck that read—Salvestro knew only because he had asked—"Coward." Two days before, he had watched a middle-aged man, a soldier, being frog-marched down to the dyeing sheds, wearing just such a sign. The nature of the offense was unclear. The men were beginning to turn on themselves.

Now the four men entered the San Marco district. The men lounging on the corners or idling past them were more ragged and watched the quartet suspiciously; only their arms marked them as soldiers. The Free Companies ruled here. At the far ends of the streets branching off to their left, Salvestro saw little barricades manned by uniformed men, Medici's and Cardona's. The Cardinal and Viceroy maintained their *famiglias* in the two fortresses whose turrets poked above the clutter of meaner houses. Medici was in the older castle, with Aldo, who was dying. Aldo was Prato's ruler, and now he was dying of a kind of plague.

Salvestro had heard, *That old goat Aldo.* . . . And, *They should go ahead and kill him,* *that old bastard Aldo.* . . . He knew who this "Aldo" was, and he knew the barricades were to keep the men outside out, the rabble, the animals. A double row of walls—the *cassero*—linked the establishments, and messengers passed back and forth, mobile interruptions of the darkening pink of the western sky. Minutes later it was dark.

Rabble. Animals? They spat on the ground and pissed against walls, ate, slept, rose . . . They wrenched the genitals off old men at spear-point and broke the legs of their old wives. Killed children. They were murderers and torturers. Salvestro looked at their faces, all red in the torchlight and firelight. They were men who wondered where their supper was coming from, who scuffled about in stables looking for straw on which to bed down, who shivered or sweated. He thought of the Teeth. Terror wrote itself over the countenances that looked upon him; it was invariable. Where was the mark on these men? They appeared ordinary: dirty, tired, disheveled, bandaged, and bedraggled. He looked no different. *I took no part in this,* he told himself. Groot and the sergeant still conversing in a whisper just ahead. *I reached down my hand to pull another out, a girl in a silent street, quite ugly. Whisper, whisper. But she died.*

The streets narrowed again, the frontage bulging like the sides of great ships drifting heavily together. A few men were huddled in the archways beneath the steps running up to the upper floors. The four of them passed through dead-eyed fields of vision, emerged unscathed, continued. He did not know what this quarter of the town was called, but it was meaner than those they had passed through already. There were no orchards or gardens to break the drab rows of houses that snaked and wound toward their destination. Even the stinking canals were fewer. The whispering ahead was dismembered and senseless: *Remember this if nothing else.* . . . *Of course, but what if* . . . *Count on it.* . . . *Depend on me for that.* . . . *The very worst* . . . *No, not before he* . . . At the end of one of these streets stood three men, soldiers better dressed than the others they had seen, more alert or more sleepless. The sergeant nodded to them, and the trio nodded back. A light showed for a second in a house farther up. The air was sharp with wood-smoke from a fire somewhere.

"Within this house is Aldo's family," the sergeant told them. "His wife, Signora Anna Maria, her maid, two children. They are safe here, and your duties are to keep them safe. Admit no one, unless it is myself. Tell no one. You are the Colonel's men and will answer to him if any harm befalls them." He repeated these commands twice more in different terms, the three of them nodding dumbly. They could smell food cooking within now. Another trio of soldiers was just visible at the other end of the street. Salvestro saw that every house in it had been ransacked, doors and shutters swinging off hinges, smashed chairs and beds and pots piled against the outer walls. Ransacked and then meticulously cleared. Where, he wondered, were the people who once lived here? "You will be brought food." The sergeant pointed to the men they had just passed. "There is no need to step outside."

There were grilles over the windows. The door was studded and banded with iron. It was opened as they reached it by a man who nodded to the sergeant, then looked warily out into the street before closing it softly behind them. Two other men rose from their cots at their entrance and, barely glancing at the newcomers, joined their comrade by the door. A fire burned slowly in the hearth at the far end of the room, a pot suspended above it from which rich meaty smells were wafting. A partition had once divided this space from the one behind it. Now the planks were stacked neatly in a corner, and the backroom was open to view. Lines were strung across it, and sheets thrown over them formed a kind of curtain. A woman emerged from behind it, looked at the four of them contemptuously, then retreated again. They heard whispering start up. "You are not to touch them, do you understand?" the sergeant said. He brushed a speck of muck from his sleeve. "Not a finger."

Just then the sheets were flung aside and a second woman strode forward. Salvestro registered billowing skirts, simple jewelry, a stiff-backed carriage. Her eyes swept over the three of them. Salvestro saw that though her clothes were rich—silks, lace, gold thread—they were also filthy.

"So," she addressed the sergeant coolly, "the murderers have arrived. Is my husband dead so soon?"

"You frighten your children for no reason, Signora," the sergeant replied. He turned to the three men, saying, "Remember your orders. You will be well re-warded if you follow them. If not . . ." He did not finish the sentence but walked toward the door.

"Wait!" exclaimed the woman, a new note in her voice.

The sergeant ignored her. The door was closed. Groot moved to bolt it while Bernardo flopped down on the nearest of the cots.

A boy's face appeared from behind the curtains, then a little girl's. The boy looked at Salvestro, then strode forward, his sister's hand in his. A miniature empty scabbard dangled from his belt. He looked ten or twelve, no more, the girl per-haps half his age.

"Did you kill my father?" he asked Salvestro.

Salvestro smiled halfheartedly. "No one has killed your father," he said. "He is as alive as I am."

"He's a traitor," the boy said coldly. "He surrendered the town. You should kill him. I'd kill him, if I got the chance."

"Silence!" the Signora shouted at him, which brought the maid out again.

"Chop him up and feed him to the pigs," the boy went on. His mother seized him and pulled his head to her breast. The boy suffered himself to be led back behind the curtain. That left the daughter. And Salvestro.

She stood waist-high to him, wearing a white linen dress or nightdress that reached to the floor. Salvestro had the feeling that he was being assessed in some way; he tried to think of something to say, but his mind was still mired, submerged underwater, where the silence roared and bubbled in his ears. The little girl stared at him curiously. Suddenly she reached down, grasped the hem of her dress, and with a single abrupt movement pulled it up to her neck. Salvestro saw bare legs, her bald cleft, a rounded belly, the white cloth bunched about her throat.

"Look," she commanded. "I'm a virgin!"

Her name was Amalia. She believed in God.

"God isn't big," she confided to him. "He's as small as an ant. If he wanted to get out of here, he'd crawl through the keyhole."

"There is no keyhole," said Salvestro.

"Yes, there is. Back there." She led him past her sleeping mother to the far end of the captive's room. Behind some furniture piled there was a low hatch, cobwebbed and with a thick sill of dust. "See in there—" She pointed between chair-legs and crates. "Keyhole."

Apart from that time, he never ventured into the quarters of Signora Anna Maria and her family. Nor did Groot or Bernardo. The maid emerged to cook their meals, standing spoon in pot with her back to them in grim silence. She retreated with four platefuls as soon as she was done, and then the three men would scrape the pot for their own supper. After his initial outburst, the boy remained sullen and immobile. His mother sobbed quietly, slept, and looked at the three men with disgust when she had to look at them at all. They lived behind the curtain. That was all, and the three men lived in the kitchen.

Food arrived in the morning, announced by a single blow on the door and left on the step outside. By the time they drew the bolts, its deliverer had disappeared again. Groot or Salvestro would glance up at the open sky, grasp the basket and two pails of water, then withdraw again into the oily light of their jail. The windows being shuttered as well as grilled, they had no means of telling whether it was day or night outside and drifted through the time like sleepwalkers. A day or two of this reduced them to near silence, grunting to one another as they awoke, passing comments about the food, dozing irregularly and at odd intervals, despite Groot's attempts to establish a roster. Their movements grew sluggish and heavy. Only Amalia rose above it.

She skipped about in her white dress, chattering mostly to Salvestro, occasionally to Bernardo, never to Groot. She drew elaborate diagrams in the ashes of the fireplace and explained the different orders of angels and how small *they* were. ("Even smaller than *God.*") She recited things, played intricate imaginary games. One day was occupied with counting the stones in the wall, aloud. There were, in the four long low walls that enclosed them, two thousand eight hundred and seven stones, exactly. No one, despite her entreaties, was willing to challenge this figure. It was several days after the stone-counting (but how many?) that Salvestro noticed how clean she was.

The white dress was not gray or brown, not smudged, stained, smeared, or smirched. It was white, and stayed white. Salvestro puzzled over this. Then he noticed her hair, which was not matted as his was, nor thick with grease like her mother's or the maid's. It floated and bounced behind her like skeins of silk. When she walked, he saw the soles of her feet were white, too. Ash from the fire, dust, dirt, the house's general filth . . . nothing touched her. Or nothing seemed to stick. He could not account for it, or did not want to try. It sank at last into their general torpor, the seeming pointlessness of what they were doing. How long would they be here? He didn't know. Groot didn't know, either. This day followed that day. The mother sobbed. The boy sulked. The maid cooked. The three men waited. One day the bells rang. The little girl skipped, and chattered, and floated. One day the bells rang and rang.

"Do you remember the bells?" he asked Groot. Sunlight streamed in through the open windows from the little yard at the back of the bakery.

Groot nodded. "They were for Aldo."

Sheep-bells, Salvestro thought later. The bells of the Pratesi, their one protest at the horrors visited upon them. It began with a single distant peal, answered by a carillon from a nearer church. Soon from all about the town the bells hanging in every campanile swung and clanged out of time and tune, and in the jail their exorbitant din brought Salvestro's head up in wondering shock, roused Groot from his cot, stayed Bernardo in his pike-practice, One, two, *three; one two* . . .

Amalia was placing very small white stones in a pattern by inserting them in the loose mortar of the wall. She stopped and turned at the noise. Her mother appeared from behind the curtain and stared at them wordlessly, her face drained of blood.

"What is it?" Groot demanded of her. She shook her head and turned away unsteadily as the clanging gained force, solidified, shook the brains in their skulls with its waves of percussive sound.

"You'll have to go and see," said Amalia. "Off you go." She returned to her remaining stones.

The three men looked at each other.

"We're supposed to stay here," said Bernardo.

Minutes later the door slammed shut behind Salvestro. Two loud knocks, five soft ones, he reminded himself. Night. Up the street, the three soldiers guarding the entrance were huddled together, talking, pointing, thirty or forty yards away. Their counterparts at the other end did likewise. As he watched, a man approached the first group and spoke to them quickly, and all four marched off at the double. He looked over his shoulder. The other guards had disappeared. Salvestro frowned to himself, then slipped down the alley dividing the jail from the house next to it. The street he emerged on was dark, empty. He hurried down it, then the next. Soon he was approaching the quarter of San Marco.

The bells chimed away, jangling and echoing down the streets. Clustered about their bonfires, the irregular soldiers looked about them in alarm. A few shouted over to him, asking what had happened, but the same question was on his own lips. He shrugged his ignorance and moved on. Everyone was in the street, only the drunkest slumbering through the racket. Bands of men were drifting toward the old fortress, but the guards on the barricades were admitting no one. Salvestro saw horses being saddled by torchlight behind the row of pikes. He struggled through the crush.

"What is it? What's happened?" he shouted over the noise. The guards ignored him.

"Mama. Where's his mama now?" A chuckle followed, behind him. He knew the voice. He turned, and Cippi's smiling face stared into his own. "Mamamamama . . ." Cippi had his knife out, and there were men pushing past him now.

"What has happened?" he demanded.

"Don't you know, mama's boy? The old bastard's dead. Aldo the Great. No more. . . ."

Salvestro backed away. Cippi looked up at the fortress. "They'd kill us if they could. Shovel the lot of us into a hole, the bastards." Salvestro turned from him and ran.

He lost his bearings in the shambles of little streets and alleys that sprawled out from a long windowless building, once a granary, which he arrived in front of twice before finding the road back to the jail. Soldiers milled about in a disorganized fashion, and the bells rang on above their heads, jarring the air with great clanging blows. A few men crouched on the ground with their hands over their ears. The word was spreading now that Aldo was dead, but no one knew what this portended. Except Salvestro. Salvestro thought he knew what it meant.

The guards had not returned when he regained the street. He had been gone more than an hour. Perhaps two. Too long, he told himself. The house showed no lights, but the shutters and door were closed. Two loud knocks, then five softer ones. At the first blow, the door swung open a crack. Inside, darkness.

"Groot?" he hissed. "Bernardo?"

Silence. Only bells, near and far, and from all directions. He said their names again. Nothing. He pushed the door farther, but he already knew that he would not enter. This was one of the things that the bells meant that night. The dead were in there.

"They went away."

It was Amalia. She stood not ten feet away in the middle of the street, spotless in her spotless white dress.

"Mama, and Agatha, and Cesare, though . . . Oh dear." She mimed a child crying, pouting with her knuckles in her eyes. "All dead and off to heaven. Come on now. Time to get Big Bernardo and Grotbag Groot."

Salvestro stared at her, unable to take in her presence there and the words she was saying.

"Come on!" She stamped her foot and set off down the street. He followed.

Groot and Bernardo were three streets away, walking casually with the three guards. It seemed to Salvestro that Bernardo was practicing his pike-drill.

"I'll stay here," whispered Amalia, though they were fifty yards away. "You go and get them." She crouched in the nearest doorway. "Well, go on," she scolded him.

All five stopped as he trotted up. The guards were dressed in dark clothes and watched him warily.

"So there you are!" Groot greeted him. "We've been looking for you. You should have stayed like I said. Those bells are for Aldo's death. Good news for us. We've been relieved. They've got some regular troops guarding them now."

"You've done a good job," one of the soldiers said then. "Fat purses all round."

"Hear that, eh?" Groot chimed in.

Salvestro grinned. "Fat purses? Well!" He looked down at his feet. "Unfortunately I left my things back there. You and Bernardo better come and give me a hand with them."

"That's all taken care of," said the same soldier as before. "No need to go back."

"What 'things'?" asked Groot. "You haven't got any 'things.'"

"Come on, Groot," he said, but Groot did not move. He looked at the soldiers, then at Bernardo. "Bernardo?" Groot and Bernardo stared at him. "They're all dead," he blurted out.

One of the soldiers put a hand to his sword. Another shook his head in bemusement. Salvestro stood rigidly.

"His wits have turned," Groot said at last.

The nearest of the soldiers edged sideways and began circling behind him. Salvestro kept him in the corner of his eye. "You're right," he said, backing away. Bernardo had his pike up and was looking from Salvestro to Groot and back again. Salvestro walked backward until there were twenty yards between himself and the nearest of the soldiers.

"Salvestro!" called Groot. "Don't be a fool!" He shook his head and kept walking.

Amalia was still in her hiding place. "Don't they want to come?" she asked.

Salvestro looked back. The five were where he had left them, indistinct in the darkness. The bells clanged on, tuneless and out of time.

They walked quickly, Amalia leading the way back toward the house. They had barely gained the next street before they heard footsteps, a man or men, running. Amalia skipped ahead of him, her dress bouncing up and down. Her pace quickened at the sound of pursuit, and Salvestro found himself breathing hard to keep up. They took the last corner before the house, the footsteps fading, then returning into earshot, nearing and falling back. He was strangely calm, being led in this way. As the house came into view the girl rounded on him suddenly, a whirl of white cloth; he felt a tiny hand grasp his own and pull him sideways.

Outside the house were more soldiers, torches, men shouting orders with an edge of panic in their voices. A tumbrel was being wheeled up to the door. For the bodies, thought Salvestro. He and Amalia crouched in the darkened *quintana* between two derelict houses. Directing the activities was a man mounted on a powerful roan, helmeted, and wearing a breastplate, who cursed the slowness of his men: the Colonel. Amalia began pulling Salvestro farther down the alley. He squeezed past a chimney breast, feet sliding amongst the refuse accumulated there. "Hurry up!" Amalia scolded. They had almost reached the far end. He sensed the ground sloping down steeply as the walls of the houses gave out. He heard water. And then:

"Salvestro!"

From the street, late, coming into view through the narrow slat of the *quintana,* pike up and bellowing. "Bernardo's here," remarked Amalia, clambering crablike down the slope, Salvestro above her and looking back to see the big man judder to a standstill, mouth agape at the soldiers farther up—they have seen him now, and he has seen them see him (Salvestro's sinking heart registers successively the Halt, the planting of the Foot, both preludes to the one, two, *three* of the well-drilled pikeman). Shouting, a horse's hooves, and then again, "Salvestro!" more plaintive this time. He's frightened, thought Salvestro.

"Poor Bernardo," said Amalia, who had reached the bottom of the ditch and was wading into the evil-smelling stream of black liquid that flowed there. Bernardo was looking about, confused, seemingly rooted to the spot. "They'll chop his head off," said the girl.

"Bernardo! Bernardo! Down here! Here!" It was his own voice.

"Silly Salvestro." Amalia was floating on her back in the current, a wheeling white agent against the darkness. "He'll lead them down here and then they'll chop all our heads off. Except mine."

For a heart-stopping second it seemed that Bernardo could not hear him, then he turned and lumbered down the alley, feet thudding, pike striking sparks off the walls, his body a great black silhouette. He was more than halfway when, with a thunder of hooves, the Colonel's horse appeared at the far end, the Colonel himself spurring the beast forward like an engulfing shadow, metal glinting, nostrils snorting, the animal gaining more ground than seemed possible. Bernardo seemed to slow and slow until Salvestro realized that the big man would not make it.

It was the chimney breast, he realized later. Horse and rider appeared to stop dead. Full gallop one second. The next, stopped. The horse let out a terrible scream, but it was as nothing to the howl that issued from the Colonel. Horse and rider were jammed tight, but it was not pain in the Colonel's voice. It was rage and want, the desire to sink metal into their skulls. The soldier was staring at him, mouth open, shouting his hatred as Bernardo shot forward and both men tumbled down the bank and landed in three feet of sluggish dark water.

The ditch rose steeply on either side. The backs of the houses rose higher still. They heard the Colonel shouting to his men, "No! No! Get back!" Amalia was waiting for them, a boat of immaculate white afloat in the stinking flood.

"Poo," she said, batting away a turd. "This way."

They waded in her wake.

The boy brought them mugs of beer in sullen silence. "He's not a bad lad," Groot said as he retreated. He turned back to Salvestro. "So the girl got you out. They asked me about her later." He toyed with the fingers of his gloves. "They asked me about you, too."

A ditch and water within it. Two men, themselves. Amalia. The ditch received tributaries, similarly foul ones, which deepened and darkened it and quickened its flow until Bernardo was struggling along with water up to his chest and Salvestro was half-wading, half-swimming, choking every time he took a gulletful of the stuff. They passed under little bridges, waiting beneath one in panting silence while men and horses passed overhead. Amalia floated effortlessly, spinning on her back, facing up to heaven. They reached a wall that climbed out of the water and rose forty feet above them. The water gurgled and whorled at its base. Salvestro eyed it in despair, but before he could frame the question, Amalia answered him. "Not over it, silly Salvestro. Underneath. . . ." She ducked beneath the surface and disappeared.

"Well, that's that," Bernardo said after a minute of silence. "She's dead."

"She's out," Salvestro replied. "She's on the other side of that wall waiting for us."

"I can't," muttered Bernardo. "I'm going back. I can't. . . . Not underneath."

"We can't go back," Salvestro told him. "They'll hang us if we go back."

"I'm going back," Bernardo said. "We should have stayed with Groot."

"Forget Groot. We'll start with your head. . . ."

"My head?"

"Pinch your nose shut like this, close your eyes, then . . ."

He could not remember how long they spent there, Bernardo shaking his head and insisting that he could not do it, himself insisting the opposite, finally shouting at him, finally threatening to leave him there. "Groot doesn't care about you, you fool!"

A few seconds of blind terror, the big man's thrashing, his panic, the weight of the stones piled over them, and the submerged tunnel stretching forward. . . . He was an eel curling about Bernardo, nudging him, punching him once or twice, sensing the panicked hands that reached for him, the legs kicking and scything, long seconds that stretched like hours, and then there was air again, the same wall towering above them, air in his lungs, and Bernardo spluttering and choking beside him. They were out.

"Poor old Bernardo!" Amalia was standing above them on the bank of the stream. She looked concerned. "You can climb up there. It's easy." The two men heaved and gasped. "Hurry up! There's miles to go yet." She struck out across the rough pasture, hopping over the hillocks and swinging her arms. The two of them stumbled behind her.

"Where are we going now?" panted Bernardo.

"Away from here," answered Salvestro. Anywhere but here.

The first torches appeared soon after. Four of them, away to their left. They seemed to fan out as they drew nearer. More appeared ahead of them, and soon they heard the soldiers' voices, which were sharp and angry-sounding. They are frightened, thought Salvestro. The Colonel would be out there somewhere. They pressed on, but cautiously. He could not judge the distances. Amalia was silent. The ground grew wet underfoot, and an old memory rose in Salvestro, a familiar fear he could not grasp.

There was a shout, sudden and frightened. Some of the torches seemed to bunch together. One disappeared. Then another. More shouting, but distant. He could not make it out. Amalia was a shapeless beacon, white in the blackness. She had stopped hopping and skipping. Another shout came from behind them. He glanced back. Nothing. Still Amalia walked on, but the footing was odd, something strange about the ground. "We're nearly safe now," said Amalia. "Just a little farther." Then, almost simultaneously, a soldier started screaming for help, near them, perhaps—he saw nothing—and Salvestro brought his foot down in water. His leg sank in above the knee, and he knew the memory that had teased him. "Stop," he said quickly. "You've led us into a bog."

First the child, a tottering tot, then the siblings, smaller to the fore and larger to the rear, mother, then father, a horse, an ox, a fully loaded cart, yes, you could drive a cart across a bog, with care. But you needed the child. He had seen such processions traversing the bog around Koserow, watching from whatever scant cover rose above the bouncy waterborne sphagnum. Intricate zigzags and doublings-back were the norm as this or that patch of the moss-crust bobbed and bent under the increasing weight and the hesitant parade ground to a halt, turned on itself, and moved off in search of the one path, the singular safe passage, the invisible winding line that the bog-surface concealed. Underneath was the bog proper, a peaty soup of earth and water that waited hungrily for the incautious foot or leg or wheel to puncture the surface, when it would suck and pull, and then drown. So you needed the child, to find the way. And you needed the load that followed to increase gently and steadily. Going through the moss meant dead. . . .

He lay back slowly, stretching out his arms and trying to free himself from the bog's grip. Somewhere behind them he heard the soldier cry out again, then the sound he dreaded, a muted splashing as the man began to thrash. Never thrash in a bog. Be calm. The shouting ended very suddenly. And then, thought Salvestro, the moss closes over the face. His leg was slowly coming free, gently now. "Lie down on your back," he told Bernardo.

"What are you doing?" Bernardo demanded.

"Lie down!"

They had the child, he thought. They would not die here. The voices of the soldiers were thin and distant, the odd shout as they retreated: victory to the bog. He felt the moss bend as Bernardo lowered himself onto it. Leg almost out now. "Amalia," he said, "don't move. Just lie down and reach out your hand. Don't be frightened."

"I'm not frightened!" She sounded indignant. "It's you who's frightened."

"Just lie down, Amalia."

"No!" She stood there, an irreducible ten feet between them. "You're too heavy," she said after a pause. "And I have to go now."

"Wait! Amalia wait!" She had turned and was walking, no, skipping deeper into the bog, into darkness. "Wait! What about us!" he pleaded.

"God will save you," she called out over her shoulder. "Good-bye, Salvestro!" She was gone.

"A bog." Groot shuddered. "No wonder they never found her body. How did you get out?"

"On our bellies. It took us most of the night. . . . We thought they'd hanged you, Groot."

The boy had disappeared somewhere, and they were alone.

"Hanged, eh?" Groot chuckled. "Well, you've been wide of the mark before. No, it was just as I said it would be, in the end." He grew quiet, inspecting his gloved fingers. When he looked up again, he was trying to smile. "They wanted to know where you and Bernardo were. Rather insistent on it." He pulled the glove off his left hand. Salvestro stared at the hand that Groot held up to his face. "This one"—Groot indicated the gap where his little finger should have been—"they took off with a small knife. This one, though"—he wiggled the next stump feebly—"this one they used pincers."

There was a long silence.

"I'm sorry for it," Salvestro said eventually.

Groot nodded. "One finger for you. One for Bernardo. It wasn't so bad. Rufo saw me all right, in the end. . . ."

"Rufo?"

"The sergeant, the dressed-up devil himself. Had me out of there in no time. As soon as I told them who I took my orders from, they were throwing food down my throat and gold in my pocket. Bought this place with it." He put the glove back on.

"He's here," said Salvestro.

"Here? How do you . . . He's not. I know for a fact he's not . . ."

"I saw him. The Colonel."

"Oh, him! Yes, well, I've seen him myself. You don't have to worry about him. They pulled his teeth after Prato. *Captain* Diego trots around on a pony now and wouldn't dare harm a fly on his own account."

Salvestro looked about him at the moldering sacks and dough-encrusted instruments of Groot's trade. "A bakery, eh? Very nice."

Groot accepted the compliment and looked curiously at Salvestro's clothes
but said nothing. Salvestro fiddled with his neck chain. "There's one more thing I
should tell you. It's not important, but I'm not calling myself Groot these days."
Salvestro looked at him expectantly. "Grooti," he said, "I'm a Roman citizen
now."

They talked on. It was not until "Grooti" asked after Bernardo that Salvestro
remembered his companion. Hurried farewells and promises to meet at the Broken Wheel were offered and accepted. Salvestro rose to leave.

"Where are you staying?" Groot asked casually.

Salvestro was already in the outer room. "A dump. You don't want to know.
In the Via dei Sinibaldi." The door slammed shut.

Groot sat quietly for a few seconds. He scuffed his toe on the floor. It made a
line in the dirt accumulated there. "Ought to sweep," he murmured to himself.
He sighed and raised his eyes to the ceiling, which bulged above his head.

Then he raised his voice. "He's gone."

First the boots, buffed to a high sheen, then the hose, laced to a doublet of
shot silk with ballooning sleeves, buttons, and badges, a belt, and hanging from it
a scabbard worked with gold. The face that topped this ensemble eyed Groot
coldly.

"You'll have to do better than that, old friend," he said.

"Yes," said Groot.

"Wouldn't want to meet those pincers again, eh? Eh, Grooti-the-Baker?"

"No," said Groot.

Rufo squeezed the imagined instrument. "You'll do better next time."

Once great, now this: a yawn-inducing acreage of alluvial dullness, a river-
riven floodplain that shelves at the rate of one vertical foot to the horizontal mile,
the drop corresponding to the land's sinking self-esteem and the coast to its despair. The land has been creeping slyly out to sea for the last twenty centuries or
so and meeting zero resistance en route, the Tiber flopping about like a sciatic
drunk, this channel, that channel, a delta briefly. At present the river's flattened
tongue gasps its way seaward in baffled meanders, accepting the indignity of sandbanks and sandbars, deferring politely to the town's token flood-control measures, a river of sloppy shallows and directional silliness, unrigorous in summer
and sulky in winter. This is Ostia, where the malaria-resistant locals busy themselves with viniculture, offshore sardine fishing, or the rearing of farinaceous
food-crops; they point proudly to the ruins from former and greater times, which
are magnificent, amphitheatrical, sadly overgrown with undergrowth, and invisible, their existence often disbelieved.

There is a castle, though, La Rocca, a three-fat-towers-and-bastions affair that the river passes on its left bank a mile short of its mouth. Its walls enclose a pleasant jousting-ground and the cathedral of Sant'Aurea, which the Cardinal of San Giorgio and Vescovo di Ostia of four years' standing, being Raffaele Riario, is refurbishing to his own exacting standards; lighters are often seen off-loading artisans press-ganged or bribed in Rome together with their equipment (paint-brushes, bits of wood, wine because the local stuff is undrinkable, paint). The lagoons are picturesque but useless.

Farther upriver the coast comes into view, curving, scything in from the left. Straggling lines of cottages bunch up on the riverbank, fronted by a second landing stage where more lighters, barges, rowboats, and pirogues jostle for mooring space. The coastal quayside is less choked; big sheds and warehouses stand at odd angles to one another, attended by little flotillas of huts. A thinning triangle of land is shaved and squeezed between Tiber and Tyrrhenian, which meet and take swipes at each other over an outermost nub of mud-flat. The road from Rome, and Ostia itself, grinds to a halt at a tavern wedged into this last corner of land, known locally as the Last Gasp. Beyond is nothing but water.

Look left: the harbor. Ships wallowed there, in the mucky shore-swill, the green and swelling slop where rot-softened fish exposed the white of their bellies in a heaving lawn of algae. Ships? Two, to be precise. The sardine fleet was out and its leavings littered the quayside: drifts of fish-scales, amphibious filth-mounds, steaming bouillabaisses of suckered and tendriled monsters with their yellow spillage and purple spurts. Useless fish. Refusenik refuse. The crud that will not budge.

So, their leather creaking and pinching, darkly crimson as a choking drunk, and tight as the skin on a sausage, Don Antonio Seròn steered his pewter-buckled pumps between stolid bollards and oily pythons of rope, eyes alert to the dockside dreck and dross and pulp. He passed the proud brig *Alleluia,* now used mostly for storing the harbormaster's firewood. He passed the empty mooring pins of the sardine smacks. He passed maggots feeding on jellyfish and seagulls feeding on maggots, and nothing smirched his shining shoes as he stepped down to the jetty that stuck its arm out to sea, ten, twenty, fifty feet, rearing, rising, falling, failing . . . It gave up there, just waved its splinters and stopped, a wooden hiccup that had belched a ship.

Or a ship that had shat a jetty, depending on the point of view, mused Seròn, looking at the vessel that squatted low in the muck-choked waters. Seventy tons, two and a half masts, and three and a half mortgages pressed hard on the *Santa Lucia.* A Genoese had bought her, renamed her after his mother, loaded her up in Naples, and sent her off to Ostia with a cargo of sardines. Bad choice. Times are hard in Ostia, and a harbormaster's perks are few. Mooring fees add up quickly. By now, by rights, she should have been confiscated, cut up, and aboard the *Alleluia.* Money had intervened. Seròn's money, doled out in large sacks on his two previous visits: five and a quarter mortgages paid out of existence already, only three and a half to go, and there she was afloat, her integrity maintained, her dignity intact. She was built of oak that two decades on the Tunis–Genoa run had turned into a mush of ratshit, ship-rot, sawdust, and salt held together by a hull-size scab of barnacles. Sagging, bending, creaking, rotting, the *Santa Lucia* looked like the morning after the night before when the night before was the shipworms' annual banquet and the shipworms were the size of eels.

From somewhere belowdecks came the stench of the ballast, a warm soupy wave of every liquid that had ever been spilled on the *Santa Lucia* and soaked its way through the sodden timbers of her decks to reach the gravel slopping in the dungeon of her hull, chiefly and most pungently the mingled discharges of the seven hundred and forty-three crew members who in the course of eighty-three voyages had contemplated swinging their buttocks out of the heads on the end of a greasy rope, shaken their heads, and found a quiet corner instead, trousers down, *aaaaaah*. . . . Forewarned and forearmed by previous visits, Seròn fluttered a cologne-soaked handkerchief before his nose, a flag of smelly surrender doing no good at all because this kind of armor-piercing reek ignores the nostrils, spurns the mouth, and goes straight for the guts. Seròn churned. Where was the captain of this floating piss-pot? Belowdecks.

Where. . . .

An eye opened, took a direct hit of daylight through the open door, and closed again. A nostril twitched at a strange and tarty aroma. A cough escaped, ungumming a phlegm-filled mouth. Fat and fully clothed in the fastness of his bunk, Captain Alfredo di Ragusa registered an alien midmorning presence in his cabin. A quick internal check: Still drunk? Yes.

Captain Alfredo? . . . Are you awake, Captain Alfredo?

He waited for this to stop. It did not.

Captain? . . . Captain Alfredo?

Yes, he thought, I am Captain Alfredo. Then he went back to sleep.

Reemerging on deck, shoes still gleaming, stomach heaving soggily in time with the soggy lurching of the ship, Seròn looked about for the mate.

"What'd I tell you?"

The voice came from behind him. The mate was lounging on the foredeck, arms folded. Lank black hair swung about his ears, while his lips curled and bunched in a range of sneers and smirks. "He's a sot," the mate went on. "Wring his guts and you'd get a bucket of brandy."

He'll do it, thought Seròn for the fiftieth time that week as the feckless tirade sprayed bile over the deck. He had considered the mate, assessed his suitability, weighed him up. Now he was sure. The mate's voice was bored and spiteful with boredom. He didn't care one way or the other. He was perfect. Almost as perfect as the ship. Almost as perfect as the two buffoons back in Rome, and they were *absolutely* perfect.

"You bought this piece of shit," the mate was saying now. "I mean, you actually paid actual money for . . ." He swallowed, looking over the vessel, searching for the right word, digging deep for squalor and stupidity, not finding it. "For . . . this?"

"I paid her debts. She's mine, or will be," said Seròn.

"You want us off, then."

Resignation, a dash of despair. It's good, thought Seròn. This is the man. This can work. "Not yet," he said. "Maybe not at all. How many men are needed to sail this ship?"

"Sail her? She hasn't got any sails. Harbormaster took 'em."

"They will be returned. With sails, how many?"

"The minimum?"

Seròn nodded.

"Twenty. Fifteen, at a pinch."

"And what, in your opinion, would need to be done to make this vessel sea-worthy?"

The mate stared at him in disbelief. "Seaworthy?" Seròn nodded again. The mate choked back a laugh. "Well," he said, "let's begin at the beginning. The keel . . ."

The keel, it turned out, was sound. Unlike the ribs, the stem-post, and the stern-post. The planking was warping off the frame, and ragged fringes of caulk-ing were coming loose from the top of the wales to somewhere below the water-line. How far below? No one knew. The *Santa Lucia,* having been tied down by the masts and careened in the Italian style once a year for two decades, had finally protested this brutal, shallow-water scraping by snapping off her own foremast, and Captain Alfredo had not dared repeat the procedure since. The bilges were choked, the pump cracked, and her rotting timbers had rotted her nails. She was iron-sick and creaky and coming apart at the seams. She had no sails. A sad, sad ship.

"The sails don't make much odds," the mate finished up. "Any wind stronger than a sparrow's fart would snap the masts in any case. Might as well rig that handkerchief of yours."

Seròn thought briefly, then pointed to the quay. "If a group of people were seated over there by the *Alleluia,* on a platform, for instance, how many of these, ah, defects would they notice?"

The mate considered this. "So long as they were upwind, and so long as they weren't sailors, they wouldn't know a thing. Except for the sails. Why?"

"This ship could be yours," Seròn said softly. "If you do as I tell you. . . ."

"Mine? This magnificent old woodpile? Well, thank you *so* much. That smell you try to keep out of your nose, you know what it is? It's rot. This isn't a ship, it's a coffin. . . ." And so on and so forth, up and down the list of the ship's past, present, and future failings from keel to crow's nest, from cracked rudder to sprit-less prow, until at length this sarcastic tirade exhausted itself just as the earlier one had. "If I do what?" he asked.

You are a whiner, thought Seròn. An ingrate, a thug, a mutineer in the making. Perfect, perfect, perfect. He said, "You may have heard talk of an expedition. . . ."

The mate was called Jacopo. He had crawled out of a swamp a little way south of Spezia twenty years ago with the conviction that he was born to be a sailor. The *Santa Lucia* was where this belief had fetched him up. As Seròn talked on, skepticism, then disbelief, then appalled amazement, then appalled and reluctant credence passed across his face. A heavily pregnant rat scampered up the jetty, paused, sniffed at the *Santa Lucia,* then turned and scampered back to shore.

"What about Alfredo?" he asked finally.

"The same way as the others," Seròn said without a pause.

Jacopo thought about this.

"Well?"

Jacopo nodded. "Very well," he said.

A minute later, Seròn was again picking his way through the *cordon salissant* of the quay, head panning left to right, the Tiber, the Last Gasp, stables behind it, cottages, more cottages, sheds, more sheds . . . Huts and then a shed that was larger than its neighbors, barn doors on the seaward side, high-sided and windowless: the sail-loft.

Seven or eight aproned men eating their lunch outside looked up as he passed. He ignored them. The barn doors would not budge, so he continued around the back to where a smaller door was propped open with a sawhorse. He strolled in and found himself at the bottom of a huge well of light.

The floor was smooth and planked with light wood. Nails driven into the beams of the walls held knives of varying lengths, strange tongs, other tools whose function he could not guess. The roof forty feet above his head was slatted, and waterfalls of light poured down. Before him, hanging from wall to wall and floor to ceiling, making this end of the shed a little square courtyard, was a vast single sheet of crackling white canvas.

There seemed to be no one about. He slipped around the side of the huge curtain, only to find himself faced with another. Then another. And another. The canvas hung from thick poles suspended with pulleys from the joists high above, sheet after sheet, each one interleaved flush with its neighbors. Seròn involved himself busily in their folds, openings, and cul-de-sacs, wrestling the canvas this way and that, working his way through the floppy walls of the maze. The cloth seemed to go on forever, winding back on itself to confuse him, tempting him with openings that led only to more cloth. He was sweating and growing irritable when he finally emerged in an airy square of the workshop identical to the one he had left except for a number of strange windlasses anchored to the walls. There were ropes and pulleys, too, the ropes running up the walls under tension to tackle-blocks in the roof, then down again, down the walls, into the windlasses, out again . . . They seemed to be converging on him. He looked down. He was standing on canvas. One of his shoes was scuffed. He frowned.

"You! Get those brothel-slippers off that canvas! Go on! I said, *Go on!* MOVE!"

It appeared that a woman was requesting his absence. A rather foul and loud one. She made the same request again, in subtly different terms, then a third time, at which he moved off the canvas as per her suggestion. She was blousy, fifty, red in the face, with a mop of curly hair that flopped like a mad rag doll on the top of her head. She marched up to him. Down the open top of her dress he could clearly see her nipples, which were big and chewed looking.

"I am Don Antonio Seròn," he announced. "Master of the *Santa Lucia*. . . ."

"No, you're not. You're Don Antonio Seròn, *owner* of the *Santa Lucia*."

"And I am in search of the sail-master," he continued smoothly.

"Wrong again. You're in search of the sail-*mistress,* and that's me. Unfortunately. And before you start telling me what I know you're going to tell me, which is that you need a full set of sails for that tub by yesterday, let me tell you, Don Antonio Whoever-you-are, something about sail-lofts. Sail-lofts are not 'calm,' they are not 'airy,' they are not 'havens of peace' amongst 'the bustle of the docks.' They are places of *work*. Canvas gets cut here with shears and knives, and shears and knives are *sharp*. It gets pierced with *awls,* and they are sharp, too. Canvas is stretched under tension, and tension is *dangerous*. . . ."

She was fond of emphasis, or perhaps just shouting. Seròn was undecided.

"For instance, while you were admiring your stupid shiny face in your stupid shiny shoes, if I were to accidentally knock out the wedge in this *windlass,* and these ropes were to release their *tension,* then *this* would happen."

Her elbow jabbed, something flew across the floor, a sudden deafening clatter as the windlasses spun, and Seròn fell back. The four corners of five hundred square feet of canvas sprang from the floor with a *whump!* and shot up into the ceiling. The cloth hung like an enormous sack, gathered at the corners, bobbing gently six feet above the ground. The sail-mistress looked down at him.

"If that was you in that canvas, you'd be in the market for a new pair of legs," she said. "Now, Don Antonio Idiot-Seròn, what can I do for you?"

She had not liked it. She had frowned and tried to dissuade him. The men trooped in from their lunch and they had not liked it, either, also tsking, shaking their heads.

"They'll shred with the first gust of wind," she protested. "You'll be sailing a bag of washing."

They were standing out the back, contemplating a brown heap of brown cloth that had once been the *Santa Lucia*'s sails.

"I took 'em off the harbormaster for three scudi. They're worth about two, as flour sacks, perhaps. But as sails . . ."

"I'll pay ten," said Seròn.

The woman whistled slowly. "Does Alfredo know about this?"

"Captain Alfredo lives on my charity, and aboard my ship," said Seròn.

She shook her head. "You really are a nasty piece of work, aren't you?" she told him frankly.

He counted out the money.

Road dust, dock-dross, ship-stench, now insults. Seròn shuttles back and forth between the city and its port, tiring himself with nocturnal and early morning flitting about, juggling headachy logistics, watching the mimosa come into bloom through the late Roman summer and sweating under its sun. Nothing's going wrong, which worries him. He has the ship. He has Jacopo. He has Diego, or Diego has him; it comes to the same thing. He has his "Master Explorers." Only Vich's lack of curiosity gnaws at his hypertrophied paranoia. There he stands on the trapdoor, the noose about his neck. Why doesn't he ask awkward questions? Seròn has answers prepared for them all: budgetary constraints, the draconian timetable, the very nature of the whole project. . . . Two days later he is back in Rome, on the treadmill again, round and round, for it never ends, this beastly business. Across the table in the Broken Wheel, Bernardo launches himself into the end of his account.

". . . and in the morning there was no sign of her. She just ran off and left us there. So we started walking. There were patrols after us, too, we saw them. Salvestro saw them, anyway. We had to hide. We walked a long way. . . ."

Bernardo shook his head. Sitting opposite him, Seròn cursed himself for the twenty-eighth time. What had he been thinking? How could he possibly have thought that humoring this imbecile might serve to while away the time before the other imbecile returned from whatever fool's chase had sent him scurrying out of the tavern in the first place? The giant droned, repeated himself, lost the thread, whined, went on and on and on. . . .

"You shouldn't worry yourself," he reassured Bernardo. "I feel quite certain that all that is behind you now, and this, this Colonel, what was his name?"

"Diego."

"Diego. Well, even if he is in Rome, he would not dare harm men in the employ of the Spanish Crown. Certainly not such illustrious servants as yourselves; no, it's inconceivable, out of the question."

"Anyway," Bernardo resumed, "it was a very long walk. And we were running away, too. From the Colonel. So when Salvestro just . . ." He struggled to find the word he sought. "Just *went,* well, I thought, It's the Colonel. He's here, see, in Rome. . . ."

The Colonel was what he feared. Other things, too, being left behind, being alone. Events had taken place, things had happened, and he had to keep quiet about them. There was no clear distinction among these things. He was not stupid. He knew he was not stupid, but things went wrong, became troublesome, and sometimes he lost his temper or grew so frightened of losing his temper that it was just as bad. He had to keep quiet, but he found it hard not to say these things. Don Antonio's questions . . . What did you do if you had to keep quiet and someone asked you about the very thing you had to keep quiet about? What did you do then? Dogs and rocks. It was always one or the other.

"What do you do then?" he asked Don Antonio abruptly.

"I think"—Seròn spoke carefully and slowly—"that I can personally *guarantee* that you will not be bothered by this Colonel Diego." This seemed only to confuse the man further, for he went off on a completely different tangent involving running away (again), something about "keeping quiet" and a little boy who, halfway through the story, turned into a little girl. Aldo's brat Amalia? He hardly cared and could sit there no longer.

"I will call on Salvestro in a day or two," he said, rising from his chair. "Or perhaps this afternoon, but if I do not, you may tell him that the ship is ready to sail. His Holiness himself will bless her. Two weeks. . . ." The giant's face was a picture of confusion and alarm. He repeated the message. It did no good.

It never does, he thought later, lying fully clothed on his bed, waggling his feet so that the candlelight reflected off the leather of his shoes. They hurt, but he did not take them off. Eventually he had scribbled a message in simple signs on a scrap of paper and left it with the oaf. After returning from his encounter with Bernardo and the fruitless search for Salvestro that followed it, he had come upon Vich patiently searching through the papers in his study. Loose pages, bound accounts, papers tied with string or wrapped in cloth, and rolls of cracked parchment were off the shelves and on the floor. He was leafing through a volume of charts as Seròn walked in.

"I have mislaid the small portolan," he said. It was the larger one that he held before him. A brown water stain at the bottom of the book added the same fanciful continent to the ragged coasts and seas on each of its pages. "Do you remember it, Don Antonio? The one with the likeness of Don Francisco de Rojas carved on its boards. . . ." He had closed the book and asked after his business at Ostia, but he was uninterested, abstracted, most urgently concerned with seating arrangements and the order of precedence. "Place Faria next to me," he told Seròn. "I want to watch his face when the vessel sails. The *Santa Ajuda,* is it?"

"*Santa Lucia,*" Seròn corrected him, then asked if the dispatch had arrived from Spain.

Vich shook his head resignedly. "They have forgotten we exist," he said. "But we continue anyway, we loyal servants of Fernando. Two weeks, do you say, before she sails?"

The days that followed were taken up with correspondence and accounts, for which Don Jerònimo seemed to have developed a sudden, brief, and inexplicable passion. He was eager to leave for the hunt at La Magliana and told his secretary that he would travel to Ostia directly from there, with the Pope. Idiot Vich, thought Seròn, yawning on his bed. He cocked an ear to the footsteps that padded about in the room adjacent to his own. Diego's room.

Since the soldier's first grim outburst he had confined himself to curt nods and the occasional inquiry. Seròn's stock of replies rotated between "As it should . . ." and "Satisfactorily . . ." and "Well . . ." delivered flatly but with conviction: the song of the competent functionary. The soldier would nod and pass by him, accepting this without further question. None of them see it, he told himself. The thought was almost melancholy. Idiot Diego, too. The footsteps paused.

And there was Salvestro. Another idiot? A fool? A fly in the Seròn-spider's web? These terms shaded into one another. Men drifted within them and between them. Some escaped.

After leaving the big man at the tavern, he had gone in search of the absent Salvestro. He rode the towpath on the west bank of the Tiber to the Borgo. Skirting the foot of the Janiculum, he had cast his eye over the city that bulged from the opposite bank. The land rose. The city fattened on its slopes. Steely rolls of late morning heat ground the roofs and terraces into shimmering mirrors or melted them to a liquid mirage. Streets thrashed and flopped in the furnace, curling and twisting, sweeping churches and towers of melting stone before them. Sweat pooled and squelched between his toes.

Even so, the cool of the Borgo was unwelcome. The lurching shambles of Santo Spirito overhung an irregular path that narrowed to squeeze past improvised hovels and shelters. The stench of their inhabitants brought out his handkerchief. The air was thick with damp stinks and stenches that spread and collided to become doubly and triply noxious.

"Pilgrim's Staff?" he inquired of a better-dressed passerby.

"God help you," came the reply. "Halfway down the Via dei Sinibaldi."

Its entrance breathed sweat and stale urine, a mouth blackened with decay. Flaking stone and unidentifiable muck lined its gullet. He tied his horse next to another already tethered to a broken boot-scraper and entered. The owner was on him immediately, a thickset ruffian with a collapsing face.

"Salvestro," Seròn announced. "He resides here, I believe?"

"Him again? Master Popular, ain't he? In the back, if he's about." The oaf pointed, snuffling and growling around him. "Need a candle?"

He took the candle.

"That'll be two giulii."

He paid for the candle.

A passageway tunneled back into the guts of the hostel. Distant noises that might have been moans or stifled shrieking drifted down from the upper floors through stairways hacked out of the building's interior mass. The floor seemed to have been laid with tombstones. The hostel's inhabitants had scraped their marks in the damp-softened stone. The last door stood open. Absolute darkness and a faint sound, a soft scratching. He ventured in.

The light from his candle would not reach the roof. There were pillars and pallets, loose straw, a chest, illumined by the yellow stain of his light. The air was dead and musky; its stench curdled the contents of his stomach. In the midst of this sat a cowled and habited man. Salvestro had mentioned "the monks," some of them by name. He should have made a note, but he already knew that his errand was futile. Salvestro was not here. The monk had not looked up yet. He was bent over a piece of parchment, scribbling furiously. Seròn moved closer and the man started, letting out a startled yell. A face smeared with dirt stared about wildly, its sightless eyes rolling in search of him.

"I am looking for a man named Salvestro," he hurried to reassure the wretch.

"I told you! He is not here. I do not know where they are." He tried to cover the pages before him with his arms. Seròn glanced at them curiously, then at the inkwell that was placed on the floor beside the monk. It was dry. The pages were blank.

"Forgive the disturbance," he said, backing away. The monk was feeling the floor, hands outstretched and fingers splayed. He found a piece of paper and grunted to himself before taking up his pen once again.

It should have been funny, Seròn thought now, boots twinkling, buckles undone. Pewter was a fine metal with its powdery sheen. Why was it not funny? The other horse was gone when he'd reemerged. The monk's words struck him then: *I told you.* . . . I told you before? Or already? Had someone else been searching for his Master Explorer? It did not matter. He would find Salvestro at the Broken Wheel the next morning. Diego's boots resumed their soft tattoo. Would the soldier pursue his own purposes, slip the leash and simply go after them? No, no, no. . . . Just a mad monk in a cellar, nothing more. Join the other idiots, Idiot Seròn.

In the next room, the pacing stopped and started and stopped again. A muted creak would be the handle of the door and the soft knock that followed the carefully damped closing of that door. The passageway was cheaply planked and squeaked like a choir of mice, but on this occasion the mice declined to sing and Seròn listened to the sound of a man not wishing to be heard as Diego padded past his door.

Two minutes later, noises off: a creak, a clunk, a rustle, a whisper. Saying what? Only that Diego was back, scraping and scratching, gravid in his soundbox. He was wide awake, straining his ears. Next door a wheezy organ rattled its pipes, footsteps beat an irregular measure, the bed supplied the air. In major and minor keys, the bed boards groaned, then groaned again. The bed feet first tapped, then jiggled, then scraped. Then thudded. And accelerated, and Seròn could no longer disbelieve the evidence of his own ears when a heavy grunt sounded the theme and was answered by a low drone that rode the scales up to wailing, then dispersed itself in a series of high-pitched squeals. The crescendo was a single resounding unambiguous crash: the bed itself being driven into the wall.

Silence. Then, again, the padding of feet. He counted, one, two, three, four. The door, the passage, the door once again. In the silences interposed between these sounds he heard only the reverberations that shook their way through his frame. He lay there, incredulous, reluctantly accepting, persuaded only for want of any other explanation. It seemed somehow unimaginable, but why not? Why would he not? Diego had a woman. Seròn had listened. Seròn had heard. In the room next to his own, Diego had had a woman.

Now the palazzo was silent, all the idiots asleep. He masturbated noiselessly and joined them.

The light came and went, a trembling glow in the dark distance. Whole days went by when he did not see it. His eyes were useless to him; he did not see it with his eyes. On the days when he was left alone he waited for a dim flicker to reappear. Sometimes it came. Sometimes not. He waited. He prayed. He wrote:

"*I . . .*"

Only poets sang themselves, Jörg thought. Contemptible pride drove them to it. Augustine of Hippo sought the footprints of the Trinity in the mud of Man's soul and found Memory, Will, and the Power of Thought. The Holy Spirit walked in everyone, being Love, the hungry Will. Christ walked in everyone, being the power of God's Thought. The double procession bound each man to both, two grinning shepherds guiding their flock down from the mountain, all galloping toward God. And memory is who we are, he thought, being all we know of ourselves and the traces of the Trinity within us. The ground was churned now, plowed under, almost illegible. It was late to be searching for footprints. Perhaps too late. Augustine too wrote of himself, but humbly, as a penitent. I, the solitary upright, the bare bar, the drawn and driven appetite for God.

"*I, Jörg . . .*"

Prior, and scribbler of these lines, the *Gesta Monachorum Usedomi,* and petitioner of His Holiness the Pope: the Trinity or succession of himself. Gather the scattered glass beads and restring them on the thread of "Jörg." He was a rope of rounded mirrors, mouth spread wide, eyes slewed and stretched: a hopeful novice, then a monk in orders, then a Prior and a recorder of these images. Observe—he observed—the graying and silvering of the hair, the lines cut in the skin, the dimming of the eyes, a man becoming the pieces of a man. Mad old Jörg. He chuckled to himself, pen paused. He was one of those who waited on the Pope, one of the desperate, clamorous, and grasping. And therefore one of the faithful. Before honor is humility, as Solomon knew, and wrote twice.

"*I, Jörg of Usedom . . .*"

Of? Or merely from? And which Usedom? Its first jagged contours were bastions shielded by natural moats, sea and river mouth; beech-wooded and untransfigured. An ur-Usedom, notional, not his island, or anyone's. The heathens came and marked their presence with the groves of their barbarous gods and the piles of a great city: Vineta, which was torn loose from her foundations and sent to the bottom of the sea. Henry the Lion built a church to stand guard above it, to stand firm against the suck and pull of its patient vengeful tides, or to mark his bloodless consummation. The island cared nothing for conscience. Then the silly simple islanders with their plows and fences. But this was not his, neither the island he was of nor that which he was from. Last of all, the Usedom of his return with the different greens of its tree mosses and bog mosses, the low humps of its fields and their straw-colored crops, its beehives and pigpens, cow-sheds and barns. Come winter the icicles hung like swords from the eaves. Look, a church rises on the seaward coast, its spire stabbing the sky's blue and its bells bringing the men and women running across the fields to praise God, its impregnable walls and high windows founded on granite: the miracle church of a miracle island. He would never see this Usedom, though it was his.

I, Jörg of Usedom, though blind, write this chronicle of the deeds of the monks of Usedom in Rome. Our lodgings here are mean, though no meaner than a stable, and we are tested daily by new affronts and impieties. Suspicion creeps among us like a jackal, or the serpent in the garden. Brother HansJürgen and I battle together for his conscience, which is assailed by doubts and fears and weaknesses of faith. It is a twisted and wretched thing that he comes to me with accusations, for he is sincere and bears witness sincerely in his belief. Still we wrestle. . . .

In truth, what else was there to do during the long hot mornings spent waiting in the courtyard of San Damaso? A few days after their first attempt at an audience, crushed and downcast, he had listened as HansJürgen whispered of Gerhardt's scheming and plotting. What did Gerhardt do, during the day, taking the rest of the brothers with him, whoever would go? HansJürgen stayed, but the others went, even Florian. He asked, naturally, and Gerhardt told him, "Building churches, Father, as was our purpose."

He was aware that he was mocked.

But dusty clothes and Gerhardt's daily absences constituted no sin, and HansJürgen's voice was strained with worry. It came to him suddenly that this was a task he might perform, and his own heart lightened as the other's disclosed the weight upon it. That Gerhardt should employ his brothers in good works, turning their hands to the business of mortar and stone, that was beyond his reproach. But HansJürgen was lost in a maze of dark suspicions. He, Jörg, would light his way out. Besides, it hardly mattered how Brother Gerhardt employed his time in this place, this city of Rome, their sojourn being less than an eye blink in the sight of God. When they returned, surely all would be as before? He lowered his pen once again and was about to write this when a voice sounded, suddenly loud in the chamber.

"I am looking for a man who goes by the name Salvestro."

The voice came from the door, or a little way inside the chamber.

"As you see, he is not here," Jörg replied. He could hear the man's breathing. From somewhere within the hostel itself came the noise of someone shouting, the sound echoing oddly. The voice was unfamiliar to him. The man did not reply. Jörg heard another sound as he turned, as if a tin cup were being scraped against the rough flagstones on the floor, more slithery, perhaps, more sibilant. Then the man was gone.

Jörg gathered his thoughts: Gerhardt's antics, HansJürgen's suspicions, his own mediation. And now Salvestro. Salvestro, who slept not six feet away from him, whose nightly returns were marked, still, by a sudden awkward hush. Salvestro, who did not fit. He considered this for a minute or so. He should write about Salvestro. Bernardo too. The pen began to fly over the page once again. Then, suddenly, he jumped and cried out. The man had come back.

"I am looking," he said, more softly this time, "for a man named Salvestro."

"I told you! He is not here. I do not know where they are." He covered the page before him, but others fell to the floor. He moved quickly to gather them, sensing the man move nearer.

"Forgive the disturbance," the man said. This time there was no strange scraping sound, only footsteps growing quieter as he turned and walked away. Jörg gathered the rest of his papers. HansJürgen would put them in order for him. He took up his pen once again, but now he was disturbed and his thoughts disorderly. Why would anyone, other than himself, be concerned with Salvestro? HansJürgen had mentioned new suits of clothes. Had the two men sunk themselves in debt? Or something worse? The idea swelled in his mind, vexing and goading him. Baseness of birth and ignorance were not obstacles on the path to grace. Salvestro was not beyond salvation. A heathen, yes, but not irredeemable. . . . The next notion came to him unbidden, so preposterous and unexpected that he laughed out loud. He tapped his finger on the page before him. Of course he must write about Salvestro. How narrow of him to have doubted it. He scratched a line beneath his text and began:

Might a soul appear as a small yellow light? I have seen such a thing from time to time, or believed that I did. That amongst the deeds of the monks of Usedom should be counted those of a heathen is no more shocking than Christ's love for Magdalen. It is for him that we are here.

He stopped there and thought on what he had written. He had presumed that the light he saw was a beacon, the Magi's star, a burning bush. But why then was it inconstant? It was a soul, wavering between salvation and damnation. Yes, he thought, for who was our guide to this place of testing, and who will guide us back? He wrote:

We are his test.

How dark the design that this pilgrimage should be not theirs but his. A thousand candles would not light it, a million eyes not see it. He had to sink deeper, breathe it in, eat it and sleep it. Blind? He was not blind enough! His guide was a flickering yellow light, his to follow blindly. He would tell HansJürgen as soon as he should return, for at its unguessable end there would be their church, built again, its bell tower chiming the little hours of Prime, Terce, Sext, and None, the greater hours of Matins, Lauds, Vespers, and Compline, when he would smile to himself in the prayers against darkness and sing with the others the *Venite* when that darkness was dispelled, and within such hours and within such walls they would pray together, as they had before, as they would again.

He sat alone in the darkness, his own and the chamber's. From time to time he scratched his pen in the inkwell and bent his head to the paper. He used his finger to measure the lines. *I, Jörg of Usedom . . .* He began each page of his chronicle with the same formula, and when the bottom of the page was reached he sheaved it carefully under the others.

Apollo sawed on a fiddle held upside-down on his shoulder. Winged horses pranced in the background, and a woman scratched in the soil with a bent stick, or perhaps she was stringing a bow. A headless figure propped itself on one elbow beside her. The severed head had horns. The walls of the *sala* were broken by doors, windows, and at the far end a fireplace as high as himself. Between these were other paintings of women against identical soft, monotonous landscapes. Woman with a stylus and tablet. Woman playing a flute. Another woman playing a lyre. Woman pointing at a globe. Four or five others.

Art, thought Rufo.

The southern corner of the lodge overlooked a laboriously leveled pasture that would be planted with limes next season. Beyond that was the river, which aimed itself at La Magliana, then recoiled, curved ninety degrees to flow away toward Ostia, six hours downstream by barge. Three by galley. Rome was an hour or two in the opposite direction, by river or the road that ran alongside it. He had ridden and arrived to find the stables in uproar. Tool-garlanded workmen clothed in tattered habits hung amidst beams suspended on blocks and tackle from the bare upper-floor joists, while the ostlers shouted insults at them from the floor below. Oxen and horses were corraled in the yard. None of this interested him. He could hear their shouting now, though the huge and shambolic stables was out of direct sight. A man in a gray felt hat walked slowly across the pasture, cradling a heron, its beak tied shut. Three hatless colleagues followed. Ghiberti had gone in search of his master almost an hour ago. Rufo idled, gazing out of the window. Grass. Stands of trees. The minutes passed. His Holiness's passion for hunting was well-known.

Footsteps. Voices. Door, the one behind him and to the left. He turned, knelt to kiss the proffered hem, rose. Leo squinted, red-faced and puffing from the climb up the stairs. Ghiberti hovered near the door.

"You may leave us," Leo said.

The door closed behind the secretary. For a few pregnant seconds the Pope said nothing at all, only peered at him as though weighing him up. "You have found them?" the robed prelate asked at last.

"I have," said Rufo.

It seemed for a moment that His Holiness might jump with happiness and clap his hands. His robes flopped about him as he hunched to spring up, hands floating out in general benediction, flying together in applause. . . . But no. He steadied himself. The leap became a bobbing double curtsy, the clap a considered and prayerful handclasp. He touched his lips to his united fingertips. "How?"

"Your pensioner. Groot. One of them was bound to fetch up there sooner or later."

"Ah, Baker Groot. Yes, of course. Bound to. Bound to." He was pacing now, back and forth in front of the fireplace. Rufo began to relate what he had overheard at the bakery.

"Her body was never found," Leo said when Rufo reached Amalia's part in the story. "Poor little mite. One presumes she died in the bog, or was savaged by animals. . . . Poor, poor little girl. The wretches! To use a mere child. . . ." It seemed to Rufo that the man might be on the verge of anger. "Even the charity of the Pope knows limits," Leo declared finally. He gathered himself. "And you followed this monster back to his lair?" he asked abruptly.

"It was not possible," Rufo replied. "But I have found them. They share a cellar in a hostel. I called there. The proprietor knew them by name, and another man." He recalled the old man crouching blindly in the stench of the chamber. "He was weak in his wits, but he knew them."

Leo was nodding. "Good. Very good." He walked over to the window, calm now, unreadable. "There will be a hunt here in twelve days. Do you like to hunt, Sergeant Rufo?"

He shook his head. Leo eyed him neutrally.

"Well, there will be a hunt in any case." He paused and thought. "Did you see this Salvestro? His dress?"

"He was dressed as a gentleman," said Rufo.

"As a gentleman. And how do you think he came by his costume?"

Rufo shrugged. Costumes. Hunting. None of this interested him. He did not care. He dressed himself expensively, and it gave him no pleasure.

"Spanish gold," said Leo then, and began to chuckle.

"I will kill them and then it will be finished," Rufo said. "It should have been done at Prato."

"There is more to it than Prato," replied Leo, though he seemed almost unaware of the other man, gazing out of the window at the river's fat bend half a mile away. "Much more than Prato," he murmured. Then, "They think they can make a fool of me." He said it softly. Rufo barely caught it.

"They are the fools," he said. "Though they will know it only briefly."

"What?" He looked about as though suddenly awakened. "The cutthroats? Yes, them too. Mere instruments. Mine, and others'. You must leave Groot until last, until you are sure of the other two. He knows more, does he not?"

Rufo nodded. The unfamiliar sensation of curiosity had gripped him. Them too? So who else? He choked back the urge to ask His Holiness to explain himself. Curiosity was a poison. Men died of it. Instead he said, "I return to Rome tonight. It can be done then. Tomorrow at the latest."

"No!" The Pope's voice echoed in the high-ceilinged room. "No, it must be the day of the hunt. Or that night."

Rufo kept his silence, waiting for an explanation of the delay, but Leo offered none. "Very well," he replied. "I will attend you here when it is done."

"Not here," said Leo. He was smiling now. "Ostia. The day after the hunt is the day the Spaniards launch their expedition. The court will be at Ostia. To bear witness to its magnificence." The smile was broader now. "To salute the brave men who serve the whims of their foolish Pope."

As Rufo walked down the main stairs, he heard the Pope's laughter rise and echo in the Sala della Muse behind him, inexplicable and of a piece with the questions that had arisen shyly out of Leo's careless hints. Riding back to the city, he allowed his mind to dawdle amongst them: the two men he was to dispose of were shadowed now by two whose role he could not guess at. Two specter-men. It was all undefined and unpursued. Did he like to hunt? No. Who would kill for pleasure?

He waited twelve days in Rome. On the last of these, he settled himself behind the broken wall opposite the Pilgrim's Staff and waited for the two men to appear. He had a flask of wine, and every hour or so he would empty a little of its contents onto the ground beside him. If anyone should ask what his business was there, he would pretend to be drunk. But no one asked. An ever-thinning stream of men and women walked past without seeing him. A dog sniffed his boot at one point. He kicked it on the nose and it fled howling. The spilled wine smelled putrid in the heat, resinous and plummy. He was not clear on how he would do it. He had killed his first man by waiting half a day on a roof, crouched behind its parapet until the man he sought had walked beneath. He had smashed his skull with a brick.

What if he had looked up? He was a big, powerful man. What if he had looked up and seen him, rising to his feet above with the weapon in his hand? His victim had been well liked in the village, better liked than Rufo. What would he have done then? He had been fourteen years old.

Flies circled erratically and lighted on the spilled wine. It was better to think nothing, plan nothing. The opportunity came and was taken. He walked away from the cadaver's twitching mess. Contemplation of a killing clouded the judgment, and the moment blunted itself, or stretched, or fattened into minutes. Sometimes it seemed like minutes. His mind was perfectly blank and the act perfect and clear within it. They struggled often enough, knees and elbows, the smell of their sweat while he pulled them about or pushed them up against a wall. They were awkward, their cow-bodies heavy and difficult to maneuver on the way to death. People trudged up and down the street. A few disappeared inside the Pil-

grim's Staff. No one had come out yet. The afternoon sun was falling off now. He
had his sword and some short knives with him. Two men were driving a mule up
the street. Four monks followed who hung about at the entrance to the hostel.
They talked for a few minutes before one walked off. The other three went in.
He thought about this for a while, then rose, stretching and yawning theatrically.
He walked across the street, dawdled at the door. It might be better inside.
Quicker and neater. The two of them would be sun-blind, easily marked in sil-
houette. He would not be seen. Then Groot.

A woman passed carrying a bundle of rags, old clothes, perhaps. Her movements seemed slow and heavy. His heart beat a dull monotone. He thought about
the quick focus and moment of concentration that would turn this collection of
limbs and organs into the instrument of the act, the sensation like seeing a pattern
in a jumble of shapes, quick like that. Inside was better. Then he would walk away,
slowly, not looking back, already outside the ugly flurry of a second ago and suddenly innocent, for nothing preceded the cadaver's twitching and nothing succeeded it, either. The entrance was black as the mouth of hell. He picked a strand
of dead grass from the breast of his doublet, its velvet a deep rust with designs cut
into the pile. Its sleeves were unpadded silk that shimmered in light. He wore
rings of heavy gold, chains too sometimes. A peacock's gaudy feather bobbed
above his hat. He shone and sparkled and glittered and dazzled. He swaggered and
cut a fine figure. No one remembered his face.

"Where in hell have *you* been?"
"Me?"
"You."
Rodolfo was standing at the door to the kitchens. Anjelica and Pierino
flanked him, the latter just arrived. The trio turned as one to indicate the main
room through which, it seemed, a small wind storm had passed. Chairs were scat-
tered about the floor. The tables were piled in one corner of the room in a defen-
sive heap that rose most of the way to the ceiling.
"He won't talk," continued Rodolfo.
"Who?"
"Him. Bernardo. Your friend Antonio was here. Then he left. That's what hap-
pened next." The tables shifted slightly, in the manner of a tortoise scaling a wall.
Salvestro approached, accompanied by Rodolfo.
"Bernardo!" he addressed the table-pile.
There was no response.
"Bernardo! Come out!" barked Salvestro.
A long silence followed in which Salvestro noticed that the tables were not
perfectly still, but quaked slightly, little creaks and knocks accompanying this
movement.

"No," said Bernardo's voice eventually from somewhere in their midst.

"No one's going to hurt you," Salvestro went on.

"I know," said the voice. (More creaking and quaking.)

"Then come on out."

"No."

"Come out! Now!"

"No!"

He tried shouting, then cajoling, then threats, then promises, then bribes, then shouting again. None of it worked. Bernardo remained stubbornly immured behind his tables and sullen "no's." Patrons drifted in, stared at him curiously, asked what was up, then offered advice. Lucullo arrived and wafted tempting fumes from a large bowl of hot fish soup into the cracks and crevices of Bernardo's makeshift carapace. Rodolfo was on the point of pouring boiling water over the whole contraption with the purpose of flushing out its architect when Salvestro realized that his approach to the whole problem had been wrong from the start.

"Well, Bernardo, you won't come out," he began. "I respect that. If you won't come out, you won't come out, and that's that. No point in my trying to persuade you otherwise." He left a pause. "So I'll be off." The table-pile maintained a wooden silence, its denizen a fleshly one. Salvestro walked back across the room, watched now by Rodolfo, Anjelica, Lucullo, Pierino, and nine or ten of the Broken Wheel's other patrons. "Good-bye, Bernardo," he called.

He had not reached the foot of the stairs before the heap began to shift and jiggle, the topmost tables teetering on those below. The whole pile shook, seemed to rise, split, and then with an enormous crash Bernardo erupted from its midst.

"The rocks," was all he was later able to get out of his friend by way of explanation. That, and a resentful, "You left me on my own." He paid Rodolfo for the damage and found himself left with less than twenty soldi.

"Why didn't you ask Antonio for more money?" he demanded of the big man as they walked back to the Stick.

"More? I never got any in the first place," protested Bernardo. "We didn't talk about money."

"What, then?"

He listened to Bernardo ramble through the confused wreckage of something that a few hours ago had been whatever Antonio had said. The greater part of it concerned his own absence. Most of the rest did, too, although recurrent references to Antonio's having just got back *from* Ostia slowly began to reshape themselves into Antonio's having soon to go back *to* Ostia. With them, it would appear. In fourteen days. Or ten, he was unsure. It might have been the day after tomorrow. When Salvestro pressed him on the point, Bernardo reached into his doublet and drew out a carefully folded sheet of paper. A row of marks lined its top edge. Below was a winding line, crossed through at two points with a crude sketch of a castle and an *X* next to one of them. Salvestro counted the marks. There were fourteen.

"He gave it to me to remember," said Bernardo. "But I forgot."

Salvestro nodded. "Did he tell you to cross these marks off, one a day?"

"Yes!" Bernardo exclaimed, amazed at this.

"These are days. This curly thing is the river. Bridges over it, see? We meet him by the *X*." Bernardo was openmouthed in admiration. Salvestro was pensive. "It means we're off," he said. He banished the frown gathering on his face. "Off at last. Good news, eh, Bernardo? We'll be out of here in two weeks."

"Good," said Bernardo. "Now you can tell me why you ran off like that."

He had not recognized the boy leaning against the damp wall in the alley leading back to Via delle Botteghe Oscure. A thin leg swung out casually to block his path, bare from the knee and the foot shod in sacking tied about the ankle. Arms folded over his chest, a straw dangling from the side of his mouth, he looked out from under the brim of his hat to assess Salvestro.

"What's it worth?"

"What? What do you mean?"

He knew him then, though his manner was completely changed; no longer the cowering scurrying boy-shaped silence who had served him wine at Groot's bakery. Gangs of street-hardened urchins hung about in the alleys and courtyards off the main streets, shouting, fighting amongst themselves, knocking off hats, and torturing cats. Groot's boy was one of these.

"What I know," said the boy. "About you and Sweat-Bucket back there."

Salvestro moved as though to push past the boy, the small shock of recognition receding and being overtaken by larger anxieties centered about Bernardo. The boy planted his foot more firmly.

"You. Sweat-Bucket. And someone else." Salvestro stopped. "C'mon, what's it worth?" The boy was looking at the chain around his neck. "Gimme that. Looks stupid anyway. Go on. I'll tell you what they're up to."

"Who?"

"Gimme." His hand beckoned.

"You don't know what you're talking about," said Salvestro. The urchin made no reply, simply kept his hand outstretched. There was a short silence. Salvestro reached to unfasten the clasp.

"Nice," said the boy. The chain sparkled as he dangled it from his hand. It disappeared inside his shirt.

"So?" Salvestro demanded.

"Rufo," said the boy. "Old friend of yours. Turns up a few weeks ago, asking about you. Sweat-Bucket starts sweating, but he doesn't know anything, so he can't exactly say anything, can he?"

"Rufo," said Salvestro, his heart sinking. He had not thought of Rufo. "What did he want?"

"You." The boy shrugged. "Where you're staying. What you're doing here. That kind of thing."

"Groot doesn't know anything," Salvestro murmured to himself.

"Doesn't know his dick from a dog-turd," agreed the boy. "You've gone white, by the way. Go ahead and puke if you want, I don't care. No, he doesn't know a thing. Then again he doesn't need to, seeing as how this Rufo was sunning himself out the back while you were gabbing on. . . ."

"I have to go," Salvestro said weakly.

"Hang around," the boy retorted. "He'll probably be strolling this way in a minute or two. You could talk about old times, all jolly soldiers together. . . ." He was laughing as Salvestro pushed past him and hurried away up the alley.

"Anyway, when I caught up with the fellow I was already past that church at the end of Ripetta. He moved pretty quick with that sack. Turned out to be some villainous Tiburtine, never set eyes on him in my life before."

"Oh," said Bernardo.

Salvestro looked at him sideways and saw lingering clouds of doubt in the big man's face. He pulled his biretta down a little farther. "So what did you think had happened? That I'd just dump you there?" Salvestro shook his head in theatrical disappointment.

"I thought it was the Colonel," said Bernardo.

"Disguised as a baker?" Salvestro made no effort to conceal his incredulity.

"No. Just, when you didn't come back, I thought, well . . . Well, what would *you* think?"

They had taken the path along the west bank and were nearing Santo Spirito, the saggy clutter of its roofs rising above the wooden-walled hovels.

"Let's stop and have a drink," said Salvestro.

"Where?" asked Bernardo. "There aren't any taverns here."

They walked on in silence.

"I've been thinking we should change our accommodation," he said as they were passing the hulk of the hospital. "I'm sick of Lappi and his shouting. We should get somewhere better, over on the other side of the river."

"How? We haven't got enough money," said Bernardo. "Anyway, we're leaving soon."

"True," said Salvestro. They walked on.

"What's the matter?" Bernardo asked when Salvestro stopped at the end of the Via dei Sinibaldi. Clouds of doubt began to gather again. "What is it?"

"Nothing," said Salvestro. His eyes swept up and down the street. "Come on."

Salvestro got no rest in the days that followed. Each day began with elaborate excuses designed to dissuade Bernardo from heading back to the Stick. Rodolfo's supposed wrath at the broken tables sufficed for a while, but as the incident faded in Bernardo's mind and became part of the hazy jumble that he called his memory, Salvestro was forced into ever more desperate inventions and distractions.

These culminated in Salvestro's sudden fascination with the shrine of a minor saint, prayers to whom were said to safeguard the mendicant against death by shipwreck, banditry, and falling roof-tiles, whose name Salvestro claimed to have been told by Brother HansJürgen and then forgotten, whose shrine was, by his own account, "somewhere to the north of the Campo de' Fiori." Francesco di Paola? Stephen of the Seven Deacons? They did not find it.

A similar charade was played out on their return to the Stick each evening, when Salvestro would once again insist on elaborate routes through the Borgo and long periods of circumspection before actually stepping foot in the Via dei Sinibaldi, with the difference that having already let this precaution lapse once, he found it increasingly difficult to justify its resumption to an exasperated Bernardo. They would eventually regain the safety of the Stick, and Salvestro would fall exhausted onto his palliasse amongst the already sleeping monks, but his mind remained obstinately alert and most of the night would be spent awake, trying to think of a reason why it would prove impossible to revisit the Broken Wheel on the morrow, just as most of the day was spent inventing reasons why they should not go back to the Stick before nightfall. He grew distracted and short-tempered. Behind his prevarications was the urge to spew what he knew into Bernardo's lap, *Yes, Bernardo, it is just as you said, Groot is alive as we are. More so, if he has his way.* . . . Let the big man deal with Groot's treachery himself. And behind this urge was the fact that soon they would be setting sail, soon they would be clear of it all, free of danger, or at least free of these particular dangers. And behind this vista of escape lay an obligation of which he was at first insensible but whose weight settled itself upon him a little more firmly with each and every one of the days that brought them closer to the departure for which he longed. It should not have mattered. He told himself that it did not several times a day, and the days passed, and the date drew nearer, and he felt the obligation more keenly with every one. He had not told the monks.

No, he corrected himself that night as the notion flitted through his mind for the first time, he had not told Father Jörg. The bodies of the others were stertorous mounds of breathing sweating flesh in the darkness around him. When awake, they were bundles of cloth topped with shaven heads who avoided his eye. They did not speak to the two of them and did not acknowledge either his or Bernardo's presence any more than they would mourn their absence once they were gone. Salvestro felt rather than understood the contagious nature of their disfavor. Invisible walls surrounded him and Bernardo; of suspicion and distaste. He did not question this isolation any more than he had his ostracism from the islanders or from the other soldiers at Prato. Private Salvestro. Explorer Salvestro. He was neither, never had been. He had to wrap himself in a swagger to be offered a seat. Play the fool in his gaudy motley. The boy had been right. The chain looked stupid. None of his costumes truly fitted. He did not belong, and any who belonged with him, they did not belong, either. He would not taint Jörg with his overtures, not with the others looking on. That at least was what he told himself that first night. He told himself the same on the second. And the third. On the fourth the monks were gone.

HansJürgen looked up as they entered. Palliasses lay scattered about as usual, but of their occupants there was no sign. Salvestro looked about but said nothing. Gerhardt and sometimes one or two of the others had kept late hours before, arriving back at the Stick long after everyone else, usually covered in stone dust. Since the day he had seen the monk at the lime quarry Salvestro had discovered nothing as to how his days were spent. But all of them gone? An hour or more passed in awkward silence, but it was already clear that they would not return that night. Salvestro, Bernardo, HansJürgen, and Father Jörg heard Lappi slam the door of the hostel shut at midnight. No one said anything. The Prior mumbled a prayer, and HansJürgen blew out the candle.

They did not return the next night or the night after that. Accustomed to fixing his eyes on his feet and keeping them there when it seemed an offense so much as to glance in the direction of the monks, Salvestro began by engineering glimpses of the Prior, affecting head-scratching and restless rollings-over. His first task on reentering the chamber remained checking the stuffing of his mattress for the scabbard, but once its presence was confirmed he turned his attention to Father Jörg. He found himself governed by odd inhibitions or afflicted by a sourceless timidity. Embarassment? He could not put a name to it or a reason, but he watched Jörg. He noted the changes he had not noted before.

Dirt. The Prior's habit was stiff with it, his face streaked and darkened with the same. The dirt was everywhere, of course, but it seemed to concentrate itself about the Prior. That a man should or should not wash his face had never been a concern of his before, yet Jörg had appeared to him not as flesh but as bone, hard and smooth so that the stuff of the world should fall away from him. . . . It had gained a purchase now. His head shook oddly sometimes, when he seemed most remote from the chamber, the hostel, the whole city, perhaps. He would sit in silence for hours on end. Sometimes he wrote, his finger inching down the page, his lips moving soundlessly. He prayed, in silence, sometimes with HansJürgen, but more often alone. Once, Salvestro came across him squatting in the passage outside their room. The sight disturbed him, the blind man grunting and straining on his haunches and his feet shifting awkwardly on the damp flagstones, oblivious of any who might be watching. He could not tell him then.

So it was HansJürgen who was the cause of his delay, not the monks already departed. (Why? When he finally inquired, HansJürgen answered only that Gerhardt's business had taken him from Rome for a few days, then looked away as though the conversation pained him, as though the real reason for their absence were the continued presence of himself.) He thought resentfully of the chest of silver trinkets and the exchanges he had made with Lucullo, two more since the first. Who would do that for them when he was gone? Every day he made promises to himself that he would tell the Prior that evening, and when the evening came he spent the hours before the candle was snuffed out turning that promise over, bending and twisting it this way and that until it broke beneath his attentions. And he did not tell the Prior.

Then came the morning when he woke late to find HansJürgen already departed for the market, Bernardo fully dressed and insisting that even if he, Salvestro, would not do their friends at the Broken Wheel the courtesy of a simple visit, share a cup or two, and perhaps another two or three after that, and perhaps get blind drunk as the occasion demanded, then he, Bernardo, would be happy to leave him here, bleary-eyed and groggy from a night of troubled sleep, to be as miserable as he wished, but to do it alone, to which Salvestro nodded and may have grunted something before falling back on the scratchy sacking as Bernardo stomped out in a victorious huff, listening to the inevitable slamming of the door, the stamping down the passageway, then other noises within the hostel, an argument somewhere, raised voices, the cranking up of a bucket of water, his own breathing, soothing sound, wakeful human breathing, his own and Jörg's. They were alone. The Prior's voice sounded then, the words distinct and clear; he did not dream them. It was the eve of his departure.

"Salvestro. Will you hear my confession?"

Head down and elbows out, moving brusquely through a crowd that only Rome's summer heat could uncompact and atomize into these obstructive bodies and loose clods of citizenry through which he barged and bumped on his way down the Via Alessandrina, Lucillo's cheery wave ignored as he passed the *bancherotti,* uncaring of the wake of ill temper that trailed him down the street: Salvestro in flight again. He stopped at the bridge. Amongst the porters who shuffled toe to toe across the river, carrying boxes, barrels, crates of pigeons or apples, he was the porter who had shucked his load and found himself pursued by it, the vengeful baggage of the thing he had not done. Kneeling with Jörg in the darkness of the the Stick, he was the Prior's unconfessed confessor.

"I would not be the first," he said, "if foolishness is a sin. A great general once stood where I stand now, called the Lion by his men."

"I know of him," Salvestro said. It was unsettling to listen to a voice so close to him but the speaker invisible. Their heads were almost touching.

"Don't interrupt," said Jörg. "The Lion too saw the thing he most desired sink and disappear beneath the waves. The Devil too works miracles. You were mine, Salvestro. You were the pin to winkle out my brothers from their broken shell. You were the miracle sent me. . . ." He began to ramble then. The island and their journey from it took shape in the chamber's darkness, but broken into fragments and the fragments themselves frayed, unraveling in the Prior's preamble. "But I have proved very foolish," he resumed. "Foolishness is a sin I readily confess. Have you seen how the brothers laugh at me now? The other petitioners mock me, too. I hear them, though the saintly HansJürgen would deny it and have me afflicted with deafness. It is just that they laugh. I submit to the fool's penance which is mockery. I was blind before. It is only now that I see."

He paused there, and Salvestro wondered if he should say something. He heard the other man shift on his knees, drawing nearer to him, perhaps.

"I know of your trials before you led us to this place," Jörg said quietly. "On the island. HansJürgen thinks I know nothing of these things. I believed then that you were sent us to aid us in our labors, more fool me. . . . It was exactly otherwise. Our church crumbled to admit you, Salvestro. It was for you, not us. We are your last trial, do you see? Sometimes I see a little light, like a candle-flame, flickering and distant. It is your soul, but your soul as it will be. I know this. We are each other's sternest tests, you and I."

There was a short silence while Salvestro again debated whether he should speak.

"As it will be? As it will be when?"

"When you take us up again, dear Salvestro," Jörg replied. "When you lead us home."

So there was the Castel Sant'Angelo, crennellated and squatting on its slab. There was the crowded bridge below it and Salvestro on the bridge. He was leaning over the parapet at the point where he and Bernardo had spied Wulf, Wolf, and Wilf mudlarking amongst the pilgrims on the landing stage below. They had not been seen at the hostel in weeks now. He looked for them amongst the beggars and rowdy boys milling about on the riverbank. Little boats spilled out and lurched in the loose grip of the water, dark green and surfaced with glass. There was the Castle of the Squatting Toad and the Bridge of the Creeping Pilgrims and below them the rolling swelling river telling him, *tomorrow, and tomorrow, and tomorrow* . . . He quit his station there and walked without purpose or direction through the streets of Parione. He must have walked for hours, but his very aimlessness seemed to lead him inevitably to the river and westward along its banks to the Borgo, for there were no more tomorrows. Tomorrow they would be gone, and he had not told Father Jörg. The day seemed endless.

At the end of the Via dei Sinibaldi there was a short red-faced man sitting on a tall open-weave basket of pears. The man sweated and mopped his brow. Salvestro sat in the shade opposite. They exchanged glances and did not speak. The short man's partner arrived presently, and they toted the basket away between them. There was that. Then some women walked past and stared at him, sitting there on the ground in his finery, waiting. One spoke in an undertone and another one laughed. At him? Waiting for what? A gang of boys with a dog?

No. Though the dog sniffed his foot. He patted it on the head, and they all ran off up the street. He rubbed his knees and got to his feet. He had only to walk fifty yards to be in the hostel. The old fountain. The broken wall. The door to the hostel and the interior beyond the door. He had only to deliver his message and leave. In the Via dei Sinibaldi the armies of the sun were being routed by lengthening spears of late afternoon shadow. Chimneys, washing lines, and parapets cast

shady swords and shields on the ground. He advanced on the hostel. Two men
passed him. They were driving a mule.

It appeared that Lappi had concealed himself in some other part of the building, for the various alcoves and niches in which he was inclined to lie in wait for
his nerve-racked guests were empty. Salvestro peered about him at the staircases
on either side of the passage. The light from the doorway gave out after twenty
feet, and thereafter his progress was the usual fumbling grope, a cautious stumble-
with-handholds. Plaster crumbled at his touch and rattled on the flagstones. Salvestro's footfalls ground them to dust. Presently his fingers felt the wood of the
chamber door. It stood open. No lights. No sounds, either. He entered gingerly,
feeling for the tinderbox and candles that were kept beside the chest. The door
should have been locked, he thought, inching forward into the darkness. If there
was no one to safeguard their belongings, then the door . . . It was the tiniest of
sounds, the merest disturbance of the air, unseen, unguessed. A wall of muscle
seemed to strike his head, chest, legs, lift him off his feet, and hurl him back, the
floor slamming into his back and knocking the breath out of him. His head rose
dizzily. A leathery hand clamped itself to his face.

The crystal-moment is in here somewhere.

There are corridors and passageways, curves and corners, stains, stairs, intrin-
sic difficulty in the obstacles. But clarity will be found amongst these coordinates,
this lapsed geography. He is inside, and the darkness does not help.

Three men blocking the entrance to the back-chamber. Problem. He moves
sideways, up a flight of stairs. Think of the passage at the top as an overhanging
gantry and move quietly, with appropriate humility. Nothing is clear yet.

A door. The door? Surely yes. In here, then, wait for the clarity to come,
which it will, Salvestro-shaped and unsuspecting. He kits out the darkness with
remembered details: palliasses, a chest, pillars (no sweeping cuts with the sword), a
mad old man who is not here now. He would hear the breathing and the rustling
of his clothing as he breathed. No one here. Except himself, Rufo. Rufo waits.

Soon, the terrible cutting, the panic and struggling, blood and piss running in
their breeches . . .

Let us dispense with that. The approaching footsteps can be counted as they
intrude on his awareness and advance on his racked-up fury, twenty-two of them.
He is in the door now. Wind him first? Yes, but smother him, too, just in case.
Stick him in the guts and throat and leave. He is not quite himself when he does
these things; coincident with the man who pounces and stabs, but not the same
man. It has taken place, already happened, is done. He walks away and leaves his
man twitching in a flood of blood. He leaves a murderer brooding over a corpse.
Calm now. Someone passes him on the stairs. Someone rages in the back of the
building, "Out! Out, you barbarian!" Outside, the soft and fading sunlight is

blinding after the darkness in which he has ensconced himself, days or years of the dark and now this searing light, this heat-drenched Roman light.

He will wait for the big man where he waited for his companion. He might even sleep. Someone will find the cadaver, and the cries that follow will draw him to the small, ghoulish crowd that always gathers on occasions such as these. The lumpish weight will be hauled out in a blanket to be inspected by the sheriff or his man. There will be brief municipal formalities. Someone will identify the dead man.

All these things happen in the next hour, the shouts, the crowd, the body wrapped in a dirty sheet and attended by flies. He is calm, leaning over with the rest of them to get a look at the victim's face, no different from anyone else. An old woman is being led forward by officials. She looks bewildered and angrily defensive, as though they have accused her. She pulls the sheet down, and for a moment he thinks the light has thickened to pure heat, to a furnace that melts the dead man's face, for it is featureless at first, then deeply lined and creased, old. . . . The woman is sobbing now, and he searches the dead man's face for his chosen victim, tries to dredge those features from the cadaver, pull that face from this face. The heat will not have it, smoothing away eyes, nose, mouth, submerging his quarry in this ancient cadaver, encasing him in its transubstantiating inferno, a Romish mirage in which nothing lives save his error.

Sometimes the Shouting Woman would pull her smock over her head and parade naked for the petitioners of His Holiness. The Switzers would run to remove her, slapping her to the ground and carting her off, still shouting, then screaming, then silence. Sometimes Battista would follow the ill-natured cortege, offering alternate advice and abuse to the dimwit foreigners and their baggage. No one touched Battista. He was licensed, anointed somehow. (By whom?) On better and braver days he had attempted to interest the man in Mass at San Croce. He had discontinued these attempts, for Battista's laughter burned his ears and scalded his womanish soul. Sometimes Jörg would walk about the courtyard, conversing amicably with the other petitioners who knew and liked him. Sometimes he sat out the hours in impervious silence. Sometimes the doors opened, and sometimes there were alms. The sun burned and they bought water from a man who slung two churns from opposite ends of a yoke carried on his shoulders. They waited for His Holiness, and His Holiness did not come.

That then was the contract. A little one-sided, perhaps, HansJürgen observed to himself and in private. Today a loutish youth had shouted down from the loggia overlooking the courtyard that His Holiness was hunting, had not been in Rome at all for the past two weeks and would not be returning for another two days, so why didn't they all just bugger off? A calumny. Or the truth. Impossible to know: hence the contract.

"At present," said Jörg, "we are a little more than seventy paces from the gate of the Cortile di San Damaso, and soon you will be able to glimpse the Chapel of Saint Cecilia on your left. The water-trough for the herdsmen is ahead of us and to our right, thirty paces away, perhaps."

"Yes," said HansJürgen, and slowed his pace. They had already passed the water-trough and in fact were not in the piazza at all. It was late in the afternoon. The streets were emptying.

"The alley already? Brisk work, Brother HansJürgen!"

He had attempted, some weeks before, to persuade the Prior to place a hand on his shoulder for guidance. The suggestion had been rebuffed. The commentary on their whereabouts had begun shortly after, and he strode along, pointing left and right with such confidence that HansJürgen found himself looking vainly at the indicated hovels or open patches of sky for some trace of the palazzo of the Cardinal of San Giorgio or the campanile of Santa Maria, which his own eyes told him were not there and never had been. A second city had grown in the Prior's blindness, a place of shifting landmarks and whimsical streets, of walking churches and galloping palaces: Jörg's Rome. Its apex was the Stick.

"Well, here we are," Jörg said, still ten feet shy of the entrance, necessitating a discreetly managed diagonal from HansJürgen. Within, their roles reversed, and he found himself being guided by the confident footsteps of the blind man as they moved through the darkness of the passageway.

"Do you hear that, Brother HansJürgen?"

A muffled grunt issued from the chamber. A fat wedge of candlelight showed through the part-open door. A thud. A grunt. Another thud, some scuffling. Jörg threw open the door and swept in. He followed.

Hanno was holding him down with one hand over his mouth while Georg dealt the blows. The grunts came from Salvestro, whose eyes bulged as the fists dug into his stomach. Gerhardt stood over them, looking up from the beating only when Georg stopped.

"Thieving!" he exclaimed in explanation, his outrage directed as much at Jörg as the floored victim, who flopped about on the floor, retching and trying to catch his breath. "Caught him red-handed with his nose in your precious chest."

HansJürgen saw that the chest stood open. He walked across the room and rummaged within, rousing a tinny clatter from the cache. It was almost empty, and he said as much. Salvestro gasped and choked, trying to signal something to him.

"Your monkey's turned on you, Prior. You were warned it would happen." Gerhardt made no effort to mask his satisfaction.

"Nonsense," Jörg replied calmly. "If you are speaking of Salvestro, then I am sure he has not acted without good reason."

"Where's the silver, then?" Hanno spoke up, his jaw jutting aggressively.

The three of them stared at Jörg, who answered, "I am sure if he has taken it, then it is for safekeeping. He is our loyal servant, is that not true, Salvestro?"

Salvestro coughed and tried to say something. HansJürgen heard "sem," or "sthem"; some unintelligible gurgle. Coughing followed, then, more clearly, "It's them. I caught *them.*"

Georg raised his fist at this piece of insolence. A shake of Gerhardt's head stayed his hand.

Jörg's voice was tolerant, almost genial. "Come now, Salvestro. Simply replace what you have hidden."

Hanno released him, and Salvestro got to his feet. "I took nothing," he said.

"He's lied to you from the start, you stupid old man," Gerhardt spat.

"Stop this foolishness now, Salvestro," said Jörg. Then he added more gently, "Do you forget how we spoke this morning?"

"Ask yourself why he's here at this hour. Ask that," said Gerhardt.

"I don't have it," said Salvestro.

"I shall ask one more time only . . . ," Jörg began.

"You thought he'd stop at this?" Gerhardt held up the silver scabbard, which Salvestro lunged for. He was knocked to the ground by Hanno. "This was in his mattress."

"It's mine," protested Salvestro.

Gerhardt looked down at him. "We pulled you out of the sea, fed you, clothed you, and this is how you repay us? You're the same savage you always were. Thief! The islanders should have drowned you at birth."

"Give it to him," said Jörg. His voice was cold and hard. "Now let him up."

HansJürgen watched Salvestro take the scabbard and rise. The other three monks held their tongues.

"Come here," said Jörg. He extended a hand, which rested first on Salvestro's head, but then slithered gently over the man's face. "Do not think I cannot read you," he murmured, though this seemed directed principally at himself. Then, "We have come a long way to fail here." HansJürgen could see that he was struggling to control himself. Then, "I shall ask you for the last time. . . ." Salvestro was already shaking his head. Jörg's arm dropped and his face hardened.

"Go," said Jörg.

"I came back to—" Salvestro began to say.

"Go!" repeated Jörg.

Salvestro protested again, his face contorting oddly to HansJürgen's eye. Jörg erupted then, his mouth twisted with anger, bellowing at the wretch as though his mere presence were suddenly unendurable, "Out, out! You barbarian!"

The five men watched Salvestro hang his head for a second. When he looked up again his expression was as blank as ever. He paused at the door, but Jörg did not turn around. There was silence. The barbarian made a quick, contemptuous movement, and the scabbard clattered across the floor. HansJürgen bent to pick it up. When he straightened, Salvestro was gone.

Ah, the deer-nibbled verdure of La Magliana and the Campo di Merlo, its fuzzed and furred undulations, its grassy creases and meadows cropped close as the pubic scrub of a Venetian courtesan. Such turf! Such happy ground! Heat-sopped by day, it now repays the sun's largesse with nocturnal emissions of warming air that blanket the *campagna* in earthy fugs and fogs: the night air and its pleasant smells. The fatly black and languid, bendy Tiber advances and recedes, the flowing moat of abandoned bastions and never built castle walls. A barge is moored there, pennanted and decked with bunting embroidered with the *pallia* of the Medici, ready for the passage downriver to Ostia on the day after tomorrow. Little stands of trees stand in stooks, stalkily bundled and clumped by giants. And—hark now—a dulcimer.

Or a hackbrett, perhaps. Tinkling plinks and plonks drift and twist, fading and returning, the very gentlest of bugles heralding tomorrow's slaughter. The windows of the Sala dei Muse are glowing slabs of light hung high in the blackness, a row of luminous interruptions emoting the jingle-jangle of high spirits and homey entertainment. Cowering in their copses and thickets, giddy deer tremble at the papal merrymaking, rabbits scrabble, and squirrels scramble for cover. The badgers are inconsolable with dread. An ominous python of ox-drawn baggage carts topped with the prelates belonging to that baggage, of noisy pike-bearing Switzers in their green-and-gold livery, of horses, of the Pope's carriage, this dragged itself here two weeks ago for the purpose of having fun. Now horses whinny in the part-built stables, the ostlers bury themselves in straw, and the workmen hired to finish the upper story wrap their habits tight about their limbs and sleep the sleep of the blessed, arranged in a snoozing defensive semicircle about their trowels, lines, plumbs, and picks. (Builder-ostler relations have been vexed.) Tomorrow is a day of idleness, their foreman being in Rome, his two sidekicks, too. . . .

Across the fosse with its slimy trickle of water, westward a few hundred yards, the *gazzara* is softly astir with billings and cooings, feathery palpitations and columbine heartache. The heron retains his cool, sitting for hour after hour on his perch while all around him the cages of partridges, woodcocks, snipes, landrails, pheasants, and magpies rustle with their occupants' apprehension. The dulcimer, or hackbrett, plays on. The killing-ground was cordoned with white sailcloth earlier in the day, two thousand braccia of brilliant, animal-blinding white to funnel the game onto the arrows and lances of the huntsmen. Leo likes to hunt in the French manner, and firearms are forbidden.

And there will be a surprise, a bristly and bad-tempered one. Boccamazza is attending to it now. He looks down on the beast, snorting and snuffling there in its pit, squealing vilely as half a dozen brawny and leather-clad farmhands tussle and grapple with it, wrestling it down and pinning it still while the paint is hurriedly applied, the appendage tied on by his skeptical helpers.

"Are you sure we've got this right?" one calls up as the animal flexes and strains.

Boccamazza looks again at his master's sketch. Monstrous. He nods. "It is intended to amuse," he says.

He is unamused himself, this Pope's chief huntsman, preparing elaborate practical jokes in the middle of the night. Come first light there will be the beaters to marshal: an unhappy mix of resentful Switzers and overexcited peasants. The hawks have yet to be chosen (gyrfalcons and sparrow hawks, some peregrines, kestrels?) and the hunters themselves graded diplomatically with the least inept to the fore and His Holiness, naturally, foremost. The men climb out of the pit in a scramble of arms, legs, sweat, ill feeling, bafflement, and droppings. He has an eye for droppings, the wormy slicks, pellets, piles, and spatters of the quarry. These are gray-brown smudges on the leather jerkins of his men, a crumbly paste. Technically, Boccamazza thinks to himself, remembering the fumbling chase of a few minutes ago, these would be fumets. He strides across the springy turf, his brain busy with the roles of tomorrow's players and the vagaries of the hunt. The dulcimer—or hackbrett—winds down. The lights go out. The palazzo and adjacent stables are black mausoleums against the lightening blue-black sky. A mile away, the staked screens of sailcloth are luminous ribbons defining the V of the killing-ground. A happily preeminent knoll stands at their thwarted junction. Put the Pope on that, thinks Boccamazza.

The next morning dawns, burning fog out of the hollows, lifting dew off the turf. A line forms at the back of the woods with a *Hey*, a *Ho!* and many a rustic whoop. We're off—*Forward!*—our whereabouts being hereabouts, a-hunting in the greenwood.

There are bushes and trees—myrtles, oaks, elms, and elders, willows nearer the river—juniper-scrub and patches of thorns. The beaters are armed with skillets and sticks, which fill the air with clanging and banging; there's hardly room for their shouting, let alone their clumsy footsteps. So, a noisy peroration: the leaves hang like shriveled bags of washing or superbly camouflaged bats. A ferret is sighted. Hooray! And there's a pigeon. . . . Yahoo!

Yahoo-ooo. . . .

Faint cries and irregular shouts reach Leo's ears, the singing of the beaters to the accompanying clangor of pot and pan. *A dulcimer? A hackbrett . . . ?* Perched atop his knoll, he squints through a tubular eyepiece at the sailcloths that run to left and right, widening until they embrace the khaki bulge of the woods. Set before him on their cadges, the hawks of the lure bate and flutter, still hooded but sensing the killing to come. The hawks of the fist are calm for the moment, goshawks for hare, rabbit, and pheasant, sparrow hawks for mice. His fellow huntsmen surround him in a semicircle, settled on faldstools and cushions: Cardinals d'Aragona and Cornaro, Bibbiena and Dovizio, three visiting bishops, their chamberlains and valets, the ambassadors Vich and Faria, who are only here on sufferance, until he conceived his masterly joke, that is. . . . Now they are as indispensable as Fra Mariano, or Baraballa, who last night accepted Dovizio's wager of twenty scudi to swallow a headless eel, then vomited it into the fireplace, still wriggling. What a good sport. *Otium, negotium, otium, negotium . . .* What fun it is to have fun!

Soon the first magpies show as black-and-white flurries in the cover of the trees. A snipe shoots out and flies south over the advancing line of beaters, descending to settle behind them. But the din is unstoppable, an impenetrable barrier sweeping up voles, ferrets, rabbits, hares, wild goats, roebucks, driving teal and heron alike to the meadow, where thistles shiver in the light breeze and the huntsmen wait. The hawkers are already swinging their lures, an array of mad windmills blowing the scent of dead pigeon across the field. Leo pats his cuirass through his robes. He wriggles his toes.

"Send in the hawks," he shouts as a lone heron flaps sadly up into the sunlight, followed by woodcocks, more snipes, two ducks, and a superabundance of pigeons. Some pheasants amble out of the undergrowth, take one look at the greeting-party, and amble back in again. A cast of gyrfalcons is unbrailed for the ducks. Leo follows them through his scope, which he glues to his eye and waves this way and that like a thick brass wand, tracking upward as the birds reach their pitch, then seem to hang for a second before stooping out of the sun. A midair explosion of feathers, and the four birds are suddenly only two. A brace of dead ducks thumps on the turf as the predators return, exchanging their pelts for the perch. The heron, meanwhile, rings upward, ever higher to the empty spaces of the air where even the hawk's wing will not reach. He's not there yet, old yellow-beak, but flapping hard, climbing high, still unruffled by the ridiculous commotion below.

Partridges, magpies, teal, larks, several crows, landrails, more pheasants, and lots more pigeons, all are shortly clattering reluctantly upward into hawk-infested airspace. Some jays, too, and the first, most panicky of the game (rabbits). The goshawks and tiercels are set to work, shuttling back and forth between their airy playground and the hawkers themselves, who whistle and call to their charges, swing lures, and hold their arms at odd, falcon-enticing angles. Two half-tamed haggards are caught crabbing and leashed to their cadges in disgrace. The feathery dead become a pile, then a mound.

Well, this is a jolly prelude, thinks the Pope. He beams at his courtiers, who beam back. Leno waves. He does not wave back. Leno arrived this morning, uninvited, under the pretext of checking on the quality of the work on the stables. The work on the stables has been pronounced satisfactory. Why has Leno not left? Apparently Leno's foreman has disappeared with two of his henchmen, os-

tensibly to find Leno in Rome. Leno's foreman has not been paid. He would like
to ask the man why his workmen are dressed as monks, but Leno has not been
paid, either. Leno is waiting for his foreman to return, so he says, but mostly he is
waiting to be paid. So the Pope does not wave back. Enough of that. Where's
Vich? He scans amongst the little marquees erected to the rear of his knoll. . . .
There. Talking to Faria. Rufo will report tonight, perhaps. Or tomorrow at Ostia.
He will ask the man the exact time of death; it might be now. A mere fifteen
miles away in the Borgo, it might be happening right now. He gazes happily at
the neatly staked sailcloths, the grassy meadow, the trees, the blue sky with its
blazing sun, and the hawks wheeling and hovering in perfect silence. He is happy,
for he loves to hunt. *Loves* it.

Aloft, the slaughter continues.

Below, an unbidden popish *pensée* appears at the edge of his thoughts like the
single black cloud portending a storm: Amalia. Did they drown her in a bog,
those cutthroats of his? Or was she torn apart by wild beasts? By bears, perhaps.
Or wolves. Poor little mite.

He catches sight of the ambassadors, who have moved a little way forward of
his knoll and now stroll in the meadow to his left, Vich's movements more graceful than he remembers, while Faria's stocky figure plods at his side. Are they arm
in arm?

"Fatso! Fatso!"

Bibbiena and Dovizio swagger across the grass carrying jugs of wine and
crossbows, of which he disapproves and yet reluctantly permits, being no bow-
man himself.

"Good morning, Supreme Pontiff!" They hail him cheerily and resume their
chant, singing it out across the thistly sward. He eyes the woods, then reaches for
his scope, scanning left and right. Something's wrong. . . .

"What is going on!" he shouts, suddenly perplexed. Heads come up, but no
one answers. "Well?" Still no one speaks; is he really so fearsome? "Nothing is
going on!" he elucidates. Puzzled faces turn blankly to the woods, and then Boccamazza appears at his side, assuring him that a lull in the beaters' progress is for
the best, allowing the beasts of the wood to spread out ahead of the marchers and
shouters; ensuring a gradual serving up of furry and hairy victims, a steady stream
is better than a glut. Besides, the beaters are having their lunch. Should not he be
having his?

Lunch. Yes.

Strolling back to his knoll, he coopts Boccamazza and Vich, asking the former if the wind has not changed, the latter if he is enjoying his day out here on
the Campo di Merlo, hunting with the Pope.

"No," says Boccamazza.

"I only hope our plainer entertainment will please you as much at Ostia tomorrow," says Vich.

Clever, thinks Leo. But clever enough? Vich bows politely and walks away.

"Did you prepare the beast as I commanded?" he inquires of Boccamazza in a whisper.

His huntsman nods, adding, "You have only to give the signal, Holiness."

A second later, the dolorous clanging starts up again, the dinging and donging more distinct than earlier, the first shouts coming into earshot as the unseen beaters shake the ants from their laps, loosen their belts, and advance. Wildlife flees in the general direction of Leo.

Presently, a premature goat emerges hesitantly from the trees and eyes the sailcloth, the little marquees, the Pope enthroned on his knoll, the idle courtiers and members of his *famiglia,* hawkers and their hawks, servants carrying water-churns and weaponry, cardinals, ambassadors . . . The goat retreats.

Then reappears, standing there for a little longer the second time. Then it retreats again. This happens several times until capricious ill temper gets the better of caution; it springs forward with a frisky gambol and takes its stand in the middle of the field, back legs planted rigidly, front ones digging at the turf, curly horns at the ready for the spindly adversaries milling about fifty yards away. Someone shoots it with a crossbow.

This sets the pattern.

Rabbits are particularly entertaining, scampering about in maddened circles pursued by hunters trying to dash their brains out with clubs. Ferrets too demonstrate a certain low cunning, lying doggo in the longer grasses until squished underfoot, and three more goats provide a midafternoon highlight by butting d'Aragona so hard, he has to be carried off on a stretcher. Someone cuts a badger in two. Quite interesting.

Naturally there are lulls and *longeurs* in which no rabbit deigns to poke its twitching nose out of the undergrowth, when the brachets and tracker dogs roll about on the grass soliciting belly-scratches or run around sniffing one another's behinds. The hawks keep themselves occupied by picking off small rodents, but for the huntsmen themselves these are disconcerting intervals, not really long enough for a game of checkers or even a cup of wine. They find themselves making awkward conversation, toting their bloodstained swords and crossbows like murderers caught red-handed by a chatty and oft avoided neighbor. "Nice day." *"Lovely* day." That kind of thing. The ground has become quite marshy in places, and the servants picking up the kills slide about in bloody, muddy morasses. Bibbiena and Dovizio have stuffed some pillows under their tunics and parade about with eyepieces protruding from their heads, introducing themselves as "the Anti-Popes of the *Campagna."* Everyone finds this very amusing.

Including Leo, who claps and laughs with the best of them while his thoughts drift between Rome and Prato, back and forth. . . .

Amalia was eaten by a wolf; he is more or less convinced of this, there being a scarcity of bears in the Florentine *contado.* A wolf, yes. . . . Or foxes! A good-size fox would make short work of a poor little helpless girl. He shifts awkwardly on his chair. His buttocks are sweaty. The old trouble flared up again on the journey from Rome, two nights of horrid internal itching and several torturous sessions on the pot. With howling. Very bad. But foxes, there was a thought. He trains his eyepiece on the bloodstained meadow. Not a fox in sight.

Suddenly a massively antlered stag bursts out of the woods. It pauses for a moment, looks to its left and right. No one seems to have noticed it yet, but how can that be? Leo stands up and shouts. A few heads turn. The dogs look up. The animal stamps, once, twice. Someone raises his crossbow, but hesitantly, for no one else is doing anything, just looking dumbly about as the stag stamps again, then hurtles off to the right, leaps cleanly over the sailcloth, and is gone. The huntsmen stare at their shoes. A baffled silence descends on the killing-ground. Now how did that happen?

And the girl would be unconfessed. . . . Meaning limbo, though surely she had reached the sunnier slopes of purgatory by now. How many sins is it possible to commit before one's eighth birthday? For the knaves who led her there, the hellish inferno. Forever. And beginning tonight.

"Holiness?" Boccamazza stands before him, broad-chested in a leather jerkin. Leo gestures for him to speak. "The beaters are almost through . . ." The sentence is left hanging.

"What?" He is blank for a moment, then understands. Of course, the finale. His splendid prank. He raises his eyepiece. The dogs are being recaptured and leashed. His men are gathering the last of the rabbit carcasses from the small blood-puddles that dot the meadow. Vich and Faria are inconspicuous amongst the twenty or so huntsmen who have drawn closer together in some obscure re-action to the stag's escape. Boccamazza's back appears, a large leather curtain as he moves across Leo's line of magnified sight. Leo snorts and chuckles. The hunts-men look to Boccamazza, then to him as the man points back to his knoll. He stands, and a ragged cheer goes up. Then another, the second containing ironic and perhaps derisive grace notes, led as it is by Bibbiena and Dovizio, who wave their eyepieces about with renewed vigor and thump their pillowed chests. With cautious steps he descends from the knoll, takes horn and lance from a waiting serving man, and advances on his fellow huntsmen. A third, very complexly nu-anced cheer reaches into the air and disperses into its several impulses: welcome, mockery, formal politeness, vague recrimination at his tardiness, now rectified. The Pope will take the field.

"Let us give thanks to God for this fine day's hunting," he announces as he draws near. They form a crescent around him. Behind them he can see Bocca-mazza disappearing into the woods. He talks of God's bounty and camouflages a giggle beneath an unconvincing sneeze, then continues, pointing to Vich and Faria, who are skulking near the back. "Tomorrow begins the quest for a beast stranger than any we have chased today. Our beloved allies Dom João and Fer-nando the Catholic, through their loyal officers here, Dr. Faria and Don Jerònimo da Vich, have pledged to bring their Pope an animal. . . ."

Soon his little audience catches the mood, chuckling along as his description of the animal mutates and imaginary beasts run riot through their minds' eyes, their bizarre appendages and improbable limbs flapping and flopping about. The servants pass around cold meats and cups of wine. Everyone is enjoying this, except perhaps the ambassadors. You think I am a fool, thinks the Pope, catching Vich's eye. He smiles and waves his hunting-horn.

Behind the juniper bushes, behind a stand of flowering elders behind the juniper, behind a thicket of peeling ash behind the juniper and elders . . . in the woods, in effect, Boccamazza kicks his way through clinging undergrowth, sidesteps fallen timber, watches out for ankle-twisting hollows concealed by deceptive depots of leaf mold, looks up now and then at patches of late afternoon sky that appear brighter in the shade of the forest, and arrives at the pit. His men are sprawled around it. The animal snuffles and turns as though chasing its tail.

"Ready?" he says.

"It's rubbed most of the paint off," says one of his men in a bored tone.

"Well, put some more on," Boccamazza snaps crisply.

The men look at one another.

"Just pour it on from up here. Come on. Jump to it. . . ."

The animal does not like having the paint poured on it. It gets angry.

". . . and although there is little in the sight of man or beast that can still surprise a Pope, the actions of his predecessors perhaps excepted" —wary laughter— "I confess myself amazed at the discovery of such an animal, not in the deserts of the Indies, nor in the wastes of Africa, nor in the hot and pestilential swamps of the New World, nor in any of those unimaginable territories whose jurisdiction—it is no secret—will be settled by this creature's procurement. . . . Portugal or Spain? Our suspense is boundless, almost unendurable, and to leaven the wait the Lord, or the Devil, has, well . . ." He raises his arms in helpless acceptance of his good fortune, of all their good fortunes. "Well, let my own happy amazement now be yours. . . ."

The assembly signals its titillation and ticklish puzzlement in sidelong glances at the two orators, who are reduced to pretending that they are in on the joke (whatever it is), nodding and smiling complaisantly. The Pope raises his horn to his lips. A strangled fart squirts skyward and is carried on mild zephyrs over the meadow and into the woods to buzz euphoniously in Boccamazza's ears. The Pope waits. They all wait. The same mild zephyrs ripple the topmost edges of the sailcloths, jiggle blood-soaked and stainless blades of grass, cool the brows of the spectators now staring expectantly at the trees, pass away. Vague crashing noises sound from within the wood. Getting louder and more distinct, branches snapping and whatnot. The specifics are unimportant, for a moment later it's there, in plain view, and in the moment following, every one of the huntsmen, the servants behind them, the hawkers and men of the *gazzara,* are silent, the same question framing itself silently behind every one of those furrowed, sweat-beaded, or zephyr-cooled brows: What is it?

To begin with, it is big. Not cow-big, but certainly bigger than a goat. It stands its ground, fifty yards away in front of the trees, being big, or fat, or obscenely well-muscled, and thus dangerous. Let us call it dangerous and add deceptively dangerous, for it also looks ridiculous and mirth-worthy, as the reaction of the huntsmen (two ambassadors excepted) shortly proves. Boccamazza, emerging cautiously from the trees, sees several of the huntsmen bent double with laughter. Cardinal Cornaro has collapsed altogether. It is gray—this too is an important clue—and very bristly. More huntsmen fall over and start rolling around on the grass. Perhaps this angers the animal further, or perhaps it was the paint, or perhaps it is naturally angry. Anyway, it has tusks. And from a standing start it seems to reach an extraordinary velocity in less than two seconds, which is when Boccamazza and Leo have the same simultaneous thought: that this is a big, bristly, dangerous, angry animal, and it is charging toward the main body of laughing and nonlaughing ambassadorial idiots, armed with teeth, tusks, and—perhaps this should have been mentioned earlier—a horn on the end of its nose. A wild boar, with extras.

The beast swerves, cantering through a tight circle before gathering speed and charging again. The horn wiggles and shudders, clearly affixed by an agency other than Mother Nature. Glue, possibly. It swerves again, as though it cannot hold its line. . . . Has it been drugged?

No, it's simply trying to get this ridiculous stump of wood off its perfectly good snout, get back into the woods, and recommence snuffling about, scraping up roots, and terrorizing the wildlife in preparation for eating them in the winter. The boar is not really interested in the sticklike creatures who have now decided to chase it about the field (their interpretation) or hide from it by following its tail (the boar's interpretation), led by a somewhat blubbery specimen with a telescope stuck to its face. A comforting boar-thought: You're never alone in your humiliation, even one so recherché as having an unwanted foreign object sticking out of your head. There's always *someone*. . . .

Amalia, thinks Leo.

Again. So obvious, how had he failed to see it? Not a bear, not a wolf, not a—perish the thought—fox. Rufo will be killing them now. Telling him later. Not cold, not hunger, not drowning in a bog. No, no, no. . . . A boar. A boar ripped her open with its tusks somewhere in the wilderness outside Prato. He doesn't care that his audience still laughs and joshes in procession behind him as he huffs and puffs after the quarry. It's heading for the sailcloth, there, dashing across the disk of vision he is reduced to by his eyeglass, reappearing, lost again, so he roves left and right, up and down the field, a bit out of breath, this pudgy Atalanta, *Father warned me of fatness* . . . then a great shout from behind him, the idiots, a triumphal chant led by Bibbiena and Dovizio: "Fatso! Fatso! On, the fierce virgin. . . ." He advances, lance held high so that its tip will glitter in the sun before plunging down, so that the beast will see it—there, caught up in the sailcloth, struggling to free itself and failing—so that it will know it was he who wielded the revenger's steel: Leo. The killer of the killer of helpless, hairless Amalia. Hobbled and trussed in cloth smirched with gray paint, the boar begins to squeal. He steadies the lance over the muscled bulge of its withers. Know that it was I who did this, he urges the entangled beast. And tell God when you see Him.

The lance comes down, all his weight behind it, piercing pelt, hide, flesh, muscle. Behind him, his courtiers have fallen silent, or he no longer hears them. He imagines the weapon's length sinking deeper and deeper, passing all the way through as one is supposed to, the point driving out the other side and finding there a second strange resistance, but he pushes harder and harder, he is irresistible, and the second hide rips suddenly, the flesh beneath is soft as cheese, the bones brittle as china, splintering with the same sound as the bones of the Pratesi. He has the two of them skewered through the neck, decoy and quarry: the beast he can see and the beast he cannot. He feels their twitching nerves and tendons shuddering through the wood of the shaft.

That evening, Baraballa is served a fricassee of squirrel spiced delicately with rosemary, which he munches bones and all. His Holiness washes down three roasted pigeons with goblets of Tuscan wine as thick and dark as blood. Carried in on his stretcher, Cardinal d'Aragona forces down a vegetable broth. Everyone else eats boar.

After supper there is, as there always is, good music to aid the digestion. Three lutes and a dulcimer (it is almost certainly a dulcimer) jangle and plink their various ways through delicate airs while the huntsmen of La Magliana burp, fart, and compare relative atrocities. Most of the rabbits have been given to the beaters and the rodents to the dogs. No one mentions the stag. As the evening grows late, candles are lit and the windows, which face southwest, darken insensibly until the rich pinks of the sunset are replaced by darkness. The talk turns to the morrow and who will sit where on the papal barge, then to the animal filling their stomachs, then to the animal that the animal filling their stomachs was presumably intended to ape. Baraballo is persuaded to do an imitation, but it is so inept that the Pope threatens to spike him for real to add the lacking verisimilitude, always a problem in circumstances such as these, when time, though it is counted with pumping lungs and hearts that tick and tock away the minutes, has no real business in hand except to pass. So time passes, and the hackbrett plays, and no one quotes Pliny, or leaves, or notices the absence of the lutes. It is almost midnight before Faria, as it were, happens upon Don Jerònimo standing alone under the fresco of Apollo.

"To beasts, horned or otherwise." Faria raises his drink. Both men take a sip, watching each other over the rims of their goblets.

"To their victims," retorts Vich. They drink again.

"Is everything in place for the embarkation?"

Vich shrugs. "Antonio is your creature. He gives me pretty answers that mean nothing. Tomorrow he gives our Pope a pretty ship with pretty sailors—"

"That mean nothing."

Vich does not reply. Faria follows his glance across the room. Leo is laughing at a joke of Dovizio's.

"We are being indiscreet," says Faria, but Vich does not look away.

Faria murmurs, "He knows. . . ."

Leo catches Don Jerònimo's eye. The Spaniard raises his goblet to the robed figure, who smiles back uncertainly.

"Of course he does," says Vich.

The river narrowed beneath the Ponte Sant'Angelo. A dank tongue of black dirt poked out the embankment and jutted into the water as far as the first pier of the bridge. Mostly invisible to the passersby above, the orange glow of small fires cast out over the water might nevertheless be seen. There might be heard shouting and sometimes fighting.

A similar shelf of land on the west bank extended farther upstream and was used as a landing stage by the watermen who ferried pilgrims up and down the river. By day the west bank bustled with activity while the east bank was almost deserted. A few crates were scattered about there, perhaps too some bundles of rags that now and again would rise, yawn, and stretch before succumbing again to their stupor. The watermen, by and large, left them alone, for the beggars of the Borgo were a rough crew, suspicious even of each other but capable of uniting against a common enemy when provoked. Having nothing, they had nothing to lose and were known to fight like animals, their crutches doubling as clubs. Julius had sent a troop of Switzers down to clear them out and had his soldiers returned to him with broken heads and, in one case, missing a nose. Under the bridge was their territory, where they shambled between the fires that blackened the stone arch above, where they fought, men and women both, where they shivered in the winter and sweated in the summer, where Salvestro, unable to think of anywhere better, brought a drunken Bernardo to spend their last night in Rome.

Stumbling down the bank, panting with effort, for Bernardo was sloppy as a bag of toads, he saw them crouching in the red glow or moving about like bears, huge and unsteady, their shadows jumbled together on the walls of the embankment and the piers of the bridge.

"Who're you?" His challenger seemed to rise out of the ground. He stood a full head higher than Salvestro, his voice thick with drink. Salvestro started to talk and was soon cut off.

"Dommi! Over 'ere! Couple of gentlemen looking for lodgings." He slurred the word "lodgings."

Murderer disguised as sheep, Salvestro thought as "Dommi" approached. Animal skins had been thrown over him. He had then been baled in string. He punched Salvestro in the face, and Bernardo promptly collapsed. Dommi looked at him curiously. "Shame," he said. "The size on him might have saved you a kicking."

Sacking flapping around their ankles, other beggars shambled over to watch the promised kicking. It commenced, painfully enough, with a punt to the groin. Salvestro leveled himself slowly to the ground. There followed a back heel to the top of the head. Someone said, "Nice clothes," and someone else growled, "I'm having that doublet," and someone else again, someone with a high squeaky voice or someone with three high squeaky voices, added:

"Hey!"

"It's Salvestro!"

"Leave him alone, Dommi!"

Wulf, Wolf, and Wilf were hopping about, sparrowlike in their cut-down habits, dancing over Salvestro while Dommi cursed them foully but with little conviction. Then they discovered Bernardo. Instantly they formed a circle, raised their arms, and began to chant slowly, "Ber-nar-do-oo! Rosserus! Ber-nar-do-oo! Rosserus!" Bernardo snored on.

Dommi interrupted the kicking to consider this. "You can stay one night," he said, feet planted to either side of Salvestro's head. "See that bit of wall?" Salvestro nodded gingerly. "You sleep there." Dommi stepped backward, reached for something behind him, then swung it over his head. Salvestro cowered and tried to raise an arm. The object landed with a loud bang an inch short of his nose. Dommi patted it. "See this crate? I'm going to sit on it, right here, and I'm going to watch you all night, and if you annoy me, I'm going to kick you again. I'm going to kick you till your guts come out your arse and then I'm going to strangle you with them. That sound fair to you?"

Salvestro nodded.

"Good," said Dommi. "Glad you see it that way."

"What about his clothes?" a voice protested. "I could use that—"

"Shut up," said Dommi.

Salvestro crawled slowly over to the wall. Small, sharp-beaked birds were hatching out his head. His groin was a cleft of floating pain that extended from his stomach to his knees. He rolled over and collapsed. One by one, the beggars too keeled over or rolled about on the earth until they found a piece of ground that suited them. A man with one arm snuggled up to an older woman, the two grunted and tussled for a few minutes, then fell silent. Wulf, Wolf, and Wilf eventually gave up their chanting. Dommi sat on his crate, watching him.

It was very late, but, watched as he was by a man for whom annoyance was sufficient cause for a brisk disemboweling, Salvestro could not sleep. What constituted "annoyance"? Snoring? He closed his eyes and listened to the rise and fall of Bernardo's snores, but his mind raced ahead to the morrow, where a ship awaited them both, passage away from this place where he had no place, this Ro-ma.

"Nobody wants us," said Dommi after an hour or more of silence. He put the accent on the first word, as though it had taken many effortful trials to achieve so complete a state of unwantedness. Salvestro, as awake as ever, opened one eye warily. "That's who *we* are," Dommi continued, growing more vehement. "We're the people nobody wants."

Some response seemed to be required. Neither sympathy nor congratulation sounded fitting. . . . Would silence provoke the promised kicking? Salvestro remembered the ruffians who made their home in the ruins and began to tell Dommi of the encounter.

"We know about them," the man cut him off. There was silence again. Salvestro tried a different tack. Perhaps he should respond in kind?

"We're explorers . . . ," he began.

"We know about you, too," Dommi said. "We know all about you two. Hear things, we do. Remember them. You're a pair of clowns hired for Fat Bastard up there." He glanced over his shoulder in the direction of the Castel Sant'Angelo. "Pair of bloody clowns."

Both men looked across the river at the dark stump of the Pope's fortress, which loomed over the river. By night it appeared more massive than ever, as though it did not contain rooms, halls, passages, and cellars but was solid stone throughout. Then something caught Salvestro's eye, a movement on the opposite bank. The ground from the embankment to the river's edge seemed to be moving, rippling and raising ridges in the mud as though it were being plowed, but from beneath.

"Rats," said Dommi. "They didn't used to come down here. Now there's more of 'em every night." The rats covered the ground in a silent blanket of furry bodies, slithering and scrambling over one another. There might have been thousands, or tens of thousands. "Look at the size of them," commented Dommi, not watching them now, but watching Salvestro. "They're Borgo rats." He spat. "Fat Bastard's rats." The river washed and sploshed against the piers of the bridge. They heard sheep-bells somewhere, far away. But no squealing. No squeaking. Clambering and sprawling over one another's bodies, the rats did not make a sound.

He must have slept. He awoke to the faintest lightening in the blackness of the sky. A solitary boat carrying a solitary passenger was passing under the far arch of the bridge. A mist had settled on the water, as thick and white as smoke. Dommi was still there, awake on his crate. He rubbed his eyes, thought about getting up, decided against it, and dozed. When he came to again, Dommi was gone and the first boats had appeared on the opposite bank. The rats had disappeared.

A tall figure wearing an elaborate hat and ornamental sword climbed carefully down the steps, where he paused to inspect the terrain. He tested the ground with the toe of his shoe, then stepped forward cautiously. The watermen were unloading planks and laying them over the worst of the mud patches to form a gangway from the steps to the water's edge. The man waited patiently for them to finish. Salvestro sat up stiffly and looked around for Bernardo. He was sleeping soundly next to a heap of tangled limbs belonging to Wulf, Wolf, and Wilf. He woke the big man gently.

"I was having a dream," Bernardo protested blearily.

"Come on," said Salvestro, gesturing across the river. "Don Antonio's already here."

There was a bridge, the river, three snoozing boys, and an empty crate. The dream was already fading. There had been no dogs in it, nor rocks. A breathing heap of rags groaned and rolled over some feet away. Bernardo looked about him in perplexity.

"Where am I?" he asked.

The foreman's mallet could still be heard, its dry reports signaling the soundness of his construction as he moved methodically along the benches, bending and tapping, gradually ascending the stepped tiers of the stand for the second time that morning.

He had begun at daybreak, and when he had reached the little platform on the top he had stopped and looked first west out to sea, then south down the quay, where the last of the sardine smacks were putting out to sea a little beyond the jetty to which the *Santa Lucia* was moored. Stanchions rose at the stand's four corners to support a trellis of joists and beams. A canvas awning would protect His Holiness from the the sun, to be draped over the frame later that morning. Lastly the foreman had turned north, toward the inn, where from the topmost room Diego gazed back at the man whose labors had awakened him.

The man had stood there for several minutes. He descended carefully, taking the benches as oversize steps, as though the stand were a staircase extracted from the vanished house of a race of titans and leading now to a phantom piano nobile, to nothing. . . . Wrong, Diego corrected himself. His Holiness would have a fine view from the platform up there, attended by a small and favored coterie. The steps led to the Medici Pope. The rest would sit below.

Then the foreman had walked around to the back of his construction, where the undersides of the tiers were so many overhangs, a sound-box from which his mallet had boomed and echoed. She had stirred then. He had reached for her in the night, and she had refused him. He was unsurprised, though there had been no warning, no particular coolness between them. It was a realignment in their relations, or in their contract. She slept naked, like a whore. He could have forced her if he had wished.

Men and women began to gather on the quay, local people. He recognized the chandler and the woman from the sail-loft. Word had got around in the past week that the Pope was coming to bless a ship—the *Santa Lucia*—and the ship would be sailing to the ends of the earth. A fisherman carrying creels slung on a rope over his shoulder sat down on the lowest bench of the stand and was shouted at by the foreman. He got up wearily and continued down the quay, past the jetty to his right, past the sail-loft to his left, eventually lost amongst the little sheds and scattered outbuildings that spilled out of the main town and were halted only by the sea. The sea was calm. Later a middling to light nor'easterly would get up, as it had on the last two days, and carry the vessel out past the breakwater into the open waters beyond.

More people were arriving, clustering together in little knots, gossiping and speculating. Sight of a Pope was better than a day of penance in warding off damnation. A mere touch of his hem guarded against quartan fever. His blessing cured certain kinds of blindness and—it was rumored—genital warts and perhaps the French pox, too. Men and women and their children had closed their shops and houses to come and be anointed by the Servant of the Servants of God. He would sit up there, amongst them in a sense, on the platform there. Above them, in a sense. Cut him down, Diego thought vaguely. He turned away.

From the east window he could see the river curling through the flat plain of the Romagna, marshy and desolate on the north bank, dotted with fishermen's cottages to the south. Two hundred paces upriver from the inn was a dilapidated warehouse with barn doors on its landward side. One stood open, and some children were wandering about outside it. Next to the warehouse, a landing stage extended tentatively from the riverbank, supported by salt-encrusted piles to which the watermen tied their boats. When the current caught them, the whole structure swayed gently. River weed collected underneath, rotted, and eventually floated into the estuary. They had arrived the night before last, a soldier on leave and his widowed sister, the latter so pious that she wore a veil. That, at least, had been the explanation he had offered the innkeeper. Concealed behind her mask of lace, Eusebia had snorted derisively.

"Her grief," Diego offered weakly. The skeptical innkeeper had nodded without replying.

A soldier and his commanding officer's wife had been the consensus amongst the regulars at the Last Gasp after they had retired. The following morning, the "soldier" had spent freely but shrewdly in the workshops and storehouses of the quayside tradesmen, directing his purchases to the *Santa Lucia*. So he was a Spaniard, like the other Spaniard, who had spent less freely, and less shrewdly, and was vaguely but broadly disliked. On any other week he would have excited more comment, but the Pope was coming, His Holiness himself, whose breath smelled of violets, whose urine was thick as honey, whose piercing gaze could cure goiter, calm storms, kill cats at a distance of fifteen paces, sometimes more. . . . He called himself Captain Diego and carried a short, businesslike sword. No one inquired further.

The previous evening, the boatman had run aground twice in the approach to the landing stage, each time pushing off with an oar. It was a Roman wherry, keeled and drawing a good foot of water to negotiate the currents and eddies of faster and deeper waters than these. The local boats were closer to punts, flat-bottomed to skim above the sandbars of the estuary. There had been three moored there the previous night. There were still three this morning. Someone had strung bunting around the rails. Diego watched the river, the morning sun full in his face so that he squinted and shaded his eyes with his hand. Still early, he told himself. Somewhere within the inn, boards creaked under stumbling foot-steps, sleep-thickened voices shouted at each other, then doors and shutters banged open as the Last Gasp took its first gulps of the morning air. The river's meanders bristled with light, a silk rope dropped carelessly from heaven. Diego blinked and rubbed his eyes, then looked again. Minutes ago it had been a dot of black floating in the glitter and glare of the water. Now it was a boat, and now a high-sided boat, with a tall stem-post and a man standing there using an oar for a rudder. She joined him at the window then, watching with him as it neared the landing stage, cutting smoothly through the water, its three passengers motionless and looking away from one another, not speaking.

"Which is the one you fear?"

Her voice broke his reverie. "Not fear," he corrected her. "I am wary of him. He is not amongst them." The landing stage was too open, too exposed, and his instincts would warn him off. The Pope's smiling sergeant would not arrive by boat. "He might be here already," Diego said. "He will not show himself yet."

Rufo's business was with the three men now stepping out of the boat, stretching their legs, yawning, and looking about. The giant scratched his stom-ach. Stay close to them, he told himself. Rufo would circle, wait, choose his mo-ment. The three men climbed the steps from the landing stage and walked toward the inn. Wary of showing himself at the window, he stepped back and lost sight of them as they drew near. They would bolt if they saw him, Seròn too, perhaps. But Seròn he could not avoid. He had business to conduct with the secretary. A sin-gular decision to inform him of.

Diego walked quickly across the room to the south-facing window, picking them up again as they filtered through the crowd in front of the stand, the big man easy to track, his companion harder. Seròn was leading the way, talking to them over his shoulder as they made their way farther down the quay and paused there before turning onto the jetty. A man watched their approach from the deck of the *Santa Lucia,* then ushered them aboard. The mate, he thought, though the distance was too great to make out his features. He smiled to himself, thinking of the conversation that must now be passing between them. The secretary's sur-prise, his anxieties and ensuing calculations. They will do you no good, Don An-tonio, he counseled. No good at all.

"Which is the traitor?" she asked. She stood behind him, so close they might be touching. He shook his head impatiently, absorbed in his own calculations. The crowd would be safe, big now and in constant movement. He could move there unseen, wait for the secretary, snatch him as he passed. He smiled again then: more anxieties and calculations, a morning full of surprises for Don Antonio Seròn.

The downstairs room was already crowded, the tables and booths all taken and men standing with mugs in their hands, talking loudly to each other. The woman from the sail-loft was there; no business would be done today. She nodded to him as he moved quickly through the crush. The sunlight outside was dazzling. Men and women were dawdling about outside, and he forced himself to dawdle with them, gradually traversing the open ground that separated him from the cover of the crowd.

"Brave, very brave. . . ." "Foolhardy, I'd say." "The one's t'other, but in my book it's brave." "Book? What book? They're fools. That ship's not fit for firewood. . . ."

Their voices drifted in and out of his ears, an irrelevant soothing noise. He was coiled tight with purpose, as if on the eve of battle. He jumped when a hand touched his shoulder. An old woman was selling apples, her whining voice pursuing him as he moved away, "Sir? Oh, sir? Would you . . ."

He calmed himself, ambling slowly among the chattering groups, looking down the quay to the ship every few seconds. Two dwarfs passed him, strolling arm in arm and blithely ignoring the stares that attended their progress. The time seemed to pass very slowly, but this too was familiar. He kept near the edge of the crowd so that their bodies might not block his view. He must have glanced at the *Santa Lucia* fifty times before they reemerged, there on the deck, then the jetty, then walking toward him, toward the crowd, all three of them together. He sank deeper into the mass of bodies, watching them approach. They stopped. A discussion of some sort? Seròn was pointing down the quay to the sail-loft. He saw Salvestro nod and then point the other way, the big man following obediently. To the inn? Surely they would part now; yes, Seròn was retracing his footsteps, away again. Diego slipped through the crowd to intercept the secretary, moving swiftly and surely, intent only on his quarry. . . .

He saw a man impale himself once. On a pike. It was a skirmish outside Piacenza, an accidental death in an accidental fight. The man had been charging full tilt and had simply run onto it. His assassin had done nothing, a halberdier frozen with fear, only stood there with arms presented. One moment, the dash forward. The next, stopped dead. Diego wondered what had passed through the dead man's mind as he'd looked down at his chest, the point in as far as the crosspiece. His legs had continued running for a second. What had he been thinking in that moment, in that absolute disjunction? Now he knew. He stared through the crowd, and the shock of recognition knocked him backward, already turning and ducking, reaching within his doublet for the short knife there, his sword useless in a crowd, stupid thoughts in a stupid head. . . . Rufo was standing directly in his path.

He caught himself before breaking into a run. He looked down. The knife was in his hand. Rufo behind him. Walk calmly, he told himself. Put the knife away and do nothing. His mind was fogged. He had lost concentration. Move slowly away—this was better—drift, merge with the others.

He found himself on the far side of the crowd, the side nearest the inn. Salvestro and his companion were nowhere in sight. Nor was Seròn, who had walked away down the quay where he could not follow, not yet. Rufo had not seen him, perhaps a glimpse of his back amongst a hundred other backs. He had been lucky. Now he must think quickly. Stay in the crowd or risk the hundred yards between the stand and the inn. Rufo in the crowd. The two men at the inn. He felt shaken and strangely relieved. The thought that the Pope's sergeant might not be waiting for him here had tempted him, taunted him. It was not fear, but it was close to that. He stepped out of the crowd's cover. Seròn would have to return to the inn to collect his men; he would have to content himself with that. The back of his neck prickled. His limbs felt awkward as they mimed the stroll to the doorway of the Last Gasp, a tiny rectangle that grew larger with agonizing slowness.

The interior was more crowded even than before. He settled in a corner, barricaded behind a group of five men too busy with their beer to notice him. He scanned the room for Salvestro and his companion, who should at least be easy to spot. It does not matter, he told himself. Seròn in the crowd or Seròn as he approached the inn to collect his charges, the two men who must be here somewhere. He scanned the room again. Then a third time, and then a fourth. . . . He began to curse under his breath. A tide of unease rose within him, growing turbulent, on its way to becoming panic. The two men were not there.

Eek.

The boatman pushed off, grunted a warning, then swung the rudder-oar over their heads and settled it in the stern row-lock. The bridge slid away and they were in midstream, the current holding the small boat steady in the Tiber's black waters. It was early morning, barely light, and the shadowy embankments appeared as extensions of the river's lightless surface, pulled up at the edges like a channel awaiting the overflow of some mightier flood. Mooring rings of weathered stone projected vaguely out of the gloom. They passed to the right of the island, watched by water buffalo whose heads appeared as monstrous busts until they swung about, suddenly losing interest. Abandoned stairways rose out of the water for a step or two, then broke off, leading nowhere. The entrance to the Cloaca Maxima was the black mouth of an endlessly patient predator, waiting for whatever the eddies might carry within its maw. Salvestro, Bernardo, and Don Antonio stared in as they passed. A dull jolt from the left was the weak summer debouchment of the Marrana. Downstream from the mouth, the buildings set farther back were a jumble of shadows that sank slowly into the sloping ground, becoming the ruins of a past city or the future of the city just passed, Rome and

Ro-ma, both quitted now as the river cut through the old walls at Testaccio and widened into a placid flood a hundred paces wide.

Eek!

A rat? A bird? Something wrong with the boat? Larches and willows lay toppled on the left bank, cut down to clear the paved towpath where, an hour hence, oxen and water buffalo would begin their trudge upriver, drawing after them barges and lighters. For now the river was almost empty. They passed a solitary fisherman, then the first of the boat-stations where men were busying themselves loading cargoes, hoisting small square sails, shouting to each other. It was still early. The sun rose and the river transformed itself, alternately a glaring mirror and a transparent spyglass through which the passengers sprawling in the boat could see the Tiber's beds of yellow sand shift and roll with the motions of the current. At Magliana a great barge lay alongside a landing stage that seemed hardly sturdy enough to secure it. Switzers stood guard on its decks. Liveried men were draping pennants over its sides. They continued on around this first and greatest of the river's bends, Don Antonio leaning out over the side to keep the barge in view until their own boat began to heel and he drew back hastily.

E-eek. . . .

The three men looked at each other, Salvestro, Bernardo, Seròn, but no one said anything, and the boatman stood there, his skin burned nut brown from the days spent under the same sun that burned down now, silently guiding his vessel past the sandbanks and their raucous pelicans, past the clamorous stations whose noise broke over them in washes that just as quickly lost themselves in the gurgling of the waters, past Tor di Valle, Vicinia, and Acilia, past a dozen nameless hamlets whose existence was signaled only by the thin columns of smoke hanging in the sky above them, the river widening almost imperceptibly as they passed the mouth of the Galeria, again when the Tiber itself forked, and rounding the thick brush of the Isola Sacra, they glimpsed the massive worked stones of great walls, smashed and abandoned now, then on the opposite bank a well-kept fortress, lagoons beyond it, the first sprinkling of huts, sheds, and houses, and then there were no more bends to round. Before them was the sea. They were at Ostia.

Eek, eek, eek. . . .

It was an intermittent squeak, sounding irregularly and without warning as Seròn ushered them out of the boat, now from the left, now from the right, a brief silence as they passed the inn, then right again as they threaded a path through the crowd that had gathered in front of the stand, erupting unpredictably but every few steps that were taken down the quay to the jetty, its source quite clear now: Don Antonio Seròn's new shoes.

He halted above the mutinous footwear. The brooch pinned to his hat, the tracery of his scabbard, and the handguard of his sword all bore the same intricate floral motif. The buckles of his shoes did, too. Without the shoes the ensemble would appear unbalanced and dissatisfying. His two charges watched him blankly.

In the picture that would surely fix this day in albuminous tempera for the pleasure of posterity, His Holiness would be shown in rich purple, waving from his platform to a beautifully detailed (a certain amount of artistic twisting would be necessary) *Santa Lucia*. The surrounding rabble of prelates, orators, and peasants would be clothed in muddy or madder reds, Vich outstanding in fugitive orpiment, portrayed as a wastrel Hercules in the poisoned skin of a lion; himself, Seròn, in durable ultramarines, the red of his shoes traduced by vairy blues, for their sedition. And these two? The dupes?

"Here she is: the *Santa Lucia*," he declared with a flourish. Their heads turned to the vessel at the end of the jetty. "Savor her name, for history will link it with your own: Salvestro and Bernardo of the *Santa Lucia*. . . ."

"A fine vessel," said Salvestro.

He watched them watching, Bernardo following his companion's motions almost exactly. The big man had fidgeted throughout the journey down the Tiber. Nerves, perhaps. He looked more closely himself. The same patchwork of new and old planking, one mast slightly askew, Jacopo on deck, the sails furled and looking whiter than he remembered. Perhaps the crew had scrubbed them, but it seemed an unlikely task for them to undertake, and as they drew nearer he saw that the canvas had not been scrubbed or even patched. The sails were new. He gaped up into the tangle of worn ropes and lines.

"Rigged 'em last night," said Jacopo. "Whole team from the loft over there. You coming aboard?"

The three men filed down the gangplank, and introductions were made. Jacopo stared at Bernardo in perplexity. Seròn slapped the big man on the back.

"Wish you had him as crew, eh, Jacopo? Fellow the size of this."

"Yes," said Jacopo after a pause. Bernardo laughed, and Seròn joined in. "Crew's still sleeping off the farewell party," he said. "Alfredo too."

"Captain Alfredo," Seròn corrected him, and Jacopo nodded acquiescence. "Sore heads all round, then," he continued in more jocular tones. "Not to worry. Plenty of time for introductions on the voyage." He noticed a number of casks stacked up on the *Santa Lucia*'s decks that had not been there before. The water barrel looked unfamiliar, too. Perhaps his expression was unguarded, or perhaps Jacopo was the type to sense another's discomfort.

"Something wrong, Don Antonio?"

Insolent cur. He shook his head. Salvestro was watching him curiously.

"I feel sick," said Bernardo. "I think I'm going to—"

He barely made the three paces to the side, from where his stomach emptied itself noisily into the water. Must be nerves, Seròn told himself. He stole a glance at the other one, who was distracted now by his companion's distress. Jacopo raised an eyebrow.

"We're hardly even afloat yet," Salvestro told the big man as he straightened and wiped his mouth.

"Let's go ashore," suggested Seròn. "I have business at the sail-loft, but you two deserve a measure of rum at the Last Gasp." He turned to Jacopo. "His Holiness will be here sometime after midday. Have everything prepared by then." He kept his tone light.

Ashore, Bernardo's sickness disappeared as quickly as it had arrived. His face grew ruddy again as they walked back toward the inn. The crowd in front of the stand was bigger and more boisterous now. A few people glanced curiously at them as they stood there, then whispered to each other.

"Imagine," Seròn told the two of them. "When you return it will be like this in every street and tavern in Rome."

"What?" said Bernardo.

"Your fame," he explained. "Your renown, so conduct yourselves accordingly. Your lives will be very different when you return. This is merely a foretaste."

"A what?" asked Bernardo.

"I will meet you for our last drink together shortly." He raised his voice above the noise of the crowd. "Over there." He pointed to the inn.

When the two men were safely lost in the crowd, he turned and walked briskly back down the quay, but instead of making for the sail-loft he turned right, toward the jetty and thence the ship.

Jacopo eyed him warily as he strode down the gangplank for the second time.

"Where did all this come from?" he demanded of the mate, who adopted an expression of baffled innocence, only goading him further. "Those casks. The sails. Where is the crew you were paid to hire?"

"Belowdecks, like I said," answered Jacopo. "And this stuff came from you, least that's what I was told. Came yesterday, most of it."

He must be lying, thought Seròn, yet the mate's resentment, his very lack of explanations, both pressed the case for his truthfulness. Not from me, he thought. So who?

"Get your men on deck," he ordered the man. "Clean them up, and when His Holiness arrives I want them standing in a line against the rail."

The mate stood his ground and stared at Don Antonio. "Haven't you got something to explain?" he said.

Seròn stared at the mate for a long moment before his ire erupted. "Me! Explain myself to you, to the villain who—"

"The big one," Jacopo interrupted him. "Bernardo. You somehow forgot to mention him?"

"Good God! There are how many, fifteen, twenty of you? Do it while they sleep."

"There are eight of us. And a carpenter," said Jacopo.

"Nine, then. Still enough, if you want to be the master of this vessel." The challenge hung there between them.

"Enough," said Jacopo. It might have been agreement, or a question. He was looking out over the *Santa Lucia*'s prow, out to sea. He was pensive now, and

Seròn knew that he had chosen his man well. "Where would you have it done?" Jacopo asked.

"Anywhere in open waters," replied Seròn. "One patch of ocean is much like another, is it not?"

Minutes later he was walking quickly back to the inn, the squeaking of his shoes piling irritation on anxiety. Someone had supplied the ship with provisions and sails. Someone had introduced a new figure in his design, disrupting it. . . . Or was he himself only a figure in someone else's plan. But whose? Vich's? Impossible. Vich was already yesterday's man, his secretary's plan too far advanced, and he was moving forward now like the huntsman for the kill. The rest was mere execution. They would know at the sail-loft who had presumed to intervene in his delicate work. The sail-loft next. He had time. The Pope would be enthroning his bargelike behind about now, the barge itself just casting off. He squeezed his way in at the door of the Last Gasp. The inn, then he would make his way to the sail-loft, then the Pope would arrive, and then the ship would sail. He looked about the crowded room, searching for Salvestro and Bernardo. Where were they?

"Sit down, Don Antonio."

He had not had time to turn before a hand clamped his neck and pulled him sideways. Something knocked the backs of his legs, unbalancing him, he was falling . . . A chair. He fell into it. A group of drinkers standing next to him glanced down curiously.

"Now calm yourself," the same voice commanded. "And smile."

He smiled. His neck was released, and the same hand clapped him heartily on the shoulder. Diego's face pushed itself into his and began talking, of people and places, of days and times within those days. He described the ship and its condition, then returned to Rome, an inn on the river, a room within that inn, a man within that room, waiting for himself, Don Antonio Seròn, then the cause that he had prosecuted through the heat of summer, admitting frankly when his store of facts ran out and speculation took their place. He knew everything. His speculations were mere details, and all correct. Antonio's head began to spin, then his whole body, as though he were being swung about by the neck faster and faster. How could he know these things? Had Vich found out and loosed his mastiff upon him? Then the soldier leaned closer still and began to speak of the only two players who had not been named, Salvestro and Bernardo.

"We had a pact, you and I," the soldier said, "and you were foolish to try to break it." His voice was calm, tinged with disappointment and regret. "You might have placed a pair of scarecrows on the deck of that hulk, dressed them up, and waved them good-bye. But you chose those two, and that was very foolish, for they are mine: your fools are my cutthroats, mine. . . ." He shook his head at this, then went on. "You told me that I would gain Fernando's ear, that you would press my case at court and I would be heard and given the justice denied me. But you intended no such thing, and that was foolish, too. You betrayed your master, Don Jerònimo, you betrayed me, your ally, and now you betray yourself. Yes," the soldier added at his expression of bafflement, "yourself, too. For I will have my cutthroats, and I will have the King's ear, too, and you will help me, you will help me, but knowingly now, just as you have these last months, imagining that I was your fool. . . ."

He spoke a few more words, and Don Antonio thought at first that he had misunderstood, or not heard, for the inn was noisy, but when Diego's intention was plain he felt his spinning head slow and stop, and he could not banish the smile, genuine now, that spread across his face or quell the sensation bubbling in his breast, incredulity mixed with ballooning mirth.

"That is my purpose and course," the soldier concluded. "Are you agreeable, Don Antonio?"

Seròn nodded quickly and rose, as much to conceal his expression as to escape the soldier's further attentions, muttering his agreement, then explaining that time was pressing, business to attend to at the sail-loft, preparations to make . . .

"Run along, then, Don Antonio," the soldier said complaisantly. "Attend, prepare. Do as you will." He watched the secretary squeeze himself among the drinkers and disappear. The contemptible functionary had accepted his decision more easily than he imagined. Don Antonio would be laughing to himself now, outside, on his way to the sail-loft, already rehearsing the maneuvers of Vich's disgrace and his own succeeding investiture: Don Antonio Seròn, Orator of Fernando the Catholic. . . . Diego occupied himself with these musings on the secretary's intrigues.

"He wasn't, you know."

The soldier's head came up. A small wiry man wearing a long leather apron stood before him. A tradesman of some sort.

"What?"

"That man you called 'Don Antonio.' He wasn't Don Antonio," the man said. "He was an impostor."

"Really? Well, that is true enough. . . ." He was about to smile. Something in the man's face stopped him. "What do you mean?" he asked sharply.

"I've just been talking to the real Don Antonio," the man continued. "Had a message for him. He's over there by the door." The man looked around guardedly. "Well, he was over there. Gone now." The man turned to go.

"Wait," barked Don Diego, his skin tightening and his fingers twitching. In the pit of his stomach he felt the churning begin again. "What message?"

"From a gentleman by the name of Salvestro. He attends Don Antonio in the sail-loft. Where I work," he added for the soldier's benefit.

"But it wasn't even moving," Salvestro protested.

"Right," Bernardo countered. "If it had been, then I'd have been all right. It was my guts, see? Moving about like this"—his arms flapped about—"and then that boat, the big one over there, it was still, so they sort of knocked against each other, and I was sick. And I was nearly sick last night, too. Pierino was nearly sick, too. Everyone was, even Rodolfo. They were asking where you were. I said you were praying with the monks."

Salvestro laughed shortly. "Right," he said.

"They'll say a few prayers for us while we're gone, won't they?"

"Of course they will," said Salvestro.

A few people stopped to stare at them as they approached the crowd gathered about the stand. Bernardo stared back. A woman selling fruit was moving among the men and women there, and Bernardo realized that he was hungry.

"I'll wait here," said Salvestro. "Then we'll go to the inn."

Bernardo edged his way among the crowded bodies in pursuit of the fruit. The woman's head bobbed in and out of view. He kept having to change direction and quickly grew frustrated, barging people aside and then, to escape their wrath, barging other people aside. The fruit-seller's head popped up, then disappeared, then reappeared, then popped down again while Bernardo charged about making himself unpopular. Eventually he felt a tap on the shoulder.

"Apples, sir? Very good apples, these. . . ."

They were, indeed, very tempting, and Bernardo was about to say, "Yes, I'll take half a dozen," when he remembered he had no money. He told her this, but she kept making the same offer, over and over in an irritating whine. In the end he shouted at her and she went away. He looked up at the stand. Something stirred in his memory, to do with the Pope, who, Don Antonio had promised, would sit up there and watch them as they sailed away. He and Salvestro would wave, as promised, but that wasn't it. He turned about to look for Salvestro, but there was no Salvestro. Salvestro was gone. Again.

Now, thought Bernardo, is the time to keep a cool head. He moved more carefully, asking politely that people should step aside, working his bulk among the chatterers and starers. He had felt foolish, emerging from beneath the tables at the Broken Wheel. He wasn't about to make that mistake again. No. This time Salvestro could do the waiting and worrying while he, Bernardo, did the disappearing. There was the inn. Salvestro was undoubtedly within it. He looked about. There was the ship, there the jetty, and Don Antonio walking upon it. Odd, though he wasn't about to worry about that, either. There was the landing stage where they had arrived. There was a large tumbledown building next to it, like an overgrown shed. There were some children outside. He liked children. He imagined Salvestro beginning to wonder where he had got to, then worrying, growing frantic, finally overturning tables in his search through the inn (where he would not be), last of all, perhaps, taking refuge beneath them. . . . He liked that, too. He would play with the children while Salvestro tore his hair out and made a fool of himself.

He walked briskly toward the shed, grinning to himself and watching the little ones enjoying themselves. Together they would play his favorite games: the how-many-children-could-he-lift-on-one-arm game, then the how-many-children-could-he-lift-on-two-arms game, finally the how-many-children-could-he-lift-on-arms-neck-head-legs-and-wherever-else game. But then, as he drew nearer, he saw they were not children at all. They were dwarfs.

Salvestro, meanwhile, was running. Arms pumping, lungs burning, feet speeding down the quay past the jetty, dodging bits of rope and mooring posts, running for the sheds and little warehouses that were safety, somewhere to hide, somewhere to escape to, somewhere to run to: Salvestro, running away again. . . .

He dived in amongst the buildings, swerving between them, tripping but up again in a second and running on. He stopped to catch his breath behind a storehouse, to listen for sounds of pursuit, to think, or try to think. He tried to remember the building Seròn had pointed to; it had been larger than the surrounding sheds. He was probably past it by now. There was no one about. He propped his hands on his knees and pulled air into his lungs, fanning himself with his hat. Don Antonio had had "business in the sail-loft." He began working his way around the backs of the buildings, moving in a half-crouch, for some were little more than woodsheds and their rooflines lower than himself. The roof of the loft soon rose above the others. Still no one about. He darted forward. The door creaked open, then shut behind him of its own accord. The only sound after that was the pounding of his heart. He should have known who would be waiting for him here at Ostia, or guessed, or assumed. He might have sauntered stupidly into the crowd after Bernardo, and if he had, he would by lying there now, a little crowd gathered curiously about him, and the short knife he had glimpsed as Diego had turned toward him, that would be stuck in his chest, or neck, or through his eye. . . . The trap had been set there. He should have known: the Colonel was the huntsman who never gave up. He had been waiting for him since Prato.

He looked about the interior of the loft. Would these wooden walls now keep him out? That curtain of canvas? He heaved it aside with difficulty, for it was stiff and heavy, suspended from poles high above. An identical sheet lay suspended behind it, then another, and another. . . . Salvestro worked his way through them patiently, sometimes finding an opening, sometimes not, listening all the while for movements, for presences other than his own. The canvas crackled. His breathing grew labored again. His feet tapped on the planking of the floor.

An identical area on the other side of this strange barrier was more cluttered than the first. Light poured down from overhead onto strange pulleys and windlasses. Taut ropes threaded their way through blocks and rose up the walls to more blocks fixed to the roof-beams. A cluttered workshop at the back seemed to have been added to the main loft, for its roof was low, extending back into a gloom broken only by the outlines of trestles, benches, and stacks of folding tables. Strange tools were hung on the walls together with coils of rope of varying weights and thicknesses. The windlasses, or whatever they were, looked to Salvestro's eye like enormous insects with their sticklike limbs projecting in all directions. He stood in the center of this workshop, looking up and around him. The light seemed brighter here.

"Hey! Get off the canvas! . . . You! Move!"

He jumped, searching for the source of the voice, already moving sideways, ready to run. There was a crash as a trestle overturned somewhere in the back of the workshop, and then a man emerged wearing a workman's apron.

"Oh," he exclaimed as he got a better look at Salvestro's clothes. "Didn't see you were a gentleman. . . . Had to shout to warn you." He pointed to the floor, where a tight square of canvas lay stretched by the insectlike machines at each corner, then began explaining the delicacy of the mechanism. "Snap your neck like a candle if you set it off," he warned. "Got to watch how you step in a sail-loft." He pointed to pins and wedges that held the contraption in tension. "One knock here, or here, and . . ." He drew a finger across his throat. "That's why I shouted like that, sir."

Salvestro recovered himself slowly and began asking after Don Antonio.

"Wouldn't know him," said the man. "I usually just come in to clean up of an evening." He pointed to a broom lying in a corner. "Everyone's off today, though. Pope's coming, so I'm here on my own."

"I would like you to take a message for me," Salvestro said then, trying to sound like the gentleman the man had taken him for. He was about to offer to do some sweeping in return but caught himself before he spoke. Instead he described Don Antonio's clothes, his sword, his feathered hat. "He will most likely be at the inn."

"I'll find him," the man assured him.

"Tell him to meet me here with all possible speed. Make sure he understands that. All possible speed."

"And who, sir, shall I say you are?" the man asked then.

"I," said Salvestro, "am Salvestro."

The man made a little salute, then disappeared behind the nearest sheet of canvas. Salvestro listened to thuds and crackles as the man made his way through the canvas. The door creaked, and then he was alone.

He found a stool and sat down. Don Antonio had been delayed, that was clear. Or he had come here, found no one, and left again, presumably to search for whomever he had come here to meet. So he would be back, one way or another. And his message would surely bring him at the double. By the afternoon they would be aboard the *Santa Lucia*, out of all this, waving as instructed while the ship pulled clear of the jetty and sailed out to sea. And then? Seròn had been unclear on that. The ship would have a captain, though, and the mate, too. He looked a capable type. And if they should fail, if the expedition should encounter insuperable difficulties or the *Santa Lucia* prove unseaworthy (she had smelled of rot, he thought), then there were always other ports, other destinations. . . . These were hazy thoughts, more or less unexamined, more or less despondent. More of the same, it occurred to him. More running away. Where did that end?

Minutes passed in this way, in vague contemplation. Perhaps, he thought, he should have simply stood there and let the Colonel come to him. He waited for Don Antonio. Then, slightly muffled by the great sheets of canvas, the door creaked. He heard a man's footsteps. How stupid his thoughts were! Of course he had been right to run. Now he jumped up and called out, "Don Antonio!" and began making his way back through the canvas. He called again. He was in one of the narrower corridors formed in the gaps between the sheets, his chest and shoulder blades brushing the rough material. He took another step sideways and heard an answering footstep on the far side, then a series of little scuffles. There was something wrong. Something missing.

Eek. . . .

That.

He stopped, suddenly in doubt as to who was on the other side of the canvas. Another footstep, on the left, perhaps. He edged the other way. If he could get behind his man, there was the door, unguarded certainly. He would run and no one could catch him then. Two sails met and overlapped two steps more to his right. He prized them apart and slipped through. Now what?

A thud, dull and percussive, directly in front of him. He froze, and an instant later he understood his error.

A rage-filled demon had pursued him through the streets of Prato. Now an unmistakable sound filled his ears: the noise of tearing canvas. The Colonel was cutting his way through.

Another thud, another slash of the sword. Salvestro began to panic as the man advanced, edging hurriedly back the way he had come, thinking how soft his skin was compared to the rough fabric shredding so easily behind him, nearer now, the blade that drove forward, then down, over and over again, piercing and ripping, and there was no Amalia to guide him now. He scrambled around the last great sheet of sailcloth. Ropes, windlasses, pulleys. The square of canvas stretched over the floor, tight as a drumskin. The crowded workshop with its trestles and tools. Was there any point in hiding back there, only to be dragged out like an animal? Better to die here, he thought, a fatal calm coming over him. He looked about the airy space, and then, in the cold midst of his calm, he saw it.

He tried to block out the noise, but the thought that he might yet live made his hands shake. He muttered orders to himself, for his fingers would not otherwise obey: Take this line, tie this knot. . . . He ran back into the workshop, trailing the line behind him. Not far enough. He worked his way under benches and cobwebbed wooden contraptions. Now he could not see. He crouched lower and listened instead, and it was at that moment that the sword fell silent. He's through, thought Salvestro. Wait now, wait to hear his footsteps change timbre, planked floor to canvas, wait and hold still, and then and only then . . .

But the silence continued. It seemed an age before he heard a sound muffled by the canvas and coming from the far end of the loft, a shuffling, or dragging, or something being dragged. He could not make it out. Then suddenly the footsteps were back, much faster, running, and Salvestro knew that the man was coming for him now. A terrible crash boomed out that could only be a man's body. A trip, a fall: I have him now. An abrupt certainty. He jerked the line, felt the wedge come loose, and the canvas hurled itself into the air.

The islanders used to carry young pigs to market like this: his first thought as he emerged and stood upright. The canvas had formed a long sack suspended two or three feet off the ground. Something struggled inside. The tools he needed now were on the wall: long awls, shears, knives, blades, and irons of all shapes and sizes. He chose a heavy spike and approached. His captive twitched and twisted about. The canvas swayed a little. He used one hand to steady it, then raised the spike high above his head.

Then lowered it.

"Bastard," he hissed. "Murderer." It felt good to say this. He said it again. "Murderer. We were your own men, Colonel Diego's own loyal men. . . ."

What else? Nothing. The same twitchy movements from within the sack, the man's breathing, hoarse and nasal, but no response. He raised the spike once more, two sweaty hands around it this time, chose his spot, steadied himself. Then—again—he let the weapon fall.

"Never easy to finish it, when the man is down."

The voice was all but in his ear. He spun about. The Colonel was leaning against the wall. As Salvestro watched, dumbfounded, Diego pushed himself forward. Three quick steps and he plucked the spike from Salvestro's hands, then pushed him backward, one hand on his chest, until he stumbled and fell.

"I am a servant of the Spanish Crown," Salvestro protested weakly.

Diego smiled. "You are Don Antonio's instrument," he retorted, "if not his fool. And now the fool has lost his master. That is whom you await, is it not, Salvestro—the Gentleman? So many imposters and imitators. . . . Your message went astray, Salvestro, but look at the quarry you have bagged. Your old commander from Prato, no less." Diego turned to the figure suspended in the canvas. "Now, would this be Don Antonio's impostor, or my own? Which would you say, Master Salvestro? It is an oversubtle point, perhaps, in circumstances such as these."

Salvestro stared up at him, still dumbfounded by this turn of events. Your old commander from Prato? What did he mean by that? The trapped man shifted again. Diego weighed the spike in his palm, then tapped it against the canvas.

"A good choice. What say you, Sergeant Rufo? A good choice? Would you have used an instrument like this?"

He looked down, then, murmuring to himself, "Better it be done quickly."

Sprawled on the floor, Salvestro watched Diego cast aside the spike. It clattered loudly on the floor. Then, with a single motion, the soldier pulled out his sword and drove it into the canvas. He used two hands, thrusting forward to push the blade in almost up to the hilt. When he pulled it out, the sack began to shake. A dark stain spread down one side and dripped, then trickled, onto the floor. Presently, the shaking stopped.

Diego bent his knees and sliced at the bottom of the sack. The sodden canvas parted like a pair of bloodied lips, a great gout of red, and then the cadaver slid partway out, slick as a stillborn calf. Across the loft, the door creaked again.

"Over here, Don Antonio," called Don Diego without looking around. He reached up to tug the sagging canvas free. "Now, let's have a look at you," he addressed the dead man.

Eek, eek, eek, eek. . . .
It was getting worse: louder and more frequent. Everything else was getting better. Much, much better. He would have to talk to Jacopo, and Jacopo would not like it. He had not liked the giant. This addition would worry him more. Money, thought Seròn. Give him money and he'll come around to the notion just as he himself had in the inn, listening in amazed horror to the soldier's insane conviction. Something had turned his mind. It was the only explanation. *There has been a change of plan, Don Antonio. . . .* All that talk of Fernando's ear, all nonsense, and the grain of truth in it only made the potion froth and foam the more. What price Fernando's favor when the currency of loyalty was diluted with use, men of arms supplanted by men of the tongue? Packs of fawning placemen scavenged in the courts at Valencia, Toledo, and Madrid, knowing that the useful were preferred above the faithful, the New Men—always—above the Old. Fernando was cold, and clever, and sick.

And Diego was unfavored by King and God alike. When earth and heaven shun you, what else is left but the sea? Seròn looked out along the jetty to the *Santa Lucia,* where a crew of sorts was at last assembling on deck, to the glittering sheet of water beyond, where Don Diego would find his appropriate fate, in open waters, alone with his absurd quarry in the kingless, godless sea. *I have reached my decision. . . .* Seròn had stared at him. Then he had nodded slowly, trying not to smile, not to break into hysterical laughter, and he'd even doubted his own intelligence, for when one's adversaries were so obliging, was it truly necessary to be clever? The man who seemed to have shadowed his every movement through the long summer, who had watched as he'd parleyed with Faria, he was gone or would be soon enough. Should he speak with the mate now? Jacopo would not be best-pleased at this particular addition to the *Santa Lucia*'s crew.

No, the later the better. He continued down the quay, shoes squeaking, *eek, eek, eek,* away from the boisterous crowd. Not long now before His Holiness arrived. An hour? It was almost midday.

"I know the fix for that."
A man had come up behind him quietly, a gentleman, walking quickly to catch up. He fell into step beside him and pointed to the offending shoes. Seròn appraised him quickly: fine hat, doublet well-cut and of good cloth, sword almost as beautiful as his own. His features were even, and a half-smile played about his face where the corners of his mouth turned up. In his hand he carried two apples. He offered one to Seròn, who declined.

"You are Don Antonio, are you not?" the man said then.

Seròn acknowledged that he was, feeling faintly aggrieved at the fellow's imposition.

"You will have received the message, then."

"Message? From whom?"

"The villain!" the fellow exclaimed then, and he explained the sweeper's error. "We are dressed somewhat alike, I'll admit, but I made the rogue swear he'd track you down once I'd convinced him that I was not your good self. Lucky I spotted you, though it seems you're going there anyway."

"Where?" asked Seròn, a little confused. The fellow's manners seemed strangely abrupt, well-dressed though he was.

"The sail-loft. One of your men is waiting for you there. That was the message. Sylvester, or Alessandro, or . . ."

"Salvestro," said Seròn.

"That's the chap!" said the other.

"And how did you know who I was?" Seròn went on, increasingly suspicious of this helpful stranger.

"How many people in Ostia dress as well as we?" he answered amiably. "You and I, we're two of a kind. We stand out like—"

He broke off in mid-sentence then, for Seròn had halted in his tracks.

"Perhaps you take me for a fool," Seròn addressed the man boldly. "I will ask again: How do you know me? What is your business here?"

The man hung his head, and for a moment he seemed at a loss. "You have me," he said, then paused as though gathering his nerve. When he resumed he spoke quickly, as though the secretary's patience might run out at any moment. "I was sent here by His Holiness to observe . . . to spy on you, in a manner of speaking, just as you suspect. His Holiness likes surprises, but detests being surprised. . . . You might have arranged singers, or some other diversion. In such an instance, His Holiness would wish to prepare expressions of delight or amusement as befits the situation. The townspeople here were of a mind to put on a masque, as another instance. I put a stop to that. Do you follow?" Seròn nodded curtly. "Of course you do," the man went on hurriedly. He seemed flustered, embarrassed at his own frankness. "I am here to learn what is to be learned, a vanguard master of ceremonies, if you like." He looked up. "An inexcusable deception. I can only offer you my apologies."

Seròn indicated his acceptance with a nod, and they walked a few more paces in awkward silence. The sail-loft came into view.

"You have business here?" he asked the man.

"Business of my own," the fellow said amiably. "I had hoped to finish it in Rome, but . . ." Then he pulled himself up short. "Perhaps my company is burdensome. I would quite understand if—"

"Not at all!" Seròn protested. The man's contrition and humility buoyed him up. In a rush of goodwill, he decided that they should introduce one another.

"I am Don Antonio Seròn, secretary to the Orator of Fernando the Catholic, King of Aragon and Castile." He made a little bow. "Now, pray tell me, sir, who are you?"

"Rufo," said the man. They were standing outside the door. "And now I would like to make amends for my deception. . . ."

Seròn tried to laugh off the suggestion, but this Rufo was adamant and persuasive, almost insistent, and in the end he complied, removing his squeaking shoes, first the left, taking Rufo's proffered hand to balance himself, then the right, wobbling a little, an awkward, incredulous stork as the man explained, "Believe it or not, Don Antonio, the instrument for this particular secret of the cobbler's art is the object here in my hand. If you have ever seen the men being shaved by the barbers of Navona, or a suckling pig dressed for Easter, you will understand my meaning now." His tone was affable, as before.

Seròn looked up in puzzlement.

"An apple, my friend," said Rufo, presenting it to the secretary's mouth. "Take a bite."

His puzzlement turned to bewilderment, and in instant later he would have cried out; but Rufo's hand forced the fruit between his jaws and, swiftly following that, the pommel of Rufo's sword descended and knocked him senseless.

"Oh, he is good," Don Diego murmured in grim admiration.

Don Antonio's eyes stared past the two men, his neck twisted strangely and his face distorted. Diego's sword had pierced his victim's back a little below the shoulder blade, the steel continuing diagonally and down through the rib cage to emerge again at the waist. Blood flowed freely from both wounds. A wide pool of it spread quickly across the floor. The apple lodged in his mouth held Don Antonio's jaws apart and pulled the skin tight over his cheekbones. He had been tied hand and foot. Salvestro noticed that he wore no shoes.

His fear became shock then, a strange light-headedness. Diego turned to him, the blood already drying on his sword. The soldier wiped it clean on a strip of canvas. The blade shone dully once again.

"Stand up."

Salvestro looked about halfheartedly, already knowing there was nowhere else to run. There seemed little point in obeying, so he remained sitting, waiting for what would follow. Diego's hand gripped him by the collar of his doublet and hauled him upright. His legs felt slack and unsteady. He twisted away, oddly irritable and nauseated, still waiting. Diego addressed him sharply, sheathing his sword, already moving toward the door.

"If I had the intention to kill you, you would already be dead. Now gather your wits, if you have any. There is very little time."

The catchers had begun by stationing themselves a round ten paces away, but that had quickly proved inadequate as Stoberin went sailing over their heads to land heavily in the dust a little way short of the door. They had retreated, then re-treated again, and finally found themselves outside the warehouse altogether, arms linked, eyes trained on the giant inside as he readied himself for the next launch. The dwarfs rotated busily between being thrown, being caught, and catching their fellows. The giant was tireless, his delivery smooth, and clearly he was enjoying himself hugely. Above all, however, he was accurate.

"*Wheee-eee.* . . . Oof!"

That was the General, who had spotted Bernardo first as the big man walked up, hesitant and confused at the sight of adult faces on child-size heads.

"Another good one, Bernardo!" he shouted back into the building. "We'll try a somersault next time."

"Right!" came the reply as the giant bent to pick up Coppernin. He steadied himself, rocked back, then launched the dwarf into space. A full rotation in midair, and, *whump!* Another perfect landing. The Pope was going to love this.

At first this Bernardo had insisted on playing a rather dull game that involved him standing there with his legs apart and arms outstretched while they clambered up and down him, two to each leg, one on each hip, and the remaining half dozen hanging from his arms and shoulders.

"I can keep this up for hours," he proclaimed proudly. Then Alberich had got back from making inquiries at the inn and had tried to complete the formation by standing on the giant's head.

"But he's not a dw—" the giant began to protest.

"Sssh!" the General hissed in his ear. "He's very touchy about that."

Alberich stood almost four feet tall. "Easy does it," he puffed cheerfully, one foot on Conopas's head. He got an arm around Bernardo's neck, then started to swing sideways. . . .

"I think," gasped Bernardo. "I think . . ."

Anyhow, a few bruises apart, no one was hurt; and dusting themselves off, they explained to the concerned and apologetic giant that dwarfs are generally a lot tougher than they look and anyone who's survived his or her mother's rubbing grease rendered from moles, bats, and dormice into his or her spine every day, well, that person will already know pretty much all there is to know about discomfort, so not to worry, and how about another game, such as dwarf-throwing?

Whaaa-hey. . . . *Splot!*

Alberich had, once again, proved problematic, protesting loudly when six of them had lined up to catch him instead of the usual four, then complaining that the amended quartet was creeping forward a few paces every time he was launched and thus denying him his full measure of airtime. He waved them back furiously whenever he spotted this happening and as a result would most often land short, just inside the door, then berate himself furiously, which seemed to fluster the giant. His next launch would often be unsteady, producing awkward uncontrolled turns in midflight and more difficulties for the catching-party, which nevertheless applauded furiously each time, for the giant's need for reassurance seemed insatiable.

"Bernardo, you're the best thing that's happened to us since we quit Magdeburg," Stoberin confided to him as he was swung shoulder-high. "We were going to stay with a cousin of mine in Rome. Rooms in the Vatican Palace itself, we were promised, introduction to His Holiness. What happens when we get there? Turns out he lives in a cupboard and the Pope hasn't set eyes on him in over a year. . . . Sometimes I think we're the unluckiest dwarf troupe in the world."

"Me too," said Bernardo. He steadied himself.

"Right," said Stoberin, eyeing the catchers thirty paces away through the door. "I'm going for a full somersault with double rotation. Give me plenty of torque."

Bernardo nodded slowly. Stoberin saw the catchers bend their knees in readiness, felt the giant tense, an odd pause before the throw, and then he was shot forward, the torque strong as promised, kicking his legs up over his head to make the somersault; but something felt wrong, yes, something was definitely wrong. . . . What?

Direction. Stoberin saw his flight-plan peel off and leave him, an invisible line aimed straight at the catching-party from which he was now parting company; there they were, crouched and waiting at the end of a smooth and beautiful curve, a fast flat arc flying through the open barn door, a lovely, lovely line. But not his. He was headed for the closed door.

Clunk!

He came to a moment later. Two sets of twins stood over him, one pair dressed plainly, the other as gaudily as the giant. Or giants, for two Bernardos seemed to be retreating back into the warehouse, a look of panic on their faces, while the gaudy twins remonstrated with them, "No Bernardo, no. Everything's changed. Don Antonio wouldn't help us if he could. Now hurry up. We've got to get to the ship. *Come on. . . .*"

The Bernardos were shaking their heads and walking forward at the same time, while twenty-two dwarfs and two identical Alberichs pleaded with them to stay, but to no avail. The plainly dressed twins said nothing at all. Stoberin felt a lump the size of an egg rise from the top of his skull. More torque, he thought vaguely before passing out.

Oboni had six fingers on each hand and six toes on each foot. He was an Igala warrior from the north. He conquered the high country of Nsukka and the low country of Idoma. He achieved this alone. He had his people build a tower high in the air so that he might make war on the spririts above. It collapsed when he climbed it, killing many of his people. Then he declared war on the spirits below. He had his followers dig a great shaft in the earth and climbed down to fight, but the shaft collapsed, too. Only Oboni climbed out alive. His name sounded like the word for a woman's parts. A lot of people laughed at him for that.

Oboni sought a wife. Usse was eldest daughter of Onitsha's King. Oboni took her while she walked alone on the banks of the River, and he made her his wife. The people around Onitsha and the Igala-people at Idah both told this story. She was named after that Usse, and she too was Eze-Ada. She was the King's eldest daughter. She *had been* the King's eldest daughter—this tongue was like a machete, cutting up lives into little bits of time: now, and then, and then *then,* and the time before *that . . .* But the King was dead. Her father was dead. And this white-faced Oboni had caught his Usse crouching by a keyhole.

Aguu was a good month for the spirits, so she waited for her father to come and tell her what she should do. The two men talking in the kitchen had described the animal badly, but she had understood. It was the enemy of the "elephant." An "elephant" was *Enyi,* she knew what that was. Its enemy was *Ezodu.*

"Not an enemy," said Iguedo when she had finished drawing the two animals in the dust of her compound. "An opposite. Like sky and land. Wise old Enyi and mad old Ezodu." Then she told her how they came to be so different, how they quarreled, and how Ezodu ran off to the desert in a rage and Enyi ambled south to live in the forest. "Just like us," said Iguedo.

"Is that where Nri-people come from?" she asked.

"Where do we come from? Where do we come from?" Iguedo mimicked her tone. "Stupid question. Where are we going? Think about that."

"Nowhere," she replied in an instant. "We're staying here." She was clever. Namoke told her that twenty times a day.

"Stupid answer," said Iguedo. "Everyone is going somewhere. How are they going, though? Like Enyi? Or like Ezodu?" More than a dozen children had sucked Iguedo's breasts until now they were as flat as her own. No one and nothing had sucked her breasts. She had tried to interest Onugu once, the youngest and stupidest of her three stupid younger brothers. He had cried.

The next year the drought began, and the year after that the famine. She began to travel with Namoke as he moved among the villages. Sometimes they were gone for weeks at a time, for Nri-men were needed now in villages that had never wanted them before. She thought about Enyi and Ezodu from time to time, but it still did not make much sense to her, and she was beginning to think that it was one of Iguedo's jokes, a little more "coco-oil to help swallow all those dry words," as the woman had once explained when Usse had confronted her with a particularly outrageous fabrication. No one else told those stories. Then she and Namoke were called to an Ijaw village that was farther down the River than they had ever been before.

These Ijaw lived by fishing and making salt, which they sold in a market on a great sandbank half a day's paddling from their village, which was a collection of stilted huts on a mangrove island. They were good fishermen, but every year one or two would be taken by the sharks who swam in the waters about their village. In return they killed as many sharks as they could, and then the sharks would take their revenge. And so on. One or two men a year.

The headman was a very stupid fellow who had a small *ju-ju* set up in his hut with some teeth and old fishing-poles in it. Usse listened as he told Namoke that the shark's power was so great that the only solution was to make it their god. If, the man explained, he could swallow the shark's power himself (he patted his stomach when he said this; Usse had to stop herself laughing), then he could use that power to get rid of the sharks. So he had made his *ju-ju,* and he had forbidden his men to kill sharks. But the sharks had taken eight men that year. What should he do?

Namoke had begun to talk about one of the *alusi.* She was called Onishe. "Big woman," he said. "Breasts down to here." He slapped his hands on his knees. "She has her place in the forest behind the point at Asaba, and at night you can see her throwing torches from the top of the cliff down into the River. . . ." They were already waving their arms and protesting that it was too far. "No, no, no!" Namoke shouted them down. "You don't have to go there. She's a River-spirit. You can sacrifice here as well as there. . . ." The headman began nodding again, then asked what they should sacrifice.

"Sharks," said Namoke. "As many as you can kill."

The Ijaws baked a fish called *odinki* for them that night. The young Ijaw men stared at her curiously, but none had the nerve to approach. Namoke and the headman exchanged an unending series of compliments and drank palm-wine, which Namoke always brought as his share of the meal. ("With enough palm-wine it is possible to eat anything," he had confided to her one night. "Even dogs' feet.") Now the headman was drunk and had forgotten she was there.

"Have you heard about the sickness on the coast?" he asked Namoke casually.

"A little," said Namoke in a tone which told Usse that he knew nothing.

"First the eyes go red," the headman said, "then the skin turns the color of this *odinki,* and then they start to sweat. At the same time, they shiver and have to wear as many clothes as they can. That is only the outside, though. The worst is here—" He thumped his chest. "Their *chis* turn into devils. They forget how to speak. A Calabari was up here telling us about it. . . ." He prattled on, absorbed in his own tall tales: outrageous breaches of hospitality and manners, blatant robberies, pointless acts of violence. "It comes from farther along the coast, plenty of days away from here," he said. "The Calabari man said you couldn't do anything with them. You had to tie them down or kill them. Nothing else to do." He shook his head.

Traveling back up the River the next day, Namoke said very little, apart from remarking that if the Ijaws could stir their bones to sacrifice at Asaba, they could barter their fish and salt there at the same time and for almost twice the price.

Ezodu's back, thought Usse, perhaps not then, but later, when everyone knew it was not a sickness, but a people. No one she or any of the Nri had yet encountered had claimed actually to have seen one of them. At present, they were on the coast. Where did they come from? Where were they going?

Stupid questions, thought Usse, grinning to herself. They come from here. Here is where they are going. Ezodu's people. . . .

She thought the same again kneeling outside a door a world away from Nri. The two men were talking inside. She understood that these people did not know where they were going or where they came from. They had no remembrance of the animal. The streets were like rivers in spate, blind and furious. The men and women were boiling surges and undertows. No wonder their Pope groped for his beast. They had traveled farther than their memories. Very dangerous, and a warning to herself, perhaps. When the soldier's hand had slid over her cheek to cover her mouth, when the thick cable of his arm had circled her waist to hoist her off the floor and carry her noiselessly upstairs, when he had released her and hissed, "What do you *know?*" his face full of a rage that had nothing to do with her, when he had expected her to stand there dumb with shock and saying nothing, a silly little serving girl, she had said, "I know everything. . . ."

She had given herself to him that night and seven times since. But not last night, she thought now, watching from the window as instructed by her fish-skinned Oboni, her six-fingered conqueror. The river was dotted with little boats, many of them anchored and waiting for the same vessel she sought in the glare of the water. Someone must have ridden down from La Rocca with intelligence of its approach, for a crowd was streaming out of the inn and making its way over to the landing stage. The people who had gathered outside the warehouse drifted across to join them. Her lover and the other two were still inside. Presently they reappeared, walking quickly, almost running against the flow of people emptying out of the inn. She glanced out of the southward-facing window. The ship that would carry them away looked indistinguishable from the one that had brought her to this place three years before. Men were moving about on her decks. Turning back, she glimpsed the three men just before the sill barred them from her sight.

She heard their footsteps on the stairs and thought of her own tramping up and down the staircase of Fiametta's house. Three years of that, but finished now. She had waited for her father's instruction in the sanctuary of her bedchamber, but his *mmuo* had never come. That was good. It meant they had not buried him. It meant her three foolish brothers yet believed she was alive: Onugu, Apia, Gboju. She told herself only the Eze-Ada might wash the body of the Eze-Nri. Only the Eze-Ada might crown his successor. She looked down again.

Men in elaborate hats were marshaling the crowd at the landing stage now, trying to push them farther back. A small boat approached from the river and was angrily waved away. Farther upstream, around the bend of the river, the Pope's barge hove into view.

The balmy airs of the broadening river, the pleasant splish-splosh of the paddles as they dip and strike the water, the padded comfort of his seat, all these contribute to the Pope's sense of well-being on this sunny morning. The number of people gathered to greet him has been described by Ghiberti as gratifying, although even at this distance—a few hundreds of paces—they appear to him as leaves shaking in a tree under strong sunlight, blurred and confused, uncountable except by God. So he places his faith in "gratifying" as the number corresponding to his perfect satisfaction, leans back in his throne, and listens to the anxious twitterings of his courtiers, functionaries, and guests, who have been herded together on the deck of the barge and are now having to be forcibly restrained from all moving over to the left-hand side, where the view of the nearing jetty is better. Capsizement would be unfortunate.

Minutes later, the barge secured, he is being carried head-high on a makeshift palanquin along the waterfront to the stand. The crowds are, as ever, importunate, shoving and grabbing, shouting for his blessing, which he distributes generally while the Switzers keep them off him with their pikes. There is a wooden contraption with a tarpaulin draped over it. A little way down the quay is a ship. He will sit and watch and be watched. The ambassadors? He cannot place them at present.

He alights from his palanquin and climbs the benches to his throne. The view of the ship is splendid, although, squinting as he does, the ship itself appears a little dilapidated. Somewhat the worse for her undoubted wear? He knows very little of ships. On the benches below, his fellow passengers are scrabbling for seats, the higher the better being the obvious principle. The spectacle is rather undignified. Leo smiles.

Then his smile disappears. There will be speeches soon that will describe his better qualities and deeds, and this artful anthology will excite no more than a wave of his hand. His titles will be recited and sweetmeats will be offered, but his titles will not rouse him and the sweetmeats will remain untouched. His smile will not reappear because now, at this instant, he looks down with the vague intention of saluting various portions of the crowd and sees amongst their excited faces one that he expected—indeed, would have been much happier to see—last night.

Standing on the ground below, Rufo is looking up at him. He is gesturing, mouthing something. He wants, it seems, to join him. He wants to sit next to his employer, the Pope.

Leo frowns. He turns away. This will be a day when he is unconcerned with the past. Rufo serves, Rufo and his ilk. They suffice. He does not want to attend to all that now. He desires only to be amused. Ah! he thinks, at last, here are the ambassadors.

The speeches that follow ruin whatever was left of his good humor, Vich and Faria displaying their leaden wits to everyone's disadvantage. They point to the shabby-looking ship, then to its crew lined up on the deck who raise their hats and bow in rough unison when it eventually casts off. They look like mismatched dolls, Leo thinks sourly: a short one, a tall one, a short one, a tall one, and so on. One so much larger than the others that the ship itself appears undersized, an oceangoing runt that the orators describe in such extravagant terms that he almost laughs. But he is too bored to laugh now and too vexed. Why has he chosen such dullards as his clowns?

And worse than that, Rufo will not go away. He stands there below him, gesticulating and remonstrating with the Switzers who bar his path. He is there alongside his palanquin when he eventually climbs back into it and is carried back along the quay. He is on the jetty too, where, seeking to avoid the man's eye, Leo gazes out to sea, where the runt-ship has now shrunk to the size of a rowing-boat. And then Rufo is in the barge, which is the final straw.

"What!' he barks across the boat to his hireling, who does not answer, or not at first. Instead he turns and points to the selfsame object of his own late evasive gaze: a speck of wood topped by a shred of canvas, bobbing up and down on the tedious patch of water he has been faced with all afternoon. He looks at it, then back to Rufo.

"So?"

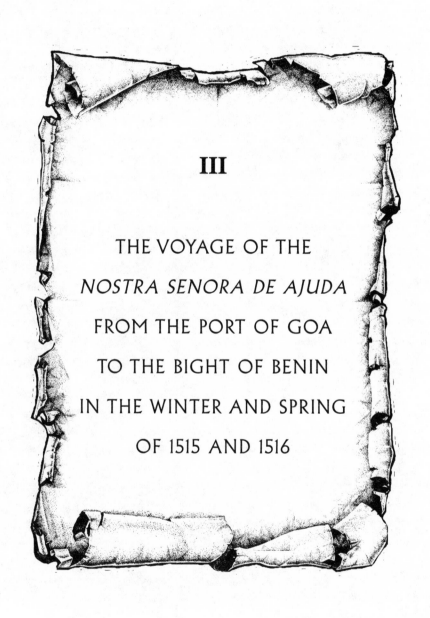

III

THE VOYAGE OF THE
NOSTRA SENORA DE AJUDA
FROM THE PORT OF GOA
TO THE BIGHT OF BENIN
IN THE WINTER AND SPRING
OF 1515 AND 1516

*F*ive more puffs of smoke appeared, hung in the air for a moment, then dispersed in the easterly wind. Seconds later the noise reached them, a series of soft *phuts*, harmless at such a distance. The alarm had been raised at first light. A force of the Hidalcao's men were marching on Gondalim. Trujillo's men had pulled back across the river to the fort of São Paolo at Benasterim. The ford it overlooked had been held so far. Later there were panicked rumors of a squadron at Panjim, certainly false, and then the gunners had appeared on the far bank of the Mandovi, but two or three thousand paces upriver of the port. The men stationed on the islands of Chorao and Diwadi had stayed at their posts, and Goa itself was secure. The river channel was another matter, passing close to the bank for almost two hundred paces and directly under the guns. The cannon-fire was a warning. The wind gusted then, and the ship's sails billowed as they were struck, a windy thud, a dull crackle of canvas as they fell limp again. The two men on the quay and the hands on the crowded deck all looked up quickly.

"This cannot last," muttered Teixeira. "This wind will die and we will be here until Saint Martin's Day."

But a second later the wind picked up again, and the men resumed their work about the ship. She was a nao of two hundred tons, tubby-looking, castled high both fore and aft. She had made the *carreira* once already, but her beams were sound, her pins still tight, so the Duc had assured him. Boxes, bales, crates, and casks jammed all three decks and even projected from her sides where they had been lashed to planks and the planks nailed to the wales. Two longboats were held in canvas slings tied aft of the chains. Belowdecks, in the hold, the *Ajuda*'s true cargo was already aboard. The hands clambered over obstacles as the sails were unfurled and their lines coiled and stowed. They seemed to work quickly, in near silence and without orders for the most part. The men were native to this place, Canarim for the most part. They kept themselves close, aboard just as ashore. The thought came to Teixeira then as it had several times before, the tempting speculation or question: Was the man they awaited necessary?

"Where is he?" he murmured, mostly to himself. His companion did not respond.

He turned away from the ship, looking down the quay on which they stood, downriver, past the clutter of the shipyard to the salt-beds where little conical piles of the crystal seemed to radiate their own painful light. The sunlight on the water was too strong, throbbing and pulsing. Everything here exceeded its measure. He could not grasp this place or its people.

The man beside him shrugged. "We need another half-fathom to float us. Another hour yet, at least that. For the tide." He held up a hand and let the wind spill off his palm.

It was a freak at this time of year. It would carry them downriver, over the bar and out into open waters, if it held, and if the Hidalcao's gunners were caught by surprise. . . . If Dom Francisco ever remembers that the ship sails today, thought Teixeira.

There was some shouting then and three shots somewhere in the town behind them. Hotheads, he thought. The Hidalcao's men could not be on the island. Frayed nerves, nothing more than that. These attacks seemed to have no end, nor any purpose save the scraping of their souls, like the heat and the fevers and the vapor-thickened air that sucked the flesh off their bones. He saw a deep hopelessness settle in the men here, either that or an appetite that gorged itself and yet found no sustenance, an unquenchable hunger. Different kinds of hollowness that the Duc would play upon or fill in some way. Without him the men here were nothing more than survivors of a shipwreck with no other thought than clinging on for fear of drowning. With him they were pioneers, vanguards, bearers of Dom Manolo's crown. . . . Affonso's spirit was the current beneath them, the wind behind them, the compass that pointed forward. But he was not Affonso's man. *You will find yourself alone, but you will not be alone.* The words of Dom Fernão de Peres. *I will be helping from Ayamonte.*

Blow hard, then, Teixeira thought sourly. Another cluster of smoke-balls popped into existence on the far bank, dispersing more slowly this time. It was a fitful wind, a matter of lulls and gusts.

"Will they take your orders, if it comes to that?" he demanded of his companion.

Gonçalo looked down at the planking of the quay. Amongst the Christians, he was the best pilot on the island, or had been. Now he farmed a plot inland from Panjim and lived with a Canarim woman he had taken as his wife. A *casador* then, his allegiances hard to read. Teixeira did not know the pact that Affonso had struck with the man to recruit him to this voyage. He went by the name Gonçalo, though the Duc had hinted that was not the name he had brought with him from Portugal. He shook his head, though whether in answer or refusal he could not tell.

"I will find him myself," Teixeira said.

The sandy path from the quay broke the stockade at Saint Catherine's Gate and thereafter broadened into the Rua Direita, the straight spine of the town from which narrower thoroughfares curved away like ribs. A few traders had set up stalls in the bazaar, but most had stayed away today. A band of frightened natives and *mestiços* were being marshaled there by a man called Mota, a *degredado* who had arrived a few months before him. Teixeira's horse was waiting under an awning, already sold in anticipation of his departure but still his, in circumstances such as these. He ordered one of the natives to saddle the animal.

"They're attacking Banguinim," Mota called to him. "Two troops of them landed by the springs. Come on!"

"On whose authority do you command these men?" he challenged the man, who grinned at him, showing a full set of yellow teeth, but he made no reply. Teixeira pulled the bridle from the hands of the native and finished saddling the beast himself. He swung himself up and shouted to Mota if he had seen Dom Francisco. Mota shrugged, insulted, uninterested. There was no force at Banguinim; Mota knew that as well as himself. And Dom Francisco was three miles away at Benasterim, for he was a *fidalgo* of the old school, and knowing nothing else, he would throw himself where the fighting was thickest. Or so Teixeira's reasoning went, knowing nothing else.

He rode past the Hidalcao's old palace and the monastery of Saint Francis, its walls already streaked with the black mold that the monsoon left on every stone in the town. The square of the *pelourinho velho* was almost deserted, the pillory there unoccupied. Soon he passed the last of the buildings and was on a track that led through groves of banana trees. The ground rose and the trees thinned, then disappeared. Two ancient pines marked the halfway point. In the aftermath of the rains, the country here was a lush heath of fibrous grass, a green mattress that hid tussocks and cracks alike. He slowed the horse to a walk, bearing right to avoid the swamp, the Zuari River coming into view as he rounded a last rise in the ground. The stockade and walls of São Paolo were no more than five hundred paces away and the river here no more than waist-high unless the tide was in. One of the men sitting behind the outermost wall spotted his approach and waved him off. He dismounted and led his animal at a half-run, crouching as he hurried toward the cover of the stockade. There was no sign of the Hidalcao's force, nor of Dom Francisco.

It erupted as he tethered his horse at the back of the fortress, a sudden volley of shots, then three or four heavier explosions, small cannon, smaller than those they would face if the ship were to sail, but sounding fearsome now, unopposable by human flesh and bone.

"Down! Down!" Trujillo screamed at him as he ran for the wall and another volley came in. He dived forward and fell in the dust beside the sergeant. As his head came up he saw one of the men down the line rise like a sleepwalker. Trujillo shouted again, but the man, a young man, only turned stupidly. He looked puzzled. More noise then, and it looked to Teixeira as though the soldier jumped, turning in the air almost like a dance step, except that his jaw exploded in a mess of blood and bone. He fell, then tried to rise again, unaware of the injury until his hand came up and found nothing, the same puzzled expression on what was left of his face as he pulled a large splinter of bone from the cavity. Then he began to scream.

"Dom Francisco," Teixeira shouted to Trujillo, who shook his head impatiently.

"Try farther down. Mendes's post." He shouted something else, but Teixeira was already on his way.

Mendes's post was a wooden blockhouse. It was deserted. Across the river, thick brushwood and scrubby trees reached almost to the bank. The breeze swung about, this way, that way. It would be stronger on the river, he told himself. There was still time. He looked left, to where the land shelved gently into the water. A swamp.

"Trujillo sent you."

Teixeira spun about. A man stood there, naked to the waist, gaunt-faced and his eyes bloodshot. A bottle swung from one thin arm. He lowered himself to the ground and grimaced, then raised the bottle to his lips. Teixeira nodded and asked again for Dom Francisco. The man started to laugh, then coughed and spat.

"Are you Mendes?" he demanded.

"I was Mendes," said the man. He began to shiver violently, then rolled onto his side, his face contorting. Teixeira began to back away.

"That's it," hissed the man. "Run, run as fast as you can. The fever's coming for you, too. Go on, run! Run!" He turned his face to the ground.

Teixeira ran. When he looked back he saw Mendes still lying there but joined by three others as emaciated as he. They stood there watching him until he turned away.

Mota had formed his men up in a palm grove at the back of the town, riding up and down on his nag before them and waving an ornate arquebus. An absurd sight to Teixeira as he cantered past, ignoring the man's salute. Mota shouted after him, "Dom Jaime! Dom Jaime Teixeira!" but he rode on. "You were seeking Dom Francisco!"

He stopped at that and turned his animal about. Mota pointed through the trees. A building was just visible between the trunks, red walls of local stone already streaked black with the local mold: the Church of Nossa Senhora da Serra had been built after the Duc's return from Malacca. But Dom Francisco praying?

"He's in the meadow behind there," shouted Mota, then he laughed at his unguarded puzzlement. "Trying to catch a horse!" More laughter, but Teixeira had his back to the man then. Amongst the trees, and shielded by the town, there was no breeze at all.

It was as promised: a man and a horse. Dom Francisco and his white gelding, the only white horse on the island, as he had never tired of reminding any who would listen since the day of his arrival. The man holding out a handful of withered grass to the beast was a little taller than he, thickset and brawny. He had a heavy face, a peasant's face, which he tried to carve into something angular and more shapely by cultivating a small beard waxed to a sharp point. He was ruddy and hearty in his manners, except when crossed. Then his close-set eyes would sink deep into his face and explosive rages would follow. He harbored grudges against many of the other *fidalgos* on the island. He had killed a man in his first week here, and the Duc had snubbed him after that. The third or fourth son of a noble family, he had never explained his presence here in the Indies, on the other side of the world. His trading had been desultory and unprofitable. But he owned the only white horse on the island.

The horse wheezed now. Dom Francisco approached with the grass in his outstretched hand. The horse took a step forward, then, as Dom Francisco reached with his free hand for the bridle, it reared about and cantered a short distance away.

"Damn!" Dom Francisco shouted, casting down the unenticing bait. The horse watched him impassively. Dom Francisco looked up as though the eyes he invoked might offer consolation. Then he saw Teixeira.

"Too much spirit in him!" he shouted, suddenly cheery. He clapped Teixeira on the shoulder. "The two of us'll have him, though." He began directing where Teixeira should stand, how he himself would drive the animal to him, then explained a few of the beast's foibles and tricks. Eventually he noticed the rigid mask that was Teixeira's face. "What is it?" he asked. "Bad news from Benasterim? Am I needed there?"

"You are needed aboard ship," said Teixeira. "You were needed there an hour ago." He saw Dom Francisco's eyes narrow for a second, but then the cheery manner was back.

"Well, ships don't run away, do they? Unlike this miserable nag. . . ." He forced a laugh. The horse bent its head and began to nibble at tufts of grass. "Come on, Don Jaime. We'll have her aboard in a minute."

Teixeira swallowed hard, biting back the thick lump of temper that was swelling in his mouth. "There is no time for this"—he almost said "idiocy"—"for this task. Nor hay for your horse on the *Ajuda*. Those bales are for the Ganda. This was decided amongst us a week ago. Have you forgotten?"

The last phrase was his mistake. He realized it as Dom Francisco colored, fought briefly with his rising anger, and lost. He began to spit words at Teixeira, who was a "jumped-up flunky," a "crawling creature of the Duc's," not worth "one hoof of his horse" or even "both of its severed balls," and his horse would sail with him if it meant waiting till the new year. . . .

Teixeira turned away from this in a cold fury. Dom Francisco was still shouting as he rounded the church and untied his horse from the rail outside.

"The wind's swinging." Gonçalo stood in the shade of the doorway. "I saw your horse here," he said in explanation of his presence. "And his." He gestured to the other side of the church. "I think we must take our chance now. And we need him, if the men are not to sit on their hands. They don't like it. . . ."

Teixeira nodded curtly. "Wait here." He rode back through the palm grove to where Mota's men were now stretched out on the ground, fanning themselves in the heat. Mota had unsaddled his horse and joined them. He raised his head in surprise at Teixeira's approach, sat up, and finally struggled to his feet.

"Did you find him, Dom Jaime?" The grin seemed to be part of his face: in-eradicable, short of violence. Teixeira assented, gathered himself, swallowed hard.

"I have a request to make of you, Dom . . . Dom . . ." He realized he did not know Mota's given name.

"Jaime," said Mota, grinning more broadly at this suddenly humble *fidalgo*. "I am Dom Jaime, just like you. What is your request?"

Something flashed across Gonçalo's face when he returned, a quick wariness, perhaps, not quite surprise. Then he was impassive again, a bystander or a recorder for some abstract court and outside whatever might happen next. He said noth-ing. Dom Francisco was trying once again to approach the horse, which was playing the same game as before, allowing the man to draw near, to reach out, then suddenly retreating.

"Dom Francisco!"

The man turned. Teixeira raised Mota's arquebus, steadying it with one hand. Dom Francisco's eyes went from the man to the weapon. For a moment he seemed not to recognize it, then suddenly he pushed his arms forward, palms out-stretched as though he might deflect the ball. His mouth opened and it seemed too that he tried to say something, though no sound came out. He took a single pace forward. Teixeira pulled the trigger.

He saw Dom Francisco stumble and almost fall. The noise thudded in his head, then throbbed as though it were trapped in there. His eyes were watering and his nostrils burned from the smoke. Dom Francisco looked down at his chest, amazement on his face. Then bewilderment. Then rage, as he turned in time to see the horse's legs fold under its belly and the animal itself collapse. The heavy ball had torn away the topmost part of its head and it was dead before it hit the ground.

He watched through stinging eyes as the *fidalgo* turned away from the corpse, then strode toward him, his hand reaching for his sword. Teixeira let his weapon fall and stood his ground, crossing his arms in front of him. Ten fast paces and the man's face was in his own, red with anger and shock, even disbelief at the enor-mity of the act, the insult. His eyes shriveled to black olives buried deep in his face; the mouth opened and closed, so close that Teixeira could smell his breath. But he heard nothing. He said, "We leave now," and the sound boomed strangely in his head. The blast had deafened him.

As he approached the quay, his hearing began fitfully to return. Odd noises cut through the wadding packed into his skull, sharp cries and loud reports that might have been gunfire or hatches slamming shut. He stood amongst the clutter of the deck, looking up into the rigging as the hands hopped about under the orders of Gonçalo and Dom Francisco. He looked for Oçem but could not see him.

"In the hold!" Estêvão Gomes finally shouted to him, when he had asked three times, pointing each time to his ears. "With the beast!" The boatswain indi-cated the open hatch-cover. Teixeira peered down, seeing only shadows moving about, but he knew well enough what it looked like. If needed, he felt, he could describe it so exactly that another might draw it from his words. He looked up once again. The sails filled and emptied, tightened and slackened. The hands were clambering down the yards now. He heard muffled rhythmic grunts, which he understood as the shouts of the gang hauling in the thickest hawser on the *Ajuda,* her mooring cable. His hearing was returning. And then, as he looked up, every square of canvas on the ship, from the great lateen sail astern to the tiny pennant on her prow, all suddenly fell slack. The wind had died.

Everything stopped, and at that moment Teixeira's hearing returned in full. The men looked up at the sails, then to each other. He heard the *Ajuda*'s thick and unbroachable silence. Gonçalo stood alone on the poop deck, looking away from all of them. Then, from the open hatch-cover a strange sound broke this hush, a kind of squealing. . . .

No, snorts that turned into squeals, the rise in pitch sounding like mockery. It was the beast: the animal that Oçem called Ganda. The image of the young man at Benasterim came to him then, the bafflement on his face, or what was left of his face. Gonçalo's voice broke these thoughts.

"Furl those yards! Hurry!" He was pointing to different sails. The men looked to each other, bewildered, not understanding. Gonçalo pointed inland, and then they saw what he saw.

A great raft of black cloud was floating toward them. Lush green hills rose in the east, their forest canopies broken here and there by bright red patches of laterite soil. The storm was over them now. Nearer, silver riverlets and irrigation channels glittered as they passed through the *sorod* paddies of the natives. This is beautiful country, thought Teixeira, now that I am leaving it. He climbed the ladder to the poop deck.

"Wind enough there," said Gonçalo. "Now we pray for water."

Soon the longboats were pulling them about, the *Ajuda*'s prow nosing blindly into the current. Teixeira waited for the mainsail to pass across his line of sight, then looked again across the river. At first he saw nothing, but then a glint of light on the far bank told him that the Hidalcao's men had moved their guns farther upriver. A shadow was racing over the inland plain as the advancing wind flattened wild grasses, reeds, and crops.

"Dom Francisco is belowdecks, raising the angle of the guns," said Gonçalo, then he shouted to one of the men to haul in a lanyard that was swinging loose from the yard of the lateen above their heads. Teixeira scanned the crowded deck, but there was still no sign of Oçem. Two men leaning out amidships were taking soundings, their arms gathering the line, then falling limp as the plumb descended, calling out the depth in rhythm with each other, one and then the other.

"Three fathoms and rising!" called one.

"Twenty degrees port!" shouted Gonçalo, and peering down from the aft rail, Teixeira saw the dim shape of the rudder turn obediently in the water. The *Ajuda* came slowly about to its new course, a gentle curve that was taking her out into the middle of the river. An answering curve would bring her in close to the far bank. He had seen the charts of the channel they must follow, split with shoals and sandbanks that the Mandovi's current carried down from the hills inland and spread about the bottom in random shifting patterns.

"Hold her there!" shouted Gonçalo, and with a nod to Teixeira he slid down the ladder, made his way over the deck, jumping from crate to bale to barrel, and took up his proper station on the forecastle. Estêvão Gomes took his place on the poop and began to relay the directions to the men on the rudder as Gonçalo shouted them aft. The linesmen kept up their soundings, but they were in the deepest part of the channel now and merely called out, "No bottom!" in the same rhythm as before. The wind found them then, and Teixeira felt the vessel's timber bend before the strengthening blow, the ship moving forward as though a giant had put his shoulder to her stern and now leaned into his task, his weight slowly overcoming the dead tonnage of the overladen vessel. Gonçalo's shouts came faster, and beside Teixeira, Estêvão's voice was the pilot's immediate echo. He understood Gonçalo's earlier order to take in sail then, for though the *Ajuda* picked up speed, she handled sluggishly, turning long seconds after the orders were given.

The headlands of Diwadi and Chorao slid astern, and they were soon alongside the far bank of the river, no more than a hundred paces out. He looked forward and saw the gun crews waiting, their horses tethered well back from the bank. The guns themselves were angled toward them. The men on the lines kept shouting out the soundings, four fathoms on the port side, clear water to starboard. Gonçalo's bearing kept them as far as possible from the shore, but then the port-side call would be three and a half and he would have to take the *Ajuda* off her line, ten degrees each time, nudging her back into the channel, nearer the waiting guns.

"They'll try for two salvos," said Estêvão, watching with him. "They'll not have time for more. If we clear the bar."

"Dom Francisco is with the gun crews," said Teixeira. "We'll not be defenseless."

Estêvão snorted. "We're overladen," he said. "If he wants to help, he should throw them over the side."

As he spoke, Teixeira saw the men on the bank gather quickly about their cannons and the guns themselves belch blue smoke out of their barrels.

"Heads down!" bellowed the boatswain, and an instant later the sound reached them, a jumbled series of dull cracks. "Impatient," commented Estêvão as Teixeira looked about for the expected carnage. "Fell ahead of us."

The *Ajuda* moved on imperturbably, and soon he could almost make out the gunners' faces as they worked frantically to tamp down more powder and balls. Now us, thought Teixeira. The vessel was alongside the gun crews. Now, he thought, you fool, you arrogant peasant, and as if in answer, Dom Francisco's voice sounded through the hatch-cover, a hoarse bellow, another, and then the *Ajuda*'s guns fired.

At first he thought they themselves had been hit. Then that the magazine had blown. The explosion crashed out of the gun deck, a solid fist of air that rocked the whole vessel, and for a second the bank was invisible behind a thick curtain of smoke. It seemed that nothing might survive such a blow, but when the smoke cleared he saw that the gunners were untouched, unharmed, already back at work on their own cannon.

"Missed," said Estêvão. "They have a clear shot at us now." Teixeira watched them manhandle their guns, turning them after the departing vessel. Estêvão crouched down on the deck. "When you can see down the barrels, that's when they'll fire," he said, grinning up at him. He dropped down beside the boatswain.

They had only to wait a few seconds before Gonçalo called again, "Heads down!" At the same moment Dom Francisco clambered out of the cargo hatch, his face blackened, cursing the gunners below. Teixeira saw him look about, then start as the nearest hand, an older man, dived at him from between two large crates. But the sailor fell before he reached his target, and then the dull cracks sounded again. Dom Francisco grinned at the miss, his teeth very white against the soot on his face. Teixeira remembered that afterward, and the strange way the sailor had fallen in midflight, as if someone had suddenly grasped him about the legs. But there was no one near. There were some splashes, a little ahead of them and off to port.

"Missed," he said to Estêvão, who shook his head and pointed to the main mast.

"Not quite."

The brace-line on the port side was swinging from the end of the yard. Below it the waist looked as though something had dented it. The wood was chipped there, and the brace-block had disappeared.

"This man's sick!" It was Dom Francisco's voice. He had turned the sailor over and was standing over him.

"I say this man's sick!" he shouted louder, but none of the hands moved. They were looking forward. Dom Francisco looked about him in disgust. He caught Teixeira's eye up on the poop deck, and his expression deepened. Then, finding no response, he left the man there and began climbing over the obstacle-strewn deck to join Gonçalo on the forecastle. The vessel was moving quickly now, moving out into the estuary and toward the open water beyond. The hands were silent, and the only sounds now were the shouts of the linesmen, who had given their soundings throughout both bombardments, their voices swinging back and forth like a pendulum.

"Clear!"

"Clear!"

Teixeira looked back and saw that the deluge had already broken over the town. The water in the river was choppy, the wind breaking up the surface in advance of the storm, whose following rains flattened the waves and dulled the water's sheen. He recalled the heavy warmth of the monsoon downpours, raindrops the size of a man's fist. Black clouds massed and piled themselves in vast towers behind them, and the wind gusted stronger than before, coming in pulses of force. He heard the masts creak and grind against the timbers below, and ahead he saw confused waters, where the choppy surface of the estuary ceded to a broad swell, the place where the river became the sea. The bar was somewhere there, invisible beneath the agitated surface.

Teixeira imagined a sweeping crescent, the burrow of a monstrous worm curled protectively about the river mouth. Such creatures were said to exist in the interior. In reality, as he knew, the bar was a thickening of the sandbanks that the Mandovi's current would push this far and no farther, an irregular submarine plateau that the flat-bottomed *paquels* of the natives skimmed over with impunity. All other vessels waited for the tide. He had watched with a growing crowd when the *Cinco Chagas* had grounded herself out here, running before a storm as they were now. The storm had caught her and beat her for hour after hour until she'd listed over, then beat her again until she had broken up, splitting open amidships and her crew spilling into the heavy seas. She had been late. The ebb tide had caught her out, plucked the men from her decks, and pulled them out to sea, where they had drowned. Only five had made it to shore. Teixeira remembered then that Gonçalo had been one of them, but no blame had attached itself to him. The Duc's doing.

Now they were almost exactly between the headlands, and their pilot had fallen silent, the bearing chosen that would carry them over the bar. Gonçalo was very still, very intent, looking forward raptly, reading the water. Even Dom Francisco at his side had fallen silent. The pilot would try to find a break, a breach somewhere in the bowed-out dike. Then, much sooner than he had expected, a soft shudder ran through the ship, a sudden slowing too quick even for the linesmen to catch, as though the hull had passed through a sump of tar. The *Ajuda* drove forward and she was clear.

"Jesu," murmured Estêvão. "Jesu, Jesu, Jesu . . ."

"We're through." Teixeira turned to the man, grinning. But Estêvão was shaking his head.

"We're aground," he said. "That was not the bar. It was hardly a shoal. We're too low. . . ."

Even as he said it, Teixeira saw Gonçalo raise his arm. It hung there for a second, then fell, and as it did so the same soft shudder ran through the *Ajuda's* timbers, the water suddenly viscous. . . . Sand, thought Teixeira. A few buckets of sand. Will we founder on that? The ship slowed and slowed. And stopped.

Instantly the hands were running for the masts, scrambling up the ladders and lines and crawling out along the yards, not bothering to use the foot-ropes. On deck they were throwing aside crates and boxes to get at the cleats and blocks then forming into gangs to heave on the halyards. Above his head, the great lateen sail was swinging loose at one corner as three men struggled up the angled yard.

"Cut the sheets!" Estêvão shouted up at them. "Let her fall!" He grasped Teixeira by the shoulder and manhandled him off the poop. A second later the huge sail fell heavily to the deck where they had stood. All about the vessel the hands wrestled with canvas, ropes, lines, blocks, tackle of all kinds, fighting to furl the sails.

Teixeira made his way forward. Two men not needed aloft were only now picking up the fallen deckhand and rolling him into a length of canvas. A quick glance at his face told Teixeira that the man was dead, though no wound was visible. He hurried past to climb the ladder to the forecastle and found Gonçalo leaning out over the waist, looking down at the water. Dom Francisco stood at his side, stone-faced at his arrival.

"Another foot of water," Gonçalo said softly to himself. "Another knot of speed."

Teixeira followed his gaze. The water under the *Ajuda*'s bows and as far back as the forecastle was deep and black. Then, abruptly, it was yellow. Sand, Teixeira realized. They were aground on the very edge of the bar, balanced there in little more than a fathom. The first spatters of rain fell audibly on the decks. All three looked up. The spars were almost bare, the last men inching back along the yards or climbing down the mast-ladders. Above, the sky was choked with thunder-clouds.

"Just a storm," Dom Francisco said gruffly. "We saw worse than this on the passage out. Emptied my belly like a chamber-pot, but we rode it out."

"In open water," said Gonçalo. "Here we will be smashed to matchwood."

He looked over the side once again. The rain began to fall harder and the wind rose, whistling about the masts and spars. When Gonçalo turned to them again his face was transformed. "There is a way, perhaps. We are not lost yet." He talked quickly, raising his voice to be heard above the wind. When he was done Dom Francisco began to bellow orders to the men.

They divided the crew according to the watches, Dom Francisco taking the lower deck, Gonçalo the upper. Teixeira climbed down the ladder with the deck-hands chattering around him. He descended into chaos.

Choking gunsmoke still hung between the decks, clinging to the under-side of the upper deck in a fat layer below which the air was hot and thick with the men's sweat and the stink of the ballast. Light entering by the gunports and the open hatch barely penetrated the fug, and the lower deck was even more chaotically laden than the upper. The partitions intended to keep the *Ajuda*'s cargo orderly only hampered the men, who now hurried back and forth in the subaqueous gloom, dim flurries of movement urged on by the shouts of Dom Francisco. They manhandled huge boxes and chests, casks, bales, and more bales. A load of hardwood was toted forward trunk by trunk like so many battering rams. A line of barrels rolled out of the aft darkness whipped along by hunched shapes, wood rumbling over wood, crashes, thuds, the grunting of cursed and cursing men. Teixeira had stepped back beneath the open hatch when the storm proper broke above them. A sheet of rain dowsed him, soaking him from head to toe in an instant. He looked up and glimpsed boiling black clouds. Another sheet caught him full in the face, sending him back again, farther into the stern.

"Jaime! Dom Jaime!" Oçem's face loomed forward out of the darkness, barely visible in the light from the sternmost gunports, even dimmer now in the green gloom of the storm. The vessel shook under a buffeting wind. "Are they mad, these white devils?" Even now, Oçem's face was fixed in a mocking grin. "What are they doing?"

He explained Gonçalo's plan to rock the *Ajuda* off the edge of the bar, shifting the movable weight forward into the bows. Oçem was already laughing quietly, bringing his hands together in a silent clap of applause. "Mad white devils! All of you. . . ." His face was a jumble of shadows back there. He seemed to revel in the disaster awaiting them, but then he went on, "Gonçalo is a clever man. And mad, like you, Dom Jaime." Then the wiry man looked back, into the pitch-dark behind him. "They will want to move him, won't they? He's heavy, old Ganda. Move him forward with the rest. . . ."

"Yes," said Dom Jaime.

"Sssh!" Oçem hissed. "He'll hear you. . . ." He was laughing now. Teixeira shook his head.

"Oçem! Where the devil. . . ."

Dom Francisco's shouts served advance warning of his presence as he strode up to them. Teixeira's presence stopped him dead. He scowled, then addressed the smaller man. "This animal—" He pointed into the darkness. "Get him forward. Quick as you can." He turned as though to reenter the chaotic activity and noise now concentrated in the bows.

"How?"

The question was Oçem's. Teixeira nodded curtly to both men as the *fidalgo* rounded on the keeper, then made his way back to the hatch, pursued by Dom Francisco's outraged voice, "How? You have charge of the beast, you tell *me*. . . ."

Water was pouring in from the open deck above. He climbed the ladder, the rain slapping his face until it stung. The wind was a gale now. He stumbled and fell to his knees. An arm pulled him up.

"Are they done down there?" Estêvão shouted in his ear.

"Almost! The beast, they're trying to—"

Estêvão nodded that he understood. "She's beginning to list. Not much time now."

The cargo piled on deck had all been shifted forward, and the forecastle seemed to have gained a story, a solid mass of crates, chests, and casks lashed together and buttressed with planks where the construction threatened to tip over the side. Teixeira saw that the deck was indeed slanted now, the starboard side of the vessel noticeably higher than the port. Rain washed over the decks in waves, overflowing the gutters and slopping against the gunwales. The sky was simply black, a solid darkness meant to crush them into the sea.

He saw Gonçalo wave him forward.

"Have they finished below?" he shouted.

"Only the beast is left," Teixeira shouted back. The wind battered them, throwing them off-balance. A series of dull bangs sounded from below, and he looked about in sudden fear.

"Closing the gunports!" Gonçalo's explanation. He nodded gratefully, looked up at the masts, which bent before the wind, the topmost spars shuddering and the loose lines thrashing. A second later he fell forward and slid across the deck.

The vessel had tipped.

For a moment the pilot seemed to freeze, then he was racing forward, gathering the hands as he went.

"Everyone for'ard!"

Teixeira picked himself up and followed. The *Ajuda* seemed to bend amidships as the bows dipped, her beams creaking and straining in protest until it seemed that she might break in two, but then, with agonizing slowness, as though the sea had congealed about her timbers and she was being pried loose with infinite care, the stern began to rise. She hung there for a moment, then slid forward. . . .

And then stopped.

Teixeira looked to Gonçalo, whose face in this moment was stripped of everything but despair. Then, from below, a noise forced its way through the din of the storm, and the men huddled together in the lee of the forecastle glanced about, nervous and distracted. Heavy thuds started up but were instantly drowned out by shrill shouts and cries, many voices all raised together, and then one voice raised itself above them all, and that voice was a scream, long and louder than seemed possible. It stopped abruptly, stifled or cut off, and any other noise that followed was buried in the cacophony of the storm.

Then the ship moved again, her whole bulk and weight sliding forward into the water, a slow unstoppable thrust. Teixeira looked up at Gonçalo, balanced precariously on top of the piled cargo. It seemed to him that the *Ajuda* was simply burying her prow in the waves, that she would dive forward and down and never rise. The vessel tilted and tilted, and he thought of the weight in her bows dragging them forward and down. He crossed himself and closed his eyes, waiting for the first cold slap of water.

But, though the bowsprit dipped as low as the sea's surface and, as Estêvão later told him, the vessel's rudder was a foot clear of the water astern, the ship slid slowly forward off the bar, the prow dipping, then rising; the stern rising, then settling finally in deep water. The vessel listed to port and starboard, rocking until she found her new equilibrium. Teixeira opened his eyes.

They were clear. So released, the wind abaft thrust the *Ajuda* forward, westward, out into the open waters of the ocean.

Two bodies were sewn into sacks and the sacks thrown into the sea. Dom Francisco stumbled through the prayer for the dead, and then the men gathered about the firebox, where they lit incense and chanted in their own tongue, a meandering drone that the hands seemed to join haphazardly, now one, now many, returning to it as their duties permitted while Oçem tended the fire and the little resinous blocks cast into it, arranging them so that each one was burned to a snow-white cinder.

"The Ganda has sand under his hide; do you know that story, Dom Jaime?"

He shook his head.

"Another time. The slightest thing will anger him, and then"—Oçem mimed the lighting of a fuse—"boom! Like Dom Francisco's wonderful cannons. Very short-tempered, this Ganda of ours. And these foolish natives, they lose their heads at the first sign of trouble, and then they lose their land too and become sailors, but that is another story again. Also very foolish."

The beast had got loose and crushed a man. There had been a frantic scramble, panic in the dark down there, and by Dom Francisco's account only the animal had remained calm, trapping his man against the barrel of the gun, then leaning forward. "With great deliberation," had been the *fidalgo's* phrase. The screams, thought Teixeira. The ship had moved off the bar, and they had recaptured the Ganda by boxing him in amongst the cargo. It had taken an hour. Not foolish, Teixeira thought now, but brave, or nerveless, at least. He did not say this to Oçem, who continued to manipulate the little blocks of resin with a pair of slender tongs, moving and replacing them with care so that they burned evenly.

The second man had fallen during the bombardment. Estêvão examined him on deck surrounded by a crowd of hands, his friends, perhaps, though they seemed more curious than sad. At first the boatswain could find no mark on the man, no spot of blood, not so much as a bruise. Dom Francisco ordered that he repeat the exam. Lifting the man's head to begin it, Estêvão let out a little gasp and let it fall. He pressed his thumb to the head again. It was soft. The skin was unbroken, but the skull at the back had turned soft as wet clay. Estêvão looked up, baffled.

"It was the ball that struck the ship," said Teixeira. He pointed to the splintering where the cannonball had hit the waist. "If it glanced off his head like this—" He mimicked the passage of the missile, and the hands understood him then, nodding their agreement.

Dom Francisco would not address him, saying only, "Then he died in my defense. I will make provision for his family. As a matter of honor." He assumed a grave expression and the men all nodded again, very pleased by this, but then looking down at the body as though it worried them in some way.

"They like this Dom Francisco," Oçem went on then. "He is a real *fidalgo*. They know what that is. To give money to Vijar's family after he has been so stupid will bring him great goodwill amongst the men. To be hit on the head by a flying stone! How ridiculous."

"I will remind Dom Francisco of his promise, when the time is right," said Teixeira.

"Do not trouble yourself, my friend. Vijar's stupidity is such that, even dead, the foolish man cannot take advantage of his opportunities. He does not have a family."

"But the men were pleased. . . ." He was bewildered.

"Very generous of Dom Francisco," said Oçem. "Even a useless gift is a gift. Do you not remember Muzzafar's gratitude at your offer of a fort?"

"I will remind him anyway," Teixeira said stiffly.

"But I do not think Dom Francisco will wish to be reminded of anything by Dom Jaime, will he?"

Teixeira eyed the smaller man narrowly. The first time he had set eyes on him, Oçem had been sitting by the side of Muzzafar and the King had been fighting to stay awake. "It is the opium," he had confided later. "Pay no attention. Tell me again why you wish to build for us this magnificent fort. . . ."

The fort, predictably, had not been built. They had returned with a gilt chair, a dinner service; less predictably, the Ganda; and least predictably of all, Oçem. It had not at first been apparent that the King's trusted minister was in effect being banished. He was "Muzzafar's Ambassador to the great Duc d'Albuquerque, servant of the great King, Dom Manolo of Portugal," but an Ambassador without the trust of his master, and perhaps in worse odor than that. This had dawned on them slowly, and Oçem had slid correspondingly in their esteem until he had reached his present station. "Animal keeper!" he had exclaimed when Teixeira had finally challenged him. "Oçem the Ganda-herd!" The man had laughed happily as though the downturn in his fortunes were the most wonderful stroke of luck, and his good humor was used thereafter to deflect even the Duc's bluntest questions. He never revealed the reason for his disgrace, alluding only to the natural enmity between the Musselmen and his own people, the conquered Rajputs of Cambay. Teixeira suspected that he knew no more than he said. In place of explanation, he offered wild tales of his former master's fondness for opium and the pleasures of the zenana. Muzzafar's mother had fed him increasing doses of poison since birth to inure him to their effect. As a result, insects alighting on his skin would die instantly, and his concubines dreaded his attentions—naturally enough, for they invariably proved fatal. Even the Duc would laugh at these concoctions.

Teixeira would remind himself that the man was not his friend, or the Duc's, or his King's. Then Peres had written from Ayamonte, and at the bottom of the dispatch was the barbed order: "And enlist this Oçem, since you speak of him so fondly." So he was here, this onetime minister of kings, tending to the brute in the hold.

"He is vexed with you," Oçem went on. "Over his horse, is it not? Why is his horse not here?"

Teixeira remembered such questions from the negotiation at Cambay, the tone of puzzlement, the fainter tone of apology beneath it. It had been his tactic to counter these inquiries with bluntness, his own version of Oçem's feigned naïveté.

"I shot it," he said.

Oçem raised his eyebrows.

"Shot it? But this is Dom Francisco's language, not yours, my friend. I fear you might have said something offensive, albeit in ignorance of local custom."

They were both close to laughter now, acting out parodies of themselves, or the selves they had been ashore. Oçem's expression grew serious. "You should soothe him, Dom Jaime. One angry animal aboard ship is enough, I think. . . ."

"His anger means nothing," Teixeira responded, a note of contempt entering his voice. "He shouts and blusters. And that is all he does."

They parted then, Teixeira returning to the tiny cabin in the forecastle, where he improvised a rough table, building it from the chests piled against the partition until Dom Francisco's voice barked, "Silence!" angrily through the thin partition. He looked about his quarters despondently, fell on his bunk, and slept.

The days that followed passed insensibly, divided from one another not by sights or sounds, which were always the same, but by the wind. With every gust the sails pumped like huge lungs, but now out of sight of land, Teixeira felt that they were merely riding up and down on the swell, going nowhere. The winds were capricious and feeble, blowing and dying, swinging about the compass, so that the men spent their days scrambling to trim sails that would need to be trimmed again within the hour if their precious force was not to spend itself in useless flappings of the leaches and lurches of the hull. They sailed west, Dom Francisco and Gonçalo alternating watches in accordance with every eighth turn of the hourglass, though it was the pilot who effectively commanded the ship. Gonçalo erected a little canvas awning on the quarterdeck and spent his days beneath it, watching the water for changes in the wind. Since that brief moment when it had seemed that they were lost and the pilot's face had collapsed for an instant into hopelessness, the man had betrayed no emotion. He spoke rarely, and though Dom Francisco had insisted as a matter of ship's discipline that they should take their meals together, these were spent in uncomfortable silence, he and the *fidalgo* avoiding one another's eyes. Sitting up there on the forecastle for hour after hour, relaying directions to Estêvão, Gonçalo was more an adjunct of the ship herself than a member of her crew. Walking the deck at night, for the heat in his cabin was often stifling, Teixeira would observe him standing erect and very still, his eye glued to a small quadrant trained on the Pole Star, waiting sometimes for a full half hour before the movement of the deck would cease long enough for the instrument's plumb-bob to come to rest. Then he would mark down the reading and hurry back to his charts and rutters. One night, Teixeira followed him.

"We are here, if my reckoning is right." Gonçalo placed his finger at the end of a line that began at a legend marked "Goa" and zigzagged forward, describing a jagged parabola. Teixeira's curiosity seemed neither to surprise nor to caution him. He spoke quietly and almost tonelessly, these matters too familiar and too ingrained in him to be of interest. "We may sight land at Guardafui. Perhaps not until Delgado." He pointed to two capes, far apart on the coast down which they would sail. "After that the Moçambique channel. We will need the right winds to get through, but our chances will be better by then."

Teixeira looked at the island of São Laurenço. "Why not sail direct?" He traced a straight diagonal to the tip of the continent.

Gonçalo shook his head. "Too early in the season, and there are the shoals of Garajos. . . . Here."

Teixeira ran his fingertip over the chart, tracing a course up the other side of the continent to São Thomé, a tiny dot in the bight of the great landmass. "We must make a landfall here," he said. "There will be orders waiting there." Gonçalo frowned but said nothing. "Does Dom Francisco understand this?" he went on. Gonçalo shrugged and was silent for a few moments.

"It has to do with the Ganda," the pilot said eventually. Teixeira realized belatedly that this was a question. He nodded quickly.

"The animal is our whole purpose. Why else would the Duc have given us leave to sail so early?" He wanted to say more then, but Gonçalo had sensed his purpose, which was to draw him in, to make of him an ally. He held his tongue. The other began to fold away his chart. Teixeira was rising to leave when the man spoke again.

"The gun deafened you, when you shot his horse."

Teixeira nodded, surprised at any conversation that the pilot initiated.

"He said that he would have satisfaction. Not aboard ship, but as soon as we reach land. That is what he said."

Teixeira gave curt thanks for the warning and walked back toward his cabin, stepping carefully to avoid the sleeping bodies of the men. He lay on his bunk, marveling at Dom Francisco's stupidity. Aboard ship he was the master, an absolute power that no later remonstrance would keep from doing as he pleased. Ashore he would be another penniless mouth returned from the Indies, scrabbling for favors, soon reduced to telling tales in the inns for the price of a mug of liquor. The streets of Belem were filled with them. And he was the envoy of Dom Manolo, protected and favored by no lesser power than Dom Fernão de Peres. . . . He smiled to himself, remembering the insults thrown in his face in a meadow behind a church in a town on the other side of the world. Then he remembered that São Thomé too might as well be considered "ashore." They might prove evenly matched there. He is a distraction, he told himself then. Remember your purpose.

Which was the animal: a distraction thrown out by Muzzafar, a tub for the Portuguese whale to nose about and sport with, then an inconvenience to the Duc and an afterthought in one of his dispatches, which had been seized upon by Manolo or Peres, then cargo, gross tonnage here aboard ship and a fantastic rumor in the slow coils of the negotiation at Ayamonte. . . . What it was now as it moved toward what it would become. Peres had speculated on unicorns, but the beast was gross, its little eyes receding into the smooth cylinder of its head, as if some delicate creature had been encased in a shell of gray plaster and now raged in there, trapped and maddened by its prison. It would be something that children would poke with sticks. The straight-faced clerks at Ayamonte would speak of it as "the other factor in our calculation" or "the subject of our private transaction" or some such, for it belittled them and was ridiculous. And His Holiness would clap his hands in extravagant delight: this was their anticipation, that he would do this and put his seal to the bull they craved, that the Pontiff and his beast would make a happy match. Teixeira thought too of the man brought up on deck with his chest staved in. It had killed a man, "with great deliberation." The Ganda had been his pretext when he'd shot Dom Francisco's horse.

Now they avoided one another's eyes as they avoided one another's presence, a transparent fiction within the confines of the *Ajuda*. They met only to eat. Estêvão carried the desultory conversation, discussing their course with Gonçalo, who seemed less inclined to talk than any of them. When addressed directly, Dom Francisco would reply bluffly, even deprecating his own seamanship. His suggestions as to the trimming of the canvas were filtered through Gonçalo before being passed on to the crew, and the pilot made subtle alterations, or delayed them until the wind changed, canceling out the *fidalgo*'s more dangerous absurdities until the flow of suggestions slowed and finally stopped altogether. At table, however, Dom Francisco was indulged by the two of them, who nodded sagely at his words on the understanding that they would remain just that. Gonçalo was the true master of the *Ajuda,* Estêvão his loyal lieutenant. He and Dom Francisco were bystanders, mere passengers, albeit with extraordinary privileges. This situation, the anomaly that bound them together, only highlighted the resentment that kept them apart. He knew better than to try to win over the pigheaded *fidalgo.* Ingratiation could bring him only contempt. So each day was punctuated with meals that were collections of long silences, stony and awkward occasions, uncomfortable tests of a precarious truce that Teixeira endured with his eyes glued to his plate while Dom Francisco chewed, and belched, and spat his leavings back onto his plate.

They changed course, swinging south down the coast, and the ship's smooth progress began to be punctuated with odd lurches. The current was weak but against them, while the wind blew from the northeast more steadily now. They never sighted Cape Guardafui, but the continent was visible from time to time, a

smudge on the horizon far off to starboard, usually indistinguishable from the
haze and the shimmer of afternoon heat rising off the water. The headlands of
São Laurenço raised a cheer from the crew and an intensification in Gonçalo's efforts, for dangerous shoals surrounded the vast island's coasts, long humps and
bars, invisible beneath the glare of the sea's surface. "The channel is many leagues
wide," the pilot said, "and once in it the currents will guide us into deep water."
He fell silent again. Dom Francisco grunted. Teixeira sensed the anxieties beneath
this unbidden reassurance. They ate.

When they were nearing the channel, Gonçalo summoned the sounders to
their stations, and once again their voices rang out in regular rhythm—"Clear to
port!" and "Clear to starboard!"—like responses in a mass. Prayers to Saint
Nicholas were supposed to guard against shipwreck, Teixeira recalled. And raising
of the host calmed storms, if a priest were to be had. They anchored some leagues
out from Cape Delgado, for it was dusk and their pilot wished to enter the straits
in daylight. The next morning, the headland grew in definition. Teixeira imagined
a crushing convergence, though when they eventually passed the jut of São Laurenço to port and Moçambique to starboard, they might still have been leagues
away from either. In the event, and in accordance with the winds, Gonçalo chose
the westernmost bearing, passing less than a league from the town of Moçambique. Caught unawares by the earliness of the season, a little fleet of *sambuqs*
swarmed belatedly out of the harbor mouth and gave chase, their sailors shouting
and waving fruits resembling huge bananas. Some sacks of rice were purchased at
bad prices, Estêvão commenting that they probably originated in the very port
they had quit a little over a month before. The merchants soon fell back, hauling
their lateens about for the slow beat back to port. Their vessel bore south, and the
coast of the continent grew gradually more distant, finally fading and disappearing altogether. The *Ajuda* was alone again.

The nor'easterly blew steadily now. Gonçalo took his bearing from the
Southern Cross each night, and the following day he bent their course a few
more degrees west of the blow. The *Ajuda*'s deck leaned a little more with each
tweak of the bearing, finally finding the horizontal when the wind was directly
abaft, then leaning again, becoming a slope so gentle that it barely brought the
port-side camber level while their course drew a vast gentle curve in the surface
of this soft sea, as Teixeira imagined it. They were making for the Cape, the very
bottom of the continent, and he spent the days on the poop deck, in idleness,
watching the men find tasks to occupy themselves, listening to the jabbering of
the men below him in the steerage. Sometimes even they would fall silent, looping a rope about the tiller and dozing off with Estêvão's connivance. Then he
would look out over the side at the sea, which was a liquid mirror smashing and
mending itself ten million times a second, or up at the sails, which bulged and
shivered, an immense white expanse, too large for the ship, surely. Gonçalo was a
rival king atop the forecastle, sitting cross-legged beneath his awning. Or an idol
erected by the Canarim. At mealtimes he would have to shake himself awake and

make his way through the cargo on the decks, sun-blind and light-headed. He felt sick climbing the little ladder sometimes. He realized that he would converse with someone if they had a mind to join him. Oçem, perhaps, but he rarely came on deck. These days, these weeks, were intermissions or intervals between deep sleeps. They could end at any second. He would jerk awake and everything would begin again: the donkey-headed Dom Francisco, or the orders awaiting him on São Thomé, or the animal Oçem tended so assiduously belowdecks. He was primed for his indolence's ending in an instant. Instead, insensibly at first and very gradually thereafter, it grew cold.

A heavy swell got up and and began rolling under the ship. Gonçalo took down his awning and stowed it below. Teixeira watched a weather front spread from horizon to horizon and rise above them, an enormous suspended wave of thunderheads. The storm advanced out of it like a tun of tar rolling down a mountainous sea, its staves the size of tree-trunks, splintering and spilling its black stain across the sky. The wind swung to a sou'westerly and increased steadily. Gonçalo had the sails reefed until the *Ajuda's* yards held no more than thin strips of canvas along their lengths, and still the masts bent alarmingly, for after a certain pitch, the wind changed its character, seeming to hold back for a second or two before pounding forward again. Then the ship would rock to leeward, for they were sailing due west now, past an invisible lee shore that was the Cape and would smash them in an instant if the wind should push them onto it. No bearings could be taken in such conditions; Gonçalo did not even try. From time to time a pale disk of light showed briefly through the clouds. The sea to windward was a chaos of precipices and crags. The ship rose and fell within them, crashing down into troughs from which Teixeira could not believe she would rise.

Teixeira realized that the storm that had almost destroyed them on Goa's bar was no more than a squall, noise without force, nothing compared with this. That was the first day. On the morrow he realized that these winds and seas were a respite or holding-off, that the sea contained depths of thoughtless rage and malevolence that he had not imagined possible and that now that bile was being brought up from a stomach that had swallowed bigger and better than the *Ajuda.* The rain came.

It came in sheets. Within the hour every scrap of clothing belonging to every man from Dom Francisco down to the boy who washed pots for the cook was soaked. Within the day everyone aboard knew that they would stay soaked for the duration of the storm. Teixeira lay sleepless in his cabin, kept awake through the night by the *Ajuda's* lurches and plunges, her sways and rolls, as the sea broke over bows and the rain raked her decks like grapeshot. In the morning he shrank from the touch of wet wool on his skin and shivered until his body warmed the sopping cloth, staggering about his cabin like a drunk while he drew the hose over his legs. His clothes clung to him like bandages soaked in brine. Opening the cabin door, he caught a falling column of spray, and then he was just as wet as he had been when he had tugged off his clothes the night before. Disdaining his flesh, the wind cut him open to suck the heat directly from his bones.

Estêvão was harnessed to the foot of the mizzen, his mouth open as he bellowed up into the rigging. Eight men were working up there. Teixeira hauled himself across deck, clinging to the ropes lashed about the cargo. At the ladder to the poop deck he looked up again. It seemed unimaginable, but there they were, clinging to a spar jutting from a wooden pole that swung, and bent, and shuddered, doing all in its power to shake them off and drop them into the sea that boiled fifty feet below them. They were naked but for strips of cloth about their loins, wrestling with a corner of the lateen that two or three of them would grasp, then pull on, while the others scrambled to tie it down. But the wind would not have it, ripping the canvas from their hands as soon as they offered it to the blast. The heaving sea, the gale, the rain, these howled together at a volume that made them indistinguishable. The vessel shuddered as he climbed the ladder, and he cringed like a child. Heavy men were beating one another to death in the storm breaking over his head, their blows thudding and impacting with unimaginable weight. Estêvão shouted something down to the men on the tiller.

"Here! Hold here."

Teixeira clung gratefully to the offered rope.

"What are you out here for?"

They had to shout to make themselves heard. He did not know. Estêvão looked up again. One of the hands had made his way out to the far end of the spar and was gesturing to the nearest of the others. It seemed all he could do to cling on there, but then an arm came free and through the rain pelting his face Teixeira saw him grip a water-stiffened rope and put a bight around the spar.

"Good man!" Estêvão yelled up, but they ignored that or did not hear it. He turned again to Teixeira. "Get below, Dom Jaime. You have no business here."

He clambered down and pulled himself hand over hand to the hatch-cover. As he lowered himself down he glanced forward. There was something on the deck of the forecastle, a man-size mound wrapped in a cape against the water that the *Ajuda's* prow smashed from the sea and sent up in cascading towers of foam. The shape made no effort to escape either the continual drenching or the biting winds. Gonçalo, thought Teixeira, and slipped below, pulling the hatch shut behind him.

The air down there was heavy with the smell of the men, of their wet clothes, their ammoniac urine, the swilling ballast, but most of all with damp. A man was vainly trying to coax the firebox into life but succeeding only in adding reeking smoke to the dead air that hung between the decks down here. A few lanterns swung from the beams and threw pools of weak yellow light into the darkness. The men nearest them turned to look at him. The storm was a dull hammering down here, but the ship's motion seemed more violent than ever, a random jolting and seesawing. He clung to the ladder for support. Oçem appeared out of the darkness.

"Dom Jaime! You have come to visit us, and already I am ashamed. No *chi.*" He gestured to the firebox. "Not even a bowl of rice, unless you prefer it dry?"

A sudden lurch threw him off-balance and he almost fell. Oçem caught him by the arm.

His eyes adjusted slowly to the gloom. More faces appeared, and more behind them, and then more still. The men were crowded together like cattle amongst the tied-down guns, crates, barrels, coiled ropes, rolls of canvas, and timber that was stacked in depots up and down the length and breadth of the lower deck. The headroom was less than the height of a man, so the hands crouched and bent their necks beneath the beams.

"You would be worried about the Ganda," Oçem said then. Teixeira glanced back quickly, but there was no light back there. He could not see. Only darkness, and neither movement nor the sound of movement. The beast might as well be dead. "We are trying to train him to piss in a bucket," Oçem went on, looking back with him now, "but this is not successful. He pisses on the deck."

It was the beast's urine he could smell. He noticed that though Oçem had swept his hair into some semblance of order, his clothes were filthy. The other men watched them incuriously. His head began to ache from the foulness of the air.

"Would you see the sick men now?" Oçem asked him.

"Sick? Which sick men?"

"We have almost a dozen now. Did you not know this? No, no, I see you. . . . And why should you, when the weather is as it is?"

His head was beginning to spin, the train of Oçem's thought a snapped cable slithering over the side, lost. . . . Sick? Sick of what? He followed numbly, grasping onto the beams overhead, stumbling after Oçem, who moved more easily. The men moved aside for them or, rather, for his guide. He leads them, he thought suddenly, already wondering why something so obvious had not occurred to him before.

"Here they are!" Oçem said with a little flourish.

Hammocks had been improvised and strung between the foremost bulkhead and the nearest crossbeam. They stretched across the width of the deck, careened like a row of small boats. Oçem called in his own language and a man hurried forward, bearing one of the lanterns. The hammocks swayed, and the men's faces stared up at him from the bottom of narrow trenches formed from the rising sides of the canvas. It would be easy to simply sew the narrow openings shut and inter them there, each in his shroud of canvas. He passed along the row. The sick men were expressionless, not reacting to this intrusion.

"What is wrong with them?" he asked.

Oçem reached down into the last of the hammocks. His fingers touched the sick man's mouth, and he said something that Teixeira did not catch. The man's mouth opened.

Teixeira almost retched. The stench that hit his nostrils spoke of decay, of flesh fit for maggots. The man's teeth were long as a dog's fangs; the gums had peeled away from them, and the remaining flesh was black. The tongue, too, which was swelled to twice its normal size, a fat ball of rot in there. He turned away, and found that the men had crowded around him and were watching him expectantly while the ship continued to pitch and roll, the sea butting her from side to side.

"What can I do?" Or anyone? Oçem eyed him for a second, then let his gaze fall. The men began to turn away. He had failed something, some test. That was why Oçem had led him here, to show that he was powerless.

"This one has stopped eating," Oçem said then, and shrugged. "Cannot swallow, you see?"

He nodded. It was intolerable, being down here with these men.

A commotion then, a rise in the storm's noise. The hatch was opening, and the men from the watch coming off duty were hardly bothering to climb down, preferring to let themselves fall and then simply lie there on the deck. Their fellows picked them up without surprise. One began shouting, marshaling the next watch. Teixeira moved aft again and watched as a score or more of them clambered out to take the places of the exhausted men. A great wash of water spilled down the hatch and doused him from head to toe.

"Dreadful weather," Oçem called out behind him. He was being mocked somehow and did not reply.

Crawling back to his quarters, he saw men from the watch just come on duty begin clambering up the mizzen. The lateen had come loose again. Spray falling on the deck barely made the gutter before the next mountain of water broke against the *Ajuda*'s sides, sending up great columns of freezing brine. The sea's violence was a kind of insanity, a thousand armies all fighting without allegiance or strategy, mere murder. Slopes of black water yawned open before them, and they plunged forward. Mountains broke apart, became precipices, hurled themselves against other mountains, smashed them, smashed against the ship. . . . That they might survive a moment in this chaos was a miracle. At Ayamonte they were trying to draw a line through this, he thought, but he could not laugh.

After that, he saw the storm out from his cabin, leaving it only to join Estêvão and Dom Francisco in the latter's quarters. There they chewed on dried sticks of meat and drank brackish cask-water and a fiery spirit that Dom Francisco tapped from a small barrel. They sat huddled in damp blankets and shivered, concerned only with the warmth of their bodies and the filling of their stomachs. Their silences were not awkward now. The storm had worn them down to this. The *fidalgo* drank moderately but constantly, and his face glowed from the alcohol. From the few words that passed between the latter and Estêvão, Teixeira understood that they were drifting in this tempest, that the winds were blowing them north and west, that the Cape was somewhere out there, and that it would wreck them if they were blown upon it.

"We might have already passed it," Estêvão said dully. Dom Francisco nod-

ded. There was nothing they could do in either case. They dared not sail any farther off the wind for fear of turning the *Ajuda* broadsides to the storm. It might
take a single wave then. Or it might take two. The ship would roll and keep
rolling until she buried herself in the sea. It would be quiet down there, thought
Teixeira. Just a few fathoms below this madness was an immeasurable silence. A
wrong turn of the tiller would do it. No more than that.

Gonçalo never joined them, and to Teixeira's eyes he never left the deck,
though that was impossible. The pilot hauled himself about by the ropes strung
from the rails, shouting directions to the men unlucky enough to be sent aloft
and cursing the teams on the tiller if they left his bearing by so much as a single
degree. The freezing rain and wind lashed at him. He cinched himself to the foremast and watched the sea's rage for hour after hour. On the splinter of tossed
wood that was his vessel, amongst the beams, planks, spars, ropes, canvas, and the
flesh and bone that wrestled and fought with these, he alone was immovable, and
irreducible. Everything and everyone else were ground down by cold and exhaustion to mere matter, failing resistances, bodies that bled their warmth into the
sea. There were twelve sunless days and thirteen moonless nights of this. And then
Teixeira woke to stillness and silence, and for a moment, shut up in his cabin and
wrapped in his sodden blankets, he believed that the sea had indeed swallowed
them and they were dungeoned on the ocean floor, at a peace beyond the slightest shudder or sound. He stood in the doorway of his cabin and rubbed the sleep
from his eyes. Sunlight flooded the deck. The storm had passed.

Every hatch and door on the vessel was thrown open, lines were strung up,
and soon the *Ajuda* more resembled a laundry than the deck of a ship as the crew
stripped and dried their clothes in the strong sunshine. Salt crusting on the drying
ropes and canvas fell to the deck and crunched underfoot. The sodden planking
steamed. Gonçalo once again erected his awning on the forecastle while the men
staggered about bare-chested, himself included, stretching and blinking, soaking
in the sun's warmth. The firebox was brought up and soon the smell of boiling
stockfish drifted about the ship. Finally the men of the lower deck brought up
their dead.

Teixeira watched as the same ceremonies were performed six times over:
Dom Francisco's mumbled prayer, the upended plank, and the sound the canvas
made as it slid down the wood. A silence. A splash. Three of the sacks had not
been weighted properly, and the winds being light, they floated off the stern in
sight of the ship for more than an hour. The hands, as before, seemed unperturbed, placing little blocks of incense in the firebox, which Oçem tended carefully. One stopped, and he and Oçem exchanged a few words. The man turned as
if to go, then changed his mind and resumed the discussion, which seemed to
grow heated, though they spoke the Canarim tongue and Teixeira did not understand a word. A few of the other men looked around, but then Oçem barked
something quickly and the man stopped in midsentence. Oçem turned away, and

Teixeira caught his eye. The keeper shrugged ruefully. The men went back to their work. Sails were unreefed, and two gangs worked their way around the rigging under Estêvão's direction, finding two spars cracked along their grain and replacing them. The lateen, not needed in these winds, was suffered to fly loose until it dried. One of the longboats had been smashed irreparably and was broken up for firewood, of which there was precious little now. Teixeira watched the vessel he had known before the storm heal her wounds with magical swiftness and become again the *Ajuda*. It was a day of ease and respite, of exorbitant luxury after the privations of the fortnight past. Teixeira allowed himself that much, and then, when the cross of stars by which they navigated appeared in the sky a few minutes after sunset, he sought out Gonçalo.

He found the pilot on the poop deck, his eye fixed on the southern sky they were leaving behind them. The man appeared to rest upon some deep stillness that he found far beneath the gentle roll of the deck or the surges of the sea that rocked the vessel, pinned there by a beam of light sought in the night sky. Teixeira watched him for long minutes before the pilot lowered the instrument from his eye. Turning, he looked unsurprised at his presence. Teixeira followed him down to the space he had cleared for himself in the steerage and waited while he pored over tables of figures and made slow calculations. After that it was quick. Gonçalo unrolled a chart and drew his finger across it east to west, cutting across the very tip of the continent and then continuing out into empty ocean. The finger roved back and forth, narrowing their position to a line of thirty or forty leagues' length. They were somewhere upon it, but, their bearings lost in the storm, they would not know where until they next sighted land. "Here," said Gonçalo, indicating a dot to the north and west of them. "Santa Helena. We can take on wood and water there, fresh food—" He broke off. Teixeira was glaring at him.

"There—" He stabbed the chart at a point due north of them. "As we agreed. As I told you. As the Duc would have ordered if he were not in Cochin when we sailed. São Thomé."

The pilot was shaking his head. "We will not reach her in time. We have water for sixteen days, food for less and much of it bad. The men we buried today will only be the first. . . ." He stopped again.

"We must talk with Dom Francisco," Teixeira said crisply. "He will resist the notion, though for no better reason than his dead nag. I expect your support in this, do you understand me, Pilot?" The man said nothing, so Teixeira went on. "Here Dom Francisco is the master. Ashore he will not prove so valuable a friend. You wish to return to Goa, to your wife, and so you shall. But whether you sail in the first vessel of the season or the last in ten years' time is more difficult to tell. What is certain is that you will sail in a ship in the service of Dom Manolo, and it is to Dom Manolo that I report on our return."

"You would threaten me on this matter?" Gonçalo murmured then. "Is this beast so important that you would risk the crew for ten days' sailing?"

"The best part of a month's sailing, as I understand it," Teixeira replied. "And yes, the animal is dearer to me than a hundred of Dom Francisco's horses, and it is dearer yet to our King."

The pilot shook his head, his face adamant. "I will not do it," he said.

Teixeira sighed. "Tell me about the *Cinco Chagas*," he said softly.

Gonçalo stared at him, his face expressionless. "She was lost."

"How was she lost?"

This time there was a long pause before Gonçalo answered. "She ran aground."

"And you were her pilot?"

Silence.

"And you were her pilot?"

A longer silence followed. The man would not meet his eye. Teixeira let it go on, knowing now how the Duc had persuaded the pilot to sail in the *Ajuda*. After a while he spoke again. "Come. Let us tell Dom Francisco where his vessel is going."

The southeast trades would be blowing steadily in a few weeks' time; for the moment they were variable, and the ship sped along one day only to find herself becalmed the next. A weak southerly current was all they could rely on then. It flowed across the face of the coast that they sighted at Angra dos Ilheos, its odd pair of conical islands identified positively by the great cross erected on the larger one. Teixeira watched it disappear as their bearing took them out again and they began climbing the latitudes to São Thomé. Dom Francisco had blustered and shouted, and finally Teixeira had fetched his own orders and laid them out in front of the man, who had squinted, his tongue sticking from the side of his mouth with the concentration required to decipher them. Then he had disowned himself from the disasters that would surely follow from this piece of lunacy and ordered both him and Gonçalo from his quarters. First his horse and now his ship, thought Teixeira. How the man must hate me.

The salted meat and dried fish had rotted in their barrels and were useless now. There was a little rice and rather more flour, which were both cooked into cakes on deck. The ship's company was put on half rations, and Teixeira felt his hunger grow and become a hard stone lodged in his abdomen. At first he sat in his cabin by day and ventured out only to eat and meet with Gonçalo, who plotted their course an hour after sunset. By his reckoning, and at their present rate of progress, they would sight São Thomé in fifteen or sixteen days, "if there were any left alive to look," he added bleakly.

It was growing hotter. Teixeira's cabin became stifling, forcing him out on deck. Much of the cargo stored there had been ruined and jettisoned after the storm. His own lading was bales of silk, twelve full quintals crated and wrapped in oilskin, stored somewhere below and most probably rotting now. He tried to calculate their worth in cruzados and reis, then his own worth, then the *Ajuda*'s. . . .

If the Ganda were not flesh, bone, hide, and horn, but silk, how much would he fetch. How many of the heavy gold coins? How many men?

As Gonçalo had predicted, more men began to fall sick, and those who were already sick began to die; by the end of the first week four more bodies had been sewn into bags and thrown over the side with no more ceremony than that. Dom Francisco's watch mustered fewer than thirty men now, and looking about the crew, he saw hollow faces and gray skin. Those still able to work moved about listlessly, taking an hour over tasks requiring a few minutes, sometimes coming to a glassy-eyed halt and staring forward at a point that seemed to be receding rather than drawing nearer. The next day those men would join the sick, and then the ship would be more shorthanded still. Dom Francisco shambled about, barking the odd order to the men on his watch, who then looked furtively to Estêvão for confirmation before carrying it out until Teixeira feared another outburst of the *fidalgo*'s temper. It never came. These slights went unnoticed, or perhaps the man no longer cared. It was the fact of São Thomé's drawing nearer, the petty defeat that that spoke of, Teixeira speculated privately. Or Dom Francisco was only biding his time. He should check his lading of silk, he told himself. He should get down into the hold with the sick men and with the beast. Oçem told him that the animal was thriving, eating its way steadily through bales of hay and straw, standing there obediently while its keeper rubbed lanolin into its hide or shoveled the dung from its enclosure. Each morning the native would stagger up on deck to empty a basketful of the beast's droppings over the side, wincing theatrically under its weight when he caught Teixeira's eye. Its contents rained down like gravel. He watched this, he ate, he slept. Their vessel continued, hour by hour and league by league, but the *Ajuda* herself was strangely set apart from them now; it was no longer the ship demanding their labors, nor the sea sucking the life from them. These were merely the places where they did this. Day after day they woke to the cloudless skies that arched over them horizon to horizon, utterly indifferent to their fate. A man drank seawater and went mad. Other men fell sick. The ship seemed hushed and the sea was calm, a bystander. The malaise was all their own.

One night there was a sound outside his door. He later calculated that this was five days' sailing from their landfall, although in its immediate aftermath he thought of it as "the night before he fell," for the five days would pass him insensibly or nearly so. He was lying in his cabin in near complete darkness—the hatch-cover to his window having swung shut and being himself unable to muster the energy to rise and reopen it—perhaps he was sleeping, perhaps awake. His memory of it was confused or blurred. There was a soft knocking at his door; he remembered that, at least. And there was a native, one of the hands, and he spoke brokenly, supplementing his words with little mimes and gestures. He whispered. He recalled the one word they held in common, which was "Ganda," and the man was saying that he should be brought up on deck. There was more, but he could not grasp it, and the man was frightened, crouched down that he might not be seen, eventually shrinking away when he realized that no more might be accomplished. It was only then that Teixeira remembered him: the man who had quarreled with Oçem on deck the day after the storm. Want of food or the bleaching moonlight had altered the shape of his face. He staggered back into his cabin, strangely debilitated by the encounter. There was a taste to his mouth, metallic, putrid. He realized that it had been there all day and he had not noticed until now. He exhaled slowly and sniffed. Rot.

The next morning he woke, rose, swung his legs over the side of his bunk, and fell heavily to the floor. He lay there for some minutes, dully surprised. His legs seemed to have lost all sensation. His arms appeared not to be strong enough to raise him. He thought of calling out for help, but even this was beyond him. His tongue felt fat in his mouth, and the taste was stronger now. He lay there for a while, then fell asleep again.

The next time he awoke he was back in his bunk and Estêvão was standing over him, trying to spoon something into his mouth. It was cold and thick, difficult to swallow. Estêvão's face became the native crewman's. He said, "Ganda," but his tongue was swollen and filled his mouth. The word sounded wrong. Then it was Estêvão again, and then the crewman's, who was not the man who had come to him but another, quite different. The face kept changing, though he understood vaguely that he was falling asleep between these metamorphoses and the arms shaking him awake from time to time, then lifting the spoon to his mouth, belonged to different men. The intervals were dreamless black silences or submergences from which he would surface briefly before sinking once more. "Ganda," he said again, but there was no one present to hear. He waited patiently for someone to return.

"Ganda."

"What of him?" said Estêvão.

He swallowed hard on the cold mash in his mouth. He said, "Bring him on deck." He had to repeat it before Estêvão understood.

"He's already there," said the boatswain. "We've built a cage for him. He's sick. Even sicker than you."

He moved more of the mash around his mouth. He could taste nothing, though it smelled of onions, perhaps. *Sick? Sick of what?* He tried to gather his energy, then asked, "When do we . . . ?" That was all he could manage.

Estêvão indicated that he understood. "Landfall? São Thomé?"

He nodded, already falling back into sleep.

"Well, let me see," he heard the man say. "That would be about dawn, and two days ago. We're anchored in Povoasan Bay."

The bay curved around from a wooded headland that sloped abruptly to a shingle shore. Two short jetties extended into the water. Canoes of various sizes clustered about one, which was crowded with Negroes either loading or unloading boxes and sacks. A caravel was moored to the other. A wide track ran along the shorefront, passing before the frontage of several long wooden buildings, roofed with thatch of some sort but mostly open at the front. Wagons waited outside these. Farther back there was a jumble of little sheds or houses, perhaps, and behind these Povoasan suddenly became orderly. Long, straight rows of flat-roofed structures extended to left and right for a mile or more, thatched like the other sheds but much larger. Behind the first row were others: seven, eight, perhaps more, ranked so closely together that it seemed a fat strip of the island had been lifted on poles and raised twelve feet off the ground. A single low hill rose behind it, up which two lines of tiny figures seemed to be ascending or descending. The *Ajuda* was anchored four or five hundred paces from the shore, and he could not make them out exactly. Apart from this interruption, the view was of the plantations, acre after acre, stretching back south for leagues in a yellowish-green monotone that rippled and swirled like a sea. It stopped only at the mountains. These rose suddenly, fifteen or twenty miles away, thickly wooded and so dark against the brightness of the sky that their greens appeared to him as blacks. He had slept again after Estêvão had left him. Another night had passed; more time lost. His legs felt weak and unsteady, only partially his own. Some of the hands were up on the poop deck, talking amongst themselves. Others were asleep on the hatch-cover. He looked about for Estêvão, but other than these men the ship was deserted. Then, through a narrow gangway between the crates and bales aft of the main mast, he noticed a structure that had not been there before. A large cubelike construction had been built out of the poop. Over this, sheets of canvas had been draped and tied down, their lower edges stopping inches short of the deck. The ends of thick wooden posts showed where they had been nailed to the planking.

"He is much happier now, in his tent. And you too, Dom Jaime. You are quite recovered. A miracle, would you say? I know very little of miracles, but this is the term Dom Estêvão used." It was Oçem.

He stared at the edifice without replying, so Oçem went on, telling him how the Ganda had stopped eating, then drinking, and finally had lain down, remaining motionless for two days before the enclosure was built on deck.

"And now? Is he recovered?" He spoke shortly, not looking at the man.

"He is different, Dom Jaime."

"Will he live?" he insisted then. The man exasperated him.

Oçem paused, then said, "We await another miracle."

The words fell on him like stones. Peres was unforgiving and unyielding. Dead, the beast was nothing. There was a long silence while he considered these things.

"I want to see him," he said abruptly. He strode toward the tented cage. Oçem caught him by the arm, suddenly distressed, asking him to wait. He shook the man off, reached forward, and pulled aside the canvas.

It was shapeless, some claylike substance shoveled into a low mound; he could not make sense of it in the shade within its cage. Then it rose, and a moment later it was the beast he knew, springing and turning on him much faster than he believed possible, the horn scything around and aimed at him, at his chest, its little eyes hunting for him in the sudden gush of light. . . . He fell back, startled, and Oçem jumped forward to pull the canvas shut. When he looked up, the hands on the poop deck were peering down at him. He waved them away angrily, an anger directed mostly at himself. What had happened? The Ganda had tried to get up. Then it had turned around to look at him. That was all.

"He can move," he said to Oçem.

"He can eat, too," the man replied. "But he chooses not to." There was a pause. "I think he will die quite soon."

Teixeira shook his head. "Where is Dom Francisco?" he asked.

"Ashore, with the others. The captain of this island sent boats for them at daybreak." Oçem watched him anxiously. "You are still weak," he said. "You should eat, then sleep again."

"Before I fell ill," Teixeira said carefully, "a man came to me. One of the hands. He said I should bring the Ganda on deck."

"But why did you not?" Oçem replied. "Dom Jaime, the beast might today be as well as yourself. . . ."

"Why did *you* not?" Teixeira turned on him. "And why did this man believe I should?"

"How would I know?" Oçem spread his hands. "We must find this man and ask him. What was his name?" He spoke vigorously and with great purpose, as if this were of the utmost importance.

But he had not asked the man's name, and though he would recognize him when he saw him, he could not give Oçem a description. He walked away and sat alone on the forecastle, sheltered from the sun by Gonçalo's awning. Across the length of the ship, Oçem and the men on the poop deck talked amongst themselves. Toward midday, two of them lit the firebox and cooked. The tented cage was quiet. The beast's deathbed, he thought bitterly. Perhaps if he had heeded the man and had ordered the animal brought up sooner . . . Or perhaps he would recover anyway. But why had the man come at all? He puzzled over this. Might Dom Francisco have made good on his threat after all, choosing the Ganda as his vulnerable proxy? Cut the mount down; its rider will follow. He thought uneasily of the white horse collapsing, a parallel that even the *fidalgo* might be capable of drawing. Yet it seemed beyond him, and there was no proof.

Glancing in to shore, he saw a few men move on the deck of the caravel. Wagons drawn by small oxen and piled high with bright green sugarcane trundled up and down the waterfront. Most of the canoes were gone now. He considered having the men lower the longboat and row him to shore. Peres's instructions awaited him there, instructions concerning the beast. An embalmer's manual would be more appropriate now. Or a missal. Before he could act on these thoughts, he saw a large rowboat set off from one of the jetties, manned by

Negroes who pulled powerfully on the oars. A white man sat toward its stern. He watched it draw near.

"Dom Jaime Teixeira! Dom Jaime Teixeira! Dom Fernão de Mello, Captain of São Thomé, requests the honor of your presence and commands me, Dom Pero de Cintra, to carry to you his warmest greetings. . . ."

His legs began to shake as he climbed down the rope ladder. Still weak, he thought. The Negroes swung the boat about. Instead of returning to the jetty, they made directly for the shore, leaping out into the water and hauling the boat the last twenty feet to the beach with her two passengers still sitting in her. Dom Pero's chatter washed over him as he staggered up the shingle, the lack of motion quite unfamiliar to him after so many months aboard the *Ajuda*. The caravel was called the *Picanço*, commanded by a gentleman of the name Dom Ruy Mendes da Mesquita, the first of the Mina fleet to arrive that year, and a full month ago at that, under license from Dom Afonso da Torres, which would—according to Dom Pero—greatly irritate Dom Christobal de Haro, who held the contract as far down the coast as Cabo Santa Caterina, the reason being the trades blowing weakly or strongly that year, or late, or in the wrong direction. . . . Teixeira listened with half an ear while they walked along the waterfront. A sound drifted in the air, audible only when Dom Pero paused to draw breath, a strangely agreeable wailing, but very faint and punctuated with brief stops and starts. Eventually he motioned for Pero to be silent and then he realized that it was singing.

"The Negroes chant while they are at their milling," Pero explained. He indicated the area behind the crude sheds they had passed, and Teixeira guessed that he must mean the roofs he had seen from the ship. But even as he listened, the singing suddenly stopped.

"Ah," said Pero. "That will be Dom Fernão. They always stop when he passes them at their work. It is a noise he cannot abide. Come, we are to meet him at the fort."

The fort turned out to be a kind of palazzo, built entirely of wood and thatched in the same manner as every other building on the island. A raised terrace surrounded it on all sides, and on each of its four corners stood a small cannon whose function seemed more ornamental than anything else. Two men were standing over one of these. One was pointing to something, and the other, nodding and laughing, was Dom Francisco. At the sight of him, the laughter stopped.

Dom Fernão de Mello approached and made a deep bow. He was of medium height, thickset, jowled and double-chinned. The heaviness of his face was offset by a pair of watery-blue eyes that made him appear strangely childlike, a perpetually swelling youth on the verge of a perpetually swelling tantrum. He spoke deliberately and generally to Teixeira, as though addressing a crowd that had gathered there only to hear his opinion. Once their greetings were done, the four men moved inside and began discussing the revictualing of the *Ajuda*. Prices were agreed, quantities and quality haggled over briefly. Dom Francisco bargained with Mello while Teixeira looked on, increasingly puzzled at the ease of these negotiations. Mello was known the breadth of the Indies as the man who had refused food to the starving men of the Mina garrison because they could not pay for it in gold. Granted, that was almost a decade ago now, but there were other stories, and worse, and here was the chandler-in-chief of the Guinea Coast humbly agreeing to whatever the lumpish Dom Francisco suggested. They would begin lading that very night and should be done in three days, perhaps two. Teixeira and Dom Pero watched them banter and bicker, the latter making no effort to hide his astonishment at this sudden transformation in the Captain of São Thomé. They were still making their final handshakes, Mello commenting with rueful admiration that Dom Francisco drove a harder bargain than King Manolo himself, when Teixeira interrupted to ask after his dispatch.

Both men fell silent. Mello turned to Dom Francisco, and Dom Francisco cleared his throat.

"That's all settled," he began gruffly. "I've already looked the thing over. We're to keep to our original course." He paused then. "Your sickness forced me to take appropriate action and being, I mean to say seeing, seeing that I am the master of the *Ajuda,* then I took it upon myself . . ." He came to a halt there, the clumsily rehearsed explanation foundering in his own ill-disguised discomfort.

Teixeira kept his face expressionless. The earlier sudden stifling of their laughter was growing clearer. Knowing that he would not see it otherwise, Dom Francisco had taken advantage of his illness to open his, Teixeira's, dispatch. Mello, no doubt, had inveigled him into it and then concocted the witless prevarication that Don Francisco was dutifully parroting now.

Outwardly he said, "Of course, Dom Francisco. In the event of my death it would have been necessary that you act in my place, and that would hardly be possible without instructions. . . ."

His voice was calm, almost toneless. Good, he thought, go on. "Nevertheless it would be awkward if Dom Fernão de Peres should learn that his dispatch's intended recipient was wholly ignorant of its contents. Original course or no, it might be best if I looked the thing over, do you not think?"

There was a short silence after he finished. Mello looked again to Dom Francisco. Dom Francisco looked back, baffled.

"The dispatch, Dom Francisco?" prompted the Captain of São Thomé.

The other reached into his doublet confusedly, then burst out, "But it's back there, where you . . ."

"Ah, you left it there. Your pardon, I thought you had picked it up."

Teixeira felt himself grow calmer while they played out this little pantomime, then Mello led him back through a series of rooms to one used as a study. The parchment lay on a small writing desk, Peres's seal instantly recognizable, its wax broken as expected. Mello handed it to him and left without another word.

Greetings, Dom Jaime. I have entrusted this to the hands of Duarte Alema, Captain of the Picanço, *and Ruy Mendes de Mesquita, her pilot, who sail from Belem to the Guinea*

Coast and São Thomé. You will receive it from the hands of Dom Fernão de Peres, Captain of that island and Dom Manolo's loyal servant. . . .

He snorted at that, then read on. Peres praised him for his tenacity in reaching São Thomé through the rigors of the voyage. There were references to the horrors of the Cape, then more praise for himself, then more exhortations. The fervent hope that they would meet soon and safely was expressed in both formal and familiar terms. He was wished good health and informed that he was remembered nightly in the prayers of both Dom Fernão de Peres and his wife. He almost laughed at this. The notion that Peres might conduct himself in private devotions was ludicrous to anyone who had spent two seconds in his company. The dispatch ended there, and his brief good humor with it. The beast had not been mentioned, nor its destination, nor . . . He put the parchment on the desk.

Then a grin spread over his face. He imagined Mello's exasperation as his patient subtleties lapped at the rocky headland of Dom Francisco's stupidity. Perhaps he changed character, swapping to a warm wash of bonhomie, two hard-living *fidalgos* on a godforsaken rock in the middle of the sea. . . . That would be better, and still, Teixeira felt sure, Dom Francisco was quite possibly unaware that his celebrated dealing to victual the ship was no more than a blind orchestrated by his sudden good friend the Captain of São Thomé to cover the fact of which he was also unaware and would have been outraged to learn, namely that he had been bribed. And Mello—Teixeira chuckled aloud at this—would be similarly unaware that there was no need to bribe the man in the first place. Dom Francisco would have opened it for a cup of Madeira and a slap on the back in any case. . . . He would have read it, and found nothing. And then Mello would have read it and found the same. It told him nothing, too, and in the manner by which it told him that it was *intended* to tell him nothing, he caught a faint sniff of the dubious statecraft, the double- and triple-blinds that were the very air that Peres breathed at Ayamonte. It was a whiff of the old fox himself. Peres and his wife at prayer . . . That was too good for words. Peres's wife had been dead for two decades.

He laughed without restraint, loud enough to bring Dom Pero running to inquire if all was well.

"Never better," he said, still laughing. He was the servant of a man who had cut him adrift in the middle of an ocean with a dying monster for company. Soon he would be the disgraced servant of the same man, who would tether him to the beast's cadaver and cut him adrift in the more treacherous currents of the court, where he would drown.

Mello and Dom Francisco had disappeared when they reemerged. Dom Pero watched him warily while explaining that the Captain would give what he termed "a banquet" that night for the gentlemen of the two vessels arrived at São Thomé. In the meantime he had been instructed to show Dom Jaime whatever he wished of the island.

"Where are Dom Estêvão and Dom Gonçalo?" he asked the man, and was told that they were supervising the transport of the stores. He considered joining them, but if Peres's "instructions" told him anything, it was that it no longer mattered what he did here or how he spent his time. "I should like to see the mills," he said. Dom Pero shouted for two horses to be saddled.

The Negroes' singing rose in waves, in fat chords of sound that swelled and stopped, then started again. A man's voice barked the chant in the intervals, and the music followed from that, twisting obediently when a new element was introduced, following until it was replaced by a new modulation and the song moved forward again, huge and low in the air. They passed through trees and high grasses that Teixeira could not identify. The track widened and they came face-to-face with the factory.

The roofs he had seen from the ship stretched away from him now in a single enormous thatched canopy. It was divided into sections only by the different tasks performed beneath it. The Negroes worked stripped to the waist, overseen by other Negroes who swaggered about amongst them, carrying long sticks or machetes. Nearest them it appeared that hundreds of cooking pits had been dug in the ground, each with a large kettle suspended above it. The men tending these alternated between feeding the fires below the pots and stirring and skimming their contents.

"We burn the water off the molasses here," said Pero. "Then it is sent to the curing houses."

"Where do these men come from?" Teixeira asked then.

"The traders buy them at Mpinde or Gató. Most are sent on to Mina or Pernambuco, but all of them pass through São Thomé. We have the pick of them," Pero said then. "Or did."

"Did?"

"The trade has slowed of late. There have been problems. . . . Not here, of course. On the mainland. The natives have stopped trading, or the Mani has banned them again. We do not know. Such things have happened in the past. Something strange. . . ." He caught himself there and forced a cheerful expression upon his features. "Shall we view the crushing?"

The workforce employed on the reduction of the molasses was dwarfed by that crushing the juice from the cane. Teixeira was presented with the same tableau reproduced a thousandfold: a Negro standing straddled over a long wooden basin, in his hands a heavy trunk of wood with which he pounded the raw cane until both it and he were soaked in the liquor. Their chants took the rhythm from this work, and the air was at once thick with the heavy smell of the juice and vibrant with the song that went on and on, seeming to have no end. The same kettles he had seen over the fires were brought around, the sugar-juice emptied into these and carried away. Men toting huge bales of raw cane would follow, empty the pulped megass, and replace it with new stalks. Then the process would begin again. As the men carrying away the megass threaded a path back through the workers, the pounding would already have resumed.

"Where are they going?" he asked Pero, pointing to one of the bearers.

"To the Hill," said Pero. "Dom Fernão has been building it for many years now. Some of the megass is dried for fuel. The rest goes to the Hill."

"I should like to see it," he said.

The overseers glared at Pero as he steered a path through the men. Emerging finally on the other side of the factory, Teixeira looked up at the Hill. At first he thought the whole pile was smoldering, for it steamed and seemed to give off heat. The steam stank of decomposition, however, and the men climbing up its sides some little way to their left showed no hint of fear. They carried loads of pulverized fiber, and as they ascended their legs sank to the knees in the cane-mulch. Each step meant pulling one leg free and planting it deep in the hot compost, then shifting the body's weight forward and repeating the process for the other leg. Teixeira was about to ask what purpose this decomposing monument was supposed to serve when a commotion started up. Four men, overseers by their weapons, were pursuing a fifth up the side of the Hill, all five scrambling madly and shouting in a language he did not understand. Two of the overseers carried ropes, and as Teixeira watched they caught up with their quarry, who was brought down and silenced for a second by a blow to the side of his head. Then he was shouting again, and Teixeira heard the pleading tone in his voice turn to panic as the ropes were produced. They had him tied in a trice and then were dragging him like a log by his ankles, farther up and around the slope.

"Thieving," said Pero by way of explanation. The men quickly disappeared from sight, but he was already moving left around the base of the Hill, forcing his horse through the line of bearers, who had not slowed their pace or even looked up at the disturbance. When he caught sight of them again, two of the overseers were digging a pit high up on the side of the Hill, kneeling to scoop out the rotting stalks with their bare hands. When they were done, all four simply upended the man and lowered him headfirst into the hole until only his legs were showing. Even bound, Teixeira could see the violence of the man's struggles. Then the four crouched to gather armfuls of the megass and began tamping it into the pit with their feet. Within a minute they were done, and all that was visible of their victim was his calves and feet protruding from the side of the Hill. The line of bearers continued climbing as before, but now the overseers were marshaling them along a new route, shouting and lashing out with their sticks as though the act they had performed excited them or provoked them to this. Teixeira watched as the first bearer dropped his load where the thief had been buried, then the next, and the next. . . . He became aware that Pero had joined him.

"What did he steal?" he asked tonelessly.

"Sugarcane. It is usually that. They eat it, you see. . . . You must understand, Dom Jaime, before you condemn Dom Fernão, you must understand that these men are valuable, that it is not greed, not greed for a stalk of sugarcane. . . ."

"How many are buried in there?" Teixeira asked, still looking up. The thief had already disappeared beneath a growing mound of megass.

"You must listen to me, Dom Jaime. When Dom Fernão first came here there was nothing. Nothing at all. I have seen him. . . . I saw him once. He knelt, it was near here, he brought his hands together like this, and he looked up as though in prayer, but then he looked down, at the earth, and he drove his hands into the earth, he plowed it with his bare hands that day, and everything you see here, he built, with those same hands, those same soft hands, and now the King he has served here would revoke his contract and send a factor to take it all away, to ruin it. . . ."

The man was babbling. He was tired, sick. He did not want to hear. So Mello feared him, took him for Manolo's spy. That the *Ajuda* might truly be here only as the barge of the beast dying on her decks? No, of course it was absurd. Mello would not give it credence for an instant. He turned his horse away. Pero came abreast of him, still talking, the apologist of a madman, his voice a nervous clatter. He listened instead to the Negroes' chanting, which was unending and vast, an unbroachable pulse that filled and weighted the air. As they left the Negroes behind them, he noticed that their horses were walking in step with it.

"Joao Afonso de Aveiro, who is the factor at Gató by the city of Benin; Dom Valentim Coelho and Dom Fernando da Montoroio, traders to the Mani-Congo; Dom Ruy Mendes da Mesquita, the master of the *Picanço;* and Dom Duarte Alema, her pilot. Myself, the Captain, yourself, and Dom Francisco. . . ."

They were walking their horses along the side of a number of large pens, all of them empty. Something in Pero's recital caught his attention then, but he could not grasp it. He asked the man to repeat the list of Mello's banquet guests and listened more carefully to the repetition.

After reaching the "fort," Pero called for men to take their horses and then disappeared after them. Teixeira sat down on the terrace and quickly reread Peres's letter, nodding with satisfaction as he confirmed his suspicion. He began to think how the encounter so obliquely signaled by the man a thousand leagues distant might be engineered, for it would have to be that night, at the "banquet in their honor," whatever those two things might turn out to be. Laid out before him, the bay was a windless bowl in which the *Picanço* and *Ajuda* appeared embedded, the water flat and gelatinous. He could not see the Hill from here, but the sight of the living man's burial was still before him. He wondered how many other such sacrifices had preceded this latest. And sacrifices to what? Mello? God? The reeking rot itself? He dismissed these thoughts, they did not help him. The bay was in shadow then, the *Ajuda,* too, and the structure on her deck. Where the Ganda was dying.

That night, the guests arrived in twos: Joao Afonso de Aveiro and Dom Fernão de Mello, the factor and the Captain, stood outside the fort to greet their guests. First him and Dom Francisco; then the slavers, Dom Valentim Coelho and Dom Fernando da Montoroio; last Dom Ruy Mendes da Mesquita, master of the *Picanço,* and Dom Duarte Alema, her pilot. They ate capons that were cooked on spits over a firepit in front of the terrace, where they sat. Negroes stood one behind each, fanning the eight men, who pulled hot flesh off the carcasses as they arrived at the table and licked the grease off their fingers. They drank sweet rum that Dom Fernão told them was made on the island.

"I only wish we could sell it," he said. "Could you sell this in Antwerp?" he asked Mesquita.

"Sugar," said the *Picanço's* master. "Sugar to Antwerp and slaves to Mina. That's our run, when we're loaded." There was a note of complaint in his voice.

The slavers sitting to either side of Teixeira shifted on their seats and scowled. "Soon enough," said the one called Montoroio. "This situation cannot last forever."

"What situation?" Dom Francisco spoke up then, and it looked for a moment as though Montoroio would speak again. Mello cut him off.

"Scarcity." He thumped the table with his fist. "That's the heart of trade. No scarcity, no trade. No one turned a profit in the Garden of Eden, did they? I remember the time when a good healthy *peça* could be had for three shaving basins and a rusty knife. No longer, my friends. The Negroes are treacherous, and we are far from home." The last phrase was spoken as a truism, familiar to the others, who smiled, all except Aveiro.

"Their treachery is the same as ours," he said. "Only now they know the value of the trade. Or did."

"Did? The situation? What is this *situation?*" Teixeira could see that Dom Francisco's color had risen, his temperament with it.

Aveiro answered him calmly. "They've stopped the trade," he said simply. "I oversee the factory at Gató, have done for thirty years. The Oba there, that is their King, sells his slaves to me. Until a month ago. A month ago he stopped the trade, then refused to see me, and then a week ago I was pulled out of my bed and thrown into a canoe and paddled down the river to the coast. . . ." He stopped there and spread his hands in bewilderment. His face, though, remained unsurprised.

"It is the same down the coast at Mpinde," said Montoroio. "The Mani speaks, the Congo Negroes obey. About a month ago. Since then, nothing. And nothing we can do about it."

"Don't be so sure," said Coelho. He was younger than the other and more pugnacious in his expression. "There's still Ndongo, and other places upriver of there—"

"I won't hear that!" Mello broke in fiercely. "I won't listen to a man talk of breaking his license. I won't have it, Coelho. Do you hear me?"

For a moment it looked to Teixeira that the two might rise from the table and come to blows. Across the table from him, Alema, the pilot, who had said nothing all evening, looked between them in alarm. Then Aveiro's voice cut through the rising heat of the row.

"Caught a real little pirate before I left." He spoke calmly, as though the other two were noisy children and would subside if simply ignored. "Walked into Benin cool as you please, tattoos from head to toe: a real old *lançado,* I reckon. I'd heard of him, of course. Been up north in the forest trading with the Warri for ten years or more. Claimed he didn't know that he needed a license. . . ." This produced guffaws of disbelief from around the table. "Anyway," Aveiro went on imperturbably, "this villain knew something about trade, and he knew something about why it was stopped, so he said."

The others went quiet at that, leaning forward and suddenly attentive, all except Mello. He sat back in his chair and his eyes roved around the table. He has heard this already, Teixeira thought.

"He was up in a village near the head of the Fermoso. A little over a month ago, about two weeks after the rains stopped, a man walks in, not a villager, a man from some other tribe, carrying a *ju-ju,* that's a kind of holy stick they have," he explained for the benefit of the newcomers. "The villagers greet him, treat him with respect, and then they hold a meeting, from which our *lançado*'s excluded. A few days after that he's woken up by the man he does business with and told to leave. Before he can even gather his goods, some more men arrive, men he knows well, mind you. They put a spear to his guts and march him out of the village. When he looks back, they're burning his hut and everything in it. That was his story."

"The same as your own," said Montoroio. "Except for the man with the *ju-ju.*"

Aveiro nodded. "So I thought. But then I remembered something from my first year at Gató, the same year the Oba there was crowned. There was a vast ceremony going on for days, eating, drinking, masquerades, and so on. And then, right at the end, a fellow turns up and, this is the odd thing, the whole thing stops. The whole city—and it's a huge city up there, big as Lisbon—the whole place comes to a halt. This fellow walks in alone, enters the Oba's compound, and when he comes out, the Oba's been crowned. What I remember is that he carried an odd-looking *ju-ju,* just like the one my pirate described."

"And this fellow crowned the Oba of Benin?" Montoroio sounded incredulous.

"As I remember it. I asked about him then, but no one would tell me for a long time. In fact, they regarded me very strangely if I so much as mentioned it. . . ."

"So you never found out," said Montoroio.

Aveiro snorted. "Of course I did. In the end I got a man drunk. He told me this fellow was from a tribe to the north and east of Benin. He was called 'Ezzery,' or 'the Ezzery,' if I remember right. No one goes up there, though. The Oba doesn't like it."

"Nor the Mani," said Montoroio. "North of the Rio dos Camarões. Have you marked that?"

He addressed this to Coelho, who nodded, saying, "The same area, only reached from the south—"

"So what are they hiding up there? This 'Ezzery'?" Mello broke in. No one answered. He turned again to Aveiro. "We must question this *lançado* of yours. Where have you got him?"

"The *lançado,* ah, a dying breed," Aveiro sighed. "There was a time we'd have called him a true *pombeiro* and had him sitting at this table with us. But that was a long time ago, eh, Dom Fernão? Before the likes of Afonso da Torres with his 'Contract for this-Coast' and Dom Christobal de Haro with his 'Contract for that-Coast,' and their licenses, and their licensees, no offense intended"—this was directed at Mesquita—"and before our King signed treaties with the likes of the Mani and the Oba. There used to be a man, and each man had a price, and that was that. . . . A long time ago, as I said. Different now." He reached for a bird from the plate before him and began pulling it apart. Teixeira realized belatedly that the factor was drunk. He had forgotten the question, and Mello had to prompt him to return to it.

"Ah yes, the *lançado,*" he said as though the matter had just then been raised. "Well, trading without a license. . . . I hanged him on the spot."

Teixeira looked across the table. Alema was staring at him.

"Let's have a song, shall we?" Mello appealed to the company then.

They sang for a while, then talked idly of the heat. Dom Ruy told anecdotes of the *Picanço*'s voyage and relayed the gossip from Mina, some two hundred leagues away on the mainland. Then he asked Dom Francisco the nature of the animal that, rumor had it, was stowed on the *Ajuda*'s deck.

"It is a kind of monster," said Dom Francisco. "And an evil one at that." He too was drunk by now, his tone sullen and morose. "It eats horseflesh," he said finally, and shot Teixeira a look of frank contempt across the table.

The banquet broke up soon after, the traders and Mello stumbling inside while the others walked off to find, respectively, the jetty where the *Picanço* was moored and the boat that would ferry them out to the *Ajuda*. Dom Francisco took Mesquita by the arm and began telling him how they had blasted their way out of the harbor at Goa: "Two full broadsides in less than two minutes! How's that for gunnery, Dom Ruy?" The *Picanço*'s master nodded politely. Teixeira watched them go.

"Dom Jaime?"

It was Alema, standing there waiting for him, hesitant. Nervous too, Teixeira saw. The man had scarcely touched his cup throughout the evening. Teixeira looked around casually, but the terrace was deserted now, except for the eight Negroes who had stood behind them through the hours of the evening and who still stood there, now fanning eight empty chairs. Dom Francisco's drunken babble faded into the night.

"You may stop," he told them. The men looked at each other but continued fanning. Teixeira shook his head, then turned back to Alema.

"You have the letter from Peres," he said, and watched the relief that washed over the younger man's face. Then the guarded expression returned.

"How did you know?"

"Mello's letter contained nothing, as you probably know." The young man shook his head at that. "You were mentioned as the *Picanço's* master and Dom Ruy as her pilot. Peres does not make mistakes like that without a reason. You have the letter with you?"

Alema reached within his coat and handed it over. "Normally we would be long gone by now," he said. "In other circumstances it would have been difficult to justify our wait here."

"Other circumstances? What is your pretext now?"

"You heard them at table. We have been waiting to lade for a month now. There are no slaves. It was the same along the coast. In the past we have put in a few leagues before Axim to take on fresh water, fresh vegetables. The prices at the fort itself are ruinous and so . . . It is harmless enough. We know the natives there, and they know to keep quiet. But this time, nothing." He shrugged, baffled. "They would not come out. We saw them watching us from the beach, but they would not come."

Teixeira folded the letter away carefully, half-listening to Alema, half-thinking of the words he would soon be poring over in his cabin. Peres's words.

"Did you meet him in person?" he asked the pilot. "Peres, I mean."

The man shook his head. "One of his lieutenants."

"Alvaro Carreira?"

"He did not give a name. A man a little older than myself." Alema paused then and looked about him hastily. "There is another matter," he began, speaking quickly and quietly. They were walking a deserted path whose curve unwound and gradually straightened, becoming the track that led along the waterfront to the jetties and the beach. Mesquita and Dom Francisco were visible a few hundred paces ahead, the latter now being supported by the caravel's captain. "Dom Ruy is of a mind to keep quiet, for if Mello knew, he would have every ship on the coast up there." He checked himself and organized his thoughts. "It was at the Rio Real. We had come too far along the coast, and drifted too far in. Even so, we were five leagues or more out, beating south against the wind. We only caught a glimpse of her, but there was a ship anchored in the estuary. That was a month ago now. Then I was thinking of what they were saying tonight, about the trade drying up. . . ."

"And so? Many ships trade here, do they not?" Teixeira could not fathom the man's excitement.

"Yes, yes, they do," Alema conceded. "But not there, and not now. When we left, the *Berrio* and *Esphera* were still looking for crews. We are the first this season. Perhaps it is a privateer, a Spanish vessel, or perhaps even French"—the latter was hazarded with a perceptible shudder—"but that does not explain her anchorage."

"This 'Rio Real'?"

"It is hardly a river," said Alema. "The coast there is a kind of swamp, or a flooded forest, the same for fifty leagues. The people there are called Ijaws, fishermen. But there is no trade. No gold, no pepper, Malagueta or tailless, no slaves."

They were almost at the beach now. Mesquita was already walking down the jetty, Dom Francisco blocked from view behind it. He listened as Alema explained that the mouth of the Real stood equidistant between those of the Fermoso and the Camarões. "If someone wished to trade with this all-powerful 'Ezzery,' then he would anchor there," he said. "Don't you think?"

Teixeira nodded agreement, but the pilot's theory seemed outlandish, a tissue of conjecture. The vessel might as easily have been blown off-course or anchored there to take on water, or perhaps to buy fish from these "Ijaws." It did not concern him. Only the beast concerned him. The pilot fell silent.

"You have done well," Teixeira said as they reached the jetty. "I will recommend you to Peres when I see him." That seemed to please the man.

"You will sail direct to Belem?" he asked.

"God willing," he replied, tapping the letter pressed against his chest. Peres willing, he thought.

They parted there, Alema walking quickly down the jetty to the caravel. Teixeira watched him board, then continued along the beach. The bay's black water broke into a white foam as it lapped and splashed up the beach, luminous in the light of the waning moon. Six tall figures were visible against it, then the boat, and last of all, a little way up the beach, he saw a prone figure. The *fidalgo* was snoring loudly, his knees tucked up against his chest.

"Horseflesh," he murmured to himself. "Monster." *And an evil one at that. . . .* He stood over the sleeper, waiting patiently for the saliva to gather in his mouth, watching impassively as it fell. The Negroes looked to him.

"Throw him in the boat," he said.

Greetings, Dom Jaime, once again,

I write in haste from Ayamonte, where our situation is perilous three times a day and the waves every bit as forceful as those you face at sea, though different in kind—I grant you that much. . . .

Peres's words, his voice, his hand. Teixeira felt the man's presence in the parchment he held before him.

The *Ajuda* had sailed two days later, revictualed and repaired. Now, closeted in his cabin, he reread the letter, searching it for clues, for the things he had missed in that first hurried reading the night of Mello's banquet. It was something to wave in Dom Francisco's face. He heard the men shouting on the deck above him. In an hour they would be in open waters, and he could not trust the *fidalgo* while they were anchored in the bay; it had to be now, before Gonçalo turned them about and they headed south to pick up the trades that would take them home. Not south, he thought. North. Not away from the great continent they had almost circled, but toward it. . . . Dom Francisco's reactions were invariable.

"What? That you can come to me and ask that, that . . ."

The man spluttered and raged in full view of the crew, the two of them up there on the poop deck with Estêvão, who tried to appear both deaf and blind to the man's ravings, absolutely absorbed in the trim of the sails. They will need to be trimmed again, he thought idly while Dom Francisco blustered in his face, for he would have his will.

I will not rehearse all how we are brought to this pass. You are not alone—I must tell you that first—though the company is not such as I would have you keep. All my efforts at Ayamonte have been directed to the safeguarding of our King's new possessions: those known, those yet to be learned of. That was my charge. Of the transactions in Rome, it was my wish that they never concern you. Our Orator there is Joao da Faria. It was he and Fernando's Orator, Vich, who were charged with procuring His Holiness's agreement to their sovereigns' treaty, for Leo has promised and yet delayed, affirmed and yet prevaricated. The bull has languished in the Camera above two years now. I believe you know the price that is required of us to drag His Holiness's hand to the inkpot. . . .

The beast: he rehearsed that to himself in the days that followed. The Ganda, the sick monster. *And an evil one at that. . . .* He looked again for the face that had appeared at his cabin door to warn him, scanning the watches as they changed with every eight turns of the glass. The man did not appear. He confided in Estêvão, who could tell him only that fifteen men had died of disease between the night of his visitation and their landfall at São Thomé. "Perhaps he was amongst them," the boatswain told him, leaving unsaid his clear conviction that the man was imagined, a harbinger of the sickness that was to overtake him, too. Perhaps it was so. There was time to turn it over, to consider and ponder as the ship made her way north, for the winds were light and contrary, the currents likewise. Gonçalo sat as always on the forecastle, silent, watching the water. Oçem spent his days on deck, sometimes adding his weight to the ropes, for they were short-handed now but usually sprawled beside the cage, into which he would poke armfuls of hay in the morning only to retrieve it, uneaten, in the evening. The beast was silent in there. Each day, at different times and without routine, he would catch the keeper's eye and the question would pass across his face. Each day, Oçem would wordlessly return the same answer, and then Teixeira would consider whether he should broach the matter that lay between them. *He eats horseflesh. . . .* The keeper looked away. Tomorrow perhaps he would ask, or one of the tomorrows that would follow that one. Not today.

Now know this: that the Spaniards too seek the animal which resides aboard the Ajuda. This much was allowed in our negotiation, it being among our purposes to entertain His Holiness, albeit as a means of making him our own. Rivalries amuse this Pope, according to the astute Doctor Faria, and thus, being good Christians, we conjure for him the image of a rivalry. A contest, between ourselves and the Spaniards to procure for him a certain beast. And so, my dear Dom Jaime, you find yourself our elected champion. I hope the picture affords you some amusement of your own, for it is no more than that. A likeness of contention, sketched by myself at Ayamonte, colored by our Orator at Rome, and so lifelike that His Holiness already claps his hands and fingers the laurels which he dreams of plac-

ing on the victor's head. But now, like a statue stepping from its plinth and swinging blindly amongst all our causes—Dom Manolo's and Fernando's, mine, your own—the image becomes the fact.

He read the letter every day, or almost every day, and came to know it by rote. Peres's "likeness of contention" teased him, framing as it did a circumstance the very opposite of his own. What of the contentions that have no likeness? he wondered. The soundless, unlit struggles . . . what of those? Fifteen men. The animal: eater of horseflesh. Oçem's little shrug, repeated day after day, until finally he sat down heavily beside the man, knowing already what his questions would elicit, unsurprised when they came, hardly even angered, the method used even exciting a vague admiration, for he had underestimated his man.

"What will you do, Dom Jaime?" Oçem asked him then. He was nervous, as close to apprehension as Teixeira had ever seen. Fearing bloodshed, he supposed.

"What can I do?" he answered frankly. What could any of them do? The animal stank. He recalled the man in the hammock, his mouth open under Oçem's gentle prompting and the breath foul with rot. He had recoiled then. Now it was familiar. Forward of the main mast, the door to Dom Francisco's cabin banged open. Oçem glanced at him again, but his expression was unchanged.

A ship has sailed from Rome, a ship captained by two fools recruited for the purpose and intended by the Spaniards to offer no more than a pretense of their intention. Their Orator claims now that a renegade captain commands her, a murderer and thief, his booty being the vessel herself and—mark this, Dom Jaime, as I marked it—a rutter containing regimens for sailing east along the Guinea Coast from Cape Palmas as far as Cape Santa Caterina. She is called the Lucia, *and the cutthroat who captains her goes by the name Diego. . . .*

There was more. The phrases went around and around in his head as the days passed and Gonçalo piloted them north toward the coast. Alema's briefly glimpsed caravel would be this caravel. Or it would not. It would be there, or it would be gone. It would be a mirage, a specter, or as solid as the *Ajuda,* whose decks rocked beneath his feet. These possibilities mingled and collided, and their different players merged within them.

The coast appeared, a darkening cut between sea and sky. They stood a league or two off and sailed west, Gonçalo gradually lengthening the legs of their tacks as he beat against the weak westerly currents prevailing here. In his mind's eye Teixeira saw the Ganda stamping and roaring again, killing his man "with great deliberation," then rooting up and trampling such objects as rotting fruit, rats, firewood, a miter, starchy vestments, heaps of shells, wooden angels carved from brittle yellow timber, a great mash of these things in which he snorted and whinnied, his trunkish feet pounding up and down. And in his wilder leaps, slipping into view at only the most abrupt kicks and twitches, Teixeira fancied he might glimpse the animal imprisoned within this one's leathery tegument, dancing madly in there. . . . He yawned and stretched. It was nonsense, of course. There were no "wild leaps" now. No "twitches," either. The stench was getting worse, and it was possible he had offended Estêvão, shouting at him when he had mentioned this. That was yesterday, or the day before.

... and I need hardly conjure for you the wreck which will follow should this renegade succeed, our careful vessel's reduction to flotsam, remote as such a feat may seem. ...

No, you need not, thought Teixeira. If he should get up and walk among the obstacles on the deck to the enclosure at its back, if he should take the canvas and pull it aside, exposing the beast as he had at São Thomé. ...

Yes?

Reading the tiny script of the legends that studded Gonçalo's chart, he traced the Malagueta Coast until it became the Ivory Coast, which then became the Mina Coast, which became the Slave Coast, which became the coast they sailed now: a twisting ribbon of darkness separating the different glares of air and water, trees of some kind, he supposed, and punctuated by beaches that they could make out only by night when moonlight shot the heavy white surf with a faint luminescence. Gonçalo's chart gave it no name. Oçem had turned against him by now. Each day he had to prompt the man to his duties, shoving hay into cage, raking out the spoiled stuff. These demands were met with neutral nods, although the keeper also shook his head in a melancholy way as he fulfilled them.

The sounders took up their places once again. Gonçalo brought the *Ajuda* nearer to the shore. Their voices called out the fathoms as regularly as ever, a lulling sound to Teixeira's ears. Whole hours would go by when they were clear on both sides, but as Gonçalo gradually edged the vessel nearer in, the men would begin to call the fathoms again, eight to port, eight to starboard, then seven and seven, six and six. They were less than half a mile out. The coast became a low flooded forest of mangroves whose roots projected clear of the water and whose canopies sometimes merged into an impenetrable thicket suspended fifty feet in the air. The water here was neither sweet nor salt, but brackish. Sometimes the trees would run out and form great piers of greenery. Sometimes they would detach themselves and form small islands, or whole groups of them, which would merge with each other and form the coast again. Egrets and gulls perched in the branches, sometimes diving into the stagnant waters and coming up with fish wriggling in their mouths. After five days' sailing, other trees began to appear, sometimes standing fifty feet clear of the mangroves. They looked outlandish after the monotony that had preceded them. But they appeared more frequently as the ship sailed east, and became more familiar. One morning Gonçalo hauled a brimming bucket over the side and declared it sweet. They were stood out three miles or more, for there was a headland forward that jutted out from the mainland. When they rounded it that afternoon, they found themselves sailing along a coast made up of islands of mangroves.

Teixeira, Gonçalo, Estêvão, Dom Francisco, and everyone else on deck crowded to the starboard rail. Innumerable creeks cut paths among the islands, meandering among the mangrove clumps, whose canopies sometimes linked in midair to form bridges or shaded tunnels. The islands were sometimes little more than a single tree, sometimes a whole wood. They sailed across the face of this strange coast for more than an hour before someone shouted and pointed. The mangroves broke suddenly a few hundred paces ahead. A channel opened and a wide, slow river flowed forward between banks of contorted trees to debouch into the sea. They moved into the center of the flood, and then the men of the *Ajuda* stared in silence. In the mouth of the river, a ship was riding at anchor.

She was a caravel, smaller even than the *Picanço,* perhaps seventy feet in length and rigged identically to the *Ajuda,* though her masts were barely half the size. Minutes later Teixeira and Dom Francisco were sitting side by side in silence while six hands pulled on the oars of the longboat. As they drew near, Teixeira saw the name *Lucia* picked out in faded paint along her prow. He scanned her decks for some sign of life, but there was none. Unless her entire crew were hiding belowdecks or in the ballast, she was deserted. Soon the longboat was bumping against her sides, and Teixeira watched Dom Francisco's buttocks strain, then flop forward as he pulled himself over the rail. He heard a grunt, then a metallic clatter, which would be the cutlass clenched absurdly between his teeth falling to the deck. He followed, unarmed. The boatmen looked up at him, not wanting to follow. He left them there.

The forecastle was no more than a platform raised a foot above the main deck. Dom Francisco was standing on it, waiting for him. Teixeira prized the lid off the water butt, which was lashed to the mainmast: almost full, teeming with tiny swimming creatures. They moved aft to the ship's only cabin, which was built into the poop. The *Lucia* smelled dank, unused. A small table, a chair, two box-bunks: the cabin air was musty. Dom Francisco knocked open a hatch-cover.

"They took everything with them," he said.

Teixeira watched the man's broad back, which shifted clumsily about the cramped cabin, the fat neck. An awl such as the men used to sew canvas would sink into the flesh there and hardly leave a wound. He was powerful and stupid, the worst kind.

They moved out on deck again. Anchored no more than a few hundred paces away, the *Ajuda* appeared huge, a wooden leviathan compared with this craft. Teixeira looked up. The mainmast had been patched. Bright new wood took over near the topmost spar. The sails were furled neatly. New canvas by the look of it. Dom Francisco was busy sticking his cutlass into the deck, then leaning out to do the same thing to her sides.

"She's rotten," he said. Teixeira did not reply.

Together they raised the hatch-cover and lowered themselves into the hold. There was barely headroom to stand down there, and they felt their way about in the gloom, ducking under the timbers that supported the deck above. The stench from the ballast was overpowering. Cracks of light showed between the planks where the caulking had dried and shrunk. Teixeira stepped forward gingerly, feeling with his feet for stray ends of rope, loose planks, whatever might trip him. A great column of wood directly in front of him would be the mizzenmast. He edged around it, and then he found the cage.

It had been built into the ship's end-timber. Thick posts had been stepped into the deck below and the beams above. Three square-cut beams formed a kind of skirting, and planks were nailed crosswise up from these to the deck above. The back wall was formed by the bulkhead that divided the hold from the steerage. The *fidalgo* clambered about at the other end of the ship. Eventually he noticed the other man's silence and joined him. They stared at the construction for a few moments, then Dom Francisco reached out and struck one of the posts with his cutlass. It bit and hung there.

"Sound," he said. "What's this for, I wonder?"

"Horseflesh," said Teixeira.

"What?"

It eats horseflesh. . . . "It was the revenge of a peasant," said Teixeira, and he saw the man stiffen at these words, astonished perhaps that the accusation should come so late and so naked. "What did you use?" he went on. "Saltpeter? Worm-wood? You dared not harm the knight, so you slew his horse. . . ."

"If you were not mad, I would kill you here and now." The *fidalgo's* tones were measured, untroubled. "Your ravings are nothing to me, or anyone. And it is you who are the horse-killer, if you recall." Teixeira felt his anxiety swell and clot, unsure how he had been prompted to this. The cage, though, the empty cage. Was he sick still, his wits deranged?

"Why would I wait until you fell sick?" Dom Francisco continued. "Do you truly imagine I was alone, climbing down there each night with my bottle of poi-son, as you put it? Do you think there is a single man aboard who would take up your cause and stand in my way? Oçem, perhaps? Dom Estêvão? Our pilot, whose name you threatened to blacken across the Indies? The men whose com-panions died with their mouths full of blood that you might read a letter from your precious patron?"

There was a man, he thought, a man who came to warn me. His name, though . . . And dead now. Dom Francisco had pushed him up against the bars of the cage. "I could nail you in this cage, we could sail away, and no one would say a word. I could saw off your head and throw it over the side. . . ."

He felt sick; the stench down there and the closeness of the air. The man's face was in his own, a clot of shadows following him as he tried to look away.

"But I will not do that," the man said then. "I will discharge my duty and de-liver you safely to your beloved Dom Peres. I will wear my stupid peasant face and threadbare clothes. I will obey you, and be blameless. But what will you be, my puffed-up courtier, with your flowery phrases and an empty cage for your ef-forts? What will become of you then?" The man was pulling him forward, then pushing him back against the cage, a little harder each time. He did not resist. "He's dead," the man hissed. "He's *rotting*. . . ."

Once back aboard the *Ajuda,* Teixeira went below. He could not watch what he knew must follow. From his cabin, Teixeira heard Dom Francisco shouting to the hands, organizing the work-party that would first pull off the canvas and fold it, then set to with hammers and crowbars. There was banging and the creak of nails being prized from the wood. The resonant reports that next echoed about the vessel and reached him sitting there alone, those would be the posts and planks being thrown into rough piles ready for storage below. A silence followed, or what followed next was silent. He remembered Oçem telling him that he had smeared its skin with lanolin. It would slide smoothly across the deck. Suddenly the voices rose, and Dom Francisco's joined them, rising above them all, "Ready, u-uupp. . . . One, two, three!" A pause, for which he held his breath, hands pressed over his face, then the great splash, and finally the cheers of the crew, which were loud, and long, and sounded to him like mockery.

His Holiness plans a tournament, according to the good Doctor Faria, a contest to try the fabled enmity of this "Ganda" toward the elephant. Many writers tell of it, Dom Manolo has already supplied him with the first of these beasts, and preparations are under way. Our Pope is resolved. Does this amuse you, Dom Jaime? As it does myself?

Oçem came to rouse him from his cabin at dusk. He lay on his bunk with the letter clutched in his hand. The two men were silent for some time.

"The Ganda died two days out of São Thomé," the native said eventually.

He nodded but did not reply. He could hear Dom Francisco and Estêvão talking on the deck above.

"You would not be told." It was offered almost in apology. He nodded again.

"He was rotting, there were maggots . . ."

"I know! I knew that!" The conversation above stopped abruptly. Dom Francisco laughed. The two men listened to this.

"Amongst the Rajputs, my people," Oçem said, "the body is very unimportant. When dead, I mean." He was half smiling, speaking lightly as though musing to himself. "Usually we burn it, or throw it in a river. The part that you call soul comes back anyway, sometimes in a stone, or a toad, a bird . . . Anything at all. It is a matter of luck, or the nature of the life led before death. Subtler doctors than I dispute this point, and their views differ, as you may imagine. Perhaps the Ganda will come back to you, Dom Jaime. As a fish, or a lizard, or perhaps a man, perhaps even someone you may meet."

"But will he come back as himself?" Teixeira asked in the same tone. He swung his legs down from the bunk. "Is that ever remarked by your subtle doctors?"

"I have not heard of it," said Oçem, considering this. "It is not impossible."

He walked out onto the deck. The corpse was floating some hundreds of paces off the larboard. Its legs and swollen belly projected out of the water and formed a platform for scavenging birds that alighted in small flocks, flapping and screeching at each other as they pecked at the animal's flesh.

"The current will carry it away before tomorrow," Oçem said.

He turned away and climbed the ladder to the forecastle. Dom Francisco, Estêvão, and Gonçalo looked up in surprise at his appearance there. He sat down, and for a minute no one spoke. It was Estêvão who broke this uncomfortable silence.

"When do we sail?" he asked.

"Sail?" Teixeira exclaimed lightly. "But we have only just arrived!"

"Dom Jaime, we understand your disappointment. Your mission . . ." Gonçalo spoke softly.

"My mission, yes. I think Dom Francisco here understands my mission as well as anyone, do you not, Dom Francisco?"

"I am at your command," the *fidalgo* said levelly.

"We all are," said Estêvão. "But you understand, Dom Jaime, our supplies are limited. The weather might change and strand us here. . . ."

"Strand us? I think you are confusing January with August, my friend. And as for supplies, we are anchored in the mouth of a river of sweet water with, unless my eyes deceive me, an abundance of fish." He looked from face to face.

"We stay," he said with sudden authority. "We stay until the villains whose ship lies anchored before us return."

His tone silenced them. Gonçalo and Estêvão exchanged looks. "And if they do not return?" asked the latter.

"We stay," he said again.

This time both men looked to the *fidalgo*, whose face had remained expressionless throughout.

"Well, Dom Francisco?" Estêvão appealed in exasperation. "Have you nothing to say about this?"

"Correct, Dom Estêvão," the man replied. He addressed the boatswain, but his eyes were fixed on Teixeira. "If Dom Jaime commands that we stay, then we stay. There is no more to be said."

Teixeira rose and returned below. From his bunk he heard their murmuring start up. They whispered to one another far into the night, but there was no more laughter.

The Ganda was still there the next day. Mobbed by scavenging birds, its limbs in tatters of flesh and skin, it bobbed about in the water, drifting through its own eccentric orbit, now nearer, now farther, but always in clear view of the *Ajuda*. Succeeding days brought more and different birds to the sharp-billed egrets and gulls: a heron, a hawk once, which carried away one unwary scavenger but dropped its prey over the mangroves. Two vultures flapped lazily out of the sky, tore open the stomach, and gorged until they could no longer fly. Teixeira watched the cadaver's flaying and reduction from the main deck. The Ganda's legs were no more than bones festooned with gristle and the belly a gaping wound black with dry blood and decay. The river should have pushed it out to sea. The weight of its bones should have sunk it to the bottom. The water threshed and foamed when the sharks found it, but still it floated, a stinking and ragged island, irreducible, going nowhere.

"There is no river to 'push it,' as you say," Gonçalo told him shortly when his curiosity finally prompted him to ask. He took it as a snub and was about to walk away when the pilot spoke again. "Rather there is the current which runs along the edge of the mouth, so weak it can hardly be called a current. This river, as we thought it, is no more than that. But somewhere behind there"—he gestured at the acreage of mangroves that stretched back inland for as far as they could see— "there is a river, and a river the like of which we have never seen or dreamed of."

"But is this not its mouth?" Teixeira persisted.

"Perhaps the very edge of it. But its mouth? We have sailed across its mouth already, a mouth choked with silt and the trees which have taken root there. It took us better than five days. Think of it"—he seemed only dimly aware of Teixeira's presence now—"a river whose mouth is sixty leagues across. It would have currents running in it greater than the Tagus. Storms on one bank might never even be glimpsed from the other. . . ." He gazed at the stunted and misshapen trees as though, through the exposed roots and branches, he might catch sight of this oceanic flood.

Teixeira looked with him, but his gaze was drawn to the *Lucia*. Where are you? he asked of her vanished crew.

That night, the silence that normally descended over the ship and the waters surrounding her was broken by a strange sound. A faint crying, bestial and distressed, prompted the sleeping lookout on the forecastle to rouse first him, then Dom Francisco, then Teixeira. They gathered on deck to listen, and soon found themselves joined by the better part of the crew. The sound grew louder, then seemed to fall away, then grew louder again. They looked to one another, baffled as to its origin and unable to discover more in the darkness.

"Animals?" Estêvão said at one point. The noise seemed to be all around them and yet no closer than before.

Daybreak explained all and yet begged questions more troubling than any contemplated in the cocoon of the night's ignorance. The sky lightened in the east, grew luminous, and the familiar line of the coast rose clear of the water like a palisade of shadow. They could make out dim shapes then, teasing and ill-defined silhouettes. The noise seemed quieter and more intermittent now. Weak wails and bleats. The men looked to each other, still puzzled. The shapes grew in definition but made no more sense than before. There were more than a score of them, and others presumably in the patches of water still in shadow. It was one of the hands who saw it first. He shouted out, or would have, but the cry had already turned into hiccups of surprised mirth.

"What? What is he saying?" demanded Dom Francisco, but his explanation was superfluous, for Estêvão too finally understood what his eyes had been telling him for some minutes now, though his mind had been unable to accept it.

"Good Christ!" he exclaimed.

They were to port and starboard, fore and aft, grouped together in twos and threes, heads bobbing up and down as though grazing, bleating in consternation.

The men of the *Ajuda* looked about them in amazement. They were surrounded by a herd of goats.

"And look there!" shouted Estêvão. He was pointing upriver, beyond the *Lucia*.

Another flotilla was advancing.

"Good God!" said Dom Francisco. "Pigs!"

And more goats, and small oxen, and whole flocks of squawking chickens. . . . They were tethered to rafts constructed from a light wood so soft that one could sink a thumb into it, the trunks bound together with vines. Soon the open water around them was filled with these craft, varying in size depending on their passengers, which bleated, and roared, and lowed, and screeched. A long raft of chattering monkeys drifted past, then one of birds with bright yellow beaks, and upriver the waterway was filled with more.

The longboat was launched and scurried about among these floating platforms, collecting two or three and then towing them back to the *Ajuda,* where men waited to slaughter goats and wring the necks of the chickens. It was soon clear, however, that they could not hope to eat the superabundance of livestock that floated down the river and now began to drift out of the mangroves to either side. The crew contented itself with watching. A large ape sat impassively on the deck of his barge, looking up at the faces that peered at him over the rail. A struggling bull capsized. The rafts seemed to get bigger during the course of the afternoon, with whole herds of animals standing rigidly, their legs planted apart against the water's motion. One ill-constructed platform struck the *Lucia* and broke apart, spilling a whoop of baboons into the water, where they drowned or were eaten by patrolling sharks.

By sunset the flow had hardly lessened. Teixeira looked about at the creatures that surrounded the vessel, then out to sea, where a score or more were wallowing in the swell. Oxen, for the most part. He turned west and shaded his eyes against the glare of the great fireball now sinking below the horizon. A little way along the coast, a lizard the length of a man had drifted amongst a squealing squadron of hogs, panicking them. He turned east: a fleet of creatures adrift on their arks.

"He has gone."

Oçem stood behind him. "You are looking for the Ganda, Dom Jaime. He has disappeared."

The man was right. He had been searching for the cadaver without thinking. "Where are they coming from?" he wondered aloud. "Whose purpose can this serve?"

Oçem did not reply. He was gazing upriver, scanning amongst the bobbing heads and bodies that even now were floating toward them. Teixeira saw that a strange expression had come over the keeper's face, nor did it change when he opened his mouth to speak and addressed Teixeira in an absent tone.

"I did not say it was impossible, Dom Jaime." His eyes were fixed on a single distant raft.

Teixeira looked from the watcher to the object that gripped his attention, not clear yet at such a distance, but growing in definition as it advanced. It appeared more substantial than the other rafts, raised a foot or more clear of the water and prevented from heeling to either side by two outriggers resembling small canoes. It was larger, too, more than adequate for the single animal upon it. Some of the hands were watching with them now, and on the forecastle above, he could see Dom Francisco and Gonçalo were standing still as statues, eyes fixed on the same object. It passed behind the spars of the *Lucia* then, inching forward so slowly that it might have been dragging an anchor. The minutes passed and the *Ajuda* fell silent, every man aboard watching. A few stole alarmed glances at him, as though he had willed this, as though his need were a hawser pulling the craft toward them. It reemerged from behind the caravel. The animal raised its head then, silhouetting itself against the water. Teixeira felt his doubts crumble to dust. He looked up and saw Dom Francisco staring not at the beast, but at him, his face slack with shock.

Estêvão called out, "Look! Look there!" He was pointing to the outriggers, which were indeed canoes, Teixeira realized now. Thick ropes had been wound around them, partly to lash them them to the raft, but also to contain their cargo, for as the whole contraption drew nearer, Teixeira saw that each narrow canoe held a captive: two men were bound hand and foot, two sentries struggling in their boxes, divided from one another by the motionless beast, a resurrected Ganda that paid no more attention to their contortions than to the wriggling of two maggots.

IV

AND THE SHIP SAILS ON. . . .

*T*he same old trouble, the usual problems. . . .

"There was . . ." is too blunt, sets off on the wrong foot entirely, soon blundering into such obvious epistemological booby-traps as "Is it at all?" and "If it is, how do we know?" "It would appear . . ." sounds a casuistic note, its tone of doubtful hauteur a perpetuum mobile of backtracking. "It would be perceived . . ." is less worse, or "sensed," perhaps, though the latter imposes a priori–type difficulties on the subject, as does "subject," come to think of it. . . . And "think"! More of the same, the same problem, the usual trouble. This is fancy footwork, sleight of hand when the thing itself demands rough handling and workmanlike brutality. "If it *were* (as it were), it would be . . ."

Well, what? How to get to grips with this? Work-shy fingers wriggle and procrastinate within the clumsy gloves of the conditional mood. The wrong questions get asked, and even with his eyes screwed shut, with his head buried and his brain pan stewing in treacly-sweet rum, even then it wells in his ducts, drips from his glands, begins to glow behind the hot screens of his eyelids. His imagined arms grapple with the rubbery corrugated skin; a wishful dream, which ends as always with his hurling it to the floor and kicking the acidic yellow daylights out of it. He wants it dead, this throbbing blob of goo-excreting gristle, so he wrestles, grunts, dribbles onto his sleeve. He's never seen it, but that proves nothing. He would know it in an instant as it oozed toward him, if he could ever get out of it in the first place. But he cannot. How many fish have seen the sea? It is enormous, and orange, and almost all gut. He knows it as "the Slug.

Resistance is futile. This slimy whopper is simply too big, too enveloping, and the most full-blooded blows only carom off its rubbery partitions—it has flanges and valves and enfilades of sphincters—redounding on the putative attacker so that his limbs thrum and bump like trampolining lunatics, so that his head balloons and bulges like a bag of drowning cats, until there is nothing to do but wedge his skull into the nearest flabby corner, press his face to the indestructible gum-smeared membrane, and weep with frustration. No, there's no getting away from this slug. No escape. All assaults begin with a fatal misconception. You, we, they, he, she, it, and everyone else are not on the outside trying to get in, but actually on the inside and trying to get out.

The slug's translucent tubes and multiple stomachs are the elasticated corridors and cells of an illimitable and eternal rubber prison. It's dulled, muffled, blurred, fogged. Siegfried has bounced his Balmung against these elasticated walls, Charlemagne his Flamberge, and Caesar his Yellow Death. Zadkiel's knife sliced the gullets of a thousand goats before blunting itself in these mucus sumps, and Occam's razor shattered on the fact that this particular entity has no desire or need to reproduce itself. Even a four-armed Mahomet wielding Halef, and Medham, and Al Battar, and Dhu i Fakar all at the same time succeeded only in wedging himself even tighter between the quivering membranes, the glandular secretions swilling about his ankles as he stabbed fourfold at the floor. It's no good. They've all been through here, all suffered the rush of this homogenized stuff, the fakery of its affects, and its dreary occupation of the senses. Ansias, Galas, and Munifican applying the most advanced technologies yet dreamed by the armorers of Nürnberg to alloys forged from Thor's melted-down hammer and the saw-blade used to quarter Saint James the Less may yet come up with some monstrous slug-shredder sufficient to the task, but in the meantime there's only the age-old program of sufferance and a fistful of well-worn pieties. These hardly mitigate the orangeness or the sliminess, not to mention the "No escape" aspect. It's so unpleasant, this "as-it-were-sort-of slug."

But being in it is also vague and tantalizing, rife with inexplicable glows and aches and sudden metallic tastes, quick sweetnesses and little sounds: dry leaves being blown across a clipped pasture, a cane scraping down a wall. Icy stillnesses intervene and—this second, that second—teetering arches again fail to topple over. There are plains so muddy and flat that there is nothing left to fall, to make the slightest impact, to happen. . . . The next moment it's a racket again, all flapping canvas, yelling, the *splish* and *splosh* of apples being thrown into the water that sits under jetties and stinks. Small boys are shouting that the old woman's a witch. Someone's going over to belt them around the ear, and parts of this are already sliding away to be replaced by other parts: a sensation of weightlessness, hands on him, sun on his head, and his brains boiling in there for hour after hour while the slug rocks him back and forth, lulling him, settling him within its chambers. He knows what that means but resists it anyway, burying his face deeper in the soft corners until the throb of orange fades to a calm darkness. This is better. Much better. He sinks, gently, deeper, away.

And then it's back! Naturally: regular returns are something it does with mind-numbing dependability. The Soft Hammer treatment quickly follows, then the Drip-just-out-of-earshot and the sensation that finely sieved flour is being sprinkled into his ears. Horrible! He resists again, but he's running out of time, that second, this second. . . . Next come the usual phantom gurgles and rumbles, a few random pangs (of what exactly is hard to say), an internal ticklishness, an itch just begging to be scratched. The slug wants him back, and he can't put it off much longer now. It's not really a slug, of course, this thing he's in, and all of us, and all the time. It's something else, something worse. Is whatever it is even nameable . . .

Captain Alfredo!

... from the rum-soaked nook he's hollowed for himself in the furthest recess of his skull, this tyrannical itch, this skintight slime-sac we're fitted with at birth? Of course it is. It's—

"Captain Alfredo di Ragusa! Wake up, you drunken sot!"

Thirst. Men shouting. He smells sea-spray and staleness, the staleness of being himself. He opens one eye. It's starting up again, as it always does. His head hurts (that being its function). Oh, it's bad. He's in it again. The sky is green as an orange. It's—

No-ooo-o. . . .

Yes.

. . . consciousness.

The sails are sloppily furled, no lookout posted, the crew hunkered down belowdecks, steering by the rear compass and a lazy lean on the tiller. Captain Alfredo would have been amongst them with a belaying pin in his glory days, but those are far behind him now and he himself, as noted, is still doing a creditable impression of a sack of turnips, dead drunk on the deck above. The giant dragged him out and dumped him there on the orders of the one calling himself "Captain Diego" half a league out from the jetty. Now all four of them are closeted in his cabin, directly above this coven of shirkers. It's dark, because they are in steerage; and it's doubly dark, because it's nighttime; and it's triply dark, because their hearts are plump with evil intentions, reluctant camaraderie, and a leaking, blackening fear. They are talking themselves up in half-whispers, nodding a lot, and thinking of the quartet above: Salvestro, Bernardo, this "Diego," and the mysterious and veiled girl accompanying him. Her too. They're all in the same boat.

The previous week, in a discreetly concealed nook of the back room at the Last Gasp, a series of near identical meetings had brought together Jacopo and a procession of local hopefuls, attracted by talk of inordinate rates of pay for service aboard the rickety vessel that had been rotting in the water off the jetty for some months. The name of a certain "Don Antonio" was bandied about and confirmed as the same "Don Antonio" who had been paying without demur the inflated prices that the quayside traders had advanced more in a spirit of combative negotiation than realistic expectation. The drunk collapsed over an adjacent table during these furtive chin-wags was identified by Jacopo as their captain. The rates offered were, as rumored, generous to the point of absurdity, and there was, as most of these prospective seamen expected, a catch. The catch concerned the passengers, of whom there were supposed to be two. Now, it seemed, there was a further catch, an unexpected development or nasty surprise. The number of passengers had jumped to four.

"Don Antonio never mentioned the girl," muttered Jacopo, mostly to himself. "Nor Diego, come to that. Don't like the look of him much. Eh, Bruno?"

"He's Bruno," said the man addressed. "I'm Luca."

"Luca, then," said Jacopo. "What do you say to chancing your arm with this Diego?"

"Not me," said Luca.

There were eight of them standing up in a wooden box no more than three paces wide and effectively divided in two by the heavy beam that was the *Santa Lucia's* tiller. The compass hung above it told them that they were headed a degree or two west of sou'sou'west. The ship rolled lazily, almost stationary in the currentless and tideless waters.

"How about you, Enzo?"

Enzo shook his head. So did Arturro, and so did Piero. Bruno and Roberto scratched at some dry lichen on the tiller and did not look up. It had sounded easy in the back room of the Last Gasp three nights ago. Afloat, it suddenly seemed daunting. There were eight of them and half that number in the room above, one of them no more than a girl, or so they assumed. She had yet to lift the veil that covered her face. Perhaps she was a boy. Perhaps this Captain Diego's tastes ran that way. It would be more palatable to kill a sodomite.

"What about you, Ruggero?"

Enzo, Bruno, Piero, Roberto, Luca, and Arturro turned to him. They were all of a piece, short thickset men with wiry black hair, drawn from the villages scattered about Fiumicino and the Isola Sacra. They might have been cousins, and they looked at him diffidently now, peering out from under their thick brows and looking away the moment he caught their eyes. Shy country cousins, suspicious and curious in equal measure of the taller artisan who had walked on board with a bag of tools slung over his back and said nothing unless directly addressed. He had wedged himself into the narrow doorway cut in the bulkhead between the steerage and the lower deck. His feet propped against the jamb opposite, he appeared to be digging dirt from under his fingernails.

"I am called Ruggero di Palma Castiglione," he replied without looking up. "I signed on as a carpenter for a foolish voyage to the Guinea Coast on behalf of a foolish man called Antonio, who I have never met. There was talk of an animal, and need of a cage, and perhaps a boat, too. I remember discussing such things with a man called Alfredo, the master of this vessel and a drunkard, as it turns out, and you." He indicated Jacopo. "Now, let me understand you correctly, you want me to cut a man's throat, then his woman's, then his two companions'. Would that be correct?"

"I could hardly declare my purpose with Captain Alfredo present," Jacopo began.

"Well, we must add him to the list, then," Ruggero said sarcastically. "Where are we now? Five?"

A short silence followed this retort. Jacopo stared at Ruggero, and the others exchanged dark looks amongst themselves.

"He'll talk," Enzo muttered finally. "He'll tell them." He flicked his eyes to the ceiling.

"Six, then," Ruggero responded immediately, "including myself, if you can decide which of you brave-hearts will do the cutting." His eyes did not leave Jacopo's.

"Don't think I won't," growled Enzo.

"Shut up, both of you," Jacopo broke in then. "It's true Ruggero here didn't know anything until an hour ago. So he's surprised, that's all. This is a sweet deal if we all stick together. It's like I said; we get rid of them. We sail the *Lucia* to Tunis. I know some people there who'll give us a fair price on her. We divide the money between us. . . ."

He got as far as that, and then Arturro and Enzo broke in, wanting to know just how he proposed to divide up the money, on what basis, how much to whom, and so on and so forth, for even if they knew little of sailing and less of murder, they understood divisions, and shares, and the practical difficulties of who should get what and why. They had been breaking their backs in the floodplain of the Tiber since before Rome was ever dreamed of and waiting for their fathers to die since before that.

"No," explained Enzo to Arturro an hour of bickering later. "You get twenty-*seven* shares. You know damn well you'll get that vine-plot behind old Isabella's when your uncle dies, and don't tell me again about that cousin up by Tolfa, he may as well be in the moon. You're not married, so you don't get the nine being-married shares, and you have a well behind your place, too, so you lose three shares for that. On the other hand, it's true that your brother's dead and you've got *his* wife to feed, but she hasn't got any brats, and isn't likely to get any if you keep your hands to yourself. So you'll get your brother's plot, too."

"I owe Piero over fifty soldi," Luca broke in. "What about that?"

"What about what?" Enzo retorted. "You've got thirty-nine shares already, you greedy little bastard. . . ."

And so it went on, the six men arguing amongst themselves, offering up their dead and living wives, their sick uncles and hungry children, their dry wells and dead vines, their fields in which nothing would grow except stones. Jacopo watched and listened and said nothing. Nothing and no one had interrupted their six-cornered dispute save the sound of the door above banging as someone left the cabin, then banging again on his, or her, return. They stopped and looked up hastily each time, but a moment later they were back amongst their hedges and ditches, their water shares and rights of passage, already busily chopping up the very ship in which they sailed. Ruggero continued working on his nails and played no part in these discussions until Luca turned to Enzo and asked, "What about him?"

Once again they all turned and stared at the carpenter.

"Well," said Enzo, "are you in or out?"

Ruggero spoke to his nails. "Put me off at Tunis," he said. "I don't want your thirty-one and a half shares or whatever it is. I cut wood and join it, that's all."

Enzo nodded. "Fine by me. Don't get in our way, though, carpenter. And don't open your mouth too wide, unless you want to swallow one of your chisels."

The carpenter smiled at that; then, pushing himself upright, he disappeared through the door.

"We should kill him, too," said Luca. "I don't trust him. He'll talk, I know he'll—"

"Shut up," said Jacopo. They were the first words he had spoken since the others had begun dividing the ship among them. "You'll leave him alone, and he'll leave us alone. We're all hanged men if we're caught. Him as much as us, and he knows it."

The mention of "hanged men" silenced them. It was hot in their little wooden box. They grew somber again, anxious and sickly-looking in the yellow light of the oil lamp. Stupidity and greed and fear, thought Jacopo. Sons of the soil, and all at sea.

"You'll divide half what we get between yourselves," he said. "The other half goes to me." He watched their outrage swell, their eyes widening, faces turning thunderous. "Unless one of you wants to strike the first blow. . . . Any of you want to be the first? . . . Luca? . . . Piero?"

He looked at each of their faces in turn. Enzo's eyes were the last to drop, but drop they did. "No takers? Well then, I must suppose that it will be me." He spoke lightly, toying with them. They so wanted to be old and fat, and ashore. "I'll kill the first, since none of you have the guts. We'll all do the others. All of us, mind you. And together." They were frightened now and relieved. He had brought them near enough.

"Which one first?" It was Luca who spoke, his lips pursed with nerves.

"The big one. Bernardo. Without him, the others will be easy." Lank black hair framed his face like a bonnet. The men watching him were apprehensive and silent. He had put himself beyond them; he frightened them now. "I'll do it tonight," he declared, "if they ever rouse themselves from that bloody cabin."

All seven of them glared up at the ceiling.

"What are they doing in there, anyway?" asked Enzo, lowering his eyes from the boards above his head and fixing them, for no good reason, upon Luca.

"Talking?" Luca replied doubtfully. "What have they got to talk about?"

Jacopo did not answer. He was thinking of Don Antonio's stray remarks about "our two fools," a phrase he had varied only rarely. Once he had dubbed them "our beast-catchers," the title bestowed with a strong sarcastic inflection; once, and in the same tone, he had called them "our licensed brigands," a phrase that he had puzzled over until he had seen the two of them following this "Captain Diego," hurrying across the quay to the jetty with the girl, unnoticed as all eyes turned to the barge and its robed passenger. They had walked in step.

Marched, as it were, and when this captain had directed them to settle the girl in the cabin, to drag out its drunken occupant and dump him on the deck, then take up their station at the stern to doff their hats to His Holiness, they had obeyed without delay or reflection. "Licensed brigands" meant only one thing to him then.

"I believe that they were soldiers together," Jacopo said eventually. "Once."

Their faces clouded, and he cursed his loose tongue. "A long time ago," he added, but they were inwardly shaking their heads, slipping away from him, back to their drudgery and digging. "Soldiers" were a black stain that appeared on their horizon, a monster with ten thousand hacking limbs that pulled them out by the heels, then their women and children. . . . No one had told them that these were "soldiers." He eyed them contemptuously. Don Antonio had somehow neglected to mention that one of the "fools" stood almost two heads taller than he, that they would be joined by their old commander, if that were the case, who had even brought a woman on board. Don Antonio would have a few questions to answer if they ever met again.

"I'll take the big one," he spat at them. "Then it's all of us together."

He tripped on the doorsill as he quit the cramped chamber. Behind him, he heard a couple of them snigger.

It began as ants. Then became worms, a ball of them the size of an apple, then the size of a small cabbage, vigorous and slithery in the pit of his stomach. His mouth filled with spit, which he swallowed every few seconds or so. The worms drank it, then lashed about with their tails and mated, producing more worms— bigger ones. It might have been something he ate, except that he had eaten nothing since the night before, when five or six of Rodolfo's pies had disappeared down his gullet at the Broken Wheel. These had shown no intention of returning. It might have been the drink, which was more likely, and it might have been his "nerves," which still jangled from the moment when he had released the dwarf in mid-heave and found himself staring into the face of the very man who had chased them out of Prato, and Rome, over mountains, through rivers, and down them, eventually to a fishing port, where a ship waited to take them to "somewhere safe"—this was how he had understood it. So here he was aboard ship.

Every few minutes, Bernardo looked across at Salvestro to see his friend was immersed in a conversation with the very man they had taken passage to escape: the Colonel, who it now seemed was not about to kill them, and who it seemed was no longer "the Colonel," but "the Captain." So it was in all probability his nerves, and if not that, then the strange musty smell that clung to the whole ship, a noxious vapor of the sort that caused fever, and if not that, then it was the actual motions of the vessel, though these were gentle and almost imperceptible. The cabin was furnished with a kind of table built into the stern bulkhead, a stool and chair on which Salvestro and Diego respectively sat, an open-fronted cupboard filled, so far as he could see, entirely with empty bottles, and two bunk beds. He sat on the lower, the girl was asleep on the upper. She had not been mentioned yet by the two men. One corner was piled with a heap of dirty rags, clothes possibly. The other held a small chest with bands of iron about it held shut with three formidable locks. Its contents clinked occasionally, usually when the boat rolled. Worms, pies, drink, nerves, the stink or motions of the *Santa Lucia* . . . Bernardo felt that he might very soon be sick. The cabin did not contain Captain Alfredo. Or a bucket.

"It was an unholy trinity," Diego was saying, shaking his head. "Aldo, Medici, myself. If it had been I who went in to parley with him, then everything would have been different. Of course Medici wasn't going to let that happen, and Aldo was sick with a wasting disease, it was eating his flesh, and I, I had little wish to breathe the air in there. Even in the antechamber, you could smell it. . . . No, they spoke alone."

Bernardo had heard this bit already and almost understood it. He remembered a lot of waiting around outside Prato. More specifically, a lot of being hungry. This had happened then. Diego and the Cardinal had talked terms with Aldo. . . . No, he'd got that part wrong. The Cardinal had talked terms with Aldo, and Aldo had surrendered the town, on terms that . . . He did not quite grasp "the terms." Then the Cardinal had ridden back to the camp with a story about Aldo's defiance, which had been the pretext for all that followed. There was something wrong with this, Bernardo felt, but whether it was his fault or someone else's was still unclear.

"The boy knew," Salvestro was saying. "Aldo's son. He thought his father a coward for it."

"Then they all knew," replied Diego. "No wonder Medici kept them hidden. Aldo was brave enough, though. He had little choice. . . ."

This was going too fast for Bernardo. He had the talking bit, the surrender bit, but the Aldo and his family bit he did not understand. Nor were "the terms" getting any clearer. He heard the girl shift on the bunk above him. He was going to have to be sick soon. Very soon, actually.

"Medici came out of that room shaking his head, lamenting his 'old friend Aldo's pigheadedness.' He was almost in tears, the charlatan. I even remember him trying to persuade Cardona not to attack. Imagine if he had acceded!" The soldier grinned quickly, but then his face fell again. "Of course, Cardona would have known everything. Even then he would have realized that Aldo had to surrender, that Medici was lying through his teeth, and there was I, standing next to him, an officer under his own command. . . . He must have known then where the blame would fall." His voice had a strangled quality to it.

Bernardo cleared his throat loudly.

Salvestro furrowed his brow. "Why?" he said at last. "Why would he wish the town sacked?"

"I await the chance to ask him. I await the chance to ask many things. Why else am I here, aboard a floating jakes on a fool's errand for the man I detest most in the world?"

The talk drifted and meandered around this question. Bernardo followed intently, certain in the belief that if he only listened hard enough, Diego's role in this whole affair and his presence here on the ship would make perfect sense to him, or at least become less inexplicable. The Beast, he gathered gradually, was central to the soldier's project, which was intended to gain Fernando's ear. Possibly the ear was central, too, but anyway, the one clearly led to the other: the beast in some sense was the key to the ear, and this had something to do with "renown." With the ear gained, the rest more or less fell into place. There would be a petition to Fernando (via the ear) against the injustice done Diego by, as he had put it, "the man I destest most in the world." This could only be the Pope, guessed Bernardo, basing this belief on the fact that every time the word "Medici" or "Leo" was mentioned, it was invariably preceded by the epithet "loathsome" or "vile" and followed by clauses portending violence such as "whose head I look forward to parading on a pole." The Pope had been the murderer at Prato, albeit through the actions of men who did not know whom they served (Rufo was mentioned here), who believed they served Diego while actually serving the Pope and thus were intended to implicate Diego when caught, except they had escaped, or some of them had, and Diego had been disgraced anyway. And these "men" had been dupes just as much as Diego, for they had been led to believe they were protecting Aldo's family, even though they were actually guarding them only so that the murderers, who were not they, could kill Aldo's family later. And then the "men" would be blamed for it, and Diego, too.

This last part had a very familiar ring to it. Being blamed for things he had not done struck deep chords within Bernardo. He watched Salvestro and Diego construct this edifice of supposition and guesswork as they faced each other over the table. Then it dawned on him that, by "the men," the murders of Aldo's family who were not the murders of Aldo's family and the soldiers in Diego's service who were not in Diego's service (although they thought they were), the two men talking amongst themselves actually meant himself and Salvestro.

There followed something about the "men" also being the "men" who would, assuming both the Beast and Fernando's ear were gained, form the first link in a chain that would drag "the man I detest most in the world" into the light, where his guilt would be clear and thus Diego's honor restored, and their own, too, it seemed, although Bernardo was far from certain that he had ever lost it or even had it to lose in the first place. Also, his nausea was growing worse. He hiccuped and swallowed.

"Cardinal Medici," Salvestro was saying.

"Yes. Our beloved Pope. May he burn in hell—"

"I'm going outside," Bernardo broke in then.

The two men looked up, and the girl too raised her head, roused by the unfamiliar voice. The other two had been talking on for hours.

"To be sick," Bernardo added, reaching urgently for the cabin door and slamming it behind him.

Salvestro and Diego looked blankly at each other, as though nonplussed to find themselves in a little wooden room floating in the middle of the sea when, only a moment ago, they had been standing on terra firma in a little town at the end of the valley of Mugnone, hundreds of miles to the north. The sound of vomiting reached them faintly: a gurgle from the deck, a soft slop over the side.

"We were amongst the vanguard, when the order to attack came. I found Aldo in the palace, the very room outside which I had waited while he and Medici talked. Only the old women had stayed with him. There was no guard, and we would have killed them if there had been. There was no defense, do you remember that?" Salvestro nodded. "He was all but dead already, rotting from the inside, by the smell of him. All he said was, 'So the stories of the Spaniards are true.' Later he asked to see his family, but they had fled, so I thought. He smiled when I told him this, and I was not unhappy for it. He already knew that his would be a miserable death. Later the Cardinal arrived and asked my permission to administer the last rites to 'his old friend.' I agreed, naturally. Another mistake. When he had gone, Aldo was transformed, almost mad. He asked again for his family, and again I told him that they were far away by now, perhaps already in Florence. This time he would not have it, and ranted that they were yet in the city, that I must find them and keep them safe, for my own sake as much as his. He was a clever man. He had already understood what was happening. I ignored him. I understood nothing then."

"But you did send out patrols, did you not?" Salvestro asked.

"Too late," said Diego. He stared into the oil-lamp. It might have been anyone putting the question to him.

The door opened again and Bernardo stepped carefully over the sill. It banged behind him, the noise bringing Diego's head up quickly, as though startled from sleep.

"I was sick," said Bernardo.

Salvestro glared at him.

"What?" protested Bernardo. "What now?"

"You know the rest," said Diego, "if what you tell me is true." He watched Salvestro. "There were no 'last rites' for Aldo. Medici had his family as hostages for his silence, and you were intended as Diego's men, so Diego's fault. Rufo was Medici's man, but you never thought to ask his name, did you?"

Salvestro did not answer, so Bernardo shook his head. He was feeling somewhat better now, though the beads of sweat on his brow were still cold. The moon was quite bright. His vomit had resembled a waterlogged shirt, and obviously he had missed several important episodes while outside. Salvestro would explain them to him later.

"Aldo died on the twenty-fifth day of the sack," Diego continued, "though no one knew until two days later, not even Medici. Another day and I would have had his family safe." He frowned then. "It was the Pratesi themselves who told him. The sheep who whistled for the wolf."

"The bells," said Salvestro, and then it was Diego's turn to nod.

"The whispers began the next day. Men I had fought with the length and breadth of Italy began to turn their faces from me. I had found their bodies, but that proved nothing. There was a tribunal later, and your old comrade Groot performed the tricks he had been taught in the cellars beneath the fortress. . . ."

"Groot!" Bernardo burst in then. "Groot's alive?"

"Alive," Diego confirmed. "Is that not what led you to Rome?"

"That was the monks, well, we led them actually," began Bernardo, and was about to begin the lengthy process of organizing his thoughts on the question of how it was that they found themselves in Rome when Salvestro motioned for him to be quiet.

"He lives, in any case," Diego resumed. "And on a pension from the Pope, I believe." His tone was of mild mocking surprise. "He confessed to the killings, carried out on my orders. It was enough."

"Groot didn't kill anyone!" Bernardo burst in. "Him and me were there alone, then some other soldiers came along. . . ."

"It does not matter," Diego said impatiently.

"But he didn't—"

"I know!" It was the first time he had raised his voice, and he grimaced as though this betrayed some weakness. He began to speak more calmly, talking of the humiliations that followed, his shunning by his peers, the mutterings from the men he commanded, finally his secondment to Rome, there to trot before the Orator "like a mastiff on a ribbon," as he put it. "No court was ever convened," he said. "Medici and Cardona saw to that between them. And Fernando's ear is an elusive organ, selective in the lips that are permitted to approach it, and in the words that such lips may speak. Sometimes Fernando's ear even appears quite deaf. Sometimes it is necessary to bang a drum in it merely to gain a hearing. . . ." He paused for a moment, lost in this thought. "And I will have a hearing. It is my right." He looked up and smiled, not at Salvestro or Bernardo, but at the figure on the topmost bunk, the girl. "It will be before the clerks of the orators and the servants of the Roman Pope, before the Portingales, and the Aragonese, and the Castilians, who knows, even the French. Two cutthroats will be my witnesses, and my advocate. . . . My advocate will be a monstrous animal."

"Ezodu."

Bernardo looked up, startled by the voice. The girl was staring at Diego, head propped on her elbow, her black face expressionless. The two looked at each other for several long seconds.

"Ess-odoo," he repeated carefully. "It is her word for the Beast."

"I think," said Bernardo. "I think that . . ."

It was the worms again, unvigorous as yet but growing more energetic with each passing second. They had already passed the apple stage and moved on now to the small cabbage stage. They were beginning to thrash and multiply. A small vanguard had formed up and were attempting the climb his gullet. Bernardo gulped, rose, and hastened once again for the door. Salvestro watched a faint smile appear and disappear on the girl's face.

"She knows this beast," Diego said. "She has seen it. . . ."

"She?" The girl had sat up.

Diego stared at her. "She is called Eusebia," he said. "Or Usse."

In response to this, Eusebia-or-Usse snorted dismissively.

"Usse," she said. "Eusebia is only fit for scrubbing people's feet."

"Usse," Salvestro echoed absently. "Eusebia" and "Usse." "Salvestro," and "Niklot," who was far away and long ago. Dropped somewhere and lost. What was "Salvestro" fit for?

The cabin was quiet and the motions of the *Lucia* were confined to a lolling motion, a shiver slowed to the swing of a bucket being raised carefully from a well. He thought vaguely of his flight out of Prato, the little girl skipping away into the darkness. Of Usedom, himself twisting away from the men who had dragged him down to the beach, then beat him to the ground. Of Rome . . . There was a boy swimming in the black water of the Achter-Wasser, diving deeper and deeper. Was that him? Or was he the one running away? "Salvestro" was fit for that.

Diego flicked his eyes toward the door. "How many stomachs does he have to empty?"

Salvestro shook his head to clear it and rose.

Outside, the sinking arc of the moon was crossing the bows of the *Lucia,* and from the stern of the ship it seemed that their vessel was being drawn down a long white corridor of reflected light. The masts were in shadow and the sails all furled save the foremain, which was reefed to a narrow strip of luminous canvas. The stepped decks were a confusing jumble of harsh angles and shadows, and at first he thought Bernardo was nowhere upon them. Then on the narrow apron of deck between the main hatch and the forecastle, a little before the foremast but obscured by the housing for the pump, he saw a humped shadow crouching down as though trying to hide. He squinted, but the moonlight through the rat-lines dropped a confusing lattice of light and shade over the hunched body. It looked as though one figure were leaning over another, which was trying to get up. He saw a hand press firmly down on . . . something. He watched intently. A head.

"Hey!" he shouted, scrambling down onto the hatch. But as he moved forward something caught him about the shins, sending him tumbling onto the wood with a loud thump. He glanced back—a large sack of something left carelessly on the deck, turnips, perhaps. He clambered up again to reach the two of them, challenging the aggressor, "What do you think you're—"

Bernardo turned around in surprise. He was kneeling beside a figure lying facedown on the deck. The figure was trying to get up and, at the same time, it seemed, trying not to. Terse grunts escaped from between clenched teeth.

"It's Jacopo," explained Bernardo. "He's hurt himself."

"Well, get your weight off his head, then," he commanded, for Bernardo had the mate by the nape of the neck and would not let him rise.

"Can't," muttered Bernardo. "He keeps trying to get up."

"Well, let him up—" Salvestro began to retort, then noticed that one of the mate's arms was extended along the deck, that its hand appeared to be fixed flat to the planks, that its fingers were splayed, and that the reason for these contortions was a six-inch spike that entered the hand at a point a little below the junction of the thumb and forefinger, then continued through to pin the hand to the deck beneath it.

"Ah," said Salvestro.

Jacopo turned his head carefully sideways. "Thought. He was. Going. Overtheside. Grabbed. Slipped," he grunted.

The cabin door opened.

"Watch out! There's a sack of turnips," Salvestro shouted back to Diego, who avoided the hazard by simply leaping across the hatch.

"Is that what it is?" said Bernardo. "I fell over it twice."

Diego reached them a second later. "Foot on the hand," he said. "Then hand on the handle. Then pull." Before anyone else had time to move, Jacopo let out a huge shout and his whole body seemed to spring up off the deck. Diego straightened and stepped back.

"Strange tool to be using at this hour," he observed, weighing the spike in his hand.

Jacopo was wincing and fishing in his pocket with his good hand for a length of rag to wrap around the injured one. For a second it seemed as though he had not heard. Then he said, "I was marling the starboard jib guy when—" He looked about as he spoke and suddenly shouted out, "What the devil . . ."

Usse had moved silently along the narrow gangway and now stood behind Diego. Jacopo stared at her in bemusement. "A Moor?" No one answered.

"Of course," said Diego, looking vaguely in the indicated direction. "The jib guys." He turned and began making his way back to the cabin. He stopped at the door and prodded the "sack" with his toe. The girl said something to him, and he prodded it again. A grunt sounded. "Tomorrow we shall wake him up," he told her.

The moon had swung to port and now was dipping toward the horizon. Jacopo left them without a word and lowered himself slowly through the trapdoor in the hatch-cover.

"He doesn't want to kill us now, does he?" Bernardo asked.

"No," Salvestro replied. "For all the difference that makes."

He thought of the richly dressed men and women who had crowded to-

gether on the benches of the stand. The tiers of faces had formed a rising pyramid, and at its top had sat the Pope. He looked different from the man who had
charged about on horseback before the gates of Prato. Fatter, possibly, or perhaps
it was the robes. He and Bernardo had waved stiffly, as directed, until the crowd
on the quay was a congealed mass of indistinguishable bodies and the men and
women under the awning of the stand had shrunk to little puppets, jostling and
clambering about under the direction of the string-puller above them. The coastline became a smudge of gray and then they were here, afloat in the middle of
the sea.

"I think," said Bernardo. "I think I'm going to . . ."

Salvestro looked out over the black waters in which the ship drifted. The
Lucia creaked gently, and the waves murmured amongst themselves. Bernardo's
stomach emptied itself in a sudden gout, followed quickly by two smaller ones
that spattered over the sea's surface, twin yellow slicks that lengthened, stretched,
and finally broke up. He yawned. Bernardo spat. The stars above glimmered indifferently. Below them the air was all but still and the ship, more or less, sailed on.

Captain Alfredo . . .

"Captain Alfredo di Ragusa! Wake up, you drunken sot!"

He had been shouting for the best part of an hour, or so it seemed. Diego felt
his throat grow hoarse. Initial gentle prods had become firm kicks to the ribs before an arm emerged and groped about in the immediate vicinity of the deck. A
brisk volley of slaps brought the head up briefly, though neither of its eyes
opened. Then the head disappeared again. The arm was retracted. The remainder
still looked like a sack.

Diego redoubled his efforts, and presently a leg made its first appearance,
shyly extending itself sideways as though the foot were searching for something
solid to rest on and the larger but more timorous member was being cajoled into
following. A second foot followed its trailblazing twin and came to rest beside it.
The sack-that-was-Captain-Alfredo paused to gather its energies. Next, fumbling, hesitantly exposing itself to the Tyrrhenian light as if this cloud-diffused
glow were a volcanic blast of skin-shriveling fire, entering wakefulness with the
circumspection of one of the sleepers of Ephesus, then wriggling quickly over the
soggy mossy boards, came a hand. The other hand followed, flopping down beside its mate with a fleshy thump. Fat, hairy fingers groped weakly at first, then
more urgently.

"I think he's looking for something," said Salvestro. The other crewmen
watched attentively.

"Bottle," wheezed the heap at their feet, still sacklike but becoming more
Captain Alfredo–ish in its responses to these unpleasant stimuli. A little moan followed, and the head began to rise again. Thinning curly gray hair parceled out the
captain's head into patches of leathery skin broken by outgrowths of steel wool
below which the skin was mottled with patches of red and striated with broken

veins. The redness intensified about the nose—an oversize purplish conk whose pimples had exploded long ago, leaving a rabbit warren of holes above the nostrils, which were cavernous and choked with hair. A number of teeth had been buried in his mouth; their gravestones leaned at odd angles to one another. After making its plaint, the mouth simply remained open, allowing this inspection, or perhaps waiting for the insertion of the requested "bottle." When it became clear that this was not forthcoming, the eyes opened.

Captain Alfredo's eyes were held in place by fat flanges of pink eyelid flesh that puckered and wrinkled as they retracted to disclose the eyeballs themselves. Their pupils were the blue that waits within the gray of stormclouds for the sun to dissolve and spread it over a cloudless sky, a startling bright cobalt, set off in this case by the equally startling scarlet where the whites should have been. The eyes peered up at the faces looking down at them. The mouth mumbled something ("Ah, the slug"?), then realized it was still open and closed. Nothing more was heard or seen for a minute or so. Diego considered a bucket of water, but before he could act on this thought, beginning somewhere in the midst of the human heap that was Captain Alfredo, a slow eruption began, a business of rumbles and grumbles, groanings and moanings, the creak of eroded cartilage and the scrape of old bones as stiffened muscles flexed and tensed, booze-furred blood-pipes squirted venous and arterial liquor to dormant extremities and vital organs tried to remember their functions. Salivary glands eked out a phlegmy paste from which the tongue recoiled, and digestive juices trickled into an empty stomach in a preemptive strike against the anticipated "first one of the day." A fart sounded its wan trumpet, and the battle with gravity commenced. The limbs began to move: a leg, another leg, an arm, another arm . . . A grunt-filled minute later Captain Alfredo's head was topmost and his feet were bottom-most. Technically he was standing.

"Is he really awake?" asked Arturro a few moments later. His fellows looked closer.

Captain Alfredo was upright. His eyes were open. He breathed. But he seemed quite unaware of those clustered about him, let alone the ship and the sea in which she wallowed. Diego reached forward and tapped him on the nose. The eyes blinked once, then stared blankly as before.

"Bottle," said Diego.

The eyes turned and fixed themselves upon him.

"This way," he said, pointing aft toward the cabin.

Captain Alfredo followed.

Salvestro was left outside with the crewmen, who scuffed their toes on the deck, folded and unfolded their arms, cleared their throats, and found things to fiddle with or lean against. No one spoke for a while. Bernardo was a little way forward, bent over the side and trying to heave. Jacopo squatted down, his arm in a sling. He winced loudly as his bandaged hand knocked against his chest and Salvestro saw the one called Enzo smirk. Nothing was heard from the cabin for some time. The door remained closed, and the men outside occupied themselves with idleness. Ruggero emerged from belowdecks with a length of planking in each hand, saw the cluster of men gathered there on the main deck, and asked what was going on. Jacopo jerked his good thumb in the direction of the poop.

"Alfredo woke up."

Ruggero stacked his planks carefully beneath the gangway and made his way forward to inspect the damaged mainmast. Three poles had been lashed to the stump a little below the break to give the appearance that the mast was whole. He glanced curiously at the still-retching Bernardo. The men on the main deck continued their mooching. Presently, from the poop cabin, a loud voice shouted disbelievingly, "A *what?*"

And, a few minutes later, "From *where?!*"

It was a pensive Captain Alfredo who paced the decks in the days that followed. His drunkard's totter evolved into a rolling swagger, an all-purpose amble that had been designed and perfected over the last three decades to keep him upright on decks rolling through anything under sixty degrees and which now propelled him about the *Lucia* to acquaint himself with his crew. Discovering that the "fishermen" recruited by his mate and pilot were of the rod-and-line rather than the boat-and-net variety made him more pensive still. Nevertheless he divided them into watches under himself and Jacopo, who was given the additional responsibility of showing them the ropes, for it seemed there was not a single man amongst them who could tell a vang from a brace, let alone a stay from a guy. Salvestro and Bernardo were posted as lookouts and stationed on the forecastle until the crow's nest directly above on the foremast could be repaired. In the meantime it reminded them of its existence by shedding pieces of wood on their heads at regular intervals and once, during Bernardo's watch, a large block of sandstone, though that turned out to be dropped accidentally by Jacopo, whose shout of "Look out!" came a split second after the arrival of the stone itself to the left of Bernardo's head and was followed another split second later by the arrival of Jacopo himself, who tumbled through the bottom of the decaying structure and would certainly have broken his legs had Bernardo not caught him. Captain Alfredo added an intermittent stomp to his swagger, and his makeshift crew began to appreciate the subtle distinctions between, say, the ratlines (which were for climbing on), the clew-lines (which were for pulling on), and the gob-lines (which were for leaving well alone because the martingale had snapped off years ago and the bowsprit was about to follow it). Under his bellowed directions, the sails went up, and after long hours spent on the poop deck with charts, compass, crosspiece, tables of declination, brow furrowed and his tongue sticking out from between his teeth, a course was set, too. Ustica was sighted, and a few days later the island of La Galita, from where hot, dusty winds blowing off the coast pushed the *Lucia* north and west. Ruggero loped about the ship with a sharpened nail which he would sink into various beams, planks, and rails, and a lump of yellow chalk, with which he would make obscure marks. Each time he did this he would hoist his tool-sack higher onto his shoulder, scowl and mutter to himself until his aspect became so forbidding that even Captain Alfredo kept out of his way. Twenty leagues south of Cartagena, two stays snapped with eerie simultaneity, sending the mizzen lateen yard crashing heavily to the deck with Jacopo atop it. Bernardo, who happened to be underneath, sidestepped neatly, then plucked the mate from the tangle of lines and canvas, and Jacopo hobbled away with a lightly sprained ankle. Bernardo continued his journey aft to the poop rail, where he duly emptied that morning's breakfast over the side: salted anchovies and biscuit. Similar deposits were made off Cabo de Gata, Punta de las Entinas, Cabo Sacratif, the Torre del Mar, Punta del Cala Moral, and many other points in between. Large yellow stains drifted in the *Lucia's* wake, proving remarkably cohesive in these tranquil waters, the wind fanning them along, still observable at distances of up to two furlongs, where small fish fed on them and died. Diego was not seen on deck much and the girl not at all. When the Rock of Gibraltar was sighted by Salvestro, slightly ahead ("For'ard," he corrected himself) and far off to the right ("Starboard"), they had been at sea for twelve days and the *Lucia,* her crew could not help but notice, was covered from bow to stern with little yellow hieroglyphs. Ruggero had completed his survey.

"I want to explain the markings to you before we start," he told Captain Alfredo. They were crouching in the nose of the ship, legs splayed awkwardly amongst the ropes and hawsers piled there. Ruggero held up an oil-lamp to the massive compass-timbers that curved about them at waist level and on which a dot with a circle about it had been drawn. "This one, that looks like a man being sucked down a whirlpool, this means worm," he said.

Captain Alfredo said, "Right."

Ruggero rooted amongst the tangled fakes of rope ensnaring their feet and pointed down to where the bow timbers passed beneath the breast-hook. Here the symbol was a simple cross. "This one, that looks like a man floating facedown in the sea after his ship broke apart in a storm, this means rot. And this one"—he rooted deeper, uncovering an irregular oval—"this one that looks like a man's mouth screaming in terror as the waves bury him beneath them, this means that I don't know the cause but the timber in question has the resilience of a wet boot-lace and the consistency of pork fat. Now, shall we begin?"

There were other symbols, too, one for iron-sickness, another for mold, yet another for the luxuriant growths of white mushrooms that flourished in the hold, and one—a circle with a line through it, indicating a man cutting his own throat, according to Ruggero—that denoted bad workmanship. The latter was a phrase Captain Alfredo found increasingly irksome as Ruggero moved back through the lower deck, past the hammocks where Enzo, Arturro, and Piero were snoozing, amongst the barrels and casks lashed down to either side of the steerage, holding up his lamp to point out gaps in the planking of the wales where the apron had lifted off the stem-piece. The sharpened nail was produced and sunk to depths of four or five inches in timbers, which, following retraction, oozed unidentifiable black liquid from the puncture-hole. Matters were no better in the hold, where more barrels, lengths of rotting rope, the detritus of a hundred concealed breakages, and a small rowboat all floated in a foot of stinking liquid. Ruggero tapped beams and planks with his hammer until the hull resounded with soggy thunks and thwacks. Kneeling down in the soupy muck, he fished with his hammer until a distinct *clang!* rang out.

"Ah," said Captain Alfredo. Ruggero raised an accusing eyebrow, then struck the submerged object again. "I suppose you'll be wanting to know what that is," began the captain.

"I know what it is," Ruggero retorted. "It's the anchor. What I want to know is, what's it doing down here? Another thing, why is it that not a single stick of wood on this ship has seen a tar-brush in the last twenty years? Another thing, how is it that this wormy, rotting, moldy piss-pot is still afloat at all? This"—he pointed to the evil-smelling slop that swilled about their legs—"has got to be removed. The pump will have to be patched and the foremast, too. I haven't even looked at the yardarms, but if the rest of this 'ship' is anything to go by . . ." He came to a halt there, his outrage being temporarily too great to contain. Captain Alfredo took this opportunity to look once again at the rowboat, which he could not remember seeing before this morning. "It's the wood," Ruggero resumed in a strangled tone, then fell finally silent, as though so deeply affronted by the abuse of this beloved material, evidenced all around him, that he could express only his own dumbfounded shock.

"Well, yes," replied the captain. "With ships, it usually is."

A voice sounded behind them. "Add a cage to that list, carpenter." They turned to find Don Diego clinging to the ladder. He addressed himself to Captain Alfredo: "We're entering the strait." He paused, then added almost as an afterthought, "And Jacopo's gone overboard," then disappeared upward.

Bruno and Bernardo were hauling him up on the end of a rope when Captain Alfredo reappeared on deck.

"I was just standing here, you know, waiting," Bernardo was explaining as he heaved the mate clear of the water, "then I leaned forward to, well, I was sick, was the problem," he continued, grabbing the dripping man under the armpits and swinging him over the side, "and Jacopo here"—depositing him on the deck—"seemed to jump over my head. . . ."

"Don't know what came over me," gasped the mate. "One minute, here. The next . . ." He waved an arm. "There. In the drink."

"No time to worry about that now," Captain Alfredo said, casting an anxious eye over the lee shore, which, though still a good two leagues to starboard, was coming up on them faster than he would like. There were easterlies, called levanters, if he remembered correctly, which blew through here from time to time, and some shoals after Tarifa, but if you kept leeward of the latter, received wisdom was that you missed the former. "We're going to put on a bit of sail in a minute, but first of all I want a man up front swinging the lead." He cast his eye over the men assembled on deck, then pointed to the rearmost.

"Who are you?"

"Salvestro," said Salvestro.

"You'll do."

The lead was a large rusted cleat tied to a line with the fathoms marked by strands of string up and down its length. It plopped into the water, and Salvestro paid out eight fathoms of line, feeling the water's drag increase, the line bow as the heavy cleat drifted under the keel. He shouted, "Clear!" and pulled it up. Thirty feet above his head the crow's nest belched a cloud of wormy sawdust and dropped a length of planking onto the deck. He threw out the lead again. The shore was a wavering ribbon of sand topped with scraggy-looking trees. He glanced aft. Bernardo was helping Enzo and Luca pull on the mizzen lateen. As the wind caught hold of the great sail they moved quickly to secure the guys, and the *Lucia* seemed to skid very slowly to port. They were moving away from the coastline, and the water became more choppy, jostling the vessel. If he were to dive right now and strike out for land, he would be standing upright on solid ground inside the hour. It must be now, he told himself. He had believed that they would put in at Tunis or even as soon as Naples. Or the Roads of Marseilles, and if not there, then certainly Cartagena. . . . He had been wrong on all these counts, and now they were in the strait that would take them from a sea to an ocean, so it had to be now, without delay, without reflection.

"Clear!" he shouted, and threw out the lead again. The coast was falling away more rapidly than he had thought. The weight tugged dully at his arm, pulling him down into the water, should he wish it. . . . He looked down at its chaotic troughs and scends. Now? He pulled on the line, turned his head away, spat. He knew he would not jump.

"What next?" Bernardo shouted up at the poop deck, where Captain Alfredo had been joined by Don Diego. The captain was pointing to the sails, then down at the water. Diego was nodding. Salvestro realized that their vessel was turning very slowly sideways. The two men spoke quickly amongst themselves, and then Alfredo bellowed down to the man on the tiller, "Hard a-port! Hard as you can!"

The ship stopped, then continued to turn.

"Damn!" cursed the captain. Enzo, Luca, and Bernardo looked up at him while he deliberated.

"For'ard, you men," he shouted, and then he was jumping down from the poop and taking the gangway at a run. The three men followed him to the forecastle. "Got to get some more canvas up there," he said, pointing to the foremast. "Got to get her nose around or we'll be on that shore in no time." The stern of the ship was pointed directly toward the coast, and they were drifting backward. Luca jumped on the ratlines, followed by Bernardo, but neither was even within reach of the mainsail when the mast itself lurched. A stay snapped on the port side, those to starboard went slack, and the remainder of the crow's nest crashed to the deck in a cloud of sawdust and splinters. Everyone froze.

"Climb down steadily, lads," said Captain Alfredo. The mast quivered again as Bernardo stepped back on deck. The captain looked warily up at the sail, then down at the water. "Eddy of some sort," he muttered to himself. "Plenty of wind, though. If we can catch it . . ." His eyes went back and forth, his brow furrowed. Apart from Piero on the tiller, everyone was on deck now, even the girl, who watched the approaching coast in baleful silence. Salvestro raised and sank the lead, glancing over his shoulder every few seconds. The sea was rougher near the coastline, he saw now. There were low cliffs and rocks below them. The sea foamed as it broke over these. He would have drowned there.

"The boat!" Alfredo shouted suddenly. "Arturro, Bruno, in the hold. . . ."

It took some minutes to persuade Bernardo, and several more to lower the boat over the side, for it seemed determined to capsize on any contact with seawater. There was a short discussion as to the proper length and weight of the rope and a vaguely panic-stricken hunt for anything forward of the foremast solid enough to take the strain, but in the end everything and everyone was in place: Piero on the tiller, Diego and Usse on the poop, a sawdusty Salvestro in the chains, a grim-faced Alfredo on the forecastle, and a dripping wet Jacopo beside him. Ruggero hammered a last nail into the most solid of the knight-heads, and Enzo, Arturro, Roberto, Bruno, and Luca hovered over the rope against the possibility that the nail would not hold. Then Bernardo began to row.

He rowed to port, which brought the ship about, and then he rowed forward, as if tugging the ship behind him. The stern of the little boat dipped to within an inch of the water, and the rope that attached her to the prow of the *Lucia* rose clear out of the sea while Bernardo churned the oars with such force that it seemed they must snap. Presently the wind again filled the *Lucia*'s sails, the rudder pushed against the strange current, and the vessel began to gather speed. Bernardo simply continued, keeping a generous fifty feet between his own craft and the battered two-and-a-half-master, and when Alfredo had led the crew in several rousing cheers for their oxlike savior and shouted for him to come in, the giant merely yelled back, "No!" and kept rowing. He rowed diagonals, then zigzags, then several wobbly circles. The rope flopped after him and the crew cheered again, none louder than Salvestro, who was also laughing uproariously. The Pillars of Hercules inched past, the last cape slid abaft, and before them was the ocean. Bernardo was standing upright now with the oars angled downward, threshing glittering droplets from the water. The rowboat bounced and spun in the heavier swell, zooming about in front of the larger vessel as though the latter were a dim-witted predator being lured out into the open water. The *Lucia* lumbered after the smaller boat, her fabric sagging like a half-filled wineskin, her masts and yards creaking and groaning, her stanchions and transoms and futtocks and poles and posts and planks all grinding squelchily against one another: a soggy, wormy, mutinous, beastless boat.

Salvestro pulled in the lead and coiled the line. Bernardo was off the larboard, keeping level with the prow and showing no sign of tiring. Two or three leagues separated them from the coast. Africa, Salvestro realized. Behind him someone shouted for everyone else to get their grub, and at almost the same moment a small splash sounded forward. He glanced curiously over the side. The bowsprit floated past.

Jacopo hopped to keep the weight off his ankle, and greasy hair flopped over his forehead. Six doubting faces eyed him. The punctured hand dangled in its sling. "Tonight," he said. "And no more mistakes."

Piero nodded, but nobody else did. Here they were again, thick as thieves in steerage. His failures had stripped him little by little of the steely aura and title they had invested him in. Jacopo the Hand of Death . . . Now, Jacopo the Clown, the dripping buffoon who spat seawater onto the deck and whined about "whatever came over me. . . ." They did not fear him, but they feared his dereliction, for that would turn their gaping faces on each other, all tense and white tonight, crated together like cattle and shifting uneasily from foot to foot. Skeptical already, they would be sneering if he failed again. They wanted to know how. He told them. More nods. More shifting about. The dank boat-smell that clung to every corner of the vessel mingled with the oily lamp-smoke and their unwashed bodies. They could smell each other down here. Lacking rats, the *Lucia* had them.

"We take Bernardo first," said Jacopo, bringing his hand down on the tiller. "Then the others, chop, chop, chop."

"Salvestro! Look!"

Bernardo stood upright in the boat, leaning back to force the nose out of the water and waiting for the next oversize trough to deliver its corresponding peak. His arms tensed, then dug the oars deep into the water, pulled heavily once, twice, thrice, and the little boat launched itself skyward up a ramp of seawater, shooting clear of the surface for a second before crashing down again in a great splash of spray. A grinning Bernardo waved triumphantly. Salvestro waved back.

Later in the afternoon Captain Alfredo had Salvestro detach the rope from the knight-heads and drag it around to the stern, where it was retied to the taffrail, so that Bernardo's antics would cease pulling the ship off her heading. Little by little she was moving out from the coast, which was now little more than a smoky blue line far off on the larboard side, dwindling and thinning. Removed to this new location, Bernardo amused himself by leaping the ship's wake, then, by stabbing down at the water with one oar while in midflight, he discovered that the rowboat might be made to pirouette. Perfecting this maneuver took several more hours, broken only by his stopping to eat. The rugged motions of the smaller boat had settled his stomach where the larger's soft yaws and pitches had upset it, and his appetite had returned in force. Salted fish and pork disappeared down his gullet, followed by bannocks that Arturro baked in the hot embers of

the firebox. Bernardo gulped a round dozen of these ashy dough-cakes, then resumed his rowing.

"A marvelous thing, to be afloat on a day such as this," said Captain Alfredo.
His pink-rimmed eyes roved over the men at work aloft, then off the stern to
Bernardo's sploshings and whoops. "That lad can pull an oar," he marveled.
"Hasn't held down so much as a herring since we left port and now look at him."
He tapped a tentative foot on the deck. "She may not be well-founded, I mean in
the conventional sense, but still she's a good ship, our *Lucia,* is she not?"

Salvestro agreed that she was. The coast had slipped below the horizon, and
the setting sun was a thin red disk slicing deep into a pink sea. The nearest landfall
would be twenty miles away, perhaps more. He heard the cabin door open and
Don Diego walked a little way onto the gangway joining the poop to the forecastle. He looked over the side, then up at the darkening sky. When he turned and
saw the two of them standing there, his gaze swept over them as if he and Captain
Alfredo were simply part of the deck clutter. Since the first night of the voyage he
had barely addressed a word to anyone on board save Captain Alfredo, preferring
to stay in the cabin with the girl, who was seen even more rarely. Salvestro realized that, disengaged from the past injustices heaped upon his head, the soldier
became vague and abstracted, a half-man, only truly animated by the choler that
darkened his face and brought the blood flushing about his throat when the
Medici was mentioned. If the Pope were to die peacefully in his bed, Salvestro
mused, on the other side of the world, Diego would relapse into a torpor indistinguishable from death. Without his anger and its object, he was as he appeared
now: mooning and idle, gazing sightlessly into the water as though he had once
lost something within and could not drag himself away. He stood there a few
minutes before offering the two of them a perfunctory nod, then disappeared
back into the cabin.

When the sun fell below the horizon, Captain Alfredo had the men take in
the sails. Jacopo supervised them. Night fell quickly, and it was almost dark before
the canvas was brailed and they descended wearily belowdecks. A fat moon hung
in the sky, its wan light disappearing altogether for minutes at a time when it
drifted behind the clouds. Salvestro found himself alone on the deck, looking off
the stern at the rowboat that rocked and seesawed on the end of the rope hitched
to the taffrail. Bernardo dozed within it. He looked around quickly, then took
hold of the rope and began to draw it in. When the boat was all but bumping
against the Lucia's stern, Bernardo stirred and woke up.

"What are you—"

"Sssh!"

"But—"

"Shut up!"

Salvestro clambered over the rail and began climbing down to the boat. He
used the end-timbers and larger beams as steps, feeling for them carefully as he

worked his way down the sheer stern. From within the closed hatches of the poop cabin, a human voice droned. Diego's. Below that, a faint light showed around the end of the tiller. He peered in and glimpsed Jacopo and the others gathered together in steerage. Then Bernardo took up his oars and maneuvered the bobbing platform directly beneath him. He waved a foot about, searching for the bottom of the boat, whose motions seemed to grow more erratic the nearer he approached.

"Jump down," whispered Bernardo.

"I *am* jumping down," he hissed back.

He fell on Bernardo, who fell back himself, and the oars clattered loudly in the quiet of the night. The little boat drifted back, away from the *Lucia,* until the weight of the rope brought them to a halt. Salvestro looked back anxiously, but no one appeared and there was no sound save the slap of the water against the boat, the creaking of the *Lucia's* masts, and his own breathing.

"I'm not going back on board," said Bernardo. "I've been sick since we left and I'm not going back, so before you start telling me, I'm going to tell you: I'm not going back and that's that."

"You're not sick now, are you?"

"That's not the point. If I was up there"—Bernardo pointed to the *Lucia*—"I'd be heaving up again in a minute, just like before. Same thing. You don't know what it's like being sick all the time. You wake up, sick. You stand up, sick. You eat, sick. Drink, sick again. You lie down, sick, so you can't sleep, still sick—"

"Bernardo—"

"—and even your dreams are about being sick, when they're not about dogs, and if they are about dogs, then the dogs are sick, too—"

"Bernardo, if you'd simply—"

"—and they're sick on you, because when you wake up again there it is all over you. Sick. You can be sick even when you're sleeping, so don't think for a second that I'm going back on board just to be sick again—"

"Bernardo, shut up. Neither of us—"

"—because I'm not. It was you that had us spend a winter in that fish-shed, and it was you that made us go to Rome, and that's how all this started—"

"Bernardo, neither of us is going back on board."

"—so this is your fault . . . What?"

There is such a sea as this, a loose-limbed body of water whose surface is a membrane of clear resin that sags and stretches under the tonnage of the hulls that slide upon it, dipping, creasing, opening deceptive troughs under blankets of spoon-drift. Fat filaments shred and fly in high winds; skeins of its fabric unravel or snap. Taut bubbles swell, then pop, becoming the mouths of deep sumps, long watery throats leading to the bottom of the ocean. The surface blisters and peels like varnish in a brazier. The water beneath is loose and molten: abruptly skinless. Its frameless mass upholds nothing, neither vessels nor the men who sail them.

This sea was once . . . This was not that sea. The *Lucia* towed a near waveless pond of wake-water, wherein a rowboat, wherein the two benighted men who sat upon her thwarts and argued.

"I said," said Salvestro, "that neither of us is going back. We're going to make for the shore, then coast up bit by bit. We can't be more than fifty miles from a friendly port. We'll do it in stages. Now, give me a hand with this rope. . . ."

"Row home? You want *me* to row all the way? . . ."

"You've been rowing all afternoon," Salvestro countered. "You didn't complain then."

"But what about the others? What about Diego? What about the beast?" Bernardo's voice had risen in complaint.

"Diego? Weren't you listening to him? Do you think the Pope is going to sit politely while we tell the world that he is no better than a murderer of women and children and brave Colonel Diego is innocent as the day is long?"

Bernardo wrestled with this new construction of the events. He was still arranging the old construction into some semblance of sense. There was the surrender-that-was-not-a-surrender, and then the question of whose fault this was, and then the men-that-were-not-Diego's. Himself, Salvestro, and Groot. Now the beast was involved in all this too and was the solution to most of these problems and misunderstandings. There was also something about "Fernando's ear" and gaining its attention.

"When we have this beast, though—" he began.

"Beast?" Salvestro cut him off. "You mean the animal with armor in place of a hide, the beast which is lured out only by virgins, which has a great horn that it uses like a sword to cut the guts out of its enemies?" He stared disbelievingly at his companion. "It doesn't exist, Bernardo. It never did, any more than dragons do."

"But Diego . . ."

"Diego is insane. This business sent him mad, or he was mad before, or he was born mad for all I know. Here we all are aboard a ship that the first storm will send to the bottom, sailing to a coast full of savages who will probably slit our throats, in search of an animal that does not exist to give to the one man in the world who most wants us dead."

"If all that's true, then why is he here?" Bernardo protested. "How come you're so much cleverer than everyone else, Salvestro? If it doesn't exist, then why is he—"

"It's a fool's errand," Salvestro hissed, checking the deck of the *Lucia* again and worrying that he had heard someone upon it. "And Diego knows as well as anyone. Now help me get this rope loose."

Bernardo did not move. "So why is he doing it? Why is he even here?" he persisted, a sulky tone in his voice that Salvestro recognized as the usual prelude to the giant's reluctant acquiescence.

Salvestro was bent over the rope, his fingers trying to dig a first bight from the stubborn and complicated knot. "Because he has nowhere else to go," he muttered, then added more loudly, "Are you going to help me with this or not?"

"Just pull it in."

Salvestro looked up and saw that the *Lucia* was more than a hundred feet away. The rope was sinking into the water. He rubbed his arms, still sore from the afternoon's lead-swinging, then hauled it in hand over hand until he held the end and saw in the fitful moonlight that it had not been untied, but cut. The stern of the *Lucia* receded, a black wall sinking into the night. Bernardo picked up the oars. Salvestro dropped the rope-end into the bottom of the boat. They were alone.

So they rowed then, Salvestro directing Bernardo to turn the boat to larboard and Bernardo pulling powerfully, soon settling into a rhythm and grunting to himself, "*One*, two, *one*, two . . ." The night tented them in darkness and reduced their surroundings to a narrow apron of water. The boat occupied this little patch of ocean, where it bobbed up and down and lurched from side to side. When the swell deepened, as it did some hours later, Salvestro gripped the sides of the boat with both hands. They climbed up and down the troughs, the nose of the boat sometimes sending up a curtain of spray. He was soon soaked, but the night was warm. Another hour and they would see the surf breaking on the coast, a luminous white in the moonlight. Or perhaps the beach would simply rise beneath them and lift the hull clear of the water before they so much as saw the land.

Another hour passed. Bernardo asked for water and Salvestro realized that he had made no provision for this. Later Bernardo asked when they would be reaching their landfall, for he was beginning to tire. The swell was no heavier than before, but now it was knocking the nose of the boat off her bearing and Bernardo would have to stop and bring her about. In the dark, in the monotony of the ocean's surface, where their only coordinate was themselves, the boat's motions were lost in the larger motions of the sea and it seemed that they were going nowhere. Bernardo would dig the nose of the boat from the troughs into which she pitched and haul her up the corresponding slope. Each dip in that sea was the mouth of a tunnel that sucked at their vessel, drawing her beneath the surface. Eventually they swapped places, but after only a few minutes on the oars Salvestro's shoulders felt that they were loose in their sockets and the cavity had been filled with burning sand. He strained against the weight and drag. His hands blistered and his numbed fingers began to slip. After he had dropped the right oar for the third time, Bernardo motioned for him to move aside.

"The sun'll be up soon," he said as they shifted places. "We'll be able to see the coast then."

They did not speak after that.

The sky lightened, but not off the stern. Salvestro watched the horizon gradually form itself to starboard as darkness lifted off the sea. Strange pink lights extended glowing ribbons in the upper air, radiating from a still invisible sun. The shadowed sea crawled about them, coal black against the dawn. It seemed an age before the first fiery sliver of sun showed itself, but by then the sky was already light and, standing precariously in the boat, Salvestro could see the horizon that ringed them as though they were the center of a world of water and its only inhabitants. Their little patch of benighted sea had swollen overnight into a sea, but they were as confined as ever and their dominion's new extent gave them nothing. Salvestro gazed east. The sun slowly hoisted itself clear of the sea. There was no coast.

The sun rose higher, the same sun that had warmed them pleasantly aboard the *Lucia*. Now it burned down on them, forcing the two men to drape their shirts over their heads and screw their eyes tight against the glare. Salvestro's mouth dried and his tongue shrank to a flap of leather. Gravel scraped in his throat when he swallowed. The boat had turned through ninety degrees in the night. He had Bernardo row due east, directly at the sun, for the coast must be there, he thought. They must have run alongside it in the darkness; it was easy to believe that. They continued, although Bernardo was at the limit of his strength and the oars that he had earlier sunk deep with every stroke, searching for purchase in the water, now skimmed inches below the surface and raised dashes of strength-sapping spray. The merest current would be enough to overcome this effort, Salvestro realized. He took another turn at the oars, and Bernardo slumped in the bows. When sleep overcame the big man a few minutes later, his head knocked against the gunwales and Salvestro did not trouble to rouse him. Crusts of salt had formed around his eyes. His lips cracked and bled. His feeble efforts on the oars grew feebler still, then stopped altogether, and he found it took all his strength to draw their weight through the row-locks and stow them in the bottom of the boat. Salvestro hugged his knees to his chest. He looked at Bernardo, who lay still as a corpse across from him. He tried to call the giant, but the name emerged from his parched mouth as a croak. The red clouds that drifted in the very periphery of his vision were afterimages of the sun, stamped on his eyes by a burning hammer. Waves slapped the sides of the boat, knocking her through a jerky circle. Bernardo's mouth fell open. The sun hit him full in the face, and his head dropped. The boat turned and turned, rocked gently by the sea's motions. They drifted.

Some minutes passed, or hours—they drifted in and out of different kinds of waking and exhaustion, time counted only by the boat's slow rotations. Angles and edges dug into their sleep-starved bodies. The boat held and chafed them, pulling them out of their stupor for a few moments at a time. Sunlight glittered and shot off the water, its stabs seeming to reach through Salvestro's eyes to the inside of his skull. A knot of inflamed flesh throbbed and pulsed there. The sun was either a few hours away from sunset or had risen only recently. He did not know east from west. Sleep wrapped him in a murderer's cloak. His head pounded, though it was painless now and sounded like the loose spars that floated in the *Lucia*'s slopping ballast when they knocked against the ship's sides. He had heard that sound while he slept. *Tap, tap, tap* . . . Another life. It came again, an irregular and muted tattoo. Salvestro shook his head. He tried to open his eyes, but they had crusted shut. He reached deep into his mouth and rubbed spit into his gummed eyelashes. Prizing one eye open, he let his head flop over the side. Jacopo's face stared up at him.

He started, which made the boat rock alarmingly. There was no doubt. The eyes were open, the hair as remembered. He floated alongside the boat, subject to the same vagaries, the water's little butts and nudges. His head bobbed loosely against the side. His throat had been cut from ear to ear.

A sound came from Bernardo, a groan. Salvestro rubbed the salt from his other eye. Water washed over the mate's face, but the eyes stared up unblinkingly. He was dressed as usual in a shirt and loose trousers. Bernardo grunted again and pointed. He looked around.

They looked like half-submerged logs, a little flotilla of them bobbing up and down in the water. Six? The nearest was no more than twenty feet away. Bernardo reached for the oars and together they fitted them into the rowlocks. The farthest was fifty yards away and the object of attentions other than their own.

The sides of the *Lucia* rose out of the water like great cliffs. Her masts were spires and her sails were flags too heavy for the wind to lift. Ruggero was alone on her deck, leaning out over the water and fishing for the nearest body with a boathook and a length of chain. He cast the chain out beyond the body and let its weight pull the cadaver toward him. He stopped when he caught sight of them. Bernardo caught hold of the chain. Salvestro rolled the body over by the shoulder. It was Luca. His throat was cut, too. They left the boat tied alongside and climbed wearily aboard.

Ruggero's face was dull with shock. They drank hungrily from the waterbutt, then turned to him.

He stared at them in silence, though whether he was dumbfounded by the events of the night or their own reappearance, the two men could not tell. A man's voice began shouting somewhere belowdecks, and Ruggero clapped his hands over his ears as if he could not bear to hear it. Usse's shriller tones rose against the bellowing, and it was from that alone that Salvestro knew the man shouting down there was Don Diego. His voice sounded thick and uncontrolled. Ruggero was crouched on the deck and was now muttering to himself, "Terrible hours, terrible hours . . ." Diego's bellowing ceased suddenly, and Salvestro gently prized the man's hands away from his ears.

"What has happened here?" he asked. Ruggero shook his head and turned his face away. They left him crouching there.

Captain Alfredo lay spread-eagle on the poop deck, an open bottle in one hand and several empty ones around him. He was holding the bottle above his face, then tilting it gradually until a thin flow spilled into his mouth. At their appearance, he swallowed quickly and tried to raise himself on one elbow but gave up after a couple of ineffectual attempts.

"Thought we'd seen the last of you," he said. His words were slurred and hard to follow. "Cut you adrift, didn't they, the poor bastards." He belched loudly. The effort seemed to exhaust him.

"Who?" asked Salvestro. An empty bottle rolled against his foot. He took the full one from the captain and sat down. The liquor burned like fire.

"Jacopo. All of them, except Ruggero. Came at us like dogs. Died the same way." He gurgled softly and his head knocked gently against the deck. "Two ship-wrecks. Boarded three times. Marooned once. More storms than I can remember. Now this." He patted the deck softly. "And who's going to sail the old girl now?" he murmured.

Salvestro's neck prickled. It was the silence that alerted him, a tautening in his attention. He turned around slowly. Diego stood there with his arms folded over his chest. His face was blank and somehow loose. He did not seem surprised at their presence. He and Salvestro watched each other in silence, then Usse ap-peared behind him. The soldier hung his head and stared at Salvestro until the other was forced to look away. When he looked again they had gone. He heard the girl's voice in the cabin below them. He knelt beside Captain Alfredo and shook him until the man's eyes opened blearily.

"We could have put them in irons," he said. "Had them tied up below, we did. All trussed up, but not"—he gulped painfully—"not for that. They screamed like pigs."

"Jacopo and the others?"

The captain moaned, protesting his drunkenness. Salvestro would not let him alone.

"You had them tied up," Salvestro pressed him. "For what?"

Something in his tone registered in Alfredo's liquor-soaked brain. His eyes opened wide, and one hand tried to paw at Salvestro or grasp his shirt. "Not for that," he repeated. "Diego promised me." He choked and wheezed as he spoke. "He went below. The girl followed him. She made him do it. I heard them, I heard how she did it. And then Diego cut their throats."

His hand found Salvestro's shirt and gripped it as he got these words out. Sal-vestro was shaking his head. "How?" he demanded. "What do you mean, 'She made him do it'?" It made no sense to him.

"She has a hold over him," Alfredo went on. He coughed, then pulled Salves-tro closer to hiss into his ear, "Who else is steering us? Who else, Salvestro? It's her. She has the hand over all of us now. . . ."

Sharks ate the bodies. Alfredo sobered up. The ship sailed on. Salvestro under-stood that they had rowed a wide and perfect circle that night, circumnavigating the as-good-as-stationary *Lucia* to rearrive off her bows. Whether they had veered westward, out into the ocean, then in again, or east, in toward the coast and out, he never knew. He considered their passing across the face of the coast, the curve of their bearing bringing them nearer and nearer until the single point in that trackless darkness, no more than a single pull from Bernardo's exhausted arms, perhaps, when they must have stood no more than a fraction of a league offshore. A cruel joke, and one that they had played upon themselves.

The *Lucia's* reduced crew improvised watches, hauled together on the ropes, pumped, steered, messed, and slept. Ruggero sawed and hammered in the hold. He built a cage and patched the pump. Bernardo spent a single nauseating afternoon pumping out the water in the hold, then returned to the rowboat that the *Lucia* towed, as before, off the stern. When the sails had to be trimmed, Usse worked with the men, shinning up the masts and swinging herself out to the ends of the yards, where she tugged on the stiff canvas, putting on more sail or reefing it in as required. Her black skin shone with sweat as she dropped down onto the deck, panting to catch her breath, then splashing water into her mouth from the scuttlebutt. The merest movement of her limbs raised small flat islands of muscle. Salvestro watched her hungrily. Then he would remember Jacopo and the others, and he would remember that Diego watched her, too. The soldier grew even more taciturn in the days that followed, abstracted, dazed. There was a madman in him, the one who had bellowed and lashed out wildly in the hold. He was silent for now, but Usse spoke to Diego in an undertone, as if she feared to break the fragile spell that chained this part of him, and the other four were careful in his presence, alert to the menacing something that was in him. Ruggero showed Salvestro the gouged beams in the hold where the soldier's sword had bitten, then the rotting ones, then the compass timbers and sprung planking through which fat waterdrops seeped and dripped before running down the sides and pooling in the bottom.

"We tied them up down here," he said, sinking his nail into the mainmast where it was stepped into the keel. "Back to back. She went around the circle of them. . . . Enzo was dead already, I think." Ruggero stared at the thick stump. "Not the others, though."

Salvestro looked about the leaking hold. Ruggero's oil-lamp cast a subaqueous light in the confined space, while the ship's timbers threw exaggerating shadows along her sides, the shadows of a vessel twice her size. Sitting with their backs to the mast, they would have been waist-deep in the water. They would have seen the girl climb quietly down, watched her wade toward them, puzzled by her presence. . . . He turned for the ladder. Ruggero went back to his tests and repairs.

They passed the Beach of White Sands and hugged the shoreline thereafter, for, mindful of Dom Manolo's ordinance to throw the sailors of all ships other than the Portuguese directly into the sea, Captain Alfredo was eager to keep well east of the Canaries. On the eve of Saint Martin's Day they watched the justly dreaded surf of Cape Bojador breaking on its northern bank and pushed out again into the ocean. The ship abseiled down the coast, bouncing from point to point in a series of flattened arcs linking the Bay of Fish to the River of Gold, though it was no river and contained no gold, then the Gulf of Gonsalo de Cintra, though it was really an inlet, and Gonsalvo de Cintra had actually been killed while swimming off the isle of Naar in the Bay of Arguin, which was some eighty leagues to the south, then the Bay of San Cipriano on Saint Gregory's Day and the Cabo Santa Ana on the Eve of Saint Cecilia, the land falling away after the long spit of Cabo Blanco and reappearing as a purplish smudge off to larboard. The soft clatter of distant herons taking wing; then, for many days, nothing. There were no capes, or points, or rivers, and the coast, when they sighted it, was a low unending sand-ridge fringed with white surf. The sun rose behind it, climbed over the ship, and fell into the western ocean. They woke, worked, and slept. Ruggero constructed a davit to raise the anchor from the hold. Salvestro clambered up and down the ratlines. Bernardo let the blisters on his hands heal and the rowboat once again bounced around the *Lucia,* its jolly sploshings pointing up the undeniable leadenness of the larger vessel's progress, while Bernardo stood in its stern and ceased clubbing the hapless water only to sleep or throw quantities of salted pork down his throat: a jovial two-legged seawolf, a-wolfing. He was better off there, in Salvestro's opinion. A desultory air hung over the *Lucia,* the pall of their mutual ignorance and incompatible wants. Their course was the sum of different routes and differently hoped-for journeys, a tangential, compromised bearing not truly congruent to any, unless that of the girl. They rounded Cabo Verde one dawn and the Cape of Masts the next, whose "masts" were a stand of three enormous and long-dead palm trees. The nor'easterlies blew steadily, and they trimmed the sails only by night. Alfredo sat on the forecastle with a compass beside him and in his lap Diego's rutter, from which he would read out ominously opaque phrases: "The Senegal is the end of the land of the Tawny Moors and the beginning of the land of the Blacks" or "The Bijagos Isles are surrounded by shoals and sandbars pushed out by the Rio Grande some fifteen miles to the north" or, bluntly, "Tanguarim. Avoid." Their bearing bent gradually more eastward as they sailed down the Malagueta Coast until, after rounding Cabo Palmas, the sun rose each morning directly over the prow and set each evening directly below the stern. That was their last sight of land, for the rutter told them that the Portuguese maintained forts at Axim and Mina and they dared not sail in sight of them. A dry wind blew off the invisible coast, coating everything and everyone on deck with fine red dust. Ruggero jointed and planed the last of the planks to fashion a new top for the foremast, and he and Salvestro spent a day balancing on the yardarm while Ruggero cut off the splintered end of the pole, sawed out a mortise, and fixed the tenon of the top-piece in place with three carefully fashioned pins. The crow's nest was judged a lost cause, as was the bowsprit, and in any case there was no more wood.

The watery wafts and surges of a gentle westerly current found purchase enough on her barnacled underside to drag the *Lucia* forward, and so, lurching, lolling, leaking, sagging, growing more jellylike with every passing league, her boards popping off her beams and the beams riddled with worm, her hold awash with a noxious liquid peculiar to the bottoms of decaying ships—ineradicable notwithstanding Bernardo's twice weekly sessions on the pump—her poles loose in their steps and their idiosyncratic divergences from the vertical creating interesting perspectival distortions for anyone glancing aloft, her ropes thin as thread and her oozy timbers dripping with damp, her supple decks dipping and flexing, breasting the waves of an unchallenging sea by thumping down soggily on the taller crests and squelching the smaller ones, galumphing toward her landfall like a gasping flatfish flapping its way down the beach, the ship sailed on.

Bernardo sported in his rowboat, Alfredo navigated on the poop deck, Diego leaned on the tiller or remained motionless in the cabin, and Ruggero fussed about belowdecks, his chalk-marks appearing now as sudden yellow rashes covering his hapless patient's skin, overnight fevers of worry that the whole contraption might simply break amidships, fall to bits, even dissolve. . . . That left Salvestro. And Usse. How long for her now?

She stood alone on the forecastle, a figurehead carved from ebony, her eyes fixed forward with such concentration on the narrow line of their bearing that had whales and whirlpools appeared to port and starboard, she would not have glanced at them. She fixed herself there and the *Lucia* followed, drawn by nothing more than the force of her will. She invited no distraction. Soon she would lead them within the vast and vague blur that they had skirted and sailed about. Its dust was already with them. Their futures were there, waiting for their lurching bodies to inhabit them and play them out while she skipped amongst them, unreadable as now. Watching her, Salvestro felt himself a thief. Only the most appalling determination could explain her. What had she felt as she'd wielded the knife above the mutineers? What gnarled and massive hand had enclosed her own as it had cut the signs of its purpose in their flesh? His observations told him nothing. Parted from her, Diego would fall into slack-faced reverie, an unwilled loosening of his fiber. With her, his purpose returned. He believed in her, and Salvestro saw the offering and withholding of her will reflected in the soldier's torpor. She inhabited him as she pleased. She was the instrument of his redemption, if she chose. Or they were the instruments of her return and of no more significance than that. He did not know. It was Alfredo who called out, "Land! Land to starboard!" but she must have seen it long before the old sailor. She did not move or even turn around. They had sailed clear past the Mina Coast and the Slave Coast. They were to the east of these. A strange forest marked the shoreline here, extending up and down the coast for as far as they could see, a forest growing out of the sea, or set on innumerable islands, or riven with thousands of creeks and channels and composed of strange trees whose roots showed high above the waterline. They sailed along the face of this coast for the best part of a day and Usse said nothing. It was almost dusk when an outcrop of these peculiar trees fell aft, and in their lee a bay was disclosed to them. Fringed with palm trees and fed by a broad river, it was the first break in the vegetation they had found. Salvestro saw Usse's body stiffen as she looked about, her eyes sweeping back and forth. Then she threw out her arms and shouted words in a language he did not understand. The men gathered on the deck and looked up at her. She was talking to herself up there, in her own tongue, outside them, already distant and as impenetrable to their gazes as the shadowed landmass that filled the horizon behind her. She whirled about, her face shocking in its sudden animation.

"Home!" she shouted at them. "Home!"

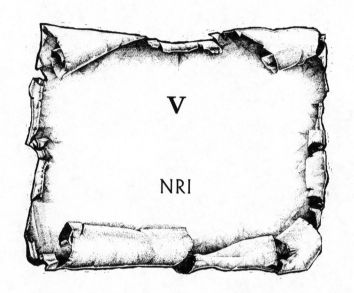

V

NRI

*C*onsider, a tiny spring spills out of the wall of a ravine, wets the moss on a rock, and collects in a pool of dark red granite. A stream flows from the pool and is soon joined by two others hardly larger than itself. They mix together, their banks no more than a single stride apart—the Tembi, the Tamincono, and the Falico—bubbling and gurgling, glittering as the shade of the ravine is exchanged for the arid savannah below, flowing north and east in accordance with the slant of the rock. An ocean waits to receive this rivulet: a tight redoubling of its infant channel and two days' westward flow would bring this watercourse to its end. . . . But, hedged between the highlands of their birth and the desert to the north, swelling with minor tributaries, nosing blindly over floodplains that have not tasted water since the greening of the Sahel, the stream becomes a wide and shallow river bouncing along, oblivious of the flattening of the landscape under the twin hammers of the sun and wind. The tributaries give out, but the river goes on. The clouds hanging provocatively over distant mountains are pregnant with nothing but dust. The mountains themselves are dunes, the degree zero of a landscape. What happens when there is nothing left to happen. Sand.

And the river happening through it. Sometimes it backtracks. Sometimes it splits and fans out into arms or throws backwaters and swamps into the stony monotony of the surrounding desert. Treeless banks rise and fall. Its channel narrows and widens until parts of it might better be considered as lakes and other parts as waterfalls. Little labyrinthine regions of creeks and sandbanks mark its suicidal progress into a desert, where dried beds, salt pans, and wind-eroded watercourses that the heat has baked to stone warn of other unluckier rivers. On it goes, north and east, an immense glittering calm traveling into dry oblivion. Then, sixteen hundred miles from its source, it turns.

Rain falling in the wet season spatters the ground with its fat drops, percolating patiently through fissured granite and porous sandstones, welling in muddy pools and puddles whose spillage trickles and drips, collecting and gathering into little sumps and runoffs that themselves regather and join forces, grow and flow through a riverine hierarchy of rills, gills, runnels, and streams to reach any one of a hundred rolling swollen floods, great muddy gurges in which uprooted trees flop and rear, beaching themselves on dwindling sandbanks before being lifted off again by the waters' increase and carried down to the confluence, which might be a lazy arm reaching back into a floodplain, or a foaming gash in the cliffside, or a trickle, or a swamp, or the dripping of wet moss. . . . Drainage being inevitable, all rivers meet in the River.

And the River turns southeast, away from the desert and down into the savannah and forests of its lower course, sucking hungrily at its lower tributaries, swelling, growing, rolling mud and rocks before it, bursting its banks and creating doomed lakes and backwashes, curving down toward the ocean like a scythe or the wound such a scythe might make if its blade were two and a half thousand miles of razor-edged steel slicing open a mile-wide vein of silver. For it glitters, despite its muddiness, and is placid, despite its enormity. And it slows, despite the nearing of the ocean that is its end. It lazes, and its meanders redouble so tautly and perversely that channels often form between their cusps. It divides, and subdivides, and sits in inert malarial pools, which leach brackish and sluggish liquids into the innumerable creeks that now make up its channel. Mud collects too, sometimes forming little islands. Were this a sea, these eyots and sandbanks would add up to an archipelago. It is not. It remains a river, though a reluctant one down here, this near to its egress and the dwarfing bulk of the ocean with its brine and its recalcitrant unriveriness. Successive alluvial washes only redistribute the landscape, and the little mud-islands it offers as a bulwark against its own momentous flood simply drift about, dissolving and accreting, disappearing and reappearing . . .

Father . . .

. . . never quite land and never quite water. It is a landscape of local compromise, lodged in its protean phase, a soupy swamp, a delta, a stubborn remnant of the unsettled soft land that Eri hardened with a blade forged for him by an Awka blacksmith.

Daughter? Have you returned?

So: a recoiling River, procrastinating and delaying behind a thick mat of mangroves and one hundred miles of accumulated river mud. Its creeks and islands make up a spongy labyrinth that the River would be happy to wander forever, drifting, stagnating, never quite emerging onto the raw and bristling coast. In the meantime there are slow fluxes and convections, false currents, leakage, all kinds of watery evasion. But the drift is always seaward. All rivers end in the sea, dissolving there and being sent aloft to fall as rain on some distant watershed, the beginning of another river, eventually another dissolution. The water of this silent floating world waits in pools and inlets, in false lagoons and deceptive lakes. The channels between the mangroves are flat brown mirrors of water where exposed and reflected root systems strive doubly upward and downward, as though suspended over bottomless ravines. The sky appears as a powder-white glare, and mirrored birds fly upside-down, fish eagles and egrets, the odd pelican, rising out of the virtual depths to scoop fat carp and perch: a splash, a glittering fillet of fish-muscle sinks wriggling into the mirror-world or rises into the sky. Surface commotions and ripples edge the mud-banks with a liquid sheen. The mud is pastel blue or black, or a marbled mixture of the two. It stinks, drowning the more delicate smell of the water. When the banks widen and this jungly sprawl opens out into a little lake or lagoon, a faint peaty scent lifts off the surface and hangs in the air, spiced with waterweed and marsh gas. Bracelets of blue-black oysters ring the stiltlike roots of the larger mangroves. Colorless crabs rest on the mud underneath. A tree drops a ripened seedling out of its dark green canopy, its heavy taproot spearing the soft mud and startling the crabs, which scatter. A heron clatters heavily into the air. The water is mostly still now the floods have subsided. The harmattan blows, but it is mild here, a watery shiver, a night-breeze. The thin poles of an *isanga*-trap project inches above the surface of a quiet, tree-fringed lagoon. Three pirogues with a man in each are maneuvering their craft to draw the trap shut. Raffia palms grow in tall stands behind the mangroves. Something caws, invisible in the undergrowth. Something moves in the water—the fishermen can hear it—splish, splosh, splish, splosh . . . Strangely regular. Their heads come up. A little rowboat rounds the bend in the creek and paddles slowly into the lagoon.

Later, a solemn-faced headman delicately lifted the charred skin off a fat *edo*-fish, prized open its belly to pull out the bones, and offered Usse the first of the smoking fillets. Through the gaps in the fence of his compound she saw faces peering in at them, though whether it was a visit from the Eze-Ada that drew them or the appearance of three white faces, or simply visitors, she did not know. The three fishermen who had guided them back to the village sat on their haunches a little farther back from the fire. The headman was very old and smiled to himself as she praised the food with polite extravagance. The fishermen glanced between her and her companions, though whenever she glanced back in their direction they would pretend to be looking at something else entirely. Her fellow travelers were another matter. They were inspected frankly and closely, as though they were intricately carved effigies whose bizarre workmanship had to be minutely appreciated. When Diego made as if to swat one of the fishermen away, the headman spoke sharply, and after that they confined themselves to watching from a distance.

"A woman from here took a man whose brother lives in a village nearer the coast. The man died and she went with the brother, down by the coast. She comes back here sometimes. She makes baskets. They have those bamboo houses down there."

The headman was cutting fillets for the rest of them now.

"Must get cold this time of year, harmattan time. Anyway, she sells those baskets at Ikolo, so she comes through here on the way. They have a market there each week. She comes through every tenth or twelfth week, talks to her family here. This brother is a good man. Plenty to eat down there. Do you know this place?"

Usse looked up at this, the first question she had been asked since their arrival. She swallowed the fish in her mouth and shook her head.

"They had Nri-men down there once. This was before she got there. The brother told her about it. They had problems with a *ju-ju* the headman there had set up. Lost some men in the River. Bad problems. It was an Ijaw village, like here. Not Nembe-people. It's better now." He made a gesture with his hand, indicating the direction, perhaps, and Usse saw that his eye alighted on a covered calabash set up behind him. He turned back to her.

"This is good fish," she said. "Not too dry."

"You are thirsty?" He clicked his fingers at one of the three men, who rose eagerly and began dipping cups into the calabash. She sipped carefully. The palmwine was sweet and thick, its fumes heady. Its heat warmed her to her bones.

"Drink slowly," she told the three men sitting opposite. "It is stronger than it tastes."

"Who are these people?" Diego demanded. "Are these the people you spoke of?"

She shook her head. The headman took a long draft from his cup, watching this exchange without understanding it.

"Sharks," she said, suddenly remembering. "This village had trouble with sharks."

The headman nodded. "It is much better now. They kill a lot of them after the rains when the water is high. We send them cutch for their nets. Good against rot. This woman says the headman has whole necklaces of shark's teeth. He thinks his teeth will never fall out." The headman grinned then, showing her a full set of shiny teeth. "Cutch works better. In my opinion."

Diego's head went back and forth as they talked. The other two got on with their fish, pausing only to slurp from their cups. More faces appeared behind the fence to the man's compound. The village had been reached through a creek so narrow that the mangroves met above their heads to form a glossy green tunnel. It gave out onto a lagoon much like the one where they built their trap, except for a low island in its center on which stood a dozen or so fenced compounds containing mud-walled huts thatched with raffia palm, each one raised four or five feet off the ground on piles. Two children busy raking embers up and down the bottom of a small half-made canoe shouted and jumped up and down at their approach until the uncertain expressions of the men in the pirogues had silenced them.

"We had good crayfish this year," the headman said. "We heard the harvest was bad again inland. They had yam-beetles. The people up there should eat crayfish. The traps are easy to make." He began to describe the traps, drawing conical baskets in the air with his long-fingered hands, then miming the trigger mechanism. She nodded in an interested fashion. Her three companions paid closer attention, their heads moving in comic synchronization as they followed the man's movements. She remembered her first weeks in the city, knowing nothing, understanding nothing. People's hands had been the only language she understood then. There was a cult of the hand, called Ikenga, but it was for warriors and merchants and all its rules concerned either fighting or wealth. There should be a cult for talking hands and for different tongues. . . . Her mind drifted through these thoughts while the headman went on to tell how snails could be caught in simple baskets. He described them in the same manner, and she understood that he was doing this partly out of hospitality for the three men who would understand nothing else, partly for the pleasure of it (the very traps he described were stacked in a corner of the compound), and partly, most obliquely, out of curiosity. There was no famine here. Their harvest had not failed. There was no war to calm, no souring of the earth to draw out, no spirit to banish. He wanted to know what she was doing down here: herself, the eldest daughter of the Eze-Nri, paddling through the mangroves with three ash-faced men. But he dared not ask. The *ichi*-marks on her face forbade his curiosity. Nri itself forbade it.

She said, "These men are mine. We have come up from the coast. Tomorrow we must go on upriver. A great boat is in the bay back there, and there are two men we left, men like these ones. They must not come to harm."

"There is a Nembe village near that bay," said the headman, clearly relieved that her business did not concern him. "Some of my people know the people, but they are very fierce. And they hear the stories from along the coast. They hate the White-men. . . ." He poked the embers in the fire. "I will send men in the morning, and they will tell these Nembe what the Eze-Ada says. It may be too late."

It was quite dark now. The whispering from beyond the compound fence had fallen quiet, though she could see a dozen or more of the villagers still waiting there, their eyes watching her and her charges. And what do *you* think of these people? she wondered to herself. She was impatient for the evening to end. The headman indicated that she should sleep in the hut in which they sat while he would sleep in the hut of his son, who was away trading mangrove-salt farther inland. He hesitated when his eyes swept over the three men, and she saw worry pass fleetingly across his face. She reassured him that they would do no more than they had done already, which was eat and drink, then sleep like ordinary men. Troublesome spirits sought out trouble and lived in the places where trouble began. In the morning she would level and cleanse the ground on which they slept in case they left a mark there. After she told him this, the man touched his right hand to his forehead. He beckoned to a woman outside the fence who entered with her eyes fixed downward, though she had been staring boldly enough before that. She scooped up the embers and began spreading them in a shallow firepit under the slats of the bed on which she would sleep. To warm her, the headman explained.

She lay down and waited for the three men to fall asleep. After a time, and when no further sounds reached her from the other huts, she rose quietly and walked down to the water. The harmattan was a cool breeze that barely moved the leaves in the trees but still raised gooseflesh on her arms. She sat down and hugged her knees to her chest. The journey behind her was no longer the force that pushed her forward. She had felt the new pull as soon as the giant had propelled them in amongst the mangroves, a troubling impatience. The journey thrashed behind her like a useless tail. She cut it off. None of that mattered now; she was being drawn by her destination. She closed her eyes, imagining the mangroves around her, then herself pushing them away, flattening a great swath of them with a single fan of her arm. That left the water. She thought of it simply flowing away. But where? Where was the place that would hold so much? Its smell filled her nostrils. She raised a dome in the earth, and the water rushed down its sides. The ground was solid beneath her. She pushed herself off it, rising, letting it fall away from her at extraordinary speed. There was nothing now. She was alone, not here in an Ijaw village, on a little island of river-mud, but where? She waited. Eri fell from the sky, or so the story went when little children were told it. Iguedo had told her there was a sky behind the sky one saw. This was that sky, not the familiar blue one, with its familiar clouds, its familiar sun. That sky. This sky. Never go too far when you dream. . . . Iguedo's cackling and hectoring. Little girls like you get lost. . . . Usse was somewhere far below, sitting by a lagoon with her prizes snoring behind her. Eusebia was dead, and good riddance. She was the Eze-Ada, eldest daughter of the Eze-Nri.

Father?

Eri fell from the sky, which was the image of where she was now. He fell to the shaking earth, the soft and thunderous earth, and calmed it and hardened it with a blade from an Awka smith. She waited for a time, squatting there on the ground, listening.

Daughter, have you returned?

Eri was the first of the Eze-Nri. He sank his blade in to the hilt and felt it shiver and twist. He clung to it with both hands, softening and opening, drawing it out, then plunging it in again until the shaking shivered up the blade and stopped in his bones. He was a strong man. He held it in and looked about him at the earth. The earth was stained. Eri grew fearful at what he had done.

Will you calm my house? Will you wake me from my dreaming?

Father, I have brought the White-men. . . .

Eri said, "Ala, Mother of the Earth, I have stained you with my work. What am I to do?" Ala heard him and spoke with the other Alusi, with Igwe-in-the-Sky and Aro-the-Year, with Ifejioku who guards the yams and with Agwu, the trickster god. Igwe sent down rain to wash away the stain, but it was deep and dry and would not wash away. Aro looked into the future, but as far ahead as he could see, the stain was still there. Ifejioku said nothing. Agwu laughed at them all. Ala came to Eri then and told him to cleanse the land, for when Aro had rolled around enough times, the earth would begin to shake again and grow soft like a sea, and his people would have to calm it and harden it once again.

Eri said, "But how will they know when this time is to come? I am Eri, and I do not know. How will I tell them?"

Ala told him.

I will bring them to you.

As you promised.

As I promised.

When she rose, the sky was already beginning to lighten in the east. Walking back wearily, she saw by this faint illumination a head lower itself gently—stealthily—onto the raffia mats that the headman had provided for the three men. She regained her bed and squinted across the compound, watching the three men under the pretense of sleep. But the three were indistinguishable: mouths open, limbs sprawled, eyes shut.

The mud changed color, exchanging its blues and blacks for a deep rust as they moved out of reach of the sea's tidal fluxes and the water in the lagoons and creeks lost its salinity. Salvestro scooped up a handful and dashed it into his mouth. Still brackish, though less so than the day before and less again than the day before that. He understood that they were moving north.

Fan palms and huge cottonwood trees with strange mixtures of red and green leaves began to show themselves amongst the mangroves. The banks of the creeks through which they passed were choked with rushes and stunted bushes at the water's edge, while a great tangle of fronds and lianas bound the screw pines, palms, and other trees that he could not name into solid cliffs of greenery. Swamp lilies covered some of the lagoons, and their craft would cut a channel of black water through the fleshy leaves, which would join together behind them as soon as they had passed, only to be cut again by the prow of the following canoe. Or canoes, for after that first night they were not suffered to travel alone. They set out each morning from whichever fishing village had offered them its hospitality with an escort to guide them to the next. The canoes were much faster than their row-boat, usually manned by four or six young men who kept a respectful distance whether trailing behind them or shooting ahead to cut away the lianas from a choked channel with heavy, razor-sharp machetes, for the undergrowth would often reach over the creeks and these waterways were cool green tunnels where the overwhelming silence of the swamp seemed to thicken into something unbroachable. Salvestro felt the urge to shout loudly and a corresponding reluctance to break the taut calm that tented this hushed landscape. Usse had warned them that crocodiles and water-snakes waited and listened in these quiet channels. His reluctance had nothing to do with that. They spoke to each other rarely, and then only in undertones. Bernardo rowed. Diego stared over the side, his face blank, as though exhausted beyond sleep. When they reached the village where they would stop the night, when increasingly elaborate obeisances had been made to Usse by the headman and elders, then it seemed a spell had been broken or temporarily lifted, for he and Bernardo would talk inconsequentially, Usse would exchange greetings with their hosts, often pointing to the three of them, there would be chatter, a human noise in the watery silence, but the soldier would say little or nothing at all.

The receptions in the villages grew more formal the farther north they went. The sun disappeared behind the green walls of the swamp, and long shadows crept across the water. Their escorts would draw a little closer then, hurrying them along. A bend would be rounded and suddenly the familiar stilted huts would appear with a small group of men standing on the bank, and the whole village behind them, all talking until their craft was spotted. Then silence. They would drag the boat up the bank and the whole village would bow their heads until Usse said something solemn in her language, whereupon they would stand normally and their eyes would rove between the young woman and themselves. Yet however cordial the greetings that passed between them, the villagers would avoid looking at her directly and would keep their arms fixed awkwardly at their sides. They feared her, he realized gradually, and this had something to do with the place where they were going, which was called Ree, or Nree. He had asked her. She had told them not to repeat it.

They would eat fish and sometimes a porridgelike dish that was gray and sticky, washing these down with the sweet liquor the villagers called *tombo*. He would gulp as many cups as he could keep down, drinking himself into a stupor. The evening would wear on and his eyes would drop, though not from the liquor. Exhaustion riddled him like fever. His limbs ached with it. His head pounded. It seemed all he could do to stay awake. Yet he could not sleep.

Ants, he had thought that first night. Winged ones.

They had come upon three men in pirogues. The three men had led them through a bowerlike creek to their village, where they had eaten and drunk. It was their first night on solid ground since Rome, since the hard-packed dirt under the Sant'Angelo bridge. Usse and an old man who seemed to be the chief had talked quietly together in their own language. He'd understood nothing until the old man had begun drawing objects with his hands: different kinds of boats, it seemed. The fishermen had looked curiously at their craft, which was broader amidships and much shorter than their pirogues. The old man would be asking about the rowboat. Later they were given raffia mats to break the hardness of the ground. Usse took the slatted bed on the other side of the hut. He remembered his head sinking irresistibly to the ground and sleep overtaking him like a great warm wave. He drifted down, away from his companions to either side of him, away from the village, away from everything and into a snug darkness. Then it began.

The first time he awoke, he examined the coarse fibers of the mat, picking at a loose strand that he assumed had worked its way into his ear and irritated him back into consciousness. He snipped off a number of coarse fibers with his fingernail and sank gratefully back into sleep. . . . Or ticks! It seemed he was awake again, and ticks had been trying to crawl into his hair, or his ear, to lay eggs that would turn into more ticks, if ticks did in fact lay eggs. It must have been his ear, for it had been a sound that had awoken him this time. Insect-feet scraping across his eardrum. He could not hear it now. He was already dropping off again. It was gone. He slept, and it promptly woke him once again: a whisper, very distant or very hushed. Ants? Winged ants? Or perhaps some larger beast crashing about in the undergrowth far away, its clumsy maneuvers amplified in the still night air. . . . Except the air was not still. A breeze blew. A breeze that rustled the leaves in the trees, leaves the size of skillets and leaves the size of thimbles, umbels, fronds, and lianas all scraping dryly together out there in the uncharted swamp. It was not that, either, the susurrating and sibilant twist of disturbance that curled itself in his ear and shivered there, a broken hiss that stopped the instant he woke and started the instant he slept. It had the character of voices, a fugitive rise and fall, different registers, but all incomprehensible and maddening. . . . He sat up. It stopped. Through the open door of the hut he saw the lightening sky, the water beyond just distinguishable from the towering mangroves, then a figure rising from the water's edge and walking toward him. Usse? Yes. He let his head fall back, knowing dawn was not far off, an hour at most. A single precious hour. The voices had fallen silent. But the next night they were back.

So their near silent passage through the silent swamp went on, glossy dark green ferns appearing amongst the various palms and taller trees and dogtoothed perch breaking the surface in the late afternoons to swallow the hatching water-flies. The mangroves stopped and the creeks became wider, the land about them higher. Black rings formed about Salvestro's eyes, and he spent these days lolling in the cramped boat, drifting in and out of sleep, knowing that only one night in two or three would be offered to him undisturbed. The creeks turned into long chains of lagoons. Then, a few days later, a stand of *abara*-trees was passing to their left, and behind them he glimpsed something glittering through the shade. The land there narrowed to a spit, then a point; the little rowboat rounded a last screen of bushes, and then there was open water: an enormous lake lay before them, its far bank visible a mile or more away. To either side there was only water for as far as the eye could see. Bernardo pulled harder on the oars, making for a ragged plume of smoke that Usse pointed to, though his course seemed to veer off the bearing the farther he went. They were traveling along a sagging arc, falling short for some reason. Salvestro looked back at the dense verdure through which they had traveled, a low hump of green, an unimpressive littoral. Their escorts had not followed them.

"It is a river," Diego said abruptly. They were the first words he had spoken that day. Salvestro looked forward again in bafflement, unable to comprehend so large a body of water as a channel extending many further miles in both directions. It seemed formless and endless. Too big to move.

Bernardo eventually reached the far bank a few yards below a wide flight of steps formed from tree-trunks split down their centers and pegged in place with thick staves. A group of women wrapped in brightly colored cotton were washing clothes in the river, kneeling on the bottom step to pummel the sodden cloth, then dowsing it again in the opaque water. They stopped their work at the approach of the rowboat, watching its occupants with undisguised curiosity until,

when their craft was no more than ten yards away, Usse turned to observe them.
Those nearest squatted down on the lowest step, seemingly frozen in place and
transfixed by the lines carved in the young woman's face, but the greater part did
not even stop to pick up their washing baskets, wheeling en masse like a flock of
birds and scattering up the steps.

They tied up the boat and stepped ashore. The remaining women watched
warily as they mounted the steps. Usse led them along a path toward the wooden
arch that marked the entrance to the village. Three young men were standing
there, and Salvestro waited for them to bow, or crouch, or lower their heads as all
the other villagers had done. Instead they grinned broadly at the young woman's
approach, embracing her and breaking into animated conversation. All three wore
the same marks on their faces, identical to Usse's, and all three carried heavy, elaborately carved staffs. Salvestro, Bernardo, and Diego stood there awkwardly while
this reunion ran its course. From time to time Usse turned and indicated them,
and the men nodded, their eyes running quickly over the three of them, apprais-
ing them. Eventually one of the three beckoned them forward, and all seven entered the village, which was larger than any they had yet seen and the mud-walls
of the compounds much higher.

"Is this 'Nree'?" Bernardo asked Salvestro.

Usse turned and told him shortly that it was not. One of the three men asked
her something and nodded when she answered. Men and women began to appear in the doorways, their eyes following the odd procession as it passed between
the huts and compounds. The three of them were led to a small doorway set deep
in a wall.

"Tomorrow the people here will take us upriver," Usse told them. "Food and
water will be brought to you. We leave at first light."

She was turning to go when Diego broke his silence. "Who are these men?"
he demanded, indicating the three waiting for her. "How do we know we can
trust them?"

"They are my brothers," Usse said shortly.

The door led to a little courtyard walled on three sides. A long low building
fronted by a raised terrace closed off the back. A cooking pit in the center of the
courtyard had been swept out. There was a hutchlike structure to one side, carefully thatched but containing nothing. The three men were left alone.

The foremost part of the building was divided into three rooms, each with
two doors giving out onto the terrace in front and a much larger room behind,
its roof supported by stakes of a dark hardwood. Two rearmost rooms were
reached across this darkened area, for there were no breaks in either the walls or
the roof. They were as narrow as corridors, placed one in front of the other and
the doorways staggered so that the last was in complete darkness and Salvestro
was able to make out its dimensions only by running his hands along the smooth
walls. The whole place was clean, but a musty smell hung in the air as though no
one had entered for a long time. A pile of mats had been stacked on the terrace.

Salvestro spread these out, and he and Bernardo lay down on them. Diego stood there for a few moments as though undecided whether or not he would do the same. Eventually he turned away and wandered back into the building.

"Diego is sick," Bernardo said when the man had disappeared. "I saw him last night. He was shaking."

"The only place Diego's sick is in his head," Salvestro retorted.

"What do you mean, 'in his head'?"

"Be quiet or he'll hear," Salvestro hissed, nodding toward the inside of the building. "He doesn't know what to do. He hardly speaks. He knows no more than we do."

Bernardo thought about this.

"And we don't know anything!" he burst out.

"Right," said Salvestro. "We don't. So what are we going to do?"

Bernardo shook his head in ignorance.

"We're going to keep our heads down and get out of this somehow. And if that means Diego leading some animal along by the nose and us following with a shovel, then that's what we'll do." His fingers minced with exaggerated caution past the tip of Bernardo's nose

"Like at Prato," said Bernardo, watching the walking fingers. "Or Rome."

Like Muud, thought Salvestro. And Proztorf, and Marne, and all the other villages he had crept away from in the dead of night. Like the island.

He said, "We'll be back at the Broken Wheel scoffing Rodolfo's pies before you know it. Who knows, we might even find a use for the bread."

"The bread," echoed Bernardo, savoring several confused memories. "And beer?"

"Beer too," confirmed Salvestro. "Barrels of it."

Their stomachs rumbled nostalgically.

The promised food arrived later, carried in an earthenware cooking pot by two old women who set it inside the door to the courtyard, placed a large calabash of water beside it, then retreated without once having glanced at the two men who watched this operation from the terrace. The cooking pot contained a gray stew in which maize cobs had been boiled whole. Bernardo dipped a finger in.

"Salty," he said. "Where's Diego?"

Diego was in the dark of the rearmost room.

"Sire, I bring greetings from Fernando the Catholic, King of all Spain. I am Don Diego of Tortosa, the servant of my King . . ."

No. The words tasted of ashes. They fell off his tongue like stones. He began again.

"Sire, my King bids me salute you in his place. Greetings, from Fernando the Catholic, King of all Spain, whose wish it is to give a certain beast to Pope Leo— to the Holy Father, Leo, our Pope—to Medici, neither holy, nor a father, my enemy and the agent of my ruin. And yet it is the wish of my King and so it is my wish too that this be done. Thus and therefore I come before you, King of Nri."

He was on his knees. He saw their shapes in the darkness of the empty room, their dissolving bodies: Medici, Cardona, the whisperers and slanderers.

"He is my enemy. I wish him dead."

His own voice sounded odd to his ears, thickened, perhaps. He curled his tongue around his teeth. When he delivered this speech, Usse would be standing at her father's side. She was a different person. He no longer knew her. The Princess of Nri.

"Sire," he began again. "It has been my great pleasure to lie with your daughter seven times, in which art she has proved most dexterous. I have had her in different places and several diverse manners, including the Turkish. In sight of this fact, I beg of you a Beast, called *Ezodu* in these parts, and hereby promise you that I will, on the horn which grows upon the end of its nose, impale a certain fat Pontiff, called Leo in my country. I am Diego of Tortosa, though I have not been there in many years and have no plan to return, and I am the servant of Fernando the Catholic, King of all Spain, though I have not served him since the butchery of Prato and his creatures will most likely hang me anyway. . . ."

He stopped again. He felt laughter rising in his throat, a strange wheezing sensation that bubbled and gurgled up from his chest.

"These, my companions, are called Salvestro the Fleet of Foot and Bernardo of the Brawny Arm. They are from nowhere in particular. I, however, am Diego of Tortosa . . ."

He stopped again. Was he laughing? Was this laughter?

"I am the servant of Fernando the Catholic."

It made no difference what he said.

"I am the servant," he began.

It felt as though he were laughing, his sides aching, his insides racked with hiccups of mirth that forced their way up to his throat. His mouth opened and closed. His body shook, but there was only silence. If this was his laughter, his laughter made no sound.

Two clean-picked cobs already lay on the ground beside the cooking pot when Salvestro emerged again.

"Mmmn?" asked Bernardo.

"He says he will eat later. We are to save his portion for him."

"Whhhth?"

"He is praying," said Salvestro, "and does not wish to be disturbed."

A waist-high conical volcano coughed thin blue plumes of smoke out of its top. The damp sods enclosing its sides hissed, and twists of steam peeled off the turf. Within, smoldering wood crackled when the fire reached the knots in the logs. The turf was to keep the air out, and keeping the air out meant the wood burned slowly, and burning the wood slowly made charcoal. Apart from watching it, there was very little to do: adding an extra sod of turf when the smoke escaped through the sides and giving it an aerating poke with a stick when the smoke began to thin. The fire must not burn too freely. The fire must not go out. Making charcoal bored him.

The boy poked listlessly with his stick, a fire-blackened pole of iroko-wood longer than himself. He added a sod of turf. He listened to the muffled hiss and fizz deep inside the cone. It would be dark soon. He would pile on the remaining sods and return to the old man's compound. Nothing grew in the shade of the crabwood trees that ringed the clearing except ground-creepers that snaked and slithered downhill, presumably in search of water. The ground fell away and formed a cut through which ran a stream. The old man's place was on the other side, outside the village proper. Earlier he had chased off a chimpanzee. Now a wood owl hooted. It was intended that he learn bronze-casting, and the old man was supposed to teach him. So far he had only made charcoal.

He gave the sods a poke, then dawdled around the edge of the clearing. His feet crunched down on the leathery leaves of the ground-creeper. His pole trailed behind him. The sky was a bowl of deepening blue fringed by the ragged canopy of the trees. The village rested in a broad-bottomed defile defined by five steep-sided hills. It was rather longer than it was wide, a place of shade and shadows even in daylight. There was a *ju-ju* on the ridge above and others to either side of it: a protective ring to warn off intruders, though there never were intruders. Only Nri-people would dare to enter Nri. The old man's place had a mud wall around it that looked as though it would collapse with one good kick. No one had ever bothered him, as far as he knew. The boy thought about creeping up and pulling down the crumbling palisade. The *mmo*-men did that if someone misbehaved, and he would join the *mmo*-men when he was older. That would show him. He looked up again and saw the quarter-moon hanging far above him. The fire hissed and smoked: a squat, grumpy little charcoal-god. It was time to pile on the rest of the sods and go home. He did not like making charcoal. He did not like the old man, either.

Below the clearing, the stream rushed between several very large cotton-wood trees. The ground curved down steeply for the last few feet on either side, but if you took a running jump, you could clear the water and scramble up the other side without wetting your feet. After that the ground leveled off, and then there were some stands of coco-palms that belonged to Iguedo. The old man's place was somewhere behind them—"somewhere" because, try as he might, he could never quite fix the location. There was a long-abandoned termite-mound and some scrubby bushes with long purplish leaves, then some more trees. . . . It was back there somewhere, though a "somewhere" he never had any difficulty finding. The old man's whiny croak scraped his ears at a hundred paces, and his cackling was even worse. Like a hornbill having its feathers pulled out. There it was now, meaning Iguedo was inside, meaning supper. He pushed forward through the undergrowth.

The door to the compound was a sagging assemblage of sticks bound together with raffia that stood permanently half-open. Iguedo was boiling yam over the fire in the center of the courtyard. He could smell the sharpness boiling away as the old woman pounded the yam to a mash.

"Yeh, the boy's back!" she called out as he slid reluctantly past the ramshackle door. An incoherent grunt sounded from the hut, then the old man appeared in the doorway: a bag of twigs with skin hanging off the elbows and a thatch of white hair on top. He was drunk again, standing there bent forward at the waist in an effort to squint through the gloom. At least he behaved as though he were drunk. The boy had yet to see him actually drinking, but there were wine-jars behind the heap of clutter that the old man called his tools. He gestured impatiently for the boy to come inside. He looked stiff-legged when he walked, yet the boy had seen him leap across the stream with two bundles of charcoal over his shoulder, then scramble up the other side like a billy-goat. He was a spry, lean, sinewy, old man.

"You think Iguedo's going to eat it all without you, eh? An old stick like her?" said the old man. "Stop looking in the pot and come in here."

Iguedo looked up and belched. The old man laughed.

There was a small mound of wet clay sitting under the old man's bench. Two palm-oil lamps flickered and smoked. The old man clapped him on the back and pointed at the object on the bench.

"What do you think of that, boy?"

The old man appeared to take great delight in pointing out his variously real and imagined defects. Thus his chest was hollow as the inside of a calabash, his legs bandy as a baboon's, his feet slow as tortoises—and with considerably less cunning. His farts were less sonorous than a fruit-pigeon's, and his penis might be taken for a rat's tail. Such remarks were doled out with only the old man's cackle to sweeten them. Yesterday he had observed that the boy walked as though he had a snake stuck up his arse, then laughed uproariously at his own wit. It was all very amusing. He was long and thin, but no more so than any of the other boys. He walked normally and at a normal speed. His penis was larger than a rat's tail. But the dried-up old man would have few pleasures indeed if insulting himself were denied him, the boy reasoned, and so, faced with the indicated object, he decided neither to give the monkey-faced cackler a good clout about the ear (his first impulse) nor fill it with goat-dung (his second impulse), but to bear such insults with a lofty fortitude and treat them with the contempt they deserved. This latest was obscurer than usual but nevertheless of a piece with all the others. He took one look at the thing, restrained himself from dashing it to the ground or throwing it at the old man, but simply curled his lip into an unimpressed sneer and said, "So?"

It was a carefully modeled clay penis, at least eight inches long, standing upright on its base with a shaft, a head, and a fat vein winding up its side like a half-submerged python.

"So? What do you mean, 'So?' What do you think of it, boy?"

"Nothing."

Iguedo walked in, took one look at the thing, and began hooting with laughter.

"What's this, then, old man?" she gasped between guffaws. "Your eyes going the same way your balls did?" She picked up the penis and began waving it around. "You make this to keep me company, old man?"

The old man was cackling away as she jabbed it at him. "Careful," he protested. "It's not . . . it's not . . ." He couldn't get it out.

"It's not hard yet? That what you want to say?" It set her off again. "Not hard yet. Oh dear, it hasn't been hard since Eri's time."

They both collapsed, laughing too hard to stand now. The boy looked down at them. It was rather disgusting, two old people behaving in such a manner. As though they were drunk. They might as well roll around naked together right there in front of him. Something like this seemed to happen every night. He stood there wondering if it would not be better just to leave, but gradually the two of them calmed down, their laughter and ribaldry turning into snorts and snuffles, grunts and groans. The old man rolled his eyes.

"He doesn't approve of us, Iguedo. Look at him looking down at us, eh?"

"Who could approve of you, old man?" she retorted, getting up to bring in the food.

They ate sitting down on raffia mats, the old man shoveling handfuls of yam into his mouth and complaining about its bitterness as usual.

"You've got a thousand years of monkey-dung in your mouth, you lazy old pig," Iguedo barked back, "that's why it tastes bitter. Why not wash your mouth out?"

The old man gathered a ball of mashed yam in his mouth and spat it out the door.

"Anyway, you'll be cooking for yourself tomorrow, if you can manage that without poisoning yourself, so eat what you like and do your complaining on your own."

The old man stared at her. "Cooking? Me?"

"Going to Onitsha," Iguedo said shortly.

The boy ate steadily, looking at the two of them as little as possible. They were going to have a fight again, he thought, so he stared at his food, chewed, swallowed, and did not look up. Most of the men were at Onitsha. There was a meeting there that had something to do with the Onye-ocha—the White-men—whom everyone had been talking about and no one had seen. If he had joined the mmo-men, then he would be in Onitsha, too, discussing what to do with the White-men, although in the privacy of his own thoughts he still muddled them up with lepers because people discussed both only in whispers and the words for both sounded almost the same. Instead he was here, idling his life away over a charcoal fire, listening to an old man bellyaching.

"What do they want with a scrawny old woman in Onitsha?" the old man protested. "Why are you going over there?" A whine had entered his voice.

Iguedo spoke more curtly than before.

"Usse's back."

The boy's head came up in surprise.

"Ooh, look at his ears prick up!" hooted the old man. "You fancy a little bit of her, do you, boy? Hmm? You'd better watch out with that one else she bites your little balls off!" He nudged the boy, which made him scowl.

"Someone bit yours off years ago," Iguedo snapped at him. "They were rotting there anyway, you hadn't used them in so long."

"That must be why your breath is so bad"—the old man laughed—"since you were sucking them as soon as you could reach." He farted loudly.

Iguedo glared at him for a second, then reached over and calmly emptied the contents of her bowl into his lap. The boy looked from one to the other, certain that this time they would come to blows. The old man looked down at the steaming mess. Then he looked at Iguedo. Iguedo looked back at him. He scooped up a handful of sludge, inspected it, dropped it from one hand into the other, and deposited it in his mouth. He chewed and grinned.

"Stupid old man," said Iguedo.

All three ate on in silence.

"I thought Usse was dead," said the boy after a decent interval.

Iguedo shook her head. "Ijaw men found her down by the coast."

The old man broke in again then, prattling, taunting him, winking as though he had confided some great passion. He ignored it as best he could, still eating, remembering how Anayamati's rather fearsome daughter would stalk about the village in sullen silence or fight her brothers until all three were bloody-nosed. He and his friends had been scared of Usse. They were little boys, and she was the daughter of the Eze-Nri. Then, one day, she had walked out of the village and never come back, and their mothers had started scolding them with her example, not to go here and not to go there because "that's what Usse did and you know what happened to *her.* . . ."

But really no one knew anything at all. "Usse" was like the boy in the story who would not hoe his mother's oil-palm patch, ran off into the forest, grew a tail, and was changed into a monkey. What happened to him? the boy wondered. He never came back. And Usse had not left because she would not hoe, or draw water, or chop wood, or even make charcoal. She had disappeared because of the White-men. And now she was coming back again. For the same reason, perhaps, or perhaps for her father, who had been trapped in his dreaming for years. . . . Or something else entirely. No one ever knew what she thought about, the Eze-Ada.

Iguedo began scraping out the pot. The old man patted his stomach and let a series of soft belches escape into the room.

"Well, we'll be eating *adu* and drinking pit-water tomorrow," he grumbled to himself. Then he addressed the boy. "How tall is your charcoal pile now? Tall as you?"

He shook his head. The charcoal was heaped in a corner of the courtyard. The old man knew very well how big it was. If today's labors produced the usual two bundles, then, he estimated, the current pile would top his head. And that would mean the end of charcoal-burning, and that might mean he could go to Onitsha, a place he had never been before. He had never been anywhere except the village.

The old man got up and went to the back wall where a lot of sacks hung suspended over stacks of wooden trays that looked like badly made *chi*-shrines with their handles and little compartments. Suddenly he turned and tossed a large white rock across the room. The boy ducked and it thumped on the floor in front of him. The old man was trying to kill him now?

"Beeswax," he said, walking back with the empty sack. "You want to make this instead of charcoal?"

The boy glared up at him.

"Calm down, calm down. With old bare-bones here out of the way we can get down to work in peace. That wax, pick it up—go on—that's for the model. You'll get the trick of it. And this"—he picked up the clay phallus—"will be inside it, just like this"—he moved as though to open his wrap—"will be inside old Iguedo. Eh, Iguedo?" He started cackling, louder and louder, and Iguedo started shrieking, though whether in outrage or happy surprise was far from clear. "Eh, Iguedo? Heh heh heh heh . . ."

The boy dropped the wax and seized his chance to stalk out. They were crude and stupid. But tomorrow, he thought, tomorrow he would learn bronze-casting. Unless the old man was lying.

"Heh, heh, heh . . ."

"Go outside and use your hand."

"What? Beat on my belly when I have a drum? Heh, heh, heh . . ."

The sounds from inside the hut grew more raucous, then gradually subsided. A low chuckle might have been either of them. A few grunts followed. He would not listen to them. Usse was the one they all had wanted and whom none had dared to approach. He reached tentatively down to his groin, but at that moment a guttural wail started up in the hut, a breathy growl that sounded as though it began deep in the stomach, then rose up the body, and erupted finally through the nose as a high-pitched squeak: "Urgh . . . *reee!* Eurgh . . . *reee!* Eeyare . . . *reee!* Aer . . . *reee!*"

It was Iguedo's voice. He tried to shut it out, but then the old man started grunting along with her, perhaps even trying to drown her out himself, for his noise was at least as loud. He recalled Usse's face, but all that came to mind were her *ichi*-scars. She would look different now in any case, he reflected. He reached down to his groin again. He had gone soft.

Her hair had been braided in locks that shot out of her head in all directions, then fell about her face like the stems of a fleshy carnivorous plant, stiff and dyed red with cam-wood. Dark blue welled in her *ichi*-marks where *uli*-berries had been rubbed into the scars. She had chewed them, too, darkening the inside of her mouth until her teeth flashed white as ivory when she spoke. Her brothers stood behind her, impassive and unsmiling.

"Come. We go now."

Salvestro, Bernardo, and Diego variously concealed their shock at her trans-formation. She did not appear of this place, or anywhere, for that matter. They trooped down to a large pirogue manned with nervous-seeming paddlers who bobbed their heads at her approach. Soon they were cutting through the water, the paddles slicing down to pull them forward, then stilled and dripping in the hands of the men, then stabbing down again, a dozen blades and a dozen wounds a second in the unprotesting liquid that healed itself effortlessly behind them.

Usse watched the first sandbanks appearing, low humps of gritty mud ex-posed by the River's falling flood. The land farther upriver sent down its flotsam, which beached itself upon them: broken branches, rafts of river weed, drowned livestock that the crocodiles would tear up and lodge in grim stores beneath the surface. The voices in the River were all jumbled and unlimbed. The gaws of Gao a few weeks upstream threw their gods into the flood each season, and they were in there now, damaged, discarded, powerless down here. She paid them no atten-tion: Baana, Gangikoy, Moussa, Mama Kyria the leper. The White-men sat for-ward of her, placed there to keep them away from the paddlers, who feared their touch but were too scared to tell her directly. All around them was the slow churn of the River, a vast slack muscle whose mischievous twitches reminded her that it might—if it chose—sweep all before it in a single wave, splintering forests, smash-ing mountains, turning the land back to its original mud. Where would Eri be then? Nothing kept this from happening, unless Nri. The White-men were a warning. Namoke had understood that and had said nothing. It was she who had dived into the blinding water, let it wrench and pummel her as it pleased. She undrowned herself and came back; the River's voice drummed in her ears, a voice she alone had dared to hear. She was painted and armored, moving her own mass against the current.

Behind her, her brothers talked obliquely amongst themselves of the meeting at Onitsha, using odd turns of phrase and obscure proverbs so that the village men would not understand. They were excited and anxious; she heard that much in their voices. Last night she had hardly slept, so insistent were they to hear of her time with the White-men, all three of them wide-eyed, asking after their shrines (vast and built of stone, but filthy), their priests (richly robed and powerful as their own), their kings (of whom she knew nothing). Were they a warrior-people, or a smithing-people, or a farming-people? They were all of these, all mixed together with hardly an idea of any of them. They lived in huge cities, al-most as huge as that of the Bini, and their houses were built of stone, but—again—quite filthy with dogs wandering in and out of them and fouling the floors. They washed only rarely. She did not mention Fiametta's fondness for baths. Their food was very rich and stank. The winters were ten times colder than harmattan time, but they could not follow her description of snow. She caught them looking at one another in disbelief, and then she realized that they had not changed at all. She spat on the floor in front of them, her three foolish brothers. There had been no time to ask what was happening at Onitsha. The village women had braided her hair, their nervous fingers tugging and pulling out the strands, then rubbing in the thick cam-wood dye. She was clearheaded now, strangely weightless. She had not sought her father's dreaming spirit, and if it had sought her, it had not found her. She had told her brothers the stories they wanted to hear, and she had told them of the men sitting in front of her now. They had nodded in the manner of wise old men, all three together.

"Yes." she wagged her finger at them. "Just as I told you. Did you believe me then, eh? Did you listen to your sister, Usse?"

She made them feel her wrist where it had been broken, the little nodules of bone in there.

So she had shamed them, and now they were all together in the pirogue, pressed up against each other with the White-men, too: cadavers and their rags. She glanced forward at the soldier, recalling the episodes she had left untold. His had shocked her, merely how hot his skin had felt when she had lain with him and the violence in his face while he'd performed the act. His sweat, a White-man's sweat. She watched his back when it showed around that of the giant. The third was the one who had watched her in the night, the first night, when she had sought and found her father in the Ijaw village. She was sure of it, and now she thought of him as the Thief. Soldier, Giant, and Thief. It was like the begin-ning of a children's tale: "Tortoise and Leopard were out walking in the forest . . ." or "Hare and Dog met one day at the water-hole . . ." She felt drowsy even with the motions of the boat, the muddy-watery smell in the air, the little grunts of the paddlers, whose rhythm never changed. Soldier, Giant, and Thief went in a boat to a strange country with a fierce princess called Usse. They wanted to catch the ugliest beast in the world. . . .

Ezodu and Enyi were walking in the forest. . . . Eh, Usse? Remember that one, my fierce little princess?

She woke with a start. River-glare. The men paddling. Apia reached forward and touched her on the shoulder. She shrugged him off, reaching into herself for the source of the voice.

Father?

Ezodu and Enyi were once the best of friends. They used to meet at the water-hole, eh? Heh, heh, heh, heh . . .

And then he was gone. She sat up quickly. Gone as abruptly as he had come. Her father playing tricks on her? Strange. Not like him. Had his dreaming made him playful? Then she noticed the Thief.

He was sitting bolt upright, a puzzled expression on his face that she could see only because he turned his head to left and right; his baffled, startled, searching head. With its spying eyes and its thieving ears. Could he have heard, too? Was it possible that a White-man could hear such voices? The Thief was the one she would watch most closely. Now he was settling back again, readjusting his ragged hat and pulling it forward until it covered his eyes. Sleep, then, she thought, or feign sleep. Nri would reveal him. Nri would reveal all of them.

Their course began to take them in toward the right-hand bank, where a single dense thicket of greenery marched up to the water's edge and rose at their approach until solid cliffs of vegetation loomed over them, the canopies of the great cottonwoods appearing as teetering shelves and overhangs. Closer yet and the wall dissolved into boughs and branches, bristling bushes decked with tiny scarlet flowers and looping lilac convulvulus. Here and there were gaps through which she glimpsed the cool shade of the forest's interior. Then the bank fell away again, and a little later the Engenni River broke through the forest to mix its brighter brown waters with the great flood beneath them and the pirogue was pushed farther out by its current. They were almost at Ndoni and the afternoon was well advanced, but they would not stop. Later, the Orashi would come into view in a similar fashion, sweeping in from the right with its bunched meanders seeming to recoil from the greater mass of the River, and beyond that confluence would be Osomari. And they would not stop there, either. The paddles rose and fell, rose and fell. The backs of the men bent and strained, yet they did not slacken their pace. Atani was where the River widened and the far bank dwindled to a distant puny ridge, where years ago, in another life, a boy had fished in a pool of shadowed water and she had sat digging her toes into the cool earth, watching him. They stopped there.

At first the White-men were a sickness and no one knew what to do. They came across the sea in great white-winged boats, and their mouths were full of blood and lies that they spat on the people whom they met. Their weapons were light machetes, slightly curved, and fire-sticks that they held up to their eyes. There was a soft bang, some smoke, and then whomever it was pointed at fell down dead. Their chests were thick as tree-trunks, and their legs were thin as twigs. They were silent, often for days at a time, and then they would begin shouting while keeping their bodies very still. Most were exceedingly ugly and stank. They did not bury their excrement. They were quarrelsome, and powerful magicians. They had no women. Their speech sounded like coughing. The land frightened them, and they spent as little time on it as possible. When sufficiently angered, they would wave one arm and whole villages disappeared. The ground where they stood was churned up and the soil so hot that it smoked. They were impossible to insult. Nobody knew what made them so angry, or ugly, or white, or red, or whatever color they were, no one amongst the Ijaw, anyway, so it must be a kind of sickness, or madness, a bad spirit that squatted in their heads, shat down their throats, and could not be expelled. Much of this, Namoke knew, was nonsense.

The rains had come and gone four times since he and Usse had sat in the old Ijaw man's hut and listened to him ramble and grumble about the Nembe down the coast, the sharks in their fishing-ground, and then after a calabash of palm-wine the White-men. . . . Anayamati was not yet in his dreaming, but it was not far off, and he was cautious, their Eze-Nri. Too cautious for his angry, restless daughter. The titled men had sat down together, broken the kola-nut, passed the calabash amongst themselves, scratched their behinds, and talked of what these "White-men" portended. And talked more. And talked more again. She was too impatient, Anayamati's daughter, and too wild, eventually bursting in and mocking them for their circumspection, strutting before them, spitting out the suspicion that none of them would voice before storming out in frustration. Had she been right? Anayamati had shaken his head at the disgrace, then broken the heavy silence. "Sometimes I think she is Ezodu herself. . . ." He had rolled his eyes in a comical fashion, and they had chuckled along to spare his feelings, gone back to their *tombo* and their jawing. Had she heard them? They were cautious old men, proceeding as cautious old men are wont to do, making cautious old men's decisions. She would have left anyway, Namoke told himself.

Later they learned that the Bini across the River to the west had several of the White-men already at Ughoton, although they kept them out of the city, and there were more of them down on the coast, where they had built a stone fort. The famine took Nri-men farther afield than they had ever been before and wherever they traveled they listened now for tales of these White-men. To the east and south as far as Mpinde in the lands ruled by Nzinge Nvembe, to the west and north as far as the land of the Dyulas, they heard the same stories over and over. One day great boats hung with white sails appeared off the coast, then smaller boats rowed to shore, and within these were the White-men, who traded well or badly, and then they were gone again until the next year. Each year they would stay a little longer, and sometimes a few would stay behind (as ransom? punishment?), and sometimes build houses for themselves. According to Nvembe, they had reached Ngola of Mbundu after him, just as they had reached the Calabaris before him, and the Nembe-people and Ijaws before that, and so on west through the lands of the Bini and the Warri, then north up the coast as far as the desert, where nothing grew and where the tribes who lived there built nothing but each day woke and fled from the fierceness of the sun until nightfall, when they would drop to the ground and sleep again. The north was where the White-men came from. Usse had gone in pursuit of them. Now she was coming back. Nri-men had listened to these tales and observed the unease of their tellers. The White-men were weak and few in number, but there was something fearsome in them. Something hidden even from themselves. Perhaps the foolish Ijaws were right, Namoke thought now: the White-men were a sickness.

And no one knew what to do. Not the Uzama-men of Oba Esigie of the Bini, now picking their way like storks in their white robes along the bank of the River. Not the counselors of the Alafin of Oyo, nodding wisely to one another a little way ahead of them. Not the Aworo of the Esie, closeted with the petrified images of half a hundred of his ancestors in the elaborately constructed *ju-ju* shrine that his retainers had raised behind the ridge and that they would disassemble and carry away when the palaver ended. (When would they all lose patience? Namoke wondered. A week? a month?) Not Tsoede, the Eze-Nupe, who had arrived on a litter as tall as a cottonwood carried by sixty slaves and had yet to descend from it. Not the Achadu of the Attah of Idah, permanently veiled by a brimmed hat whose hangings reached to his ankles, nor the Oni of Ife, who had sent his eldest and youngest sons. Not the delegates of the Mani Kongo, one of whom claimed to have been carried to the house of the White-men's King but would say nothing of it except that it was cold, nor those of Ngola Ndongo, who allowed them to trade from the mouth of the Dande. Not the Odum of the Awome Calabaris, who was permanently drunk. Not the Aro-people, nor the Uratta-people, nor the Ekwerre-people, nor the Etche-people, nor the Asa-people, nor the Ndokinor-people, nor the Awka-people, some of whom were already drifting back to their villages a mere three or four days away. Not the Anam-people across the River at Asaba, nor the Ndi Mili Nnu, who had waited for the sand-island that appeared in midstream at this time of year to rise slowly above the surface before suddenly materializing upon it one morning, Ijaws and Nembe camped peacefully together—a miracle of sorts. And not the Ozo-people, whose village this was, or had been before the word sent out from Nri had gathered more than a thousand men from some three dozen peoples within a camp that spilled along the bank of the River almost to the bend where the broad flood was joined by the Anambra. None of them knew, any more than they knew where the rain came from or went or why the yams would grow one year and fail the next. So they had turned to Nri, and Nri-men had gathered them for the palaver that had turned Onitsha from a village into a transitory city.

The ground rose slightly at both ends of the encampment to form gently humped ridges of rain-smoothed, sun-hardened red mud that ran out of the forest and broke off abruptly at the River's edge. From his vantage point Namoke looked down on a sprawl of makeshift huts, shelters, and shrines roofed with raffia mats or thatched with the long grasses that grew in abundance after the recession of the floodwaters. The men moving among the homes of this flimsy city were counselors, headmen, priests, princes, title-holders, their numbers swollen further by retinues of servants and slaves. All of them, in one way or another, had wanted this palaver. Now, a mere twelve days after its commencement, they were growing impatient. Those who already had trade relations and treaties with the White-men had broken them off in deference to those who believed the strangers were no better than rats in a hen coop. None of them agreed on anything, except a desire that Nri should answer the questions arising out of their disquiet. . . . They wanted the Eze-Nri to appear in a thundercloud and tell them what to do, which was very foolish, for Nri-people had never told anyone what to do. Nri was the condition of their meeting, no more than that.

Namoke's sandaled feet scuffed the new shoots of grass forcing their way out of the baked laterite earth. Pirogues were hauled up on the shelving mud-bank below him, two scores of them, at least. On the bank behind them stood the *obiri*, its roof raised high off the ground on thick *abara*-wood poles, open at the sides, its floor covered with raffia mats. A few Ikwerre-men were already sitting there, waiting for that day's palaver to begin. His *ofo*-staff, a collection of sticks bound around a short branch, was balanced on a small, elaborately carved stool at the far end of the *obiri*. It seemed innocuous, sitting there on its stool—a little bundle of kindling wood or a ramshackle bird nest—yet if he were to advance through the encampment with it raised above his head, if he were to plant it in soft earth, then rip it up again by its root and scatter the soil as though it were seed, then they would take to their heels and flee in terror, every last one of them. They would flee it as they would their own deaths. . . . Tempting.

A kingfisher whirred over the boats in a blur of green. Namoke turned to look downriver. Two days had gone by since Gbujo, Apia, and Onugu had got word from the Ijaws that their sister was traveling through the mangrove-swamp and had set off downriver to meet her. But there was nothing on the River now except some fishing canoes and the pirogues setting out from the island bearing the chiefs of the Ndi Mili Nnu, crossing over for the palaver. He turned and walked down to the *obiri*, watched by the Ekwerre, and the strutting Bini, and the delegates from the Mani, and those from Ngola, and the Awka-men, and the Nupe-men, and the eldest and youngest sons of the Oni of Ife together with their (separate) retinues of servants. . . . They were waiting for him, and waiting for the palaver, and waiting for the words of the Eze-Nri.

The soft white glow of the harmattan sky intensified to a harsh glare. As the hours went by, men gathered slowly, speaking softly at first, but then more emphatically, clustering in little groups, which quickly became factions, knots of disagreement and argument, until Namoke overlooked a forest of waving arms and pointing fingers and the noise was an angry din of grievances, resentments, obscure insults, pleas falling on skeptical ears, rejected lines of reasoning, rivalry, pigheadedness. . . . How, he wondered, moving calmly among the squabblers, will agreement come of this? He looked toward the River again, his view partly obscured by three Nupe-men browbeating a hapless Calabari, who was protesting that three men from his village had been killed by White-men, or at least had set out one morning to trade fish and had never come back. The River was very broad here, the long paddle over to Asaba broken only by the sand-island where the Ndi Mili Nnu were camped. Usually a large market was held there. Namoke contemplated its annual appearance in the midst of the River's turbid waters, hard ground rising out of mud-choked floodwater, where the traders could meet in amity to buy and barter. Perhaps agreement would come like that? Then he remembered the phenomenon that the Idah-people called *yangbe:* a brief swelling of the River that was due in a week or two and raised the water level the height of a man's knee. The *yangbe* lasted only a few days, just long enough to wash the island away.

The afternoon wore on and the debates in the *obiri* grew sullen and ill-tempered. An Awka-man called Jiofo was arguing fiercely with a tall Bini who stood impassively in front of him, his long arms folded inside his robes.

"They want gold and slaves, Enyi-tusks, pepper. Very well. . . ." Jiofo was waving a finger in the air. "That is only today. What about tomorrow? What do they want then? More of them come each year—you say as much yourself—and the Bini give them land to live on, protect them even when they have stolen from the people on the coast. . . ."

"Oba Esigie has banished them for the time of the palaver, just as he promised. Besides, they are very weak and most of them die of fevers," the Bini interjected.

"Yes!" Jiofo shouted. "Even the air hates them, and nothing grows in the earth that they touch. The land they touch is stained! Dead!"

Namoke looked from one to the other, the Bini man shaking his head in exasperation, Jiofo still shouting at him. Similar confrontations were breaking out throughout the palaver, and the racket sounded to him like angry hornets. What good would come of this?

"Just wait," Jiofo finished up, turning now to Namoke. "When the Eze-Nri makes his judgment, you'll see!"

"When the Eze-Nri speaks," the Bini man said as though speaking to himself, "everything will be clear. Your head, too, perhaps." He stalked off contemptuously.

Deprived of an opponent, Jiofo redirected his complaint to Namoke.

"These Bini people think they are so much better than everyone else, eh? All they do is sit around and twiddle their lovely long fingers, and what good is that? Look at these." He held up his own hands, whose fingers were short and thick. "These hands have smithed a hundred blades since last harvest, and before that I lose count. Bini people, huh!" He made as if to spit on the ground, which was taboo in the *obiri,* and then resumed his complaint while Namoke nodded calmly and waited for a chance to slip away. But Jiofo droned on and on, his voice boring into Namoke's head like arrow-worm, and there were so many voices trapped in there already, twisting and gnawing away at him. When the Eze-Nri speaks . . .

Where was that voice? The voice they all awaited with the dwindling patience that fueled Jiofo's vehemence now, still hammering away, repeating himself, the man's bitterness growing out of the same anxiety that had brought them all here, and the anxiety out of ignorance. *The iron is broken. . . .* A smith should relish that particular turn of phrase, Namoke reflected grimly, though not the fact it concealed: *And no one knows what to do.* A little oil to help the dry words down. He realized with grateful surprise that the man had at last fallen silent. There was a group of Idah-men talking amongst themselves. As he watched, they fell silent, too. An eerie hush was gathering and swelling behind him, an unsoothing silence as of rivals catching sight of each other through the jabber of the marketplace and breaking off in midsentence to stare at one another, the corridor of their attention growing quiet and thickening until it silences the whole assembly. So mouths closed, or hung slackly open, and seconds later the whole *obiri* was silenced, everyone peering forward to the very spot where he had stood earlier. He sensed her presence then. "So," Namoke murmured as he turned with the rest of them, "she is back."

Usse stood at the very edge of the *obiri*. The sunlight fell on her there, and to the eyes fixed upon her, grown used to the shade, her hair was a headdress of bright scarlet and her face a mask of ebony slashed with blue. The line of the ridge cut her in two, the red sun-baked earth and the white sky set above it. She took a single step forward, and those nearest fell back as though she exerted a physical force upon them. Still no one spoke. Namoke began to move forward through the silenced crowd. Her eyes widened as he broke through the bodies that were pressed together in their efforts to keep a protective distance between themselves and her, a living *ju-ju* that confronted and dazzled them. He sensed the force of her through them, how she lay coiled inside the painted body, strong and untouchable like a python's muscle. Her breath filled their lungs, pumping them full so that if she were to hiss and suck, they would collapse, fall to the ground as sucked-out skins, Nri taking back their spirits. . . . She was more powerful now, Namoke realized. She stepped forward again, raised and extended an arm, the movement carving her own shape out of the stony air. Her fingers corked their straining ears, and she had only to pull them out for the words to flood their heads and come pouring out of their mouths. They were caged apart from one another and bound together only by the snaking arm that reached out of her and gripped them, each one held singly—she was pivoting, her limbs motionless, as though her spine were a stake stabbing deep into the earth, where Ala grasped and twirled it slowly between the strong white pads of her fingers. So she turned slowly between the River to her left and the forest to her right and had she spoken an instant sooner, Namoke reflected later, they would have formed the shape of her compulsion, falling beneath her shadow in exact congruence with it; her image casting a hard island of darkness into the bright soft soil of the palaver, where they were all sinking, the Eze-Ada's redoubt. . . . And yet.

They were lucky, Namoke thought later that night, when she sat before him as only Usse. She was the child of his brother and recognizable as his own flesh, a little girl who had chattered and made up stories of meeting Iguedo in the forest. He could recognize her now. In the *obiri* she had been a stranger, too changed for him to see her beneath the apparition who had addressed the assembled men. They were lucky not to have been torn limb from limb. Or perhaps the Alusi had reached down from the sky and firmed the crumbling walls that held the men there before the specter of the Eze-Ada, just long enough for her brothers to arrive and drag away the three intruders. For an instant he had thought that the one she called "the Soldier" would draw the blade that he wore in a long metal pouch at his side. His hand had wavered there, but she had seen and hissed at him in his own language. Gbujo had gripped the man by the shoulder. He had suffered himself to be turned about in that manner, and the other two, the Giant and the one she called "the Thief," had fled.

"You were to keep them with the pirogue," she scolded her brothers contemptuously now. "Fools, all three of you. Nothing has changed." Her glare challenged them to deny it. The three of them scowled and said nothing.

It had happened very quickly. The ragged clothes had confounded the men in the *obiri,* and for a moment they had simply not understood what their eyes told them was before them. Then they had looked up to their faces and comprehension came. Namoke recalled the sound in the men's throats, a gasp that came from their stomachs. Three White-men had walked into the *obiri,* and the Soldier had stepped between the Eze-Ada and her audience and begun speaking in his own tongue, sounding as though his mouth were full of earth. He had seemed to be addressing . . . himself. Namoke.

The other two had hung back, sensing the hostility that was gathering in the faces that stared at their own, recognition rippling back through the press of bodies, a horrible amazement. Gbujo and his brothers appeared, panting, flustered, and it was that which seemed to trigger the men. They had moved forward, and Usse had turned. Then it was his own turn to be amazed, outraged, shocked out of a trance. She had snatched up his *ofo*-staff and brandished it like a weapon while her brothers pulled the intruders back. How long before the crest of the men's anger toppled and broke, raining down fists on their swaddled bodies and their baffled red faces? And how long before they might have been pulled to safety? A heartbeat? Two? He had lost his head, Namoke admitted to himself. He had acted without thinking.

Now an oil-lamp sputtered. It was dark outside, gloomy in the hut. The three brothers avoided their sister's eye.

"So?" Gbujo challenged her sullenly.

"None of them know anything, except this 'Pope.' Why else does he send these White-men? What does he tell them to bring him, eh? Tortoise? Baboon?"

"They remember nothing because there is nothing to remember."

"So Nri-men want to forget, too. There are ashes in the fire outside. Rub them on your face and you will look like White-men as well as forget like them.

Such forgetful brothers I have. Forget to keep White-men in the boat, forget their sister, forget Ezodu. And now look, White-men in the *obiri,* sister come home, and Ezodu. . . ."

"Ezodu is a story that mothers tell their children. . . ." Gbujo's voice was dismissive.

"Nri-women remember. Nri-men run around like chickens with their heads cut off. They want to feel important, round up all the other chickens, and have a big palaver together. Very nice, all squawking through the neck and strutting about together. You know what White-men are. Nri-people have known what White-men are ever since Eri took a blade from an Awka-man. Nri-people have been waiting for the White-men since Enyi and Ezodu. . . ."

"Enough, Usse! These are old stories, taboo stories. . . ."

"Taboo stories? Children sing them! And don't you plan to tell them to the Bini-people? The Ife-people? And what about the Ijaws? They like stories, too. Why this big palaver when Nri-people already know what these White-men are? This is Nri business; it began with Nri. Now it comes back to Nri. You want to tell all of them about that? Think how big and important you could look. 'O Forest-peoples! Nri-men once broke their own taboo. O Saltwater-peoples! It was long, long ago, in Eri's time. O River-peoples! Nri-people stained the earth. . . .' It makes a good speech, eh, my brothers? Everyone listening with their ears pricked up." She glared at the four of them.

"You are so certain, Usse?" Namoke spoke more gently than her brothers. "You are so sure this is why the White-men have come? So sure this is truly what they are?"

"Why they have come?" she echoed him. "They do not know themselves. What they are? Yes, I am sure. I have lived amongst them, as you have not. Why should I care if believing it makes your head ache?" She turned to her brothers. "Believe our father. He sees them even now in his dreaming. Soon he will know them, too. And when he knows them, you will know them, too. Or do my three wise brothers see further than their father, more clearly than the Eze-Nri himself?"

She fell silent then. Namoke watched her pull her legs from under her and stretch them out on the mat. Whose curiosity, he wondered, would compel him to ask her to explain this? Her feigned indifference was laid over a true one, he thought, so certain she was, so certain of what she knew or believed she knew. The palaver seemed very far away and himself clear of its noise now: insects buzzing on the far side of a stream she had led them across. She does not need to understand herself, he thought. It would only sap her strength.

"It is nonsense," Gbujo said calmly. "Our father. . . . You know this, Usse. The iron is broken. It was broken before you left. Our father was already . . ." His words petered out.

"Dead," she said bluntly.

Namoke heard Apia suck in his breath sharply. His own shock surprised him,

at the blow dealt by the word itself—to spit such a word on the face of the
Eze-Nri.

"What you say is nonsense," Gbujo repeated coldly. "The iron is broken, as I
said, and as my sister must have said, for I do not hear my sister when her mouth
is clogged with dung. It is nonsense because our father never saw the White-men,
and never will, and if you brought those three at his bidding, as you claim, then
that proves only that you are his dutiful daughter. . . ." He stopped again. "You
did well, our sister, to bring them this far. We your brothers salute you, you, the
Eze-Ada. To bring them so far only to see them perish is a hard blow. To carry so
heavy a load only to spill it at the door—"

And there he was forced to break off, for his sister's drawing up of her knees,
the clasping of her arms about them, her rocking back and forth, and the escape
from her lips of little mews and sighs, all these signs broke out of her then not as
sobs of her bitter disappointment—they had been waiting for that—but as harsh
guffaws of mirth. She was laughing at him. She was laughing at all of them:
Gbujo, Apia, Onugu, even himself. Namoke frowned in puzzlement, recalling
how he had lunged for her, fearing the power in the *ofo*-staff she brandished
before the seething crowd, thinking it would burn her hands to stumps, impale
her, seed itself within her, and its branches would burst out of her flesh, rip her
open. . . . He had reached forward, and the great mass of men had reached with
him, the wall she held them behind crumbling and their bodies pouring forward. . . . They had chased the three men into the forest, where they would die.
White-men did not know how to live in the forest. All she had done was for
nothing. And now she was laughing at them.

"Poor Gbujo!" she burst out. "You think I do not know that you led them to
the *obiri*? Poor Apia! You think I did not hear you when you shouted for the men
to chase them? And you, Onugu, my baby brother, you think I did not see you
hand them clubs over there behind the coco-palms? You think I did not guess the
clubs would be there? Oh, my foolish, foolish brothers: you do not listen, so how
can you understand? Imagine that what I say is true—let your heads ache just a
little now—imagine that they are just what I tell you. Do you think that the Alusi
will let you spill their blood? Do you think they will let Nri-men stain the earth
again?"

The three of them would not look at her. Yes, Namoke thought, she is indifferent. She knows they do not matter. Try as they might, her own brothers would
play no part in this. She leaned forward, talking into their faces, choosing to take
their shock for incomprehension or stupidity.

"Two hundred men chase three sweating White-men into the forest. And the
White-men escape. Tell me now, my clever brothers, how does that happen? Do
they run like leopards? Fly like birds? Disappear? Three ignorant White-men,
who can hardly walk without falling over, who crash about like buffalo. . . ."

She turned between them, barking the question at each of them in turn.

"Tell me how?"

Her brothers were silent.

"Iguedo has them," she said flatly. "It does not matter what you believe. They live. And soon they will be in Nri."

Every nastiness has its pathology. Minor streams and tributary rivers spill off distant uplands and watersheds, then branch through the forest watercourses carrying and depositing meager alluvial washes of precious black mud along their lushly vegetal banks, a rank double ribbon of rushes and reed-beds where herons and red-legged ducks blunder about in search of fish, a green and stringy palisade, a fertile fringe rooted in fine-grained friable soil. And thus a deception, for three strides back the dirt turns thin and sandy, the forest starts, and outlying knobbly cables of vast shallow root-systems undulate, rise, and plunge back into the leached and gravelly ground in a long-distance quest for phosphates on behalf of massively trunked sasswoods and greenhearts, mahoganies and ironwoods, gumcopals and *obechi*-trees, the forest giants and their enormous sucking appetites that drain the already poor soil for miles around and feed nothing more useful than an overweening urge to be taller than their neighbors.

The roving roots of these hydra-footed monsters (Salvestro is about to trip over one) pump tree-food a hundred feet or more into the sky, where a glossy canopy of leaves soaks up supplementary sunlight like a fat green sponge and produces brightly colored flowers, most of which are small and exquisitely engineered. Birds enjoy these very much. Everything else is underneath, groping around in the gloom for whatever gleams and glints of growth-promoting sunshine drip down from the light-hogging canopy high above, the strongest contenders here being fifty-foot balsams, smooth-grained satinwoods, locust-trees with feathery leaves and long pendant seed-pods, densely packed stands of false date palms, fibrous *aji*-trees, crabwoods, all of which sprout sun-hungry leaves of their own, sopping up the remaining little rays and fugitive shafts until the forest floor is lit only by the vaguest dapplings and glows, the leavings and leakage of those on high. Ferns grow here and sometimes cotton-plants. Lianas lassoo their way up, entangle themselves, and rappel down again. Lichens and mosses actually thrive, and the trees themselves drop seeds whose saplings barely have time to form thickets of impenetrable scrub before their parents starve them to death. The soil down here is overcrowded and sucked out by the competing hungers of these monsters, while the sun far above plays expertly on their edaphic insecurities to lure them farther and farther from their washed-out foundation, reaching higher and higher in a desperate competition to choke off everything around, until finally the roots can no longer supply the crown, the leaves turn papery, then brown, then fall off and drift slowly down to the forest floor, where mulching promptly begins at the foot of one hundred feet of perfectly useless already rotting tree-trunk, which sooner or later—the inevitable finale—crashes through its victorious neighbors, a thrashing smashing catastrophic scaffold of dead trunk, branchwork, twigs, and epiphytic trailers: a gigantic tree-corpse. Termite food.

But sometimes—or rarely, or hardly ever—the canopy breaks. A sunlit haven opens. Speargrass springs up and lives in happy amity with little shrubs and flowering bushes, bright red rhododendrons, for instance, the odd wild yam. Things flower and run to seed, and a respectable percentage of these seeds produce puppyish versions of whatever flowered in the first place, not enough to choke the neighbors, but sufficient for a modest self-perpetuation. The nutrient problem is solved by unspoken subsoil negotiations resulting in a just apportionment satisfactory to all parties. Unhurried bees buzz and bobble about, pollinating without fear or favor within this little paradise—albeit walled in by the scowling cliffs of the surrounding, pressing forest—this happy ecotopia where cowbirds hop about regardless of the absence of cows, where lovely flowers might be gathered by the armful but never are, where the parasitic liana fails to worm its way in and so never strangles or corrupts anything, where all is pristine and peaceable and nice.

Then twenty-five tons of rotting tree-trunk wielding a fifty-foot scourge fashioned from its own dead branches and six different species of creeper crashes down from nowhere and flattens everything in sight, vicious little saplings shoot up to tent the area in a light-absorbent leafy mattress, killing everything underneath, and the nasty norms of the forest reassert themselves; these, from the insufficient soil to the inadequate sun, from taproot to topmost crown, being slow starvation, infanticide, arboreal cruelty, and greed. Thus the vertical.

Sideways, though, sideways. . . . Giant black trunks rise out of the mottled humps of the lower tree-crowns and support the hollow domes of those above. Fruit-pigeons and guinea fowl drill through the groundless and skyless slice of airspace suspended between these sub- and supercanopies. "Above" is somewhat lighter than "below," but both are composed of insubstantial greenery, as though one were the identical reflection of the other, mere images stretching the length and breadth of the forest. Dimensional confusion reigns in this interstitial zone (what exactly *is* height?), where squirrels, lizards, the smaller monkeys, and chimpanzees climb and descend without making any obvious distinction among these radically different maneuvers and, far from providing the missing coordinates, the orgulous trees carry on obliviously with their decades-long games of homicidal leapfrog. Small wonder that the fruit-bats sleep upside-down: "up" and "down" themselves are all adrift and a-quiver, swapping position, pulling the vertical axis out of true and into serpentine loops, kinky twists, lemniscate turns and returns. . . . The vertex is no good up here, and it's not much better down there, either.

Which is where Salvestro is, under the underneath, at ground level, or even level with the ground, having just tripped over one of those troublesome gnarly hard-to-spot tree-roots. Alerted by the thud, a chaffinch peers down and sees what appears to be a very large and unconvincing brown-and-white crab lying motionless in the dirt. A small hamsterlike creature with tufty ears extends a twitching nose out of its burrow and notices a single grimy toe visible through the hole in the sole of Salvestro's shoe. Salvestro has winded himself, and somehow managed to get soil in his mouth, which tastes acidic and extremely gritty. Lacking for the moment the breath to spit it out, he swallows it. The hamsterlike creature retreats back into its burrow. The chaffinch realizes its mistake and loses interest. A lost soldier-ant carrying a piece of twig in its mandibles encounters a large and particularly confusing obstacle. Salvestro coughs. Earthquake? wonders the ant. It jettisons the twig. Starting with the toes, Salvestro begins to move his various limbs, checking each in turn for possible cuts and fractures, taking his time over this primarily because he is still winded and could not stand up if he tried, also because the last sounds of pursuit faded into silence several hours ago, and last because ever since that moment he has been hopelessly lost in the middle of a forest thousands of miles from home (whatever that is), and having no idea where he is at present, he sees no urgent reason to go somewhere else, where he will similarly not know where he is. Being found appears to entail being clubbed to death by a small army of shouting black men led by Usse's brothers. A lynch mob. He seems to attract them.

So he lies there for a while, facedown in the dirt, gulping air, wiggling his feet, while the similarly lost ant, deciding that something this much larger than itself might reasonably be assumed to move correspondingly quicker, clambers up the arm of his shirt, enters by a small rip in the fabric, and gets tangled up amongst the wiry hairs sprouting in the dimple of Salvestro's armpit, where it will bite him exactly eight minutes from now. Time to be getting on, think Salvestro and the ant simultaneously, even though one patch of forest is much like another. . . .

He gets up and gazes into the gloom. Amorphous thinnings and halfhearted lightenings of the forest's subaqueous shade float and drift like wobbly clouds, hovering over the ground and nosing about in random fashion, sometimes bumping into one another and merging, sometimes swelling or contracting out of existence. There are no shadows—the light is too vague—only a murky chiaroscuro that furs the forest and blurs its denizens, breaking outlines and bleeding hues so that they muddy themselves in one another, producing a homogenizing surfeit of hessians and khakis. Seen in the sublight of the forest floor, one patch of forest really is much like another. Viewed sideways, most of what's in it is, too. Along the lateral axis of homologue and homage, the massive flanged buttresses of the cottonwood trees might as well be twenty-foot termite nests, or the rotting stumps of dead cedars, or creeper-strangled satinwoods, while the creepers and lianas themselves resemble—rather obviously—snakes both large and small, the little yellow ones also disguising themselves as young palm fronds and the young palm fronds as bamboo and the bamboo as various strains of elephant grass (which do not, however, look like elephants, although there is a certain beetle—rather tangy when roasted—commonly found in the wormy logs whose wood it relishes and which it digs out using the curved and pointed horn on the end of its nose). Seeping sap trickling down the trunks of the copaiba-trees ferments and smells like forest orchids, or would if the orchids did not smell of carrion. Leopards at rest look like (and are as rare as) cloudy dapplings of sunlight falling on damp black earth. Leopards in motion look like a swarm of dying drone-wasps plummeting down from their podlike nests, the latter reminiscent of the highly prized but toxic *tololo*-tuber. Flightless insects imitate sticks, leaves, poisonous fruit, and inedible lichens. The forest spreads sideways by processes of imitation and analogy. Parrots are its heralds and the primeval chameleon is its king: there he goes, mottling and marbling in accordance with the terrain, lifting one articulated leg at a time and putting it down again with exaggerated care, as though the land were still soft, as though one false step would see him sink burbling into the mud that covered everything in the days before Eri hardened it and made it the land whose nature determines everything here, being its pathology and washed-out grammar. . . . Everything here eventually breaks off at the roots, topples, falls, returns to the waiting soil from which it rose. And in the meantime everything looks, or tastes, or smells, or sounds like something else.

"Ow!"

Except Salvestro. Hat lost, toes stubbed, legs scratched, dirt in his mouth, hole in his shoe, ragged, sweaty, hungry Salvestro as yet looks like nothing else in the forest. There was a time—a long time ago and a long way away—when he would have been at home here. The trees and bushes, thickets of cedar-scrub and thorn-breaks, evoke another forest, damper and colder but still recognizable in this monstrous and exaggerated version. Can he sink back into that? Can this forest in some sense be that one? He's dirty and disheveled, his hair wild and clotted with burrs. If he could just forget how to speak again, blend and merge with the little rustles and crashings, the *whoosh*es and *whirr*s, the creaks and croaks and coughs, lose himself in this forest as though it were that one . . . Can he go back to what he was then? What exactly was he running from a few hours ago, when all three of them charged into the forest, split up to confuse their pursuers, and crashed forward with not a whither or whence between them? Salvestro, fleeing the scene of the crime yet again with the righteous mob in full cry after the thief who stole himself away from under their very noses. He cannot go back, can he?

No, it's either too far or not far enough. If he's going back anywhere, it's not to the forest. Not that one and not this one, either. He owes himself elsewhere and to different creditors. . . .

Anyway, the ant bites Salvestro, and Salvestro squishes the ant. Then, the afternoon waning, the cool interior of the forest growing even shadier, he wanders among the giant trunks or clambers over their finlike buttresses, kicks his way through banks of ferns and drifts of bright yellow cotton-plants, clambers up and down little ravines through which tiny creeks *splosh* and gurgle, looks up to see the branchwork high above festooned with lilac convulvulus and webbed with woody lianas, follows the little bare-earth paths that lead in all directions to junctions from which more little paths set out, not really going anywhere as far as he is aware, just moving through the forest, sniffing and misidentifying the fleeting odors of earth, tree mold, pig dung, fungal spoors, wild garlic, sour-sweet ground peppers, the ground rising in a long shallow slope that he seems to have been climbing for eternity, then leveling off, and some new scent comes curling through the trees, sharpish, familiar, filtering through the forest to fill his twitching curious nostrils with. . . . Wood-smoke.

The scent trail twists and turns, leading Salvestro by the nose around a copse of flowering bushes twice the height of himself. He creeps and advances, carries on sniffing. Then he stops.

Ten thousand dangling men hang in the branches of the *ofo*-tree. Their arms and legs and heads and trunks are sticks joined together by nodes and swollen boles approximating elbows, knees, ankles, knobbly shoulders, groins, the body's junctions and twiggy terminals. Corpses of the fallen lie in heaps around the moderate trunk. Small black flowers grow sparsely amongst the branchlets. *Ofo*-trees bleed when cut, but no one cuts them, or touches them at all, or even approaches the groves where they grow.

But Salvestro does not notice the *ofo*-trees. A long plump lizard is roasting over a cooking fire attended by an ancient woman, a lively bag of skin and bones who hops about prodding and clucking, alternating between the lizard over the fire and, sitting on the ground, two men who seem to be doing nothing at all except staring blankly into the flames. It is almost completely dark now, but the fire casts an adequate light over the two men's faces. He walks forward, toward the old woman, the lizard, and his motionless companions. The lizard smells surprisingly good. Red-faced from the fire, Bernardo and Diego both look rather glum. No doubt his reappearance will cheer them up, thinks Salvestro.

Afterward he came to believe that it began with the wax. Of course it really began much earlier than that, but for him it began with a lump of off-white wax. The old man chipped at it until he had two pieces the size of his fists. They looked yellow in the lamplight, then red when he carried them nearer the firelight, and in the melting-bowl they took on the color of the earthenware, which was black as soot. He peered in from above and saw his own face staring back at him.

"Such a pretty boy," cawed the old man. "We need a bucket of water now. Go admire yourself in that."

The boy waited for the usual accompanying cackle, but this time it did not come. The old man had grown quieter and less annoying in the past few days, though still annoying enough. His mockery had become halfhearted, almost sullen. Without Iguedo he had no one to play to; perhaps that was the reason. Or perhaps it was because they would soon begin casting, for unlike wood, or clay, or wax, bronze lasted forever, so casting was a serious matter. The Eze-Nri could find one another when they finished their dreaming, first to last, Eri to their own Anayamati. Their *mmuo* never died, but their bodies did. They had to shed them to end their dreaming, so the bronze-casters made an image for Nri-people to remember them by. The Eze-Nri carried his ancestors' memories in his head and their bodies in a piece of bronze so they would not be lost in that way, either. Bodies were important, too.

He walked beneath the canopy of the trees, swinging the bucket by its handle. The leaves on the bushes looked black instead of purple. It was almost dark. He gave the termite mound a good clout. Anayamati's sprawling compound was several hundred paces downstream from here, though no one had entered it in three years or more and the council of the Nzemabua met in Namoke's place. He had always thought that the Eze-Nri lived at the very back of the village. He was in there now, waiting for Usse to come. Drawing the water, he looked back through Iguedo's coco-palms. Beyond the termite mound the bushes and trees appeared as an impenetrable thicket, although the passage through them was quite easy. Perhaps that was why he had never known of the old man's compound before his strange apprenticeship had begun, although the deceptive thicket did not explain how he invariably arrived at the ramshackle door no matter what path he took. Bronze-casters were secretive and odd. It was well-known.

"Fenenu."

He looked up, startled as much by the use of his name as by the sudden appearance of Iguedo. She was standing by the edge of the coco-palms.

"For the wax?" she asked as he drew nearer. The heavy bucket pulled him sideways with each step. He nodded. They began to walk in silence between the enormous trunks of the cottonwoods.

After a while, his curiosity overcoming him, the boy asked, "Have you returned from Onitsha, then?"

Iguedo looked at him quizzically before grunting that she had, but she chose to say no more.

The boy held his tongue for a minute or so. He was hungry for news of the palaver there, of the Nri-men and the other peoples or anyone else who might have arrived.

"So what are they saying about the White-men?" he inquired lightly. The query sounded ridiculous for some reason. His voice, perhaps. Iguedo began to chuckle softly, and the boy felt the familiar rush of annoyance mixed with bafflement. It was tiresome to be mocked whenever he opened his mouth. The village boys would form little gangs and chant insults at one of their number, himself sometimes, or sometimes he was one of the gang. Singly, however, no one acted in this way. Alone, he had thought vaguely, the old woman would behave differently. He flushed and looked away, stomping through the bushes with the bucket slopping water onto the ground. Then the old woman confounded him.

"Do you want to see one, Fenenu?"

He turned sharply, at first suspecting that a joke was being played on him. Iguedo put her hand on his shoulder, and both of them came to a halt. She was not laughing, or not at himself. He nodded warily.

"Not yet," she said, "but soon." Then, seeing the mistrust on his face, she added, "There are three of them. Three men that Usse brought."

"Where are they?" he asked. They were whispering for some reason.

"Here," she said. "Here in Nri."

The old man looked up from the melting-bowl as he carried in the bucket. His mouth was already open to deliver the customary insult when Iguedo appeared in the doorway.

"So you're back," he said sourly. "Took your time, didn't you?" It was unclear whether he was addressing one, the other, or both of them. He waved his hand as though wafting away flies, clearly torn between complaining further and getting down to work. The bowl hung over the fire was now full almost to the brim with melted wax. His other hand held the obscene stump of clay, with which he thumped the floor beside.

"Get these mats out of the way and set the bucket down here," the old man commanded. "Hurry up, boy, if you want us to get any sleep tonight."

He did as he was told, glad of the chance to rest his arm. If he rubbed the muscle, the old man would make a comment about his puny shoulders, so he folded his arms stoically and waited to see what would happen next. Iguedo was still standing in the doorway. He thought he heard her speak, but when he looked up all he saw was a glance passing between them, a question and its answer, but wordless and in the blink of an eye. He turned and looked askance at the old man. The old man grinned and raised the clay stump, waggling it in front of his nose.

"To work."

His role in "the work," it soon transpired, centered not about the melting-bowl, or about the wax in it, or the clay stump, or even the fire. His role was centered about the bucket.

The old man took the stump and, holding its base with his fingertips, dipped its length very quickly into the melting-bowl, as though he were stabbing the molten wax; then, keeping its "head" pointing downward, he brought it straight up, swung his arm sideways, and plunged it into the bucket. When he pulled it out again the clay was coated with a thin sheath of wax. The old man held the shaft still while drops of water slid down its sides, shook the last few back into the bucket with a single motion of his wrist, then dipped the stump back into the wax to begin the procedure again. The wax formed a sheen over the dark red clay, then a milky coating as the wax thickened. The old man dipped, swung, plunged, raised, and shook the object, while with his other hand he fed the fire, burying the new wood under piles of embers to keep the flames low under the melting-bowl.

The boy's job was to watch for droplets of wax that would drip off the shaft before the old man could plunge it into the bucket. When these hit the water they formed smooth white beads and quickly sank to the bottom. He was supposed to fish them out and throw them back into the bowl without interfering with the movements of the old man or interrupting his rhythm. Iguedo was somewhere outside, he assumed, for she had shrugged at the old man's cantankerous greeting and when the boy looked up again she was gone.

The old man rocked back and forth, his arm moving forward and back, and the two of them fell into a rhythm that hardly wavered and that lulled the boy. The hut was warm. The fire glowed and faded between red and black in accordance with the movement of the air over the embers. They worked together in a silence disturbed only by the faint hisses and crackles of the fire, so the boy thought, until he gradually became aware of a murmuring or mumbling, at once very faint and very close. The old man's lips were moving, but whatever he was saying was quite inaudible or too jumbled for his ears to disentangle and make sense of. It distracted him. He looked over at his work-partner and slid a hand into the bucket for the hundredth time. As he retrieved the little bead of fallen wax his wrist knocked against the old man's arm. The old man stopped and looked him in the eye. He was expecting a comment on his clumsiness or inattention.

"Layers," said the old man. "Smooth even layers."

The clay stump was the core, and the clay in which they would later encase the wax was the mold. The wax itself was the image of the casting, and the casting was of the Eze-Nri, who was not one man but many, each one encasing the last all the way back to Eri.

"Difficult to get them all in," he grumbled. "Gets more difficult every time."

When the layers had reached the thickness of a man's arm, the old man had dipped the wax into the water for the last time and bade the boy fetch the basket that held his modeling tools, which were little sharpened sticks and short-bladed knives as far as he could see. It was very late and his head ached with fatigue, though the old man had done almost all the work and seemed as lively as ever.

"Eri sat on an anthill," said the old man, "and all around him the land was soft as mud. Useless. Couldn't grow a thing in it. . . . Are you listening, cloth-ears?"

"Yes," he mumbled. "Eri sat on an anthill."

Everybody knew this story. He was supposed to be learning bronze-casting, not listening to tales his mother had told him when he barely reached her knee. The old man's hands were moving busily around the wax, turning it this way and that while he hacked and pared at great speed, barely glancing at what he was doing.

"So the Eze-Nri sits down, because of Eri and his anthill. Look"—a fat plug of wax flew off—"this will be his lap. Knees here. What happened next?"

"He took a blade from an Awka smith. He used the blade to harden the land."

"How?"

He recited by rote, "Eri cut rivers to drain the land, one to the east and one to the west, and where they met he cut a third to the south, which is the greatest River of them all."

"So he did, so he did. Hard work, eh, boy? Harder than carrying a bucket of water. Harder than burning charcoal." He turned to the door and bellowed, "Harder than boiling yam, too!" No answer came back. The old man shrugged. "Anyway, he cut the rivers. So?"

The boy thought. "We give him a blade."

"Where?"

"In his hand."

"Which one?"

"Right."

"*Otonsi*-staff goes there. Without *otonsi* the yams won't grow."

"Left, then."

"Enyi-tusk goes there. That story comes later."

"When?" He felt his curiosity struggle up through the numbing fatigue, but the old man shook his head impatiently.

"Later. And you're thinking like a wood-carver." He spat in the fire to indicate his contempt. "Eri's already cut the rivers. He doesn't need a blade, and the Eze-Nri carries no weapon, and anyway, casting something like that is too difficult. It always looks like a stick. Forget the blade. We give him big shoulders instead, strong spine down the back. All that hard work. . . ." The old man chuckled. "Now, what about his ears?"

So it went on. The old man picked, scratched, gouged, and whittled, swapping the wax from hand to hand, working usually with two tools gripped between his fingers and the rest in his lap, keeping up a constant commentary on the significance of this or that feature and prodding the boy to respond. A seated figure emerged gradually from within the smooth wax. To the *otonsi*-staff and Enyi-tusk the old man added a bundle of *ofo*-twigs, which were placed between the figure's feet. A breastplate in the shape of a leopard's head grew out of the chest, and a headdress of coiled and braided cord strung with beads sprouted from the top of the head. The old man added wristbands and necklaces, or rather scratched away at the wax until they suddenly appeared as though he had dug them out of the ground.

"Eri is always there," he murmured. "Scratch the land, you find Eri underneath."

But the boy's head lolled. His eyelids drooped. The night, and the work that filled it, seemed endless. He no longer answered the old man but only nodded whenever prompted. He did not understand how he could still be awake.

Eventually the old man took a tool he had not used before, a knife whose blade was worn so thin that it more closely resembled a needle. Holding the figure in his lap, he began cutting long thin lines, each one beginning at the ear, running over the cheekbone, and stopping only at the edge of the mouth. He turned his wrist to widen the lines into grooves. The boy watched as the *ichi*-marks multiplied to cover both sides of the figure's face.

"Eri had two sons," the old man said. He might have been addressing the face that stared blindly up at him. "You remember their names, boy? Hmm?"

He blinked and struggled to clear his head. Two sons? Eri had *one* son. These were stories that everybody knew. One son. He was sure.

"Ifikuanim," he answered. "He was the second Eze-Nri."

The old man was nodding, gazing down at the image he had created. "The other had no name. Has a name now. But back then . . ."

He lifted the knife clear of the wax and placed it carefully back in the basket, then he held up the figure to the light. As he turned it slowly in his hands, the glow from the dying fire and the oil-lamps played over its scarified surface. The boy's eyes ached, yet privately he marveled at the cleverness of the design. The tusk curving up the line of the chest was hardly more than a ridge and the *otonsi*-staff mostly obscured by the arm that held it. The detail in the headdress was more suggestion than reality, and the leopard's-head breastplate seemed to leap forward even though it was little more than a bulge with three holes in it. He counted fingers and toes. The *ofo*-twigs were a lump of wax with some grooves in it and yet uncannily realistic. It was the shadow that revealed these details, for when the old man moved it nearer the light, the figure appeared almost feature-less. He *tutted* and frowned as he peered at it.

"Something wrong here," the old man said. "You see that, boy? You see what's wrong?" When he eventually shook his head, the old man regained his usual ill temper and began mocking him as before. "Can't see it? It's staring you in the face! What does the Eze-Nri look like? What do all Nri-people look like? Answer's in front of your spotty little nose. . . ."

And so on and so forth. He was too tired to care. His eyes closed, and he knew that if he did not open them, the old man's voice would drift away and the yammering, whining, goading mockery would fall silent. He wanted only to sleep now.

"What color is wax? Eh?" insisted the voice. A new tone, anger. At what? He did not care. Then the answer to his own question, spat out and succeeded by the silence of sleep:

"No color at all! Wax is the color of *nothing*. . . ."

They walked in single file, for the paths they followed were narrow channels cut through waist-high ferns; and they walked in silence, for each time any one of them uttered a word the old woman would stop and clench a fist in front of her mouth as though to catch the sound and strangle it. Diego never spoke in any case, but Bernardo seemed unable to comprehend this simple interdiction. Every few minutes he would turn to Salvestro, who was walking behind him, and the first syllable of some pent-up query would burst from his lips and be instantly quelled by the old woman's increasingly vigorous gesture, so their conversation was effectively limited to "Wh . . ."

There was little to say in any case, and what there was had been said the previous night:

"She's probably just keeping us here till the rest of them arrive."

"Or fattening us up."

"Or poisoning us."

"We could just leave."

"She'd follow us."

"We'd have to kill her."

"Or tie her up."

"With what?"

"And where would we go?"

Silence. The flames of the fire, an eye-aching orange in the encircling darkness.

"So we'd better stay here?"

"At least till morning."

"This meat isn't bad."

"What's left?"

"Just the head."

Chewing noises followed. Then some crunching, then sleep, and the next morning found all three following the old woman through the forest, up to their waists in a sea of ferns, arms flailing like three hapless canoeists: Salvestro and Bernardo without the least idea of where they were going or why they were going there, Diego locked in silence. Since attempting his speech by the river, he had not said a word. Monkeys chattered and crashed about in the branches high above their heads. Raucous birds shrieked and flew from perch to perch. The forest whirred and buzzed and chirruped and growled, and the little procession thrashed its way forward through fleshy fronds and tendrils, their sore feet padding down the path.

After an hour or more of this the ferns began to thin, then gave out altogether. The men's legs reappeared, and the dim sunlight brightened as gaps opened in the topmost canopy, hard shafts and beams lancing the leaves of the lower trees. The forest grew quieter and the land rose in a gentle slope. At its summit the trees stopped and a vista opened before them.

Two diverging ridges ran forward in front of them, and between these the ground fell away, forming a ravine that deepened and widened, becoming a long valley whose wooded sides fell steeply to the floor far below. A ravine identical to the one they now overlooked formed the distant end of the valley that was thus shaped like the hull of a sharp-prowed ship, or so it seemed to Salvestro. The canopies of the trees merged together to coat its sides and bottom in green. Like moss, he thought. Or, remembering the *Lucia,* mold. Here and there thin plumes of smoke rose up. Something glittered. Water?

"Where are we?" Bernardo asked finally, and this time the old woman did not gesture for him to be silent.

He looked to Salvestro for an answer, but Salvestro only shrugged. They had not crossed the river, which meant that they must be east of it. The back of the valley was still in shade, and from the position of the sun they were facing east now. The river was behind them. A steep valley was in front of them. Apart from these facts, he knew nothing. The old woman was beckoning for them to follow her down a path that ran at an angle off to the left and then disappeared into the trees lower down. Salvestro and Bernardo turned, but Diego simply stood there, motionless and transfixed. The woman beckoned again.

"Here," Diego said.

Salvestro looked around in surprise at the breaking of the soldier's silence. The old woman said something in her own tongue. Diego gazed into the valley.

"This is where I will find the beast," he said.

Daughter . . .

Almost there now. The men had drifted back out of the forest in twos and threes, their fruitless pursuit abandoned and its fury expended. Their trails and noisy passages were wounds in the cool of the forest that healed as soon as made. She ran a finger down her cheek. They were shallow cuts, made for show.

Later still, when her brothers had stalked out of the hut and she and Namoke were alone, she turned her painted face to the older man, to her father's brother. The residue of her contempt hung in the air between them.

"I had thought there would be a festival for your homecoming," Namoke said eventually. "I imagined the *mmo*-men performing a masquerade for their Eze-Ada and the Nri-people sitting down to feast together. A great celebration. At other times I imagined you were dead. I could not see you. I could not see your life." He shrugged wearily. "It was hard to believe you were dead, but it was harder to believe you were alive. And amongst the White-men. . . ."

"Yet you have not buried my father," she said. "As the youngest son, Onugu might have washed his body in my place. It is permitted if there is no Eze-Ada, and if the men of the Nzemabua agree. My brothers wished it so, did they not? Who opposed them?"

"Anayamati would have wanted his daughter to wash his body, to calm his house. He is waiting for you now."

"I have heard him," she said. Namoke brought his head up sharply. "You are the leader of the Nzemabua," she went on, ignoring his surprise. "Who else would speak for me? Alike? Ewenetem, perhaps?"

Namoke smiled. Alike and Ewenetem were notoriously taciturn.

"I need you to speak for me again. Nri-people need you to speak for me. Do you remember the Ijaw who told us of the White-men? The old man with his necklaces of shark's teeth? You suspected even then, I know you did."

Namoke was shaking his head. "Your brothers did not lie to you. It is an old story, hardly even a story. Our children chant it at each other, not grown men and women. If I were to stand before the men of the Nzemabua and speak as you ask, they might think fondly of their childhoods, but they would not act. They would laugh, and I would laugh with them, all of us together at my foolishness."

"And who will be the fools if it is true?" she demanded. "I know it, and so do you."

"Even if it is true, who is to say these White-men are what you claim? They are few, and far away, and weak. . . ."

"So you call a palaver to talk about nothing? The Bini did not come here to fish in the River. The Ngola did not send his men to hunt pigs in the forest. They come to Nri-people as they always have, and what do we say then? That White-men fall from the sky? Anayamati sees them already in his dreaming. Soon they will be in Nri and he will know them as I do. What will Nri-people say then? What will they do?"

The vehemence in her voice had increased throughout this speech until she was almost shouting at her uncle, and at its conclusion the silence in the hut was heavier even than when her brothers had left. Namoke waited several long seconds before replying.

"Good question," he commended her. "You always asked good questions, Usse, even as a little girl. Suppose the old story is true, and suppose the White-men are what you say they are, what will Nri-people say then? What will they do?"

He paused then, and she saw a strange expression pass across his face, recognition mixed with something else. Disappointment, perhaps.

"I do not know, Usse. If what you say is true, I do not know what Nri-people should do. I am not your father. I am not the Eze-Nri. I know of no rite that would cleanse this stain."

"Yes, you do," she said quietly.

Namoke shook his head, puzzled by her now. There were rites to make the yam grow, and the coco- and oil-palm, rites for the rain, and the drought, and the flood. There were rites for the birth of children and the death of old men. There were rites to erect taboos and others to demolish them, thousands upon thousands, which only Nri-people knew and only Nri-people might perform. There were rites to cleanse the land of any stain that might fall upon it. . . . But not the one she urged on him now. His eyes narrowed in concentration, watching her across the fire as she began to recite the chant that he had not sung since childhood, speaking the words at first, then intoning them in a singsong voice, like a child, gradually adding emphases until the simple rhythm asserted itself by force of repetition, for every verse was identical in form: a question followed by a response, and the latter growing more insistent as the chant went on, for although the questions were all different the answer was always the same.

"Enyi knows, Enyi knows," Usse sang to her uncle, over and over again.

Daughter . . . ?

The Ndi Mili Nnu cared more for their boats than their homes, Namoke reflected, looking across the water. The low windbreak they had built on the north side of the sandbank only goaded the harmattan, which gusted down the River, met the inadequate obstacle, and tumbled over it chaotically to assault their roughly thatched bivouacs. Raffia mats used to patch holes in the roofs flapped and luffed in the stiffening breeze as though threatening to carry off the ramshackle shelters and send them skidding over the River's glare or lift them high into the haze-white sky, a flock of lumpish, disintegrating birds molting bamboo poles and palm leaves. Their inhabitants disdained them, except to sleep. They preferred to gather about their boats, for which they had driven heavy stakes deep into the sand of the temporary island to serve as mooring posts. The Ndi Mili Nnu were wary of land. Rains would dissolve it and redeposit it elsewhere. The River's flood was more constant than its banks, its annual destruction more dependable. Soon the late echo of that flood would wash away the island on which they were camped just as it always did. The sand was a distant and colorless strip against the prickling glitter of the River, visible at all from this bank only because of the antlike figures shifting about upon it as they readied their craft for the daily crossing to the palaver. The first of them were already pushing out into the water, angling their pirogues counter to the current and directing them along a shallow arc that brought them invariably to the exact mud-flat that they favored. Namoke watched them until he could see the water spilling off their paddles. Behind him, the *obiri* was already loud with the mixed pidgins that the tribes used amongst themselves. He felt his unease rise again. The men of the Nzemabua would meet in Chima's compound, in the village itself and out of earshot of the palaver. He had told Usse that the decision she sought would mean nothing without the Eze-Nri. It had been his last argument. She had smiled and said only that the Eze-Nri was not so far away as he thought. Anayamati's successor already chosen? Her words might mean anything or nothing, but they had unsettled him all the same. Now he was waiting for Aguve and Ilonwagu and turned anxiously every few seconds to search for them amongst the men milling about below the ridge. A covered litter bobbed amidst little knots of people who stepped aside impatiently. The first of the Ndi Mili Nnu had landed and were dragging their pirogues up the mud-bank.

"Uncle."

He turned quickly. The two men he awaited were standing before him. Usse stood between them. They exchanged greetings formally, and then he led the way along the short path that led to the village. Usse walked behind all three. This is how goats are herded, thought Namoke. Was this how she brought the White-men here? If all she had pressed on him was true, the three of them were already at Nri. And if that were true, it had already begun and there was no more time. She would sit beside him when he addressed the Nzemabua. She would not speak.

Although, ringed with the impassive countenances of his peers, men whom he had known since childhood, finding himself almost unnerved by the unfamiliar stoniness of the expressions on these familiar faces, he reached for Usse's words, not his own. The sound of them as she had modulated between scorn and cajoling, pulling him forward only to push him away, then pull him in again, drawing him slowly toward the core of her belief. . . . He needed that now, not the words themselves, but the shape of them, that they should fit the world the silent men of the Nzemabua saw with their own eyes, stitch it together, and patch the rents in its fabric. To convince them. He began by speaking of Eri and his first son, which they would take for a conventional piety, nodding slowly as the story unfolded. Then he spoke of the second son, which was a story reserved by the men of Nzemabua, a secret they shared. It would draw them tighter together. He told them of the fight in the mud by the water-hole, speaking lightly as though he himself were unsure how much credence the tale deserved and moving back and forth over the protagonists and their actions, pointing out this or that detail or implication, recasting the story slowly, and even signaling that he was doing this by the repetition of stock phrases until their meaning began to shift and grow slippery; he would discard them then and adopt others. He spoke softly so that they would lean forward to catch the words. Usse sat at his side, motionless and silent as she had promised.

He said, "When the White-men came, the Ijaws knew what they were. The Bini knew too, and the Calabaris, and the Ife-people. The Ngola and the Mani Kongo were in no doubt. Nor the Aworo of the Esie, nor the Attah of Idah. They all knew. . . ." He paused there and looked around the ring of faces. "But, as we know from the wise discussions in the *obiri,* they all knew very *differently.* . . ."

Most of the younger men smiled. He caught Onugu's eye on the far side of the circle. He could entertain them now, if he chose. He could tap their frustration at the quarrels and shouting matches they had endured in the thick of the *obiri.* Or he could touch on their unease.

"Only Nri-people were mystified, asking, What are these White-men?" He said this in a wondering tone, weighing the moment, gauging their readiness. "Only the people who most should have known, as though we had forgotten our own oldest stories. As though we no longer believed them and left them instead for little children to sing and then discard when they come of age. Well, we are all of age now. Some of us a little more than that. . . ."

This time no one smiled. They were wavering between caution and curiosity, and underneath Namoke sensed a strange eagerness. Had they been waiting for one of their number to break the silence? He could not stop. This was the last part, the piece that fitted exactly with all that he had already said and all that they had accepted. He felt their different attentions variously sweep over him or fix upon him or float freely, uncaptured as yet. The words themselves were almost beside the point. He guided himself forward by the ebb and flow of his audience, its sympathies and antipathies, feeling his way forward. He began to speak of Ezodu. His gaze moved steadily around the circle—Alike, Enweleani, Obalike, Ewenetem, Usse's brothers next to him, Onugu, Apia, Gbujo, then Nwamkpo, Oniojo, Aguve, Ilonwagu, and so all the way around until the only member of the Nzemabua he could not see was its speaker: himself.

He had not been able to read them, he remembered later. He had believed he had lost them, although his voice had held the level note he had first struck, held its suasive equilibrium. And the resolution they were coming to was inevitable in any case and independent of his efforts. With hindsight, the rite had already begun, the call to gather the beasts was already ringing through the *obiri,* already unstoppable. Anayamati and his willful daughter. . . . But, in Chima's compound, their faces had told him nothing. He talked and was heard. He saw eyes flick sideways rather than meet his own. He sensed distraction. They were drifting, or being drawn away, as though a malevolent *dibia* were at his invisible work, burying chicken claws and muttering gibberish. They were not watching him. In fact, he realized with a start, they were paying him no attention at all.

Their eyes were fixed on Usse, who had not moved or uttered a word. At first he thought she was staring at her brothers, for her face was turned to them, but her gaze either stopped short of their faces or continued on past them, through the mud-wall behind their backs and the village outside. Or it was turned in upon herself. She was sealed off from them, an echo sounding to herself, and they could do no more than press their palms to the walls of her chamber in search of its resonance.

It was then that they had come over to him. Her painted face was rapt and abstracted. He had not believed her before, Namoke realized.

Father . . . ?

She was confined, her privacy loud with great thuds and crashes, the din of something trying to get in or something trying to get out.

Gather the animals.

Her lips echoed the command, forming words the men of the Nzemabua no longer needed to hear, and which they would echo themselves until they amplified and magnified, their noise drowning out the bickering voices of the palaver. Their legacy was an old mistake; an ancient stain. They were choiceless custodians, debtors to an old story, victims of a prank played long ago.

Heh, heh, heh, heh . . .

"Wet clay, dry clay, water, ashes, chaff, and goat-hair," said the old man. "My pig-bristle brush, Iguedo's stirring stick, sunlight, the iron rings hanging on the wall back there, two thin bronze rods, and a large store of patience. We will need all these things."

He had attached two strips of wax to the wax model that projected at a comical angle from each of the figure's knees. They would serve as "sprues," apparently. The boy had not yet decided whether knowing what "sprues" were was worth the mockery that the question would provoke.

"Clay, bronze, and iron are the materials which every Eze-Nri must gather for his coronation," the old man went on. "Bronze must come from the Nupe, who trade with the peoples of the desert; iron must come from Awka; and the clay must come from the bed of the Anambra River. There are things he must make in secret."

He turned the model about, indicating creases and depressions, the eye-holes in the leopard's face, the thin grooves delineating the arms. "This part will be difficult," he said, stabbing the end of his little finger into the irregular space formed between the figure's legs and the *ofo*-bundle between the feet. He held it up and squinted, eventually nodding to himself as though to say that whatever problem he had diagnosed was soluble.

"Grinding now."

The old man began measuring out substances from the calabashes arrayed on the bench, and the boy set to work with pestle and mortar, grinding dry clay and ashes to a grayish powder in which the pale red of the clay was all but lost. The old man rummaged in his basket, emerging with a thin awl. Holding the figure in one hand, he began to bore a narrow hole a little below the breastplate, withdrawing the tool at intervals and peering closely at its point until, when he rubbed it between thumb and forefinger, a dull red smudge indicated that he had reached the clay core. He bored a second hole in the figure's back, then inserted the two bronze rods, twisting them in until the slick resistance of the wax gave way to the granular abrasion of the clay.

"What are these for?" he demanded.

The boy frowned. There was the clay core, then the wax, then more clay, which they would apply to make the mold. The wax would be displaced by bronze, and the rods were made of bronze, too, protruding less than a finger's length. The clay would cover them, he thought, so they could not be for lifting the mold. The wax would melt and run out. . . .

"The rods are to hold the core in place when the wax melts," he said.

The old man stared at him, at a loss for words for once. "Yes," he said eventually. "Without the rods the core would sink to the bottom of the mold. That is what the rods are for." The stunned expression began to fade from his face.

"What are 'sprues'?" asked the boy.

"Go outside and make water. Good example of a sprue," the old man snorted, recovering from his surprise. "Where does the wax go when we pour in the bronze? How does piss get out when your bladder's full? A sprue is an outlet for hot liquids." He took the powder from the boy and dipped his finger in it. A half-ladle of water and some stirring turned it to a heavy black paste. A splash or two more and it was a thick liquid. The old man picked up his brush and dipped it into the mortar-bowl. "Bronze breathes," he muttered, painting the smooth liquid over the figure, using the end of the brush to work it into the crevices and indentations. "So it needs a skin to breathe through."

"Like the sprues," said the boy. "Or else where's all that breath going to go?"

The old man grunted sourly. When he was finished painting, he handed the glistening black figure to the boy. "Put it outside, but not in the sun. Let the air dry it slowly."

By midafternoon the slick coating had dried to a shell of matte gray. The old man mixed clay in a calabash, working in the goat-hair and chaff. The boy's task then was to roll out little strips, about the size of his thumb and as thin as he could make them. The old man fashioned pellets and began by kneading them carefully to the shapes of the wax figure's various cavities. He began tamping the smallest pieces into nooks and crannies with a tiny wooden spatula, then took up the first of the boy's strips and wound it about the head. Already blunted by the first coating, the model's details disappeared entirely as he plugged, wrapped, and overlaid them with the pellets and strips of this new admixture. The boy yawned.

"Bored?" the old man inquired. "You think you have learned enough about bronze-casting now?"

When he was finished, the figure was barely recognizable as a seated man with two short rods sticking out of his chest and back, some inexplicable lumps on his shoulders, and a bulge between his feet. The boy took the object outside again. He had chosen a spot in the shade of the compound's south wall, next to his charcoal pile. A breeze supplied the air that the old man had demanded. Some stones had been piled there, and he placed the clay-encased figure on the topmost. Then he sat back and waited for it to dry.

So it went on: waiting, carrying the object back inside, rolling out strips of clay and watching the old man apply them, carrying the object back outside again, waiting again, and each new application blunted the outline of the seated man further. It became a vaguely indented anthill, then a smooth one, then a squat log stood on its end, and the only clue to the clay's contents was the projection of the waxen sprues, poking out like a centipede's feelers, and the nubs of the bronze rods on the top. The old man built up little walls of clay to either side of these, widening and thickening them gradually until they formed two bowls set at an angle to the mold with a channel leading to the rods themselves. Now, thought the boy, it looks like a tree stump with ears. He carried it outside again. More waiting. More drying. Finally the old man slapped on the last of the clay, which was a single fat strip rather wetter than the others, smoothed it off, and told the boy to fetch the iron rings.

"He's in the clay now," the old man said grimly. A new note; it brought the boy's head up. "Know what these are for?" He took the rings and knocked them together. They rang dully, and the boy shook his head.

"They're to keep him in while we cook him."

The old man had lost him. There was a lump of wax in a lump of clay, and the old man was forcing the iron rings over both ends "to keep him in." Now he wished he had not asked about the sprues. If he had not asked then, he would have asked now. But he had, and so he did not. Only so much pride could be swallowed in one day. The old man smeared more clay over the rings, embedding them in the mold. He was hunched over, working quickly. Abruptly he unbent and jumped to his feet, lifting the mold and thumping it down on the bench.

"Not one," he announced. "Two."

He paused.

"Two!"

The boy tensed. The old man was unclean in his habits, ill-natured, his tongue rough as sharkskin and wagged in a mouth fouler than an old fish-basket. He was a drunkard. His breath smelled like a dog's. But up till now he had not seemed mad. The boy readied himself to run. Then he remembered the old man's ramblings as he had carved the *ichi*-marks on the Eze-Nri's face, the last details. He had been all but asleep.

"Eri's sons," he hazarded.

The old man nodded, forgetting to react with his usual insulting surprise at this evidence of thought. He was standing with his palms flat on the bench, but now, as he turned, the light from the door caught his face oddly, and it seemed to the boy that he was older than before. Much older. It lasted only for the moment it took him to squat down.

"Ifikuanim and his nameless brother. When Eri died they cut his land in two. East of the River was Ifikuanim's land. West of the River was his brother's. You know this story, boy?"

The old man seemed to have forgotten his earlier speech, or at least the boy's professed ignorance then. He shook his head and listened as the old man told how on his side of the River Ifikuanim cleared the forest and planted yam and coco-palm, how he caught goats and tamed them, then cattle, even dogs.

"Ifikuanim worked under the open sky, under the sun which burned him, so that people might eat what he grew."

Everybody knew this, thought the boy. But when the old man began talking of the brother, the boy began to realize that the old man might indeed be weak-witted, or simply a liar. Eri had one son. One, not two. There was no "brother."

"But the other brother didn't like the hoe, didn't like the ax, didn't like felling, or clearing, or planting, or weeding. He didn't like the sun, either. What he liked was hunting. He kept his land as forest, and he kept himself within it."

The old man was jabbering away.

"He was a good hunter; even the leopard feared him. Every time he killed a leopard he took just one tooth for himself, and he had twenty necklaces of leopard's teeth. He made himself a horn from the tusk of a boar that stood taller than himself. Every day he filled his game-bag till it took ten men to lift it. But he still could not feed his people. So he began crossing over the River."

The boy understood now. He understood perfectly. He nodded eagerly at each sentence and made little noises of assent. He listened intently, respectfully, raptly. It was quite clear what the old man was doing. He would leave here and tell all his friends that Eri had two sons; that's what the old man was counting on. He was trying to make a fool of him again. And his friends would think him an idiot. . . .

You don't fool me for an instant, he thought, smiling encouragement as the old man began telling how Ifikuanim tracked his brother and how he could never catch him.

"Until he went to Enyi," said the old man. "Ifikuanim found Enyi by a waterhole, his trunk sucking up water to spray on his back. Enyi was happy to help. The brother hunted him, too. He told Ifikuanim to stop chasing around, his brother would be there soon enough. There was plenty of game at this waterhole."

"What happened next?" asked the boy, dutifully wide-eyed.

The old man fell silent for a while. To concoct the rest of this ridiculous tale, his audience of one surmised. When he resumed, his tone was more brusque, as though he regretted having begun the story and now wished only to conclude it.

"What happened next was they caught him. They caught him by the waterhole, just as Enyi promised, and they rolled him in the clay there till he was covered from head to foot. Then they rolled him some more, until the weight of the clay was so heavy that he could not stand. He fell on all fours like an animal. They stripped off his necklaces of leopard's teeth. They took his hunting-horn and stuck it on the end of his nose. Every time he tried to run back into the forest, Enyi and Ifikuanim herded him back to the waterhole and rolled him in the clay again. They held him down until the sun had dried it hard."

That was when the boy recognized the story. Enyi, the watering hole, the tusk stuck on the nose . . . It all came from a children's song. He barely remembered it. The old man must take him for a simpleton.

"He was trapped in it like a turtle in its shell, and he was too ashamed to go back to his people like that, so he tried to rub off the clay against a tree. Then he tried to break off the horn they had stuck on his nose, so he hit it against a rock, but it would not break. It was stuck there in front of his face. That is why he is called Ezodu, which means Tusk-hater. It was his own hunting horn. A boar's tusk. They put it there to mock him."

Yes, yes, yes, thought the boy. They had sung it as children. Even the most dull-witted could manage it. One group would sing out questions like "How did Ezodu get his horn?" Or, "Why is Ezodu the color of mud?" Then the other group would sing the answer, which was always the same: "Enyi knows! Enyi knows!" It always ended the same way, too. One group would sing, "Why did Ezodu run away?" Then the other group would answer, "Ezodu will be back one day!" That was it.

The old man had stopped speaking and nodded to himself as though confirming that this was the end of the story. Now he was lifting the damp mold off the bench. The boy realized that some response was required of him.

"What happened to the brother after that?"

The old man shrugged. "That is the end of the story. Ifikuanim was the second Eze-Nri. He planted his brother's old hunting ground with yam and coco-palm. He claimed the beasts that his brother had hunted for himself. Good story, eh?"

The boy agreed that it was.

"Never tell it to anyone, understand?"

The boy nodded, but uncertainly, for the old man was staring at him with an odd expression on his face.

"Want to know why?" asked the old man. He took the boy's silence for assent and continued, "Because they will not believe it then any more than you believe it now."

He raised his hand before the boy could protest and looked down at the mold balanced precariously in the crook of his arm. "Different story now. Shorter. What do Nri-people say when the Eze-Nri ceases his dreaming? What do they say when his daughter washes him and lays him to rest?"

He was scrutinizing the rings around the mold, not looking at the boy.

"The iron is broken," the boy replied.

The old man nodded.

"They do, they do. But the iron is never truly broken. Now take this outside. When it is dry, we will cast bronze."

It or them? Specimen or species? The Beast is plural, its components oblivious: Salvestro, Bernardo, and Diego; a triple-humped dromedary or elasticated amphibrach, zigging and zagging, skidding around the angles of a slalomed path whose obliquities not only mitigated the steepness of the valley's sides, but also turned its travelers' heads this way and that, spinning them about and throwing off their senses of direction, perspective, proportion. . . . Where were they going, apart from down? The forest canopy closed again over their heads, blocking out direct sight of the sun. The root problem resurfaced, and there was the constant hazard of mutual collision, for the trio tended to bunch when the track took one of its many abrupt turns, the rearmost shunting the foremost into ankle-snagging ground-creeper that lurked beneath the amorphous off-piste greenery. The lithe old woman hopped ahead, more surefooted than them. This, Salvestro soon understood, was a path to be negotiated rather than followed. Crashing, tripping, bumping, scrambling upright, and continuing, it took the course of an afternoon for Salvestro, Bernardo, and Diego to descend into Nri.

Eventually, however, the ground leveled out and the three men stopped to catch their breath, hands propped on their knees while the old woman stood there unperturbed. Salvestro felt the throbbing in his head begin to recede. He had lain down by the fire the previous night and sunk into a black sleep, his relief that at last he might rest pulling him down, his memories of the day closing over his head and burying him. Then, once again, the voices had started up, more insistent than ever before. He had tossed and turned under their assault, trying to shake them out of his head, but they were trapped in there, and there was no means of escape. Not for them. Nor for him. The old woman had woken him at dawn, and as he rose the throbbing had begun. Now she waited patiently with her arms crossed flat across her chest. The throbbing came and went in waves. She beckoned them to follow her, then led them into the forest.

Salvestro soon realized that the view from the rim of the valley had deceived him, for the forest down here was broken by little groves and clearings where plots of land had been planted, all quite invisible from above. Where the land had been cleared, the soil was piled up in large regular mounds, as though monstrous turnips were swelling there. Groves of young palm trees were hung with bright red fruit. The path snaked between these little sunlit plantations, darting in and out of the shade of the forest, which was quieter than the forest they had left. The noise of the birds was muted and sporadic.

To begin with, a few smaller paths would lead off to left or right, but after only a few minutes' trudging, these ceased. A little farther on the plantations ceased, too. The path continued, winding its way between the trees that supported the canopy above, running along the northern edge of the valley floor, according to Salvestro's observations, curving slightly and broad enough for the three of them to walk abreast if they should so choose. In the event, the old woman led, Diego followed, and the other two dawdled behind him. They saw no one.

"Where are the people?" asked Bernardo.

No one answered. Presently the path began to narrow. Encroaching shrubs and clumps of grass squeezed it to a single line that appeared and disappeared, its breaks growing longer and longer until they were once again walking through forest that betrayed no sign that humans had ever set foot there. They weaved their way through the tree-trunks with the old woman, who seemed as certain of her destination as ever. With her as their guide, Salvestro surrendered to his ignorance. He was going wherever she was taking them. They all were.

To their right, and insensibly at first, the ground began to drop. When it leveled out again they found themselves in a clearing. The steep slope that enclosed the valley to the north was visible through the gap in the canopy. In the center, the soil was charred and gray with ashes where someone had once lit a bonfire. Salvestro put his hand to its remains. Cold. The old woman was already beckoning them on. He heard water, a little stream. The ground fell away on the far side of the clearing to form a little scarp, no more than the height of a man, which the stream below had presumably cut and then taken as its near bank. They jumped down one by one, landing heavily and having to scramble up the other side. In front of them were several huge cottonwood trees, then some coco-palms, and behind those a forbidding thicket of bushes with dark purple leaves. The old woman turned away. They were to follow the water downstream.

"What's that?" Bernardo said a few minutes later.

Earlier, Salvestro had only shrugged at the giant's question. He had no more idea where all the people were than his companion did. Perhaps there were no people. The plantations might be some freakish caprice of the forest, the paths worn by animals. The old woman might be leading them around and around for no better reason than her own amusement. Now his gaze followed the giant's outstretched arm. To the left of the stream the trees were beginning to thin, and between their trunks, perhaps a hundred paces away, he saw sunlight falling directly on some smooth surface, a high wall, perhaps, or an unnaturally smooth bank of earth. The vista was interrupted, broken up by the tree-trunks into segments that his eyes could not make sense of.

"I don't know," he replied.

The old woman had not waited, nor had Diego. They were standing a little way ahead. The two men quickened their step to catch up and, when they reached them, found themselves standing at the edge of a dusty apron of cleared ground that served as a kind of forecourt to the structure behind.

The object they had glimpsed was indeed a wall, made of smooth mud and fifteen or even twenty feet high. It formed one side of a rectangular enclosure whose extent they could only guess. It stretched from the apron back into the forest until it was lost to view. Its frontage, if it was a front, was broken only by a small door set so deep into the wall that the shadowed recess appeared at first to be a tunnel. After the jumbled lines of the forest, the scale and regularity of the walls seemed shocking, a disruption.

"I think we're here," said Bernardo behind him.

The old woman began chattering in her own language, its strange sounds and rhythms only reinforcing the alien character of the structure. Still chattering, she led them to the door. Carved faces pushed their features out of the wood. She pressed her palms against two foreheads as though trying to force them back into the timber. She was trying to explain something, but they could not understand her. Then she buffeted the massive door with her shoulder, stepped aside, and pointed to Bernardo.

It took the big man two heavy blows before the barrier so much as shuddered. All three set their shoulders to the task, forcing an entrance inch by inch, dislodging clods of dry mud that rained down on their heads, and gouging a semicircular weal in the ground. The door turned out to be fashioned from a single slab of hardwood, no higher than Salvestro but thicker than Bernardo's chest.

Time, damp, and heat had warped the frame in which it was set until its sagging hinges had deposited its weight on the ground. They set to again, heaving and pushing, sweating and cursing, until eventually the crack widened to a gap through which even Bernardo might squeeze. He gave it a last tremendous buffet and turned to the old woman in triumph.

She was gone.

The ground was cleared for fifty paces or more in any direction. The three men looked around them, but she was nowhere in sight. The trees stood in a half-circle around the open area as though they had advanced that far and then been stopped abruptly by an unseen force or prohibition. An hour ago the men had been walking beneath their canopies. Now they appeared forbidding. Something was different, Salvestro thought vaguely. The old woman seemed to have disappeared into thin air. A door that seemed not to have been opened in years had been forced. . . . Something else. He looked about uneasily and saw that Bernardo was still looking about anxiously.

"She guided us here," Salvestro said uncertainly. "Now we're here, why would she stay?"

He addressed this last remark to Diego, but the soldier only stared at his boots, nodding to himself with a half-smile on his face, at once resigned and amused at some private realization.

"But what now?" Bernardo burst out. He looked about him at the encircling forest. "What do we do now?"

There was nowhere else to go. Diego was already sliding around the door.

A courtyard: a wide strip of open space stretching widthwise between the side walls. At its center stood a structure that reminded Salvestro of the one Diego had entered after they had climbed out of the boat. A roof fashioned from intertwined palm branches had been raised on stout poles, but the fronds had dried and shredded, and now they lay scattered on the ground. Its sides were open. The three of them stood beneath the bare lattice on which the roof had once been laid and stared at the wide front of a building that as far as they could make out filled the entire remainder of the enclosure. A number of low doorways punctuated the forewall at irregular intervals. They were quiet. Salvestro realized that the source of the strange apprehension he had felt only a few minutes earlier was, in effect, an absence. This courtyard, the great low building that squatted before them and stretched back out of sight, the clearing outside, and the surrounding forest were all perfectly silent.

He looked again at Diego, but the soldier was intent on the doorways, his gaze sweeping over them as if whatever he sought might suddenly flicker in the interior darkness, disturb it somehow and reveal itself. Salvestro recalled the man's last words, spoken on the ridge overlooking the valley. The certainty he had invested them with. The soldier was lost, adrift, clinging to the fraying thread of his quest. It had happened on the river, or in the rear room where he, Salvestro, had discovered him "at prayer." Or on the ship. Usse could bring him back, perhaps, or the Beast. He would find neither of them here.

Instead chambers. And more chambers. And more chambers again beyond those.

They entered the building and began moving through its divisions. Sunlight entering by the open doorways illuminated the foremost rooms, but as they moved deeper into the structure the three men were reduced to squinting into a darkness lit only by the faint glimmers that penetrated the thatch. The chambers varied only slightly in size and were linked by unframed archways that seemed to have been carved directly out of the same smooth mud that formed the walls. Their angles and corners were curving planes, and their floors bowed up so that it was impossible to say exactly where they stopped being floors and started being walls. Only the roof was constant, uniformly flat and suspended out of reach above their heads. Gradually their eyes adjusted to the gloom, and, advancing hesitantly through the irregular enfilades, they began to realize that the building was not simply uninhabited. It was empty. None of the chambers contained anything.

To begin with they drifted through together, one leading the way, then another, one poking his head through a side opening while the others went ahead, then reconvenings, then more individual detours, which grew longer and longer until Diego grunted and marched off to the left and, a little later, Bernardo seemed to forget his earlier unease, simply wandering through the opposite door to Salvestro. They went their separate ways, not so much by design as by the fact that there seemed no compelling reason to stay together. Soldier, Giant, Thief: a disbanded trio or dissected amphibrach: a humpless dromedary trudging in three different directions at once.

Salvestro found himself alone in a space rather longer than it was wide and tapered at one end. The next was narrower, and the next almost triangular. A dead end. He moved on. The hardened mud that formed the walls and the floor deadened the sound of his footfalls. He had a vague idea of continuing forward until he reached the building's outer wall. He would then follow it around until he reemerged at the front or discovered some other entrance at the rear. He was not sure what benefit this information might confer on him, but nevertheless he advanced, passing slowly through the chambers and taking careful note of the angles at which they were set, for the building itself seemed to resist straightforward passage, its skewed honeycomb bending him away from his objective and forcing him to guess at every turn whether he was still maintaining his heading or had been subtly turned or diverted somehow. His steps grew hesitant, and realizing that this was adding to the problematic nature of the task, he strode forward more boldly, forcing himself to walk quickly. He passed briskly from chamber to chamber, almost running now, thinking that the very next dead end must indicate the building's limit. Then he stepped confidently into one of the largest chambers he had yet seen and pitched forward into space.

"Bernardo!"

The structure was not, after all, quite empty. Or even uninhabited.

It took some time for the giant to find him. Guided by Salvestro's periodic shouts, Bernardo moved in haphazard fashion toward the source of the noise, growing increasingly confused and impatient as he did so. He had been quite content to drift aimlessly among the chambers, but now they seemed arranged for no other purpose than deflecting him. Salvestro's shouts increased and decreased in volume, booming out one minute, stifled the next, as the chambers trapped or amplified the sound. Several times he stopped to try to clarify his predicament, allowing Salvestro to yell away for a minute or two before resuming his search. His predicament grew no clearer. So he blundered forward through the gloom, calling out what he hoped were encouraging phrases such as "Over here, Salvestro!" and "Almost there!" and "Not long now!" until the variously muffled or resonant answering voice, instead of shouting his name, said quite clearly and distinctly: "Stop."

Bernardo stopped.

He was standing on the edge of a smooth-sided pit. The chamber's floor, though concave like the others, was hollowed to a far greater depth and the consequent depression shaped like the inside of an enormous inverted bell. Its impatient clapper was Salvestro, standing there looking up at him. And there was something else down there. . . .

"Come on, Bernardo! Get down here. Just sit on the edge and slide."

"Then we'll both be stuck," he objected.

"What do you mean, 'stuck'? I've been up and down half a dozen times already. It's easy."

Bernardo peered at the slope mistrustfully, then squinted into the pit.

"What's that?" he demanded.

"Come and look for yourself," retorted Salvestro.

Bernardo scrambled down.

It was a man, or one who once had been a man. He was seated upright on a chair that seemed—the light was even weaker than before—to have been carved from a single tree-trunk. He wore a headdress of some sort and a long robe that was open at the chest, disclosing some necklaces and a pendant carved with an animal's face. Part clasped by and part resting against one arm, its base resting on the hard mud of the floor and its tip extending a little higher than his shoulder, was a massive ivory tusk, while the other arm held a thick staff with a few disks stuck on the end. A tightly bound bundle of twigs lay on the ground between his feet.

Bernardo stared into the man's face. "He's not breathing, is he?"

"No," said Salvestro behind him.

The face, indeed the whole body, appeared in so perfect a state of preservation that both men had hushed their voices for fear of waking the seated figure.

"He's dead, isn't he?"

"Yes," said Salvestro. Then he added, "Touch him."

Bernardo poked tentatively at the robe. It crumbled where his finger touched. He nodded his satisfaction.

"No," Salvestro said. "Touch *him*. His skin."

The giant approached the body again, hesitating as he decided which part to touch. The forehead, it seemed. Yes. He extended his arm to press the palm of his hand against the figure's flesh.

"Urgh!"

He recoiled in horror, springing back and crying out, "You told me he was dead, damn you, Salvestro!"

"He is dead."

"But he's still *warm*. . . ."

Salvestro said nothing. Performing the exact same act, he had jumped back himself. But then, conquering the strange mixture of fear and revulsion that had risen in his throat, he had pressed his hand to the figure's chest. It was still. The heart had ceased beating, the lungs had stopped pumping, and long ago judging from the state of the robe draped over his shoulders. The man was dead. Yet his flesh was warm. Bernardo's face was a mask of appalled incomprehension. He seemed unable to tear his eyes away.

"What is he?" he whispered.

Before Salvestro could say he did not know, a third voice broke the chamber's hush.

"King of Nri! I bring greetings from Fernando the Catholic, King of all Spain. I am Don Diego of Tortosa, the servant of my King. . . ."

The two men stared up in amazement at Diego, who stood poised on the edge of the pit, one arm folded across his chest, the other extended to lend emphasis to this peroration.

"Sire, my King bids me salute you in his place. I have traveled here to beg of you a Beast, called Ezodu in these parts, for it is the wish of my King to have him and so it is my wish too that this be done. Thus and therefore I come before you, King of Nri.

"These"—he pointed at the two men staring up at him but did not look at them—"are my companions, called Salvestro and Bernardo. They are from . . . I do not know where they are from, but they are my servants. And I am Diego of Tortosa, servant of Fernando the Catholic, King of all Spain. . . ."

He paused to draw breath, then his voice sounded again.

"King of Nri! I bring greetings from Fernando the Catholic. I am Don Diego of Tortosa, the servant of my King, the King of all Spain. . . ."

Different cacophonies. First the animals: chattering, roaring, lowing, and screeching, their cries all jumbled together in a meaningless panic. Bleating goats

were being herded along the bank of the River. A man forced his way through
the crowd with a brace of squawking chickens.

Were the men any different? Their accents battered her ears, a fabulous mess
of cluckings and cries, random shouts, pointless yelling: excitement and its noises.
She was in the thick of it, in the press of their bodies as they formed up. She had
only to stand firm now and their orbits would wrap them about her. She thought
she glimpsed Gbujo. His defeated face. Men were streaming out of their huts and
compounds. She heard hammering, axes striking wood. Yes, she thought, send
them the forest if that is what the Eze-Nri decrees. In the middle of the River,
the Ndi Mili Nnu were ripping up their bivouacs. The dwindling island would be
flooded soon, the *yangbe* already driving down the River, swelling it again. The
Nri-men around her pressed closer. Namoke was near the front, she thought. The
hunting-party was long gone. Noise, and more noise, hammering at her skull
until it hummed, her very bones quivering under the assault. They were almost
ready. There was no more time. She let the racket pound her.

Then the swarm took flight, a distant buzz at first, a million sounds all blurred
together. She could not pluck a single voice from the increasing roar, a massive
wave of urgency and appeal, *hurry, hurry, hurry* . . .

Wait, she told herself.

Ezodu *is stepping on our graves*. . . .

She ignored their complaints, sifting through the mass of voices that now descended on her, each one striving to rise above all the others.

"Nri!" shouted a voice that might have been Namoke's.

They were moving off. Nri, she echoed to herself, and the spirits parroted it
back to her: *Nrrurrreee-eee*. . . . Mocking laughter rose above their wail: *Heh, heh,
heh* . . . She knew who that was. Eri was the one who would not reveal himself,
the only one who did not care. They were your sons, she thought. The laughter
subsided. Her feet were moving her forward. Torches somewhere. There were too
many voices, too many generations, and going further and further back, thickening and weighing on her: a wall of mud she could not break. She could not find
the one she sought.

Daughter? . . .

The voice was distant but distinct, set apart from the others. She could follow
it, a single insect, a feather glued to its back with a dab of resin. She could run
after, chase it until it chose to stop.

She followed, and the men around her seemed to carry her along, keeping
close to her and watching her while she drifted and darted after her playful
quarry. She knew they saw nothing of this. The swarm was no more than a murmur now. She moved farther away, or sank deeper, or reached back and felt herself
stretch after the one she pursued, who eluded her with such ease that it seemed
she was not following but being led or even dragged away. The men around her
were so close, she could feel the warmth of their skin. They would surround her
as they moved from Onitsha to Nri: a village by the River, then the paths through

the forest. The slope of the valley that led to the village. Nri's plantations and the course of its stream. They would find themselves before an apron of dusty ground, before a door so heavy that no one man might open it, before a compound that stretched back, and back, and back. . . . The chambers of the Eze-Nri. She would leave them there. She was the Eze-Ada, and these names were familiar, these places known. Yet within herself she was so far away now that she feared she might never be able to return. What if she could not find her way back? The voice sounded again then, the voice she chased after colder now than before.

Too late. . . .

The boy dug a calabash of charcoal from the pile in the courtyard, then carried it inside and handed it to the old man, who grunted and began distributing handfuls about the fire, more where it burned hot and less where the glow had yet to penetrate the fuel.

"Fire must be even," the old man said, sprinkling the last few pieces over a tiny flame that had sparked into life a moment before. "Even this way"—he swept his hand out horizontally—"and even that way." The same hand cut slices of air, moving downward as it did so. "You have to build it up slowly. In layers, like clay. When you need more heat, you peel off a layer, and there it is underneath. More heat. Simple."

The boy nodded. His fetching and carrying had begun before midday. Burning charcoal, the boy decided, was much like making charcoal. There was no sign as yet that they were doing anything but building a fire. No indication that they were there, at last, to cast bronze.

"Stop nodding. You're standing there like your mother's about to boil yam and you don't have the first idea what I'm talking about. Everything even. Have to keep everything the same. Hot clay and cold clay, or the bronze when it's running and the bronze when it's still. Things that are different don't like each other. They crack. Can't have a cracked Eze-Nri, eh?" He glanced over at the mold that sat on the bench next to several short rods of metal. The boy suppressed a smirk: the bowls affixed to its top still resembled ears. "If the bronze comes apart, those iron bands won't help. They're just for the mold. . . ."

The boy almost nodded, stopped himself.

"Yes," he said. He picked up the calabash and went outside to fetch more charcoal.

"I haven't finished telling you about the fire!" the old man called after him. "We don't need any more charcoal yet!"

The boy ignored him.

He was getting tired of the old man and exasperated with his whining, with his boring "jokes." Even his insults had become dull. He simply ignored them when they came, though they came less and less frequently and grew weaker and weaker. When was the last? Had it been something to do with the "sprues"? He dug the calabash into the charcoal and carried it back to the hut.

Late in the afternoon, Iguedo returned. As the sun sank, the ridge high above threw a shadow over the forest below, advancing down the valley like a soundless flood. She seemed to simply appear, leaning against the doorpost with her arms folded as though she had been there all along, watching them for hours. The old man looked up hurriedly, then turned again to the fire, a flat dish of heat spreading over the floor of the hut, pulsing black and red. He had an iron rod for a poker whose tip glowed dull orange. When he dipped it in the water-bucket there was a little hiss and a puff of steam. The hut was stifling, and the weak gusts of air entering through the doorway felt icy by contrast. The two of them sweated. Breathing burned their throats. Iguedo seemed indifferent, simply standing there, watching them, making no comment.

"Ready," said the old man at last. Then, "Now we've got you." He seemed to be talking to the mold.

The fire throbbed, pumping slabs of flameless heat into the two faces that squinted above. The glow seemed to reach behind their eyes, throbbing and aching, but they could not look away now. They had the mold between them, maneuvering it with heavy tongs into the very middle of the fire. They settled it there, and the old man piled coals up the sides. He began placing the bronze rods one by one into the bowls on top of the mold. Not ears, the boy told himself. Crucibles. The old man was moving the dull rods with the tongs, fussing over their arrangement and muttering as he did so. The boy frowned in puzzlement and moved closer to catch the words.

"Got you nice and tight in there now. And you can't get out, can you? Clay too hard? Of course it is. . . ." There was a pause then, but a few seconds later the old man took up the theme again, seemingly oblivious of his audience.

"Struggle all you like, you won't get out like that. Tried scraping it off, didn't you? Didn't work. Only one way you're getting out of there. Thought you could run around the forest like an animal, keep the sun off your back, keep your nice white flesh soft as cheese, leave the work to your brother. . . . Let half the people starve before you'd pick up a hoe. Well, now we've got you, and there's only one way you're coming out. Going to cook you out, we are. Going to melt you. Going to burn you out. . . ."

There was no doubt: he was addressing these remarks to the mold. The boy glanced over his shoulder at Iguedo, who shook her head at this foolishness.

"Stupid old man," she said. There was no affection in her voice. "You'll be in the clay yourself soon enough."

The old man did not look up. He was fiddling with the bronze rods, which in the heat of the fire were now beginning to bend and loll within the crucibles. His arm shook a little as he reached over the heat to give one of them a poke. The boy saw that he was grimacing from the effort. He thought about the insults heaped upon him by the old man, his own patient silence, his humility, if that was what it had been. Stupid. Why had he ever accepted that? And from a doddering grayhead who could talk about nothing unless it had to do with Eri or Eri's sons. He thought about the stupid story the old man had made up. It was stupid even if it was true.

"Ifikuanim *stole* his brother's land," he declared abruptly.

The old man's head came up.

"You said it yourself. He was the thief, not his brother."

The old man looked surprised, almost dazed. Good, thought the boy.

"Ifikuanim was the one who was wrong. And after he was wrong he was stupid. Rolling his brother in the clay and driving him out of the forest. . . ."

"Didn't drive him," the old man muttered. "He did not do that. Ezodu ran away."

The boy ignored this. It changed nothing. "He was stupid. Stupid to do that. He should have driven the horn through his neck, not stuck it on the end of his nose. He should have *killed* him. . . ."

"What do you know, boy? Eh? What do you . . ." It was the same tone as before, but now the old man's contempt only sounded querulous. An old bleating goat.

"What happens when the clay cracks, eh?" he pressed on. "Old man? What happens when Ezodu comes back? When the brother comes back for what was once his own, what happens then?"

The old man straightened. He turned and faced the boy. Apart from the dull hiss of the fire, there was silence. They stared at each other, and the boy began to think that he had gone too far. He wanted to goad the old man, that was all. Now there would be some crushing answer, something he had not considered. He would be the stupid one. But the seconds stretched and lengthened, and still the old man remained silent. Because there was nothing to say, the boy realized. The old man mumbled something, but too low for him to hear. He moved nearer. The old man picked up his tongs again, still muttering away.

". . . never happen. Never will. He's in the clay. Come back? He can't come back. Crack the clay? The clay won't crack. He's like a maggot in there. Wriggling and writhing, trying to worm his way out. But he can't. He won't. Never. . . ."

The bronze began to melt. The boy looked over the old man's shoulder and saw the taut surface begin to quiver. For a second it deepened in color, then the whole heat of the fire seemed to pour out of the metal, an unwatchable glare, one moment the color of honey, the next no color at all. It was light, a pure blinding white light that the boy could not look upon directly any more than he could stare into the sun.

"Now we dig him out," murmured the old man, and as he spoke the molten mass of light seemed to swell. Suddenly the topmost sprue began to spit. A colorless liquid spurted out into the waiting fire, which turned it into twists of acrid smoke.

"Smells bad, doesn't he, boy?"

The boy did not answer. The old man took up his heavy tongs and gripped the mold around the middle. The iron bands glowed red and white as he began to lift and tip the mold, pouring the molten metal, draining the contents of the crucibles into the groove of each opposing channel until the streams of light and heat met. The old man's arms shook from the weight. Cords of muscle rose on his back. Inch by inch the old man tilted the mold, his whole body rigid with effort. Slowly the bronze sank into the mold. Then it seemed to flow more quickly. And then suddenly it was gone.

The old man fell back, his chest heaving. Water bubbled in the bucket as the tongs sank within it. The boy pushed past Iguedo and stumbled outside. His skin seemed to burn and meeting the cool night air was like diving into cold water. His legs felt weak, his whole body feverish. He sat down next to the remnants of his charcoal pile. He may even have slept then, but for how long he could not guess. He did not know if he heard or dreamed the sounds that erupted out of the hut. When Iguedo shook him by the shoulder it was still dark.

"Fenenu. Fenenu, get up. Come inside."

He rose and shook his head in an effort to clear it. In the hut the old man was slumped on the ground. Shards of the mold lay scattered about him. He looked up at the boy's entrance, and the boy saw his face had changed in some way. There was a dullness to it, and behind that was something else: age. Before he had been old. Now he was ancient, and the boy was at a loss to explain in what exactly the change inhered. The boy approached, both fascinated and appalled at the old man's transformation.

"Eri cut the rivers," the old man mumbled. His voice was little more than a whisper. "Eri hardened the land. He planted yam. . . ."

"Yes, yes, yes!" Iguedo broke in, her voice harsh and impatient. "Eri made the sun shine and the grass grow and the birds sing and the fish swim. All these things, and yes, Eri hardened the land. And yes, Eri planted the yam. But now the land is hard. Now the yams grow. The rivers are cut. What good is Eri now?"

"Old woman . . ."

"What good, eh? Time to put Eri in his pit. Give him an Enyi-tusk to remind him of his sons. . . ."

"And his daughter? The first of the Eze-Ada?"

"Mind your mouth, old man!"

She shouted this, taking a step forward and even raising her arm. Caught between them, the boy tried to shrink back into the recesses of the hut. The old man caught him by the wrist. His grip was feeble now. The boy could have broken it easily if he had wished.

"Ifikuanim was not wrong," he said. "Not wrong. Not right, either. He made Ezodu, him and Enyi together. . . ."

"Yes?" the boy prompted. He understood none of it. There was something wrong with the enmity that had sprung up so suddenly between Iguedo and himself, something old and tired in it.

"It's for you to decide now," the old man said.

"Decide? Decide what?"

The old man shook his head. He felt Iguedo's hand on his shoulder.

"Come with me."

"Decide? Decide what?" he insisted.

"Usse will tell you. Now come with me," said Iguedo.

The old man looked away.

He got up and moved toward the door but found when he got there that Iguedo had walked to the back of the hut and was rummaging about in the darkness there. She gestured brusquely for him to join her. The old man kept his tools somewhere here. A great pile of old baskets, broken bits of furniture, worn-out raffia mats, coconut husks, odd sticks, and other unnameable rubbish were heaped up against the wall. Iguedo was clearing it away, throwing it all behind her, where it formed a new heap in the center of the hut. He bent to help her, and soon all that was left was a rickety frame of some kind in which palm fronds had been interwoven to form a screen. Iguedo knocked it aside to reveal a low doorway.

"Through here."

He had expected to find himself amongst the bushes that, he had assumed, surrounded the compound on all sides. Instead there was another room, very narrow this time. He could feel dried leaves underfoot, packed earth beneath those. The wall behind them was a kind of partition, then, and this one in front of them was the real exterior. Iguedo led him to the left, and they ducked down again. Another room. Or a chamber. Underfoot, the leaves had disappeared. Above, the roof seemed to have got higher.

"You can see?" she asked him.

He said that he could, although he was not at all sure how this was possible. An archway to one side led via a raised threshold to a chamber larger than the last, and the next one was larger again. Several smaller ones followed. Their walls and floors were made of hard mud, smooth and cool to the touch. The floors dipped and curved up to meet the walls. He ran his fingertips around the arch of the next, and it was only then that it struck him that the old man's compound could not possibly contain so many rooms or extend this far. How far was this? Where was he?

He stopped, suddenly apprehensive. Something knocked against his leg. Iguedo was carrying a basket. Heavy, by the feel of it. He knew what must be in it.

"Where are we?" he asked. "Where are we going?"

Her face was impassive, calm. "You wanted to see the White-men," she reminded him.

"White-men?" He shook his head, and as he did so he saw a smile spread across her face. "I've changed my mind," he said quickly. "I want to go back."

. . . too late . . .

"No, it's not," he protested. "We just turn around, go back through there, then turn. . . . He tried to remember. We turn . . ."

"Can't go back," she said. Her hand closed about his wrist. Her grip was like iron. "River only flows one way. Take this." She handed him the basket.

"What is it?" he asked, the weight of the bronze confirming what he already believed.

"You know what it is."

True, he thought, I know. But it cannot be for me. Only the Eze-Nri carried his image in bronze.

"Give it to Usse," the old woman said. "And do not ask me questions to which you already know the answer. Only the Eze-Ada may wash the body of the Eze-Nri. Only she may crown his successor."

"Usse? But she—" He broke off. Another question to which he already knew the answer. He looked away, taking in the implication of what she said. He knew he would hear no footsteps in those moments, no movement, no sound at all. All he could hear was the beating of his own heart. And he knew when he turned that she would be gone; that when he eventually decided to move on he would not find her; that when he called her name she would not reply. Questions and their answers. All known. None of them understood. He could only blunder forward, advancing through the chambers of his ignorance.

"Iguedo!" he shouted, and he kept on shouting until her voice sounded in answer:

"Iguedo? That's a story only women tell, Fenenu."

Her voice, but not her.

". . . and so, sire, it is this manner and for these reasons that I bring greetings from Fernando the Catholic, King of all Spain. I am Don Diego of Tortosa, as I mentioned before, the servant of my King, who bids me salute you in his place. So greetings, King of Nri, from the King of all Spain, whose wish it is to give a beast to Pope Leo the Holy Father, our Pope . . ."

So it went on, so-this and therefore-that, louder, then softer, and for hours, it seemed to Salvestro. Diego stood above them and delivered an address that swelled and stretched, turned back on itself and jumped sideways, offered paraphrases and explanations, repeated itself and took tangents that had so far encompassed Diego's deeds at Ravenna, his betrayal at Prato, his humiliations in Rome, and his journey to this place, which was Nri. From time to time it would rearrive seamlessly at its opening salute, and the words "King of Nri!" would signal its beginning again, although as time went on—and the speech with it—this reference to the dead man seated next to him in the pit assumed more of the character of a punctuation mark or an anchor by which Diego and the freight he carried might swing themselves through the current of this diatribe, the better for it to carry him off again. There was within it, however, a certain progression, or intensification, Salvestro thought, or imagined, or dreamed. Diego was waving his sword about now.

"And therefore, King of Nri, I stand before you now as a cipher of my master, the King of all Spain, Castile and Aragon and Navarre and Granada and the Kingdom of the Two Sicilies, as I described them to you earlier, called Fernando the Catholic. My so-called master. And the master, it would seem, of the Pope, who far from being holy is a murderer, and my enemy, too, and the agent of my disgrace. I would spit him on this sword if I could. And . . . And Fernando, too, for my fealty to him is broken, and not by me. He threw me to them through the efforts of his creature Cardona, that puffed-up coward, that aptly named 'Viceroy,' and he will have me hanged, if I return, for the murder of a preening courtier, which was a mistake. Yes, King of Nri, the injury done me was done by all of them. I imagine them wriggling together like skewered snakes on the point of this blade. . . . Anyway, King of Nri, for all these reasons and injuries and slanders, I stand before you now and offer myself as your servant."

He must have dreamed this, Salvestro decided. It was not so much this last bizarre conclusion, or the exhaustion overtaking him, or even—for all its fire—the lulling monotony of Diego's speech, that convinced him he was actually asleep. It was the voices.

They hummed, then buzzed, and then the buzzing grew louder, with odd shouts and cries rising faintly above the general noise. These were muffled, though, or blurred, smoothed over, or weighted down and unable to rise high enough for him to distinguish them, and whenever they grew louder the groundswell of noise beneath would rise to match them. It was getting closer. Coming toward him. He was alone—nothing new about that. But where?

He remembered skies like this, milky hazes of diffused light too bright to look up at directly. He seemed to be in one at present, with no discernible up or down, no extent in any direction. He must be standing on something, though? Yes. Grass. So there was that. And a pond off to the side, and beyond it some beech trees and then a little orchard of wild greengages. An eel slithered past. These things appeared not as though emerging from mist, but as though his eyes had been sun-blinded and were now returning to normal: these things had always been here. He had not been able to see them, that was all.

Next, the source of the noise appeared, which was a crowd of men, or an army, or a vast mob, for more and more of them came into view the farther he looked, their bobbing heads and waving weaponry—short thick swords, pikes, weighted clubs—rippling forward like a human sea . . . Toward himself. Time to run, he decided vaguely.

Too late. . . .

True, for they were already upon him, the time for running was gone, and yet, far from falling upon him like a pack of hungry dogs, their clubs thudding into his flesh and splintering the bones beneath, as he expected, the army of men flowed around and about him, swept him up and carried him along, burying him in their midst, where their noise engulfed him, their din pounding in his head, where each individual voice was drowned out and dulled by the volume of all the others: a cacophony of muddled need, each and every one of them lost within all the others. For they seemed to have been marching for so long, and so far, and they were desperate for it to end.

He looked about and began to spy faces he knew amongst the sea of heads about him: Diego first, shouting along with the rest, his face red with excitement or the cold; then Father Jörg, his sight miraculously restored, waving a silver cross and yelling out a field Mass for the men who were to die, Bernardo, too, although he seemed to be the same height as everyone else; then others of the monks, Gerhardt spitting against the heathens, HansJürgen beside him; and beyond him were some men he recognized from the Broken Wheel but had never spoken to in his life. And then, on the far edge of the mob, he saw her, separated somehow from the ragged men around her and skipping along quite unconcerned, hopping over the tussocks in her spotless white dress: Amalia. Impossible. For one thing, she was too short for him to see her over the bellowing cursing heads that surrounded him. Also, he thought, she had no place here. No role in what was to come, for he knew now where this army was marching and what they were here to do, or fail to do.

The ground began to rise. He looked along the coast and saw flat marshes broken by stands of saplings, beech and ash, but no sign that the island had ever been inhabited, no huts or fences. That was wrong, he thought to himself. There was a people here before this. He saw the great holm oak in the distance, the curve of the strand. He looked forward again. Ahead, the army had formed a line. They could march no farther, and their noise was changing in character, the war cries and boasts breaking up and becoming low groans, baffled anger, disappointed sighs: the sounds of failed purpose, of frustrated need, of their lack. Little by little, their voices died in their throats. They were halted there on the edge, at the limit of the point. They were silent.

He fought his way through them and looked down into the yellow-gray waters that crawled lazily about the cliff. The Water-man looked up at him, aping the motions of his limbs. He looked ridiculous, his arms and legs flopping about, his body hanging in the water down there while his own teetered on the raw edge above, amongst the serried ranks of the Lion's men. He watched the shape of himself stretch and distort. The Water-man was breaking up, coming apart, his mouth widening impossibly. To swallow him?

Niklot!

Not yet. The men around him are silent, their long-sought coordinate invisible, unreachable, as they search for missing walls and ramparts, listen for the hum of voices, clatter of footsteps, for the clangor of drowned Vineta. . . .

Salvestro!

But they see nothing, hear nothing. They will turn away. They will carry stones from quarries as far away as Brandenburg to build a church here, as a monument to their bafflement. . . . The Water-man was telling him this. He glanced down at him again, then stared. Now how had he failed to notice that before? The Water-man was black.

"Salvestro! Salvestro, wake up!"

"Niklot," he mumbled, coming blearily awake, "I am called. Or was."

There was a face staring into his, a black face, not old, not young, and not the Water-man's, either. A youth, he decided. Diego had fallen silent and seemed—he blinked, one arm searching for the floor to push himself upright—to be kneeling in front of the corpse. Bernardo was standing beside him, looking up. Then the youth said something he did not understand, turning as he did to the one figure not in the pit, whose reply he also did not understand but whom he recognized, beneath the thick lines of her facepaint and the braided coils of her hair.

"Get up," said Usse.

Bernardo looked at him anxiously. Salvestro rose slowly to his feet, but Diego remained kneeling in front of the seated figure.

"All of you."

Again, the youth addressed the woman standing above them. When he fell silent, Usse shook her head.

"I am the servant of the King of Nri," Diego said suddenly, still kneeling, speaking as much to the dead man as to the living woman behind him. "I attend him. I remain with him. My fealty is owed him."

There was another short exchange in their own language between the two of them. At the end of it Usse merely shrugged. Salvestro wondered how it was that he was awake, that he could dream the island and yet wake to this.

"Then stay," she told the kneeling soldier indifferently. "You two"—pointing first to Bernardo, then to Salvestro—"follow me."

The dust in the courtyard looked like white sand. The roof of the Oba cast a sharp black shadow under the moon's glare. Outside the compound a faint orange light wavered, just visible above the wall. The torches of the waiting men, he thought. Fenenu watched the two White-men slide hesitantly around the massive wooden door, the smaller one first, then his companion.

"Where are they going?" he asked the woman standing beside him.

It was she who had commanded them, speaking to them in their own language.

"Where have you sent them?"

"The River," Usse replied.

There was some shouting then. He heard the White-men's voices rise above the hubbub. They sounded harsh, like the roaring of animals.

Consider the tripartite nature of rivers. Source, course, and mouth. Rivers fatten as they approach the sea; they widen, or deepen, accumulating the donations of their watersheds, which have in turn accumulated rain. Rain falls. Rivers flood. The relationship is directly causal—hydraulic simplicity itself—and as, hereabouts, at least, the rains come once a year, so one might expect a correspondingly singular annual flood. Instead the river offers two: major and minor, a full-blooded bank-bursting walloping torrent followed about ninety days later by a sort of bore-in-reverse, a watery bump or weak echo that raises the water level by a foot or two, then falls away. . . . An anticlimactic and unengaging mystery, known around Idah, where it sometimes carries away the odd unmoored canoe, as the *yangbe*.

Consider the triply troubled nature of this particular river, the disjunctions and segments of its upper, middle, and lower courses. Top and tail flow through forests and savannahs, gurgle through ravines, and spread themselves over beds surrounded by greenery and growth. The wet season here is genuinely wet. The middle, however, flows through a baking desert, meandering and evaporating under a blazing cloudless sky. No clouds mean no rain. No rain means no flood. This part of the river is a noncontributor, a sponge, the sagging center in a fluvial amphimacer, mere delaying distance that the upper course's flood must negotiate to reach the lower, whose own flood is always long gone by the time of its depleted late arrival some time after the departure of the harmattan. It's not much more than a swell by then, a local curiosity for the remainder of its passage. In a good year it might raise a little spray around the rocks at Ansongo, but this apart it is more or less ineffective, a sad and somewhat useless little water-bump, unable to raise itself above anything except the lowest lying of the river's sandbanks. . . .

Not too high but satisfyingly broad, the sandbank that sits midstream between Onitsha and Asaba is usually the venue for a noisy market. The *yangbe* races down from Idah as though already anticipating at last getting some land underneath it, sweeping away the market women, rolling up and over the gentle hump, and doing some proper *flooding*. . . .

But usually the market has already gone, its traders happy in the knowledge that the *yangbe* never lingers long. Usually the sandbank is an empty gentle hump, but not this year. This year—tonight—it is crowded with livestock tethered to rafts.

There are goats, hogs, dogs, and rats. There are squirrels, geckoes, monitor lizards, and fruit-bats. Crates of varying sizes fashioned from interwoven sapling-branches and elephant grass hold chickens, crested guinea fowl, hornbills, parrots, and fruit-pigeons. Other crates hold toads, frogs, hermit-, ghost-, and hairy mangrove crabs. Special submersible baskets hold fish. There is a raft of baboons, and several of chimpanzees, and one that supports a solitary morose gorilla. Three antelope share a shifting platform made of balsa logs, and small hornless cattle are corralled in groups ranging from two to seventeen on pontoonlike structures with rails. There is a bull. There is a turtle. There are snakes tied to sticks.

And, in consequence, the benighted sandbank is loud with bleats, oinks, barks, squeals, chatterings, hissings, squawks, caws, tweets and twitterings, croaks, roars, pules, screeches, chirrups, wails, mooing, and ultrasonic whistles, for, weak as it is, the *yangbe* is now creeping up the edges of the fragile island, raising the water level and lapping at the outermost of the makeshift rivercraft. Three trays of chaffinches have already floated away, their feathered crews cheeping plaintively before being audibly devoured by waiting crocodiles. Several baskets of toads will soon follow. The cacophony began even before the men who had towed them here had climbed back into their pirogues and disappeared into the darkness. Now, as the cattle stamp, the chickens flutter, the snakes writhe, and the dolorous ape ineptly attempts to free itself from its bonds, it seems that every animal capable of sound is making as much of it as possible. Except one.

The largest of all the vessels assembled here sits in the very center of the sandbank. Perhaps this accounts for its passenger's calm. Or passengers. There are three of them, though only the most massive is visible, standing proudly erect on a raft built of whole tree-trunks lashed together lengthwise and widthwise with a pair of canoes extended one on each side as outriggers. So far, he has not made a sound or moved a muscle. He simply stands there in the midst of the din, waiting for the water to lift the raft off, and the other two passengers with it. They are in the canoes. Tied up.

"Salvestro?"

The two men had emerged from the compound and come face-to-face with the waiting mob. They had been seized, trussed, and bundled into two tapered coffins, or so it had appeared to Bernardo. He had lost sight of Salvestro as he was raised up and carried head-high through the forest, the men's shouts ringing in his ears and his head knocking against the wooden sides, for his captors moved at a prodigious rate. Suddenly the canopy had broken and the men had fallen silent. Bernardo had heard water and then felt his coffin being lowered into it. He was afloat. Men were splashing about in the water around him. He felt the tug on his craft as it was towed away from the bank. At first there was only the rhythmic slaps of the paddles in the water, but gradually these were superseded by a stranger noise and more mixed: unrecognizable wailings, shrieks, and growls.

The canoe was too deep or his bonds too tight for him to raise his head above the sides, but as the silent men had dragged his canoe ashore and hauled it over the sand to tie it to the raft, they must have passed directly beneath the animal. One minute, he was staring helplessly up at the stars. The next, a huge head swung over and blotted out the sky. A head the size of a water barrel. Eyes like a snake. A horn on the end of its nose. It looked down at him. He looked up at it. Then it swung back out of sight, the men dragged his craft around to the side of the raft, and he was left with his earlier view of the stars.

"Salvestro?" he tried again.

Over the last hour, the noise of the panicking animals had risen gradually to an earsplitting din, then—just as gradually—it had subsided in a manner he did not understand. Until now. Now he could hear the water lapping at the sides of his canoe. One end was rising as the water tried to lift it off the sand. There were other movements, too, but he did not want to think about those. They were coming from the raft. From the Beast.

"Salv—"

"Ssshh!" hissed Salvestro. "What if our voices startle it? Keep quiet, Bernardo."

He tried to keep quiet. Salvestro was scared, too. He heard it in his voice. His canoe was more or less floating now. Only the raft prevented it from drifting down the river like the animals. Where were the animals? The last sound he had heard was desolate mooing, growing fainter and fainter. Then nothing. . . . Silence. Just the water. He listened to it for a while.

The raft jolted.

He shouted, "Salvestro! I can't swim!"

"Keep calm, Bernardo!" Salvestro called back. "We're moving off the sandbank, that's all."

The raft began, very slowly, to scrape along the bottom. After about a minute of this, Salvestro called out again.

"Don't worry, Bernardo!" Then he added, "We've been in worse scrapes than this, haven't we?"

Bernardo felt the raft wheel about, his canoe swinging with it, shuddering as it scudded over the sandbank. Worse scrapes than this? He recalled running out of villages with the rest of the Christian Free Company in the middle of the night. Then, cowering in a ditch under the guns at Ravenna, and after that the woman at Prato . . . the one in the street. Then their own escape, Salvestro making him dive under the black water, choking down there. He was frightened. He hid under the tables in the Broken Wheel because Salvestro had left him there, and he couldn't pull the barrel out of the water because it was stuck somehow. It wasn't his fault. The monks arrived and lifted it out. Anything else? He had lain all night in a bog after a little girl dressed in white had skipped away and left them both there. . . .

Now he was floating down a river, in the dark, trussed up in the bottom of a canoe tied to a raft on which the very beast that had lured them here was now shifting its weight, bouncing his canoe up and down as though it wanted to capsize all three of them. Had they been in worse scrapes than this?

"No, Salvestro," said Bernardo, "we haven't."

VI

NAUMACHIA

$\mathcal{V}$ioletta's worn leather slippers padded quietly over the cold flagstones. Drafts chilled her ankles where the threadbare gown she had worn throughout the winter fell short. She recalled the chests that, in previous times, would be lowered from the attics, her ladies-in-waiting cracking open their lids and brushing away the wax used to seal them against the moths, then lifting out her winter gowns and shawls. Rich velvets and woolens, their laundered folds falling heavily open. The mere sight of them had warmed her. It would have been more practical, she now told herself, to have plugged the gaps beneath the doors, to have shuttered up the windows, to have paid fewer milliners and more masons. The palazzo was a low and ramshackle sprawl, standing alone on the low rise of the foreshore. The sea sat before it and the marshes behind it. Winds whistled down from the mountains to the north and east, or off the sea, or along the coast. She shivered, walking down the passageway. Two more women had arrived the previous night, and there was nowhere for them to sleep as yet. She heard the cart being pulled about in the courtyard below. Its iron-banded wheels grated on the cobbles, more of which had lifted after the frost got its fingers underneath them. An airy thud would be the stable doors closing. Perhaps the new arrivals might sleep there, if more blankets could be found? Violetta climbed stairs. She considered the realignment of her circumstances.

A door opened somewhere and the cold waft of air made her clutch her elbows. The coarse voices of the women quartered in what had once been her dining hall reached her ears in dulled bursts of noise. The wind plucked a shutter open and banged it against its frame. She turned a corner and walked past rooms that had once played host to her friends when they had quit Spezia's pestilential summer and gathered here for the *villegiatura*. She had taken her lovers from these rooms. Amongst her new companions she was the oldest woman in the house, though many of them appeared more aged than she. Their profession exhausted them, coarsened their features. Each repetition of the act was vulgarly supposed to shorten one's life by a day, which was a silly superstition, thought Violetta. One might grow old from a season of such work. The sort of nonsense peddled by her brother. She reached out to pull the shutter closed. The seaward vista was darkening, and the wind had swung around to blow directly inland. Thunderheads were piled up on the western horizon. Violetta shivered again. Herself, the child, and bracketed between them a houseful of clientless Christ-less Magdalens. Her

brother had grown exasperated, then furious when she had reassigned her revenues, withdrawing them from his bishopric and pouring them into the maintenance of this hospice. It had taken a year to persuade him to send a priest to hear
the poor creatures' confessions. A drunk had finally arrived, snored his way
through the absolutions, watered his mule, and succumbed to his stupor in the
stables. Faced with her fury and to make amends, her brother had traveled, improbably enough, all the way to Rome to petition His Holiness on their behalf
and returned with a grant of three hundred ducats, which the child had then refused for reasons she would not or could not explain. Another small mystery to
add to the others. She had appeared in the courtyard, a waif found wandering
amongst the wagons loaded for the autumn return to Spezia three years before,
and had been brought before the mistress of the palazzo herself. Her account of
how she had got there was a confused and impossible fantasy studded with the
gruesome incidents that little girls loved to frighten themselves with and peopled
by the improbable saviors who saved them. She was well-spoken. Some of the
words she used were peculiar to Florence, but that meant little except that she
had heard and remembered them. She had refused all inquiries and had asked for
nothing. She spoke to God in a familiar way, and God spoke back in kind. Violetta's brother, on being told of her, had declared that she was a charlatan, but her
brother was a peasant, a carnival-Bishop at best. Violetta had taken her in. And
then others, which had turned out to be a more vexatious and less mysterious
story altogether, whose continuance plumbed the depth of her charity and as yet
had found it bottomless. Her childish charge was a kind of mirror that reflected
only good, and Violetta's image of herself transfixed her. This was her current
understanding.

A little turret at the southern corner of the building had once stood alone.
The palazzo had encroached upon it steadily—first a gazzara, then a cottage of
ill-defined utility. Her grandfather had added a small chapel and a gallery projected over or through the roofs of the foregoing—until the gallery had succumbed to the inclemencies of the Genoese winter and been replaced by the
closed passageway Violetta now traversed, and the earlier buildings became piers
to raise it a somewhat purposeless distance above the ground. It met the turret
halfway up its height and broached its wall by means of a low doorway. Violetta
contemplated a spiral stairway of flagstones. The wind blew in by the superfluous
doorway below and whirled up in freezing gusts. She climbed slowly and steadily.
The room at the top was little more than a platform, and although the winds that
blew through its windows were refreshing in the hottest months of summer, at
any other time of the year they bit and sucked the warmth from her flesh until
her bones felt as though carved from ice. Its tenant, however, seemed not to
notice.

"Whoosh!"

She was standing in front of the seaward window, looking out over the water.

White crests were forming farther out from the shore, and the wind was blowing harder.

"Whoosh!"

She jumped, throwing up her arms, sending her white dress flying about her as she turned in midair and crouched in front of the older woman. Sometimes, Violetta thought, she was like an animal, angelic and undomesticated. Sometimes she was only a little girl. Today she did not know. The girl turned again and stared intently out at the troubled sea. Violetta waited a few moments before speaking.

"Amalia."

"Have they been fighting again?" asked the little girl in her singsong voice.

"No," she answered.

Amalia nodded without looking around.

The two newcomers had arrived cold, soaked by a late afternoon shower and in a foul humor with each other. Violetta had suspected that they would come to blows. Rightly. It had begun in the laundry room, where they had sat wrapped in blankets while their clothes—the usual brightly dyed rags—had been dried. She had left them there and gone in search of bedding. Suddenly two naked harridans had spilled into the courtyard, screaming and scratching at one another. She had seen them from an upper window and hurried down. Fights were not uncommon. After the noisy violences of the town it was the calm of this place that set them off. She had arrived in the courtyard only to find a ring of silent women surrounding the pugilists, who were now separating and feigning modesty at their nakedness, appearing cowed and oddly unresentful. Amalia was within the ring, peering at them in a curious fashion, calming them in a way Violetta did not understand. It had happened many times before and in many different circumstances. The women did not question it. Only she remained puzzled.

"Amalia, what are you doing?" she asked now.

By way of an answer, the little girl suddenly jumped up again, making the same exclamation as before.

"Whoosh!"

Her feet thudded on the wooden floor as she landed.

"I'm watching the shipwreck," she announced.

Startled, Violetta hurried over to the window. The wind was blowing full in her face, and her eyes stung from the cold. She peered out over the gray sea, which was laboriously piling up dark mounds of water, then flattening them again. Beyond these, crests of white water were breaking out of the dark liquid, and beyond these she could see only turbid brine. The thunderheads were nearer and blacker and higher. There would be a storm tonight, that much was obvious. She would have to marshal two of the more trustworthy of the women and have them check the doors and shutters before lights out. She looked left and right, up the coast to the low headland of Punta Bianca to the north and down to where the strand fell away, curving inland until it met the waterway to Massa. In the very distance she thought she could see the first of the rain, an advancing curtain of gray. But there was no ship.

She looked down curiously at the child, whose eyes did not seem to be fixed on any point in particular but whose face showed every sign of animation, as though she were indeed witnessing the catastrophe she claimed. Her mouth twitched, her hands jumped halfway to her mouth, then fell to her sides again, she leaned forward, then seemed to be pushed back by some ghastly detail. She jumped and shouted again:

"Whoosh! Oh, the poor sailors! Their souls are like . . . like rockets! They look *beautiful*. . . ."

Violetta watched with her for a minute or more. In the first months after the child's arrival she had frowned in puzzlement at the odd pronouncements that issued from Amalia's lips. At times, the child had lacked propriety. At others, she had seemed to descend into a matter-of-fact insanity. When her brother had arrived with his three hundred ducats, the child had spent the whole period of his visit laboriously dividing the coins into piles. She had then informed him that the amount was seven ducats short, that Jesus had been sold for thirty pieces of silver, not twenty-three, and that her brother's lips looked like sausages. After his departure Violetta had gently upbraided the child, who had skipped away, singing, "A sausage is a sausage is a sausage. . . ." What was one to make of this?

Amalia counted things. There were seven thousand five hundred and thirty-one blades of grass between the stables and the gatehouse, or had been over a certain two days last June. She invented languages all of whose words rhymed with each other, outlined extraordinarily complex descriptions of God and then forgot them the next day. When confronted with such inconsistencies by Violetta, she would dismiss all objections by saying that God had been like that yesterday, but today He was quite different, and then launch into a yet more incredible account. In her childlessness, Violetta felt, a child had been sent to her. The wrong one, possibly. Children were troublesome beings. Her brother's initial false concern had not veiled his customary and unctuous malice, but still it had pricked her skin. Ask yourself what she is doing here, he had urged, a familiar hand upon her arm. Why is she here, dear sister? For want of anything better to say, she had parroted the latest of the child's burblings to the prelate. Amalia was waiting for her savior, and her savior would come from the sea. This phantom ship was part of that, perhaps. In the failing light, the sea crawled and slithered like a nest of snakes.

"There is no shipwreck," she told the child flatly.

"Whoosh," replied Amalia. "Not yet, no. But tonight it will be too dark to see anything except for their souls. I wish you could see them, Violetta, all of them shooting up." The child paused and looked up at her. "Nearly everyone goes to heaven."

Violetta resisted the temptation to ask archly if "nearly everyone" included herself. She was the eldest daughter of one of the oldest families of Spezia, a town where she was known for her charity, her vigor, and her levelheadedness. Her father had distinguished himself in three campaigns against the French, and her brother was Spezia's Bishop, albeit a venal one. Her love affairs were discreetly managed and had given her much pleasure. It was difficult to understand the changes that had so transfigured that life. Perhaps the women she took in, most of whom would leave again in the summer to resume their trade in town, were only the rudiments of a new mode of existence. Goodness was a maze through which she craved guidance. Was this humility? Weakness? To be pitied would be the pariah-hood she could not bear. . . . Silly woman. The child was only a child, painting her imaginings and observations, her heart's desires and soul's registerings, willy-nilly on the same fantastically jumbled canvas, where cows roamed freely with monsters, where unnamed "saviors" blew the water out of their lungs and arose from the sea to claim her, where invisible ships descended from the sky and smashed themselves on waves made of granite.

"Ooh!" Amalia clamped her hands to her ears. "The masts have snapped! She's starting to break up, Violetta!"

With that, the child spun away from the window and began to stomp maniacally in a circle around the room, her windmilling arms punching the air, her voice imitating the creaks, groans, and crashes of the stricken ship. She made one circuit, then a second, then a third, and her movements grew more and more violent, her feet pounding more and more heavily. She was lost in the privacy of her game, Violetta realized as she dodged away from the child's mad progress. But it was nothing more than a frightening game. Amalia shrieked and shouted and stamped and stabbed, now and again interrupting this ugliest of dances to leap into the air, each time calling out, "Whoo-oosh!" or "There goes another one!" while Violetta, determined not to intervene, stared at her with ill-concealed alarm. The room resounded with the child's cries, which, after they had grown as loud as her lungs would permit, became more anguished, more piercing, as though something that had lain concealed within her uncanny but blunt-spoken self-possession was now cutting its way out. As though, Violetta believed or realized, it was not a ship that was breaking apart at all. Nonsense, she admonished herself. One of her brother's better barbs: You think too deeply for a woman, sister. Amalia was a little girl and no more than that. She had feelings after all; it was only now she chose to exhibit them. Grasp hold of her. Comfort her, a child in a child's pain. *If only you could see, Violetta.* . . . Violetta did not see, or not then, nor did she move to comfort the child.

And yet there would be a shipwreck, in the night and less than a league from the shore and invisible as foretold in the child's grotesque performance, in a storm that smashed the vessel and drove her down, pounding and ripping at the corpse of its enemy. Tattered flesh and splinters of bone. Exorbitant victory. That she should "think too deeply"? Pah! Not deeply enough, she would decide then. Brother Bishop was the silly and greedy fool he had always been and would always be. The child had been right in her rudeness and in her strangeness, and she had been right about the ship. Her mad circuits had narrowed until she was almost marching on the spot, her little head jerking from side to side, her half-controlled limbs twitching like a puppet's. Violetta turned from this vision in distraction, which, she told herself later, was only the prelude to her running to the child. . . . She turned to the window, the encroaching night, the rising sea, the thunderclouds descending like hammers to smash whatever might fall to them.

To a ship. At first she saw only a distant speck or mere interruption of the darkening storm that, it seemed, was about to overtake it. Violetta stared as the speck grew in definition. A vessel under near bare spars was running before the wind in a hopeless dash to drag itself out from between the great black plates of sea and sky that met like millstones to crush it. But it was still leagues away from landfall. She turned back to Amalia in amazement. The child had fallen silent.

"You knew?" she demanded softly. "But how could you know?"

"Whoosh," Amalia mumbled. She sat down quickly and bent her head. "Whoosh, whoosh. Three more souls."

She appeared crumpled, skeins of her black hair scattered about her face. Violetta glanced out the window, and at that moment the wind blew the first spatter of rain into her face. Even at such a distance the vessel seemed to lurch as it toiled north and east in the heavy sea. Making for the gulf, she supposed. Night would fall within the hour.

"Oh," the child said behind her. She repeated it, as though she had just remembered or realized a fact that now surprised her.

She was picking at the linen of her dress, face still mostly covered by her hair. She hiccuped, then sniffed. Violetta watched her curiously. The mad marionette of a minute ago was a limp ragdoll. The ragdoll sniffed again, then wiped her nose on her dress.

"Amalia," she exclaimed, never having witnessed the phenomenon before, as much surprised by the sudden realization of its earlier absence as by its appearance now. Why had she never remarked it? "You are crying."

But the crying seemed to end as suddenly as it began, and when the child looked up her eyes were hardly reddened.

"Whoosh," Amalia said quietly. "Bernardo's going to drown."

"Who is Bernardo?" asked Violetta.

"Bernardo is Salvestro's friend," replied Amalia.

Violetta awoke to a monotonous endless drumroll, the sound of rain beating against the shutters. When darkness had fallen she had closed them, and the two of them had sat in silence. There was nothing more to be seen or done. The storm began to batter in earnest, a shrieking gale driving it onto the coast. The seas rose up and pounded furiously on the beach, the normally inert gray waters releasing their store of noise for hour after hour. Eventually the din had numbed her and driven her down into an exhausted stupor, where thought of the fates being suffered in the watery turmoil outside had been unable to find her. Now the predawn light, entering through the cracks in the shutters, etched the room's roughly hewn stones and roof-beams in cold bluish-gray light. Her neck ached. She looked blearily about her: a small wooden chest, a crucifix hung high on the wall, a small puddle of water where the rain had found an entrance. The nest of blankets in which the child made her bed was empty. Amalia was gone.

Outside, the rain fell in sheets, each new gout of water slapping down onto the beach and disappearing there as though the surface of the gritty mud were a taut sheet of gray silk that the pelting droplets pierced insensibly, driving on into some airy emptiness beneath. The sea's surface prickled under the same assault. Violetta's shoes sank into the mud as she climbed down the scarp. The blanket she had thrown over her head was already soaked through, and rain trickled between her fingers where she clasped it bunched beneath her chin. When she looked back, the turret was no more than a thickening of darkness through the rain, the eastern sky a steel gray screen behind it. The palazzo sank into the foreshore. They would not have seen it, she thought, if any had made it ashore. She stood on the rain-lashed beach and shivered. The bare sea heaved and stretched away.

The vessel, or the pieces of a vessel, was all around her. Up and down the beach as far as she could see, embedded in the sand at strange angles, were broken spars and beams, massive curved compass timbers, smashed planks, and barrel staves. A section of decking the height of two men seemed to have been peeled off entire and driven into the mud like an ax-blade. A splintered line of railings pointed jaggedly out to sea, appearing now as futile late defenses against the slopping waves. Farther down the beach a single massive pole with a crosspiece near its top stabbed the shore in an exact vertical as though a huge hand had wielded it like a sword. She tried to grasp the force that had snapped it off and planted it here, a great mocking cross to mark the men who had died beneath it. They were here, too, or some of them. Scattered amongst the detritus were low and irregular humps, unexceptional accumulations of tatters and rags: the ship's human jetsam.

A light caught her eye then. A door had opened in the palazzo, and three or four of the women were making their way out to the beach. She saw them hesitate and huddle together beneath their shawls as the rain greeted them with its first cold slaps. The wreck's transitory monuments studded the strand to north and south: rope-ends and flapping canvas snagged in splintered poles and planks, the timbers themselves set in mud, water, and sand. Amalia emerged from behind one of the larger piles of wreckage, heaped up and dumped some two or three hundred paces away. She was carrying a stick. Violetta squinted. The child seemed oblivious of the rain, moving about in a methodical fashion between the low humps and using the stick to poke at them. Two pokes, a short wait, another poke, and then she would move on to the next. Violetta was already thinking of the work to be done before the tide swept in that afternoon. There were twenty corpses, at least, and each one would have to be dragged up the scarp. The tide would probably fetch up more. It might go on for days, she realized grimly. Down the beach, Amalia came to a halt. The ground about the palazzo was marshy even in summer. Now it would be waterlogged. How would they bury them? she wondered. Amalia had sunk to her knees now, as though she were prostrating herself. . . . No. As though she were wrestling. But with a corpse? Violetta took two curious, wondering steps, then broke into a run. Beneath the child's clumsy assault, the corpse had moved.

It was lying facedown, trying to rise. The feet scraped and scratched, searching for purchase in the mud while its hands grasped handfuls of the same stuff as though trying to pull itself up hand over hand. It was naked except for the rags of something that once had been a shirt, and the cleft between its legs opened and closed with these spasmodic efforts. The limbs were emaciated and spattered with mud that seemed ingrained in the flesh, for the rain did not wash it off. Where the skin showed through the filth it was either bone white or broken with rashes and sores, and when the "corpse" at last managed to raise its head its face was that of a blind man, staring ahead and seeing nothing. Amalia was trying to turn the body onto its back. Him, she forced herself to acknowledge, for it was a man, though he seemed bestial somehow, something that had yet to become human or had been driven beyond that by his privations. She came to herself with a start, took the sodden blanket from her back, and knelt beside the child. The man was trying to speak, but his incoherent mumble made no sense. With her own help, the little girl rolled him over onto the blanket. The man grunted again, struggling to speak.

"I've told you three times already," Amalia said in a tone of girlish exasperation. "He's drowned. They're *all* drowned, except you, Salvestro."

The man's eyes closed. The eyebrows that wolves have, thought Violetta, instantly shaking her head at this irrelevance. Practicalities, she insisted to herself. The child's discovery had unnerved her. How to carry him inside.

"He's going to die," said a voice behind her. "When they stop shivering, that's when they die. I've seen it before."

A woman who called herself Minetta was standing behind her. The three others she had seen were beside her, all four looking down at the still body, which had indeed stopped shivering. Had he been shivering before? Violetta could not remember.

"No, he's not!" Amalia sounded outraged at the suggestion, as though it were a personal slight.

"We'll get him up to the house," Minetta said then. She was moving to wrap the blanket around their burden when one of her companions let out a little shriek.

"Urgh!"

She was standing on something that Violetta had taken for a large, gently rounded stone. It was gray, oddly textured, and when the woman offered it a prod with her toe, it gave beneath the pressure. She jumped back.

"It's soft!"

"What is it?" asked Minetta.

The first woman looked helplessly to her companions, who looked back at her, then down again at the stone-that-was-not-a-stone.

"Well?" the woman appealed with an edge of hysteria in her voice that was as much a product of the rain and the cutting wind as the enigma buried in the sand.

For a moment or two no one spoke.

"I know what it is," said Amalia.

She was smiling delightedly, hands clasped behind her back, her shoulders swiveling as she rocked with pleasure at their bafflement. She pointed to the creature in the blanket, who seemed to be trying to rise and perhaps move toward the object of their consternation. His efforts were too feeble to be sure.

"He knows what it is, too."

The man croaked or coughed.

"What, then?" the woman demanded.

"Not telling," replied Amalia.

A ship is marching on Rome: a three-master, square-rigged, pennants a-flutter to signal plague, which perhaps explains the paucity of reliable eyewitness accounts. It finds its dry docks a little way outside the walls of the cities, which it assiduously skirts, bedding itself down each night in the furrow of adjacent knolls or lodging itself within an impromptu scaffold of burly tree-trunks. Its topmost spars are glimpsed surmounting low hills, its fabric passes more or less concealed behind this or that copse of evergreens. So many planks are sprung off its frame that it seems to bristle with stubbly feathers. Presumably it once had wings, too. Four hatches cut in its barnacled underside allow its peculiar method of locomotion. From its punctured underside protrude four enormous gray legs.

Alternatively, far from being contained in the ship, the Beast is actually carrying it. Disassembled, naturally, but with cabins fashioned from its timbers to protect the heroic crew from the inclemencies of the Ligurian, or Tuscan, or Sienese, or Umbrian weather. It is said to be gray, rotund, and approximately the size of a cathedral. Some versions have it rescuing children discovered en route from under waterwheels or the tops of tall trees. Others have it laying waste the countryside in the manner of the Calydonian boar. Others still dispense with the ship, and some with the crew, too, though the latter version is rare. Vich and Faria are active in the city, and the nature of the crew is the main focus of their attention. Is this a Spanish Beast or a Portingale? The purveyors of rumor would hardly be so stupid as to exclude the minor but lucrative diplomatic market. But the deepest pocket is known to be papal, and his familiars in the inns and taverns, in the salons, streets, and naves, have made it more than clear that papal interest is focused on the Beast.

In consequence, the Beast changes shape and size with bewildering rapid-

ity—the rumor-market is nothing if not liquid—responding day by day to What
His Holiness Wants, understood as a direct correlative of What His Holiness Pays,
and a medium-size gush of soldi drawn from the Apostolic Camera and secured
against the latest of a series of loans made by Filippo Strozzi, dispensed in dribs
and drabs from the grubby purses of a motley collection of ambitious curialists,
poetasters, costermongers, ne're-do-well minor nobility on the slide, and well-to-
do social-climbers on the make, has so far bought only the vague consensus that
it is gray, that it is big, and that it has a horn on the end of its nose. If it exhibits
any greater degree of vacillation and duplicity, His Holiness has observed to
Ghiberti, they will have to invite it to join the League of Cambrai.

Anyway, the Beast has landed and is on its way to him. Has been for weeks
now. A triangular swath of possible-Beasts with a base stretching from the Ligurian Alps to the Comacchio valley has found its inevitable apex in Rome, a
funnel of dwindling diameter down which the "real" Beast has been washed on a
sea of specie along with its imitators to arrive, after a final sifting-out, here. Or almost here. The trend is clear even if the exact location is not. There was a rash of
sightings around Montepulciano ten days ago and a speckling a little below
Viterbo after that. The market in southerly and easterly reports has all but collapsed, and Beastly-possibilities in the west are going from bad to nonexistent.
From the north to Rome is the most likely course, if it does in fact exist.

"It will be here before tonight," says Ghiberti, who is standing behind him. It
is not hard to divine the Pope's thoughts. Of late, he has only had the one. "Here
in the city, if it is not arrived already."

"Arrived already! Impossible. How would I not know if it were in Rome? If
it were to roar in Trastevere, I would hear it in my sleep. If it shat on a stone of the
Via Appia, I would have the droppings in my possession before they so much as
stopped steaming."

"No one has seen it," Ghiberti answers bluntly. "Everyone has heard of it
only because it is so profitable to do so, Holiness."

"Not true," counters Leo. "Size, color, distinguishing features? Gray, big, horn
on its nose. All the reports agree in these particulars. How do you explain that,
my cynical secretary?"

"By the fact, Holiness, that your agents have been offering to pay between
three soldi and a full gold scudo for any and all information relating to a beast described by them as gray, big, and having a horn. . . ."

"That was later," Leo answers tetchily. "The first reports were clear enough.
The ones from Spezia. . . ."

"From Massa and Carrara, Holiness. As I recall, those reports mentioned a
hay-cart that floated miraculously above the ground suspended by a single golden
thread from the ankle of an angel of tender years and attended by anything between one and a score of vagrants. The animal itself was said to be in the cart.
Something of an afterthought, I recall thinking. At the time . . ." He stops there,
for the Pope is glaring at him. "It is the orators, Holiness," he continues more

humbly, once again the self-effacing keeper of ledgers, the docile butt of his master's wit. "Vich. Faria. I have men in both their camps, and they know no more than we do. For the Portingales, a ship named the *Santa Ajuda* arrived from the Indies and took on supplies at the mouth of the Tagus more than two months ago. Since then, nothing has been heard."

"And Vich?"

"The little charade he played for you at Ostia seems to have been the only act of the Spanish comedy. The local fishermen were of one mind. That ship was only afloat because it lacked the decency to sink. There will be no gift from the Spaniards, and there is no evidence of one from the Portingales. It was you yourself who proposed this contest, Holiness. And it was you who linked it to the question of the bull—"

"Dear Ghiberti, do not trouble yourself," Leo breaks in airily. "The bull will be published tomorrow, and I will hand it over in person, sealed *sub plumbo* with the heads of Peter and Paul, signed Leo Episcopus Ecclesiae Catholicae in my best Lombard hand on parchment thick as board. As promised. And the Beast will be here to contribute his hoofprint. There now, does that reassure you?"

It is apparent to Leo, peering solicitously at his secretary, that it does not. Ghiberti is more troubled than he calculated. It makes no difference whether they have their bull or not, he wants to tell him. They will draw their fantastic frontier. They will form a battle-line the diameter of the globe and sail east and west to kill each other on the other side of the world. Perhaps they will slice the world north to south next. Perhaps they will upend the two halves and join them at the poles to form an hourglass. They are in league with each other, in any case—he would especially like to tell Ghiberti that. But the bull is his word; *Praecelsae devotionis et indefessum fervorem, integrae fidei puritatem, ingeniique in Sanctam Apostolicam observantiam. . . .* Sadoleto presented it for his inspection in the Cancellaria with the air of a singer who has somehow resolved a cacophonous and conflict-ridden sheet of music into clear and effortless harmony and now condescends to return it to its composer, its knots untied and puzzles solved, more obviously beautiful and yet tainted by the implication of the improvement. He wanted to tell Sadoleto, too. At root, the exquisite tissue of compromise and half-truth was theirs, not his. He was merely the place where their separate parts met in dissonance and discord. His word was the Pope's, and the Pope was the Servant of the Servants of God. Did Vich and Faria serve God?

"Do not trouble yourself," he repeats vaguely, turning to look out of the window.

The sheet of water now covering the lower courtyard of the Belvedere had spread with miraculous rapidity: a puddle, a pool, a lake . . . Now a little sea, three hundred paces by two, bounded by the loggia to the right, the steps leading up to the next level in front of him, the palace itself, and on the left—Leo pokes his head out of the window—a rather unsightly palisade of sandbags now being gradually concealed by tiers of outsize steps. Leno's men are hard at work sawing timber under the direction of their foreman, many of them standing up to their waists in the freezing water to maneuver the longest lengths into position. Others, similarly bedraggled, habits tucked into the toolbelts slung about their waists, are sizing up the fountain in the center. Leno has designed an ornamental platform that will sit above it. A throne will sit on the platform. He, Leo, will sit on the throne. Or rather, he, Leo, will sit on the throne in effigy, for someone else will actually do the sitting. Standing in for him, as it were. And probably—at the climax of battle—falling in for him as well. Splosh.

He leans farther out of the window to see if he can catch a glimpse of Hanno in the gardens beyond the workmen's sandbags. Hanno will be his champion. Last night he improvised a little prayer for his victory, although as the ultimate arbiter of the battle, he will be careful to keep this partiality to himself. If only it had been possible to enlist the orators. . . . Faria equipped with a trunk. Vich with the addition of a horn. Or perhaps the other way about.

"Of all the water-fights ever staged in the palace of the Pope," a voice offers from behind him, "this will undoubtedly be the most splendid."

"Naumachia!" he snaps back automatically. "It is not a 'water-fight.' It is a naumachia. My predecessor had bullfights. Commodus cut the heads off giraffes. I, on the other hand, a lover and patron of the gentler arts . . ." He stops there, for the voice behind him is laughing. Ghiberti does not laugh.

Whoever actually is laughing then slaps him heartily on the back, causing him to jerk forward into space and his belly to extrude over the sill, where the narrowness of the casement pinches it tight. Thus bisected, he reaches down to maneuver it back inside, but as he does so a second voice begins declaiming from the loggia below:

> O Leo! So low were we
> 'Ere thee. Now none say no
> Though there are those decline our fee
> Not ye! A mere giulio? No, a scudo d'oro!

A poet, dressed in the inevitable black, one arm folded across his breast (indicating sincerity), the other extended at full stretch toward him (an aiming device), bows deeply from the arcade below him and to his right.

"Very good," he calls back. "Very nicely done." He waves his thanks one-handed while the other tries to lever his stomach back inside. He attempts a discreet wriggle, but he is stuck tight as a cork, and the poet has now been joined by another, who is taking up position to deliver his own encomium, when suddenly, from behind him, two enormous arms shoot past his ears, bend at the elbows, then retract with tremendous force, knocking him bodily back inside. He finds himself on his back in the bearlike clasp of Cardinal Bibbiena.

"Poets?" the Cardinal inquires sympathetically.

Leo nods unhappily.

Ghiberti hovers over them, appearing faintly ridiculous with the plump un-opened ledger clasped protectively to his chest, unsure what to do. The inexpert tumblers look up at him.

"Take a seat," Leo says innocently. "You could join us down here on the floor."

Ghiberti purses his lips and shakes his head. He is waiting to be dismissed now, thinks the Pope. How fickle I am with my servants: the servants of the Ser-vants of the Servant of God.

"You may go."

Ghiberti and his ledger glide away, leaving the two of them still sprawled on the floor. Through the crack of the closing door, he glimpses groups of black-capped curialists and notaries, two veiled women nodding to one another, indo-lent youths leaning against walls, scaffolding for the painters. The Sala di Constantino hums with their noise, which stops as the door is opened, then starts again as the door booms shut. Leo nods in the opposite direction, and the two men struggle to their feet.

More painters perched on scaffolding are at work in the Stanza di Segnatura. Indeed, they seem to have become a fixture there. Last summer the ceiling was predominantly green. Then, for a few brief weeks, it was yellow. Now it seems to be green again. An outsize seagull is dropping splats on the floor as they pass be-neath. Several paint-spattered faces peer down at them.

"Storm at sea?" hazards Bibbiena, pausing to look up. "Marsh gas over the Borgo?"

Leo ignores this and gestures shortly for him to continue into the Stanza di Incendio, which is painterless, and poetless, and where the Pope turns on his striding Cardinal, bringing the big man up short.

"So, will Hanno be performing solo tomorrow? Tell me now, is the animal in the city or not?"

This surprises Bibbiena, Leo observes. Directness is a rarity in their ex-changes, its meaning unfixed by usage.

"It is."

The quick confirmation rattles between them, the red-robed Pope and his ermine-trimmed prelate. Dumpy stomach almost pressed against the bearlike man, Leo clasps his hands in front of him and Bibbiena takes a step back. The cleverest of his cardinals, the most alert to the feints of his bonhomie. He has a fi-brous quality that even Dovizio lacks. As for the rest of them, the old warhorses like Petrucci and Serra, his onetime peers Riario and Farnese and d'Aragona, they are stateless princes, all glitter and pomp. Bibbiena, he suspects, understands this well. Does he then understand the Beast? At mass today he had recalled the whiff of taper-smoke mixed with burning flax, Farnese's hands extending toward his head, bearing the pearl-encrusted tiara. What had caught his eye, then? A little

gleam of silver in the lime green of the Cardinal's cap, a tiny finely detailed
brooch. A prancing horse . . . No, a unicorn. Lover of virgins, who were able to
tame the animal with a Marian caress of their long white hands. Lurking in the
matted fringes of his purpose is the slash of tusk or horn along the adversary's
belly and then, tumbling down from the denaturing birth, unsteady at first on its
fawnish props but quickly regaining the strength lost in its long interment, white-
haired, soft-skinned, bright-horned . . . unshackled at last from the coarse prison
of its hide. . . . But what? He believes only, and fondly, that the battle will be a
kind of negation, that between the two adversaries lies a third truth, a pristine
creature preserved within their caked and coarsened skins, for just as there are
truer Romes beneath *Ro*-ma, so God's ciphers grow filthy with handling and the
accretions of use. How to uncover the infant in its chrisom, the soft nerve cased
in its scarred and stinking armor? He has never learned to wield a sword, so a
piece of whimsy in its stead, Bibbiena's water-fight. The Beast is here. It is a bright
and beautiful day, the sky cloudless, the air cold and perfectly still. When Lucifer
was thrown from heaven, he thinks, it would have been air like this through
which he fell. Leo pictures him blazing, his angel's flesh melting and hardening
into a prison of nerveless scars. Whose hands would strip it off? Where would he
find his enemy, the one whose cuts and slashes would free him? Bibbiena shifts
his feet uncomfortably on the patterned floor. The Pope concentrates. Where I?

"Where?" he asks abruptly.

Bibbiena shakes his head, mildly surprised after the long silence. "I do not
know exactly. Perhaps Ghiberti . . ."

"Ghiberti did not know it was even in the city. How do you?"

His tone is abrupt, even harsh. He softens it, musing aloud to himself on why
Ghiberti would not know. Soon the cadences of mockery are bubbling happily in
the roof-space of the *sala,* constructing there a flattering comparison between his
secretary and the Cardinal, an unvoiced apology. Bibbiena loves him after all.
Haughtiness was his brother's preserve. Poor Piero.

"I only wondered"—rearriving at last where he left off—"how you came by
this intelligence? Assuming, of course, that you did not simply reach into your
own omniscient mind and divine it there unaided."

"My mind?" Bibbiena arches his eyebrows. "I hocked my mind to Chigi ten
years ago. For the price of my horse, if I remember correctly, which I do not. My
memory paid for its shoes."

"And your soul?"

"Sold for this—" Bibbiena touches his Cardinal's hat. "Cheap at the price."

"A Cardinal with a soul would be an unnatural beast in Rome," offers Leo.

"Unnatural beast, yes."

There is a short silence, which quickly becomes oppressive.

Bibbiena says, "The source of this intelligence is Rosserus."

At this, the silence resumes and bifurcates. The pair digest the implications of
this in separate contemplations. Rosserus rarely means exactly the same thing to

any two people, and Rosserus-as-the-source-of-a-rumor adds a further twist, for Rosserus himself (or herself, or itself) is only rumored to exist, and only then in the most tenuous and loose-tongued discursive practices, such as idle chitchat, nostalgic reminiscence, confessions swapped amongst drunken strangers, lies, slanders, slips of the tongue, snitching, grousing, whining, and loud slanging matches conducted in public among people with serious speech impediments. Rosserus is not a subject for polite conversation or even meaningful dialogue. Likewise it is impossible to be witty about Rosserus; the subject rasps like sackcloth and sticks like mud, these being the most obvious affects of its (his? her?) constituency, a certain subsect amongst Rome's beggars, neither the most gruesome (self-mutilation and the maintenance of open sores) nor the most wholesome seeming (the horribly perky, bright-faced urchin and its adult counterpart, the gentleman "temporarily down on his luck"), but rather the middling sort of vagrants, intermittently violent but more inclined to torpor, cussed, and invariably caked with filth. They seem to know more about this "Rosserus" than anyone else, and at any given time Rosserus seems to know more or less anything and everything about Rome's ground-level activities, diffusing this intelligence through the infinite removes of someone who heard it from someone who heard it from someone. . . . Backtracking along any one of these reports to their source is slightly less feasible than stalking a shrew through the aftermath of a stampede by a herd of aurochs, for Rosserus is decentralized, operates by seepage, makes no sound, and is unimaginable, if by "image" is meant something hard, sharp, and bright, such as a silver brooch in the shape of a unicorn. Its memes are everywhere and nowhere at once, a blackening swarm, multiplying their way through *Ro*-ma. . . .

"Ah," says the Pope.

They proceed through the Stanza di Incendio, turning left, then right. Leo peers anxiously down a stairwell. The chapel choir is rehearsing; thin harmonies reach the two men's ears mixed with the dull clanging of a distant church bell and the nearer squawking of parrots from the courtyard. The stairwell seems deserted, but when they reach the first landing, two figures glide out of the shadows, right hands moving smoothly to their breasts, left extending toward him. . . . Poets. The black is not a uniform at all, Leo realizes suddenly. It's camouflage.

"*Dum iuvenes poppysma rogant, tu, Lucia, nasum,*" recites one.

"*Inspicis et quantum prominet ille notas,*" continues the other.

"Splendid, splendid," mutters Leo, turning in a mild panic to Bibbiena.

"*Hoc perpendiculo virgas metire viriles. . . .*"

Bibbiena edges between his master and the pasty-faced declaimers, reaching into his purse for coins to press into the outstretched hands and turning to cover the Pope's retreat as the latter scurries down the stairs, adopting a gait he has developed for situations like these, suggestive of gratitude, whose full expression is baffled only by the irresistible demands of his office. It involves a number of decelerations and half-turns while quick expressions of joy pass across his face and are overtaken by regretful remembrance of unspecified pressing business: such a finely turned iamb, it seems to say, if only I could stay to hear more. . . . Bibbiena clatters down the stairs after him, pursued by *"Ut iam ego me fieri rhinoc,"* which line gains a sudden rude caesura as they exit into the Cortile di Sentinella, where the situation is worse. They are hardly out of the door before five or six black-garbed collections of angular limbs are moving in on them like hungry crows, thin arms moving to their breasts as though to contain the inner swelling of song. The courtyard grows loud with a macaronic gibberish in which comparisons between himself and various celestial bodies vie with rhymeless testaments to his liberality and several acrostic constructions loosely based upon the word "Leo." He favors a stout gray-bearded individual with his most beneficent smile, some vague association between age and the production of epigrams prompting this decision, between epigrams and brevity. . . . Instead the old man smiles back, reaches down, and propels toward him a boy of six or seven.

"Holiness, let me present my little Pierino. Even from the crib his wails had a poetical character. . . ."

Little Pierino beams up at him. Leo looks about in desperation but the Switzers guarding the doors are confused by the joyful rictus plastered over his face. Little Pierino takes it as his cue to begin:

> You were born, O Leo, in fair Florence town,
> Where the fields are green and the earth beneath brown. . . .

Notwithstanding his tender years, little Pierino has already perfected the poet's stance. He varies it at the end of each line by throwing out his left arm in an expansive gesture and making a little skip to emphasize the anapest. Leo flees.

More poets are encountered in the passageway leading along the outer wall of the chapel (the singing louder, the barked orders of the chapel-master as he mimes the actions of the Mass), but Bibbiena precedes him, blocking their view until the last minute, when he dances sideways to dip his head beneath the far door and escapes with no more than two heroic couplets and the fragment of a Horatian ode ringing dissonantly in his ears. The two men move farther into the palace, away from his apartments (an obvious focal point for petitioners of all kinds) and deeper into the cells and chambers of his *famiglia* and their servants. Here, a bedchamber means a screen of sacking and an apartment is a curtained section of corridor. They pass dim shapes, slumped against the walls or hunched over smoking oil-lamps, whose heads follow the progress of these finely robed figures as they stride forward out of the fug, pass by, and are swallowed by it again. Rotting rushes squelch under their shoes. Bibbiena offers an elaborate salute to a woman relieving herself in the gutter that runs down the center. Leo notices that not a few of the creatures they pass carry or keep within reach short, ugly-looking clubs. He frowns. Soon, the sweat-and-urine stink of the "apartments" is augmented by several new odors: salty tangs and creamy steams, beef broth, vegetable water, charred fish-skin, hot fat, the complexity of stocks. The scent of oranges somehow struggles through this gallimaufry of stenches. Leo's nose is tickled, tantalized. He sniffs appreciatively. They are on the outskirts of the kitchens.

Through the aromatic fog of a large vaulted chamber known as the Boiling Room, Leo sees Neroni and his new chef, Guidol, deep in conversation. The latter mumbles something as they approach and hurries off in the opposite direction. Neroni turns to greet them.

"Had to go and check the *corquignolles,*" he offers in answer to the Pope's curious glance. Leo nods, still peering after the rapidly retreating chef.

"Some dish he's working on for tomorrow."

Neroni too carries a short, weighted club, "for the rats," as he explains. The *maestro di casa* hauls sturgeon out of baskets and slaps them onto the table. Leo prods one gingerly.

"You have a problem with rats?" he inquires, looking up from the fish.

"Problem!" roars Neroni, then, remembering whom he is addressing, lowers his voice. "No, Your Holiness. A 'problem' is what we used to have. What we have now is a plague!"

"A plague?" murmurs Leo, looking about him at the boiling pots, whose steam billows up, condenses on the ceiling, then drips down to form small puddles on the floor. "My dear Neroni, I see no rats. If rats there are, they seem . . . how should I put it, too reticent to constitute a plague. . . ."

Neroni stands there for a second. He wants to say something light and witty. This, he has been told, is the language the Pope understands. On the other hand, he also wants to make his point about the rats. He is crude, he knows, but the habitual utterances of an effective *maestro di casa* are directed not upward toward popes, but downward at lazy scullions and underchefs, at thieving butchers and grocers, down even so far as pot-boys, for whom the most effective language is kicking. He thinks about this for a while. Then he throws back his head and unleashes a great roar of laughter. Next, directing a jovial wink to both Leo and Bibbiena, he snatches a cleaver from a passing minion and with a single swipe cuts off the head of the sturgeon. The Pope appears a little alarmed now, but he presses on by hurling the fish-head into the corner of the room.

"Now watch this," he says.

He is still worrying that what he should have said was, "Now watch this, *Holiness,*" when something moving like a rocket-propelled ink-spill shoots across the floor and seems to simply erase the fish-head from existence.

"There," says Neroni. "Your Holiness."

Leo looks at him blankly. "That was a cat," he says.

"They ate the cat," says Neroni. "Poor old Towser." He looks grief-stricken, briefly. "Mozzo!" he bellows. "Bring me the rat-basket!"

A plump steward presently appears, straining under the weight of a two-handled basket rather wider than himself, which he places at their feet.

"That's just from this morning," says Neroni. "Pull out a nice one, Mozzo."

The basket is full of black-haired bodies. Mozzo rummages amongst them, emerging with a rat-corpse that he holds up by the tail. The belly, as it swings toward the Pope, appears to be a collection of open sores and scabs. Green fluid drips steadily from the nose. By Leo's conservative estimate, it is approximately ten inches long.

Neroni says, "That's one of the smaller ones."

Someone else begins whispering in his ear:

> *There once was a Bishop of Rome*
> *Who got lost in his very own home. . . .*

Rome? Home? It rhymes. . . . Worse, it scans. He turns about in a panic, but instead of the expected black-garbed figure, left hand planted on his chest (the fetters of the heart) and right arm extended (for money), he sees a more moderate version of Bibbiena topped by a familiar face, now grinning into his own: Dovizio's.

"Found you at last!" Dovizio exclaims. "What an evasive Pope you are!"

"I am?" Grinning sheepishly.

Relieved.

"You are indeed, but now I have tracked you down. Today, in fact, I have tracked you down *twice*. . . ."

Dovizio will not as yet be drawn on the meaning of this enigmatic declaration. Instead he tells him that the beast probably entered by the Porta del Popolo some three or four hours ago ("Yes, yes, Rosserus. . . ."), somehow passing undetected under the noses of papal, Spanish, and Portuguese "welcoming parties" composed of low-level functionaries and thugs.

Outside, the brilliant afternoon shades itself in ever-deepening blues. In the courtyard of the Belvedere the water level rises at the rate of an inch an hour in a futile chase after the sunlight, which drops below the tiers of seating on the western side. The monks wring out their soaking habits. The business of the day is halted and the paperwork assembled. Palatine secretaries present their findings to the Cardinal Nephew; abbreviators and protonotaries apostolic seal them beneath the ring of the Fisherman. It is more or less the hour of the day when brecciated marbles look their best—*traccagnina, corallina, samesanto*—when their stalagmitic whorls and schistose veins seem to pump a little of their formative heat into the cooling interiors, where candles are now being lit and evensong sung. The Pope peers at his cardinals through a feathered fan improvised from the wings of a plover. He samples a quail's egg. Dovizio sniffs a plate of pâté, and Bibbiena reaches into the dark red carcass of a part-gutted boar to set the soggy viscera hanging there swinging like the clapper of a big meaty bell. They are stocky and heavy-fleshed men, three beardless Olympians sporting in the busy squalor of the kitchens. After battle is joined, and won, there will be a banquet in honor of the victor, so, scurrying around them, pastry chefs are busy fashioning little horns that will be filled with a variety of sweetmeats, subchefs are rolling up slices of ham

for Hanno's trunk and debating whether cabbage leaves or fillets of skate most
nearly resemble his ears. Around the kitchens, the horned and trunked combatants face each other in the guise of modified poultry, mutant suckling-pigs, carefully carved butter-sculptures, and racks of bulbous meringues. The "Hannos" are
more or less uniform—trunk, tusk, big flappy ears—but their opponents appear
to be the victim of the cooks' internal dissent over what exactly this beast is
meant to look like. Pig-with-Additions seems the most popular guess, but Very
Big Mouse has its supporters, as does Foreshortened Drayhorse and Bull with
Reshaped Head. Others look like the victims of drunken surgery. Rosserus has
been at work down here, too, as anywhere where the absence of dogma demands
answers that the usual channels cannot or will not supply. Clouds of steam and
smoke, shouting, banging, running around: out of this chaos comes regular fodder
for six hundred people three times a day, but even the *Dauer im Wechsel* of
kitchens cannot hold forever. These botched bestial concoctions gesture at deeper
failures, an undiagnosed lack probably too late to treat by now, a fissure already
slicing through the center of the earth. . . .

"Yum," says Bibbiena, reaching for a third handful of little frosted sugary
things.

"Mmm-hmmth."

Dovizio swallowing melon.

The trio quits the kitchens in high, oblivious spirits. Leo is a taut wire strung
between his cardinals, humming a tune composed for him the week before by
Gian Maria to accompany his favorite *frottola, "Il Grasso Porco di Cattivo Umore,"* a
title widely touted as his epithet. His favorite verse is the one in which the cunning librettist finds five perfect rhymes for the metrically awkward *occhiata.* Leo
appreciates polish. They march three abreast past the bivouac-clogged corridors,
Leo content enough with his central position to straddle the gutter while his co-
horts bluffly hold forth on the expected opulence of tomorrow's entertainment.
Apparently Dovizio has secured the gondolas that Leo so desired as the craft for
his rival navies, and they are being gilded with the Medici emblem of the Pallia
even now. More important still, he has managed to engage the services of King
Caspar and the Mauritians, an ensemble consisting in lute, sackbut, several viols,
and dulcimer, famed for their suavity and a facile diminuendo ranging from the
lachrymose to the sepulchral. They are expected to arrive late tomorrow afternoon. Now, arm in arm up a stairway to the antechamber battened onto the side
of the Chapel of Saint Nicholas, where Leo notes happily the absence of the
mooching poets who thronged it earlier. Departed, he presumes, for dinner.
Dovizio has a surprise for him and is trying to inveigle him into guessing what
it is.

"You have written a play to be performed tomorrow in which I feature as
my earlier namesake, Leo the First, and the Dauphin of France plays Attila. I halt
his advance at the Mincio, then return to Rome in triumph and am adored until

my death, which scene is affecting but free of sentimentality. A tuneful dirge played on goatskin drums accompanies my passage to heaven," hazards Leo.

He thrums and twangs between them, his querulous treble rising, then sinking, as Dovizio informs him that his guess is incorrect, and the Dauphin of France does not, as far as he knows, yet exist. "I gave you a clue earlier, Holiness. Remember? Today I have found you twice. . . ."

This is obscure but happy banter. They swing around corners and swoop down corridors. Clerks bow low, then press their backs against the walls to let them pass, and stewards burdened with tureens take little staggering backward steps. The dinner din of the *tinello* is a softened roar, a distant clamor, the barbarians corralled in their camp. No poets are encountered, not one. Retailing the choicest of the recent pasquinades against the hapless Cardinal Armellini, Bibbiena knocks over a dwarf.

Dovizio punctuates his companion's theme with directional jolts and jabs— "This way" and "Turn left" and "Just around here"—a segmented antiphon that bowls them along and around and up and down while Leo's happy, fun-stuffed head nods and chuckles and wonders where he is. They seem to have been walking for quite a long time now. He had not realized his palace was quite so big. The cardinals exchange their tunes along the buzzing cord that joins them. Leo Vibrato. Then big black thumbs give the tuning pegs a twist. Leo conceives of a thick hairy rope passed through his glistening guts and bluish translucent tubes, his buttocks *thwock*ing in time with the strikes of the bow against the lacquered fingerboard of a tree-size violin: His Holiness the Highly Strung. Now that would be a martyrdom, grisly as Erasmus', musical as Cecilia's wedding song with its latent squawks and pain-filled screams, the cries of martyrs giving birth to saints. Such a tortured music, and strangely familiar. Now where would he have heard that song before, sung to the accompanying clank of tongs in the braziers, the grating of saw-blades on bone, toneless peelings like the tearing of dry cloth . . . Ah.

"Here we are," says Dovizio, providentially but too late.

Prato. Again.

"Where?" asks Bibbiena. "And what?"

"Him," answers Dovizio, pointing into a sunken side-chamber so narrow that there is barely room for the bench that runs down one side. The Pope's expression is quite vacant. "Your Holiness? Are we boring you?"

"No, no, not at all." He shakes his head gently, regrouping. "No, this is all very interesting and instructive. Very good, dear Dovizio. I presume that this is my 'surprise'?"

"Isn't he perfect?"

An old man is sitting on the stone bench, supping from a tin bowl, rocking forward to take each sip with so minute a motion that Leo, observing the bow of his back almost touch the wall behind and then—a generous second or two later—almost not, is put in mind of the mechanism of a clever water-clock built for his father. A palsied cantilever would hang, then quiver, and finally tip itself over a pivot to trigger something or other. It was the hesitancy of the thing that was so maddening. Piero had smashed it eventually, and both of them had been glad.

"Perfect? Well, Dovizio, I am not at all sure I would have reached that epithet without your aid. There is, for instance, his beard. . . ."

"Matted, unkempt, irregularly cut if cut at all, stained, and probably lice-ridden, too."

"Yes, and he is rather gaunt, almost emaciated. As to his rags, might we agree not to dwell overlong on the subject?"

"Their filth and stench urge my prompt concurrence. Let us pass them over in silence and move to the pronounced rattle in his lungs or, if you prefer, the cough which seems to accompany his least movement or—"

"Perhaps later," Leo interrupts, a vague curiosity now overtaking the fading pleasures of this exchange. "What I should like to know now is what he is."

"He is one of your petitioners," Dovizio replies, shooting Bibbiena a quick grin of complicity. "I found him this morning in front of San Damaso."

At this, the old man, who has shown no sign of having paid the slightest attention to their words up to this point, or even of having heard them, lowers his tin bowl from his lips and places it carefully on the bench beside him. He does not, however, alter his expression or turn his head to look at the three heads crowding the narrow doorway to peer in at him. Rather, he folds his hands in his lap and directs his gaze to the bare wall opposite him.

Leo frowns. It is not unwelcome to find himself unregarded from time to time. No, he is not displeased, but puzzled, perhaps, at the old man's lack of curiosity and also at the purpose behind his display. Dovizio is grinning again. They are making fun of him, but how? Leo feels his patience ebbing.

"What baffles me is your interest in this graybeard, Dovizio. Why is he here?"

"My interest? It is your interest that he engages, Holiness." A snort of mirth escapes through Bibbiena's nose at this. Leo is about to lose his temper with them. Today has not been an easy day. . . . Then it comes to him. The filth. The rags. All that business about a "surprise. . . ." He knows. He nods his head sagely, turning to the two of them and reaching out so that they might each clasp an elbow in comradely fashion. They do.

"This," he announces with absolute, fatal conviction, "is Rosserus."

They stare at him for a second, faces frozen. Then melting. . . . They start laughing, beginning with a succession of nasal explosions, then some half-stifled hiccups that quickly develop into full-throated side-aching guffaws. Soon, Bibbiena can stay upright only by leaning against the wall. Dovizio has to sit down, wall or no wall.

"Rosserus!" Dovizio gulps between roars of laughter. He glances in at the seated figure. "Rosserus? Him?" (More laughing.) "Oh dear, Your Holiness . . . he's not Rosserus. He's *you*. . . ."

"Put him," attempts Bibbiena, but his own hilarity thwarts him.

"On the," tries Dovizio before mirthfulness gags him with giggles.

"Platform. On the fountain. Tomorrow. Got a tiara for him. And everything," says one or the other or a combination of the both of them.

The pair have almost calmed themselves when Leo sets them off again by stating huffily that, actually, he knew all along and was simply pretending not to for their amusement. Then he makes matters worse again by beginning a new topic of conversation—"So, my friends, what about these rats of Neroni's?"—in a blatant and clumsy attempt to divert them from their task, which is laughing at him: what else are cardinals for? Their hearty derision springs and bounds down the empty corridor, slowly breaking up into sniggering and intermittent titters. Eventually they shut up.

"Since he is to be me, I am going to speak with him," Leo announces to the pair's mild surprise.

He begins maneuvering himself through the narrow entrance. The chamber itself is barely wider, its floor a mere three flagstones laid end to end. His belly squeezes into the aperture. Has he gained more girth through the winter? A solid belly aids balance. Footing is related to the center of gravity, especially when hunting. Look at Boccamazza, although his equally generous middle is found a little higher up. More in the chest region, really. . . . Leo is still trying to get through the doorway. Perhaps by using one arm to lever the protuberance while squashing it in with the other. . . . Yes.

The old man has not moved. He does indeed stink, Leo notes, but the smell is musty rather than acrid. His hair is indeed matted, the beard stained and stringy, but he is not gray, or not naturally so. Has someone deposited ashes on his head? From time to time, when bored, and from a suitably discreet vantage point, he has watched the rough pranks of the petitioners waiting in the Courtyard of San Damaso, their brutish japes and capers. Anyway, old "Graybeard" is actually fair-haired. He stands before him, waiting.

"Stand up, old man," commands Bibbiena from the doorway.

The creature turns his head at this, and there follows an outbreak of the promised coughing, which racks the old man for a minute or so and is succeeded by the similarly promised lung-rattle.

"He doesn't have to stand up," Leo tells Bibbiena. The Cardinal shrugs.

Then more waiting. It is rather awkward standing there, a mere arm's-length away, while being ignored. Usually by now there would have been a grab for his foot, or at least the hem of his mozzetta. The situation is drifting. He gazes airily about. He considers the possibilities. A decision.

"My son," he says to the presumably weak-witted creature. The old man turns his face to the voice issuing from above, and Leo sees first that the old man is really not so aged after all, hardly older than himself, in fact. And then, the strange immobility of the upturned head, its fixed focus on someone who seems to have drifted free of Leo, a shadow-Pope . . .

"He's blind!" he exclaims.

"Did I not mention that?" replies Dovizio from behind.

"He does not know who I am," continues Leo. He looks down again in a more kindly manner. "My son, I am your Pope."

The not-so-old old man appears to find him then. Dead though they are, his eyes widen, his face loosens, and an expression passes across it that might be wonderment, or amazement, or even joy. Leo never identifies it, something promised and snatched away, for in the next instant the brow wrinkles, the face hardens, and its fleeting unguardedness is replaced with resignation. His voice, when he speaks, is surprisingly clear.

"You are not."

Dovizio snorts, or perhaps it is Bibbiena. Leo looks down in consternation, ignoring them. He puts his hand on the man's shoulder.

"I am," he insists. "I am your Pope."

But the figure seated on the bench is no longer paying attention to him. He seems to be coming to some comfortless realization of his own. His reply, if that is what it is, sounds weary and dismissive.

"I have been mocked long enough."

Pebbles, wood chippings, apple peel, dried horse dung, old nails, walnut shells, melon rinds, and spit. These were the objects and substances that made the most regular appearances in his bowl.

At the other end of the scale, having appeared only once so far, were a small perfume bottle made of blue glass, a chipped knife-blade, a turnip with a smiling face cut in it, a milky-colored mosaic tile, a spinning top, a playing card (the seven of spades), another playing card (oddly, also the seven of spades, but a different design), and an ear.

The bowl rested on the ground between his feet. The shape and size of the bowl mattered. Too large a bowl attracted all kinds of rubbish, while too small a bowl was ignored. Wooden bowls were better than tin bowls (no one used a tin bowl), and the bowl must be shallow enough for passersby to see its contents. Not too much, for that argued lack of necessity, but neither should it be bare, for potential donors needed guidelines. The bowl therefore was "seeded." A wizened apple and a worthless copper disk were his items for this. He would accept food and coin. The most ambitious beggars would seed their bowls with nothing less than a fat silver baiocco, but they were the ones who worked in the piazza or on the city side of the bridge, and those were the richest pitches in the whole of Rome. In front of the bridge on the Borgo side was where he had started himself, where he had had what remained his best and worst day. He had sat a little way down from another beggar, or rather three, for they rotated the pitch among them. One had greeted him with a cheery salute: "First day?" He had confirmed that it was. It had taken him ten days to bring himself to this, ten days of racking his brains for any other way. . . . And there was a way, of course, but it was even worse than this. So he sat there on the bridge, shaking with shame to begin with, but gradually resigning himself as the coins clinked steadily into his bowl. When the crowds began to thin, the two teammates of the beggar to the left of him reappeared, and they began to divide up their spoils. He counted his own, which came to eighty-seven soldi. "Good day?" inquired one of the three beggars, saun-tering over toward him. He was the largest of the three, and he was the one who, a moment later, punched him efficiently in the stomach while the second banged his head on the ground and the third poured the contents of his bowl into their own. He recalled lying on the ground, dazed, with hundreds of boots and shoes stepping around him.

He moved to a pitch south of the bridge. There were fewer beggars there and fewer passersby. From a little after dawn to a little before sunset, he accumulated three stale rolls and fifteen soldi. The three men reappeared as he was counting out the coins. He handed them over without protest, and he did the same the next day (seven soldi) and the next (twelve). They did not take the food. He moved still farther down the river, into the neighborhood of Santo Spirito. It was cold, sitting there motionless on the ground, so he found a piece of sacking to in-sulate him from a chill that seemed to travel up his spine and freeze his brains to ice. He watched men more ragged even than him scouring the mud-banks that ran along the river. Once he nodded to one, and the scavenger nodded back. A good day.

A bad day: his three oppressors found him and beat him. They explained to him between blows that since he was so evidently untrustworthy—the move-ment of his pitch downriver was offered as evidence of this—he would in future present himself to them at the bridge each evening, there hand over his earnings, and thus save himself this (what they termed) "bother." The "bother" at that point took the the form of an agonizing blow to the ear, so he heard only the end of a strange ululation that rang across the river, something like ". . . ss'rus . . . !" and which seemed to give them pause, for they then threw him bodily over the em-bankment and ran off. He landed in freezing mud. The oarsman of a passing wherry glanced at him curiously and passed on. The river looked like treacle. He lay there for a while, then, when he was picking himself up, eyes watering, blood and snot still bubbling in his nostrils, he looked across the river and saw the scav-enger of a few days before joined now by two of his companions. All three were watching him. They must have seen it all. They stood shoulder to shoulder and raised their arms high above their heads:

"Rosserus!"

It was their voices he recognized. It was almost dark, and begrimed as they were, the faces of the former novices were anonymous masks of mud. He pulled his hand free of the ooze and lifted it toward them. Something caught his eye then, a movement over the mud on his own side of the river. Rats? When he looked across again, Wulf, Wolf, and Wilf had disappeared.

The next day he presented himself in front of the bridge as promised, but the three beggars were not at their pitch. Leaning against the wall in their place was a broad-chested man wrapped entirely in sheepskins. His head was shaved, and on the top of his head sat something that he first took for a bird's nest but which, as he drew nearer, revealed itself as a covering of mud shaped into the approximate form of a hat.

"You're the monk," said Mudhat, glaring at him.

He nodded, glancing about nervously for his extortioners.

"If you're looking for who I think you're looking for, don't waste your time," Mudhat told him. "You won't be meeting them again. Leastways, not here. This here's your pitch from now on. Everyone's been told, so there's no argument and no excuses, either. You can start here tomorrow."

With that, Mudhat pushed himself off the wall and began to walk off. He put a hand on the man's arm and was opening his mouth to thank him when Mudhat rapped him hard on the knuckles.

"That," Mudhat cut him off, "is just the kind of thing which irritates me. When I get irritated, I usually get annoyed. And when I get annoyed what I usually do is pick up whoever is annoying me by the ankles and pull them apart like this"—he demonstrated the motion—"till he splits down the middle. After that, I examine the two halves carefully to see which has the head on it. Often it's the left side. Sometimes, though, it's the right. Whichever side it is, I find it makes an excellent tool for beating the other side, the headless side, to a pulp. Am I making myself plain?"

It was late November. The next day, as promised, he gained his pitch by the bridge.

Without it, HansJürgen thought now, counting out his day's earning under the grim turret of Castel Sant'Angelo—twenty-five, twenty-six—he and his Prior would in all probability not have survived the winter. Twenty-seven soldi, which was about average. The amount he had taken on his very first day had proved to be a fluke, and his somewhat wild speculations walking back to the Stick after his encounter with his brutish savior—that he might hoard enough one day, perhaps, to escape from the city that had effectively become their prison—were quickly quashed in the succeeding days. There was firewood to buy, lamp-oil or candles, bread, and from time to time there was Lappi's widow to be placated, for they were the only tenants left in the Stick. After the murder of her husband, she had appeared in the entrance hall enthroned on a chair stuffed with horsehair that leaked from a rent somewhere on its underside and that Signorina Lappi tried to restuff by gathering the stray wisps off the floor and forcing them back in, all this without moving from her seat. In fact, she seemed never to move at all. HansJürgen would come upon her bent sideways over the arm and uttering great groans of effort. He had tried to help her once, and she had hit him with her broom. There was a box chained to her chair. The box was where their "rent" was collected. Sometimes he would put in the full four soldi. Usually rather less. Sometimes an old nail or a piece of glass. It was a charade, in any case, for the real tariff on their entry each night was paid in a quite different coin, and it was paid by Father Jörg.

Lappi's widow hated him. She detested the very sight of him. At his appearance each evening after his fruitless sojourn in the Cortile di San Damaso, she would scream and bellow at him that he was a ruthless trickster, that he only feigned his blindness, and when this ritual of rage had built itself up to the required pitch, she would accuse him of her husband's murder. Lappi, according to his widow, would still be alive if it were not for Father Jörg. No evidence or reason explained her conviction beyond the facts that the murderer had never been discovered, that the only people with whom she came into contact, so far as HansJürgen could see, were himself and the Prior, and that an antipathy so fierce and so cherished as that which she harbored against the latter could hardly subsist without the foundation of her heartfelt faith that it was justified. She believed in his guilt because she must. She had a leaking chair and a blind man. Sometimes she waited for him to hesitantly mount the steps, treading quietly, stealthily, into the hallway, where the similarly silent, wakeful widow would be waiting for him with the broom handle. . . . She bloodied his nose once. Her frustrated yelling would continue for long minutes after he had scrambled past her and made his escape.

Jörg endured this without comment, as he endured everything without comment. He had fallen sick that winter: a disease of the lungs. Now, rounding the corner that led him into the Via dei Sinibaldi, he recalled the admixture of forebodings he had fallen prey to every evening at this point in his journey home. Listening night after night to the coughing and choking, he had come to realize that the Prior would die. That thought was the gate to the rest. He had dreaded it, and yet, shivering on the thin straw mattress, sleepless with the cold and the gruesome noise, he had been drawn through it nonetheless. Jörg kept the silver scabbard in his chest with the papers on which he poured out his ramblings. There were *bancherotti* in the piazza who would change it into coin. The coin would pay their passage away from here. It would pay their passage home. But Jörg would not pawn the scabbard. Perhaps it was the accusations he had flung in the heathen's face or his dismissal of Salvestro's own accusations—shortly after proved abundantly true—or perhaps it was the scabbard's provenance, for it was of the island and in the Prior's mind perhaps a last link with that. In any case it did not matter, for Jörg would not go and would only chuckle when HansJürgen urged this on him night after night, replying, "But you do not understand, Brother. Darkness is not a force, nor a power to be fled from. Our fears will only rebound on us if we retreat back into them. Our ignorance is where we are needed. . . ." Or, when he had described their lives as hopeless and foolish, "My foolishness is only the truth, Brother HansJürgen. Look at the candle, since I cannot. Does it not flicker? Are there not moments, very brief ones, when it gives no light at all?" Finally, when he had ventured to recall the church that they had left to the mercy of the elements, "But why did it crumble in the first place? Better to ask yourself that, Brother. . . ."

These mad heresies, and others equally incomprehensible, were what had come to mind as he walked toward the entrance to the hostel one particular night, as he wondered whether he would find his Prior hunched noisily over a phlegm-filled bowl or curled up in a corner, motionless and cold. He counted soldi in his head, this much, then that much. Thirty-one yesterday. Seventeen to-morrow. Never enough. Never, ever enough. And then the dirty thought. Or worse even than that: a hope. It had found him here, just a few yards short of the doorway, where he was now. Farther up the street, some small boys were playing a game that had grown popular over the winter, running about chaotically, then suddenly freezing at a shouted command. A dog was wandering around, sniffing at their legs. Beyond them, a cart with splayed wheels and high battened sides stood uncoupled from whatever beast had drawn it there. Some hovering men would be the gang hired to unload it. The driver appeared to be asleep. In the depths of winter he had seen such a wagon rumble very slowly through the streets, its load gradually growing heavier as the men who drove it stopped to search down alleys and passageways, behind low walls, or in the doorways of abandoned buildings. These seemed to be the favored places for those with nowhere better. The bodies they found in these miserable refuges were typically frozen solid. The cart's drivers were able to roll them out like logs. His prayers seemed to offer no consolation. Rome, this particular part of Rome, this exact street, and this stone on which he now stood and ground the wooden sole of his sandal, were where he had stopped and thought that if Jörg were dead, he could leave. A slick, gritty sound. The scent of manure drifted in the air. Jörg had lived. Their existences went on as before. He had collected close to forty soldi today. A good day.

Lappi's widow said nothing as he dropped four coins in the slot of her box. He added a fifth, and she nodded her satisfaction. The passageway emerged from darkness, the light from the lamp revealing walls of cracked and crumbling plas-ter. Small islands of the same fell daily from the ceiling and shattered on the floor. The smell of damp was more pronounced back here. He heard Jörg scrabbling amongst his papers in the chamber at the rear of the building. This was usually how his evenings were spent. He scraped lamp-black and mixed ink, scribbled and scratched, using and reusing the sheets of parchment that they could not af-ford to replace, covering them with his minute script left to right, then turning the sheet to cover it again, sometimes a third time along the diagonal, until the page was black with his near indecipherable handwriting. The ink alternated be-tween its constituents. Water and soot.

But the scrabbling was not Jörg. He ran forward and five or six fat black bodies froze for a second, then fled from him, or perhaps from the unfamiliar light, scattering around the chamber and disappearing into the shadows. Chewed pages of the Prior's manuscript were strewn about the opened chest. Opened, HansJür- gen realized, by the rats. He frowned, then stooped to gather them up. The rats were growing bolder and cleverer. They were still in the room, he knew. That was the game the children had been playing—the Rat Game—which was based on exactly this tactic. Instead of disappearing down their holes, the rats would hide in some dark or inaccessible corner, keeping still and silent until they judged that the danger was past, then they would move forward again. Their entrance to the chamber was a crack in the wall that they had enlarged somehow, choosing to chew through solid stone rather than attack the door. A puzzling decision. HansJürgen secured the chest and walked out to the back courtyard for a clod of earth to block their egress, a vague plan to hunt them down in the chamber forming in his mind as he walked back in. He would need a stick or something. He was tamping the soil into the crack when Lappi's widow started shouting. The usual rage. Jörg had returned. He worked the soil in with his thumb, but it crum- bled and would not stay in. A dash of water, perhaps. The woman was still shout- ing. He would have to go out if it continued much longer. Sometimes his presence seemed to abash her. Sometimes it raised her ire to a new level entirely. The shouting grew no quieter, and after a minute or so he rose reluctantly to investigate.

Again he was mistaken. The widow was raising her broom as he appeared. Before her stood not Jörg, but a brown-faced man, quite old, his face wrinkled. He knew him from somewhere. The old man dodged the broom-thrusts with ease, looking up as HansJürgen emerged from the hostel's darkness.

"Murderer!" shouted the old woman.

"Murderer yourself," retorted the man, seemingly unconcerned by the accu- sation. "Remember me?" he addressed HansJürgen. "I'm Batista." He gestured in the rough direction of the Pope's palace. "I remember you. Last summer."

HansJürgen nodded.

"You look different, if you don't mind my saying so. Or even if you do. Will you shut up?" This last was directed at Lappi's widow, who, rather surprisingly, did. "Anyway, say good-bye from me, that's why I've called. I'm Batista. Don't for- get. Had some good chats we did, me and old Jörg. Never a cross word. Then again, I never understood a word he said."

Batista made a little salute and turned to go.

"Wait," said HansJürgen. "Where shall I say you've gone?"

"Gone?" Batista turned again but continued walking, backward, away down the street. "I'm not going anywhere. It's you two who'll be off, won't you? I mean, now His Holiness has heard that petition of yours. Building a city under the sea, wasn't it? Something like that. . . ."

"A church," HansJürgen called after his departing back. "What do you mean, the Pope has heard his petition?"

Batista waved without turning around. HansJürgen watched him dodge his way through the children playing the Rat Game and pass the cart still waiting up the street. Its driver woke as he walked quickly past. One of the children ran toward him.

HansJürgen went back inside and resumed his work on the rat-hole. They would dig it out, of course. Clay would be better, or plaster. Or best of all, cement. Batista was talking nonsense. It was quite clear that Jörg had been delayed by something this particular night. He knew that the petitioners played tricks on each other. In the early months, Jörg had several times returned covered with chalk dust or soaked with water. He presumed it was water. By this standard, Batista's would be quite a sophisticated trick. He began smoothing the earth flush with the surface of the wall. Once or twice they had directed Jörg down to the Porta Pertusa or into the sea of mud behind the palace, where, on the basis of four stone piers and several hundred waterlogged trenches, the new basilica was rumored to be rising. It might take him hours to find his way out of there, and he, HansJürgen, would probably have to go out and look for him soon. Yes, a silly trick. No doubt at all. Or almost none. Although, perhaps, barely possibly . . .

"Filthy murderer."

No. None, for this surely was Jörg. The widow seemed to have already expended that day's store of hatred, for after this single weary expletive she fell silent. HansJürgen settled himself to his task once again. He played the oil-lamp over the surface of the patch. Quite smooth. Next would come the shuffling footsteps. Then, "Brother, are you there?" He would reply that he was. The Prior would go to his chest and take out his papers. Later he would unhook the palliasses that they now hung from a rope fixed to the wall. He would have to suspend the chest up there, too, or devise a more resistant lock. They would pray. They would sleep. He smoothed the earth in the rat-hole. Perhaps he would try to kill the rats. Quite smooth. There was no "petition." No petition "would be heard." Quite, quite smooth. He moved the lamp away from his handiwork, placing it a little way behind him. Then his heart jumped.

A pair of boots.

He turned back to the wall. Someone was standing behind him, at the very edge of his vision. He felt strangely weightless. Perhaps this too was part of Batista's trick? He ran his hand over the wall for what must have been the thirtieth time, feeling his heart thud in his chest.

"You can't pretend I'm not here forever, Brother HansJürgen."

He swiveled clumsily on his heels, ready to rise and . . . And what? Defend himself? The notion was almost comical, but he seemed to be getting up anyway. Before he could do so, the intruder placed a firm hand on his shoulder, squatted on his haunches, and joined him on the floor. A face moved forward into the ambit of the lamplight.

Later, HansJürgen would realize that the question he blurted out in the shock of that instant more properly belonged to the other and, later still, that the smile

that flitted across the other's face was in consequence not of his knowing the answer, but of an odd pleasure taken in the momentary confusion of their roles. He
should have known that it would never be the Prior who would come upon him
like this. Not only should the question have been the other's, but the answer
should have been his, and the smile, too, for only minutes earlier the answer he
received now was precisely the one that he had rejected then for fear that his
hopes raised to such a height might not survive the fall if dashed. He had felt
nothing in the black mud by the river, nothing at all. Not even despair.

"Where is Father Jörg?" he demanded more sharply than he intended.

"With the Pope," answered Salvestro.

Two or three times a day, women arrived with basins and cloths to wash his
sores with warm salt water and, after that, to force a vile-tasting gruel down his
throat. He was turned this way and that as they swabbed the rawest patches of
flesh. Then one held his head and another wielded the spoon. He coughed and
spluttered but otherwise neither helped nor hindered them in their ministrations.
They always looked the same, although he knew that there were several of them.
They kept the shutters open so that the sea air should dry the worst of his sores,
those that exuded a colorless fluid and stubbornly refused to scab. Most of his
waking hours were spent with his head bent back, watching the upside-down
view out the window, which was the same as the view through the open hatch-
cover: a sky scrubbed to a raw blue by high freezing winds. A sky strung with
white filaments like wool on a loom. A sky dark and heavy with rain, prowling
silently forward, belly low to the ground. A storm sky.

"They cut us out of the canoes and threw us in the cage with it."

He thought of the expressions on the Portingales' faces as they were lifted up
on deck.

"They believed it would crush us. Or devour us, perhaps."

The animal's blunt mouth and lips would curl and pucker when it ate, briefly
animating the expressionless head that swung low over the planking in search of
food-scraps that it would deftly pluck up and then chew with a placid roll of its
jaw. It seemed too delicate a maneuver for so bulky an animal. The brown-faced
crewmen called it *gomda*.

"All it ate was hay, though," he said.

Amalia waited politely until she was sure that these latest ramblings were
finished.

"Do you know how to play leapfrog?" she inquired brightly.

At night the sea sounded soft and endlessly patient. *Wish, wash, wish, wash . . .*
He was on the beach, white as a fish and festooned with dark green seaweed.
Bernardo was out to sea with a good thick rope cinched diagonally across his

shoulder and a further loop around his waist. He was quite a way out and swimming very powerfully, enough power there to tow a fleet. The rope rose slowly to the surface as it tautened. Bernardo's arms were going like windmills. He watched the hawser pop up out of the smooth wet sand and run past him to tug at the embedded corpse, which lifted like a great tree-stump, its roots snapping under the tension of huge winches. Then it was free and being dragged down into the water, where it rolled and flopped, legs showing briefly above the surface, four comical stumps, before turning on its side. Bernardo was swimming along an enormous arc, raising a ridge of water before him and cutting a deep, turbulent wake. The animal hardly disturbed the surface at all. He watched them dwindle and disappear: a giant towing a small gray island out into the dwarfing sea.

Amalia staggered through the door with a pile of clothes that she dropped on the floor in front of him. Some shirts, thick breeches, a kind of coat made of cowhide. He pored over these, turning them over, pushing them about. A pair of boots.

"Hurry up, Salvestro," she said when it seemed that he might continue his inspection indefinitely. "Violetta's made crosses for all your friends, but she doesn't know what to write on them."

He looked up at her, standing over him impatiently. "Your dress has a stain on it," he said.

"I blew my nose on it," replied Amalia, sounding pleased. "It's snot."

They had laid out the bodies in the stable. Two of them were Portingales. The rest were crewmen, eighteen in all.

"One of these two was the vessel's commander," he told the older woman who hovered at his elbow. "But I do not know which one, nor either of their names."

Violetta frowned but desisted from questioning him further. He continued on down the line.

"This one I know. The native men called him Ossem. He was the one who gave us food." He looked down at the body, which, unlike many of the others, had been spared disfigurement in its passage to shore. When the first mast had snapped it had been on the orders of this man that two of the natives had tried to break open the cage.

"There were no others?" he asked.

Violetta shook her head. The two of them stood in silence over the dead men.

"Where is the animal?" he asked.

The woman looked up from her contemplations. She led him toward a door at the rear of the stables.

"It was Amalia's doing," she said dryly as they emerged. She pointed to the source of the ammoniac reek now wrinkling both their noses. "Or at her insistence."

So Rome, scabbed and raked-over Rome, where night is falling, the dipping sun giving the fabled bumps of her topography the chance to throw casts of shadow eastward over their rivals. The pink-lit ridges of the Quirinale, Viminale, and Esquiline are briefly a three-pronged claw closing about the wreckage of the Forum before the Palatine lops off the last of these and is eclipsed itself by the Janiculum. The Aventine and the Coelian go the same way, doused in black, sunk in the shadow of the long hump on which they will take their corresponding revenge in the morning. Goats scuttle down the sides of the Capitoline, followed quickly by the shrinking hill itself as it buries the jagged angles of its abandoned ruins in the chaotic tessellations of the city's blocky houses and stumpy towers. Grassed-over heaps of broken pottery ripple and flatten into the contoured sweep up from the kinked river to the Porta del Popolo. Rome, for the moment, is the place where deer nibble the trees in the Baths of Diocletian and cows graze in the Forum, where the cinerary urn of Agrippina is used as a grain measure and the marble bas-relief of a fish on the Palazzo dei Conservatori is the pretext for a tax on sturgeon. Around the wreckage of the Flaminian Circus, tonight as every night, Parian and Porinian marbles are being crushed and roasted for lime, the kilns of the Calcararia pricking the night with little glows. Subterranean Rome is burning, too, the same lime eating out cadaverous vesicles, soft body-shaped cases of earth that riddle the porous subsoils, a ransacked gallery of empty aedicules and niches cut to the exact dimensions of absentee river-gods and emperors. Things sink into these waiting spaces, these obverse-statues of Rome's builders and rulers and demolishers. Foundations sag and tip houses into the unsuspected urban churn. Successive Romes collapse under their own accumulated detritus and rise out of it again and again, reconsecrating themselves to the greater glory of Roma, a cannibal with the palate of a gourmet. Pasquino's missing head, Marforio's arms, the lower halves of innumerable Tritons . . . There are good reasons why the gazes of statues are almost always directed down. Planted outside the Convent of the Blessed Virgin inserted into the erstwhile Temple of Minerva is an enormous marble foot. It has not taken a step in fifteen hundred years.

And into this city, or swallower and regurgitator of cities, plods the Beast. Of the various semiofficial "reception committees" stationed respectively by the obelisk (the Portingales), the print-shop of the Cinquini (the Spaniards), and the Porta del Popolo itself (the delegation of the Apostolic See), perhaps one, at least, should have known that very little of value is obtained in Rome without either the aid of a shovel or a willingness to get one's hands dirty. They are all meant to be there incognito and as such are busying themselves with the usual inconspicuous activities: picking at their fingernails, hailing imaginary friends, trying to read the inscription on the obelisk, retying the laces on their sleeves, lining up to buy goat's cheese or a reproduction of the Crown of Thorns from one of the stalls set up on the north side of the piazza, strolling about singly with their arms folded over their chests as though deep in thought, or standing on one leg while trying to find a particularly elusive stone that has worked its way into their shoes. All these precautions come to naught every five minutes or so when guests invited by His Holiness to tomorrow's water-fight, aware that one of the combatants has yet to arrive and anxious whether they should attend so lopsided an event, arrive on horseback and direct indiscreet questions toward these master dissimulators, such as "So, has it arrived?" or "Any luck yet?" Perhaps most dispiriting of all is the thrice daily appearance of the secretary of Cardinal Armellini, who, no doubt through some clerical oversight, has not been invited at all. The secretary is the proud possessor of a powerful baritone. He stands up in his stirrups at one end of the piazza, directs his roving eye over the unhappy agents already scurrying away, fills his lungs, and simply bellows, *"WELL!?"*

They have been waiting here a week now. Their guts are running white with the goat's cheese. Most of them have two or three copies of the Crown of Thorns. There is no inscription on the obelisk. Even the neatherds know who they are and why they are here. The word was out before they even arrived because the exact same word was what got them posted here in the first place: Rosserus.

So all three camps miss Salvestro and his ox and cart. One or two take note of a little girl skipping about in a brilliant white dress, remembering their instructions, "Anything out of the ordinary." "Anything at all. . . ." But then, checking her happy gambols and eye-catching attire against the issued description—"large, gray, horn on end of nose"—they dismiss her from their minds. The cart rumbles on, out of the piazza and south along the Via del Popolo. However did they miss it? A few hours later the same question will be asked by a double column of pike-bearing Switzers who trot up the same road and practice complicated drill-maneuvers in front of the gatehouse while their commander makes inquiries amongst the hapless spies. Loitering neatherds applaud a slick transition from the defensive square to the double-crescent with pincer movement, and it is left to the lone apprentice in the print-shop working late to fold in quarto the fourth and final printing of Brandolini's *Simia* to tell the vexatious officer that yes, the Beast passed through this afternoon, and no, he did not actually see it himself, nor did anyone. So how does he know? Oh, well, it's simply one of those things. Rather like the supposedly incognito delegates. *Everybody* knows. The Beast? It just *did*. . . .

And does. By this point, having trundled past the noisy quays at Ripetta—the light fading and giving the distant tin-topped towers of the Palace of the Senators a milky oxidized sheen, darkening further the already treacly trickle of the river, which swings away only to be met again at the end of the Via del Panico—the Beast is in the Borgo, a hundred paces west of the now defunct Pilgrim's Staff in the Via dei Sinibaldi on the left side of the street, to be exact. More Switzers are soon milling about there, together with a small cadre of hunted-looking Palatine secretaries, although it is they themselves supposed to be doing the hunting. "Murderers!" shouts a mad old woman from farther down the street. The Beast is gone. Where? Artisans working late in the Via delle Botteghe Oscure look up from the pile of beast-brooches they are whittling for sale to the crowds expected at tomorrow's event in the Belvedere and are struck by the strong sensation that, had they just peeked out their doors about an hour ago, they would have seen the subject of their labors ambling down the street. How odd! They look out anyway. Their neighbors look back at them. They have all had the same simultaneous thought, all missed it, sighing, waving, shaking their heads, and then back to gluing pins on the backs of their brooches, worrying now over details that never bothered them before, such as whether its hooves are perissodactyl or merely cleft, and the position of the second horn. All of a sudden their products look somehow wrong. (Second horn?) Absurd doubts, for nobody actually saw it, and by now it is probably mingling with the cattle in the Campo Vaccino or the buffalo on Tiber island, which soon and sure enough are lowing grumpily on being awakened by torch-bearing Switzers, who prod them about to no good purpose, acting on information received from a gang of stonemasons inspecting the crumbling keystone of the Ponte di Quatro Capi from a cradle anchored to the underside of the arch. The stonemasons will not be dissuaded that, yes, it was here about an hour ago. No, can't say that anyone actually saw it, but . . .

But nothing. It's gone, and Boccamazza is digging a pit in Trastevere with the help of two dozen Corsicans. "Netting over the top," he tells them. "Leaves, stuff like that." The Corsicans indicate surprise on learning of the pit's purpose, it being unlikely that the Beast would return to the exact same spot, and even though Boccamazza is His Holiness's chief huntsman, renowned for the wiliness of his trapping, this strikes the Corsicans as an elementary error. Should they have offered Boccamazza this opinion before digging the pit? "What? Here? An hour ago . . . ?" Which is confirmed by the youngest of three priests sitting down to a late fish supper in a waterfront tavern on the opposite bank wedged between the Dalmatian hospice and the Church of Santa Lucia Infecundita where they have just finished celebrating a particularly turbulent mass. "I did not see it"—Brother Fulvio rises suddenly from his seat, his voice thick with fervor—"but I believe it was here. And it is a loving Beast!"

The other two are dividing up a splendid steamy tench. "Then why don't you find it and sit on its horn?" replies Father Tommaso. "Where would you say it is now, Bruno? The Pyramid of Cestius?" Brother Bruno nods.

Inevitably it is not, although—equally inevitably—it was, just as it was overlooked in Arenula, disregarded in Trevi, missed in Monti, skipped in Ripa, unheeded in Pigna, and pretermitted in both Campitelli and the Campo Marzio. The Beast does not enter Rome so much as materialize out of it, leaving the shadows of its sloughed former selves on plastered walls and iron-braced doors, in broom-choked porticoes and rubbish-filled vaults. It wipes itself off the travertine and tufa of Rome's *rioni,* leaving not afterimages, but only the surprise occasioned by their disappearance, a déjà déjà vu.

"Twenty-nine," says Amalia.

"Tighter," commands La Cavallerizza.

"Then show him up," commands Vich.

"Ouch!" gasps Colonna.

"Too big," opines the Pope.

"But why fish?" wonders Grooti the Baker.

"Just. One. More. Notch." Vitelli bends obediently to refasten the buckles. The strap's deliberately-roughened leather chafes pleasantly in the cleft between her nates. "Good," decides La Cavallerizza. Vitelli falls back on his haunches to admire her, admiring herself in the pier-glass. La Cavallerizza wears raffish fox-furs, thigh-boots, and a phallus. She turns this way, then that way. It juts nicely in quarter profile. The rising curve. The tapered point. Grooves to channel the blood. "Tighter."

"Thirty."

"Hush," Vittoria soothes her father. She tousles his gray hair (a martial basin-cut) where it sprouts about the nub of the arrow-stump. The barb, she thinks, made of iron and embedded in his brain. The consequent pain when she does *this.* (Another howl from Colonna.) How many daughters can boast such access to the insides of their fathers' heads? Her thumb massages its way in concentric spirals, creeping closer to the little boss of wood. Her father does not love God, so the Beast gored him at Ravenna. Everything is clear, now that the Beast is here. Or it was: she never caught sight of it herself. She jabs down again in frustration.

"Argh!"

"Thirty-one."

"My dear Faria!" exclaims Vich, arising naked as a satyr from the squalor of Fiametta's bed. A broad sweep of his arm takes in peeling velvet hangings, grease-stained sheets, wine-jugs, goblets, a finger-gouged bowl of dazzling crème fraîche. "This Beast's act of coition lasts upward of six hours." His swiveling arm halts above the shuddering humps of his mistress. "Shall we?" Little Violetta's soot-blackened face retreats behind the door, the blacking applied each morning by her teary-eyed mistress, "for the memories. . . ." She scrubs and scrubs in the scullery while the house reverberates with the cries of the rutting ambassadors, bucking and bouncing on either end of their fleshy sweaty seesaw. This not-so-secret meeting—their last—already has a valedictory feel, which they dispel with wild conquering shouts.

Africa!

India!

"Thirty-two."

"You see, he will not be able to walk in them. Do you see that?" Leo explains earnestly to a trio of carpenters and one shipwright. Mooching about in his pen behind them, Hanno sneezes loudly. *Absit omen,* thinks His Holiness, pondering the four miniature galleons careened at his feet. He had wanted something more like gondolas, but it is too late now. He has promised to address the poets, too. At some point they will have to be told the precise nature of the "Poetry Contest" in which they expect to compete tomorrow. Surprising, really, he reflects, that none of them have put two and two together yet: isn't that what poets are supposed to excel in? "You need straps," he tells the still-silent artisans. "And much more padding. The elephant is noted for the delicacy of his feet. Haven't any of you read Plinius?"

Atchoo-oo!

"Thirty-three."

The flour gets up his nose. The yeast, too. Groot trickles the remnant of his latest consignment of flour through his fingers, then sniffs the tips cautiously. Fish? And that strange purplish tinge. . . . The results of three days' labor more or less fills the bakery. He hates the kneading. The boy used to do it, but the boy has left and he can't find another. He knows why. They whisper about him. They know about Groot around here. Somehow they have found him out. Idolators and Christ-killers, the lot of them. He used to blame it on Bernardo, when it happened. Marne, Proztorf. And Prato. Two more there. It was one of the problems with Groot, one of the reasons he got rid of him. "Groot" is the past. Now he's Grooti the Baker, whose bread comes out flat and hard and inedible. Yesterday he nibbled a few crumbs of the latest batch. It was strange-smelling, oddly colored, and made him feel tingly. The problem with Grooti the Baker, thinks Groot, is that Grooti the Baker cannot bake bread. "Groot," on the other hand, from time to time, had killed children. That was the problem with "Groot."

"Thirty," repeats Amalia. *"Three."*

"Thirty-three what?" Salvestro asks at last.

"Thirty-three people following us," replies Amalia. "Thirty-four now."

Salvestro peers back over the cart. They seem to have attracted a ragged tail. A small, rather aimless mob is traversing the little square at the western end of the Via Pelamantelli in ones, twos, and threes. The nearest is a good thirty paces away, hardly any kind of threat, thinks Salvestro. Indeed it appears that, far from trying to catch up with the oxcart, most of the mob are having difficulty walking slowly enough to avoid overtaking it. There are lots of pauses and little detours, hitchings-up of their smocks, inspection of the soles of their feet, some rather overdone limping. Also, Salvestro cannot help but notice, they are all incredibly dirty. He faces forward again as the ox turns into the Street of the Jews. Something— Salvestro squints—is coming toward them. Marching, actually, and at a trot, pikes held high, the familiar livery, yes, more Switzers. *Hup, hup, hup* . . . Oxcart (hup). Large? Yes. Gray? Yes. Horn on nose? No. Salvestro watches the squad divide a few paces short of the ox's nose, flow about the cart, then, peering backward, re-form into two perfectly aligned columns, which make a cambered right-hand turn, *hup, hup, hup,* up toward the Chapel of Saint Ambrose and out of sight. Very impressive, but while he was watching them the oxcart's straggling escort seems to have disappeared. . . . No. They're still there, drifting out of doorways and simulated conversations, re-forming just as impressively, albeit into something looser and harder to define, more Rosserus-like. The Switzers never saw them. They never saw the Beast, either, although that particular sin of omission might be ascribed to a fatal flaw in their instructions: large, gray, horn on nose. This is splendid and succinct as far as it goes. A helpful coda might have added: "and artfully disguised as a pile of manure." An enabling subcodicil: "by virtue of being deceitfully buried therein."

Having neglected the question of what spidireen vessel spilled this Beast ashore in the first place, no one has yet essayed either the nature of its landfall or the concomitant unfortunate possibility lurking within this unasked question. Namely, that the animal is dead.

It has swelled alarmingly since Spezia. Twice now he has stuck a knife in its stomach to release a jet of stinking gas.

"Oh, I know where we're going," Amalia says as ox, cart, Salvestro, herself, manure, and Beast all turn right into a dank side street a little way before the arch of Septimius Severus. There is a sudden silence as the wheels of the cart pass from stone to hard-packed earth. Tall dark tenements press in on them from either side.

"He's not going to be very pleased to see you, Salvestro," warns Amalia, shaking her head.

Salvestro grins. "No one ever is."

"Bernardo was," she answers reproachfully.

But Bernardo is dead, he thinks, crushed under toppling walls of water, driven under by the same sea that had tossed him about and spat him out. All dead or lost, except himself. There had been minutes or seconds when the water had tugged him down, but then released him to bob back up to the surface like a cork. It had dashed him toward rocks, and then sluiced him around them. He had sunk and risen, breathed water, then air. His skin had puckered and peeled, separating and loosening as though he wore it like a smock. He had shucked it off and dived into a calm darkness, where everything was quiet and still. The storm capered and crackled harmlessly a mere fathom above his head while his arms pulled powerfully, a bone-white diving body, a choiceless visitor. Yes, he reflects, Bernardo was happy at every one of his reappearances. Who else? He turned and darted deeper, his head turning about, knowing already. The Water-man was there on the very edge of his vision, waving to him and retreating. The figure turned white, then black, slate gray and bottle green, dissolved into ripples and emerged again. What color is he? wondered Salvestro. And what color himself, when water will take on any color offered it? The flat grays of near tidelessness and near saltlessness, a dull tinge of yellow. He is not long for that now, although there are no "true colors" and it will not—cannot—happen here. Tonight he is invisible, the color of *Ro*-ma, which will forget him the moment he is gone.

The ox stops.

Behind, their escort stops, too, although more gradually and chaotically. Those toward the rear shunt into those toward the fore, who turn on them and push back so that little clumps and clusters form, then spring apart gently, a disintegrating vanguard. People start sitting down. Later a contingent from the Ruins will arrive bringing firewood. Little campfires will be lit. It appears to Salvestro that a loosely organized sea of heads is breaking on a gently sloping beach. Amalia's head-count now looks woefully outdated. There must be two hundred of them and more still drifting in. He wonders if he should offer some greeting, address them, perhaps. They seem to require nothing, simply to be here. For the Beast? Himself? Amalia? He climbs down from the cart. For the ox?

"Is he in the dung?"

"He is, isn't he?"

"Why isn't he in the dung?"

Their voices startle him. He had not seen them approach. Wulf, Wolf, and Wilf are regarding him expectantly through face-masks of thick dried mud. Behind them stands their more easily recognizable protector. And his own once, he recalls. After a fashion. The latter seems to be wearing a heap of mud on his head.

"Who?" he asks innocently.

"Rosserus," growls Dommi. "And are you going to knock on that door or are we all going to stand here all night?"

It takes a long time for Groot to answer.

A saw, thinks Salvestro. And wood. A knife, an awl, strong thread. A needle as thick as a poker.

"Told you so!" sings Amalia at the expression of dismay on the face that peers through a miserly crack in the door. It changes to terror when Dommi kicks the rickety barrier off its hinges, then bafflement as six or seven of the most vigorous beggars leap up on the cart and begin digging bare-handed in the dung. They are tugging at something, all of them scrabbling for handholds and heaving together. Slowly it slithers out and half-falls, half-pours itself out to land with a thud on the ground, something vast, lightly smeared with the manure's liquids.

"No," protests Groot as they begin manhandling it through the door.

Salvestro lights as many candles as he can find. A gutter runs along one edge of the floor. That's good. There is the oven, some large bowls stacked in a corner, empty flour-sacks, oversize spatulas . . . Anything else?

The bread. Mountains of it. He watches as one of the beggars picks up a loaf, sniffs at it, and puts it down again. He wonders if Groot realizes yet the operation he intends to perform here. Probably not. After all, he hardly knew himself, until now. The bread decided him. It will be perfect. And plenty of it, too.

"Get out!" shrieks Groot from the doorway. He seems to have lost his temper. His next shriek sounds rather strangled, however, for Dommi has picked him up and is patiently explaining that since bakers are one of his least favorite forms of life, noisy ones in particular, in order to shut them up what he usually does is take a few of their own proudly baked loaves and shove them down their throats. "Sometimes it takes only three or four before they come to their senses," Dommi continues, reaching calmly for the first. "Sometimes as many as eight." Amalia observes this procedure with a mixture of forensic detachment and glee.

"Right," says Wolf.

"We're ready," says Wilf.

"Let's go to work," says Wulf.

Dawn is less than four hours away. It is the second week in March. Groot is on his third loaf already, and the pace is hardly slacking.

"Begin the first cut underneath the tail," directs Salvestro. "Then continue up as far as the throat."

> *Fummo gia come voi sete*
> *Voi sarete come noi*
> *Morti siam come vedete*
> *Cosi morti vedrem voi. . . .*

Just a little song to pass the time.

Squarely, promptly, in perfect silence, and from unimaginable height, continuously from just before the donging of the campanile of nearby San Damaso onward, without pause or respite in the spread of its measureless glow, rather subtly in the corners but quite unabashedly elsewhere, with neither fear nor favor, warmly, finally, and inevitably: thus sunrise dawns on the Field of Honor. The sharp-shadowed angles of the steps to the north and the benches on the east dissolve in soft beiges and creams. The triple-decked arches of the loggie to the west admit congruent arches of sunlight whose skewings produce interesting ogivelike intersections on the back walls. The palace radiates warm yellows and whites. A limey-smelling breeze wafts in from the east and jiggles the pennants hung from the underside of the little roofed deck whence the Pope will watch the battle, itself hung rather precariously from the modillions of the palace's third-story cornices. The breeze passes on. All is pastel. All is still, the Lake of Mars so flat that it mirrors everything around in perfect detail down to the brutally pollarded willows and the parasitic lichens on the stone pines in the wilder gardens behind the sandbags that restrain the water from flooding down in a torrent of mud and shallow-rooted squills to the Porta Pertusa. The substructure of the benches doubles as a subaqueous frame. The benches hold the sandbags in place, and the sandbags uphold the benches: solid, simple engineering, an elegant piece of load-bearing construction. The surface of the water is milky brown, or silver, or glossy and green as a fern. Ah, a ripple now. Is something about to happen?

A little boat pushes its nose out of the ground floor of the Palace of Saint Nicholas. It is a rowboat, rather too small for three people. Nevertheless there are three people in it. It is being punted toward the very center, toward the fountain, or what used to be the fountain before it was enclosed inside a tall and boxy plinth with a ladder up the side and one of His Holiness's best chairs (upholstered in green silk with silver knobs on the armrests) perched precariously on the top. The little boat wobbles and bobbles its way to the foot of the ladder, its inexpert punter sending it left and right while his companion deals with their cargo, which is chiefly old curtains and table linen, strings of bunting, a hammer, tacks, two pennants sharing a representation of the world divided by a line running one hundred leagues west of the Cape Verde islands, a papier-mâché miter, a wooden staff, and Father Jörg. They have been ordered by Neroni to "bedeck the podium." Costumed approximately as a Pope, Father Jörg is part of the bedecking.

"How we going to get him up there?" demands the manager of the cargo, eyeing the narrow ladder. The gurgling fountain resonates inside the box.

"Dunno," says the master of the boat, assessing Jörg's probable weight. Not much, he decides. "Poor old devil."

Silence.

"Carry him?"

This turns out to be the preferred option. Halfway up the ascent their gaudily robed captive suffers a violent coughing fit, which continues until they deposit him on his "throne." They impress upon him the dangers of the drop and the coldness of the water, then get on with their bedecking, hammering and hanging, pinching and cinching, until the makeshift podium is dressed in a jolly motley of mauves and light greens, the Medici emblem of the Pallia picked out in gold and all the edges neatly tucked in behind a ruff of crimson velvet whose dags dangle a finger's width short of the water. . . . Which dips. Like a shallow bowl.

Then undips—*plop!*—catching the eye of the master of the cargo.

"What's that?"

"What's what?"

"The water. It sort of, well, dipped."

The master of the boat hangs out from the ladder.

"Looks all right now."

"It dipped. I saw it."

"Probably a fish."

The master of the cargo looks doubtful. "Funny sort of fish."

They climb down into the boat and begin the punt back to the palace, calling out a final warning to the lone figure sitting on the podium before they disappear inside. Father Jörg hears the gentle plash of their departing boat, then,

"Whatever you do, don't stand up!" then nothing. He is alone, undistracted. Outside, it would seem, and in some sense "aloft." The bells of San Damaso are silent. A crow caws, but far away. And there is a kind of bustle. Voices?

Possibly it is the languorous awakening groans of the denizens of the dining-hall or the more plaintive ones of those bivouacked in the passageways below. It might be the poets, limbering up with a few macaronics before breakfast, or perhaps the rumbling stomachs of King Caspar and the Mauritians, arrived last night but too late for supper, or the shrill yips and yelps of His Holiness, who ate his own later still and is now enduring some difficult negotiations over his ermine-padded chamber-pot (a gift from an anonymous donor, although Bibbiena is strongly suspected). Indeed, it might even be the latter's snoring, for he has over-slept deliciously and later will be late to a degree just this side of fashionable. Or Guidol's muttering? There is something peculiarly penetrating about his rolling *r*'s and elongated diphthongs. He is up already and busy in the kitchens, piping intricate whorls of oyster-cream over the *corquignolles* while keeping an eagle eye on a bubbling pot of thick orange marmalade to which he will shortly add the six braces of plucked pigeons resting in a basket beside it. A wailing or screeching noise reaches his ears, a stringy ululation. The musicians, Guidol thinks balefully. He caught them literally red-handed last night with their fingers in his blood sausage vat and, unable to bear their whining (nothing to eat since Montepulciano three days ago, faint with hunger, the usual nonsense), chased them out of the kitchen with a meat cleaver, shouting after them that Montepulciano was less than two days' walking away, even encumbered with violas. A chef must be feared above all else. He has a disturbing tendency toward diffidence but has been exorcising it through his regular encounters with the poets, who are even worse, turning up bright-faced in the morning with paeans to his "honest toil." More nonsense. Cuisine is the art of deception, and the rest is elbow grease and heating. None of them have yet appeared this morning. Whatever His Holiness told them last night seems to have rather cowed them. Guidol finishes up the oyster-cream and reaches for the bucket of pike spleens. *Corquignolles* are a demanding dish worthy of his talents. Now, how many spleens?

He looks down, and there, his gaze passing over the rim of the bucket, he notices a little stringy thing, white and wriggly, perhaps a sinew cut from a fillet of pork or a fragment of blanched asparagus. However, the important thing is not what it is, but *where* it is, for it is on the floor. Guidol frowns. As a test he picks up one of the pigeons and hurls it into the corner. Then he waits. He watches, and then, looking around the kitchens, he notices all kinds of detritus on the flag-stones that normally would not have lain there more than a second: cabbage hearts, bits of gristle, snippets of intestine. . . . He glances back to the pigeon. Still there. He should be joyful; after all, no chef worth his salt wants a plague in his kitchen. But instead the continuing presence of the pigeon worries him. He feels strangely unnerved. Where have all the rats gone?

Plop!

The water dips again.

Not voices, or not human ones. Something is shifting down there. And it's not fish because there are no fish. Father Jörg can hear it, but nobody else can. He cocks an ear. He puckers his brow. What *is* it?

Well, hard to credit without at least a dry sob, it's actually Towser the cat. . . .

Yippee! Yahoo! Over here, Towser! Come on, Towser. Towser! *Towser . . . !*

Boing. . . . And up on the worktables, paws in the fish-basket, paw-prints in the pastry: Towser, a long-haired ginger tomcat. In the kitchens of the Vatican, no one and nothing walked prouder than Towser. Watch him spring. And hiss! Fangs bared, claws out, Towser stalked the corners, a terror to all. Towser could leap the length of the boiling room, traverse the scullery with a single bound, fling himself though fires, scale impossible heights. On his birthday, the pot-boys would weave him a garland of rat-tails, which Towser would destroy in under a second. The mere sniff of a rat was enough for Towser, sending him into murderous frenzies. He would froth and foam, sometimes even vomit with anger, and when he had a dead rat beneath his paw he would not be content with merely biting off its head; he would skin it, too, and eviscerate it, and drag its guts around the floor to loud prolonged cheers before stowing them safely in somebody's boots. From the most elderly of the sauce-stirrers to the youngest of the carrot-peelers, all were agreed: Towser was the greatest ratter of them all. The cooks knew it, and the sub-cooks knew it. Pot-boys, wood-carriers, fish-gutters, meat-trimmers, and stock-boilers harbored no doubts. From Neroni all the way down to the amazingly decrepit old man whose job it was to carry away the excrement squeezed from the bowels of freshly slaughtered cows, anyone in the kitchens asked to identify the most tireless, talented, hardworking, and popular exponent of his or her allotted task would point directly to the same furry candidate: Towser the cat, Ratter Supreme.

Except, unfortunately, the rats.

Observation. Report. Response. Via devolved command chains and relay-systems, an ultrasonic klaxon of squeaks carried the usual warning from beneath the kitchens through the culverts, crawl-spaces, and geometrically planned tunnel-system of the colony to the outlying subsurface bastions and outposts as far as the garrisons by the river. Cat alert. Location: kitchens. Designation: Towser. Decision: Assess risk.

Accordingly, a few mice were released by night into the kitchen and Towser's performance gauged. Next some shrews. Then cockroaches, finally woodlice and worms. Stage one of the assessment was ended, and from the result the Vatican rats might have predicted what would happen next. Towser's capture rate was nil, and stage two was a rat. Neither the largest nor the smallest, although possibly the most fearless, for the rat's mission was to scamper about in front of Towser, as close as possible and as slowly as possible, to get nearer (Towser watching), nearer (Towser rising), nearer (Towser tensing), and nearer yet . . .

Towser running away.

The rats dubbed Towser "the Executioner." (Even the Vatican rats have a sense of irony.) Towser never actually caught a rat. Instead the rats fed him their old and sick, their recidivists and degenerates, those hopelessly wounded in skirmishes with the Rome rats guarding the river, and the failures from their selective inbreeding programs, limbless two-headed monsters and the like. They killed them first, then tossed them out to him. One day, they reasoned, they would have a use for Towser. Strategically, in the long view, Towser was best left in place. The Vatican rats can afford to wait, for a cat as easily as a kingdom. The habit is ingrained in them as the counterweight to rattish impatience, the tendency to rush and dart, the impulse to be impulsive when the best policy is to advance slowly and methodically, to discipline their racing hearts into slower rhythms, to watch and wait. Sometimes, very rarely, in the early hours before dawn, one or two of them will scrabble up the eastern wall of the Belvedere and gaze out over the city of their rivals. Colonies weaker than their own are waiting for them over there, over the dark flood of the river. They watch, and sniff, twitching as strange blends of adrenaline and glucocorticoids roar through their arteries. They want to run forward and rip and bite and kill, but they do not. They observe. Conquest will come with discipline and restraint. They wait, just as they wait for Towser and the day they find a use for him, for it will come just as surely as the day when they break out of the Borgo and sweep through the city to unleash their dammed-up rage and bloodlust, killing every alien rat in their path. And then, with a drip, and a drop, then a trickle of water into one of the highest and driest chambers of the colony, the point one would choose if armed with a blueprint of its every tunnel and junction one wished to wash every rat in the Borgo clean into the Tiber, Towser's day arrived.

Plop!

Here, boy, over here. Here, Towser. *Here!* There, then; yes, there. . . . Oh, forget it, Towser, wherever you've got to. . . . Anyone seen Towser? *Towser!*

Poor silly Towser, lured down a tunnel with a string of cow-guts. Throat slashed, tail trimmed off, lugged north toward the Belvedere. The most artifice-ridden artificial lake in Christendom has sprung a leak. For the sub-Vatican colony, the leak is a potential catastrophe. For Towser, a final fatal flaw. The Vatican rats are using him as a bung.

Plop! Plop! Plop!

Stop.

An hour passes, or several, time in which the seconds drift in and out of synchronization with the twitches of Jörg's sinewy heart, advancing, overtaking, recurring, coinciding. He too is waiting, and his faith is like coal, a patient black crystal guarded in a battered body. The little light appeared last night, a little time after the three mocking impostors left him to his contemplations, which were of winter and the memory of stones falling into placid black waters far away and long ago. No church protected him from the soaking and freezings then or now. No buttress held him upright, or gaudy-colored window lit his way. His little chunk of coal will burn briefly and brightly when the flame is put to it, this being adequate and in due proportion to the needs of a faithful fool. His inner pilgrimage is almost ended. His followers have almost all fallen away. HansJürgen remains, but who else? He smiles to himself, enjoying the fine irony of his elevation after his long confinement in the monstrance of the Pope's palace. Little breezes play about his feet. Little sounds play in his ears. A dulcimer tinkles, or a hackbrett, perhaps. The silver knob that terminates the armrest grows warm under his sun-warmed palm. He listens to the silence of the water and then the disturbance of that silence. The crow starts up again, then men's voices, things being dragged, and dropped, and coaxed, and cursed. Various splishings and sploshings.

Plop!

This is something he does not hear. So far, the soggy moggy is holding.

The commotion grows more complex, new sounds arising out of a general background hum of activity, intermittent tapping and bangings and squeaks. And hoots! Someone on his right shouts, "Poets over here!" and from the direction of the palace he hears a strangely rhythmical mumbling start up. He is surrounded, he realizes. A fanfare begins and is cut short in midtoot. Oranges thunder out of buckets and thud into barrels. "Will half the poets please move over to the other side of the water! Now!" Footsteps and massive murmurings. The cries of commemorative brooch-hawkers. A single colossal splash followed by many smaller ones. His own slipper-clad foot taps softly on the podium. He grips his staff. He adjusts his miter. Jörg hears the noise made by a city inured to spectacle and pomp, a dull and watery wail overlaid with grumbling and shuffling, jostling and elbowing, thousands of voices ringing him with their jabbering, their wit, their well-turned bon mots and badinage. It fills the registers, swamping everything except itself and clogging his ears until, seeming to arise from somewhere exterior, or anterior, somewhere primitive and shorn of trimmings and ornament, he hears a chant. Rather crude and monotonous, but vigorous, too: a guttural grunt sung out to a simple one-two rhythm, an aural battering ram that seems to pick up speed as it gets louder and nearer, finally bursting into the arena by the spiral stairway with its champion held high, its champion's deliverer perched on top of it, and their chanting followers following in an unstoppable charge of mud, rags, ropes, sticks, vigor, bad temper, and rudeness.

"Ross'rus. Ross'rus! Ross'rus! *Ross'rus! Ross'rus . . . !!*"

"So that's Rosserus," murmurs the Pope through the din, enthroned on his deck and ensconced amongst a selection of his favorite cardinals. The ambassadors too have gained places in this most favored vantage-point, along with those there by merit of precedence: senior curialists, the more powerful conservatori, a scattering of old barons, the more patient and generous of his bankers. "And that thing he is sitting on," he continues. "That, I presume, would be the Beast?"

For a moment, Ghiberti does not answer. His eyes, like those of the robed dignitaries around him, the capped curialists, the bejeweled bankers, the black-garbed poets waiting in their bobbing gondolas below, Hanno lurching amongst them, vainly attempting to coordinate the four floating rowboats disguised as miniature galleons that have been attached to his feet, the hoi polloi and lower members of His Holiness's *famiglia* jammed together on the benches and crammed into the loggie to either side, everyone's eyes—the eyes of *Ro-ma*—are fixed on the animal that stands amidst the mob of chanting, mud-encrusted beggars like a gray rock rubbed smooth by the tossings of a rubbish-choked sea. The plan, Ghiberti realizes, is already going awry. The naumachia was to have been a sedate and balletic affair with poets rowing out in twos and threes to face each other across a notional battle-line in allusion to the demarcating bull and there to declaim poetry at one another as loudly as possible and perhaps to hurl things if this were to become too boring. Little floating arsenals have been set adrift on the water stocked with decorous missiles: oranges, grapefruit, the odd melon, caged doves. The parody-Pope was to have adjudicated from the podium (with considerable guidance from the real one), while the two animals were to be maneuvered about until one or the other decided to attack, and then . . . Well, the plan was silent after that, but there were to be winners and losers, honor and disgrace, various ironic prizes. Commemorative medals might be struck. Now, however, taking in the Beast—its lumps and bulges, the ragged stitching criss-crossing its belly, the silly horn and ratty tail, but above all its immobility—Ghiberti is realizing a fact that should really have been rather obvious before, a fact that has already voided the plan and is now turning what should have been a triumph of popish whimsy into a day that almost everyone connected with it will probably want to forget. So, for a moment, Ghiberti does not answer.

"Dear Ghiberti, please correct me if I am wrong." The Pope sounds almost genuinely puzzled. "My eyes are weak, my understanding poor, but would I be mistaken in believing that this much-vaunted Beast—forgive me, but there is no delicate way to put it—is dead?"

Vich and Faria stare forward, their faces immobile. La Cavallerizza scratches at her enormous codpiece and hisses to her husband that, just as she suspected, the animal's horn is two or three times the size of her own. "Look to the other one," Vitelli whispers back. "The one on its withers. That is the one it uses to rip the elephant's belly open. Sharper and crueler, the very image of your own. . . ."

She sees and nods, whispering back, "Tighten me again. One more notch. . . ."

Arriving late, Cardinal Bibbiena slaps her on the behind as he passes by. "Dead?" he inquires of the Pope.

Dovizio puts his finger to his lips, but Leo nods slowly, his mood crystallizing about the fact. Abruptly, he heaves himself upright. "I do not care!" he exclaims defiantly. "In fact, I prefer that it is dead. Let the naumachia commence anyway! You lot!" he shouts down to the massed poets. "Go and attack it!"

"You were born, O Leo, in fair Florence . . . *unk!*" says little Pierino as his father clouts him around the ear.

Ross'rus! Ross'rus!

"Right," Dommi shouts over the racket to Salvestro, astride the Beast. "That's Fat Bastard up there on the platform. The scum frothing around him are Fat Bastard's friends. That's the elephant underneath. The bunch dressed as crows in the boats are poets, they've been arriving for weeks. Don't know who's the lunatic on that wooden tower-thing, but he's dressed the same as Fat Bastard. What d'you want to do now?"

Salvestro shifts uncomfortably. They had worked through the night, hacking at the cadaver he now sits astride, breaking up the cart and constructing from its timbers a frame. Dommi had knocked off the smaller of the two horns by accident, and they had nailed it to the crosspiece running across the withers to serve as a pommel. Groot had watched mutely after his force-feeding. Toward dawn he had begun to twitch. Then sweat. When they left him he was on his feet and dancing, perhaps with happiness at the fact that his bread had found its true use at last, although the rictus on his face was more suggestive of abject terror and the blue tinge to his skin of necrosis. The Beast is not just dead. It's stuffed, the leathery products of Groot's bakery proving ideal for fitting into those difficult niches and corners with which the Beast's awkward gutted interior abounded. Salvestro spent several hours in there. A particularly rigid loaf is now digging into his left buttock. He looks across the lake to where the crows in the boats are being prodded forward on the end of pikes wielded—*hup! hup! hup!*—by a squad of Switzers, then back to the mud-masked beggars now improvising a badly coordinated war-dance to the rhythm of the Rosserus-chant, up to the faces peering down at them from the loggie, the hapless trumpeting elephant sliding in four different directions at once—is that Lucullo up there? Father Jörg is dressed as a pantomime Pope in the center of the water; Salvestro spotted him almost as soon as they got in. He is unsurprised. Nothing surprises Salvestro now. If the beast came to life and started walking beneath him, he would simply cling more firmly to the improvised pommel and bump up and down on its back. Fat Bastard on his platform. The water. It's the wrong water, but it will have him if he wants. He smiles, not at all sure what will happen next, determined only, whatever it is, whenever and however it ends, that it be large, chaotic, noisy, with boats to overturn, barrels to smash, flailing men to hurl through the air: feats worthy of a giant.

"Salvestro!"

"Wake up!"

"What now, Salvestro?"

Salvestro looks down at the trio, then left and right along the battle-line of his army. They are silent now, all waiting, stalled there in front of the water. He clambers to his feet and balances precariously on the back of the Beast. A little flotilla of poets is advancing hesitantly, a boatload of the boldest almost at the podium. Salvestro gestures to the motley collection of punts and rowboats before them. He raises his arms, cries, "To the boats! Attack!" and plunges headlong into the water.

ROSS-err-oooss. . . .

Say this much for poets: they do not lack for nerve. Unnecessary to the well-ordered society and mostly incomprehensible to its citizens, they know all about advancing into the void of public indifference and hostility. This serves them well as their gilded gondolas paddle forward to the rhythm of Saturnians and hexameters chanted by their metrically minded coxes. Two or three adopt stately alcaics and drop back toward the rear, while the foremost whip out brisk heroic couplets, arms and lungs pumping, lobbing up the odd orange as a covering bombardment, speeding forward to meet the vanguard of the forces of Rosserus, half of whom are still struggling to get afloat while most of the others are manhandling the Beast into two of the least leaky-looking punts. Imperfect logistics will be the besetting fault of Rosserus, compounded by confusions at the level of command. Of their three potential strategists, one insists on saying three things at once, another submits entirely to his penchant for elaborate and unmanageable violence, and the third spends most of the battle underwater.

"That's Rosserus," the Pope informs Bibbiena smugly.

"Where?"

"Underwater."

Salvestro dives and skims the floor of the lake, pulling himself forward through the cold drag of the water in a smooth glide. The lines of the flagstones slide under him and tumble away. This is dead tideless water. He is an arrow moving through vacant space, toward the center of the Lake of Mars, toward Jörg. His lungs burn the last of their oxygen. Time to rise.

"There!" shouts the Pope. "Look, Bibbiena! Rosserus!"

Bibbiena and Dovizio exchange glances.

Below, it appears the battle has now been joined in earnest. Most of Rosserus are afloat and punting vigorously to engage the enemy fleet. A detachment under Wulf, Wolf, and Wilf is already occupied in restraining Dommi, who has upended a scrawny rhymester and is emphasizing the gravity of a perceived flaw in the latter's metrical technique—"How would you like it if I reversed one of *your* feet, *poetastro?*"—while Hanno seems to have achieved this already, fourfold, galumphing about in circles directly in front of the Pope's platform and unaware as yet that his mortal enemy is at last being launched from the opposite side of the Lake of Mars, teetering and lurching away from the waiting punts, the unevenness of Salvestro's stuffing making itself felt as it rears, twists, topples, and—*kersploo008h!*—crashes down into the water. "Hooray!" shouts little Pierino. A melon floats past. He tries to pick it up and hurl it. It's too heavy. He starts sniffling.

"Try a grapefruit!" shouts King Caspar. "Yes! Over here!" join in the rest of the Mauritians. (No supper. No breakfast. They can hardly hear themselves think over the rumbling of their stomachs.)

Salvestro looks up at the faces looking down at him. He seems to have veered to the left and has surfaced beneath the crowded loggie. "That's Salvestro," Lucullo remarks with quiet pride to the *bancherotti* standing next to him. "Old friend

of mine." They nod in agreement. Salvestro sees four gray legs sticking up in the
air, the Beast's stitched-up bobbing belly, a Rosserus-squad paddling furiously to
the rescue. Motionless in the dross of his finery, Jörg might as well be carved out
of stone. Salvestro dives again.

The black bodies of the punts pass over him like huge fish. He twists under
gondolas whose paddles are the legs of scurrying watercranes. Pressed between air
and stone, this sliver of water is his domain; Salvestro is the only thing alive in it.
He kicks off his boots, then shrugs off his jerkin. He ripples forward noiselessly,
the slick liquid running over his skin. Faster, he tells himself, for the surface is a
fragile sheet of perfect ice. Find the depths. . . . There are no depths. The surface
breaks about his head.

Krekk-unnch! Splosh! Arrgh!

Dommi is breaking boats with one hand and poets with the other, beating
the latter rhythmically over the head with fragments of broken boat and melons,
awkward but serviceable implements: "Now you've got the hang of the amphimacer." *Bish, bosh, bish!* "Let's move on to the mysteries of the amphibrach, shall
we?" *BOSH! BISH! BOSH!* The poets are wisely giving him a wide berth—it
seems to be their ineptitude that enrages him—and most of the Rosserus-boats
are, too. He is unrestrainable, now breaking a melon over the head of Marinano:
"There! Now you know how Baldus felt!" Little Pierino is still plucking up the
courage to grapple with a grapefruit, King Caspar and the Mauritians are still
dying with hunger, Hanno is hooting miserably and clog-dancing through a watery hell, when to add to his anguish he sees that the Beast is up and heading toward him, towed by a flotilla of coracles and punts captained by mud-masked
desperadoes waving sticks. Hanno panicks, tries to turn, and finds himself reeling
through a medley of chaotic Sicilian folk-dances. The Beast looks as though it's
getting bigger and lumpier, as though . . . Its pilots look nervously over their
shoulders. The spectators rub their eyes. It's undeniable. The Beast is growing. Or,
more accurately, it's swelling. Inside its tautening, tightening hide, the impossible
is taking place: Groot's bread is starting to rise.

"There he is again!" shouts the Pope over the noise of the crowd in the adjacent loggie. They have begun chanting again. His Holiness points to the wet head
surfacing like a seal to the left of the podium. "It's Rosserus."

Bibbiena drags his eyes away from the ballooning Beast. "No, it's not," he says
flatly.

"Listen to your unwashed flock," adds Dovizio.

Even as they watch, the head ducks down again. The chanting only gets
louder and clearer, resolving itself into a vigorous anapest—*BISH!* (ow!) *BISH!*
(ow!) *BOSH!* (argh!)—as Dommi explains to Pierino senior, even though in
strict metrical terms the name that the crowd seems to have seized on as its rally-
ing-cry is actually an amphibrach by stress and an amphimacer by measure. Why?
Why—when Hanno (now capering his way through an inept tarantella) seems at
last about to engage with his long-dreaded mortal enemy (now swollen to three

times its normal size and still growing), when Dommi is picking up the very last of the gondolas and smashing it over his knee, when Wulf, Wolf, and Wilf are apologizing for his excesses in triplicate to the sodden battered poets wading to shore, when little Pierino finally hurls a wizened orange to the starving musicians, who rise as one, already calculating the probable number and division of its segments, only to see it speared in midflight and carried away on the beak of a passing crow, when all this frolicsome fun is being played out for their entertainment on the surface of the Lake of Mars—why has the crowd chosen as its champion the one creature diving invisibly through the water underneath?

SAL-VES-TRO! SAL-VES-TRO! SAL-VES-TRO!

"Yes, that's right. Salvestro," murmurs Lucullo. "Old friend of mine." He has been saying this for about half an hour now. "Sal-ves-tro. Important to get the pronunciation right, don't you agree?" Everybody does. Absolutely everyone agrees absolutely wholeheartedly, and as a result the pronunciation of Salvestro's name is just about perfect, even more perfect when the volume starts to fall off a little, better yet when it quietens to a whisper, and when the last sussuration dies away, leaving an unbroken silence, the perfection of "Salvestro" is absolute. It is not the silence of smooth water. It is the silence of ice. Every head is fixed on the lake, where the two Beasts gaze at each other and where Salvestro does not rise. Old memories tick and tock. The crowd remains quiet. Possibly they are waiting for their champion to shoot up like a vengeful Neptune. Possibly, though, they are waiting for the Beasts. Hanno takes a step backward. His enemy creaks. Another step. Another creak. The Beast is a bloated, ballooning monster, its head the size of a water-barrel, its body the hull of a ship, and still growing as the pressure inside builds to the point where this brine-drenched dung-dunked hide stretches tighter than a drumskin, until, in a fleeting instant of aghast anticipation, everyone realizes what the next moment must inevitably bring. Everyone, that is, except two.

"Salvestro? Is that you?"

"It is, Father Jörg. I'm in here. Underneath you."

Then the Beast explodes.

The force shoots fragments of Beast-skin and sodden bread high and wide into the air in a spray of gray tatters and pinkish-white clods that spatter the waiting crowds. Small brawls develop around the landing-sites of the horns, and the larger flaps of skin are quickly torn to shreds in the quest for souvenirs. The brooch-sellers pack up and go home. Groot's bread—fluffy but sodden—splats wetly down on all and sundry, who scrape it off their faces and fling it in disgust to the ground (all except King Caspar and the Mauritians, who, notwithstanding its purplish hue and fishy smell, gobble as much of it as they possibly can). When they look up again, what they see, to their astonishment, is Salvestro, their champion, standing upright on the podium with the strangely dressed old man in his arms. What Salvestro sees is the Pope standing upright on the distant platform. They look at each other across the intervening distance. From his gestures, the

Pope seems to be making a speech, and from the cheers of the crowd it seems to be a popular one, and from the chant that succeeds it, it would seem that it concerns him.

SAL-VES-TRO! SAL-VES-TRO! SAL-VES-TRO!

"Oi! Are you going to stand up there all day?" Dommi's punt bumps against the podium. "Whoa!" Dommi's punt-pole suddenly drops a foot, almost unbalancing him. "Come on. Fat Bastard's going to feed us dinner. Are these your boots?"

Father Jörg coughs hoarsely. "Have you come to join with me, Salvestro?"

SAL-VES-TRO! SAL-VES-TRO! SAL-VES-TRO!

"Come on, Salvestro!" shouts Dommi.

Plop!

No one hears it, not even Father Jörg. The crowd are shouting too loud and will still be shouting when Dommi has punted both men back to the palace, when he has questioned the manhood of a sullen band of Switzers and head-butted their commander in the face en route to the *tinello,* where Salvestro will find himself seated at the top table, wedged between the Orator of Fernando the Catholic and His Holiness himself, when he looks around and sees that Father Jörg has been seated farther away, amongst the servants, when he wonders, without really worrying, where Amalia can have got to. . . . They will still be shouting then, but only just. Thirty or forty of them at most. Finally they will be silent, all departed, all forgetful, on their respective routes back to wherever and whatever they came from. As the last one makes his way down the spiral staircase in the eastern wall of the Belvedere, Guidol will be leaning over himself and His Holiness in the midst of an explanation of a dish called *corquignolles,* the musicians will be about to play, and His Holiness will have offered him "whatever it is in my power to grant," while wondering privately when Ghiberti will return from the errand he has been sent on. (*Sal-ves-tro!* Salvestro? That name is in the ledger somewhere. . . .) It will be dark. It will be his last night in *Ro*-ma.

Plop! Plop! Plop! . . .

Poor Towser. Even his corpse is useless.

And poor little Pierino—such a difficult day for the pygmy-poet, for the producer of the Painful Paean. A clout around the ear, an immovable melon, an unreachable grapefruit, then the climactic escrowed orange, and now everyone's disappeared and left him all on his own. Little Pierino begins to sniffle again, then cry.

"Two thousand seven hundred and three. Two thousand seven hundred and two. Two thousand seven hundred and one. Two thousand seven hundred and none . . . Oh, hello, little boy. Who are you?"

Little Pierino raises his tearstained face and wipes his freely running nose. A girl is standing in front of him.

"I'm little Pierino," says little Pierino. "I'm a—"

"Little Pierino the poet?" asks the girl, an expression of incredulous delight suffusing her artless features, as it seems to the diminutive dithyrambist.

He nods proudly. "What were you counting?"

"Oh"—she gestures airily—"just the leaves falling out of the trees, or God's acts of mercy, or the saved, or the damned, or the people who will remember Salvestro."

"Salvestro? Who's he?"

"Six thousand nine hundred and ninety-nine. Never mind. Do you know any games, little Pierino? I only know leapfrog and the rat game."

"I know a poem," offers little Pierino. "It's about His Holiness. Shall I recite it for you?"

Amalia nods eagerly.

His right hand moves to his breast (plucking the Orphic lyre), his left arm extends toward Amalia (tuning it to the Aeolian mode). Little Pierino opens his mouth.

> You were born, O Leo, in fair Florence town,
> Where the fields are green and the earth beneath brown. . . .

And so on, while Amalia claps and laughs, dances and cries: the perfect audience for the pipsqueak panegyrist. She even joins in the anapest-skip at the end of each line.

"That was lovely, little Pierino," she reassures him when the final hendecasyllable has been sent rolling down the empty passage. "Although . . ."

"Although what?"

Two thousand two hundred and two, thinks Amalia. She has been counting silently and still is. Aloud she says, "It is so perfect, its numbers so smooth, its figures so ornate. . . . But you have left something out, haven't you, little Pierino?"

"Have I?" He might be about to cry again.

"His Holiness's visit to Prato, little Pierino. Of course, he was not Pope Leo then, only Cardinal Medici, but he had such fun while he was there. . . ." She stops, for little Pierino actually is crying now. She puts her arms about the wee weepy wordsmith. "Don't worry, little Pierino. We'll write the Prato part together, and then you can recite it to His Holiness. He will be amazed by you, just as I am."

Little Pierino's runny nose nuzzles her snow-white neck. "All right," he sniffs gratefully.

One thousand and twelve. One thousand and eleven and counting. Poor Salvestro. At this rate, nobody's going to remember him at all. . . .

"Poor" be damned, and "Poor Salvestro" doubly damned. Forget the saved. Forget the leaves. God's small acts of mercy? On the face of it, Salvestro's having an excellent time. Just count the number of new friends he has made: a Pope, a cook, an Ambassador, a Cardinal, an underbutler, a wine-server, a noisy man and a quiet man, a short man and a tall man, a shivering band of musicians with lamp-blacked faces, men in caps (red, black, green, and blue), a Senator, a financier, a dozen curvaceous courtesans (all, for some reason, called Imperia), a Baron, a Lord, no priests, innumerable poets (his "honest toil" is already being extempo-rized upon), fivescore mud-caked beggars, and a secretary. Everyone wants to meet Salvestro, except perhaps the secretary, weighed down by a stoutly bound folio and trying to gesture discreetly to His Holiness, who is preoccupied, as is Salvestro, by Guidol's explanation of the *corquignolles.*

"Now we come to the eleventh layer. Unlike layers one to five, which, as you will recall, nourish the natural spirits produced in the liver, or layers six to ten, which feed the vital spirits of the blood, the eleventh layer is sustenance for the animal spirits of the brain."

Guidol turns over a wafer of pastry and discloses a greenish paste latticed with stringy red things and studded with highly polished periwinkles. Both men are finding it hard to follow this explanation, for Guidol has a habit of talking into his sleeve and his accent thickens when he becomes excited. "You're not French, are you, Guidol?" asks His Holiness on a hunch.

"Alsatian," replies Guidol. "Now, these plum-flavored tendons. Any guesses as to the meat?" They shake their heads. "Wolf." The dish containing the *corquignolles* is deep enough to hold a cow's head, with horns. So far, they have excavated rather less than an inch. Perhaps, thinks His Holiness, it is time to ask this Salves-tro for the second time if he has decided what he wants yet, or Guidol just how many layers of these *corquignolles* remain.

"Four hundred and twenty-seven. Four hundred and twenty-five . . ." Amalia's skipping. Both senses.

Meanwhile, at the other end of the *tinello,* a jolly *Mohrenfest* is starting up, King Caspar and Mauritians tuning up their violas, lutes, sackbuts, and some other instrument. Hackbrett? Dulcimer? Call it an alpine zither. Dommi leads the applause by thumping vigorously on the table, which promptly splinters and sends flagons of Tuscan rotgut crashing to the floor together with platters of steamed chicken and tureens of mushy turnips. Everyone else claps, and King Caspar announces that their first tune tonight will be that old favorite *"Il Grasso Porco di Cattivo Umore."*

Soon two of the Imperias start dancing a frisky *moresco,* incorporating sly al-lusions to the simple life of the peasant girls whose shapeless shifts are the (dis-tant) models for these courtesans' taffeta-lined gamurras, bobbing and curtsying, hoeing and milking. "Honest toil," the poets murmur approvingly, wondering if the rhythmic flop of their breasts might lend itself to a tetrameter. Soon everyone is on their feet and hopping around, although King Caspar, mindful of the fact that the Supreme Pontiff paying his fee values suavity and a facile diminuendo ranging from the lachrymose to the sepulchral over anyone actually enjoying themselves, resolutely maintains a sedate tempo against the wilder riffs of his

Mauritians and the alpine zitherer in particular, whom he shoots disapproving glares whenever he runs his plectrum down the strings.

From the top table it appears that everyone below is having a splendid time. The Pope taps his finger in time to his theme tune, Guidol begins explaining the fifteenth layer of the *corquignolles* (puréed squirrel gizzards and chitterlings marinated in snake venom), Dovizio points and says, "There's Rosserus," and Bibbiena collapses in fits of giggles. "Another notch," murmurs La Cavallerizza. Vitelli reaches behind her. Salvestro notes that the Pope's book-hampered secretary is waving frantically to His Holiness, but only when he, Salvestro, is looking the other way. He waves back but gets no response. The Ambassador sitting beside him has not said a word in over half an hour. It does not matter. He has reached his decision. He has decided what he wants, leaning over now to whisper it in His Holiness's ear, rather pink and fat, he notes. His Holiness beams delightedly. "Blasphemous, my dear Sylvestro! Wonderful."

"One hundred and eighty-three. One hundred and eighty-two . . ."

"Right!" bellows Neroni, drowning out the hundred and eighty-first chorus of *"Il Grasso Porco di Cattivo Umore."* *"Shut up!"*

Seventy-nine beggars, sixty-three poets, five skiving incognito kitchen workers, eleven assorted members of the lower orders, three gate-crashers, King Caspar, the six Mauritians, and just under a baker's dozen of women all claiming to be called Imperia grind to a halt, look up, and utter a collective, "Uh?"

"Thank you. *Thank you very much!* Now, as you know, His Holiness the Pope Leo for an abiding remembrance, meditating fittingly in the inmost counsels of his heart upon the unwearied fervor of lofty devotion, the purity of blameless faith, the respect for the Holy Apostolic See, and the ardor of lofty virtues, whereby our very dear son in Christ . . ."

And there Neroni stops. He stares across the hall at the man standing beside His Holiness, the man he should be naming now. He does not really like giving speeches. He prefers just shouting, but inept though he is, this has never happened to him before. He stands there as though struck dumb while a fruitless struggle takes place between his mouth and his memory. He seems to have forgotten the man's name.

"Him!" he shouts eventually, pointing at Salvestro. "He has made himself, in manifold ways, pleasing, serviceable, and agreeable, namely by bringing here today a certain beast which His Holiness Pope Leo greatly desired. And thus His Holiness deems it fitting and expedient that, that this bringer of the beast should be granted a gift, appropriate in measure to the magnitude of the task, which has now been chosen, and granted . . ." Here Neroni pauses; his speechmaking is not completely inept. "And is"—another pause—"that he should hear *His Holiness's confession!"*

Raucous applause greets this popular choice: something for everyone to enjoy. Slowly, in step, the two men walk forward into the cheers of the crowd. The beggars are already ripping the hangings off the wall, and Dommi has re-

verted to his earlier table-smashing mode while the poets bend their energies toward the task of reconfiguring the wood fragments and tattered strips of velvet.
With miraculous speed, a ramshackle but serviceable confessional rises in the
center of the dance floor. King Caspar beats out a stately measure, and behind
him the violas go to work, pounding out a thunderous flattened fifth, a two-note
earthquake that they privately dub "The Confessional Processional; Music for Fat
Bastard and Whatever-His-Name-Is to Stroll To":

Leo smiles at Salvestro. Salvestro smiles at the Pope.
"After you."
"No, after *you.*"
They enter together.

To hear His Holiness's confession had seemed an inspired notion just a few
minutes before, but now Salvestro is unsure how to proceed. There is a dull ringing in his head, muffled and somehow distant. Inside him and yet far away. The
cries of the Pratesi? Of the soldiers who had slaughtered them? It was hard to
hear the victims under the noise of their aggressors. He thinks of Bernardo's terrified face as the water poured into the hold. His mouth had been open to say
something, but the sea had drowned him out. Confess to that, he thinks, but it is
hard to connect the plump and jolly Pope to Bernardo's fate, or that of the
Pratesi, or even Diego's a thousand miles away in Nri. A mad white soldier kneeling before his dead black King. Should the Pope confess to that? And what of the
corpses tossed up on the beach? He must say something now, mark the ended
lives that have carried him like so much cargo to his landfall. At Spezia he was the
one the sea would not take. There was a place for him, but it was not there. He
thinks of a boy swimming in the near tideless waters of a near saltless sea, bone
white, silent, diving for Vineta. Ashore, an identical creature creeps ino the forest.
Behind him, the torches muster for the chase and dot the night with their red
glows. He might as well be outside the palace at Nri, or in Rome, or Prato, or on
the shore of the mainland, looking back at the island. The torches of his pursuers
are always there, gathering behind him, driving him forward. Who awaits him at
the end of his circuit? For Salvestro there is only the Water-man now, and the
Water-man is himself, the self he fled long ago when he pulled himself out of the
Achter Wasser and stumbled into the forest. He is always there, hanging in
the water, waiting to coax him forward down the ramp of ice that leads to
drowned Vineta. The ringing in his head is her bells.

He sits there pondering these matters. A sharp yelp sounds from the other
side of the curtain. His Holiness has sat on a splinter. The music outside seems to
be getting louder and faster.

"Twenty . . . Come on, little Pierino. You don't want to be late, do you?"

Little Pierino shakes his head uncertainly. The girl is much stronger than she looks. She is more or less dragging him toward the source of a noise that started up a few minutes ago and now sounds like a thunderstorm.

"Nineteen," mutters Amalia. "Come *on!*" They run though a long, low chamber. There is a small door at the end of it. The door is shaking. Amalia pushes him forward.

"What on earth can they be doing in there?" asks Cardinal Bibbiena, peering over the heads of the dancers to the confessional marooned in their midst.

Dovizio shrugs.

"I imagine they are remembering their time at Prato." Ghiberti has appeared behind them, ledger closed now.

"Prato? Where he had Tedaldi's family killed?" Bibbiena snorts. "Who cares about that now?"

"His Holiness, apparently. And this, this"—Ghiberti flicks quickly through his ledger—"Salvestro."

"And me!" protests a child's voice behind the trio. They turn, searching for the source of this impudent intervention, and that is the moment when, on the other side of the booming *tinello,* the alpine zitherer raises high his plectrum and brings his hand down on the trembling strings with a sound like trees being ripped out by the roots.

At this, the music reaches a new and horrendous pitch. It would take every oak in the bear-haunted forests of the Gargano Mountains to build the glockenspiel, which sounds as though it is now being smashed in the *tinello,* and all the iron in the Harz to forge the hammers to do the smashing, but who would have thought the men to wield them would be suave King Caspar and his diminuendo-adept Mauritians, those first fiddles of the lachrymose, those wizards of the sepulchral? Their shuddering leader stomps the floor, the sweat beading through the blacking on his face, whipping them through the diabolical tritone while the alpine zitherer slithers up the scale and slaloms down in a scorching zigzag that the violas and sackbut name variously and privately as "Death by Shrieking," "Zither in Flames," "Slaughter of the Innocents," and "Music for Fat Bastard to Bang His Head against a Wall To," although it should more properly be called "The Purple Spur," for that is the bit of biochemical grit around which this pearl of song is forming. Groot's meal was spurred. The bread was spiked. Now two dozen church organs are trampolining on a drumskin the size of the erstwhile Lake of Mars (*plop!* the last drop), and one hundred and eighty sweating, mudcaked, drink-fueled, tipsy Terpsichoreans are dancing the carmagnole, all jammed together thigh to thigh, except for Cardinal Armellini (protected as always by the

six-foot cordon sanitaire of his own unpopularity), La Cavallerizza (because anyone who touches her thighs seems to come away covered in blood), and Father
Jörg, who is sitting down in a corner.

No, he's not. He's up, pulled to his feet by two childish hands as the alpine
zitherer raises his instrument to his face and begins playing it with his teeth, as
King Caspar brings his staff down on his toe, doesn't feel it, and carries on, while
Vich scratches at the itchy ring of teeth-marks scabbing around his member and
Faria reaches for the *corquignolles,* chews, swallows, and falls choking to the floor,
while the black flood courses down the rat-tunnels and the crow perched atop
the eastern wall of the Belvedere wonders which it should eat first: the orange?
the leathery gray tail it found wrapped around the weather vane of the spire of
San Damaso? or the sodden cat-carcass lying on the mud-streaked flagstones of
the courtyard below? The crow has just noticed that the cat lacks a tail when a
small boy shoots it dead with a catapult.

Thock! That's the crow.

Thock! That's His Holiness, who is indeed banging his head against the wall
of the confessional in frustration. Valentino? Zoroastro? He cannot for the life of
him remember this fellow's name.

Contrition? wonders Salvestro. Remorse?

The door is flung open: bodies, noise. Father Jörg and a little boy. What are
they doing here? muses Salvestro. He is quite calm, quite quiet in the midst of the
uproar, simply waiting there, quite content to listen to whatever the Pope might
want to tell him and in the meantime drifting on his own watery thoughts.

"Five!" shouts a furious Amalia, jerking him out of his reverie.

Alessandro? Venturo? *Thock! Thock! Thock!*

"Begin," His Holiness says, wincing. "Begin anyway."

But the voice, when it finally does begin, sounds squeakier than he remembers, familiar somehow but not attached to, to . . . He cannot be sure. He has forgotten the sound of the man's voice.

> *You came, O Leo, to fair Prato town,*
> *Where the grass is green and the earth beneath brown,*
> *Where the gutters ran red and the hair turned white,*
> *Where the people so loved you that they danced through the night.*
> *They threw off their clothes and they stripped off their skin,*
> *They tore off their flesh to the white bones within.*
> *They danced till they fell and with their very last breath*
> *They sang a hymn to you, Leo, called the "Triumph of Death."*

There is a pause then. Leo sees the glowing braziers, the tools of black iron.
The smoke from the burning flax, he remembers now, smelled of hair.

"Would you like to hear the hymn now, Your Holiness?"

He says nothing. The voice will continue whatever he says, hanging in his memory like the reek of burning hair. The voice sings:

Once like you we were,
Our corpses now you see,
Such as we now are,
Such you soon shall be. . . .

"Four!"

Running and running and running and running . . . Is Salvestro running away again? If so, it is more of a hobble. Father Jörg weighs heavily on his arm. A few figures are dragging their shadows across the piazza. They look tiny and distant in the emptiness of the square. The towers and tenements of the Borgo are silent as mausoleums. Father Jörg coughs, and the sound echoes in the street. HansJürgen will be at the gate through which they first entered this city. He will be cold and anxious, waiting out the hours alone. The moonlight skates over stone and plaster, travertine and tufa, pepperino and pozzolana, wood, slate, brick, the fabric of Rome. Amalia skips ahead of them, a bright banner of white. The two men can hardly keep up. She turns, plants her hands on her hips, and eyes them impatiently.

"Three!"

They are almost at the river when the flood begins. From drains and gutters, scrambling out of walls and scurrying out of doorways, a black wave gathers in the Borgo and flows forward through its streets. Salvestro stops, rooted to the spot. He takes a tighter grip on the man at his side as the silent rats advance and the last paces between them and the unstoppable army disappear. They are upon him. He screws his eyes shut. He sees nothing. He feels nothing. They are two blind men standing there while the dark bodies flow about their ankles and pass on. They have not been touched. When Salvestro opens his eyes, Amalia is already skipping across the bridge. They are losing her. She is slipping away. She will not stop for them again.

"Two!"

The rats scramble down to the water, the river they have waited so long to cross. Thousands upon thousands of them line the bank, serried there behind their commanders, waiting in silence and staring across at the thing they have come to confront. On the opposite bank, a matching army stares back, waiting like themselves, silent like themselves. The roads do not lead here, they only end. From here they can only lead away again, from a tar-black river, or from a tideless sea, or from Rome. Salvestro leans out over the parapet of the bridge and sees the lines begin to waver and break. On both sides of the river, black bodies turn and start clambering over those behind them as the ranks break and retreat. The rats are turning back.

"One!"

He looks up. Amalia is a scrap of white disappearing into the darkness, calling back to him, "You're on your own now!" Her voice sounds light and mocking. "God will save you, if you can find him!"

"Amalia! Wait!"

Only her final shout finds him, sent high and clear into the night air.

"You know where to look! Good-bye, Salvestro!"

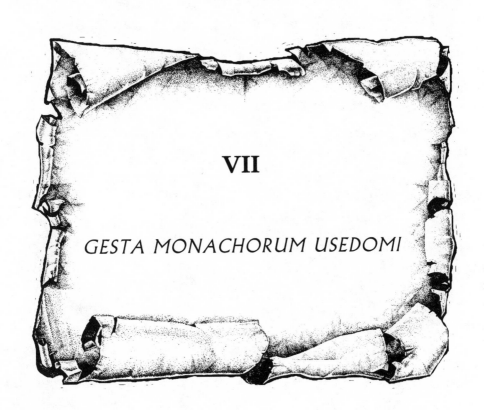

VII

GESTA MONACHORUM USEDOMI

*T*o the greater glory of God and the remembrance of him who founded their church, the present writer dedicates these tattered and unbound leaves, the whole chronicle of the deeds of the monks of Usedom, which was begun by the first Abbot of Usedom in the year that the church was founded and continued by each of his successors until the last, who was Father Jörg. It falls to a humble monk to conclude it, and, by a fitting circuit, this will the last of the deeds of the monks of Usedom. A monk without a monastery may yet be a monk, but the Church Fathers state, if the present writer remembers it truly, that there can be no such thing as a singular monk. Father Jörg died in the year of Our Lord fifteen hundred and thirty-two on the Eve of Saint Bernard and was buried on the Day of Saint John. He who writes these words is the last of the monks of Usedom.

Many of the leaves which precede this last one are not legible to these eyes. The Prior of Usedom struggled against the blindness which was visited upon him in Rome and which is recorded in these leaves but could not save the neatness of his hand. The ink has faded and in places has been overwritten many times. Too, many of the leaves have embarked on misadventures in emulation of those recorded upon them. Some were lost to rot, others to the hunger of rats, still more went missing on the journey from Rome to Usedom, and more again on the less perilous route to this place, the monastery which gave shelter to the last two monks of Usedom. It is only by God's grace that we found ourselves here, as it is that we left Rome. God worked through us to guard us safe, and He worked through Salvestro, our guide, who is mentioned many times in the script of Father Jörg, even if the likeness in certain passages is a confusing one.

It is the present writer's purpose to conclude the account, which ends as it began on the island of Usedom, for, as it was the wish of Father Jörg to be buried there beside his Abbot, so he was conveyed there, as he had been many years before by Salvestro. Father Jörg never spoke Salvestro's name in the years after his final departure from the island. His habit was ever to shoulder the burden of guilt himself, although it would accord with his character if he intended by this last return to recall that other and more difficult one.

He stopped there and laid down his pen. Outside his window he could hear the distant town bells tolling the end of the market, footsteps and voices in the nearer cloister. It was the hour when, had he been alive, Father Jörg would be ushering the novices through the door of the chapter-house for instruction in geography. Brother Jörg, he corrected himself. He had never accustomed himself to his Prior's insistence on this mode of address. Five days before, standing before Jörg's grave in the August heat, he had looked out over the flat gray sea and wondered why the Prior should have wished to be buried in the very ground that had caused him so much hardship. For it had all begun with the earth, he realized, which had failed Jörg as surely as it had failed his church. The priest, an unlettered clerk from the church at Wollin who mumbled the words to conceal his ignorance, droned his way through the rite attended by himself and the gravediggers. They were all the company. It began with the earth, he thought to himself, but it had ended with the sea and the journey to that sea from Rome.

He remembered carrying the chest to the gate at the Piazza del Popolo. He remembered the two of them appearing when he had all but given up hope, and then the journey, which was a scattering of memories bound together by the cold. They had traveled with whoever might take Salvestro's outrageous stories of his adventures in lieu of payment for their passage: a company of pilgrims returning to Trentino, a Moravian printer traveling to Nuremberg, others beyond the mountains. Carters, drovers, boatmen, and when there was nothing else to be done they would walk, Salvestro supporting Jörg, the winter seeming to deepen with every step taken north. They had reached the island on the Eve of Saint Rupert and found there a wasteland of ice. They had believed, or perhaps only hoped, that Salvestro would turn back then, but it was their strangely cheerful guide who had led the two of them across the ice to their church. He and Jörg had prayed together. Salvestro had built a fire and then had gone out in search of more wood. They had been strange hours, as he remembered. A kind of limbo. He did not know how long they had prayed or when they had stopped. They had sat there alone, waiting for Salvestro to return, the same realization dawning on them both. Outside, the light failed, and when it was dark they had understood that whatever purpose outside themselves their guide had had in returning here it was being fulfilled now.

But Salvestro's purpose confounded him now. For many years afterward he had believed he had understood it, that he knew why the man had come back. Or for whom. There is one I seek here, Salvestro had said. Or one who seeks me. . . . They had looked out over the frozen sea, which glowed a dull white in the moonlight, but when the priest had bade him farewell and left him there alone at the grave, he had decided to seek out the man who might confirm it, for who else on the island might Salvestro have come back for? Unfamiliar faces had greeted him suspiciously at the man's dwelling and directed him along the foreshore and through the beech woods. Bonfires were burning in honor of the Baptist, and no one was at work. It had taken much of the afternoon to find the foul pond, the ramshackle shed beside it. But the old man who lived there stared at him dumbly, like an animal, and would not answer his questions.

Jörg had first heard the shouting that night. A line of torches had formed along the beach. He remembered the strange shapes and figures formed in the ice of the frozen sea. The torches were being held up by the islanders, who were all facing out from the shore. Salvestro was on the ice, shaking his fist at them. The monk picked up his pen.

The church of the monks of Usedom still stood that night, though much damaged. No boat or boatman was needed, for the water was frozen over and might be crossed by walking. The last two monks had not thought their guide would cross the water once he brought them in sight of the island. Many years before, in the darkness of their superstition, the inhabitants of that place had drowned his mother as a witch. They feared her son, for he was a heathen and different from they, and it was certain that they would come for him.

When Father Jörg was laid to rest, and the clerk was gone, it suited the present writer then to seek out an old man who lived alone on the island, for he and Salvestro had been friends once. Salvestro had let it be known that someone awaited him on his return to the island, and in consequence for many years the present writer believed it was this man who lived alone in the herring-shed. These matters were the subject of the questions put to the old man, of which he affected to understand nothing, even though the accents of Brandenburg are not so different from those of Usedom, and the events of that night are not so distant.

He stopped again. There had been the torches, and Salvestro on the ice, gesturing at them. That was the the image that had stayed with him, with which he had wrestled. Salvestro was not shaking his fist. He was waving or beckoning to them. The islanders carried clubs and scythes, and they waited for him in silence, not daring to follow him out there. It was as though he were mocking them, for they feared the sea off Vineta Point, as they always had, and they feared what lay beneath it. They feared Vineta. The shouting Jörg had heard had been Salvestro's. He remembered watching for a long time. Eventually Salvestro dropped his arms. He turned and began to walk away, out onto the ice, growing smaller and smaller until the darkness swallowed him and he could be seen no longer. The islanders had waited there through the night as though, in their ignorance and superstition, they thought he might appear again out of the darkness. He had watched and waited with them. But Salvestro had not come back. And he had not come back to the island for the creature in the shed. He did not know how to write this.

Now the church of the monks of Usedom is gone. Perhaps it fell entirely into the sea, or sank into the poor earth, or simply crumbled into dust, although several cottages have risen in the years since that night, and some fine new walls, built of a dressed stone which appears familiar to these eyes. The monks of Usedom are no more, and the last Abbot and Prior lie side by side in their graves. May they rest in peace, and Salvestro, too, wherever he lies. His people were drowned many years ago when the heathen city of Vineta was torn from the island and sank into the sea. It was from those waters that the monks of Usedom first plucked Salvestro, and it was to those same waters that he returned. The islanders drove him out onto the ice where the cold overtook him or the ice broke beneath him. Now only I, HansJürgen, remember him. He was the last of his kind, just as I am of mine. Let this remembrance be the last of the deeds of the monks of Usedom.

ABOUT THE AUTHOR

LAWRENCE NORFOLK was born in 1963. His first novel, *Lemprière's Dictionary*, was critically acclaimed on both sides of the Atlantic and has been translated into twenty-two languages. He lives in London.